THE MESSAGE TO
THE PLANET

THE MESSAGE TO THE PLANET

IRIS MURDOCH

VIKING

VIKING
Published by the Penguin Group
Viking Penguin, a division of Penguin Books USA Inc.,
40 West 23rd Street, New York, New York 10010, U.S.A.
Penguin Books Ltd, 27 Wrights Lane,
London W8 5TZ, England
Penguin Books Australia Ltd, Ringwood,
Victoria, Australia
Penguin Books Canada Ltd, 2801 John Street,
Markham, Ontario, Canada L3R 1B4
Penguin Books (N.Z.) Ltd, 182–190 Wairau Road,
Auckland 10, New Zealand

Penguin Books Ltd, Registered Offices:
Harmondsworth, Middlesex, England

First American Edition
Published in 1990 by Viking Penguin, a division of Penguin Books USA Inc.

LIBRARY OF CONGRESS CATALOGING IN PUBLICATION DATA
Murdoch, Iris.
The message to the planet / Iris Murdoch.
p.   cm.
"First published in London by Chatto & Windus in 1989"—T.p.
verso.
ISBN 0-670-82999-4   I. Title.
PR6063.U7M47   1990
823'.914—dc20   89-40352

Printed in the United States of America
Set in Garamond

TO
Audhild and Borys Villers

Contents

PART ONE *page* 1

PART TWO *page* 67

PART THREE *page* 112

PART FOUR *page* 199

PART FIVE *page* 273

PART SIX *page* 483

PART SEVEN *page* 550

THE MESSAGE TO
THE PLANET

PART ONE

'Of course we have to do with two madmen now, not with one.'

'You mean Marcus is mad too?'

'No, he means Patrick is mad too.'

'What do you mean?'

The first speaker was Gildas Herne, the second was Alfred Ludens, the third Jack Sheerwater.

'I mean,' said Gildas, 'that by now Patrick is mad. That Marcus is mad goes without saying.'

'Marcus is not mad,' said Ludens, 'and Pat is very ill, not out of his mind.'

'Gildas is just expressing his frustration,' said Jack.

'We are certainly frustrated.'

Gildas who was sitting at the piano, played some melancholy chords. The open window of his flat admitted smells of springtime from not too distant Regent's Park. There was to have been, as usual, singing; but tonight, although it was late, the other two were still sitting at the supper table with the whisky bottle. Of course they should have kept off the subject of Marcus Vallar, but as Patrick Fenman failed to recover, indeed was visibly sinking, the question of Vallar became increasingly inevitable.

'As we don't know where he is,' said Ludens, 'and my God we've tried hard enough —'

His friends usually used his surname, except sometimes when expostulating or for rhetorical effect.

'It's ridiculous,' said Jack, 'how can someone vanish, how can someone famous like him vanish?'

'He vanished before,' said Ludens.

'Anyway, he's not famous now,' said Gildas. 'There's no reason why he should be, he hasn't done anything notable for years. Anyone who's heard of him probably thinks he's dead.'

'Perhaps he is dead,' said Ludens.

'What happened to the little girl?' said Jack.

'His daughter?' said Gildas. 'No idea. Didn't she run off to Paris or somewhere, I wouldn't blame her for clearing off, Marcus was *intolerable, insupportable.*'

'No, no!' said Ludens.

'You're sentimental about him,' said Gildas. 'You're too anxious to please people and be pleased by them. He was a destroyer.'

'He damaged you,' said Jack. 'He was a bit of a cold fish. But he didn't harm Ludens, and he positively helped me, he set me up!'

'Oh, *you,* you'd survive anything!'

'I don't think he really damaged you, Gildas,' said Ludens. 'You'd have lost your faith, or whatever it was that happened, in any case.'

'For Christ's sake, let's sing,' said Gildas. They often sang together, fancying themselves and recalling the Finches of the Grove. Gildas was the musical man, a talented pianist who had been a choirmaster and had even imagined himself to be a composer. He had a fine high tenor voice. Ludens was a creditable baritone and Jack an impressive bass. Patrick, now absent from them, was what Gildas called, not always warmly, 'an Irish tenor', meaning by this something more than that he was (which he was) both Irish and a tenor. Of course they never let the women sing.

Jack and Ludens ignored the suggestion.

'We could advertise,' said Jack.

'He'd be furious, he'd make a point of not answering.'

'Yes, but someone else might.'

'The trouble is, if he's to be any use we mustn't offend him. We must arrive on bended knee. All right, Gildas, you hate him, but we don't.'

'You evidently revere him,' said Gildas.

'Yes,' said Jack, 'I revere him. I'd give a good deal to see him again, even apart from Patrick.'

'It's better you don't,' said Gildas, 'you might be embarrassed to find yourself feeling sorry for him. He could be pathetic. He's fallen out of sight because there's nothing more he can do. He may be fading away in some mental home.'

'Thinking he's Superman? Well, perhaps he is.'

'How is Patrick?' said Ludens to Jack.

Patrick Fenman was extremely ill, now said by some to be dying of a mysterious disease. Earlier on, when Patrick emerged from a first visit to hospital, Jack Sheerwater had removed his friend from his shabby digs into his own house. After further visits, further tests, Patrick was back again in Jack's house.

'He's thin and white and transparent.'

'Does he still talk to Franca?'

'He utters a lot of rhyming doggerel like nursery rhymes –'

'And "speaks with tongues"? That would interest Marcus!'

'He babbles in some unidentifiable language.'

'It's Irish,' said Gildas, 'nothing more mysterious than that.'

'You don't know Irish, Gildas,' said Jack, 'you just thought it sounded like a Celtic language. You don't even know Welsh. Why don't you come and see him, or are you afraid? Franca is marvellous with him, and Alison's pretty good considering how she hates anything to do with illness.'

'Alison is certainly the goddess of good health,' said Gildas, playing a few more irritable chords, 'and Franca is famous for being an angel.'

Franca was Jack's wife, Alison his mistress.

'Women are so brave,' said Ludens.

'I suppose it *can't* be Aids,' said Gildas.

'Of course not!' said Jack. 'That was settled ages ago. The doctors are still talking about an obscure African virus.'

'And the psychiatrists are saying it's psychosomatic.'

'One doesn't die of something psychosomatic,' said Ludens.

'Doesn't one? What about Aborigines who die because someone has pointed a bone at them.'

'They're primitive savages, Pat is a civilised European.'

'No, he isn't,' said Gildas. 'He's a wild man from the west of Ireland, his ancestors were seals.' Patrick had explained to his friends that, where he came from, the local girls had used to mate with seals.

'Well, we must hope it *is* psychosomatic,' said Jack, 'provided we can find Marcus.'

In the earlier and more lucid part of his illness Patrick had several times said that he had been cursed by Marcus Vallar and was dying of the curse.

'Oh, what's the use,' said Gildas. 'Let poor Pat die in peace. Why should he be tormented at his last moments by that nightmare figure? Why do you imagine Vallar would want to help him, remove the curse and make him better? He might curse him all over again, and us as well!'

'That Catholic priest came, didn't he? That did no good.'

'Marcus was dangerous,' said Jack, 'he could throw poisoned darts. We all parted on bad terms with him. He told Gildas he was telling lies about God, he told me I was a filthy lecher *and* a rotten painter! Actually he never quarrelled with you, Alfred, you were the lucky one.'

3

'We just drifted apart,' said Ludens. 'I began to find his company *extremely tiring*.'

'It was extremely tiring, but we were all addicted to it.'

'Actually,' said Ludens, 'although I agree that Marcus was dangerous there was also something naive and childish about him, as if he meant no harm.'

'Didn't he just!' said Gildas.

'You have to admit,' said Jack, 'that he was the most remarkable person we ever met.'

'We admit it,' said Gildas. 'Now do stop drinking whisky. You won't be able to sing properly.'

'We shall sing better. But perhaps not that Tallis motet.'

Supper had consisted of fishcakes and boiled potatoes followed by bread and cheese, followed by chocolate biscuits. This feast was by now so far in the past that Jack and Ludens were hungry again and were tearing up the brown loaf and hacking off chunks of cheddar cheese. Red wine, brought by Jack, had preceded the whisky. Gildas and his piano occupied a flat at the top of an office building off the Marylebone Road. The building was empty after six in the evening, which made piano-playing and even lusty singing possible until far into the night. The flat was small and smelt of ancient things with which Gildas had not contended. In the sitting room shadowy photographs of Italian lakes had been hung high up by a previous tenant. There was a deal cupboard containing sheet music, always untidy, always open, a table covered with (usually fresh) newspaper, and a fierce little upright sofa upon which no one sat. Gildas possessed, apart from his radio, no modern technology: no typewriter of course or word processor or hi fi or television, but also no vacuum cleaner. Even the brooms and brushes, also inherited, were old and bald. Nothing was cleaned, except (imperfectly) plates and cutlery. Anything which fell on the floor stayed there and was dealt with by passing feet. The floor of the bedroom was covered with tangled garments. Jack and Ludens deplored and pitied but did not exactly disapprove of Gildas's chaos. They worried about him. Since parting company with the priesthood he could almost be said to have become demoralised. Almost, for somehow he remained someone, a slightly mysterious someone, whom they respected, and they gave him the benefit of every doubt.

Gildas was said to be a solitary man, but he depended very much, or so Jack and Ludens told each other, upon his few close friends. He and Jack were indeed very old friends, having been at school together in Yorkshire, whither Gildas's Methodist parents had moved from

Wales in search of elusive employment. Gildas could not be said to be a successful man. His musical aspirations had dwindled, he never became a composer, and he had lost his choir. He had, after being ordained an Anglican priest, also lost his faith, whether or not by reason of Marcus Vallar's criticisms. He worked in an evangelical bookshop in Bloomsbury. Jack Sheerwater, on the other hand, was a success, he was a well-known painter and had even become a rich one. There was some truth in Jack's claim that Marcus had 'set him up'. Marcus had quarrelled with Jack as he had quarrelled with Gildas and with Patrick; but before he disappeared from their lives he had, it seemed, given Jack a 'vision' with which he had lived ever since. Alfred Ludens could not, as yet, be classified as either a success or a failure, and did not himself know which he was or whether he was moving up or down. Ludens had met Jack, who was a few years his senior, and through Jack Gildas, in London at a series of lectures on Italian painting. Ludens, then twenty, was studying history at University College. Jack had lately been appointed a teacher at the art school where he had been a student. Gildas, not long ordained, was a young curate with command of a choir. Patrick Fenman was a penniless poet from Ireland whose aim, successfully achieved, was to become a penniless poet in Soho. He had published some poems and was able plausibly to style himself 'a literary man'. He met Jack, and then Gildas and Ludens, in they could never remember which Soho pub, perhaps the Fitzroy, perhaps the Wheat-sheaf, perhaps the York Minster. They adopted the Irishman and were already a little 'group' when Marcus Vallar burst upon them, as Jack said, 'like Halley's Comet'. Some time had elapsed since that event.

Gildas, the Welshman, was very thin and not exactly deformed but twisted, his nose crooked, his head inclining to his shoulder, his hands (although he played the piano so beautifully) seeming to be put on back to front. Jack compared him to a parched contorted tree off which little dry things were always falling. His ill-shaven face, textured like old brown faded paper, was wrinkled, often with suspicion or anxiety or quizzical doubt, or with sadness. His head was rather small, his dry dark hair was fuzzy, over mild brown eyes he wore spectacles with small round lenses. He was the one who stood in corners and watched. Jack Sheerwater was never in a corner, he came from Yorkshire where his father was a self-made businessman. He was built on a large scale, soon to be threatened with stoutness, but still self-confidently handsome, blond, his bright untidy hair falling with careless charm almost to his shoulders. He had a fair, glowing complexion and promi-nent blue eyes. He dressed stylishly in an old-fashioned Bohemian mode

5

and dyed his own shirts. A pre-Raphaelite painter might have posed him as Sir Galahad, or more likely Sir Lancelot, but his face was harder than that of an Arthurian knight and he could equally well have passed for a latter-day soldier, some calm commander, and, with his authoritative nose and powerful staring eyes, had been said to resemble the Duke of Wellington as portrayed by Goya. His voice, retaining some northern vowel sounds, was authoritative and deep. His success as a painter still surprised him and, if he had not met Vallar, he might well have been content with less provided he could be happy. This he certainly was, and was talented too; and enjoyed making others happy, glad to be well off not least because he could be generous. The remoter ancestors of Alfred Ludens were Jews in Poland, his paternal grand-parents had come to England as children. His second name, also considered amusing, was presumed to be a Latinised version of a Polish name. He knew little of his forebears. His father, now retired, had taught classics at a minor public school in Somerset where Ludens had been educated free of charge. His mother vanished when Ludens was an infant and was later reported dead. A stepmother (gentile) took her place and presented Ludens with a halfbrother. This pair, unpleasing to him, also vanished when Ludens was fourteen, by which time he had developed the mysterious speech impediment which troubled him at rare intervals. His father still lived in the house where Ludens had grown up, had no Jewish friends, never spoke of Jewish matters, and had never visited the synagogue. Ludens, becoming as he grew up aware of Judaism as a historical phenomenon, attempted to feel Jewish, but usually preferred to say that he had no sense of identity, a claim which astonished Jack and was envied by Gildas.

Ludens was a fairly tall, thin, long-legged young man with a good deal of straight dark hair which, rising above his brow, swept behind his ears and bestowed itself neatly down the back of his neck. He had high cheek-bones, a long nose, expressive nostrils, long narrow brown eyes and a sensuous mouth with a large lower lip. He had a kindly benevolent though clever expression and what Gildas called a daft Jewish grin. He suffered from an intermittent stammer. He had had, so far, a successful academic career, with a first-class and a doctorate, and now held a coveted though not lucrative 'readership' at a London college, which involved some teaching and some time to write and study. In the small circle where his talents were known, much was expected of him. Ludens belonged firmly to the old school of historians who believed that a historian must know the whole of history. He was criticised by some for scattering his talents too widely, and for being, as one of his teachers put it, a 'romantic', fascinated by attractive personalities (such as Hannibal, Leonardo, Peter the Great, Stonewall Jackson). The same teacher told him, 'not being a genius, Ludens, you should attempt to do something, not everything'. Ludens settled down to a steady attachment to the Italian Renaissance, though without forswearing either his polymath ambitions or his romanticism. He had published two short but respected books, one called *Giordano Bruno in Oxford*, the other on the sun symbolism of Dante; and had just now been granted a sabbatical term in which to pursue research for some more lengthy work. But Ludens was still dissatisfied with his position and with himself, although he could not readily explain why, or what he desired instead. Perhaps it was just that he had always thought of himself as capable of 'some great achievement', but could not yet – and meanwhile time was passing – establish what kind of thing this might be. He felt that his father, with whom he had a close though extremely strained and laconic relation, was disappointed in him. Was he really a historian, ought he to be doing something quite else, being an anthropologist, or a philosopher, or a novelist, even a painter? He had no 'native tongue'. He felt an anxious diffusion of energies which belonged to a younger age. Moreover, was it not time to think of getting married? Though not without experience, he had no one in view. Women were always a problem. Also, he had been seriously unsettled by Marcus Vallar.

They could all remember when, at the beginning of that momentous, perhaps fatal, year, they had first set eyes on Marcus. Jack and Ludens saw him simultaneously as he entered a studio at the art school, searching for Jack to whom he was to 'report'. It was an amazing fact, upon which Jack frequently remarked, that Marcus had appeared in his life as *his pupil*. Marcus, who was ten years older than Jack, was of course already quite a famous man, Ludens had even heard of him from friends at Cambridge, where Marcus had spent his years of glory and where his legend still lingered on. Vallar was a great mathematician, a genius at nineteen, indeed, as Ludens and his friends, meditating upon the Vallar mystery, pointed out to each other, a genius at *three*, since he had been a mathematical infant prodigy. At nineteen he discovered something amazing called the Vallar Theorem which shook the mathematical world and interested astrophysicists. After that, after the great explosion of intellectual sovereignty, and fame, less was heard of Vallar. He was after a few years said to be 'burnt out', as such precociously brilliant thinkers often were. He amused himself by becoming a chess champion. He showed no interest in physics or mathematical logic, he despised computers, he was briefly fascinated by philosophy but soon 'saw through it' – he had found, as they said, intellectually speaking, 'nowhere to go'. The small area upon which the laser beam of his intelligence had so effectively concentrated afforded him no new insights. Jack and Ludens and the others, who later became his 'associates' (scarcely his friends, he seemed to have no friends), never encountered (perhaps Vallar himself saw to that) any of his old mathematical colleagues who might have, not unmaliciously, bemoaned or explained his downfall. People less 'in the know', who discussed it all later on, sometimes blamed Vallar for lacking the humility to continue as an academic mathematician of more ordinary, by comparison, though of course still considerable, talents. 'He had to be king or nothing', a former colleague was reported as saying, and Ludens understood this and, after he met Vallar, sympathised, silently of course, with the anguish of that dethronement. However, as it rather slowly dawned on the group of people who then came to know him at, or through, the art school, Marcus had no intention of ceasing to be a genius. He was diligently and ingeniously finding out how to be one by other means. He had decided to learn to paint. He unfortunately lacked the deep understanding of music which many mathematicians are said to possess. If anything he rather disliked music. But he had already discovered, perhaps through an early interest in geometry, an affinity with the visual arts, or at least, as he might have put it, an interest in certain problems of visual cognition. He wished now to learn some relevant techniques, and with this end in view appeared suddenly before the amazed eyes of Jack and Alfred.

Marcus was at that time, or certainly seemed to his stunned admirers to be, extremely good-looking. He was as tall as Jack, just over six feet, and looked as young, with plenty of longish curly reddish-blond hair. He had a long pale face with a clear almost feminine complexion, and when his long locks fell about and looked like a wig Jack said that he resembled some eighteenth-century beau or famous scholar in a contemporary portrait. Ludens preferred to compare him to a Renaissance prince. He was certainly dignified. He was at that time something of a dandy, wore high collars and cravats and well-cut expensive clothes, and an unobtrusively smart green overall for painting. He had large long grey eyes which could express some almost supernatural degree of attention. Sometimes these eyes were cold or gleamed dangerously, sometimes they just stared. They could compel people to run from the room. He was credited with hypnotic powers. He had a thin, faintly aquiline, nose. His mouth in repose was shapely and pensive,

8

longish, the lips perfect, Botticelli-allegorical as Jack styled them; his features generally chiselled as with authority by some Greek sculptor to be expressive of some universal, more than human, charm. It was Ludens who, studying the mouth and eyes, at once perceived that Marcus was Jewish, and must be, from the reddish hair, Sephardic. Marcus had a deep soft voice, slightly sing-song, slightly roughened, thickened like crystalline honey, which emerged with an arresting slow deliberation. His utterance was emphatic and precise, and although having grown up mainly in England and having acquired a Cambridge accent, he spoke like a foreigner. He was not given to autobiography, but Ludens, later, managed to learn that he had been born in Switzerland, where his parents, with whom he seemed to have nil relations, still lived; some remoter ancestors had lived in Romania. He had evidently spent his early childhood in a polyglot society and spoke several European languages fluently.

Ludens, also later on, endeavoured to 'explain' Marcus to his friends as a 'Jewish puritan'. He did not drink or smoke, never talked about sex or about women, was easily shocked, even angered, by swearing or loose talk, and never mentioned money (with which rumour said he was loaded). While assuming, perhaps unreasonably, that everyone knew he was Jewish, he did not talk about Judaism and was, Ludens suspected, not interested in Jewishness. Nor was he interested in politics, or topical matters generally, or gossip or 'news'. He abominated television. In company he was often abstracted but could listen attentively in silence. If he joined a conversation he did not necessarily dominate it, but directed it firmly toward his own concerns. Whether speaking or not he had an unobtrusive, unselfconscious, air of superiority. Even as a pupil he was, while docile, instinctively superior, as if aware that he had only to work hard in order to grasp principles which would soon set him free to excel. He retained in all this, perhaps simply through being *deeply* interested (he would not attend at all to anything which did not interest him) an air of self-confident modesty which somehow mingled felicitously with his assumption of superiority. Men who met him were usually fascinated, often captivated, never other than deferential. Women, though sometimes inclined to fall in love with him, were usually more suspicious and one or two (including Ludens's then girl friend Sylvia) found him in some ineffable way *awful*. Marcus, known to be married but not living with his wife, seemed to have, and Ludens was certain had, no sex life. Later on when Jack and his friends got to know Marcus better and had discussions with him on various matters they saw the handsome face touched by some less

attractive emotions. Marcus did not suffer fools gladly and was prepared to make frank and often adverse value judgments. He quickly
assessed individuals and did not keep his views to himself. Nor were
Jack and his friends exempted from what Jack later called the 'poisoned
darts'. A group of the students in due course became frightened of him,
turned against him, said he had the 'evil eye', and refused to mention
his name. There was no doubt that Marcus was, as Ludens agreed with
Jack, Gildas, Patrick, Sylvia, Franca (who was by then living with Jack
but not yet married to him) and others on various evenings in Soho, a
fearful egoist, the *biggest egoist* they had ever met. But they also agreed
that he was a colossal human being whom they were very fortunate
indeed to know.

Something that amazed them exceedingly was that Marcus was
becoming before their eyes quite a talented painter. He was a very
diligent student. He was a natural draughtsman, had, Jack said, a
'beautiful line', and attended the life class daily. He quickly learnt all
he could from Jack about colour, paint, oil, brushes, how to prepare a
canvas, how to mix, how to apply, surfaces, media, lightness, darkness,
and indeed subject matter. He liked drawing but had no interest in
water-colour. At that time Jack, who had of course 'gone abstract'
during his student days, had returned to figurative painting, favouring
interiors, tables or mantelpieces in the style of Vuillard or Bonnard,
but with a 'Euston Road' light. His labours in this sober style were
even having a certain influence on his pupils. Marcus did a few creditable
tables and mantelpieces and then began to find his own style as an
abstract painter. He was particularly interested in space, about which
he questioned Jack without much profit. 'He wants a *theory*,' Jack told
the others, 'and I haven't got one.' Marcus spoke of developing his own
theory, offered various ideas found to be incomprehensible, and then
began to produce large brilliantly coloured abstract works. These
paintings, some of which were later exhibited in a gallery in Cork Street
and sold for quite large sums of money were, as Jack publicly admitted,
the origin of Jack Sheerwater's new style, which he had been developing
ever since and which, since he went on painting and Marcus did not,
he could claim to have 'taken over'. (A particular remarkable colour,
which had originally been called 'Vallar red', was later known as
'Sheerwater red'.) Meanwhile, as Marcus diligently and furiously continued to paint, and Jack discussed his pupil with his painter and dealer
friends, Marcus's work became the victim of interpretation: it was
labelled the 'new Tantric', and taken to represent, in the Indian tradition, the creation of the universe, heaven and hell, sexual intercourse,

lingams, vulvas, lotuses and so on. Marcus (who never told a lie) replied, amazed, that he knew nothing about Indian art, and that his pictures did not represent anything or derive from anything. Questioned about his geometrical mandalas, orange objects floating in seas of red, red globes in seas of blue-black, circles, triangles, ovals, knotted lines, shapes suggesting seeds, trees, flowers, fishes, flames, he said that he was 'simply painting', experimenting with colours and shapes and space, and could 'see nothing' of the so-called 'meanings', some of which shocked him very much.

Then suddenly it all stopped. Marcus had been allotted his special corner or alcove where he worked all day, evidently taking pleasure in the process, but showing no interest in the finished product. As the canvases multiplied Jack carefully removed them, stowed them, catalogued them, and (later on), organised the exhibition at the well-known gallery and wrote the (at the time) much-quoted introduction to the catalogue. This exhibition (which Jack said Marcus had agreed to and Marcus said he had not) was one of the causes, together with the 'new Tantric' business, of the rupture between them, but that too was later. During his 'life as a painter' Marcus had been living, presumably alone, in a lodging in Acton which existed only as an address, no one was invited there. The discussions during which Jack and his friends became so spellbound took place at the art school, or in certain quiet pubs which Marcus tolerated as a meeting place. One day Jack arrived at the school to find Marcus's corner empty, all signs of occupation missing. Courageously, Jack took a taxi to Acton. Marcus was packing suitcases. He explained that the period which he had decided to devote to painting was now over, that he was most grateful to Jack, that he was now returning to live (he did not say where) with his wife, and to devote himself to other studies (he did not say what). Then he vanished.

There followed a period of eclipse. Ludens was at the university. Gildas was busy with his music and his pastoral duties and with the 'crisis of faith' which led to his leaving the priesthood, Jack was developing, out of Marcus's style, his own style, and the commercial success which later enabled him to give up teaching and devote all his energies to painting. About this time too he got married to Franca. Franca, older than Jack, had studied dress design and more perfunctorily painting, at a polytechnic. She was half Italian, born in England. Patrick, said to be now subsidised by Jack, published a book of poems. Time passed. Ludens's father retired, but continued to live in Somerset in the stone-built cottage in which Ludens had grown up. Ludens acquired his doctorate, then a teaching post and a flat in St John's Wood. It was

Patrick who first got on the trail of the vanished genius who thereafter, for a period of a few years, remained intermittently visible. Jack and Ludens had been, in the interim, active in seeking for news of him; there had been alleged sightings in France, in Germany, even in America. It turned out, however, that Marcus, when discovered, was not far away, was living in London, in Richmond, again devoid of wife and daughter. Jack and Ludens had pursued simple rational methods of search, such as telephone books, libraries, galleries, bookshops, academic institutions. Patrick, following some instinctive Irish intuition, simply walked about (like Wordsworth, he composed poetry when walking) different parts of London until he met Marcus one day in the street. The idea, not new, that Patrick was psychic was revived and refurbished at this period.

Of course they had all speculated about what had happened to Marcus and what he was doing now. What he was doing now, it soon emerged, was learning Sanscrit and Japanese. He actually had his Japanese teacher, a threatening figure with long black hair, living with him in his small flat. After the encounter with Patrick, reported as amicable, Ludens and Jack, and later cautiously Pat, visited Marcus. He surprised them by treating their reappearance in his life, after a considerable interval, as something perfectly natural and unsurprising, and he talked to them in his familiar manner as if their discussions had ceased only yesterday. At this stage in proceedings, as became even clearer later, the attitude of Ludens to their hero began to diverge from that of the others. They remained fascinated, in Pat's case positively attached, but agreed that whatever Marcus was up to was 'far above their heads', and that it was now impossible to talk with him on anything like equal terms. What, in any case, had they talked about in those old art school days? They could not clearly remember; then they had all been so young. Now it was different. When Jack asked Marcus if he still did any painting Marcus said 'No!' in a surprised tone, and Jack did not pursue the matter. They could not now, they felt, trace or follow Marcus's path. There was no doubting his tremendous energy, his concentration, his power, in which they heartily believed, to master whatever he wished to learn. But now they felt themselves no longer fellow-seekers but awe-struck spectators of a mysterious phenomenon, deeply affected by his person and presence but no longer able to communicate. Whereas what had happened to Ludens, who was certainly 'attached', was that he had begun to take a deep and passionate interest in Marcus's *ideas*, in which he clearly 'saw' something which the others did not. He was not content, as they were, to admit that he did not understand. This interest later on became an obsession, as if Marcus were the possessor of an intellectual secret, some master-key, talisman, password or radiant lump of deep fundamental knowledge which, if it could be acquired, would shine through all other knowledge, utterly transforming it.

Marcus now looked somewhat older, though his red-blond locks were undimmed. His clothes were shabbier, but with a colourful scarf at the neck he could still look like a poor student in an opera who is of course a prince in disguise. He complained of his asthma which had not been heard of before. A faint frown had been sketched in above his large grey eyes which were so wide apart and could express anxiety and deep puzzlement. He sometimes even looked *tired*. Ludens often, and Jack and Gildas and Patrick less often, now came to Marcus in the early evening, after his day's work (he rose, and went to bed, early), and were gratified to find how ready he was to talk to them. The 'talk' in fact consisted of a monologue by Marcus in which he rehearsed various problems, evidently finding it useful to do so, even to a silent audience. Ludens, concentrating hard, attempted to frame intelligent questions which Marcus sometimes picked up and sometimes ignored. Gildas, concentrating less hard, ventured a question or two. Jack and Pat, not concentrating at all, simply enjoyed the show. On two occasions the sessions were also attended by a Cambridge mathematician called Raymond Schutz, an old associate, who made a few incomprehensible remarks. The threatening Japanese was sometimes silently present, making no secret of his disapproval of the intruders. Another, perhaps surprisingly tolerated, spectator was the landlady, a Miss Helena McCann, who delighted in calling Marcus 'the Professor' and said she could not understand a word but just loved to hear him holding forth. It did not occur to Ludens or Gildas or Pat or even Jack to speculate about Marcus's sex life. It was somehow still obvious that he had none. The Japanese? Impossible. The persistently absent wife was quite sufficient, somehow appropriate, as if his sexual being must be a matter of absences and ideas.

Ludens's obsession with Marcus's thoughts was encouraged by Marcus's own evident sense of an urgent quest. He was 'on the track of something'. He spoke (and Ludens felt he *almost* understood) about deep foundations, pure cognition, the nature of consciousness, a universal language underlying the tongues of east and west. He gratified Jack by seeming to take his experiments in painting as an element or stage in his journey whereby he had discovered something about perception or space. This was never explained, but triumphantly taken by Jack to prove something which he had often preached to the others, that painting was the most fundamental, and so the greatest, of the arts. During this period Ludens was constantly frustrated by not managing to be alone with Marcus. He wanted to seize him by the lapels of his faded green corduroy jacket, drive him against the wall, and *shout* questions at him: not the neat carefully-phrased queries which he cautiously offered when the others were there, but the real deep crude muddled questions which, if Marcus could at all respond to them, might *get him somewhere*. As it was, even when he arrived early or lingered late he would find, if no one else, the Japanese installed, or else running up the stairs in front of him, hissing softly, or Miss McCann ('Don't mind me, I'm just a little mouse!') sitting in a corner acting as chaperone. When Marcus did attempt a reply to one of Ludens's 'official' questions Ludens would find, however hard he listened, that he would soon lose the thread, and was unable to check his mentor at those crucial points at which his understanding failed. Although it was evident that Marcus had read the great philosophical works of the past, references to other thinkers (which might have afforded clues) were never taken up. He showed no interest in contemporary philosophers and evidently despised them. It was as though the conceptual space in which Marcus's mind moved did not anywhere connect with that of Ludens – and yet it *must* connect, there *must* be a way through. What Marcus was after must sometime, somewhere, be explicable in lucid intellectual terms, there must be a way of putting it which would at last make all things clear. Meanwhile he had to console himself by a strange intuition which made him connect Marcus's reflections with something dark, almost morbid, in his own interests, and preferences: certain arcane historical problems, certain mysteries of the Renaissance, and the third and fourth centuries after Christ, and among the ancient Greeks, and indeed elsewhere and everywhere since *that* was an aspect of human nature itself. Yet what was it? What could be more respectable than 'deep foundations'? What *was* Marcus after? When Ludens mentioned this line of thought to Gildas he was ill received. Gildas shuddered, said he would not be at all surprised to find out (except that one would never find out) that what Marcus was seeking was actually magical power. He even said (which upset Ludens very much) 'There's something evil there'; and went on to question the motives of Ludens's obsession. But Ludens had already decided to leap over his motives.

However, before he could find any satisfactory clues or footholds, or analyse what Gildas called 'the smell' of it all, the second manifestation of Marcus Vallar came to an end just as abruptly as the first.

Ludens arrived one day to find Miss McCann in tears. The Professor was leaving London and retiring to live 'in the country'. It was true. Ludens and the others agreed later that the situation had been poisoned by the possessive jealousy of the Japanese disciple. This person now announced with odious satisfaction that he and Mr Vallar were indeed departing to the seclusion and privacy of a quiet country retreat. ('He was always bothered by the motor car noise here,' Miss McCann admitted.) The Japanese did not say where this was. Miss McCann did not know, and Marcus was pointedly vague or perhaps actually was uncertain. 'He's being kidnapped!' said Jack.

Marcus's departure was in fact marred, certainly marked, by sudden volleys of the 'poisoned darts' later referred to by Jack. Ludens explained this to the victims (he himself was exempt) by saying that Marcus had realised that they (Jack, Pat, Gildas) were 'tourists' who were simply amusing themselves. Whatever the reason, Marcus engineered quarrels wherein he denounced them, individually, insulted them and 'washed his hands of them', causing serious damage in two cases. Marcus did not accuse Jack of having copied his style, but did accuse him of being a facile commercially-minded painter with a vile promiscuous sex life. Jack became angry and left in a rage, banging the door (to the horror of Miss McCann). However, his generous sanguine temperament remained unwounded by Marcus's venom; soon afterwards he could cheerfully laugh, and say 'Maybe he's right!' Gildas, who had still (Ludens believed) not recovered from being roughed up by Marcus, was more easily demolished, since Marcus had simply to harp upon the doubts which the poor priest already possessed. It was pointed out that Gildas, as an intelligent rational man, could not believe in the old personal God or the divinity of Christ. And what about the oath which he had taken when he was ordained? Was he not, among his simple superstitious flock, living a lie? Gildas agreed. Yes, he, Gildas, was a deceiver, a charlatan, a false priest, a merchant of false consoling superstitions. He added that nevertheless, for reasons which he did not think Marcus would understand, he did not intend to lay down the burden of the priesthood. Marcus replied that naturally he preferred a pleasant vicarage and his prestige and his choir and easily earned salary to the ordeal of facing the truth! Gildas retired from the contest and not long afterward left the church. The case of Pat was more mysterious. The others were ready to assume that what Patrick meant by a 'curse' was simply some piece of instant savaging which had accidentally struck a nerve. No doubt some cruel words had been uttered which had sunk into the superstitious soul of that playboy of the western world. But

Patrick, saying darkly that 'he knew about curses', maintained that a 'poetic rhyme' had been spoken, and 'words in a foreign tongue', and that Marcus's face had become 'quite other' as if he had put on a mask. Pat's friends did not take this too seriously; Pat himself, unable to explain what had occasioned Marcus's attack, fell silent about the matter, and it was assumed that he, like Jack, had suffered no deep wound. Ludens at this time, sympathising with his friends, made no attempt to excuse or analyse Marcus's destructive conduct; but he had silently made a vow that henceforth he would follow Marcus wherever he went until he could satisfy himself whether Marcus really possessed a secret, and whether he, Ludens, could come into possession of it.

The first difficulty, to find out where Marcus was now hidden, proved fairly easily overcome. It did not at once occur to Ludens to return to see Miss McCann, as he assumed she also had been kept in the dark. However, when he did, on the off-chance, go to see her it emerged that the Japanese had, at the very last moment, divulged the coveted address to her under a terrible seal of secrecy. (He was expecting a letter from Tokyo which she was to forward.) Miss McCann, also capable of jealousy, had never cared for the oriental disciple, and now felt she was being bullied. So when Ludens appeared with his urgent questions she was soon persuaded, telling him that *he* had always been her favourite and was the 'only really nice one' who had genuinely loved and revered the Professor. Ludens did not hesitate to profit from her disclosure and, without telling the others (whom he hoped to surprise with his success) presented himself, after what he felt to be a decent and tactful interval, at the door of the country retreat, a cottage in a small village near Sevenoaks in Kent. He did not write beforehand since he assumed the Japanese would censor the mail. What happened after that, and will be related later, was something entirely unexpected and so awful that Ludens had never spoken about it afterwards to anyone.

Not long after this catastrophe, which effectively ended Ludens's then friendship with Marcus, Marcus left England, bound, it was rumoured, for America, and then Japan. News of Marcus's later adventures did, at this period, reach England at intervals. An American ex-pupil of Ludens, called Ephraim Baker, now studying in Los Angeles, reported that Marcus was in California and involved with some kind of spiritual or religious group who went in for meditation and for physical feats and exertions designed to stir up the unconscious mind. Later news said that, perhaps as the result of some excessive feat, Marcus had had an accident, but had recovered. Ludens's informant, who had become something of a Vallar-watcher, sent some newspaper cuttings as evidence that Marcus had attained some local fame as a guru, or at any rate as an amusing eccentric. The same informant later wrote to say that Marcus had disappeared, some said to Japan, some to India. After that nothing was heard for some time. Then another source, one of Jack's students, now an architect, who had known Marcus slightly, wrote to Jack reporting that Marcus was back in Europe and living in Germany. By this time, however, Ludens and his friends did not expect, nor for their various reasons wish, to meet Marcus Vallar again. Ludens even ceased to want news of him, so painful was it to think that Marcus existed somewhere and might sometimes remember Ludens. Those who had found him so impressive spoke of him less and less, except sometimes to refer to him as a crazy eccentric and marvel at the power he had once exerted over them. Only as time passed did Ludens revive, and rediscover in his heart, in spite of the horror which divided them, a deep secret curiosity about Marcus and a wish, which he thought would never now be satisfied, to know whether he had discovered the thing he was seeking. He wondered too, as he had wondered jealously in the old days, whether in some other place Marcus were surrounded by disciples who understood him – or worst of all had found at last the *only one* who understood. This state of affairs had existed for some time when the mysterious illness of Patrick Fenman made them all wonder where Marcus Vallar was and whether he were destined once again to play a part in their lives.

'Of course he may be dead,' said Gildas.

'I somehow think we'd know if he was,' said Ludens.

'I don't see why. You are superstitious about him. Do you think an angel would inform us?'

'The basis of this conversation is superstition,' said Ludens. 'We think he can perform a miracle.'

'Well, perhaps he can raise the dead. By now it's probably the only thing he hasn't tried!'

'I wonder if he's still worrying about pure cognition.'

'It means knowledge without concepts,' said Ludens. 'But what does that mean?'

'I believe it's what angels do,' said Gildas, 'Marcus would regard that as a challenge.'

'And the universal language, and consciousness and all that, these things must connect.'

'Why should they?' said Gildas to Ludens. 'You think Marcus's mind is one great organic whole. It may just be a cluster of random whims.

17

As for deep foundations, what a hope! Our lives rest upon contingency, rubble, rubbish. There aren't any foundations except mud and chaos.'

'Of course mathematics is a universal language,' said Ludens. 'He thought he could do the same with natural language. It's not a completely crazy idea. Like Pat thinks poetry is a universal language.'

'Pat doesn't think,' said Gildas, 'he is. And Marcus's trouble is that he is not. He's a restless insubstantial being. And he just can't stop imagining he's a genius – such a man is dangerous. He wants to model all spiritual and intellectual life on mathematics. No wonder –'

'He didn't want to talk about other philosophers,' said Ludens. 'He thought he could do it all himself.'

'Is philosophy still possible?' said Gildas. 'I doubt it. It's all a matter of temperament anyway, like some people love Aristotle and Dante and other people love Plato and Shakespeare.'

'I think he got there in the first move,' said Jack. 'Pure cognition is what painters have, and the language of the planet is painting, pictures, what everyone understands! Painting is pre-conceptual. Painters just *see* what's *really there*!'

'It is true,' said Ludens, 'that Leonardo thought painting was the king of the arts, it was where science and art overlapped. He likens it to mathematics, which depends on intuition, and cannot be taught if not innate. He calls it a fundamental science.'

'There you are! No wonder Marcus came straight to an art school when he decided to look for the Absolute!'

'It may well be,' murmured Gildas, 'that we shall all end up looking at simple pictures which everyone understands. A very small number of mathematicians will organise everything else.'

'He may have got at the other arts by now!' said Ludens. 'Perhaps he'll crop up in a year or two as the author of some massive best-selling novel.'

'Never!' said Gildas. 'In order to write a novel you have to notice a few human beings.'

'Not now you don't!' said Jack.

'Music?'

'No,' said Gildas, 'Marcus had no music in his soul. Though I remember he once said he liked the late Beethoven quartets.'

'Actually he was near the answer in his *very* first move,' said Ludens. 'Mathematics, atomic physics, molecular biology, DNA. *There's* foundation for you.'

'A horrible answer,' said Gildas, 'but doubtless correct, even obvious.

I prefer to think of the music of the spheres. Or love, which is said to make the world go round.'

'Sex is what makes the world go round,' said Jack.

'You're drunk.'

'Sex is the fundamental energy which produces everything that's good, it joins flesh and spirit, it's the only spiritual thing that is available everywhere. Painting is based on sex. Why are there no good women painters? After all they've had every chance to practise *that* art! It's because women don't have sexual fantasies.'

'Don't be silly, Jack!' said Ludens. 'What makes you think they don't?'

'I just know. Don't you agree, Gildas?'

'I prefer not to reflect on the matter,' said Gildas. 'In fact, what's deepest is the idea of goodness, without which we would not survive.'

'Music,' said Ludens, 'cosmic rhythm. He probably got into Taoism in the Far East. Breathing exercises. Zen. *That's* about smashing conceptual thought to reach the non-conceptual or the pre-conceptual or the particular or something which is also supposed to make you selfless, though I don't quite see why. Koans would have suited Marcus down to the ground.'

'Marcus *is* a koan,' said Gildas.

'Someone told us,' said Jack, 'you remember? that Marcus went round India disguised as a Muslim woman! From behind a black veil he saw everything!'

'He should have gone to Greece,' said Gildas, 'the gods are still there I'm told. He'd get on well with the Greek gods, omnipotent egoists always doing geometry. Actually I doubt if he got farther than California. I bet he's still there, half crazy and stuffed with drugs. If we met him now we'd think he was pathetic, we'd be embarrassed.'

'That's what you want to think,' said Ludens. 'I see him as a god from elsewhere who has lost his way, or more like a holy man, a sort of mystic.'

'Nothing that Marcus was pursuing had anything to do with morality,' said Gildas. 'He didn't understand morality, *that's* a concept he hadn't got. A dose of ordinary morality would have killed him.'

'Well, who says mysticism has to do with morality?' said Jack. 'Pass the whisky, Alfred.'

'He wanted to be a universal man,' said Ludens, 'and I suppose that isn't possible now. He belongs in fifteenth-century Italy. This age doesn't suit him.'

'Oh, I don't know,' said Gildas, 'this is an age of demons and amoral angels and all sorts of deep fears, like the first centuries of the Christian era, it's an age of extreme solutions.'

'That's right!' said Jack. 'Marcus is a demon, and he's certainly extreme! Extreme solutions are *forced* upon us now. This is just his time. Marcus is beyond good and evil!'

'Beyond good and evil equals evil,' said Gildas.

'Pat said he was like an elf or a leprechaun,' said Ludens, 'something weird or uncanny.'

'Yes, distinctly *unheimlich*,' said Gildas. 'But perhaps we are being too ingenious. Ludens said Marcus was childish, and there's something in it. Because he was a mathematical prodigy he didn't have a proper ordinary education, or a real ordinary childhood. He's cold and unsocial and self-centred and awkward and absolutely lacking in common sense and sensibility. He's become a grown-up child who's amazed at everything and wants everything. He wants to draw the whole world into himself and make it identical with his will. It was that amazement which impressed us so, and that *greed*. But maths was the only thing he really understood, at everything else he was tenth-rate, he simply lacked savvy, he lacked *sense*.'

'But the paintings –'

'We were just surprised he could do it at all.'

'That's not fair,' said Ludens, 'there's something heroic about him, there's something so brave in not giving up, being determined to become another sort of genius!'

'It's mad all the same,' said Jack. 'It is hard luck of course. If you're a genius at nineteen it's downhill all the way. It must be awful, famous at nineteen and done for at twenty-four.'

'Like Newton,' said Gildas.

'Yes, it's the Newton complex! He looks a bit like Newton actually. Wasn't Newton over at twenty-four? He spent the rest of his life writing theological prophecies or something.'

'I expect that's what Marcus is doing,' said Gildas. 'It's megalomania pure and simple. I see him as a false prophet, pseudo-scientist, pseudo-philosopher. He got a whiff of determinism from his scientific friends and it was too much for him, he thinks he can see deep structure by pure thought. Alchemy, Hermes Trismegistus, Solomon's ring, it's always been going on, the cheap quackery that dresses up power as wisdom and promises instant salvation, now it's scientology and astrology and spiritualism and psychoanalysis and –'

'Intuition,' said Jack, 'that's what mathematicians live by. How can one imagine that kind of thought? It's like Mozart. Marcus was used to those vast leaps and having immense systems packed up inside his head. Then he imagined he could apply it to everything. Pity he didn't stick to painting, all right he wasn't *great* –'

'He's not really an artist,' said Gildas. 'If he were that might save him.'

'Of course all sorts of things might save him,' said Jack, 'like the love of a good woman!'

'His wife?'

'I don't see her as amounting to much – no one ever even saw her. He needs someone else.'

'On your theory,' said Gildas, 'every man needs two women, a quiet home-maker and a thrilling nymph.'

'Yes,' said Jack, 'and that suits them too. Women are an alien tribe, they are not like us, they understand themselves through us, like plants and animals, we make them exist, they are, quite unconsciously, terrifying, they are sibyls, priestesses, queens of the night, they are frightened of themselves, they need a man to calm them and make them into friendly deities.'

'What tosh you talk, Jack,' said Ludens. 'All you mean is that you like to have a wife and a mistress.'

'It's the principle of the Trinity, like in Christianity and Hegel. It works, you've *seen* it work. In every woman there is a calm principle and a restless principle, you have to intuit which to encourage, which role they want to play. Some women want to be earth goddesses, others want adventures.'

'You disgust me,' said Gildas.

'Your arrangement works because Franca will put up with anything,' said Ludens. 'And I don't believe that women are an alien tribe.'

'Until you understand that you will never get on with them,' said Jack. 'By the way, your announcement that you now want to get married has caused quite a stir in some quarters.'

'I didn't announce anything,' said Ludens irritably. 'I don't *know* anybody!'

'Alison says she's got exactly the girl for you, a friend of hers called Heather Allenby, she's dying to introduce you.'

'I've changed my mind.'

'Has it ever occurred to you, Alfred, that you don't really like civilised educated women? Some men are like that, they want coarse sturdy unrefined creatures who will rescue them from culture. A dark brutish gipsy girl would be just your type.'

'About Patrick –' said Gildas.

'"Upon the poet now rests the responsibility for the continuance of metaphysical wisdom as lived experience." Who said that? Pat used to quote it in pubs.'

'If only we could find Miss McCann.'

Of course they had gone to the house in Richmond, but it had changed hands, been turned into self-contained flats and no one there knew where Miss McCann had gone or who she was; nor could the telephone book yield up her whereabouts.

'I wonder if Pat knows where he is. He found him before by psychic means. If we could only communicate with Pat –'

'It's no use,' said Jack. 'Why don't you come and *look* at him, for Christ's sake? Even Franca can't get any sense out of him now. The Catholic priest has been round again like a vulture.' Jack put his finger on the rim of his glass and moved it round and round producing a humming sound, then a ringing sound rising to a scream.

Ludens covered his ears. 'Stop that!' said Gildas. 'Now will you sing or get out?'

They came to the piano. The Tallis motet was voted to be too difficult. Various glees and madrigals were considered and rejected. In the end they sang their usual medley of favourites: 'Hearts of Oak', 'The Road to Mandalay', 'Jeanie with the Light Brown Hair', 'Whistling Phil McHugh', 'Pale Hands I Loved', and 'Abide with Me'.

Franca had seen the pale white moon in the evening, and now again pale white in the early morning. Jack had come in, as she expected, late and drunk. He sang, very softly however, 'The Little Turtle Dove' as he came up the first flight of stairs. He fell silent as he mounted to where Franca slept now in the room next door to Patrick. Franca, who had put out her light, pretended to be asleep. The door opened, giving a little light from the landing, and Jack looked at her. She pretended to be asleep because she was too tired to have a, perhaps long, conversation with her husband, but also because Jack had told her once that he loved to see her sleeping. There was something peaceful and benign in that silent looking, better than his whispered talk, always excited after an evening with his friends, and the whisky breath of his good night kiss. He also liked to see her sewing or cooking or doing anything quiet and rhythmical in the house. He had watched her for a while in the dim light and then gone into the next room to look at Patrick. She heard his footsteps go downstairs as she fell asleep.

She rose early. The sky was clear and from a landing window she could see the moon, first gleaming, then paling, soon to be as pallid as a Wensleydale cheese. She could also see, from that particular window, between other houses, the Thames, or rather at that moment the mist that covered it. Jack and Franca lived in Chelsea. She dressed quickly. Now, since only a few days, she wondered each morning whether Pat had died in the night, and saw with a painful relief that the bedclothes still rose and fell. There was now a dire sense to the saying that 'our breaths are numbered'. Since she had been looking after him she had felt bound to him by a strange silent love. Of course she had known him for many years, but had felt shy of him, made nervous by his bouncy ways. He had treated her with a comical deference or with a facetious teasing wit to which, having no gift of repartee, she was unable to respond. Now he had become another being. He was already seriously ill when Jack moved him back into their house, and he had at first been polite and grateful to her as to a stranger. Perhaps he did not recognise her. He was polite in just the same way to Alison Merrick and to the nurse. Now, when she felt so deeply connected to him, they were finally estranged. This period had passed however, and Patrick was now alone with himself, tossing and murmuring and rambling, not seeming in pain but endlessly restless, shifting his limbs and moaning softly, clutching the sheet and at times stretching out his hands piteously in a way which brought tears to Franca's eyes. He was docile, could still sit up a little when prompted, move a little when they tidied the bed, and swallow the liquids which were tilted towards his lips. There were bedpans and routines of a functioning human being. These would cease soon, according to Doctor Hensman, he would cease to respond to stimuli, would fall into a coma, and pneumonia would bring about a peaceful end. Franca had become used to the thickening smell in the room which all the summer air could not dispel.

While he was still able to communicate Patrick had had a quiet mumbling talk with Father O'Harte, the Irish Roman Catholic priest, but whether he had (as the priest wished) made a confession Franca did not know or ask. She doubted whether anything as formal could have taken place; though perhaps any imagined willingness might serve on such an occasion. Pat had, according to his own account, abandoned his religion long ago; but he had not rejected the black-clad figure when he suggested himself. How the priest had discovered Patrick never became apparent. Jack did not hesitate to lead him to the sick man, hoping that if the ailment were really 'psychosomatic' religion might cure it. This did not happen however. Patrick continued to sink. Now the persistent priest was anxious to administer extreme unction. Franca, without asking anyone else, forbade this. She felt, superstitiously, that if the priest gave Patrick the last rites he would be prompting Patrick to die. Franca's Italian mother had been a Roman Catholic, though the circumstances of her marriage had prohibited religious observance and she had not managed to instruct her daughter. Franca had never attended that or any other church, but felt an uneasy affinity all the same. Few people came now to visit Patrick, or rather to look at him. The specialists had given up, Doctor Hensman looked in occasionally, the nurse Miss Moxon (who asked to be called 'Moxie') came every day to relieve the vigil of Franca and Alison. At the beginning of his illness various friends had arrived, Jerry Locke and Sidney Brett, both aspiring writers, Barry Titmus, a fellow-poet, and Ned Oliver, an elderly Irish friend; but these ceased to come, Ned because he was ill too and the others, Franca believed, because they were afraid of catching whatever it was Patrick had, which they had now come to believe was fatal. Even close friends like Gildas and Ludens appeared less often. They think he's done for, she thought, they assume he's as good as dead. And perhaps he is, and indeed she thought so herself.

Franca patted her hair and looked at herself in the mirror. She had put on weight, but only a bright light showed the very faint wrinkles. She always confronted her reflection with a kind of startled expectancy as if encountering someone who was to give her some message, reprimand or shock. Her lips parted, her dark large eyes grew larger and more eager, she put one long hand up to her throat. It was as if her face were new every day, inspected with anxiety in case it might be found to be disfigured in some way, pockmarked, scarred. At such moments she thought of her mother. Franca had long dark hair which when unconfined, curled a little and reached below her waist. It was not however, except in bed (Jack liked to lie upon it) granted such liberty, and Franca usually wore it drawn back into an exceedingly complex bun which her swift fingers could manufacture with almost miraculous speed. She thus had for Jack her 'Ingres look' or else, especially when she wore black, her 'Italian peasant look'. Her complexion was sallow, her mouth mobile, expressive of doubt and (even when she was happy) sadness, her eyes bright, questioning, but also gentle and timidly reserved. She possessed, Jack told her, the quality he valued most in a woman: repose. She made her own clothes and dressed with a smartness so unobtrusive as to render her (he told her) almost invisible. To please him she always wore very elegant expensive shoes. Franca's father, sitting at a café table in Perugia, had selected her once so pretty mother as she passed by in the evening *passeggiata*. He took her to England and later married her. Franca's father, who sold cars and drank a lot, was never very well off and became steadily less so. The marriage was not happy, her parents' endless quarrels tormented Franca's childhood, she saw her mother's tears and shed her own. Her mother was bullied, occasionally knocked about. Franca, mouse-like, kept out of her father's way. He had wanted a boy, but no other child was forthcoming. The mother died suddenly. Franca resolved at once not to speculate about that death. The father then married a young woman who was certainly not a recent acquaintance and disappeared to Canada, leaving Franca an eighteen-year-old student at a polytechnic in north London where she did a little painting and studied fashion and dress design.

In this student world, when she was twenty-one and he was eighteen, she met Jack Sheerwater and fell perfectly in love. Perfect love healed Franca of her damaged life, simply her loving him so much transformed her, and she became beautiful and happy. Suddenly she could do everything, dance, paint, sing, invent wonderful clothes, even write love poems. She tasted for the first time honey-sweet and dangerous happiness: dangerous because, as she before long began to learn, precarious. Could one forever be so virtuously in love that one expected nothing and did not even know of jealousy? Jack, beautiful, generous, joyful, sweet-tempered man-boy, the child of a happy home, was clearly framed for women's pleasure and had many female admirers. He appreciated Franca, apprehended her love which she certainly did not conceal, and was grateful. He resorted to her as to a friendly Sibyl, he sought her wise advice, he found in her company a haven of rest. He was fond of her, he valued her, he loved her, later he lived with her, later he married her, to the surprise of many, breaking numerous hearts. Of course all this happened before the days of Jack's rise to fame. Disappointed ladies said that he married her simply out of gratitude for her love and because she was a mother figure who promised him *complete security*. 'A base for operations', someone maliciously suggested. The difference in their ages was freely exploited and exaggerated. Franca had a modest job, making clothes for a small firm set up by two of her friends, Molly Stein and Linda Blane, from polytechnic days. Later she gave this up, did some dress-making at home, and devoted her life to happy love. Jack soon gave up teaching her painting, but did succeed in changing her handwriting from its original sloppy scrawl to the elegant italic hand which he had early taught himself. When Jack was earning more money they travelled, always to picture galleries, and on this basis went to Holland, France, Italy, even America. Franca felt sad in Italy, especially when she saw young girls walking in the evening. But this sadness too was a part of her happiness.

When, some time after their marriage, Jack told her that he loved her eternally, that they would never be parted, that she was not to worry, and that he had taken a mistress, Franca thought she would die of grief. Her life seemed to be at an end. She saw now the difference between the joy that expected nothing and the joy that presumed to have everything. In a special way, she wept over a change, which she tried to resist but could not, in her estimate of her husband. Then too she began suddenly, she dared, to think about her mother's death: suicide, murder? Franca starved, she became sick with misery, but she survived, she had to, her love (and what else had she in the world?) forced her to. Of course she uttered no reproaches and learnt to conceal her unhappiness, to conceal it even from herself, when Jack explained to her, after the first girl had been succeeded by another, that this was how it was going to be, but *she* was the permanent, the real. He said that he hid nothing, that if 'there was anyone' he would make it crystal clear that he had a dear wife whom he loved and would never leave, and who 'knew about it'. On this basis many things were possible. Sincerity was all. The bad thing about adultery was the lying, that was the poison. He would never deceive anyone, truth was the key, the girls knew where they stood, and Franca would always know where he was. He developed, for her, concerning these matters, a whole philosophy, a warm poultice for the wound. He said, 'You are order, they are chaos.' He did not say that he wanted both, but she came to see that he did. He said, 'I love you eternally, I could not say that to any other woman.' She believed him. It did not occur to her that she might be pitied, she did not think of herself as a wronged or defeated woman. Her love connived at what she now took to be inevitable. Jack's activities, though generally known, were not in Franca's presence discussed or mentioned, and this significant lacuna made a difference to Franca's social life, she became more enclosed and solitary. But she had always felt, with him, solitary. In fact the episodes were brief and not all that frequent. Jack, saying he was not a Don Juan, even jokingly made a merit of 'telling' about so little, though of course they agreed that telling was crucial. He offered sufficient, but minimal, information about the girls, they were usually students, sometimes Jack's students, they were immensely young. They did not come to the house. She did not reflect about what these very young women might think or feel about the complaisant wife, nor wonder whether they too suffered. Franca disciplined her thoughts. Her resource for survival was an adjustment which she came to recognise as an increase in her love for Jack. Sometimes she felt like someone on a strict diet which it would be death to alter. Sometimes, but not often, she recalled what it had been like before the girls, and imagined what it might be like after them. She remained permanently in love, her heart turned somersaults for Jack, he retained for her *absolute charm*. She became used to a pain which she concealed, clasping it into the cloud of her marriage.

So, she was the tranquil haven to which he returned after peril on the sea: 'stormy weather', as he called his sorties. She gave him what he needed, a tranquil orderly house in which he could work. She made space and quietness for him. He said once, staring at her, 'To restore silence is the role of objects.' She had learnt, when he stared in *that* way, never to smile, being for him, beneficently, life-giving, a thing. Was it the key that she was three years older, and that that had laid down the pattern when they first met? She had apprehended him as a boy, he her as an older woman. Perhaps indeed he *had* chosen her just for that, choosing security, choosing mother with whom the bond is never broken. Jack's mother, who was dead now, had been jealous of Franca, and had been visited by Jack alone. Franca had seen Jack, and saw him still, as innocent, the only child of loving parents, blessed with a happy temperament, unfailing good humour, gentleness and tenderness, someone always forgiven. He redeemed for her the idea of man. They never quarrelled. Surely she could accommodate in this large felicitous whole the fact that she did not fully satisfy his desires? She loved the golden boy who could not say a cross word, she chose peace; but not on the terms expressed by her mother who said, 'always give in to men, they are physically stronger' (advice which the poor woman did not always follow). Franca thought of 'the girls' as part of Jack's dream of himself, a dream that had a place in reality but was not quite part of it. Yet is not reality, perhaps her own, but a dream of oneself? However that might be, Jack himself was huge, substantial, and crammed with being, the most real thing she knew.

Now Franca patted the heavy but secure coiled-up mass of her dark hair, and questioned in the mirror her dark eyes which gave back to her a quick ray of life-energy. Then she went through into the back bedroom which was still dim. Moving quietly she pulled the curtains back a little. Outside the window, in the bright green fuzz of trees and gardens, the birds were singing. She looked at Patrick. She knew that he was still alive since she had heard through the half open door his sleeping breath and the soft sigh of his awakening. One morning, one day, perhaps soon, she would come to him and find him gone; and she knew how much she did not want to see him die, and yet how much she also wished that he might die holding her hand. These thoughts induced tears, which he must not see; and she tried not to think too much about the terrible mystery which was to be enacted, the extinction of a conscient being, now here, now absent, a mystery as deep as its conjoined mystery, how can there be such beings at all. Patrick was awake. What does he awake *to*, she wondered. For a moment now as she looked at him, he looked at her and seemed to recognise her and be about to speak to her. But the spark vanished, there was no longed-for recognition, no dawning sign of recovery. The love she had learnt in tending him was an enclosed love, muted and maimed, already mourning. They would never communicate now. She loved him as she might have loved a dumb animal. Jack had once suggested that she should have a dog, to be *her* dog, not his. A substitute for Jack? They laughed about that. A representative, a guardian, a protection during his absences? Perhaps Jack simply wanted her to have a consolation, an interest, something new to love. They had not had children, at first accidentally, then by design. Jack did not want children and Franca soon felt that, for her, it was simply too late. Jack was enough of a child, a third person between them would have caused friction and jealousy, and by now Franca had enough trouble with 'the girls'. Only later did she reflect that if there had been children there might have been no girls. She had rejected his suggestion of a dog. She could not bear the tenderness which a dog would evoke, she did not want the pain of another love. She knew how very much, how desperately, she would love her dog; and dogs are vulnerable and short-lived and die. But then there was Patrick, the wounded dying Patrick, suddenly given to her, as if he had been thrust into her arms.

She went to him and began to lift the pillows. Gazing at the window he lifted his knees, pushed with his feet, wriggled to sit up a little, while Franca, helping, held his shoulders, feeling them through his pyjamas so bony, so thin and so frail. She went to the window, which was left a trifle open at night, opened it more and pulled the curtains further back. The song of the birds sounded loud. Pat seemed to be listening. She said, as to a child, 'The birds. Listen to the birds.' Illness had so transformed him that she could scarcely remember the whole man, all his crown of dark curling hair, and high-boned rosy cheeks and radiant smile and crazy laugh. His hair, cut very short, was limp and damp like a fungus, revealing the skull, his face, emaciated, peeled as to some unseemly under-skin, a very pale brown. He had a slight beard, clipped by the nurse, as it was pointless to shave him now. His 'pretty' (Jack's word) mouth from which so much ornate wit had flowed was dim and lipless, and his fine dark blue eyes were wet slits between discoloured lids, the wetness seeming not tears but the sad secretion of a vital fluid. Yet he could move himself in bed, and speak audibly, sometimes uttering long rigmaroles composed of rhyming doggerel and the foreign speech which Gildas said was Irish. He began to speak now, staring at the green window, perhaps hearing the birds.

'The bird in the morn, the hare in the corn, deep is depth, sleep is slept, shining one, moon my sun, come, my swan, my swan song, my swoon song, my silver spoon song, so forgive me, live me, raise me, praise me, I died, I lied, oh make me good, oh let me see the sun, words and blood run from my side.'

'You'll get better,' said Franca. These rhyming monologues frightened her. Gildas had said they were just the raw stuff of poetry, but they sounded to Franca like evil magic.

'Better, fetter, later, fate, too late, he come, I dumb, poor Pat, poor cat, poor dog, the sound, the wound, the wounded side, the poor dog died.'

In spite of the efforts of the three women the room was beginning more and more to smell of urine, of sweat, and with another ill smell, perhaps an odour of decay. 'The very deeps do rot, oh Christ that ever this should be,' had been uttered by Patrick on the previous day. So we go on, Franca thought, cleaning and tending and washing and mopping an unclean body that was so soon to be given over to dissolution. She was intensely conscious of the physical presence of that long thin restless body, and she felt for it something like desire, as if she would have spread herself softly over it like some huge powdery healing butterfly or indeed like the merciful lethal angel that would so soon put an end to the failing organs and the suffering consciousness.

'Oh help me, help me, help me!' Suddenly now he was stretching out his hands.

Franca sat on the side of the bed and captured his thin clammy hands in hers. She leaned over him, breathing his breath. 'Pat, it's Franca, don't worry, I'm here, I'll help you.'

But he seemed not aware of her and jerked his hands away, wiping them together as if in disgust. 'It's the snow, it covers everything.'

'Pat, there is no snow, it's springtime.'

'I tell you, snow is general over Ireland.' He turned away from her, sinking lower in the bed.

Franca rose and opened the window still wider, letting in the smell of leaves and flowers to freshen the room. A faint breeze stirred the curtains, catching Patrick's attention, and he fell silent watching them. Franca breathed the tranquillity of the house, yet it was not tranquil, she breathed its goodness, but it was not good. She thought, I shall never tell it to Jack, the strange love which I feel for this doomed man, as if he were a dog lying in the road with a broken back. I feel it like someone in a concentration camp who daren't weep in case the torturer should see the tears. But who is the torturer? There is no torturer, only mortality. There are violent things in my heart. Perhaps they have been festering there ever since that *change*. And now I have run in here to find some different pain, some mystery of myself to keep secret, something which, for this short time, is absolutely not Jack.

The door opened and Alison Merrick came in.

'You're early.'

'I thought I'd come.'

'Moxie is coming.'

'I know.'

'Close the door.'

Alison softly closed the door.

Franca did not want Jack to hear her talking *tête-à-tête* with Alison. Not that their conversations were secret or other than amicably banal. Franca just did not like the idea of Jack overhearing how, in what tone, she and Alison spoke to each other.

'How is he?'

'The same.' They said that every day, though every day he was worse.

Alison had first been mentioned by Jack to Franca as 'the girl in the sailor-suit' or 'the girl with the hoop'; and Franca retained this spirited and evocative picture of her as a child of twelve. The picture was by now, however, overlaid by other images.

Alison Merrick was taller than Franca. She was slim and lithe and exceedingly graceful. She had long elegant perfect legs. She had been a ballet dancer and until Jack had ordered her to grow her hair had looked, close-cropped, very boyish. The growth of her hair measured, Franca thought, the length of the liaison which had now gone on for some time. Alison's hair, which was very fine and silky and of the pure cinnamon ginger known as 'red', was now down well over her ears, almost to her collar. She wore no make-up, being in this respect unlike most of her predecessors whose extreme artificiality amused and captivated Jack. In a way, she was indeed not too far removed from the sailor-suit and the hoop. Gildas had rightly called her 'the goddess of good health'. She was twenty-four. Her eyes were an extremely pale lucid blue. Her complexion was milky pale and very clear, given to freckles in summer. She had a clever face, a strong Scottish face as Franca thought. She was capable of solemnity, gravity, even *gravitas*. She came from Edinburgh where her father was a solicitor. She could herself be imagined as a lawyer, a woman barrister, even a judge. She spoke in a precise manner and with a slight accent, an Edinburgh accent as she had informed Franca on their first meeting. She was certainly the most apparently intellectual of Jack's girls, though she had disappointed her father, who had quite other ambitions for her, by becoming a dancer.

She was in fact quite ambitious for herself. She had begun her training in ballet at the suitable age of five, and had by hard work and talent become a professional, a member of a distinguished *corps de ballet*, tipped to be perhaps a star, although some said she was too tall. A year ago however she had suddenly given it all up. Why? Fear? It was a terrifying profession, and Alison was not a girl who cared to fail. Better to leave abruptly before some dismal demotion. Alison explained it more prosaically. It could be physical agony. Ballet, she explained, is contrary to nature, it offends against human physiology, the limbs are continually strained, even damaged. This discipline is military. Too much is expected. One has to be a sylph. When one is already starving one is told to lose weight. She was becoming anorexic. She could not go on breaking her body in two by placing her leg in some position which God never intended or adopting a stance which deranged her organs and deformed her feet. She had wanted to be a dancer not an acrobat. Whatever might be thought of all this, Alison was clearly through with ballet. Her father urged her to return to Scotland and study for the law exams. But Alison had now decided to become a writer and was writing a television play about a ballet school. Moreover she had met Jack.

Jack's 'stormy weather' life may have been chaotic in content but it was orderly in form. With Alison, as with her predecessors, the form was as follows. Jack worked all day from early morning till about four in the afternoon. Then, on some days, he went to see his girl, returning to Chelsea about seven or eight. On some, less frequent, other days he spent the night with his girl, leaving home about seven or eight. There were usually days when he did not disappear at all. When there was a girl, Franca slept alone. She never queried these arrangements, which were never discussed or even mentioned. The girls had never, or never hitherto, appeared in the house. Alison had been introduced to help Franca to nurse Patrick. Jack had indicated that Alison had been reluctant and he had had to persuade her. Whether she was mainly afraid of infection or of Franca was not indicated. However that might be, Franca surmised that she had been, in this case, invited because she was deemed to be in some way superior.

Franca and Alison stood in silence looking at the sick man, conscious of him, conscious of each other. Alison stood back a little. Her nose was wrinkled. The sickness-unto-death odour was stronger today. Of course Alison *was* afraid of infection. She prized her health and strength, her handsome perfect youthfulness. Jack himself now kept his distance. Alison, as nurse, had arrived with rubber gloves and a mask. Soon after watching Franca she had set these aside. Nothing was said. But Alison could not conceal her fear and horror of what lay on the bed. Franca was almost ostentatious in her avoidance of precautions. In doing so she imitated the neat brisk movements of the professional nurse. Her strange terminal love of Patrick was her own secret. She felt intensely possessive of her patient, was jealous of the nurse, and would have been jealous of Alison had Alison not so clearly manifested her aversion.

Patrick, who had been lying flat once more, his head slithering low upon the pillows, suddenly rose, supporting himself with his elbows, and looking at the door cried out in a loud clear voice 'Marcus!' The women jumped, turned round, Franca even opened the door. Of course there was no one there. Patrick was now sitting up, his moist eyes widened, his nostrils distended, his pale mouth thrust forward. Through the open door the nurse could be heard below talking to Jack, then mounting the stairs with her customary quick cat-like tread. Alison had already retreated. Franca held the door open for the nurse, the confident expensive young woman called Suzanne Moxon. Pat, resuming his weakness, had fallen back and was whimpering in an unusual way which Franca found hard to bear.

Alison had already taken refuge in the front bedroom. Franca followed her. This room, where Franca now slept for Pat's sake, had never been properly colonised. As 'second spare bedroom' it had been a receptacle for poor unwanted objects. Now Franca had also filled it with things removed from Pat's room which, in accordance with her idea of a sickroom, she had stripped austerely. Buying knick-knacks was one of Franca's occupations. Jack decreed an elegant plainness in the drawing room and the dining room, in his view only two or three good things should be allowed in any room. But Franca indulged her cluttery taste elsewhere. Often she bought little objects simply because she was sorry for them. Instinctively she began to rearrange some pieces of china on the crowded mantelpiece, then desisted and sat down on the bed. She wanted a cigarette. For Pat, she had given up smoking altogether. She had also, which she had wanted to do for some time and now found possible, given up watching television; she felt that it was bad for her, a bad idle consciousness, a false consciousness into which she was being quietly and easily absorbed. Jack disapproved of television because he said its awful clarity spoilt our vision of the beautiful misty ordinary world; but he watched it all the same. Franca looked round the room, it was senseless and comfortless, it looked like a shop, it was ill too. I'll tidy it, she thought, I'll tidy the whole house, *afterwards*. She hoped that Alison would soon go away. It was not her time to be here anyway.

Alison was standing at the window looking out at the street, which was a small quiet side street. Both women were dressed, in accord with their present occupation, soberly. Alison wore a straight blue jacket and skirt of fine cotton and a white blouse pinned high at the neck with a gold brooch. Franca wore a simple light grey dress, which she had made herself, in her unobtrusive invisible style. The days were still cool in spite of continued sunshine. Alison had taken off her jacket and thrown it on a chair. Unconsciously she undid her cuffs and rolled up her sleeves a little. Then with more deliberation she took off the golden brooch and pinned it inside one of the pockets of the discarded jacket. She undid the buttons of the blouse at the neck and thrust a long hand in to her throat, perhaps to her breast. She rippled her body slowly like an animal or like a dancer about suddenly to move. As she turned from the window Franca contemplated her straight brow, her determined not quite too long nose, her clever mouth and long neck, her lucid light blue eyes, and the glossy lively mass of her bright red hair, which, though growing as fast as it could, still showed the shape of her head. She was remarkably strong, physically strong, Jack had told Franca. He also said that she was an Indian goddess, and if you looked closely you would see that her feet did not touch the ground. He did not often describe the girls, but made introductory remarks before Franca met Alison. Franca, sitting at her sewing, had nodded her head. In fact, although prepared to dislike Alison, she liked her.

She's so restless, thought Franca, there's something the matter, there's something wrong with her. She isn't usually like this, and she doesn't usually come so early. She's nervous, she's frightened.

33

'What do you think of this Marcus Vallar idea?' said Alison almost sternly in her precise Edinburgh voice.

'Do you mean about the curse?' said Franca, 'or about the cure?' Something about Alison made Franca adopt a certain meticulous air of precision herself.

'This notion that he could cure him somehow.'

'I suppose it's worth trying. Anything is.'

'But you don't like it.'

'I don't like *him*. I don't believe he could help Pat, he might harm him, frighten him.' He might harm Jack too, thought Franca. This idea had been with her for some time. After very brief meetings, in company, and having nothing to say to him, Franca had taken a strong dislike to Vallar. She thought him conceited and likely to hurt people casually.

'What's wrong with Marcus, why don't you like him?'

'I scarcely know Professor Vallar,' said Franca, 'but I think he's dangerous, perhaps unconsciously, he's rude, he's – *sinister*. Perhaps that's putting it too strongly. Anyway they can't find him so it doesn't matter.' She did not care for hearing Alison refer to Vallar as 'Marcus'.

'I'd like to meet him,' said Alison. 'Gildas says what you say, but Ludens thinks he's wonderful. Do you know, Ludens wants to get married.'

'Did he tell you he wanted to get married?'

'No, but I heard Jack teasing him about it. I've got a friend, Heather Allenby, who wants to get married. I'm going to introduce them.'

It was news, and not pleasing news, to Franca that Alison knew Gildas and Ludens. This privilege, as far as Franca knew, had not been previously extended to any of Jack's girls. Franca had, as they all agreed, a special relationship with Jack's two closest friends. Gildas had known Jack longer than Franca had. Franca had become very fond of them, and of inviting them to dinner with her and Jack, and having long conversations. Then Gildas and Ludens had taken to inviting Franca out to lunch. Jack, working all day, had a sandwich in his studio. However, perhaps after Ludens had made an unfortunate joke, in the presence of Jack who was not amused, about the 'free Franca society', these invitations came more rarely and then ceased. Franca, at home, still saw Jack's friends but not quite so often. It hurt her very much to learn that Alison had evidently visited them with Jack. Jack had said nothing about this. I don't want to hear about what happens elsewhere, thought Franca. Of course Jack talks casually and vaguely about the girls to demean them and reassure me. I mustn't start thinking and worrying about this. It was a *mistake* of Jack's to ask her to help with Pat. I've got to put up with it, and I *don't like it*. Yet I like her and I get on with her, but I'll be relieved when she's gone. But then – Patrick will be gone too: Patrick who was sinking, leaving, scarcely a person now, not a man, certainly not the man she had known, a hurt dog, a dying fish, a blind twitching worm lying in the earth. How, when *this* was happening, did she have to be annoyed by another woman!

Jack's deep loud voice was suddenly heard nearby talking to the nurse. Then the door of Pat's room was closed and Jack appeared, putting his head in and then entering. He was wearing his 'romantic' painter's smock, a genuine embroidered smock with a floppy collar, elegantly stained with paint. As he explained, he had worn such smocks long enough when he was pretending to be a painter and was not going to abandon them now he was one – it would be so ungrateful, even unlucky. Franca felt her body jolt, her breasts dilate with the warm startled rush of love which she felt even after a short absence from him. Alison stepped back and her pale face and neck flushed.

'Hello you two,' he said. 'How nice to see you together.' This remark seemed forced, odd.

He said to Alison, 'Have you –?'

Alison replied, 'No.'

Franca thought, they're both upset, there's something wrong between them. I'd better move off. She said, 'I'm just going to help Moxie.'

She made for the door; trying to pass Jack who was standing in the way she actually pushed him, pressing her hand against his shoulder, feeling the warmth as she touched him.

Jack said, 'Wait, Franca, wait.'

Alison said, 'I'm going.'

'Don't go, Aly.'

Franca turned to look at her and was surprised to see her face frowning, almost angry.

Jack let Franca pass him on to the landing, then said to her, 'Darling, go up into the studio, I'll follow in a moment.'

Franca did not go up to the studio but stood surprised, pressing her hands now to her breast. Jack hesitated, was about to enter the room, then closed the door leaving Alison inside. He took Franca's hand and pulled her to the spiral staircase which led to the studio. He ran up first, still holding her hand and pulling her after him. Once in the great light space, Jack released her, then with some deliberation walked away, then turned to face her.

Franca suddenly thought: Alison's pregnant! Not hastily, she drew a chair towards her and sat down. 'Alison's pregnant.'

35

Jack said, 'No, no – good heavens no!'

'What then is all this – *nonsense*?' She feigned anger, feeling fear.

Jack fetched another chair and sat down opposite to her a few feet away.

Jack's studio occupied the large loft of the house. A window offered a view, or narrow glimpse, of the Thames. The room was mainly lit however by skylights which were dimmed by adjustable blinds. It was sustained – perhaps that was the word since it seemed to have floated up into a realm of its own – by an unusually airy light, a rivery light, a kind of faintly bluish silvery brilliance, a kind of muted clarity, which was achieved partly by Jack's adroit management of the blinds, their position and colour, and partly (as Ludens asserted) by magic. There was a curiously clean exciting smell of paint and wood. Franca felt an awe of this room as if it were, not exactly a temple, but a revered workshop where even the tools were works of art. The beams of the roof had not been covered and the ceiling maintained its uninterrupted slope to the floor. A number of compartments, slotted into the triangular spaces, housed plain canvases and also some works in progress, as Jack often serviced several pictures at the same time. Contrary to what his adverse critics maintained, Jack's style and subject matter did evolve and vary, and 'seen one, seen the lot' was certainly unfair. He had had a long phase of painting floating objects, bright round shapes in seas of very dark colours, and vivid mandelas in Sheerwater red and green. More lately he painted knots and spirals, extremely intricate designs composed (he alleged, since they defeated the eye) of a single continuous line. Human figures did not appear, but recently shapes rather like fishes could be discerned. (Ludens, who was always urging Jack to evolve from 'blobs' up the scale of being toward humans, had bought one of these shadowy 'fishes'.) There was no doubt that Jack's pictures were very decorative and attractive and wonderfully colourful. They failed however to be 'great', were called 'unambitious', and their author accused of 'failing to develop'. Jack did mention at intervals that his work had been inspired by Marcus Vallar, but as time passed people forgot who Vallar was. At the far end of the studio, opposite to where Franca was now sitting, was a large reproduction of Picasso's *Demoiselles d'Avignon* which had been with Jack since student days and had travelled with him as a superstitiously treasured icon. Franca, who never of course said so, particularly disliked this picture.

Jack, still answering Franca's previous question, said slowly, 'No – my dear – it's *simpler* than that.' He paused. Then said, 'You like Alison, don't you?'

'Yes. What is it? Are you leaving her?'

'No. It's rather – the opposite.'

'What –?'

'I've decided to keep her.'

For a moment Franca could make nothing of this. Give her money? 'Set her up' somewhere? 'You mean –?'

'I want – have promised her – a permanent relationship.'

Franca said automatically 'I see.' With these two words she seemed to close down a curtain behind which she must now be able to control her feelings absolutely and conceal her thoughts absolutely and think quickly. An image which came to her then and upon which she reflected afterwards was that of being down inside a sinking ship in the dark and having to keep her head and concentrate on finding a way out.

'Franca, clear your brow.'

This was something Jack sometimes said to her. She drew her hand over her brow. Her face had remained composed. Jack was staring at her with his startling blue eyes. He had ruffled his blond hair back behind his ears and his white shirt hung open through the unbuttoned smock. Franca looked at him, at his face directed upon her burning with will and authority and love; and she saw all at once his sweet happy youthful beauty and the intelligent loving calculation with which he now beseeched and commanded her.

'I don't *quite* understand,' she said in her cool voice.

'As I said now,' said Jack, leaning forward and speaking slowly, 'it is simple. After all something like this happens to many people. Only here nothing will change except for the better. Happiness, Franca, happiness, we have it, we'll keep it, *you* must keep it. You have been perfect, you will be perfect, you are the guardian of the world, the central point, the pillar, the pivot, the powerhouse. The power is yours. I know you understand this. Because of you we shall be *good* enough to be happy. My love for you is eternal and can never change. What is now will be better than what has been. Alison loves you and admires you –'

'Oh, really?' said Franca, having hold now of a sustaining rhythm, the shelter of a rational conversation.

'Yes, you must have seen this. And I know you like her, you have spoken so warmly about her. That is essential, that you care for each other. Alison understands, she is an exceptional person. You see how very much I hope for here, something fine which can be created, a happiness and stability in our world. I admit that there has been in my life – a certain disorder –'

'Stormy weather,' said Franca. 'You mean, Sally, and Penelope and –?'

'I'll tell you anything you want later,' said Jack, adjusting his shirt. 'It is lies which poison people's lives, lies and fear and muddle. Lying makes people demoralised and morally careless. You know that I have never lied to you about the situation and I never would. But – disorder – you know what I mean – yes. What I want now is *order* all the way through, continuity and stability. You must want these things too. We are free people and how we deal with each other is our affair. You have accepted what some would call my infidelity. You have not seen it as infidelity because you love me and you *know* that my love for you will never cease. Our pact with each other is deep and eternal. Absolute love precludes jealousy. You know what I think about jealousy and why I have never felt it. If one embraces the whole world one is never jealous. Perhaps it's something to do with being a painter, as if the world was *offered* to you. It's all here. Love itself is an end, a creative force. Jealousy is totally illogical and purely destructive. You have wonderfully understood this too, you too are blessed with this freedom.'

Franca said, 'I know what you mean.'

'I knew you would. You see, it *is* simple. All our arrangements which have become so easy and habitual remain the same, except that instead of different girls whom you don't want to meet, there will be one girl whom you like and who loves you. And when you get to know Alison –'

'Do you want children?' said Franca, clearing her brow again.

'Children? Well – no – that's not in question. Alison isn't interested in children. She, we, you and I, are not concerned with conventional domesticity, that's not what this is about –'

'What is it about?' said Franca. 'I'm sorry, I just don't entirely understand. I've heard what you say but there's something missing –'

'You mean about how Alison sees it? Don't worry about her. Listen, my darling –' Here Jack left his chair and knelt on one knee, leaning forward, close to her but not touching her. 'This is about happiness. Happiness means being above resentment, and jealousy, and anger, and remorse. We have a talent for it, we can achieve it. I rely on your love. Franca, my life rests on your love.'

'It rests securely,' said Franca.

'I know! Peace and tranquillity and stability – I feel now – it's a revelation. My dear heart.' He relaxed his posture, now sitting cross-legged on the floor. 'We'll talk of all this, we'll live it, we'll talk it. All will be well.'

'*Does* Alison agree to this plan?' said Franca, with the slower tempo moving her shoulders and pulling down her skirt. Of course Alison agreed.

'Of course Alison agrees, otherwise the plan wouldn't exist! And the point is that she accepts it all. I never dreamt I'd meet someone like Alison —'

'You mean someone so considerate and understanding. But it's still not very clear. You mean you and I will live in this house, and you'll go and see her in her flat, like you did with the others?'

'Yes, though of course —'

'But won't there be differences because your relation with Alison is permanent, because you love her more than you did the others, in a quite different way?'

Here Jack actually smiled. Franca contemplated this smile with amazement and awe, staring as if at some briefly exhibited marvel. 'My darling, there will be differences, precisely those differences not other ones! Of course *we* shall live here exactly as before.'

'Won't Alison come here more than the others did? Well, they didn't come at all.'

'It will depend entirely on you how much she comes. But you'll want her to come.'

'Well — yes —'

'You said you like her, I can *see* you like her. You'll like her even more. It's all just the same except better, deeper.'

'I see it's deeper.'

Franca then did a strange thing, quite unpremeditated. She suddenly pulled all the pins out of her hair and let the dark glossy mass tumble down over her shoulders and down to her waist. She shook her head violently to and fro, then drew her hair over her face and pressed it against her eyes. After a moment she drew it back, parting it and combing it with her fingers. She looked up at Jack who had risen quickly to his feet. He looked at her gravely, then stooped to pick up the pins which had fallen to the floor. He gave them to her, she put them in her lap and began with thoughtless cunning fingers to control and divide the dark curly veil of strange stuff, which had so suddenly covered her, so as to pin it up again.

'Franca, my love, my life — it is all right, isn't it?'

'I put up with the others,' said Franca, beginning to pin up her hair, 'because I thought you'd stop some day.'

'No, you didn't,' said Jack calmly. 'How could you know whether I'd stop?'

'You mean I put up with it because I loved you?'

'Yes.'

'Well, I see. And I do. So I suppose it is – clear – and simple as you said – and all right.'

Looking up at him as she spoke she saw for an instant intense anxiety succeeded by relief. She thought, he is afraid, he was afraid, how strange. I have power over him but I can't use it. I don't want power, I cast it away. He wants me to make him perfectly happy, and how can I not?

She stood up and gave him her hand and he kissed it several times, closing his eyes. Then he put his arms around her and hugged her violently. After that they stared at each other with composed, almost stern, faces.

'Please,' said Jack, speaking softly, coaxingly, 'will you come and see Alison now?'

Alison? thought Franca. Oh yes, Alison. She had almost forgotten Alison during the last part of their argument which had seemed to be all about love.

'I don't think I want to,' said Franca, 'you can tell her –'

'Please come. She's afraid. Just be kind and smile. You don't have to say anything.'

It was suddenly plain to Franca that she must *get it over*. She had to see Alison, the new Alison, the absolutely different larger and more brightly coloured new Alison. After that she would think. 'Yes, all right.'

She followed Jack down the stairs. Pat's door was closed. Franca followed Jack into the front bedroom.

Alison had put her jacket on and, as Franca at once saw, had combed her hair. She stood where she had been near the window, as it were at attention, her face very cold, looking intently, even fiercely, at Jack, not at Franca.

At this fateful moment Jack, who could usually talk fluently in any situation, seemed lost for words. His face expressed some extreme emotion as he turned his head to and fro between the two women.

Franca took charge. 'Well, Jack has told me all about it and of course I'm not going to make any tiresome old-fashioned fuss. You and I have always got on well together and I hope we shall continue to do so, and to get to know each other and like each other even better, I see no reason why that shouldn't be so. That's all I can say now. I expect we're all suffering from shock. I'm just going away, I'm going shopping, so I'll just leave you two together to have *your* talk.'

Franca, who had stayed near the door, now tried to get out quickly;

but the tall Scots girl crossed the room in a leap and seized hold of her arm.

'Franca, Franca, I must tell you –'

Franca pulled herself away and ran down the stairs. No one followed. Later she saw a bruise upon her arm where Alison had gripped it.

'In faith I know not why I am so sad.'

Ludens did not reply to this remark which Gildas often uttered.

Shortly after the day which had changed Franca's life, Ludens and Gildas were drinking and arguing together at Ludens's flat. They had argued about whether to go out to a restaurant or eat what Ludens had in the larder. Ludens wanted to treat his friend to a good dinner, but as their discussion of other matters became more heated they had decided to stay where they were and had eventually consumed an omelette and were now eating bread and butter and raspberry jam. They were onto their second bottle of claret.

Ludens's flat, on the second floor of a pleasant white terrace in St John's Wood, was unlike that of Gildas. To begin with, Ludens kept it very clean and orderly. His friends likened it to a modest hotel, but this was not quite fair. The previous owner, leaving England in a hurry, had sold the flat fully furnished for a 'quick sale' price. Ludens, without in fact any clear ideas about interiors, had at first intended to sell 'all that stuff' and start again. The furniture was indeed not what he would have chosen: a rather plump three-piece suite in pale blue, pink lampshades with long fringes, an imitation Cotswold stone fireplace with an imitation coal fire, a white plastic table in the kitchen-dining room with chairs to match. What preserved the suite, the fireplace, the plastic table and so on was the fact that the previous owner (about whom Ludens sometimes speculated) had possessed some fine pieces of *art nouveau* pottery and glass. Ludens (who after all did not know everything) did not at first recognise these. They were very dirty and stowed away in a dark cupboard, together with china decorated with red roses and even dogs, but when washed and seen for what they were, served as the few just men whose presence saved the city. Ludens accepted the scene and hung up Jack's mystical fish picture over the fireplace. He even started in a modest way to collect *art nouveau* objects himself. The flat finally looked much as it had done before only distinctly happier. There had been something sad and shady about his predecessor's sudden departure.

'If we could only *do* something.'

They had been talking about Patrick, wearying themselves with fruitless lamentations.

'People always want to do something about something,' said Gildas. 'Well, lighting a candle in a church is something, saying a prayer is something. But one can't expect results. As Our Lord said, the labourer who works twelve hours gets no more than the labourer who works one hour.'

'A tiresome saying,' said Ludens. 'So because God is whimsical we are not supposed to try? You ought to write a book about all that.'

'All what?'

'Religion and morality.'

'It's too difficult.'

'Write simply.'

'That's hardest of all.'

'Well, write seriously then, write something.'

'I suppose I could write a comforting popular little book about faith and salvation designed for farmers and their dogs sitting in kitchens in the stormy fens. Actually such stuff is now selling as well as cookery books.'

'Don't be frivolous. I know you think a lot about God and so on. All right, write some decent popular theology. Pop metaphysics, pop theology, maybe that's what the age requires.'

'A new prayer book.'

'We've got that. *Concentrate*, Gildas. Or are you drunk?'

'I am concentrating. You persist in not believing me. To get past the soft stuff into the hard stuff in the subjects you mention so lightly –'

'Not lightly!'

'Is extremely difficult. Why don't *you* get on with writing a book? You've only written two. Your friend and colleague Christian Eriksen has written five and he's younger than you.'

'History is extremely difficult too.'

'At least it's about something real, not about "deep foundations", all that stuff is nonsense, and so is solemn talk about morality and "this nuclear age" and "the destiny of Being" and so on. Human beings live on top of total jumble, mess, chance, they understand nothing, they are surrounded by darkness, they've just got to keep on walking. *Ambulent, ambulent, ne tenebrae comprehendant.*'

'Or you could write about politics, you're always complaining –'

'Politics? Our parents did that for us. No, no, you can't argue with God, and you mustn't cry in front of your dog either. The best you can hope for is a little peace and not too much remorse. Thoughts at peace under an English heaven.'

'Don't be so *listless*, Gildas! Did Marcus break your back? He set Jack up, he put you down.'

'He didn't set Jack up,' said Gildas, looking more lively. 'He gave Jack a magic formula which Jack has used intelligently. But now he can't get beyond it. He has this infertile facility, he wants to do new things but he can't, he's under a spell.'

'It's not all Marcus. Those knots and tangles he's doing now, he must have got them from Leonardo.'

'That's a spell *you're* under. No. Jack doesn't *know* anything, he doesn't know the history of art, they didn't teach it in art schools when he was a student. He got those images from some of Marcus's mathematical drawings. He says he wants to portray the human figure but he can't –'

'He can when it's pornography.'

'Did he show you those drawings?'

'No, I found some lying about. I was shocked and surprised.'

'At least it shows he can still draw. I like your being shocked, dear Alfred, that's right. He showed me the drawings. I was fascinated.'

'Perhaps they're a protest against Marcus, an exit from Marcus.'

'You are a puritanical boy. Jack's always been like that. He likes to think he's living in a palace full of bedizened captives waiting for him to arrive, girls dressing and undressing, kicking off their skirts, pulling up their stockings, hauling down their knickers – it's a permanently available visit to the underworld. He thinks it stirs his imagination.'

'But fantasy *kills* imagination, pornography is death to art. It's all part of Jack's myth about women being an alien tribe full of sinister magic.'

'Is it a myth?'

'And he thinks women don't have sexual fantasies! That's supposed to be an aspect of their inferiority! Anyway it can't be true.'

'How do you know? Do you have sexual fantasies? What are they like?'

'Shut up, Gildas.'

'Precisely. Of course Jack's real life is a bit more orderly than his fantasy life.'

'If only he'd go on painting fishes, like *that* one, that might be a way out.'

'He says it isn't a fish.'

'Of course it's a fish. As for his real life being more orderly, it just seems so because Franca is so quiet and good.'

'I said a bit more orderly. So you think Franca is a simple person, an Italian peasant woman, who accepts what happens as what has to be?'

'No! Christian said that. I see her as heroic, saintly.'

'Not secretly seething with rage and hate? You may be right. They say that duty is easier when the spirit is not awakened. As for Jack, I believe he genuinely doesn't feel jealousy. Why mar one's happiness by unavailing resentment? He doesn't understand how anyone could feel anything so pointless.'

'For Jack happiness is all. His way of life ingeniously precludes jealousy. And it's convenient for him to think that Franca is as generous as he imagines he is. But everyone feels jealousy. I'm sure Franca does, but she treats it like a headache and takes an aspirin and thinks how much she loves her husband.'

'And that's saintly?'

'Yes. Maybe Jack thinks he enlivens his relations with Franca by having other women. Maybe he actually does.'

'We keep trying to analyse Jack and reassure ourselves about Franca,' said Gildas, 'but the main point is it's not our business. We can't go near Franca, she's unapproachable, she's immured, we can't consider comforting her or encouraging her to confide in us, it's out of the question. "Free Franca" was just a joke.'

'It was a stupid dangerous joke. Jack saw it wouldn't do and closed the shutters. Marriage is awfully private.'

'Actually,' said Gildas, 'every marriage is an irreversible mistake. *That's* the secret which they all keep. I can't think why you go on about wanting to be married. You haven't ever met anyone you wanted to marry, you have no one in view, you just have some vague idea about warmth and comfort and home. It's an admission of defeat. You say you want to do some great thing. But it turns out that all you really want is marriage and babies.'

'Children.'

'*Babies.*'

'Alison says she's got a girl in stock, she's called Heather Allenby.'

The mention of Alison's name made them both pause and look at each other. Each was wondering how much Jack had told the other. Ludens knew about jealousy all right. He felt possessive about both Jack and Gildas, and was perpetually jealous of their closeness to each other, a closeness which could not, in either case, be his. On the other hand, high principles kept the green demon in check, and he was helped, though also annoyed, by the way in which the age gap between them, which had mattered so much when he was twenty, had been somehow perpetuated by the other two for whom he remained 'the young chap', or 'the boy'.

'Alison,' said Gildas. He stared at Ludens, twisting up his asymmetrical face into a puzzle picture of mocking wrinkles. He was capable of hurting Ludens even to the point sometimes of deliberate malice. This time however all he said was, 'Sometimes you look like a small silly child.'

'He's going to hold on to Alison,' said Ludens.

'Yes, he said to me, "I am sick with love for this woman."'

'Poor Franca.'

'Well, many people live *ménage à trois*, secretly or openly. Don't *you* worry about it, boy. You get on with your *work*. Don't be so restless.'

'We're all restless,' said Ludens, 'how can we not be, because of poor Pat, and —'

'Marcus.'

'Yes.'

'You think he'd cure Pat, and perhaps cure us as well? Ludens, I passionately want never to set eyes on that fascist anti-Christ, ever again.'

'I'd like to see him again,' said Ludens. 'I'd like to know what it is he's after, I mean, is it an experience or a thought, is it something you'd put in a book, or die for, or die of? Aren't you even curious?'

'No. He's a lost soul. He is sunk in the magic into which religion degenerates, what he wants is a spiritual power which has nothing to do with goodness. He wants to live forever. He probably will. He thinks he's God.'

'You forget he's a Jew,' said Ludens primly. 'No Jew can think he's God.'

'*Tant pis.* Eckhart said we all could. You imagine you understand Marcus because you're both Jewish. Let me tell you the amazing fact that Jews are just ordinary people and just as various.'

Ludens did not think that Jews were just ordinary people, but he let that pass. 'All right, Marcus isn't interested in Jewishness. And neither am I.'

'I think he's interested – but perhaps only in the way we all are, now.'

'What do you mean?'

'You remember those books Marcus had on the shelves at Miss McCann's place?'

'All those grammars, Chinese and Japanese and Sanscrit, and linguistics and Saussure and *Science Formalised as a Global Language* and –'

'He had several books about the Holocaust. They were hidden behind the other books.'

'Hidden. Maybe he was questioning his motives! It's easy to be fascinated, very hard to *think*, to think justly.'

'As a historian, you ought to be concerned. Never mind. I'm going home. I played the piano almost all last night.'

'Marcus told me a story about someone in a concentration camp,' said Ludens.

This checked Gildas who was making real or feigned movements as of someone about to rise and go.

Ludens went on, 'It was very short. It was a woman he knew, Polish or Czech, I forget, who'd been in Auschwitz. He asked her what she did all the day. She said *tricotage*.'

'I doubt if there were any knitting needles in Auschwitz. There may have been a factory where –'

'I thought she must have meant something like "make do and mend". I never discussed it with Marcus. He seemed to attach some importance to it.'

Gildas's face untwisted and unwrinkled itself, becoming smooth and sad. 'Useless people didn't last long in the camps. Marcus's people were never near one, they died in their beds in Switzerland and left him a fortune. That's why he was able to set out on that Dilettante's Progress.'

'Why do you hate him so? I remember when we wanted you to do an exorcism on Pat and you refused –'

'I funked it. Anyway I'm not a priest any more. I thought it might come out backwards. I'm superstitious about that man.'

'You mean you felt that the curse was *there*, like an invisible shield which would change anything which tried to go through it?'

Gildas did not answer. He suddenly began to sing. What he sang was:

'*Wide wide as the ocean, high as the heavens above,*
Deep deep as the deepest sea is my Saviour's love.
I though so unworthy still am a child in His care,

*For His love teaches me that His love reaches me
Everywhere.'*

Ludens knew this song, which had a fine tune, a relic from Gildas's evangelical childhood, but he did not join in, he listened to Gildas's beautiful voice, which seemed in the quiet of the night to be so full of thrilling meaning.

In the pause which followed, Ludens found his own face relaxing. When he thought of his great veiled project, when he meditated upon Leonardo, he experienced himself as heroic, noble, brave, almost beautiful; but sometimes he felt upon him that face of a silly small child, wide-eyed and anxious to please. He looked humbly at his friend.

Gildas went on, perhaps he was really drunk by now, 'The Christian symbols, yes, we seek holiness, what is sacred, we brood upon the death of that man. Baudelaire worshipped Edgar Allan Poe. "Absolute" as in absolute value is mystical, we know that. But empiricism, decent Western empiricism, honest truth-bearing ordinary language, *that's* what we've got to save. There's no cosmic shamanistic nonsense in Shakespeare, no Arthurian mysteries, no Grail – just the beauty and the horror of the world, and love – love – love. Well, I must go now, only I've got something to tell you first. Are you a strong man or a weak man, Ludens, remind me? Have you had any more dreams about those women?'

'No.'

'All dreams are sinister.'

When Ludens was sixteen he had had his fortune told by a gipsy at a fair. Ludens had asked whether he would get married and when. The gipsy had said, 'When there are three women, the time will have come. But be careful, one is a witch.' After this, for a while, Ludens had dreamt of three women.

'You said you were going to tell me something.'

'Well – yes –' Gildas, who had not risen, stared down at the table. He ruffled his dry frizzy hair, then pulled at it savagely. He took off his glasses and rubbed his eyes and moistened his lips.

'What is it, Gildas?'

'I have found out where Marcus is.'

'*Gildas*! – Where – where –?'

'He's living in Suffolk at the house of someone called Lord Claverden.'

'Oh heavens, oh, my dear, why didn't you *tell* me, why –'

'I'm telling you now. I've only just found out. I'll give you the address. I feel – well, you know what I feel. But get this clear – it's all yours now. I'm not going to be involved in any way. I fear that this may bring *no good* to Patrick or Jack or you or me – or other people of whom we still know nothing.'

Gildas had gone home. Ludens had cleared away the remnants of supper. He was sitting now at the table, gazing at a piece of paper upon which Gildas had written *Lord Claverden, Fontellen, Edmarsh, Suffolk*. So. The door was open into the dark and he had but to walk through it.

Gildas had made the discovery by accident. He had seen a reference in a newspaper article about personalities in the House of Lords to an eccentric Lord Claverden, described as a Communist peer. Under his family name, Sedgemont, his Lordship had, it appeared, when young, written a now obscure book on politics. The name gave Gildas a quick, at first inexplicable, emotional shock. Then he recalled that Marcus had, in a rather embittered argument about Communism, mentioned this name, Alexander Sedgemont, implying that this person was a friend of his, and had praised the book, saying it was one of the few sensible books on Marxism. Gildas had felt a ('superstitious', as he said to Ludens) compulsion to pursue the matter. There was a Sedgemont in the London telephone directory. Gildas rang the number and said to a pleasant male voice that he was trying to get in touch with Lord Claverden. The pleasant male promptly, and without asking questions, gave him the address. Gildas discovered the telephone number from directory enquiries. He then rang the house and asked for Lord Claverden. A less pleasant male voice said he was abroad, and, no, he could not divulge his address, and who was Gildas anyway and what did he want? Gildas, with no particular hope but with nothing to lose, said that actually he wanted to get in touch with Lord Claverden's friend, Professor Marcus Vallar. The other voice then uttered the fateful unexpected words, 'Oh, the Prof, he's here, but he's in the cottage and there's no telephone.'

This for Gildas explained the situation. Ludens, trembling with excitement, now wanted him to stay, to discuss a plan of campaign, to imagine and speculate: but Gildas would not. He repeated, 'It's all yours now,' declared that he did not want to know what Ludens might or might not decide to do, disclaimed all responsibility, and departed.

Ludens fetched an atlas and discovered where Edmarsh was. Writing a letter was out of the question, getting no reply would drive him mad. He would have to go straight there and blunder in. He would go tomorrow.

Gildas had expressed uncertainty as to whether Ludens was a weak man or a strong man. Ludens shared this uncertainty. He was also unsure whether he was a happy man or an unhappy man. He was cheerful, but that was different from happy. His satisfaction with his two books, both of moderate length, and their gratifying reception, had been brief, and was now succeeded by anxiety as to whether he would be able to deliver, to go on, to become a far better scholar, a much wiser historian. He was not afraid of hard work, and not averse to becoming famous. (Fame would impress and please his father, whom Ludens deeply cared for but rarely saw.) Yet at times these goals seemed empty, and he yearned for some nebulous 'other thing'. Then there was the woman question. Ludens was not a novice, there had been girls after Sylvia, though in more recent times none. He wanted to love and be loved. Would 'women' lead to love and happiness or to the 'irreversible mistake' referred to by Gildas? Did he want children? He did not know, sometimes he shuddered at the idea. He was annoyed and upset by the rumour that he was now 'out to get married'. His colleagues at the college had jested about this, there were even bets in the Common Room. All this had the effect of paralysing him and making him shun female society lest, being seen with this or that young woman, he be gossiped about.

Even the question of whether he had had a happy or unhappy childhood was unclear to Ludens. Fortunately he held no theory to the effect that the early years of one's life irrevocably establish one's temperament and one's destiny. He could be said, from an outsider's point of view, to have had an unhappy childhood, and be marked by it. He was left-handed, having survived the vigorous, even aggressive, attempts of school teachers to make him right-handed. As a child he had developed the stammer. This affliction had waned as he grew older, but still lurked in the caverns of his speech-mind, could very occasionally render him suddenly speechless and had to be overcome at times by a drawling hesitation, characteristic of Ludens's way of talking, and found by some to be charming. His first memories were of seeing a woman sitting with a baby on her knee. This woman was his stepmother, holding his halfbrother Keith. His stepmother (her name was Angela) was kind to him, but Ludens was aware that she was *not* his mother and that he was, lacking a mother, a second-class citizen. Much later his father said that he had told Ludens as a small child that his mother was 'away'. Ludens could not remember this telling, which he had evidently taken in, together with the conviction that it was no use asking, where is she? When will she come back? Attempts to make him call Angela 'Mummy' failed. Equally, he did not call his father 'Daddy', but, when still a child, found a beautiful name for him in a story. Later, when he was perhaps six, his father told him that his mother had died. Ludens, who had already formed the view that she was dead, nodded silently. He made no comment and asked no questions. He recalled how his father had stood before him as before a judge, hesitating, struggling silently for more words, hoping for the boy to speak, then assenting to his silence. Ludens was continually aware of his father's distress. He treasured his silence, not exactly as a weapon against his patently guilty father, but simply as a resource of strength for himself. The tension between them was a ceaseless pain to both. Yet this mutual grief, far from dividing father and son, united them as in some secret pact. Sometimes they looked at each other, Ludens with cool calm eyes, his parent with humble diffident caring eyes. What made Ludens calm, and able, in this curious form of combat, to confront his father without fear or anger, was his certain knowledge that his father loved him very much indeed, more than he loved Keith or Angela. Attentive looking and listening also provided the information that relations between the wedded pair, though not actually at breaking point, were far from perfect. Ludens, in spite of his stern impassive front, returned his father's love with equal ardour, and was sometimes persuaded that his father knew this.

In due course Ludens went to the junior part of the small public school in the senior part of which his father taught the classical languages and Greek and Roman history. Among the things which young Ludens soon learnt at school was that he was Jewish and that his father was Jewish but his stepmother was not. When Ludens was fourteen this lady suddenly decamped to Portugal taking Keith with her. Ludens and his father were alone together. Still the boy said nothing. Then, though not at once, it all came out. Ludens was born out of wedlock. Ludens found this information devastating. He knew he ought not to mind but he did. When Ludens was born, his mother and father had already parted company. It was agreed that the father should take the child. Ludens intuited that his father had left his mother, rather than she him. Was it a brief episode, a *faux pas*, perhaps a matter of one imprudent night? He felt that it was. He imagined the unwelcome news of the inconvenient pregnancy, the 'agreement' about the child. Had his mother wanted to keep him? He pictured her weak, his father strong. Or had his father reluctantly obliged her by promptly removing the scandalous unwanted infant? The story told to the then fourteen-year-old boy was understandably vague. Ludens did not ask for details and later could not ask. He did not know how his birth related in time to his father's marriage. His father revealed to him then, and clearly attached importance to this, that his mother was Jewish. It was only as an adult that he learnt her name. He gained, and sought, no information about her family. As Ludens knew later, his father had been made aware of his Jewishness by Hitler, though he never observed any Jewish ritual or spoke of his parents as having done so. These parents, evidently estranged from their son, in any case invisible, were said to live 'in the north of England', and later to be dead. Ludens recalled his father going away 'to a funeral', after which there was a quarrel with his stepmother.

So Ludens, as a child, both imposed and assented to an agnosticism which was part of this silent pact with his father. Later he acquitted himself of any charge of – what could it be called? – resentment, cruelty, pride. His instinctive prudence had been, he later felt, wise. He had had the strength to check abject confessions which both might have regretted later. He loved his father, here they were, all the others were gone, there was no more to be said. Later still he sometimes felt a nervous craving which he named curiosity. He even felt then that he had been disloyal to his mother, as if he should have set out to look for her when he was five. Yet what could he discover either by interrogating his father or by his own researches which would not be ambiguous, dubious, fruitlessly distressing? He was afraid of seeming, by any question, to accuse his father of something, and he dreaded any further guilty revelations. His father must know that anything that needed forgiveness was forgiven. Better not to know. Was that courage or cowardice, strength or weakness? Angela and Keith, mercifully still in Portugal, were evidently doing well. Angela was living with some Portuguese man, Keith was earning big money in computers. Angela occasionally wrote, Keith and Ludens exchanged cards at Christmas. Ludens had always got on quite well with Keith, after an initial sneer on the subject of mothers which was not repeated. Ludens's father remained in Somerset in the same little stone-built village house, with the little apple tree garden. Ludens's relations of silent mutual love with his father continued in a timeless tension which evidently suited them both.

These merciful dispensations did not prevent Ludens from developing his own private 'complex'. He pondered, especially in relation to the question of matrimony, upon the case of his father. He knew that his father was a disappointed man: parents mislaid, two women fled or discarded, one son alienated, the university post not gained, the intended book not written. Could Ludens's own life, for all its fairly promising start, escape some destined overthrow? While still at school he had read Freud's observations about Leonardo da Vinci: also born out of wedlock, son of a servant girl, adopted into his father's house at the age of four, the real mother absent, the present stepmother. Ludens attached himself to Leonardo as to a beneficent and inspiring patron. He felt he could see the story of his own life in the great pictures: the two mothers, the two little boys, the pointing angel, the mysterious smile. Leonardo, who 'awoke too early in the dark when everyone else was asleep': scientist, inventor, engineer, painter: gentle, kindly and withdrawn: fond of animals, vegetarian, left-handed: puritanical, frigid, and said to be incapable of sexual love. How did Freud seem to know more about him than the historians did? Because he had left Freud a message: 'I recall as one of my very earliest memories that when I was in my cradle a kite came down to me and opened my mouth with its tail and struck me many times with its tail against my lips.' Freud, having (Ludens was shocked at this) read the account in a German translation and failed to consult the Italian, took the bird to be a vulture (*Geier*), not a kite (*nibbio*). However, apart from this blunder and some wild speculations based upon it, Freud provided much to meditate upon. Ludens at sixteen took what he needed from this mixture, persuaded that he could remember his mother's breast, her passionate kisses and her sad strange other-worldly smile. For himself, Ludens was content to be puritanical and withdrawn and left-handed and fond of animals. He was not a vegetarian. His sexuality was 'normal' but late (Jack said retarded) and unpromiscuous (Jack said unambitious). He did not mind being called 'timid', sex was not a great subject for him. He did not want to mess up his life. He was certainly 'romantic' and hoped to meet *her* one day. When time passed and he did not, he was not unduly perturbed. He was not drawn to psychoanalysis. His great patron led him toward the sceptical disciplines of history. The 'mythology' was something secret and personal. Yet there was something else, something strange, even as if 'forbidden', which Ludens had, perhaps from long ago, acquired from his wanderings inside the mind of Leonardo; and which was connected with his persuasion that he, and he especially, was able to understand Marcus Vallar.

There was a terrible episode in the relations of Ludens with that remarkable man which Ludens had never revealed to anyone. He had been careful when sympathising with the plaints of his friends about Vallar not to admit that he himself had also been damaged. He was prompt to say that *he* had escaped unscathed, and had stopped seeing Vallar of his own accord, because he found him tiring, even boring. But such was far from being the case. What had happened was this. After Marcus's departure from Richmond, and his 'flight into the country', Ludens had, as has been recounted, persuaded Miss McCann to yield up Marcus's address in Kent, where, after a suitable interval, Ludens presented himself. He had an immediate shock. The Japanese disciple had departed, whether after a quarrel or in order to 'prepare Marcus's way' for visits to California and Japan was never clear. The door was opened for Ludens by Marcus's fourteen-year-old daughter Irina. There was no sign of the mother who was evidently abiding elsewhere (and was a little while later reported to be dead). Ludens, who could have done without this complication, was treated reasonably courteously, though rather absently, by Marcus who seemed quite pleased to have someone to talk to. Ludens, during his brief stay with them, frequently cursed the intrusive presence of the girl, without whom he could have had, what he had always wanted, a really prolonged and peaceful *tête-à-tête* with Marcus. Irina however was everywhere, tidying, dusting, bringing in cups of tea, even sitting in the same room and listening. Marcus did not seem to mind, perhaps, when talking, scarcely noticed her presence, but it irritated Ludens very much, especially as she took to staring at him. The conversations were, and not only for this reason, unsatisfactory. Ludens had determined beforehand to *pin Marcus down*, to orient and manoeuvre the discussion so as to *force* him to reveal, at least to name, his deepest, ultimate conception, the *thing itself* which he was really after.

Though not very long had passed since that last meeting (including Ludens's failure to question Miss McCann and his tactful or timid hesitation before risking a visit) Marcus seemed already to have passed into another phase. He still had something of his student prince look but his clothes were even shabbier and more careless and his hair, cut shorter, was tangled, more limply curly, and less bright. He was thinner, very erect and austere. His undiminished presence and his soft authoritative gritty honey-voice made him seem like a distinguished actor playing the part of an impoverished statesman in exile or a famous leader in disguise. He was slower in argument, often pausing abstractedly, his alarming grey eyes, which could hold Ludens breathless and motionless, gazing elsewhere, widening and narrowing, while his whole face grimaced with the effort of thought. In answer to some rather blundering questions by Ludens he said that, no, he had come to no conclusion about a universal language, and that even at Richmond he had begun to doubt whether anything would be gained by studying the common roots of natural languages. His approach had been, he said, 'hopelessly mechanistic'. He had even, in a way, learnt more by painting, although he had, he admitted, confused at that time the idea of pure cognition with the idea of pure perception. Painting had led him, as he put it, to the brink of a void, which at that time he had been quite unable to deal with or understand. What he must now attempt was to evolve (and of course this would take many years) an entirely new mode of thinking which would take as its starting point an intuitive grasp of the errors of traditional philosophy, but would also be enriched by many other elements. It now emerged that soon after his abandonment of mathematics, Marcus had actually spent some time studying philosophy, and having grasped its fundamental mistakes and seen it 'wouldn't do', had set off on the course that led him through painting to what he called 'metaphilology'. Now he felt ready to return to the philosophers but only, as he put it, to learn from their illusions and place his feet upon the rubble of their arguments. What was necessary was a kind of deep thinking, which would involve new concepts or perhaps no concepts at all, and which was not philosophy, or science, and was certainly not mythology or poetry (*that* road was a dangerous dead end) or morality. This mode of thought, whatever it might be (and he was still not sure) was, according to Marcus, the only possible escape from the technology which would otherwise destroy the planet if not by an explosion then by a total deadening of the ability to think. When Ludens, trying in an agony of attention to frame the questions which would flood the discussion with light, asked what the new mode of thought would reveal, Marcus answered impatiently (as if this were obvious) that it would uncover what the philosophers had utterly missed, the true nature of consciousness, the deep reality which the clumsy devices of philosophy had been concealing, piling up over it their masses of futile machinery. At this point Ludens asked the only question which Marcus found at all interesting and made him hesitate. 'I understand why not science or poetry, but why not morality, isn't *that* deep enough?' After a pause Marcus said, 'Ultimately morality must be discovered to be a superficial phenomenon.' When Ludens, feeling himself for a moment on the track of his mentor's thought, asked about the 'other elements' which would 'enrich' this new world-vision, Marcus said (as if Ludens would at once understand this), 'Yes, you are right. There must be *discipline*, there must be *experience*. One must live one's work. That is why I am going to Japan.' When at this point, and also at others, Ludens eagerly requested more information, Marcus would break off and murmur, 'But it won't do – something is missing – *it* is missing – I can see it, but it's under a cloud – it's all got to depend on one thing – if it doesn't it can't be true.' Asked by Ludens whether he were now writing a book Marcus said 'not yet', but he was 'making notes'. Then Irina would come in with tea and biscuits.

Irina, for all her importunate ubiquity, was a shy awkward girl. She was given to blushing and rarely spoke either to her visitor or to her father. Ludens, in rare intervals of his frustrated excitement, did manage to reflect how extremely odd it was for Marcus to have a daughter and how extremely odd it must be to be that person. He even spared a thought for the absent mother, not mentioned. The little brick-built house, it could scarcely be called a cottage, rented by Vallar was on the outskirts of the village, at the end of a terrace of similar houses, adjoining some abandoned allotments. Next to the house was a small fenced enclosure of exiguous grass and healthy nettles containing a single dirty shaggy elderly-looking sheep with beautiful sad yellow eyes. Ludens's first conversation with Irina concerned this sheep, which the child was evidently fond of, and which she fed regularly with fresh lusher longer grass plucked from the verge of the road. On the afternoon of the day after his arrival Irina asked him to come and look at the sheep, which he did, and even gathered some grass for it. He asked Irina where she was at school and she mentioned the name of her boarding school, but of course now it was holidays. The tiny room where Ludens talked with Marcus (their knees almost touched) looked out on a tiny garden occupied by a large shiny myrtle bush. The bush was covered with white waxy flowers which placed the scene in Ludens's later storm-torn memories of it as summer. It rained much of the time he was there, drenching the sheep and the garden and Irina who presumably went shopping and sometimes peered in at them from the garden through the glass doors. Like the sheep she seemed to like getting wet and would rush in tossing her hair wildly (she never wore a hat) and dripping water on the carpet. She did not smile or laugh. She rarely spoke to her father or even looked at him. Perhaps there was an intimacy which did not need words, Ludens was not sure. Marcus eyed her with a reflective open-eyed vagueness which seemed to denote affection. She was in the charmless stage of semi-childhood, neither a little girl nor a maiden. She had a round plump shiny unformed face, a downy upper lip, long straight greasy dark hair, sometimes plaited, sometimes stringy. Her clothes were ostentatiously dowdy and messy, her skirt lop-sided, her cardigan inside out. Her dark eyes, when she gazed intently, seemed sometimes to squint. Ludens, vaguely invited to stay, had by now spent one night in the house and intended to spend another; more would be inappropriate on a first visit. For of course he hoped to come again. In fact he had already planned a whole relationship between him and Marcus stretching away into the far future.

The terrible thing that was to happen to him happened in the later part of the session with the sheep. This sortie, close to the house yet outside it, provided the first period of privacy, in which Ludens was able, at any rate felt bound, to talk to the girl and in some way make her acquaintance. They were standing (Ludens remembered it all so clearly later), having fallen silent, watching the sheep eating a pile of fresh long grass which Irina had tossed over the fence. It was not raining but had lately been, and there was a brilliant lurid evening light, a flight of white pigeons was suddenly sunlit against a thickly dark pewter sky, a momentary rainbow was fading. The sheep's enclosure was muddy. The low fence which surrounded it, raggedly broken at the top and rotting and now very wet, began to come to pieces in the nervous hands with which the two spectators were now clutching it. Ludens and Irina, first unconsciously and then intentionally began to break off little bits of the fence and drop them into the nettles. At that moment Irina said something inaudible, and Ludens said, 'I'm sorry, what did you say?' and Irina said, 'I love you.' Ludens clearly remembered the conversation which followed and how instantly he felt a detached and slightly aggressive annoyance. He replied at first 'Oh really!' and gave a little laugh and took his hands off the fence. Irina repeated 'I *love* you.' He now replied, 'Come, come, you are a child. If you *like* me, that is nice. Now let's go in, shall we?' Irina, not moving, still clutching the fence, said, 'Wait. You don't understand. I'm *in love* with you. Please take this seriously and don't go away, or I shall *scream*.' As they spoke they both looked at the sheep not at each other. Ludens said, 'I don't like screaming children, please don't make a scene.' 'I'm not making a scene. I'm telling you something deep and awfully important which has changed my whole life.' 'That's not possible, you've only just met me, this is our first conversation. Now, don't be *silly*, you're talking nonsense, pull yourself together!' 'I love you, I want you, I'd die for you –' 'Please *stop*, you're becoming hysterical, I don't want to hear about these schoolgirl emotions, what do you expect me to do. I'm years older than you, you're a *child*, and I don't find you in the least attractive!' 'Oh, I love you so much!'

At this moment Irina actually fell on her knees upon the wet muddy pavement and threw her arms round Ludens's legs, leaning her head against his thigh. Ludens was horrified. He felt the warm weight of her head and her wet hair soaking his trousers, he saw her skirt spread out and darkening in a pool of water. It was beginning to rain again. The sheep had stopped eating its grass and was watching the scene with its calm mild golden eyes. '*Get* up, you silly little fool,' said Ludens, 'someone will see us!' He leaned down and touched her shoulder, then gripped her arm, pulling her up. Irina cried out, she did not scream but uttered a strange non-human sound, a kind of soft raucous roar. Then she clambered to her feet and fell with the whole length of her body against him. She did not put her arms around him, but let them hang, gripping the hem of his jacket with her hands and leaning heavily forward, her head against his shoulder. He had to hold her for a moment to prevent her falling to the ground. The warm wet feel of the long soft animal pressed against him filled Ludens with disgust. He pushed her away with an exclamation of aversion and stepped quickly back. She staggered, standing now facing him, her feet wide apart, and he saw her face properly for the first time. It was crimson and awful, her mouth wet and open, her eyes beginning to spill tears. The rain was falling. Ludens's face too was blazing hot. He said quietly, 'We'll go in now. I'm sorry about this. I hope I haven't upset you. I won't say anything to your father.' He turned and ran back and into the house. Marcus was standing in the hall. As Ludens stopped abruptly and tried to think of something ordinary to say, Irina ran in after him weeping hysterically.

Marcus immediately seized hold of Irina who was trying to run past him, and hugged her tightly in his arms, gazing over her head at Ludens, his face flushed with rage. As Irina wailed and Ludens tried to say something, it was clear that Marcus assumed that Ludens had made some improper advance to his daughter. He shouted at Ludens, 'You vile beast –' Ludens shouted back, 'I didn't do anything. She said she loved me, she threw herself at me, I told her to shut up and clear off!' Irina could then be heard shouting, 'I love him.' Marcus released her. In a moment's silence, broken only by Irina's sobbing, Marcus stepped forward and Ludens stepped back. Marcus's face, usually so calm or else loftily puzzled, was glaring with loathing and horror, and his words sounded strangely foreign as if an ancestor were talking. 'So, you were cruel to the tender child, you rejected her childish affection, you defiled it with your base vulgarity, you trampled upon her innocence, you worthless –' Irina had followed her father and now seized his arm which was upraised as if to inflict instant punishment upon the villain. Ludens took this opportunity to race past, up the stairs, and grab his coat and suitcase and down again and out of the door, while Irina was once more weeping in her father's arms. He ran all the way to the station and sat in the train trembling with shock all the way to London.

When, late in the evening, he got back to his lodging, he sat for some time over a glass of whisky trying to compose a letter of apology. He felt then how much he loved Marcus Vallar. He had never put it to himself so clearly. It was not just an intellectual quest, it was the man he valued more than anything in the world, and had now lost for ever. How could this awful thing, this accident, have happened so suddenly, in a matter of minutes – because he had been so unkind, so rude, so thoughtless, so *ungrateful* when Irina had declared her love? He had made her cry and fall on her knees in the mud. He should have been gentle and tender, not scornful and dismissive. Surely he could have been kind and firm without giving her false hopes. And he had uttered those stupid boorish words to Marcus about 'telling her to shut up', he had shouted them out. How could he now redeem what had so suddenly, so rapidly, occurred? He laboured long over the letter. 'I deeply value her gracious words . . . I am very sorry I upset her . . . I hope she will forgive . . . pardon my blunders . . . please understand . . . I humbly trust . . .' Ludens found a little comfort in writing the letter, but when he read it through he tore it up and simply despatched a few plain words of apology. What, after all, did Marcus finally believe had happened? He did not expect a reply and did not receive one.

All these things Ludens was now remembering as he sat at the table after Gildas had gone and looked at the address: Fontellen, Edmarsh, Suffolk. He had to go there because of Patrick; and because it was fated. Yes, that gave him courage, to feel that he had not sought it, it had come upon him, and however fruitless or disastrous that journey might be, he had to undertake it, because it was his fate.

Franca and Ludens stood at the foot of the bed looking at Patrick. He lay on his back, his eyelids drooping, his face paler, moister, more sunken to the bone, his long thin skeleton hands outstretched, he looked ancient. He had become more remote. The nurse and Doctor Hensman had discussed whether to put him on a drip feed, or to let him sink. It was eight o'clock in the morning. The curtains were drawn against the sunlight. Jack, who had spent the night at Alison's flat, was not yet back. Ludens had just arrived and told Franca that he had discovered where Marcus Vallar was and was going to see him to try to persuade him to come to see Patrick.

Franca found this news, which Ludens seemed so pleased with himself about, obnoxious. She had become absorbed into Patrick's dying, she now saw this bed as a death-bed and his remoteness as a sleep into death. She almost dreaded his occasional signs of animation, the opening of his eyes, his mutterings. Once he seemed to smile and it was the most terrible smile Franca had ever seen.

'Please don't go and see that man,' she said to Ludens. 'It's too late. His life is at an end. Don't bring that horrible person here, let him die in peace.' She imagined a scene, the room full of people, Patrick screaming. She said, 'He's seen Father O'Harte now, that is enough.'

'You mean?'

'He's had extreme unction or whatever it's called. I didn't want it, but it doesn't matter now. I thought it might make him despair of life, but he has despaired anyway. The nurse wanted the priest to come, even Jack wanted it, and Alison thought it would calm him, Alison thought – He didn't seem to understand what was happening, but Father O'Harte said it made no difference. I just want him to go in peace now, to *go*, and not to suffer.'

Tears came into her eyes. She had been trying in the last days to get used to this inevitable death, to pre-enact it and think about what she would do later. When he is dead, I shall go to Kew Gardens. But what could that mean. She had indulged herself by loving him, in the guileless days when she had imagined that he would recover. Perhaps some premonition had led her to seek refuge in that innocent love. Now she had been trying to apprehend, to gorge herself with, Patrick's death, his soon nothingness, and in doing so to contain and stifle and utterly disappoint and undo her feelings for him. After all, it was already him no longer. Yet too, it was not the old him that she had chosen to love. How terrible to will death and to dismantle love. She said to Ludens, 'Oh, it's been so awful.' She felt his hand seek hers and squeeze it. She said, 'Does it smell terrible in this room? I'm so used to it.' She thought, when he is dead I shall enter *the nightmare*. For now it must wait.

'Does he speak to you?' said Ludens. 'Can you still communicate?'

When he had told her, in the other room, that he had found out where Marcus Vallar was, he had looked so bright-eyed and hopeful, a proud childish look that was characteristic of him. Now he looked full of grief, suddenly foreign, a mourner.

'You're welcome to try,' said Franca. 'He sometimes murmurs a bit.'

'Does he still talk poetry?'

'No, yes, he sometimes says something which sounds like a line of poetry. I wish he wouldn't. It's uncanny.'

'Have you written down any of the things he's said?'

'No, of course not.'

Ludens went to the side of the bed and knelt down. He cautiously took hold of one of the long skeleton hands. It was limp and damp and cold. 'His hand is cold.'

'Yes.'

'Pat,' said Ludens, and his voice trembled, 'dear Pat. It's me, Ludens, Alfred. Please speak to me.'

The sick man's eyes opened a little more. He did not move his head but his eyes turned a little in the direction of his visitor. He murmured something.

'What – what is it?' said Ludens.

'The sea –'

'Yes –?'

'Their grey faces dead in the sea water.'

As Pat said no more Ludens rose. 'We ought to have taken him to the sea.' He rubbed his hand on his jacket.

'You say such silly things!' said Franca. 'What's the use of saying that now? Why didn't you come and see him more? Gildas was here yesterday morning.'

'Oh, was he?'

'Jack comes in and stares at him, Alison comes – she's very good –'

'Yes, it is uncanny,' said Ludens. 'Grey faces, seals perhaps, or –'

'Come.' Ludens followed Franca into the adjoining room. She sat down on the bed, uncoiled one long dark snake of hair, then deftly wove it back into the massive bun and pinned it. Ludens stood watching her, still with his old grieving look. Then his face was animated by a more personal and sympathetic gaze.

Franca felt a sudden strong urge to talk to Ludens, and felt at the same moment his prompt desire to receive her confidences. His compassionate face became rueful. He looked down for a moment. Then he looked at her questioningly.

In the last days Franca had felt an urge to talk, to tell, to tell somebody else. But whom could she tell? Not Patrick or Molly Stein or Linda or Ned Oliver (whom she liked) or Moxie (whom she had grown fond of) or any other of her increasingly shadowy women friends. It would have to be either Gildas or Ludens – but which? She could not tell both and have them discussing her together. Yesterday she had almost said something to Gildas. He had been so gentle with Pat, and with her. But I *can't* talk to them, she thought, to either of them, it would be black treachery – and besides I've got to *think* first – and I can't think until – after Patrick.

And what did she want to tell, what could she say? It was as if she were looking for a substitute, a symbol of her secret, which she could soothe her soul by communicating, without giving away what it was a symbol of. So I can't *ever* tell that? she wondered. It's a life sentence to silence – after all marriage is a life sentence, *my* marriage is anyway, whatever *his* may be. The agony was of suddenly feeling herself so separate and so secret. Yesterday too she had felt an urge to whisper it all to Patrick, knowing he would not understand. But it would be an affront to poor Pat. How could she drop such poison into his ears; and how could she take even that risk of anyone ever knowing? Franca had discovered evil in her soul, and was appalled. Had it always been there, that evil? Jack had said no lies equalled all was well; had she herself now become a liar? Surely the past had been innocent, had possessed some indestructible innocence untouched by time. So now she had transferred her own past being into *that* fortress which was after all not herself – but contained herself as its guardian. She was the guardian of that past, which was also the present and the future, keeping it safe from the evil in her soul.

'You look tired, are you getting enough sleep?'

She thought, he wants me to talk to him, he will lead the conversation that way.

'Oh yes. I never sleep much. I wake, I sleep, I dream. And Moxie's here sometimes at night.'

'Not bad dreams, I hope.'

'Not –? No. I sometimes dream about my mother.'

'I dream about my mother too – only she's in disguise.' Ludens stood before her, his hands behind his back, his feet slightly apart, his sympathetic face bent thoughtfully towards her, his eyes narrowed with attention.

Franca, sitting on the bed, thought, how young he looks, he's scarcely changed since we first met. How did we get onto mothers so quickly? Did I dream about my mother last night? Then she remembered she had dreamed not of her mother, but of her wicked cruel father. She said, 'Were you close to your mother?'

'No –' He opened his mouth, seemingly anxious to say something else. 'I'm – I'm – I'm sorry, you must forgive my s- my speech impediment.'

'You haven't got a speech impediment,' said Franca. 'I mean, yes, of course I know you had one but I thought it had gone away.'

'Oh, I have, and it mostly has gone away, but it comes back occasionally like hay fever. "Stammer" was the word I was trying to say. Sometimes you see a word coming and it stops you.'

'What was the other word that stopped you?'

'I was going to say that I never knew my mother – she went away, then she died.'

'Oh, I'm sorry,' said Franca. She now remembered that Jack had told her something about Ludens's childhood. She added, 'My mother was unhappy. My father was a difficult man.'

She thought, perhaps this is the symbol I was looking for, the thing that I can say instead of the evil thing. Perhaps he was looking for a symbol too, something, anything, that connects us. But of course he's just curious. He's so close to Jack, he must know what's happened, he wants to find out what I think! She drew her feet up onto the bed, pulling her skirt over her slippers. To avoid a pause she went on, 'I think Gildas was happy with his parents, they all sang hymns together! I'm sorry he stopped being a priest, somehow one is always sorry when someone leaves the priesthood.'

'Oh – yes –' The spell was broken, the moment passed. Ludens changed his pose, wriggled his shoulders, fiddled in the pockets of his jacket. Sounds came from downstairs, voices, laughter. Jack had come back with Alison.

Ludens said, 'It's Jack, I must go and tell him!'

'I'll follow you down.'

He vanished, leaping down the stairs, eager to tell Jack his news.

Franca went back to look at Patrick. He had turned on his side, he was still mobile. One arm was half under the pillow, the other across his breast. His eyes were closed. She came close, as she often did now, to see if he were still breathing. The bedclothes rose and fell, he was still there. One's breaths are numbered. After a while she followed Ludens down the stairs.

The sun was shining into the kitchen where Jack and Alison and Ludens seemed to be talking all at once. The room smelt of coffee. Jack came to her and kissed her, putting his arm right round her and lifting her off the ground. Alison watched, smiling. Franca smiled, laughed, holding his hand for a moment. Jack was 'in majesty', broad-shouldered, erect, gracefully fingering back his blond hair, his prominent blue eyes, like luminous gemstones, seeming to gaze beyond the human scene, those of a fearless commander. He emanated a confident authority of which everyone in the room was conscious. Franca thought, how healthy and strong he and Alison look! I look like an overworked nurse, and Alfred looks like a starving intellectual!

Alison was making some coffee at the stove, using the percolator which Franca never used, having forgotten how it worked. She made a gesture to Franca which meant: do you mind? I'm making coffee. Franca gestured a smiling assent. She had laid the table earlier. Bread, butter, honey, marmalade, milk, were now in evidence. She said to Ludens, 'Would you like something?'

'Oh, no thanks.'

'He's too excited to eat!' said Jack. 'He's off to Suffolk to find Marcus Vallar.'

'Yes, he told me.'

'Franca disapproves,' said Ludens, who could not help smiling at Alison.

Jack sat down. Alison motioned Franca to sit. Franca said, 'No, thanks.' Alison sat. She gave Franca an emotional look which Franca could not interpret, indeed did not try to. Alison was nearly as tall as Jack. She wore a blue- and white-striped cotton dress which, as Franca watched, she buttoned high up at her long neck, turning up the collar. Her milky-pale complexion, now very slightly pink from the sun, was scattered with the faintest of golden freckles. Franca could see her breathing, see the blue veins on her arm. She smoothed down her glossy healthy fast-growing red hair and patted it into shape. Then one long slim hand posed unconsciously across her breast. She was wearing a gold bracelet.

She addressed Franca. 'I think I saw a cormorant fishing in the Thames. Is that possible?'

'Oh yes. I have seen them.'

Jack was talking to Ludens, who was leaning against the dresser. 'When are you going?'

'Tomorrow. Better get it over quick.'

'Are you nervous?'

'Yes!'

'But you're immune, he can't touch *you*! At worst he'll be bloody rude. I just hope – if he does come – it won't be some sort of horror show.'

'Horror show?' said Franca.

'We don't know what we're in for!'

'But you were so keen that he should come,' said Ludens.

'I'm very anxious to see him,' said Alison, 'he sounds so weird.'

'Then we'll produce him for you!' said Jack. 'Ludens shall bring him captive, Ludens our hero! We'll be waiting!'

'I must be off,' said Ludens.

'I suppose you will spend the day in meditation!' said Franca.

'I meant to go today, but I wanted to tell you, and I must make sure the car is OK. I'll leave very early tomorrow morning. I don't know how long it will take to find the place. I don't want to arrive when he's having lunch.'

'Good heavens,' said Franca, 'Marcus doesn't *have lunch*.'

'Why, is he always on a diet?' said Alison.

'No. I mean human beings have lunch.'

'You must forgive him, Franca,' said Jack.

'Forgive him? What for?'

'He was rather rude to you.'

'I don't remember.'

'Well, goodbye,' said Ludens. 'I'll hope to see you all again!'

'I'll see you out,' said Jack. He rose. Alison rose too. Franca opened the door.

Ludens, awkward, touched Franca's shoulder, then, with a little rush, moved to Alison and bowed. Then with long steps glided out. Jack followed.

Alison, still standing, said, 'Oh Franca.'

Franca, keeping the door open, said, 'What's the matter?'

Fortunately at that moment Moxie's voice was heard in the hall, together with Jack's deep tones. Then Moxie looked into the kitchen, saw Alison, and stepped back. Moxie disliked Alison and disapproved of her. Of course she knew what was going on, of course she said nothing. But, out of solidarity with Franca, she sometimes made her feelings plain.

'I'll go up with you,' said Franca to Moxie. She made an apologetic 'excuse me' gesture to Alison. Franca and the nurse mounted the stairs together. In silence they entered the twilit room. Patrick's position had not changed.

'Do you mind if I open a window?'

'It's open,' said Franca.

'He's not long for this world,' said Moxie. 'He'll soon join the silent majority.'

Grey faces dead in the sea water, thought Franca.

Jack and Ludens had walked down the road in silence and were leaning on the embankment wall and looking at the Thames. The tide was in, perhaps on the turn, lapping very quietly against the wall, not far below the reach of their hands. The quiet water was a very pale radiant blue, its surface smooth and glossy like enamel. There was a fresh watery smell, a pleasant faintly rotting smell perhaps, but there could be no serious pollution now that the cormorants had come. Perhaps one day there would be salmon. The river breathed gently, exuding coolness into the warm day.

Ludens had taken off his jacket and rolled up his sleeves. Jack, who was wearing a mauve shirt, considerably unbuttoned, also rolled up his sleeves. Jack's chest was covered with closely curling golden hair. Copious long golden hairs swarmed on his brown arms and large hands. Jack had put on weight, his chest, now visible, was broader, his head seemed larger, his arms more powerful. He seemed, not fatter, but more substantial. As they leaned there together, looking at the calm, now almost motionless, river, the dense strong hairs on Jack's brown arm brushed the scantier darker hairs on Ludens's pale arm.

'We went swimming early this morning.'

'Who's we?' said Ludens disobligingly.

'Me and Alison. The tide wasn't so far in, but it was good, the water was warm. She swims like a dolphin.'

'Of course. Have you joined that tennis club? Yes? So you may now anticipate being beaten at tennis also.'

'I look forward to it.'

'Do you usually bring her in to breakfast?'

'No, it's the first time.'

'The first of many times.'

'I don't know. It depends on Franca. Do you think I'm mad?'

'Yes.'

'You underestimate Franca. She's very strong, she's a powerhouse of strength. She can *think*, I can *see* her thinking. She likes Alison very much and Alison adores her.'

'It's all in your dream.'

'You'll see. It's got to work, so it will. Franca will make it work. She's the boss.'

'I think you're a cad. But it's none of my business.'

'Don't use that dreary phrase at me. And don't use such brutal terminology either. When you marry will you never look at another woman? You don't *understand*, you're not *thinking*. Of course it's your business. I've got to have both of them, how can I not try? You've met Alison. I don't deserve her. But the gods sent her. And I can't live without her. Franca knows that she, she herself, is safe, the safest thing in the world, pure gold, the Bank of England. They fit, they perfect each other.'

'They fit you, they fit your old dream of the calm *hausfrau* and the merry young mistress, only now, as you wave your wand, it's for ever.'

'You don't see how *enormous* this thing is for me, the whole world is made of it, I've *got* to succeed. Please don't quarrel with me.'

'I'm not quarrelling, brother. Perhaps you *will* succeed. You've got nerve enough. Perhaps you *will* make them happy. Two women. I can't even find one.'

'Oh I forgot to tell you, Alison says Heather Allenby will be in London next week. So don't let Marcus eat you.'

After a pause Ludens said, 'I saw Pat this morning. I think he's going. But I've *got* to see Marcus now – that's what *my* whole world is made of.'

Jack turned away from the river. He murmured, 'Forgive me.'

'Forgive you for being happy? I can forgive you for that – probably for anything.'

PART TWO

FREE BICYCLES. Ludens contemplated the notice which was prominently set up inside the gates on the side of the gravel drive. Free bicycles? Unwanted bicycles offered gratis? Bicycles released to wander like free-range hens? Or a protest: unjust to bicycles, bicycles lib?

The small wicket-gate at the side was, he noticed, padlocked. Formidable stone walls stretched away on either hand. But the two halves of the very tall and handsome cast-iron main gates stood awkwardly, one tilting slightly, perhaps unhinged, failing to meet in the centre, allowing a small space for a slim person to slip through. Ludens slipped through.

It was the evening of the day which had begun with his visit to Jack's house, his talk with Franca, his talk with Jack. He had indeed intended to spend the day in meditation, working out a strategy, deciding when best to arrive, what exactly to ask Marcus about his work, what exactly to say to Marcus about Patrick. But of course this had proved impossible: Ludens found himself, after leaving Jack, far too agitated to put off his journey any longer. He was tormented, for instance, by the not unlikely possibility that Marcus might simply refuse to talk to him and might close the door in his face. He had taken a taxi from Chelsea back to St John's Wood and sat for a short while gnawing his fingers and brooding upon the necessity of immediate action. After this he leapt up, realising that there was no time to be lost. He then spent half an hour trying and failing to buy a new up-to-date motorway map. When he gave his attention to his car (a Volkswagen) it turned out that the petrol tank was nearly empty and he had to spend more time driving to a garage and waiting in a queue. When he drove back to his house there was no room to park. When he had parked he thought he had better test the lights, windscreen wipers, and indicators. One of the indicators failed to work and he had to drive back, first to his usual garage, who were too busy, and then to another where he had to wait for a mechanic's attention. He drove back (still no place to park) feeling very hungry (he had had no breakfast). He ate a quick lunch in his flat and studied his out-of-date road map. Edmarsh was visible, in the smallest print, unclearly marked, almost obliterated, in a fuzzy mass of tiny remote roads. How long would it take to get there, given that it was Friday, and there would be more traffic on the motorway? Would it be wise to visit Marcus in the afternoon, when he might be resting, or in the evening, when he might be tired after a day's work? If it came to that, would it be wise to arrive in the morning, interrupting his work in full flow? Ludens decided, since yet more time had now passed, that he had better leave at once, drive to the area, find Edmarsh, book into a hotel for the night, and face Marcus on the following morning, when, however Marcus might feel, Ludens would be feeling, if this were possible, fresh and strong.

He set off and decided as he drove along that it might be prudent not to stay in Edmarsh itself, where he might encounter Marcus in the street, but to stay at a nearby village, in rather larger print, called Clinten. He pictured Edmarsh as tiny, almost a hamlet, and Fontellen as a fairly conspicuous village house near the church, possibly an old rectory, with small cottage adjacent. He would have no difficulty finding it in the morning, so there was no need to reconnoitre Edmarsh that evening. After finding himself capable of making all these rational decisions Ludens felt better, and was not too dismayed by, as he expected, losing his way in a maze of unsigned Suffolk lanes, in a flat land where, in what was now just discernibly an evening light, nothing broke the horizon but a few distant church towers. It was here, in one of these lanes where there were no other landmarks of human habitation, that, turning a corner too fast and bumping violently against an unexpected stone, he burst a tyre. He directed the limping car onto some grass and switched off the engine. The comfortable sound ceased, the silent evening countryside came uncannily into being round about him. He climbed out miserably, praying that he had not mislaid the jack. He opened the boot. The jack was there, but, as was immediately evident, the spare tyre was flat too, Ludens having intended, but forgotten, to have it changed. Ludens quietly closed the boot, looked at the map again, locked up the car and set off on foot in the direction, so far as he could judge it, of Clinten. He walked for a short while, passing no house and meeting no one. A car passed but he turned his head away, shrinking almost guiltily off the road. The landscape here was different, more wooded, not exactly hilly, but certainly less flat. The large sky was full of lines of small white clouds which were being hurried along in the direction of the (distant) sea, and the slanting sunlight came and went. Ludens reached a crossroads with a clump of trees and a telephone box and a signpost. The road he had just come along was signed to Clinten, the road ahead to Edmarsh. No mileage was given. The other names, strange to him, he judged to be of places farther away. He listened, now that the sound of his tramping had ceased, to a silence which contained the song of a lark. As he stood there tired, exasperated, conscious of hunger and unsuitable shoes, uneasy, beginning to feel frightened, a man appeared walking towards him. The man carried a trowel in his hand. To Ludens he seemed an almost allegorical figure. Ludens raised his hand in a solemn manner and the man stopped. He proved to be ordinary, friendly, was sorry he could not offer Ludens a lift, and informed him (in answer to a question) that Edmarsh, four miles away, was the nearest village. Was there a hotel there? Well, there was the Claverden Arms, scarcely to be called a hotel. It was then that Ludens, impetuously, in order perhaps to make the best use of an available informant, or simply to prolong the conversation, asked the man whether he knew of a house in Edmarsh called Fontellen. The answer, in a surprised tone, was, 'Fontellen isn't in Edmarsh! It's just here, down that road, about a quarter of a mile! You'll see the gates.' The man then asked, 'Are you looking for a job?' Thanking him and saying no, and hurrying away in the direction indicated by the pointing trowel, Ludens wondered what the question meant. Perhaps simply that he was not wearing a tie. He soon saw the wall, shaggy with plants, with trees behind it, and in a few minutes reached the gates and the intriguing notice.

The drive turned away into trees, no house was visible. The condition of the weedy gravel and the gates, whose feet were sunk in the earth, suggested that the entrance was unused. Nearby, beside the drive, was a little wooden hut with a sort of guichet. Perhaps for charging admission in some now past era? The board saying *Free Bicycles* was beside this hut, and Ludens now saw, disguised by tangles of profusely flowering wild clematis, a long shed, toward which an arrow on the noticeboard was pointing. Moving nearer and peering into the dark interior between the long strings of flowers he discerned a row of bicycles all painted white. A bicycle ride for free round the estate? Having come so far it was now, he felt, impossible not to set eyes on the house before walking on into the village. Something to do with the size of the gates suggested that the house might be some distance off. But it was even clearer that the state of the drive precluded cycling. He returned to the hut and considered leaving his bag there and decided not to. He decided to go a little way along the drive. Walking through a sea of blue flowering forget-me-nots and speedwell he reached the curve and looked ahead into a dark tunnel through a dense wood. He walked a little farther, then felt daunted. He returned to the daylight, reflecting that it was late, he still had four miles to walk to the village, it was no moment for an indefinite promenade in a dark wood. He was returning toward the road when he saw something which put another complexion on the problem. The gravel drive was rough and humpy, covered in wild flowers. But running beside it was a hard smooth flowerless track whose clean dark tarmac surface had made it invisible. A bicycle track. There was even a foreshortened painting of a bicycle upon it near the hut.

Looking at his watch, Ludens hurried back to the bicycle shed. Something to do with those bicycles had captured his imagination from the first, and not in vain. He would speed through the wood, glimpse the house, then return and – why not? – borrow the bicycle to take him into the village. He would then return it tomorrow. That kind and generous notice was surely open to any reasonable interpretation. The shed was long and dark and contained about twenty male and female machines, not, as he now feared, in chains, but indeed free. However, as Ludens soon realised he might have expected, they were but poor broken-down creatures, more in tune with the neglected gates and the drive than with the impeccable cycle track. Their white paint was still, in some cases, glossy, but they lacked here a chain, here a saddle, here handlebars, here a wheel, and all without exception had flat tyres. Other accessories, such as pumps, bells, lights, baskets, if they had ever possessed them, had probably long ago been removed by the local citizenry. Indeed it was remarkable that so much of them remained. Intensely disappointed he turned away. Then he noticed adhering to the wall of the far end of the shed, a little wooden compartment or cubbyhole with a closed door. He opened the door. Within was a beautiful shining white bicycle, a fine male machine complete with all its members, with new hard tyres and regulation lights and a bell. Boldly Ludens wheeled it out and led it to the track. He mounted, hung his bag on the handlebars, and set off.

The wood, not as dense as it had at first seemed, afforded vistas here and there where magnificent very tall conifers spread their arms over twilit clearings, and nature and art felicitously mingled their contributions. At one point a wide grass pathway crossed the drive, but it afforded no views, and Ludens stayed with the bicycle track. Further off a thrush was singing its piercing repetitive evening song, but nearby there was no sound except for the very soft singing tone of the bicycle wheels. Ludens felt excitement, fear, elation. Suddenly the wood ended, not tapering away in a lightening straggle of separated trees and saplings, but cut off abruptly at a sharp line where meadowland met woodland. Ludens dismounted, staying just within the shadow of the trees. The sudden light, vivid with late evening, dazzled him and he shaded his eyes. Cow parsley, coming into white flower, fringed the wood and touched his knees. A large meadow of pink tufted feathery grass with a glittering scatter of buttercups, lay before him, traversed by the drive and the cycle track. Beyond it, and beyond some appurten-ances of a garden, such as dark hedges and lawns, upon a slight eminence, stood a long grey eighteenth-century house with a green dome in the centre. Further away on one side a sheet of water reflected the light of the setting sun while above a low horizon a pale greenish sky entertained streaky terraces of red and golden cloud. Ludens, dismounted, stood entranced, breathing deeply, his anxiety eclipsed as he felt sudden pure pleasure at the proportions of the house and the intense glowing detail of the many-coloured scene. Then he realised that he was not alone.

A man was standing close beside him. Ludens turned in quick shock and saw a tall man with shaggy brown hair and side whiskers, dressed in tweeds and leggings and a collarless shirt and carrying a stick. The sudden proximity of this male presence made Ludens step abruptly backward, almost falling over his bicycle. He felt menaced and guilty, wondering for a moment whether this apparition might not be the eccentric Lord Claverden in person.

'What the hell do you think you're doing? You're a trespasser and a thief. What's your name?'

More likely a gamekeeper. Ludens disliked being asked his name, particularly in such a tone. He felt hostility to the whiskered man, but felt even more his own guilty situation. Adopting a mild tone he replied, 'I'm so sorry. I do apologise, I did borrow the bicycle. The fact is I have an appointment to see Marcus Vallar, he's expecting me, but I was delayed, so I took this liberty.'

'Was it you rang up?'

'Yes.'

'You're a liar, the chap who rang up had a Welsh accent.'

'That was my secretary, he rang on my behalf.'

'That bike belongs to me. I said what's your name?'

'Dr Alfred Ludens. As I said, I'm a friend of Professor Vallar and —'

'That bike was locked up, you must have broken the lock.'

71

'It wasn't locked up –'

'It was. Anyway you can leave it here and foot it back to the road.'

'Oh all right,' said Ludens, anxious now simply to get away. 'I'm sorry.' He took his bag off the handlebars and leaned the bicycle against a tree.

'I thought you wanted to see the Prof.'

'I do, but I've decided it's too late, I'll go back –'

'No, you won't, you're lying and thieving.'

'Look,' said Ludens, 'be rational. If I'd wanted to steal the bike I'd have ridden it away down the road, not straight up to the house! I just wanted to be sure Professor Vallar is here. I'll see him in the morning.'

'You said you had an appointment.'

'It's tomorrow.'

'Anyway, he's not here.'

'What?'

'He ain't here, the house is empty, his lordship is overseas.'

'But –'

'All right, you don't know where he is, do you? And I do. He's in the cottage. But you don't know where that is, do you? It's called Red Cottage. And if you really want to see him I'll show you the way now.'

'Please don't trouble, just tell me where –'

The tall man had already turned and was walking along a bumpy earthy track which bordered the cow parsley and the edge of the wood. Ludens followed, not sure whether he were not now under arrest. The evening light was fading, the sun had set leaving a red glow against which the land stood out in silhouette, while in another quarter an intensely blue sky was rapidly gathering the atoms of darkness. The interior of the wood looked black. A small path turned away among scantier trees. Ludens's companion pointed to a light ahead.

'There's his place. I don't know what to make of you. He can't be expecting you. No one ever visits him.'

'I was his favourite pupil,' said Ludens, 'I'll just say hello to him, then I can find my way back, please don't wait. Thank you very much. Sorry about the bike. Goodnight.' He turned his back on his guide and walked in among the trees toward the light.

Ludens, as he walked along, had reflected on the mess he had got himself into. He had no intention of calling on Marcus, that was out of the question, he couldn't appear suddenly out of the dark! Now at least he knew where he lived; and his immediate wish was to get rid of his censorious guardian. After that (and his heart sank at the thought) he would have to walk back alone through the dark wood and then for four pitch-dark miles through empty countryside to the village where he might not find anywhere to stay. He was also conscious of being very hungry and tired and rather cold. When he came near to the cottage he stopped, intending simply to look, to feed and indulge his emotions and then turn away. He then became uneasily aware that his guide had followed him and was standing under a tree waiting to see what he would do. Ludens moved on, nearer to the house, to the pale light, allowing himself to grasp that he was now *very close* to Marcus.

Red Cottage was, it seemed, a long thin red-brick building with a high-pitched slated roof, doubtless originally two cottages, since it had two front doors. There was a very faint glimmer up above, perhaps on a landing; while the light which he had seen through the trees, dim, suggestive of an oil lamp rather than electricity, was on the ground floor. The window was uncurtained. Ludens very slowly approached, setting each foot down with elaborate care in the dewy grass. With a few more steps he would be able to see into the room. He moved on. The room was extremely small. The lamp was on the far side of it, placed upon a chair. The window was dirty and difficult to see through. Ludens came close, trying to see more. He stood there with his mouth open and his eyes round with fear, and his hands upon his breast to contain the violent acceleration of his heart, while his bag still dangled unnoticed from one arm. Someone was in the room, an elderly bearded man, opposite to the window, beside the lamp, sitting cross-legged on a bed. He was wearing some kind of small hat and was dressed in a light-brown robe, or perhaps draped in a blanket. He was sitting awkwardly, his body twisted, close to the lamp, writing upon a pad or notebook, while a tray with a cup and plate on it lay tilted upon a heap of jumbled clothes. Ludens, looking in with intense concentration, decided at first that this bizarre person could not possibly be Marcus. The posture, the exotic garb, seemed that of a foreigner, perhaps an Indian, the complexion too looked dark, the face, surly with anxiety or concentration, unlike Marcus's. Then as the man moved, laying down the notebook, relaxing his face into weary vagueness, looking upward, he suddenly did look like Marcus, but as if disguised, in fancy dress. At that moment Ludens's forehead touched the glass. Instantly the figure jerked forward, unwinding from the robe a pair of bare legs, and glared toward the window with frightened but unmistakable eyes. The tray fell to the floor with a crash. Ludens's first instinct was to turn and run, but a second later he tapped hard upon the glass, crying out 'Marcus, Marcus!'

The figure vanished, in a moment the adjacent door opened and

Marcus's tall form appeared in the doorway, visible only, since it was now dark outside, in the light which came into the hallway from the open door of the room. Ludens stepped quickly back. Marcus said in a low penetrating rasping voice, 'What is it? Who is it?' Ludens, almost speechless with terror, said, 'Marcus, it's me, Alfred Ludens. Forgive me. It's Ludens.'

Marcus, now half closing the door, said in a voice which quavered with fear or anger, 'What? What are you doing here? Why are you here at night? What is the matter?'

'Marcus, I'm very sorry, I meant to come tomorrow, I didn't mean to come at night, someone showed me the way, I just wanted to look —'

'Who did you say you were?'

'Ludens.'

'Who showed you the way?'

'The gamekeeper.'

'How did you know I was here?'

'I found out, I wanted to ask you something —'

'To *ask* me something? How can you, how *dare* you, come like that at night suddenly banging on the window?'

'I'm terribly sorry. I'll go away now. I'll come back tomorrow morning like I meant to.'

'No, you are not to go, come inside, I want to look at you.' He retreated, Ludens came into the narrow hall, closing the door behind him, then followed Marcus into the lighted room where they stood and stared at each other.

Marcus looked strange yet the same, more burly, formidable, dangerous, like a bear who might with one swipe of his vast paw destroy what he feared or hated. The curious cap he had been wearing had fallen to the floor revealing his head much changed, as it were unclothed, at first seeming bald, his hair being shorn and cut very close, looking in the lamplight as if it were grey. What had seemed a beard was a several days growth of stubble. He was bare-legged and barefoot, wrapped in a longish brown robe, not exactly a dressing-gown. He looked toward the window, then, with a quick gesture which made Ludens flinch, drew a curtain across.

'Are you alone?'

'Yes,' said Ludens. 'The man who guided me has gone. I think.'

'Have you no one with you, no confederate?'

The word sounded odd, it was as if Marcus's mode of speech had relapsed into some primordial foreignness. 'No.'

'Are you armed?'

'No! Marcus, it's just *me*, Ludens, you do remember who I am?'

'Yes, yes, I remember. But – you can't have come – it must mean something – someone sent you – and late at night – it's *terrible, terrible.*'

'I'm sorry –'

'You said you came to ask me something? Who sent you? What is your question? What is demanded?'

Ludens only at that moment, and felt shame for it later, remembered the purpose of his mission! The 'question' he had just mentioned was of quite another kind. He hesitated. Should he pour it all out now, should he not wait till the morning? But would he be received in the morning? He said, 'Jack Sheerwater asked me to come, you remember Jack, the painter.' He named Jack as someone with whom Marcus had less positively quarrelled. 'Well, it's – Jack and I felt – it's to do with Patrick Fenman – you remember Patrick, the Irishman, the poet – he's very ill, he may be dying – and he terribly wants to see you, he keeps calling out your name like a charm, because he thinks you cursed him, and that if you would come to see him and take the curse off he might recover.' Mad, mad, thought Ludens as he uttered those words, Marcus mad, I mad, Pat mad.

Marcus seemed calmer however, as if he found the explanation satisfactory. His face relaxed. He sat down on the bed and passed his hand over the short cropped fur of his skull. He said thoughtfully, 'I cursed you. I don't remember cursing Patrick.'

Looking back later on this weird evening Ludens recalled what an extraordinary effect these words had on him. They acted like an exorcism or absolution. Ludens had had a long nerve-rending day, crammed with frustrations and fears and an increasing anxiety amounting at last to terror. He had been ready to imagine that he would never find Marcus, or that Marcus would refuse to speak to him. Now at last he was actually inside a room, holding a conversation. He ventured to sit down on a chair near the window. He wondered if the gamekeeper were standing outside listening. He said, 'Marcus, I'm terribly hungry, is there anything to eat?'

'There's something here.' Marcus retrieved from the floor the fallen plate upon which he put the fallen bread and cheese. Ludens took the offering, but too embarrassed to eat it, wrapped it in his handkerchief and put it in his pocket.

'I'm sorry I disturbed you. May I come back tomorrow? I'll go now, I can find somewhere to stay in the village.'

'No, no. You are not to go. You must stay here. I must find out more. I am tired. I have been thinking all day. You must not go. You will stay next door.'

'Next door? Who lives next door?'

'No one. You will be alone.'

Ludens was alone. He was in an upstairs bedroom where a candle was burning. The next-door house, evidently separate, was reached by its own front door which Marcus, armed with an electric torch, had unlocked with a large key, led Ludens upstairs and into the room, where he hastily lit a candle, and then vanished. Ludens at once ate the bread and cheese, his eyes closed with ecstasy. After that he considered his surroundings. The house smelt of cold and mould, and lack of habitation. The bed had been made, but certainly not recently. The sheets in one place seemed to be speckled with mildew, though it was difficult in the dim light to be sure. Everything, including the heavy tarnished brass candlestick, was covered in a faint greasy deposit. The floorboards creaked and wavered underfoot. A glass up-ended on a dusty decanter tinkled like a bell.

There was a viable bathroom and a tiny room empty of furniture from which he could see the full moon. He decided to investigate downstairs to see if there were a kitchen which might contain food, at least a tin and a tin-opener. But the kitchen was derelict. There was a larder, but nothing in it except a mouse, who blinked at the candle and refused to run away, perhaps because faint with hunger. Thinking of the warm summer night outside he tried to open a window, but the windows were jammed. He cautiously lifted the latch of the front door and pulled. The door resisted. He pulled harder. He examined the door for other handles or catches but there were none. The door had evidently been locked on the outside. Ludens reflected on this. Was he then being *kept* as a prisoner, as a trapped animal to be eaten later? (The image suddenly occurred to him.) His sense of relief had not lasted long. There had been something creepy, even uncanny, about the way Marcus had behaved, as if, though he scarcely knew who Ludens was, he had expected his arrival and been prompted by it to strange thoughts and schemes in which perhaps, whether he willed or no, Ludens was destined to play some part.

When he reached the upper landing he was startled by the sound, very close, of a footstep. He stood still. Then he heard someone, near to him, sigh deeply. Then a door was closed. The sound, of course, came from the other house. But it sounded so clear, so loud. Ludens went into his bedroom and sat on his bed. He felt sure that this was a night when he would never dare to sleep. He took off his jacket. He touched, behind the bed, the wall which adjoined the other house. He did not dare to tap it. Then he went out onto the landing. The landing ended in a cupboard and it was, he now thought, from beyond the cupboard that the sound of the step had come. He opened the cupboard. It was large and deep. Trying to step in, his foot encountered a thick obstacle which turned out to be a pile of blankets. He stepped over the blankets which were evidently old and coagulated together, and ventured to place the candle on top of them. Dark things, perhaps old coats, yes, certainly old mildewed coats as stiff as boards, were suspended in the air, upon heavy old-fashioned wooden hangers, from a rail which ran lengthwise toward the back of the cupboard, so that Ludens could not thrust them away on either side but had to slide past them, losing the light of the candle. At one moment, however, as he stood braced against the swinging coats to make a pathway for the flickering light, he glimpsed at the far end of the cupboard what he was searching for, the metal handle of a door. Bundling the stifling musty garments aside and taking a long step, he stretched out his hand and in the darkness of his own shadow reached the handle. Steadying himself against the wall he turned it. The door opened silently. At this moment Ludens, asking himself *why* he was doing this, paused. Had some spirit compelled him, some very old wilful ghost who cared nothing for him or for Marcus, some creature perhaps that inhabited the cupboard? Or was he being irresistibly tempted to immolate himself by the breaking of a taboo? Perhaps this compulsive spellbound sense of the uncanny was simply the effect of the proximity of Marcus and of his latest metamorphosis.

Ludens stood motionless, hearing his own quick breath and blinking into what first seemed another darkness. The air on this side of the door was warmer and smelt of human dwelling. He made out at last, in what was not a complete dark, a corridor, and a faint light issuing from an almost-closed doorway. He listened. The silence, like the dark, was not quite complete. He heard another very faint sigh. Feeling that he risked his life, Ludens stepped forward. He trembled with a thrill of danger and guilt. He dared himself to go as far as the light. After that he could give up and flee. He trod along the edge of the corridor to avoid creaking boards. The little light lay like a narrow streak of brown paint across the wooden floor. Hesitating, he put his foot into the light, he leaned against the jamb of the door, holding onto it, and moved his head cautiously forward to peer into the room. What he saw was, lying upon a low bed, a child of perhaps ten or twelve, wide awake. The child – he could not make out if it was a girl or a boy – more probably a boy – looked straight at Ludens with dark eyes made bright and shining by the adjacent candle. The child looked at Ludens with calmness, with understanding, without surprise or hostility or fear, but with a cool interested detachment. It made no sound. Ludens, after a moment, also in silence, withdrew, and made his way with long noiseless steps back to the open door into the cupboard and on into his own bedroom, closing both doors carefully behind him.

Ludens was lying asleep in bed. He had lain awake listening. He had heard a distant owl, then the near sound of the larder mouse or its relations or perhaps rats. He had told himself he would never sleep; and slept. Then there were other sounds. Someone or something was coming through the long deep cupboard from the other house. Ludens could hear the coat-hangers tapping together as the intruder pushed his way through. Ludens sat up abruptly. There was a light in the doorway. A huge dark figure had appeared. Ludens knew at once that it was Marcus, holding a candle. A moment later he thought, it *is* Marcus, but I must have forgotten, he's a freak, a *monster*, he has got an animal's head. Can a human being have an animal's head? What animal is it – a hare, or a bull – are those ears or horns? Marcus was staring at Ludens with large luminous yellow eyes. It's a hare I *think*, thought Ludens, and he's *black*, I can see his bare legs, and they're black, and his huge thighs are black, and he's coming nearer and he's sitting at the bottom of my bed with his huge legs astride. How terrifying and how *revolting* he is, and how *sad*. Marcus spoke to him in his deep roughened rasping voice – yes, that's just how an animal speaks, Ludens thought – 'Where is your friend who is blind?' 'He's not blind,' said Ludens. Ludens's voice was high and weird like the voice of a child, and he thought of course, that's what human voices must sound like to animals. Marcus said, 'To cure his sight, *you* must sacrifice an eye.' 'I won't,' said Ludens, 'I won't, I *won't* – but I'll give you a hand.' As he stretched out his right hand he saw that Marcus was holding a piece of thin wire attached to two metal rods; and he thought, he'll cut my hand off like a shop assistant cutting cheese. Marcus asked, 'Are you right-handed?' 'Yes.' 'You are lying, you are left-handed. I condemn you to death by fire.' With his bare foot Marcus thrust the candle in underneath the bed. Dense clouds of suffocating smoke filled the room.

As he struggled vainly to get up Ludens thought, it isn't fire, it's *gas*.

'The central structure is Palladian of course, by Kent, it went up about 1730. The wings were added quite soon after. Lord Claverden's grandfather intended to pull them down, but it turned out to be too expensive. Kent left designs for the garden too, but they were not carried out.'

Ludens listened with amazement to these utterances which came out slowly in Marcus's honey-rough tones. He looked with amazement at the house upon which the bright sun was shining. The long façade which had impressed him on the previous evening was, of course (he was interested in Marcus's 'of course') the back of the house. What he saw now, seeing it across the lake and charmingly reflected in the water, was the front. The central portion consisted of the dome, fronted by a high pillared and pedimented portico, from which two curving stairways led down. Between these ran an arcade surmounted by floral decorations, in front of which a curious flashing betokened the play of a fountain. The two wings which had escaped the (as Ludens judged it) ill intent of Lord Claverden's ancestor, had tall arched pilastered windows on the first floor. Ludens did not enquire whether or not they had figured in Kent's design. On either side of the house old brick walls surmounted by stone urns led away into trees. The lake, too, vanished at each end, narrowing, into woodland, leaving visible the graceful bridge over which Marcus and Ludens had crossed to reach their vantage point. Near to where they were standing in long meadow grass, the water was fringed with bulrushes and yellow irises and occasional lofty spreads of gunnera. Behind them was the vista, already commended by Marcus, where an avenue of beech trees led to a tall column upon which, according to Marcus, a statue of a former Lord Claverden had stood until brought down by a storm in 1911.

When Ludens had awakened that morning about seven, to sunlit curtains and the sound of birds singing, he had dressed quickly. He had the impression of having had a bad dream, but could not remember it. He recalled, as if *that* had been a bad dream, his extraordinary excursion into the other house. He inspected the cupboard, finding it surprisingly small compared with his candle-lit impression of it. By daylight he easily sidled past the pendent coats and put his hand upon the handle of the door. With no intention of proceeding further he pressed the door slightly, but it was checked. Evidently a bolt had been shot on the other side. He retreated. In retrospect the memory of seeing, and even more being *seen by*, the silent bright-eyed child, affected him deeply. Who could the child be? Perhaps another child of Marcus's, a *secret* child, never spoken of, not his wife's, acknowledged and adopted later? Of course Marcus never talked about his family, news of it only came by hearsay. Why shouldn't there be such a child? But that sudden vision, the result of such a dangerous trespass, unnerved Ludens and added to the alarm he felt at the idea of again confronting his powerful unpredictable mentor. He went downstairs, expecting to find the door still locked, but it was not. He opened it to reveal a wide sward of roughly cut grass, a circle of surrounding trees, and Marcus standing at the opening of the pathway, obviously waiting for him to emerge. As soon as he saw Ludens he turned and marched away smartly down the path, clearly expecting his guest to follow. Ludens ran after him.

He was hungry. He was also distressed because, having omitted to bring his razor, he was unable to shave. He did not feel at all ready for a prolonged tour of the estate which seemed to be what Marcus had in mind. When he had wakened that morning he had an immediate spasm of anxiety about what Marcus proposed to do with him. Perhaps he would be curtly asked to leave. Nor did he here underestimate Marcus's ability to hurt people he disapproved of. He was relieved when, catching up with his host, he had been subjected merely to remarks about the scenery. At the same time he had an uneasy feeling that Marcus was scarcely aware of talking to him and was, with great intensity, thinking about something else. Marcus by daylight looked a little more like his old self, or perhaps Ludens was learning to 'read' the changed man. His hair, which had looked grey by candlelight, was now seen as reddish and less shockingly short, just rather roughly cut, ruffled and untidy, giving him even a boyish air, or (Ludens thought) the look of an American filmstar of some past era. His copious eyebrows had remained a bright red. Yet he did seem older, very fine lines sketched beside his eyes and mouth, his nose thinner, the nostrils more prominent, accentuating a fastidious expression. He was dressed in a brown shirt, which had a khaki soldierly look, and creased baggy pale-brown cotton trousers. As Marcus went on talking about the house Ludens had the weird sense of listening to a recorded announcement: perhaps he was hearing the tones of Lord Claverden? Perhaps his Lordship, or some ancestor, was used to making just this speech on this spot, and Marcus (possibly this was one of his talents?) was able to pick up phenomena from the past.

As they walked on, Ludens noticed, obscured by the long grass and running along a little distance from the water, the dark line of the cycle track which was evidently making a circle round the house, and the lake. At the far end they crossed by a wooden bridge the little stream which fed the lake, and which at this point was leaving it, and turned back through an orchard of flowering trees. Stone balustrades were now coming into view, and a flight of steps led up to the garden. Here, where art and order should have reigned, nature had, not ungraciously, taken charge. Yew hedges had grown into shaggy trees, rose beds were covered with wild flowers and ground elder and undisciplined ivy concealed prostrate pillars. The large lawn in front of the house, which looked as if it had been mown earlier in the year, was scattered with white daisies and clumps of ladies bedstraw and intensely blue germander speedwell. Looking up at the house Ludens saw that the windows were blank, veiled by faded grey curtains or by internal shutters. They paused between the stairways, in front of the arcade, upon a stone pavement near to the fountain. The huge paving stones were covered over with ragged mounds of thyme and errant grass, the steps were dotted with dandelions and underneath the arches of the arcade Ludens could see stacks of ancient deckchairs, their canvas faded to a dirty grey, and cast-iron seats covered with rotting cushions. A door in the centre led into the lower regions of the house. Ludens wondered if he were now in for an equally lengthy tour of the interior. If so, he was ready to protest. He urgently wanted his breakfast and was resolved to walk to the village for it if necessary. A small band of swifts which was flying round and round the dome and screaming expressed his imminent feelings. Marcus had been ominously silent since they crossed the wooden bridge and Ludens, covertly watching him, had become convinced that Marcus was indeed simply filling in time, being unable to decide something momentous which closely concerned Ludens. Ludens kept trying to think of something apt to say about Patrick, whose critical situation after all, and not Ludens's future relations with Marcus, was the immediate purpose of his quest. But the open air, sky, clouds, birds, trees, plants, the sheer profusion of growing things all about him, stole away his thoughts and his will.

Marcus moved toward the fountain. The fountain consisted of a single tall jet whose sparkle they had seen from across the lake. It rose vertically from and fell neatly into a large stone basin, on the verge of which, their paws upon the rim, stood four large stone dogs, holding in their mouths short metal pipes from which no doubt jets of water were supposed to issue, but did not. Marcus put his right hand into the water. Ludens, following him, put his left hand. The gesture, with its benign resemblance to a religious rite, produced a moment of calm. They even looked at each other.

Marcus said, 'I see Busby has turned on the fountain in your honour.'

'Busby?'

'The gardener.'

Ludens thought, that must be the chap I saw last night, I wonder why I assumed he was a gamekeeper?

Marcus, shaking the water off his hand, moved away out of the sunshine into the darkness of the arcade, and for a moment Ludens thought he was going to enter the house. Then he was aware that the tall glittering jet of water was faltering, was collapsing, was reduced to a spurting trickle, and had ceased. Marcus returned and they walked on. Ludens took in the omen. At least they could not now be very far from the cottage.

They crossed the remainder of the lawn and entered a shady walk where brick pillars supported a wooden lattice upon which flowering clematis and wistaria were entwined together. Here and there the lattice had fallen down, blocking the path with a barricade of leaves and flowers crawling with bees and flies, and enforcing detours into the long grass and the trampling down of irises which were growing between the pillars. With the increasing warmth of the sun, the atmosphere had become perceptibly thicker, harder to breathe, full of pollen and smells of flowers and grass. Ludens, now following behind Marcus, slipped off his jacket and undid another button of his shirt. Earlier he had not been indifferent to the summer charms of the scene. Now he felt that all this floriferous mess was an idle show, a mere play of self-important phenomena, a sort of sinister *trial*, a struggle through an alien hostile enchanted thicket. Following Marcus he viciously kicked some plaited branches of wistaria out of the way, deliberately trod on some irises, and jumped as destructively as possible upon a spread of fallen lattice where at the end of the alley the pergola had collapsed completely. However he could, he thought, now see, beyond the downward slope ahead, the bicycle track emerging from the wood at the point where he had met the gamekeeper (gardener) on the previous evening. As he caught up with Marcus, who was walking ahead through the grass, Marcus suddenly said to him, 'Did you say that Patrick Fenman was blind?'

Ludens instantly remembered his dream. For a second the dream rose up like something dreadful and fatal rising through his body, and he could not speak. Breathing deeply and selecting his words, and relaxing his tongue as one of his therapists had told him to, he said, 'No, he's not blind. He's very ill with some wasting sickness, they fear he won't survive.' Ludens thought, he may be dead already. Perhaps that's what the dream meant. He had died because I refused to sacrifice my eye, and lied about my hand. Of course Marcus won't come, it's all in aid of my vanity, as if *I*, by my cleverness and courage, could save Patrick! Why should Marcus go to see someone he doesn't care for, whom he knows he can't cure, and who might infect him with something awful? Why should this obsessed and solitary thinker suddenly remove himself to London on the basis of such a peculiar and improbable story? I just felt as if *I* could bring it all about – and I so much wanted to!

As Marcus said nothing, Ludens added, speaking quickly, 'If you would just see him like through a doorway, you don't have to come close, just say some kind words, tell him you revoke the curse, I'm sorry this all sounds so odd, you see some doctors think it's psychosomatic, that he's dying *because* he thinks he's cursed, I mean because he *is* cursed.' Oh what nonsense all this is, thought Ludens.

Marcus did not reply to these flounderings. By now they had descended the slope from the house and were walking on the cycle track just beyond the point behind the house where it divided into two narrower tracks so as to circle the lake. They walked on in silence in single file, turning along the path beside the white cow parsley along the edge of the wood. Marcus slowed down. He was making nervous noises, clearings of the throat as if he were about to speak. At one point, not looking at Ludens, he even stopped. They reached the path which turned away into the trees toward the cottage, and came into the grassy clearing. The sun was shining upon the cottage, and on Marcus's side of it all the windows were open. The door was open too. Standing at the door was a strange-looking woman, an old woman, as Ludens in that instant saw her, with a hunched back, unkempt black hair and a dark complexion, with a red shawl round her shoulders. She looked like a gipsy, and Ludens thought, she must be the charwoman, or perhaps she brings things to sell.

Marcus at last managed to utter. He said, 'My daughter, Irina. Of course you remember her.'

Breakfast did occur, but it was so maimed and strained an occasion that it might well have taken place in silence had not Ludens attempted some minimal conversation. The table was laid for three: perhaps the boy (for Ludens had decided it was a boy) had departed early to school. Could such ordinary things occur here? Upon a crumpled cloth some pretty china had been set out together with sliced bread, butter, marmalade, jam, milk, sugar, tea, and (for Ludens only) an egg (hard-boiled). Hunger helped, and he ate (quickly in case only four minutes was allowed for the meal) besides the egg, several slices of bread liberally covered with butter and marmalade. Irina and Marcus ate blessedly slowly. Ludens remarked upon the pleasures of his recent walk and ventured to ask if Lord Claverden were in residence (which he was obviously not). Marcus said no, his Lordship, though expected back soon, was now at Karlsbad, which Marcus explained was now in Czechoslovakia and called Karlovy Vary. Irina said nothing and only looked very occasionally at Ludens, who avoided looking at her. One topic of reasonably human interest arose at the end of the meal when Ludens, who hated being unshaven, asked Marcus if he had a spare razor which he could kindly lend. Marcus said he had no *spare* razor, but he could lend Ludens *a* razor. He handed over this requisite, then announced that he had work to do and disappeared up the stairs before Ludens, who intended to speak, now much more eloquently and urgently, about Patrick, had the time or the wit to detain him.

Ludens felt guilt and dismay. For Pat, it was a matter of time. But now Ludens was feeling compelled to adopt Marcus's pace, to accustom Marcus to his presence, not to annoy him by urgent demands. Marcus disliked sudden changes of tempo, even of subject; and upon Marcus's good will and serenity the whole operation depended. Why should Marcus oblige Ludens at all? Marcus's behaviour so far, while not hostile, was certainly ambiguous, even consistent with an envisaging, not of reconciliation, but of revenge. And what about the mysterious boy, who complicated the existence, even the being, of Marcus, and who might (it occurred to Ludens for the first time) have complained about Ludens's intrusion? In this perspective the creature assumed, in Ludens's imagination, the form of a necessarily mischievous imp or changeling, a sort of incarnation of Marcus's anger. For that anger must surely exist.

Ludens, after trying to calm himself by shaving, was standing at his bedroom window trying to calculate how much time needed to pass before he dared to interrupt Marcus, or whether he dared to interrupt him at all. The sun was shining out of a blue sky. The air was thick with the smell of coniferous trees. Yellow honeysuckle, crowded with bees, overhanging a wooden seat between the two doors, added its fragrance. Ludens found himself looking at Irina who, almost invisible to him as he gazed into the sunlight, was standing in the shadow of the wood. Unconscious of being observed, she stood quite still with the mysterious immobility of an animal to whom, as it pauses unpredictably, one uncertainly attributes thought. There was, he reflected, her anger too, perhaps. Did it matter? Had she and her father endlessly and continuously discussed *that* episode? Or had they buried it in an embarrassed silence? She was wearing, in spite of the warm air, the red fringed shawl which she had had on earlier, but more carelessly disposed, not pulled together to give the hunched-up impression which had made her seem like an old woman. Ludens, who had not ventured to study her at breakfast, still found her appearance puzzling. She now looked fairly tall and fairly slim. Her hair was straight and dark brown, with a few faint lines of reddish brown. Earlier it had seemed to fall all tangled and bushy to her shoulders, now she had gathered it and stowed it under the shawl, drawing it harshly away from her face. Her nose was straight, almost sharp. Her thin or indrawn lips and intense eyes, narrowed as she gazed out into the bright glade, gave her a cat-like look. Possibly she had a slight squint. Her complexion was dark, no doubt also sunburnt, a little reddened. Her face had a strange surly distorted appearance which, however hard Ludens concentrated, remained hard to read, as if her features were out of temper with each other, out of focus, parts of different pictures. Beneath the shawl appeared a longish dark blue skirt with dark red flowers upon it. Her legs, just visible beneath the skirt, and her feet, just visible in the grass, were bare. As he watched she stirred, putting her hands together, kneading them together, then drawing them apart, in the movement known as 'wringing'.

'Franca, Franca, is that you? It's me, Alfred.' After waiting a while to see if Marcus would reappear, and concluding that he would probably not do so for several hours, Ludens, twitching with restlessness and feeling he must *do* something, decided to get in touch with Franca to find out if Pat was still alive. Irina had disappeared, turning away into the wood as he watched her. He left a note saying *Back soon* on the kitchen table, and set off along the track, vaguely hoping that he might find yesterday's bicycle still leaning against the tree. Of course it was not there, and he started walking fast along the drive, upon the cycle track. To go to Edmarsh and back would of course take too long, but he remembered having seen a telephone box somewhere not too far away, and planned if necessary to try to find the residence, which he felt must be nearby, of the man with the trowel. He had by now remembered his car, left derelict on the road between Edmarsh and Clinten, and intended also to telephone a garage to arrange a rescue. After reaching the road, perspiring and reducing his pace, he turned in the direction of the crossroads where indeed, half hidden among trees, he found the telephone box, and dialled Jack's number, reversing the charges.

'Oh – hello –' Franca's voice sounded remote, almost annoyed.

'Franca, how's Pat?'

'Much the same. No, a bit worse.'

'I've found Marcus, he's in a cottage, I stayed the night with him! I've told him about Pat. I think he may come – but don't be too hopeful –'

'I'm not hopeful.'

'I had quite a time getting here, my car broke down and I had to leave it. I'll try to get it mended today. Oh Franca, it's so strange here, it's like a fairy tale, such a beautiful place, all rather a wreck actually, a lovely house and a lake and Marcus living in this cottage covered in honeysuckle, and his daughter's there with him, and he's working away on his stuff, his book or whatever, he hasn't told me about it yet, he's like a hermit, it's quite weird, I'll tell you all about it when I get back, I mustn't talk long, I've just run away to telephone, I'll ring up again, I don't honestly know whether Marcus will come –'

'Don't bother,' said Franca's distant voice, 'better stay there and have a nice time with the lake and the honeysuckle and talk philosophy with Marcus. Patrick's nearly gone. Marcus would be wasting his time. You seem to be enjoying yourself, why not stay.'

'I'm sorry, I'm *sorry* – I'm not – I am just trying to persuade him – is Jack there?'

'No.'

'Will you tell Jack? When will he be back?'

'I don't know, he's spending the weekend with Alison.'

'Where?'

'I don't know.'

'Franca, I'm so sorry. I'll come back soon anyway, with or without Marcus, I'll come straight to see you –'

'Please don't bother.'

'If Jack rings up could you tell him –'

But Franca had put the phone down.

Ludens stood for a minute in the hot telephone box holding his head. How could two such different worlds co-exist, how could they communicate? Franca alone in that house with a dying man, he here in this amazing place wrestling with an angel (the image came to him, it was not quite right). He felt that weeks had passed since he had left London. Was he enjoying himself? No, he was scared stiff, frightened of Marcus, frightened of the gipsy girl with the dislocated face, frightened of failing and having to return alone to watch Patrick die.

He started back, slipping in through the gap in the leaning gates, and, at first, running along the track, now in a frenzy of anxiety in case he had been missed. Panting and sweating and walking fast with a stitch in his side he at last reached the footpath, and then the clearing and came in sight of the cottage.

Marcus was sitting on the seat, under the honeysuckle, between the doors. He looked annoyed.

'Where have you been?'

'I went to telephone to see how Patrick is. He's still alive. I'm so sorry –'

He sat down beside Marcus, trying to breathe calmly and inaudibly. The arch of the honeysuckle gave a little shade. It suffused a smell of suffocating sweetness. The sleeves of their shirts touched. Ludens could feel Marcus twitching.

'Is he really dying?'

'Yes –'

'Are you sure?'

'Well – it seems so – I mean he's *very* ill. We thought if you came – it might save him – it's worth trying – he keeps talking about you, or he did before he got so ill –'

'He talks about me, he knows?'

'He thinks it's your curse – sorry it's all so mad, I mean so odd. I had to come.'

'You had to come. I see.'

'If you could only –'

'It's too hot here, this stuff smells so. Let's sit over there.'

Marcus got up and went to sit down cross-legged in the darker shade underneath a tree, his back against the trunk. Ludens knelt down beside him in the cool grass and stared at him. It seemed all right to stare at Marcus, as you might stare at a big self-absorbed animal. Studying him Ludens could see again the radiant being whom he had revered in previous manifestations, and at the same time felt a new tenderness towards him as if he might stroke him. The short hair, now less ruffled, and seeming after his long locks like a tonsure, revealed his brow and the shape of his head. He had looked like a god, now he looked like a priest, the guardian of a mystery. I must find out what he knows, thought Ludens; and at that moment his idea of what it might be was of some small pulsating atomic kernel upon which, if he could reach far enough, he could place his hand.

At the moment however Marcus's fine brow was wrinkled with puzzlement and his 'allegorical lips' disfigured by a kind of involuntary sneer of uncertainty, as he now moved to return Ludens's intense stare.

Ludens now smiled, a humble propitiatory smile, resembling, as he even reflected at the time, the gesture of self-defensive deference which a small weak animal offers to a large dangerous one. As Marcus did not smile back and remained silent Ludens ventured to say, 'How is your work getting on?'

This mild vague question seemed to disturb Marcus very much. His red eyebrows shot up. 'What do you mean by "my work"?'

'Oh – philosophy – that sort of thing – you were writing a book I believe.'

'No. No philosophy. No book.'

'But you're going on with – whatever –? Last night when I saw you you were writing something.'

'Yes, you looked at me through the window, I didn't know you were there.' Marcus looked distressed, even agitated, by this thought.

'I'm sorry, I –'

'I was not writing anything meaningful.'

'You used to talk about a universal language, only you said philology was too mechanistic or scientific – and you said painting led to a void you couldn't cross – I just wondered if you'd – got on, got anywhere – like reaching a conclusion, or –'

'Conclusion – yes, if I could live to be two hundred. Human life is too short for the trajectory of human thought. Perhaps this is destined.'

'But you are going on thinking.'

'What is thinking, is it a possibility, can one endure it?'

'I understand –'

'I think you do not. What I refer to is an agony, a – an agonising pain, a pain of hell. And at the least false step one can fall not just into error, but into – turpitude.'

'Like what?' said Ludens, who was concentrating on keeping this elusive conversation in motion. 'Do you mean mythology?'

Marcus made a familiar dismissive gesture which Ludens knew to mean: obviously that, but much more . . . After a pause during which he searched for suitable words he said irritably, 'Corruption', accompanying this utterance with a gesture which meant, that's not the right expression but it will do for you.

Ludens, not enlightened, went on in an encouraging tone, 'But you make your way, you make progress?'

'Progress? One has to purify oneself at every step.'

'How?'

'By action.'

Ludens, not sure he had heard rightly, repeated, 'Action?'

'I told you last time, discipline, experience. Perhaps I should have said activity, a particular kind of activity.'

Ludens, gratified to learn that Marcus actually remembered their last serious conversation, and hoping that this was now the right move, said, 'What you called living your work? So you went to Japan?'

'It was not necessary.'

'You had an accident in America.'

'I fell from a rope. That was not important. A lesson perhaps.'

'But the universal language?' said Ludens, exhausted by concentrating.

'Let us say that was a metaphor.'

'And so you came back to philosophy?'

'Philosophy? Do you mean popular science or the trivial contraptions of vulgar empiricism?'

In desperation Ludens said, 'Metaphysics.'

As a look of revulsion and disgust came over Marcus's face Irina appeared in the doorway of the cottage, waved in a peremptory manner, presumably to announce lunch, and disappeared.

Marcus moved, uncrossing his legs, then rose pulling at the waist of his baggy trousers and adjusting his shirt. Ludens, rising too, groaned inwardly. The spell was broken. It evidently did not occur to Marcus that it was possible to ignore the summons and continue the discussion.

Catching at the moment, which at least might be propitious for that purpose, Ludens said, in a tone of urgency, 'Marcus, listen, I want you, we all very much want you, to come to London. Pat is very ill and perhaps you could help him – no one else can. That's why I came here, to say this.' Ludens thought, why am I wasting time, instead of just dinning *this* idea, this *need*, into his head. Of course I have to humour him, but I must get him to understand. He added, 'Please listen to me, please come, please.'

Marcus stood for a moment as if considering the uttered request. Then with a sudden magisterial grimness, and a searching stare which made Ludens flinch, he said, 'You are the messenger.'

Ludens, uncertain whether this was a statement or a question, said in a conspiratorial tone which seemed to be demanded, 'Yes. Yes.'

Marcus turned away, Ludens followed him, they went in to lunch.

Lunch consisted of curried rice and beans followed by tinned peaches and custard. It occurred to Ludens that Marcus might now be a vegetarian, though the fare might equally indicate the limitations of Irina's cuisine. He seemed to suffer from perpetual hunger at Red Cottage and ate gratefully. Conversation resembled that at breakfast-time except that there was less of it. Ludens asked inane questions such as how far was it to the village (which he already knew), was there a convenient shop nearby (there was not), were there fish in the lake (yes), were there nightingales in the woods (no). Irina, as before, said nothing. Ludens recalled that he had forgotten, at the telephone box, to do anything about his car, and wondered if he could safely rectify this in the afternoon. He also wondered, with a helpless bemused puzzlement, how much longer he could decently stay if his plea for Patrick continued to be ignored. Perhaps he was tacitly expected to leave after lunch. How could he find out? Was it possible that Marcus, totally indifferent to Pat's fate, just wanted Ludens, for the moment, as someone to talk to? Or was some act of revenge still pending, some thunderbolt long cherished and prepared? Toward the end of lunch Ludens, with no special intent but just because he needed another question, said, 'I suppose the boy doesn't come till evening.' There was a short silence during which Marcus and Irina exchanged glances. Marcus then said, 'No.' After that there was no more conversation.

As they rose from the table Marcus announced that he was going to rest, and disappeared. Irina went into the kitchen with a trayful of crockery, which she started to wash up with many sounds of clashing, even one of smashing. Ludens retired hastily, hurrying out to his own door and up the stairs to his room. He sat on the bed. Through his window he could see, on the other side of the clearing, two large heavy black crows tumbling awkwardly about in the thick foliage of a fir tree.

Normally this sight would have given him pleasure. Ludens liked crows. Now it seemed to bode ill. He recalled his conversation with Franca. She had been so hostile and angry, perhaps she would never forgive him, perhaps *they* would never forgive him, for having run away on this fruitless errand just because he wanted to see Marcus Vallar again.

He got up and went to the window. The crows were gone. But down below, and looking straight up at him, was Irina. She was standing on the grass, holding the handlebars of a fine gleaming white female bicycle. Beyond her, leaning against a tree, was a white male bicycle. Ludens ran from the room and down the stairs.

'Tadpoles.'

This was the first word uttered to Ludens by the new grown-up Irina. As it might be the second Irina.

When Ludens emerged she immediately started to push her bicycle down the path through the trees and onto the track which skirted the wood. Ludens, taking possession of the male bicycle, followed her. It was impossible to ride here because of the uneven earth which, parched by the long drought, lay about in hard lumps. When they reached the place where the drive and the cycle track emerged from the trees Irina leapt onto her machine and pedalled away so fast that Ludens had difficulty in keeping up. He saw in front of him, and the sight was somehow comforting, that she was wearing cotton socks and running shoes. Ludens's bicycle made a friendly sizzling sound. The sky was again cloudless, positively pale with the overflow of light. Ludens felt a gathering of perspiration on his brow. At the point some distance behind the house, where the ways divided, and the tracks narrowed, a large arrow on a notice board pointed to the right: one-way traffic round the lake. Irina turned right. The track here led through long meadow grass, passing the stone bridge and entering the wood, terminating (to start afresh on the other side) at a small wooden bridge like the one Ludens had crossed that morning, only here the little stream was hurrying to enter the lake, and not leaving it. Irina stopped, dismounted, letting her bicycle fall sideways into the grass where it lay with one wheel spinning, and began to walk along the bank. Ludens laid his bicycle down carefully and followed her. The woodland was not thick, and the sunshine dappled the luxuriant undergrowth, and the patches of faded bluebells. The grass here was unlike the meadow grass, it was thin-stemmed and wavery though quite tall, and of an intense luscious light green. Ludens felt it was quite a shame to tread on it. The sun shone into the clearing made by the stream, penetrating the water and showing a brown sandy bed. The stream, which was not deep, curved slightly here and there, affording, out of the mild force of the current, quiet pools, in one of which the creatures referred to by Irina were swimming about.

Ludens, whose spirits had been rising ever since the start of the ride, now felt, if not exactly cheerful and hopeful, himself once more, able to respond to the pleasantness of his surroundings, to hear the songs of the birds and the distant cuckoo, and to feel a sympathetic affection for the tadpoles. He also, in a kind of abstract way, as if he were a spectator of himself, realised that he was, on a delightful summer day, standing beside a charming woodland stream, in the company of a girl. As he recalled it later, he did not actually count Irina as a girl; it was as if she were playing a part, standing in for a girl, a girl's understudy. The image which quite suddenly arose before him, figuring the absent reality, was that of Alison Merrick. For a moment Ludens contemplated, then banished, the surprising intruder. This vision lasted seconds, while at the same time he was looking at Irina, and reflecting that her voice, which he remembered from the previous occasion as the cackling of a chicken, was now, perhaps had always been, rather deep, not unpleasant, in intonation not unlike her father's.

Irina, after announcing the tadpoles, had turned to look at him. Ludens was about to reply. But instantly his old enemy sprang up and sealed his lips. He could not speak. Round about him, like hovering birds, various words proposed themselves. But they were all words he could not utter. One by one he rejected them. At last, as Irina's expressionless stare now turned into a look of curiosity, Ludens, following some old tip offered by some therapist, drooped his shoulders, dropped his jaw, breathed out slowly and audibly through his mouth and at last was able to say, 'I'm – awfully sorry – I have a s-, a s-, a speech impediment.'

Irina said, 'Oh dear.'

'It doesn't come often,' said Ludens, having shaken off his demon. 'It just sometimes appears for no reason.'

They looked at each other for a moment or two. Irina, without the red shawl, looked less gipsyish, more school-girlish, in a white blouse and having shortened the red and blue skirt considerably by rolling it over at the waist. Below a length of bare leg the cotton socks had descended in an untidy heap upon the running shoes. Her face looked hot and greasy, her hair, which perhaps she had washed immediately after lunch, now fell straight down in a continuous thick fuzz. Her dark eyes, which he was now able to study for the first time, still seemed to have a slight cast, an effect perhaps simply of the intensity of her stare. He noticed, and remembered, the dark down upon the upper lip, a feature which Jack found attractive in women. Turning away from him she knelt down and, leaning over the drooping grass of the verge, began scooping up the tadpoles in her hand, holding them wriggling and struggling for a moment in her palm, then dropping them back. For a moment Ludens forgot everything except tadpoles. The next moment Irina was taking off her shoes and socks and had stepped down into the shallow sun-lucid water. Ludens would have liked to put his feet into the stream too, but was too shy. He felt more calm and business-like, however. He watched the lively wriggly black tadpoles swimming over Irina's feet.

Seeking something to say, he asked, 'Do you like bicycling?'

'Well –'

In a swift interlock of thoughts he went on, 'You know, Leonardo da Vinci invented the bicycle.'

'Really.'

'He didn't develop it, there wasn't the technology, anyway he had too many other things to do such as inventing weapons and painting pictures.' Another part of the interlock was that Irina in some strange way reminded him of the Mona Lisa, the elusive likeness being perhaps simply a hint of the hostile contemptuous expression which Ludens had always discerned upon the face of that great lady.

Irina said, 'Oh,' and dropped her gaze, stirring the water with her feet and digging her toes into the sandy bottom.

'Look, do you think your father would come to London to help my friend? You know, that's why I've come, to ask him to. I'm sorry to keep on about this, but I must go back soon, perhaps tomorrow, if I can stay till then. It's very kind of you to let me stay, but I must get back, he's terribly ill. You do remember Patrick Fenman?'

'No. I was with my mother when my father got to know you, and those people.' She added, 'She's dead now.'

Ludens was wondering how to say that he was sorry to hear that, when Irina spoke again.

'Is it true about your friend?'

'Yes – why should I invent such a story?'

'He thinks Dad put a curse on him?'

It sounded weird hearing Marcus called 'Dad'. Ludens noted that the father and daughter must have conferred. He had already withdrawn his hypothesis that Irina's silence betokened some mental flaw. 'Yes. His illness may be psychosomatic, so you see –'

'Yes. Did you come here by car?'

'Yes.'

'Where's the car?'

'It's on the road to Clinten, it broke down.'

'Dad thinks you're barmy.'

'*What*?'

'Deranged, out of your mind, off your rocker.'

'Why –?'

'He says you follow him around and bother him with questions.'

'But I thought –'

'And whatever did you mean about the boy?'

'The boy I saw last night. I'm sorry, I went into your house last night – there's a cupboard with a door – I just crept in and saw this boy lying in bed –'

'That was me.'

'But – it was a child –'

'It must have been me, there's no one else! You stood in the doorway and stared at me. You gave me quite a shock.'

'Oh dear, how strange – I'm very sorry – Did you tell your father?'

'No.'

'No wonder he thought I was crazy.'

'You must have a lot of faith in him if you imagine he can cure somebody just by seeing them and forgiving them or whatever.'

'Yes, I have a lot of faith. I think your father is a most distinguished and unusual man. And I feel it's my duty to try to –'

'And you imagine a distinguished and unusual man will drop what he's doing and travel to London just to pretend to cure somebody who's dying?'

'Not pretend. Yes.'

'Do you think my father will *believe* he can do this?'

Ludens did not like this question. 'I think he's a compassionate person and will be glad to try.'

'I don't think you care about this sick man, you just came here to see my father and find out his ideas.'

'If you mean steal his ideas, no! Of course I'm interested in him, I always have been. But please believe me, this is an errand of mercy.'

'Oh bloody tosh!' said Irina. She had stepped out of the stream and was drying her feet with her socks, then putting on her socks and her shoes. 'Anyway you aren't capable of stealing his ideas.'

'I daresay not! But I must ask him to decide one way or the other. I can't stay here indefinitely.'

'You haven't been invited to.'

'All right! Why did you put out that second bicycle?'

'Because Dad wants to have a serious talk with you and he wanted me to prepare you for it.'

'Oh. I'm glad he wants to talk to me.'

'He can't make head or tail of you.'

'He's known me long enough.'

'And he hates things that happen suddenly. At first he wanted me to hide, and he'd send you away at once.'

'I'm glad he's changed his mind. Maybe he thought he could discuss some problems. Do people visit him here?'

'No.'

'I could help him in all sorts of ways, for instance if he wanted to publish something or –'

'You? Help? Don't be daft. He's been thinking that maybe after all it's no accident –'

'What is?'

'Your coming here. He wants me to tell you something about what he's been thinking about in his work, about the meaning of his work, and then you're to see him about what will happen.'

'What will happen? You mean his coming to London?'

'No!'

'What will happen to what?'

'To the world.'

'You mean he's gone into science, like ecology, nuclear energy –?'

'No, *no* –'

'The world language, like he was trying to discover?'

'No – not like you mean anyway – he has discovered something.'

'Ah!' said Ludens, 'I knew he would!' And his face suddenly flushed scarlet with emotion.

'Or thinks he has,' said Irina. Ludens watching her now hitching up her skirt saw her hands pause. He turned his head. Someone, a man, was standing, some way off, under the trees of the wood, looking in their direction.

'Who is it?' Ludens murmured.

'It's Busby.'

'Oh – the gamekeeper – gardener.'

'We'd better go.'

'When is Lord Claverden coming back?'

'I don't know. The vile toad. Come on.'

'Please wait,' said Ludens, 'please tell me, you must tell me.'

'What, for heaven's sake?'

'You said your father has discovered something. *What is it?*'

'How can I say? Just something.' She walked past him and he followed her along the trodden path which they had made through the lush waterside grass. When she lifted up her bicycle he stood beside her. '*Please.*'

'Look,' said Irina, gazing at him with her intense gleaming faintly crossed eyes, 'you know what he's like. How can I expound his thoughts? If you can't understand him how can I? I know *nothing.*'

'But if you think he's discovered something, you must know –'

'All I know is how it affects him.'

'Well, how –?'

'He wants to serve mankind.'

'Yes, yes. He is a romantic, he is a noble man, I am sure he will serve mankind, in fact I have always believed it, but go on, tell me more.'

'He thinks he has a mission, a great mission, and he has been waiting for a sign.'

'Yes –'

'And he thinks you're it.'

'He – *what?*'

'He thinks you're a –'

'He asked me if I was the messenger.'

'There you are – So if you want him to do what you want, leave here and go to London, you'd better pretend to *be* the messenger!'

'But I'm not – I don't understand –'

'Look here,' said Irina, 'I'm not interested in your thoughts or your conversations with Dad or what you think he's after, or in your precious friend who may or may not be dying. What I want is to *get out of here.* So perhaps you were sent by God. I want to *get out*, I want to take my father back to civilisation and into a hospital.'

'A hospital? Why, is he ill?'

'Haven't you realised? He's stark staring raving mad.'

Ludens followed Marcus up the stairs. He had not yet been upstairs. He expected (foolishly as he realised at the next moment) some sort of reasonably cosy book-lined study. The room they entered, revealed by the soft light of the now slightly clouded declining afternoon sun, was at first sight simply empty. There were bookshelves, upon which some papers were scattered, but no books. Inspection revealed an old rug covering some of the floorboards, a small low table also with papers, an old wooden rocking-chair, an upright chair near the window. Leaving Ludens for a moment Marcus fetched another similar chair from a room opposite. Looking quickly at the shelves Ludens saw sheets covered with illegible writing and dust. The room had a uniform light brown dusty look, everything in it seemed dusty. The colour was the colour of Marcus's faded khaki shirt and of the curious cap which he had been wearing on the previous evening when Ludens first saw him.

Ludens stood until Marcus sat down. Marcus sat on the chair by the window, Ludens facing him on the second chair which had been placed against the empty bookshelves. It felt like an interview or tutorial.

Ludens said, 'Where are your books?'

'I have no books.'

Of course Ludens did not believe what Irina had said about her father being mad. Marcus had always been an extremely eccentric perfectly sane person. It was just like an ignorant uneducated girl to say that he was mad; and given that Irina was so evidently 'fed up' her words could be treated as simply vindictive. All the same Ludens felt very uneasy in Marcus's presence, not least in case Marcus were to bring up once more the idea that Ludens was something which he was not, a messenger from some significant group or person, bringing an expected message. It had even by now occurred to Ludens to wonder whether Marcus might not actually be some sort of secret agent. Such a development of his eccentric and versatile life journey was not impossible, he issued, after all, from mysterious central Europe, and was the master of several languages. On the other hand, although Ludens did not doubt Marcus's courage or his 'nerve', that he could be 'up to' anything as practical as espionage, which required mundane orderly precision, seemed unlikely; unless of course his unworldly eccentricity had been feigned from the start. It was more likely that Ludens had misheard, or misunderstood, the disturbing question.

'Why?' said Ludens (meaning why no books).

Marcus did not answer this question but, sitting upright four-square with his hands on his knees like an Egyptian statue, stared at his visitor. He said softly, as if this might be a secret, 'You talked with Irina.'

'She told me something about your – your plans,' said Ludens

97

cautiously, 'but I'm not sure that I understood. Perhaps you could tell me more.'

Marcus said nothing for a moment, breathing slowly and deeply. He said, now answering Ludens's previous question, 'I've done my reading.' The words sounded oddly childish. Then, 'Sometimes I feel I am crammed with demons.' He kept on staring at Ludens with an air of savage puzzlement.

Ludens turned his head away and held onto his chair. 'Perhaps you are keeping too many thoughts inside your head. It might relieve the pressure to write some of them down.'

'Not writing but a mode of life.'

'You mean *not yet* writing. You must want to communicate.'

Marcus leaned forward. 'If there is writing, what is written will be written in blood.'

Ludens, startled, said, 'Do you mean revolution?'

'A metaphor.'

'You mean a sort of catharsis?'

'One can only understand what one identifies with. A pure experience.'

'Experience of what?'

Marcus hesitated, as if fearing to unveil a mystery. 'Of suffering.'

'What kind of suffering?'

'The most extreme.'

'You mean compassion?'

'Deeper than compassion.'

'What is deeper?'

'I cannot name it.'

'Marcus, *try*, say something –'

'The world must be saved. We must know that miracles are possible.'

'Yes, but do you think –'

'How to have clean thoughts, that is the problem, how to separate one's thoughts from one's obsessions.'

'The demons.'

'Yes.'

Ludens, subjected to a beam of attention which was making him feel giddy, and aware that he must now *keep Marcus going*, tried desperately to construct *the* question which would prompt a sudden continuous flow of explanation. But his concentration failed, he was silent too long, Marcus looked away, coughed, shifted his chair, fluttered his hands about. While Ludens was still struggling with his failing powers, Marcus said, 'Where did you walk with Irina?'

'Oh – down by the river – at the wooden bridge – the right-hand one just beyond the stone bridge. We went there on bikes.' Ludens decided not to bother Marcus with the tadpoles.

'You got on all right together?'

'Yes, very well.'

Marcus, leaning forward and lowering his voice almost to a whisper, said, 'She is a virgin.' He leaned back with a solemn air, watching Ludens.

Ludens's first thought was, why not, she's only sixteen! Then he thought, but I'm crazy, she's *not* sixteen. She must be over twenty now. I've been thinking of her as a schoolgirl, and in the night I saw her as a child.

Marcus said in a slow grave neutral voice like someone making an announcement, 'I was very displeased with you, that time, you remember.'

Ludens said, taking this remark as a warning, also gravely, 'I'm sorry. I trust that you no longer blame me.' He wondered if he should now explain in what sense it was 'not his fault', or whether this would make things worse.

However Marcus evidently considered the matter sufficiently dealt with. To Ludens's astonishment, and as if this were the most natural topic to tackle next, he said, 'Well, when shall we go to London? Tomorrow morning?'

Ludens was following Irina through the twilight. This was no dream.

After Marcus's amazing question not much more had been said. Ludens was indeed anxious to conclude the discussion on just this note, and before he somehow 'put his foot in it' by saying something which annoyed Marcus, and before it occurred to Marcus to change his mind or to return to the subject of his 'displeasure'. Ludens had said cheerfully, and as if this were some long anticipated holiday plan, that yes, departure tomorrow morning would be fine, and he would make all the arrangements.

Even as he went away down the stairs, Ludens's mind was already darkened by the question of the car which now assumed a special urgency. He must remove Marcus tomorrow; faltering, inefficiency, delay, signs of failure, would give Marcus time to reflect, have second thoughts, doubt Ludens's reliability, even his veracity, and so lose whatever grasp or vision of the future had inspired his proposal. Ludens looked about for Irina but could not find her. He discovered the white masculine bike in a shed, hauled it along the path, rode it to the gates, manoeuvred it through the gates leaving a streak of white paint behind, and rode on to the telephone box. There was no telephone book. He rang the exchange and asked to be connected with a garage. The exchange referred him to directory enquiries. Directory Enquiries could not help him unless he gave them a name, which he could not do. As he stood in the telephone box trying to think he saw a man and a dog approaching along the road. He recognised his friend, the man with the trowel. The man was even, once more, carrying a trowel and Ludens wondered again what that signified. Perhaps he was a botanist, or simply a gardener, who dug up specimens of plants in ditches? He left the box and walked to meet the man, meeting his dog first. The dog was the sort of cheerful irresponsible collie who has no concept of work and possesses the perfect self-confidence of the much-loved household pet. The sight of Ludens filled it with pleasure and it ran to him wagging its tail with pleasure and putting up its front paws, which Ludens caught in his hands and then gently released. The dog frisked about him, the man smiled at him. Ludens loved dogs, he had yearned for a dog when he was a child, but Keith preferred cats.

'So you found Fontellen all right!'

'Yes, thank you. Perhaps you could help me again? My car has broken down. Would you tell me the name of the nearest garage? Is there one in Edmarsh, or Clinten?'

'There's one in Clinten, but I'm afraid it's closed this afternoon. They all close in this locality.'

'When do they open in the morning?'

'They don't open tomorrow, it's Sunday.'

When Ludens got back to the cottage he was at first afraid that his absence might have been noticed and would by now have had some fatal effect. Time had indeed passed. The sun had not set, but was low behind the trees. As Ludens moved stealthily toward the door he glimpsed, as on the first evening (was it only yesterday?) Marcus, wearing his curious beige cap, sitting in the downstairs room cross-legged on the bed, looking at a sheet of paper. He did not notice Ludens. Again there was no sign of Irina. He did not imagine that she would be able to solve the car problem but he felt a nagging anxious need to tell her about it. He went into the kitchen and was wondering whether he should find himself something to eat (had he missed tea?) when he saw her outside the window once again holding her bicycle. When she saw Ludens she put a finger to her lips, and pointed to the other bicycle which Ludens had left against a tree. He ran out, seized the machine, and followed her. When they reached the cycle track she set off towards the house, now taking the left-hand fork toward the farther end of the lake, crossing the drive where a large notice said *Dismount*. When they had outflanked the house and the garden the track led down toward the water. The sun had just set, the lake was crimson. A pink cloud with a red hole in it like a wound hung in the western sky. Irina stopped abruptly, leapt over her fallen bicycle, and walked quickly away across the grass toward the flowering trees whose pale blossoms glowed in the vivid subdued light. Ludens too let his bicycle fall and hurried after her, afraid she might vanish into some rapidly gathering cloud of dark. He did not walk beside her, but followed in silence. The fading twilight, already blurring and jumbling the shapes of trees and bushes, was silently disturbed above by the erratic passages of bats.

After a slight incline the ground was level. They walked upon a grass path cut between longer grass. Now there were no more trees. Thick smudges of indigo clouds obscured a sky of granular blue-grey which now gave little light. A mist seemed to be forming ahead, or perhaps it was simply the twilight itself. Ludens, walking behind the girl upon the noiseless grass, was conscious of a change. All of a sudden he was no longer walking upon earth and grass, but upon a hard surface. Concrete. A concrete path? No, an expanse. All about him, as far as, in the dimness, he could see, before him, on either side, now behind him, a vast level concrete floor was stretching away. They walked on. Where to, where was Irina so purposefully going, what was this huge level place with its smooth floor and no edges over which they were moving in darkening silence? Ludens, not daring to look up, had the eerie feeling that he was *inside* something, that he had actually entered an enormous room, a great hall, as it might be the throne room of some god, a place of judgment, perhaps of execution, where a maleficent priestess was conducting him, the chosen victim, to his death. In the silence even the sound of their feet was inaudible. The edgeless floor stretched on, the air darkened.

Ludens hastened his step and came up beside her. He spoke in a low voice.

'For God's sake, what is this place?'

After a moment, Irina replied, also speaking softly. 'It's an airfield.'

'An *airfield*? Do you mean Lord Claverden has got a —'

'No, no, it's an old airfield. From the war. There was an American airbase here. The bombers used to go to Germany.'

Irina, who had been walking fast, now checked her pace, and they walked slowly, then very slowly, on. An immense silence surrounded them.

Irina said, 'It's a special place. I like to walk here, especially when it's misty or dark and I can't see the edges, it helps me to think, it helps me to be really alone.'

'Gods live here.'

'Ghosts of American airmen perhaps.'

'No.'

'After all, what was it like, flying out in the dark? But I'm not frightened. I don't ride my bike here, it would be wrong.'

'Because it's holy – or do I mean uncanny. I feel something terrible has happened here or will happen here. Does it belong to Lord Claverden?'

'Yes, he owns the land all around.'

'Look, we've got to decide what to do, this is urgent, please concentrate.'

They paused and stood side by side, not looking at each other, as if, it occurred to Ludens, they were servants, perhaps privileged attendants, who, on near approach to some mystery, had, at a silent signal, halted.

'I talked to your father, and he actually *said* and we *agreed* that he would go to London with me *tomorrow morning*.'

'He told me.'

'Oh? Does he mean it?'

'At the moment, yes, certainly at *that* moment. But what about your car?'

'Exactly. It needs a new tyre, and tomorrow's Sunday, and he could change his mind! What about trains, could we get a bus to the nearest station?'

'No buses on Sundays. Anyway it's miles and miles and Dad *hates* trains.'

'How did you get here?'

'Lord Claverden's chauffeur – but he's gone abroad.'

'How about a taxi?'

'There aren't any local ones. Anyway they wouldn't answer on Sunday, and –'

'Has Busby got a car? No? But he must know someone who has, *you* must know someone who has.'

'I don't know anyone.'

'You could ask Busby, couldn't he help us?'

'I don't like asking favours of Busby.'

'Why? Is he hostile?' Ludens recalled the silent figure in the wood who had evidently made Irina uneasy. Unpleasant possibilities suddenly occurred to him. 'Has he ever annoyed you, I mean been too familiar, or –?'

'No, no. He just has his own work to do.'

'I can't bear to wait here till Monday or Tuesday watching Marcus have second thoughts, I'd go mad! A man's life may depend on this. Can't you suggest *anything*?'

'No! I haven't any friends around here, I haven't any *friends*. Can't *you* ring up someone you know and tell them to drive up early tomorrow, or even tonight?'

This had already occurred to Ludens, but Jack and Alison were away, neither Franca nor Gildas could drive, Pat's friends had no telephones and no cars, Christian Eriksen was in Denmark . . . 'No – there's no one who would come *at once*, and it's the *time* – so you're afraid too, that he might change his mind?'

'*Yes*! I wish it could be *now*!'

'So do I! Oh *God*, I must think, I must *think*. You won't mind being alone here? We won't be long away, *if* we go! I'll bring him back at once.'

'I won't be alone, I won't be here.'

'You'll stay with someone?'

'I'm coming with you.'

'There's no need to, I can look after Marcus –'

'You haven't understood.'

'What –?'

'I'm leaving too. We are both leaving. I hope. It's up to you now. Dad asked if you were the messenger. You may not be his messenger, but you're certainly my messenger!'

'What do you mean?'

'It's my chance to *get out*, to return to the *real world*, to get Dad looked after, and *then* –'

'He's all right, he can look after himself, he's not –'

'Look, I've been here with him for over a year, a year of my life, I've seen it all happening, I thought I'd never get out, no one could help us, no one would, everyone was afraid of him, he didn't want to see anyone and I couldn't find anyone and he quarrelled with Lord Claverden and –'

'Why didn't you write to me?'

'*Write to you*?!'

Ludens, in the darkness, felt himself blush. 'To Jack, to Pat, to any of us –'

'I didn't know any of those people, how could I write, what could I say! I kept hoping at least he'd decide to go somewhere else, and sometimes it seemed as if he would – but he's been like somebody in a trance, the *concentration* has been terrifying, he wouldn't have just left here with some semi-stranger just to please me, try to imagine it, this place suited him, I can't think why I'm not mad too!'

'You stayed, you didn't abandon him.'

'I thought if I disappeared he might do – anything.'

'But what do you envisage –?'

'*Envisage*! Fuck envisage! I don't "envisage" anything except leaving this bloody awful place and getting him off my hands! Hell's bells, what sort of *plans* do you think *I* can make? I just want to *survive*!'

Ludens was startled by her language. He did not like swearing women. He had taught Sylvia not to swear. He said, 'You must have some plans – I mean like you leave your father somewhere, that you return here and –'

'God! Can't *you* get the *message*? Tomorrow we shall both leave here *forever*.'

'But all your things –'

'Things! I've had our stuff packed up for ages, for months, ready to leave at once if only there were a chance. Once we get out we shall never see this shit-house again *ever*.'

'But where will you live? I suppose I could put you up for a while.'

'Oh thanks! But it won't be necessary. We have a London flat.'

'*A London flat*?'

'Yes, why not? At least I hope we have. I've been paying the rates long enough. Dad bought it when he got back from India, but we only lived there for a short time, he wanted rural solitude.'

Set in motion again by the invisible watchers they turned and began to walk very slowly back. It was dark now. A thin moon was visible, a bright portent, but giving no light. Ludens had lost all sense of direction, but Irina paced confidently.

'You said your father felt he had a mission. What is it?'

'I don't know! He imagines he's some sort of sage. He wanted me to shave his head, only I wouldn't. I just cut his hair and beard with scissors. He's going to save the world, we're living through a dark era and waiting for a revelation, and he's the revelation!'

'You mean like the Messiah, or Jesus?'

'No, he's just great Marcus Vallar, it's just dull old megalomania like loonies in bins believe.'

'I can't agree with that.'

'Well, try. You know, it *is* a bit of luck your suddenly turning up with that story about your friend who's blind. It *is* like a sign.'

'He's not blind, he's just very ill. Marcus had the idea he was blind.'

'Perhaps he thinks he could perform a miracle, it'll be his first one, like Christ's first miracle was curing a blind man.'

'Actually, Christ's first miracle was turning water into wine.'

'Hmm. I doubt if Dad could manage that.'

'You think he might save my friend?'

'No, of course not! Getting him out of here is the main thing. And finding someone else to look after him. He's been sitting here for ages just *concentrating*.'

'But what *on* exactly?'

'Oh just lately it's been suffering, pain, pure suffering, pure pain, how to become a god, because only a god suffers purely, and only pure suffering will cause a cosmic change! You see, to save the world a god has to die, not exactly an original idea. The problem is how to suffer if you're fearfully rich and living in beautiful scenery and waited on hand and foot!'

'One suffers in the mind.'

'He hasn't started fasting or lacerating himself, not yet anyway. He just reads about it! He once read a lot of stuff about the Holocaust, you know, the murder of the Jews, he got every book on it, read all the books and then burnt them. I suppose that was symbolic, he's great on symbols, maybe that's one way to live without actually doing anything. Well, he did visit Auschwitz and distinguished himself by fainting. He should have remembered he was just a tourist. And he went to India to look at all the suffering on show there, perhaps he thought *they* would see that he was really a god, but all he got was hepatitis. And another thing is he's got to be a great sinner and understand evil as well as good and be the victims and Hitler too and Christ and Anti-Christ. He wants to enact the spiritual or something destiny of the human soul. He wants to fall into awful depths of suffering and degradation and die a terrible and famous death and be taken to heaven in a fiery chariot, it's all in the mind, just as you say, and he still expects to get his breakfast on time.'

'Has he said all this to you?'

'Well, not like that, what he says is much more jumbled.'

'I think you haven't understood.'

'I think *you* haven't understood. Let's leave it at that.'

'Listen. I want to say something about what happened last time when we met in Kent. Perhaps you've forgotten.'

'*Forgotten*?!'

'I mean, I expect you feel it's something trivial which you've put out of your mind or not wanted to think about or to regard as – as memorable or –'

'Go on!'

'I just want to say that I'm sorry, what happened took me by surprise and I reacted rather ungraciously. It was an unfortunate episode.'

Irina was silent.

'So – I apologise.'

'It wasn't an episode, it was a disaster, it was the beginning of the end. Dad was always against me, I was supposed to be a boy, then I was supposed to be a mathematical genius, I wasn't even beautiful. Then you rejected me –'

'I didn't reject you! You were a child!'

'I'm just one long disappointment. What you did was the last straw, a sort of parable of my failure, I was permanently devalued, you were the sign of my inferiority! He despised me, he hated you!'

'It wasn't my fault!'

'Now he thinks your destiny is entwined with his, so watch out! I felt humiliated, I was miserable, I learnt nothing, I didn't go to the university, I did a secretarial course.'

'I'm very sorry, but you can't blame me!'

'Your coldness has ruined my life. All right, you didn't mean it, all right I was a schoolgirl, but you could have been kinder to someone who said they loved you, you could have been gentle and grateful.'

'I can't remember what I said.'

'I can. After that Dad wrote me off. I was something that had to be hidden. By the way, he told you I was a virgin.'

'You must have been listening.'

'Well, I'm not. There was something, one thing. Oh, all right, perhaps it wasn't all your fault, I was just doomed from the start.'

'I don't believe –'

'Oh shut up!'

They had reached the edge of the airfield. Ludens could feel the soft cut grass, now damp with dew, under his feet. The dew from the trodden grass leapt in droplets onto his ankles. Irina walked ahead, Ludens followed. He felt upset, wounded, remorseful, yet also angry. Why should he be so troubled by a girl's spite when so many other urgent matters pressed him? When they had walked a little way he became conscious of the crying of owls, near and far, long wailing cries, long fluting cries, shrieks, and thought how silent it had been on the airfield where he had heard nothing. Looking past the striding figure of the girl he saw somewhere before him a lightness, a faint glow as of small clouds floating a little above the ground. They were entering the copse of flowering trees. Cherry trees, he thought, white cherries, as he looked up into the pallor pendent above him. The fallen petals lay thick under their feet and they scuffed them aside like autumn leaves. Irina had stopped, and was gathering the petals up, compressing them together in her two hands like a snowball. When Ludens reached her and was about to speak she hurled them violently into his face, then turned and ran away through the now pathless grass in the direction of the lake. By the time he reached his bicycle she had already disappeared down the track.

The sun was already high up. Ludens's watch said six o'clock. The birds were singing loudly in the wood. Now however he was down by the lake. He had slept badly. He had not seen Irina again. He had pedalled slowly along the darkened track and even fallen off at an unexpected curve. The stars, unclouded, crowding the high arc of the sky, gave some light, or some illusion of light. As he neared the cottage, dragging his bicycle over the dry humps of the track, he was chiefly concerned with whether he would be able to get into the kitchen to find something to eat. All was well, both doors were unlocked. No lights were visible. Ludens had already worked out that Marcus did not sleep in the downstairs room, which opened out of the kitchen, but on the upstairs corridor, next to the room where he had seen the 'boy'. He could not locate a candle and blundered about in the dark finding some bread and some cake, also a dish of butter reduced by the warm weather to a sticky liquid state. Unable to discover a knife, he smeared some butter onto a fragment of loaf with his fingers, and carried the soft crumbling mess up to his bedroom where he enjoyed by candlelight an extremely satisfying feast, whose pleasures for a time even obliterated the painful anxieties which later rendered him sleepless.

Now, standing by the lake, he was wasting his time thinking about Irina. He could still feel the impact of those snowballed petals in his face. The hostility of the gesture was unmistakable; though there had been something childish, as of some implicitly proffered peace, in the gathering up of the petals. He did not believe that he had 'ruined her life', but he felt an irritating futile remorse about the way he had behaved to her in those few shocked minutes, during which he had perhaps lodged in Marcus's mind also some atom of dangerous indelible anger. The absurd 'dotty' nature of his whole present operation now overwhelmed him. It had been from the start a thoroughly *silly* idea. He should have left Marcus alone. How could he have dreamt up the notion that Marcus could save Patrick? The project was not only useless but in effect cruel, raising false hopes and leading Marcus himself into a trap of painful and inevitable failure. Why had he not thought of *that* beforehand? The purpose of it all, as Ludens now saw but too clearly, was simply the aggrandisement of Ludens. Yet even as he thought this Ludens was aware that he was thoroughly entangled in his own stratagem and not only could not withdraw but did not want to. He passionately desired to take Marcus to London, and would be bitterly disappointed if (which would be one solution of the problem) Marcus were to change his mind. Moreover he had, somehow or other, by now also contracted obligations to Irina, to whom he was appearing in the role of liberator. He did not want to take her with him, he wanted to travel alone with Marcus – but there was no use arguing. He dreaded any delay which might remove his dilemma. He had decided during the sleepless night hours that his best plan was to bicycle to Clinten and hope to discover, beseech and bribe the necessary assistance.

He had walked from the cottage and was standing beside the little stream, the one in which Irina had stood among the tadpoles, at the point at which it entered the lake. The sky, which had been a very light luminous grey, was now a very light luminous blue. The moon, which had travelled throughout the night, was a pale and milky slit. The lake water was almost white. The visible world, as if enchanted by the song of the birds, was motionless. Ludens experienced, as an extra pain, an intimation of the happiness he might have felt in such a place.

Then he noticed, quite far out in the water, a disturbance of some kind. Waterfowl fighting? More like a large dog swimming. As he watched it he became aware, out of the corner of his eye, of another phenomenon. He quickly turned his head. There had been a pale flash, a little way away, among the trees; and Ludens imagined that he saw, *dancing*, in a little glade where the sun penetrated the leafy branches, a completely naked human figure! There was no sound; but the sudden, now vanished, image transformed the whole scene, the tranquil water, the dappled sunlight, the gracious patterns of the trees, into an impressionist picture, or some more ancient ambience of a dancing satyr; for the capering figure had seemed to be male. A splashing noise now attracted Ludens's attention once more to the lake. The swimming creature, nearer, was revealed as a woman. Irina? He felt alarm, distress, desiring to hide but fearing to move. The woman, moving into the shallows, came gently to a standstill, then slowly and awkwardly rose to her feet and began to step cautiously, long-leggedly, forward toward the shore. She was entirely naked and she was certainly not Irina. As he watched she stopped and stood with outstretched arms, delighting in her nakedness, her youthful strength, her beauty, the glassy lake, the cold water, the cool air, the pure morning light. She was now so close to Ludens that he could see, in that clear light, the drops of water upon her skin. He recognised her. She was Alison Merrick.

He stepped back, and as she noticed the sudden motion he called softly, 'Alison! It's me, Ludens.'

Alison, turning abruptly and nearly losing her balance, waved, then proceeded very quickly and regardless of dignity to emerge onto the shore and dart in among the trees.

Immediately another form appeared, also naked. It was Jack. He advanced, shading his eyes and peering into the light, then stepping out into the water.

The sight of Alison had filled Ludens with a choking sensation as of swallowing some enormous draught mixed of excitement and dismay and delight and embarrassment and envy and shame. The sight of Jack's tall nude figure prompted nothing but joy. He rushed forward and, striding ankle-deep into the lake, splashed his way towards his friend. They met in an impetuous embrace which soaked Ludens's shirt and trousers.

'Jack, thank God you've come!'

'You don't mind? We were going to be very discreet, we weren't going to knock on the door! We didn't know where you were anyway. We just felt such *agonies* of curiosity, we felt we *had* to come and see! We had a very quick wander last night and it all looked so gorgeous and so derelict, and you said Lord C. was away, so we got up early, the weather's so heavenly, and then it was just *impossible* not to swim — we've been so quiet, like water rats!'

'Don't talk so loud. Where did you stay?'

'At the Claverden Arms in Edmarsh.'

'You came by car — of course you did — where's the car?'

'We opened the gates and drove it down the drive — if you can call it a drive, the Bentley didn't care for it much. We left it up there in the trees when the house came in sight. I must say, it's a darling house –'

'You opened those gates? You must be giants.'

'We are. What's been happening? Look, I'm beginning to freeze, that water's cold. Let's get back to land.'

Ludens followed him, his insubstantial shoes weighed with mud, into the shade of the trees where Alison, who had acted swiftly, manifested herself in a light blue dress of feathery cotton. Jack began to dry himself perfunctorily on Alison's scarf which she had handed to him. He showed no sign of wanting to put his clothes on. Ludens gazed upon Jack's sturdy burly white body, upon his broad shoulders, his golden-haired chest, his sexual organs and long strong straight legs, and marvelled. He felt also a curious embarrassed *frisson* at the sight of Jack unclothed in the presence of Alison who now looked so neat and so respectably pretty. Jack, pawing the long grass to get the mud off his feet, was clearly enjoying having Ludens as a spectator of his display of his charms to the girl. Prudish Ludens, indulging his mixture of emotions, felt with it a kind of despair: he would never understand women, never dance naked in a sun-lit glade, never possess a girl as wonderful as Alison. Just then he caught Alison's eye and an ambiguous signal passed between them, as if she were, at least at that moment, understanding and sympathising with his feelings.

'Well, Ludens, what's going on, tell us all.'

'Well, Jack, as you know – but of course you don't know, unless you rang Franca.'

'What? I haven't rung Franca.'

'Pat's holding out. Marcus will come to London to see him.'

'Oh, isn't that wonderful!' said Alison.

'But listen,' said Ludens to Jack, who was now condescending to put his clothes on, 'Marcus wants to leave today, *this morning*, and Irina's coming too –'

'Irina?'

'His daughter, I don't want to bring her but I've got to, and it must all happen *quickly* because of Pat and because – Oh I'll tell you later – and my car is crocked up, I burst a tyre and the spare wheel is flat and it's Sunday.'

'We'll take you,' said Jack, stepping into his trousers, 'don't worry. All is well.' He began to sing in his loud ringing bass. 'Nymphs and shepherds come away, come away, in this grove we'll sport and play –'

'Shut up! Someone will hear you. Jack, listen to me, we can't go together –'

'There's room for five!'

'Yes, but I can't have you and Alison in the car with Marcus and Irina, it just *wouldn't do.*'

'Why ever not, what's wrong with us?'

'God – you know what Marcus is like – he mightn't come, he might decide not to come at all. He mustn't see you – don't you understand, it's all *precarious.* I've only just managed to persuade him, he only just tolerates *me –*'

'Is he dafter than before?'

'No, he's not daft at all, he's just been working and working all by himself. Jack, I've got to have the Bentley.'

'And leave us with your dud car?'

'Yes! I'll tell you exactly where it is, here are the keys, you can get it fixed tomorrow morning.'

'So we'll have to foot it to the Claverden Arms!'

'Give in, Jack,' said Alison.

A little while later Ludens, not even pausing to scrape the mud off his shoes and ankles, was hurrying back to Red Cottage with the keys of the Bentley in his pocket. Now that the doors of possibility had magically opened one after the other, Ludens realised how much comfort he had derived from uncertainty. Now nothing separated him from any of several catastrophes: Marcus might not come, he might come and find Pat dead, he might try to save him and fail. Ludens only now began to imagine what that failure might be like. It looked as if only one thing was really likely to be achieved, the escape of Irina. Where to, and what for, he wondered; and decided it was none of his business.

PART THREE

Irina's hand was trembling. She thrust the key against the door several times, missing the lock. At last she got it in and turned it and pushed the door. It moved a little, then stopped. Ludens helped her push and they squeezed through. A pile of letters was lying on the floor. Ludens kicked them aside and held the door open for Marcus. Marcus marched in. 'Marched' was indeed the word. He came in with a long stride, with head erect, and calm authoritative eyes. He looked around, then made his way to the lavatory. Ludens closed the front door, then looked for Irina. She had disappeared into one of the bedrooms and was dragging clothes out of the drawers of a chest.

Time had slipped, the flat was in the past, not a particular human past, but some old ownerless past like that of a hitherto undiscovered cavern whose silence resisted the puny human sounds of the intruders. The sound of clothes tumbling onto the floor was a startling phenomenon, difficult to interpret. The rooms, painted green, were dark and damp and smelled of alien growths. Ludens tiptoed into the kitchen and was amazed to see two mugs on the table with remnants of tea in them. He then looked about, expecting to see a cage with a dead bird, the body of a starved cat in a basket. He pulled back a curtain revealing a brick wall close outside the window. Standing still he was aware of a, near or far, faint humming which he decided must be the sound of traffic in Victoria Street. The flat, deep in the inwardness of a huge mansion block, was on the sixth floor.

The departure from Red Cottage had been effected with dream-like ease. Ludens received one shock as he was returning to the cottage. He was startled to see a column of smoke rising from among the trees. He ran. The source of the smoke turned out to be a huge cast-iron incinerator behind the house which had been crammed full of papers and what seemed to be old clothes. The incinerator was tall, like an ornate pillar, with a crenellated top, and between its bars the smouldering contents spurted out at intervals in flames. Gazing at the random and momentary flares Ludens felt himself in the presence of some awful rite. What was it that had been condemned to this total destruction? He felt an urge to reach out and rescue some of the sheets of paper on which he imagined he could see writing, but the heat was extreme. Stretching out an incautious hand he burnt a finger on one of the bars. Then suddenly Irina appeared carrying a bucket. She did not see him at once, as he stood back from the coiling smoke. Ludens thought, she can't put it out now! But then, as she hurled the contents of the bucket at the huge pyre, he smelt paraffin and leapt away. The incinerator became a roaring pillar of flame, its iron bars instantly glowing red hot. Ludens shouted at her, afraid that the cottage would catch fire. They ran back together to the front. As he reached the front door he saw a strange sight. The door was open and just inside Marcus was sitting on a chair, wrapped in what appeared to be a cloak or ulster, wearing a tweed hat and holding a stick in his hand. He sat quite still, looking like a rather odd god in a shrine or a waxwork in a box. Ludens looked upon him with relief. Clearly Marcus had not changed his mind.

After that things moved fast. Ludens informed Irina that a car was waiting in the drive. He did not tell her how he had performed this miracle, nor did she ask. She began hauling suitcases out of the hall, onto the grass. It appeared that she and Marcus had already had breakfast. Ludens ran into the kitchen, finding the other half of last night's mangled loaf. He quickly devoured a few fragments and stuffed into a bag a lot of miscellaneous food which Irina was evidently leaving behind. (He thought: maybe in London I can *really* get something to eat.) Irina had already set off carrying two suitcases. Marcus rose and was following her more slowly. Ludens picked up two more suitcases and hurried after them. Jack's beautiful pale-brown Bentley was parked in the drive, at the end of the track, at the edge of the wood, with its nose pointing to the outside world, towards freedom. When she saw the car Irina uttered an extraordinary sound, a long raucous rapturous cry. Marcus said nothing, he just climbed into the back seat. Irina climbed into the front passenger seat. Ludens detached from the windscreen a note from Jack which read *Bon voyage. Take care of my lovely car.* Ludens made two journeys back to the house to bring remaining luggage, the suitcases which Irina had for so long kept packed, ready for the moment of escape. These now filled the capacious boot of the car and much of the back seat. Should he lock up the house? Irina said not to bother. All this time Ludens was in a frenzy of exaltation and terror. One thing that frightened him was the thought that, for some reason or other, Busby might prevent them from leaving.

He must resent the impertinent intrusion of the big car. He could have many reasons for being vindictive. He must *know*. Suppose they were to find the gates closed and padlocked? Arriving back at the cottage for the last time Ludens paused to look and listen. He went round the back of the house and inspected the incinerator, now full of partly glowing but mainly black ashes. He ran back and into the house, first to his own room, and then into the other half of the cottage, feeling a strange compulsion to *find* something, as if there were some crucial thing, upon which everything else depended, which was still hidden and must not be left behind. He went into the downstairs room where he had seen Marcus through the window. He picked up a piece of paper with some writing on it, could not decipher the writing, and dropped it. In the kitchen he noticed the keys of the house lying conspicuously on the table. Had Irina told Busby they were going? At the last moment he saw an apple lying on the dresser and put it in his pocket.

Leaving was after all easy. The beautiful pale-brown Bentley bumped with slow calm dignity down the drive. The gates were wide open. Only as the car approached them did Ludens think he glimpsed a figure standing in the shade under a tree. Once on the motorway Ludens was able to calm his mind by, what could not be ignored, the pleasure of driving the magnificent car. Instinctively anxious for its welfare (he had not needed Jack's admonition) he drove it carefully at a modest pace, resisting the temptation to press hard upon the accelerator. Nor was he unaware of the rays of force emanating from the presence behind his back of the fateful being now committed to his charge. No one spoke during the journey, which was marked by two events, one of them baleful. The first event was introduced by a loud and persistent hooting just behind them. Then a blue Rover drew out and flashed past them at speed, two people waving. Jack and Alison. Ludens, proceeding sedately, worked out what must have happened. Jack, used (unlike Ludens) to getting his way, had hired the Rover somehow in Edmarsh, and had (Ludens had no doubt) commissioned someone to rescue the Volkswagen and drive it to London. Jack could, in the briefest time, bring about such things, impossible to others. The second event was the sudden brutal crashing of something large and heavy, coming from above, upon the windscreen. The car swerved. The projectile vanished in a wild cloud of feathers. A pheasant, caught in a stream of air, had dashed itself to death. Its blood, streaming upon the glass, was slowly set aside by the windscreen wipers. Nothing was said. But Ludens became aware that Irina was now quietly crying, quietly and continuously her tears streamed down, not like a waterfall, but like the gentle slide of water over smooth stone. Ludens, aware but gazing ahead, felt a deep weary compassionate feeling of tenderness and pity which soothed and pacified the anguish of his exaltation and his fear.

Ludens had brought up two suitcases in the lift. The rest were locked up in the car which was illegally parked below. He had at first intended to drive straight to Jack's house in Chelsea. But he decided he must at least stop somewhere to telephone a warning of their arrival and to find out if Pat was still alive. It seemed sensible to go to the flat and telephone from there. Only now his charges seemed to be settling themselves into occupation, having forgotten the urgent purpose of their return to London. Marcus was still in the lavatory. Ludens went to look at Irina who was on her knees rummaging in a pile of clothes which now covered the floor of the bedroom. The garments exuded a damp musty smell, some were stiff, some visibly mildewed, some stuck together and had to be torn apart.

'Oh *shit*, I can't find *anything* to wear!'

'Is your father all right?'

'Yes, he sits there for hours, he thinks.'

'I think we should go at once and see Patrick.'

'Who's Patrick?'

'My friend who's ill.'

'Oh yes. I could go out and buy some.'

'What?'

'Clothes.'

'All right, but Marcus and I must go, I must telephone to say we're coming.'

'What time is it?'

'Just after twelve.' This seemed incredible. A day, days, must have passed since he stood beside the lake.

At that moment Marcus reappeared and said, 'Alfred, would you mind –?'

Ludens followed him into one of the other rooms, a bedroom, green, where an iron bedstead was wrapped in stillness. Marcus said in a low voice, 'Would you mind shaving me? I don't think I can do it myself.'

A few minutes later Marcus was sitting in the bathroom before a washbasin (the water was hot) with a towel over his chest and his face covered with shaving cream. Marcus had of course left his razor behind, but the bathroom cupboard revealed a razor, virgin blades, and cream.

Ludens, who had never shaved anybody but himself before, soon discovered that shaving somebody else required a different technique. It was in any case no easy task to remove the hard stubble which covered Marcus's face and neck, though it had been cut as short as possible by Irina's nail-scissors. Ludens, steadying Marcus's head with one hand, his fingers plunged into the short hair, and slowly and firmly moving the very sharp instrument, felt like an acolyte performing a dangerous task, perhaps intended as a test. Suppose his hand slipped, suppose he were to shed Marcus's blood? At the very thought he felt a tendency to tremble. A large mirror above the basin revealed to Ludens at intervals the progress of his toil. He was aware of Marcus watching the work of transformation. Avoiding Marcus's eye, Ludens saw his own face, his dark hair unkempt, his shirt awry, his lips parted in a grimace of nervous solicitude. His initial anxiety about the technique had postponed his astonishment at being able suddenly to *touch* Marcus, to *hold* him, feeling the shape and warmth of his head with one hand, while with the razor he caressed the cheek and throat, allowing his fingers to feel the smoothed flesh. Surely a barber didn't *hold* his client in this way, was he perhaps *going too far*? But he could not think of any other way to work safely. The finger which he had burnt on the incinerator was in addition giving him trouble and would not tolerate pressure. The basin was full of scraped debris which Ludens removed at intervals by running the water. Meanwhile Marcus's face, emerging from beneath the soiled stubble, was looking remarkably clean and young. When the task was almost over Marcus, who had been solemn, caught Ludens's eye in the mirror and smiled, and Ludens smiled too. They said nothing. When the task was finished and Marcus had mopped and dried his face and neck, they once again looked into the mirror, Marcus still sitting and Ludens standing as if at attention behind him. For a moment Ludens put his hands on to Marcus's shoulders, holding him firmly, feeling the warm flesh through the shirt. As his grasp closed he felt a shock.

'I've been thinking about you.'

'Oh?' said Ludens, removing his hands abruptly. How had he dared to put them there? No wonder he got an electric jolt. What was to follow?

'I want to ask you something.'

'Yes?'

'Could you close the door?' Ludens closed the door. 'It's about Irina.'

'Oh, yes?'

'I want you to look after her.'

'How do you mean?' said Ludens, startled.

'I may not be able to be with her.'

'She's grown up, I'm sure she'll be very good at looking after herself.'

'She is a child, she does not know the world. She may be in danger.'

'What sort of danger?'

Marcus hesitated, he actually blushed, the blood suddenly colouring the new clean skin of his face. 'All sorts of danger.'

Ludens, alarmed, began, 'Oh, I don't think –'

'I ask you. That is all.'

Irina, dressed in her petticoat, threw open the door of the bathroom.

Ludens said quickly, 'Look, we must go now to Patrick at once. All right?'

'Yes, yes. At once.'

Ludens was suddenly conscious of being hungry again. This seemed to have become a permanent condition. He could hardly now suggest lunch, nor could he, at this solemn moment, eat the apple which was in his jacket pocket. The food he had brought from Red Cottage was still down in the car. Could he ask Franca to make sandwiches for them? God, was Patrick still alive? He remembered that he had intended to telephone, but decided not to.

Irina had dashed into the bathroom and was washing her hair with shaving-cream.

At an earlier time, when the Bentley was still on the motorway, a conference was taking place in the upper rooms of Jack's house. Franca, Moxie, Dr Hensman and Father O'Harte, who had been talking softly in the front room, had now returned to the back room where the curtains had been drawn against the sun. Patrick lay on his side, one arm upon his breast, in the attitude of a relaxed sleeper. His long gaunt bony head lay heavily upon the white lace-fringed pillow which Moxie had put in place, the flesh of his thin forearms, emerging from spotlessly clean pyjamas, was like wax. The ordinary naturalness of the attitude filled Franca with a thoughtless tenderness which she felt to be entirely misplaced. She also retained her tears. She told herself sternly that the time had passed when sympathy, hope, tender care, even love could have anything to do with the figure on the bed. Pat was breathing, the bedclothes rose and fell. His eyes, very nearly closed, showed a faint grey gleam beneath the lashes. But he was surrendered, they had surrendered him, into the power of death. The bottles, pills, medicines, even the glass of water, the paraphernalia of tending and caring, had been taken away, Franca herself had taken it away. The room was stripped and tidy. Nothing was left in it except Patrick himself and he had nothing to do now but to depart. The doctor, who had now been there for some time, and was looking at his watch, had been explaining. If Patrick was sent back to the hospital he might be temporarily revived, but only briefly and perhaps in some damaged state. There was no point in adding this useless torment. He was sleepy now, he was resting. Let him have his sleep out. His body, untended, would slowly and painlessly and naturally bring about what was inevitable. In a few days' time, perhaps sooner, he would die quietly of pneumonia, peacefully suffocating as the bloodstream slowed and the deprived lungs surrendered their function.

'So there is nothing more to do?' said Franca.

'Nothing.'

'It's no use trying to rouse him?'

'No. I don't think he will regain consciousness. And anyway better not.'

Franca had in fact tried vainly to waken him that morning, stirring him a little and calling his name. Now she did not even wish to try, for fear of rousing up something terrible. It was better to let him rest. She said, 'I shall stay with him.'

The doctor bowed his head respectfully. He was a stout man with a bald crown round which a ruff of brown hair grew thickly. He was attentive but impersonal, and esteemed rather than loved.

Father O'Harte, easing his little white collar, for it was a hot day, sighed deeply. He was perspiring and would have liked to take off his jacket. He had done his part. He had performed the last rites earlier, when Patrick was at least half aware, and perhaps even knew what was happening and assented to it. God was merciful. Father O'Harte had become very fond of Patrick. Now his task was over. He knew that Franca and the nurse regarded him with hostility. He would not visit this house again.

Franca had once seen a film of a burial at sea, how the coffin slid with a curious slowness down toward the waves and entered them without a splash. She felt now as if something were slipping away, leaving her mind not quiet and empty, but suddenly filled with the black debris of her own trouble. It was as if, during the time when she had so strangely loved him, she had relied upon Patrick, hoped for him, dreamed of him, run to him as to his love for her: a love which had never existed and could now never exist. He had been, even as hope faded, her occupation. Now she would have to *think*, that was what was happening to her mind. Looking at Pat quietly sleeping away his life, she was shocked, assailed, by a sense of solitude. Patrick had been company, tending him had been a solace, hoping for him had been a hope. Now she had to think how to survive, that was what it came to.

If only she had stopped Jack in his tracks, at least made scenes, made a fuss, however mildly accused him, on the occasion of the first girl! What had her motives been for keeping quiet then, for not behaving as (perhaps) most women would have behaved? She had not colluded, but might have seemed to. Had she *deceived* him? Her main motive had been simply her love for Jack, her desire to believe him, not to question him, not to cause him any pain, but to accept as fundamental that he must be happy. Love had stopped her mouth. But had love been right? She had believed Jack at the start when he had told her that she was the pillar, the guardian, the deep essential truth of his life, the indestructible centre point. She had believed him *even now*, even after what had happened and was happening, when he had said that his love for her remained as it had ever been, something eternal. If she were to cease believing that . . . Supposing it were simply words which now meant little, something vague perhaps. Yet when she looked upon him she could not but believe that his sincere eyes could tell no lie. So shall I live, supposing thou art true.

She reflected upon, perhaps only now fully remembered, her sense, in forgiving Jack, of in some way devaluing him, accepting him and loving him as something less than the perfect being she had married. She had sided with his lower self. Should she not have fought him, fighting on the side of the better Jack, the good Jack, against the false bad Jack? She could not see him in any such clear moralistic light. Why should he not look at other women, as other men did? His *nature* was different from hers. Was this not, as she felt it, a judgment upon him? Would it have been better if, like other men, he had not told her? She could not think that, and in a way the question was senseless. She had pitied him; and that was part of the devaluing, the belittling. But would she have endured a Jack on whom she had forced her will, who would sadly, perhaps resentfully, have given up what he desired in order to please his possessive wife? So in that way, she thought, she had acted not just lovingly, but selfishly in choosing peace! That was the first weakness, the first failure, which had led on, so *inevitably*, through the series of, not after all so many, girls who did not matter, to the girl who mattered; and to the point where Franca's complaisant kindness must come to an abrupt end. Yet even here she had been so far weak, so far selfish, in concealing her violent and terrible feelings, her destructive misery, her rage.

She was confused, of course, by liking Alison, not hating her, even in a weird sense sympathising with her. Alison wanted to talk, to negotiate, to exhibit her guilt feelings to Franca and receive some sort of absolution. Perhaps Jack had even encouraged Alison to do that. So, they discussed her, they must do. But Franca while remaining seemingly so calm, friendly and kind, had refused to be led into any woman-to-woman conversation about 'how things were'. She was, in any case, not sure how they were, or how they were for her. The situation was so dreadful, so nightmarish, *their* details did not matter, they just confronted her as an abomination which was capable of driving her mad. Once she had, after she had listened with a gentle face to Jack's admission, his ultimatum, that Alison was different, Alison was 'for keeps', believed that nothing could be worse, that she had now experienced the worst. It was not so. She had been tortured by Alison's presence in the house, by the sound of Alison and Jack laughing downstairs. Now she was further reduced, twisted to screaming point, by Jack's having gone away with Alison without telling her where he was going and when he would be back. Jack had left her a shamefaced note with no explanation, a *humble* note. So it had come to her on the previous day, and came again now, the whiff, or stroke, of solitude, as her final hope for Patrick's life was extinguished. Great waves of pain assailed her heart and she gasped and put a hand to her breast.

'Franca, dear, wouldn't you like to go and lie down,' came Moxie's voice.

Dr Hensman was looking at her. He said in a kindly voice, 'I'll write you a prescription for sleeping pills, and a mild tranquilliser.'

Their solicitude made Franca feel that she was going to faint. She said, 'I'm all right.'

There was a sound from downstairs, a door banged, then voices, loud clear voices, were heard below, the voices of Jack and Alison.

Franca said, 'I think I'll go and rest now.' She made for the door, but decided instead to sit down on a chair. She could hear Jack and Alison modifying the pitch of their voices as they came up the stairs.

The new arrivals burst in. They could not help bursting in, and though they were aware of it, could not help seeming what they self-evidently were, healthy and happy. They had composed their faces, but their eyes sparkled and their mouths yearned to smile.

The sight of Patrick, and of the little assembly, sobered them a little. Jack said in a low voice, 'How is he?'

The doctor said, 'I'm afraid we cannot hope now.'

Alison said, 'Oh –' and turned to Franca and put her hand on her shoulder. Franca at once stood up, displacing the sympathetic hand.

Jack said to Franca, 'We've been having the most extraordinary time! We went to that place, Fontellen, you know, where Marcus Vallar was, where Ludens went to find him. We thought we'd go and help! Well, Marcus said he'd come and see Pat, and Ludens is driving him down in the Bentley! We'd have got here sooner only we stopped for a bite of something. Ludens will bring Marcus here, he should show up any moment, I hope he hasn't messed up the car!'

'It's too late,' said Moxie, and said to Franca, 'do go and rest, dear. I'll stay with Patrick. We needn't detain these gentlemen.'

The priest and the doctor had listened with interest. They had of course heard of the 'Vallar plan', and had joined in discussions of it at various stages. They now looked animated and alert.

'I think I'll stay,' said the doctor.

'Me too,' said Father O'Harte.

In the sun-twilight of the room Franca, the doctor, the priest, and the nurse stood as sombre figures. The doctor and the priest wore their customary dark suits, the doctor's smart, the priest's shabby. Moxie (who never 'dressed up' as a nurse) and Franca were wearing dark sad dresses. Franca, with her almost black hair and her almost black dress, felt occluded, invisible, as if she were wearing a shadoor. A little touch of brightness in the room had been Patrick's red pyjamas, where had those pyjamas come from? Franca wondered. Probably Moxie brought them. By contrast Jack and Alison were brilliant figures, taller than the others, and upright, whereas the other four crouched a little and bent their heads. Alison was wearing her dress of feathery blue cotton, bound in at the waist, her red hair was tousled, her freckled face not darkened, illuminated rather, by the sun, her pale skin delicately, milkily, opaque and her unpainted lips the faintest purest pink. Her forearms and much of her long legs were bare, visible, pale as her face. Jack, burly, untidy beside her, even taller, was wearing white trousers, a little smudged, and an apple-green shirt carelessly undone. He had rolled up his sleeves. His large sunburnt face and prominent blue eyes expressed determination and excitement. Franca, looking at him, felt the old familiar rush of feeling as if her body advanced and entered his body. The next moment she was a shocked spectator, seeing them both as something in a theatre, perhaps ballet dancers pretending to be puppets. She moved the chair and leaned on it with one hand. Jack instinctively moved to the window and pulled apart the curtains. Sunlight streamed in. The bell rang down below.

Jack immediately dashed out of the door followed by Alison. Franca moved her chair well back against the wall and sat on it again. The doctor and the priest, stepping back on the other side of the room, murmured to each other. Moxie said, 'I don't approve of this nonsense,' and walked out onto the landing. Loud excited voices could be heard below, and ascending steps. Jack and Alison came in followed by Marcus and Ludens.

Franca was immediately struck by Marcus's appearance. She had never seen him with his hair cut short, and the absence of the red-blond locks made him for a moment unrecognisable. His face looked odd, the upper part brown, the lower part white. He was dressed in a crumpled brown suit with a brown shirt and tie. He entered the room leaning forward, in a blundering awkward way. Ludens, slightly behind him, trying to hold his arm, was gripping the tail of his jacket. Ludens looked his craziest, his hair jagged, his dark eyes narrowed, the corners of his mouth raised in a ghastly contorted grin of fear. As he came in he looked straight at Franca. In that instant she realised the whole shocking weirdness of what was going on. Something terrible, horrible was going to occur, a desecration. As she felt a desire to scream there was a strange sound in the room. The priest had uttered some incoherent exclamation. Franca rose to her feet. Someone was holding her arm and pressing it hard. It was Moxie, who was leaning against the wall beside her, seemingly spreadeagled by some centrifugal force. Unconsciously she kept squeezing Franca's arm. Jack and Alison stood side by side against the door, which was closed. Their arms and shoulders touching, they stood at attention, like brightly caparisoned guards. There were now nine people inside the small room. No, ten, for a girl was also present, standing just beyond Marcus, a gipsy-like girl with fuzzy dark hair, wearing a much creased coat and skirt of light-brown cotton and a flowery blouse. She was holding up the collar of her blouse and gradually twisting it.

There was an embarrassing silence. The embarrassment might have been felt as relief. Franca, staring at Marcus, thought, he's like a scientist, no he's like an architect, if his suit were smarter he could be an art dealer, he's looking competent and ordinary – and yet he's still terrible, as he always was. Marcus, still leaning forward and clutched from behind by Ludens, was fingering his tie. No one looked at the sleeping figure in the bed. Franca thought, Oh God, who's in charge, am I?

Ludens spoke first. He said, releasing Marcus and addressing Franca, 'This is Professor Vallar.' Then he said to Marcus, 'You remember Franca. This is Dr Hensman, and Miss Moxon, and this –' He could not recall the priest's name.

Moxie whispered to Franca, 'Don't let him –'

Franca said to the doctor, 'Dr Hensman, perhaps you could explain to Professor Vallar that there is nothing he can do. We thank him very much for coming.'

Dr Hensman said to Marcus, 'My patient is in a deep terminal coma. It is impossible to communicate with him. I am sorry. We appreciate your desire to help.' He bowed, and gestured toward the door. 'Suppose we all go downstairs now?' he said to Jack.

Jack did not reply. His lips were parted, he seemed excited, agitated, almost frightened. His bared chest was rising and falling. Alison was whispering in his ear. He continued to stare at Marcus.

Franca appealed to Ludens. 'Alfred –'

Ludens, addressing the doctor, said, 'Can't he have a try?' The sentence sounded ludicrous, as if Marcus were some child who had to be humoured.

The doctor, who evidently, and not unreasonably, on the basis of conversations with Franca, thought he was dealing with a madman, said to Marcus, 'I think we should all go now and have a nice conversation downstairs. Nothing whatever can be done here. Perhaps you could open the door, could you?' He motioned to Jack, who moved slightly away from the door, drawing Alison with him. The door was opened by the gipsy girl who with a decisive movement turned the handle and pulled it wide. Franca, wondering who she was, had decided that she was some sort of secretary or servant of Marcus, like the conjuror's assistant.

Dr Hensman advanced toward the door. The priest did not move. Ludens, now speaking in an angry slightly hysterical voice, said, 'No, no! We won't go away. Marcus has been kind enough to come here. He believes he can help Patrick. He can't do any harm. He might do good –'

The doctor said to Ludens, 'I am sorry, you are evidently unaware of the facts of the medical situation. Perhaps you imagine that my poor patient can be wakened up and talked to. He cannot, it is too late, he will be dead soon. And even if he could be roused – which he cannot

– no contact could be made. Don't you understand? The mind is gone.'

'What illness is he suffering from?' said Ludens, who had managed to take charge of himself.

'Well, we don't know,' said the doctor, 'but –'

'There you are!'

'The facts are evident. It is fatal.'

'I don't believe in these "facts".'

'*Really*!' said the doctor to Ludens. 'What do you want? To disturb and shake a peacefully dying man simply to oblige your friend here who thinks he is a healer? Please be rational, please be considerate. Don't you agree?' He appealed here to Franca.

All this time Marcus was standing, now more upright, looking about him at the various speakers, with an interested air.

Ludens said, 'Jack –'

Alison said, 'The doctor's right, let him be.'

Ludens said again, 'Jack –'

Jack said, 'I think Marcus should decide. If he believes it's worth trying, then I think he should try.'

Moxie said, in a piercing furious voice, 'But this is superstition, gross superstition! Just *think*! You can't do anything to Pat, you can't help him or harm him. Do you expect us to stand and watch this idiotic charade? There are people here who love Pat and who will be deeply hurt and upset by this brutal interference. The peace of the dying belongs to the living too. What you suggest is monstrous. Don't you agree, Father?'

There was a moment's silence. Franca, stirred by Moxie's surprisingly vehement utterance, said, 'I think I agree. You might raise him up as a devil.' When she realised what she had said she blushed. Where had that extraordinary utterance come from? Of course it had belonged among those unhappy mad thoughts which she had had in the last days. Perhaps it did express something which she really deeply felt, the sort of fear which she felt. She put her hand up to the mound of hair upon her neck and a hairpin fell just audibly to the floor.

Ludens said, 'Oh, *Franca*!'

The gipsy girl with the fuzzy hair said, 'Let's go downstairs, shall we?'

Ludens said, 'Please keep quiet, Irina.'

Irina (Franca now guessed who she was) said, 'Keep quiet yourself.'

The doctor said, 'This is becoming ridiculous!' And to Ludens, 'Please take your friend away.'

At that moment the priest, speaking for the first time, intervened. He said, 'Professor Vallar has not told us what *he* thinks. Should he not be asked?'

Ludens turned to Marcus and put his hand gently against his arm. 'Marcus, do you think, you might somehow, perhaps, be able to help Patrick, to cure him?'

Marcus said irritably, 'Yes, yes, of course.' Then he moved from the centre of the room towards Franca, who moved quickly aside, and sat down on the chair which she had vacated, and leaned his head back against the wall and closed his eyes.

'Your friend needs medical attention!' said the doctor.

'He is collecting his powers,' said Ludens.

'Everyone here is mad,' said Moxie, tears coming into her eyes.

Father O'Harte then moved forward into the space which Marcus had vacated. He said, 'I think that this thing should be attempted. Nothing may happen. If anything happens I do not think it will be bad. At least let us try. I personally would like the Professor to be asked to do what he can.'

It was at this moment, as Franca recalled it afterwards, that the balance suddenly tilted in the other direction, and what had seemed sensible and inevitable suddenly began to seem trivial and irrelevant, and what had seemed impossible became not only possible but essential.

Ludens cried 'Yes, yes!' Jack stepped forward and put his arm round Ludens, the doctor made a washing-his-hands-of-the-matter gesture, and Franca said, 'Oh do what you like!' Marcus, who had seemed an almost ridiculous outsider, was now the centre of the scene, endowed, by the mysterious waft of change, with an authority recognised by all.

He opened his eyes, got up and moved to the end of Patrick's bed. The others, grouped around him, stood in silence looking down at the stricken man.

Patrick lay as before, on his side, his head deep in the pillow, one arm upon his breast, the other extended. The flesh was thinly spread upon the elongated skull, the motionless hands were bony claws. Yet the hand touching the breast now seemed like a communication, as of one who, coming to an appointed place, says humbly, here I am.

Marcus turned to Franca and said in his deep slow honey voice, with his slightly foreign accent, 'Please could you move the bed away from the wall. I'd like it *here*.'

Franca and Moxie hastened to move the bed toward the centre of the room. While this was going on Marcus took off his jacket and his tie and handed them to Irina, who was now visibly playing the part of the magician's assistant. He said to Franca, 'Please remove the covering.'

Very gently the two women drew the light quilt away, sliding it from under the arm of the sleeper, drawing it down at both sides, peeling it off and over the end of the bed. Moxie folded the quilt and put it in the corner where the bed had been. Marcus, standing now at the foot of the bed, carefully rolled up his sleeves. He stooped and took off his shoes and kicked them aside. Irina picked them up. He undid the top buttons of his shirt and pulled the shirt apart. He put one hand over his mouth, then drew it slowly down over his throat onto his chest. There was something strangely impressive about these rites. Father O'Harte shuddered and crossed himself. Marcus, putting his hands upon the board at the foot, moved the bed slightly on its casters, moving it gently to and fro with a movement as of one rocking a cradle. He stopped this and stood looking down.

Patrick, now revealed, lay, his arms undisturbed as before, seeming now like something fallen or struck down. One leg was bent, the other extended, his bare long-toed skeletal feet pallid and damp upon the white sheet. He seemed like an ancient man. A stench, which Franca now noticed for the first time, arose from the bed.

Marcus still stood looking down, almost as if he were now puzzled and did not know what to do next. There was a tense silence in the room. Franca, now gathered into Marcus's attempt, was saying in her mind, Oh let it be all right, let it be all right, not sure what she meant by this, whether that Marcus should revive Patrick, or whether simply that Marcus should 'get away' without some positive disgrace, some catastrophe or shameful happening. She did not, now, want to see him dismissed, led away hanging his head. She was concerned too for Ludens. She glanced at him. His face was composed, motionless with concentration, no longer smirking with terror, as he bent his will upon Marcus. Beyond him she saw that Father O'Harte was kneeling, his lips moving. Looking again at Marcus she was horrified to see that he had again put his hand to his throat and was trembling. Was he going to faint?

Marcus then moved round and sat on the side of the bed near to Patrick's feet. He reached out and touched the feet, holding each one for a moment in his hand. The bed was wide, Patrick was lying with his back to Marcus. With a sudden movement Marcus stretched himself out on the bed, also lying on his side, bringing his body into contact with Patrick's, pushing his knees into the crook of Patrick's knees, and his breast against his back. For a moment Franca thought that something obscene and horrible was about to happen. Then she felt horror and pity at seeing Marcus so confused and so evidently useless. Then she thought perhaps Pat is dead now, perhaps he has died even now while we have been watching this dreadful absurdity. She thought of looking at the doctor and indicating that he should interfere and stop it; but she did not.

Marcus sat up again, sitting back on the edge of the bed. He seemed to be at a loss. It seemed the end of the attempt. Franca thought, it's over. How much longer would the silence last, when would someone say, please, stop, for heaven's sake, give up, it can't be done? The unspoken words trembled in the air. Then Marcus stood up and began to unbutton his shirt further. He pulled it off and threw it behind him, revealing himself naked to the waist. He stood still for a moment breathing deeply. Then with an energy which he had not yet displayed he took hold of Patrick. Franca could feel the increase of tension in the room. Gently, deftly, as if he now knew exactly what to do, Marcus turned Pat on to his back, pulling him slightly toward the centre of the bed and laying his arms out straight beside his body. The limpness of the body as it was thus laid in place was pitiful. It seemed a kind of sacrilege thus to arrange it and pull it about. It looked so like a dead thing. Like a dead cat, Franca strangely thought, stirred by some memory. She wondered, is Patrick still breathing? She could not see. Marcus then undid Patrick's pyjama jacket and started to try to pull it off, then decided not to. He undid the cord of the pyjama trousers. Then he lay down again carefully, putting his hand and arm on the far side of the body and easing himself down so that he was partly lying on Patrick, his trunk upon his trunk, his legs upon his legs, and, as he supported himself on his arms, his face just above the skeleton face.

Franca thought, he'll lie on him and suffocate him. The priest had risen to get a better view. There was a strange irregular sighing sound in the room. Franca realised that it was Marcus breathing, slowly, deeply, into Patrick's mouth. She felt her own breathing slow down to accord with Marcus's respiration, and she could feel, perhaps even hear, the others also breathing in unison. After a while, Marcus, as if impatient, or to see if he had had any effect, stopped the breathing exercise and, half sitting up, began to pull the limp body about, almost roughly, almost angrily, as if he would *scarcely believe* that he was not succeeding. The watchers moved a little closer. Was it all going to end like this? Ought *she* to end it? Franca could feel Moxie tap her arm, but she did not turn to her, nor did she look around her, fearing to meet some significant glance. She concentrated her attention and her will upon what Marcus was doing. He lifted Patrick's hands and arms and let them fall, he shook his shoulders and moved his head to and fro, then he began to stroke his face, carefully as if he were moulding it. This movement, which went on for some time, gave Franca (and Ludens agreed with her later) the sense that Marcus was actually *creating* Patrick. Then, breaking the long silence, Marcus said slowly in his deep resonant voice, 'Patrick, Patrick, wake up, it is I, Marcus Vallar, Patrick, I command you, wake up.' Then, as Franca, who was nearest, was the first to see, Patrick opened his eyes. They opened for a moment, then closed, then opened again and gazed at Marcus's face. At this Marcus, instead of continuing his manipulation and massage, became quite still. He took hold of Pat's head in both hands and, lifting it a little and coming close to it, simply stared into Pat's open eyes.

How long this staring, during which there was complete silence in the room, lasted, Franca could not afterwards be sure. Perhaps four or five minutes, though it certainly seemed more; Moxie guessed ten minutes, and Gildas later told her that Ludens told him fifteen minutes. During the later part, or the very last part, of this period, Pat's body began to show tiny signs of animation. Father O'Harte said he saw, quite early on, a foot move slightly. Then the fingers of one hand moved, an arm moved, and the trunk seemed to shift very slightly. The body began, very faintly, in all its parts and regions, to *twitch*, as if its muscles, its very bloodstream, wished to prove that they could maintain their living functions. This scarcely perceptible but ubiquitous twitching, described by Ludens as like the slight tremulous movement of leaves on a tree or ripples on a pool, was one of the strangest, and in an odd way most convincing manifestations of the raising of Patrick. And all this while Patrick simply lay there looking with his now wide open eyes into Marcus's eyes. At last slowly, continuously, Marcus began to withdraw, laying Pat's head back on the pillow, removing his hands, and sitting in his former position on the side of the bed. From here however he leaned forward and began to stroke and caress Patrick's body, drawing his hands over his face and neck and chest. He did not attempt the removal of the pyjama jacket, but suddenly stood up and began to pull the red trousers down and get them off; and it seemed that Patrick, shifting very slightly, assisted the operation, his eyes now moving in awareness of what Marcus was doing. Now standing, and more energetically, Marcus caressed and massaged the thin white body, drawing his hands rhythmically along the arms, down the legs, over the chest and stomach, over the genitals.

Franca became aware that tears were coursing down her face. She could hear Moxie catching her breath. She too was weeping. Alison held a handkerchief to her mouth. Franca glanced to where Irina was standing, near the priest, and was startled by her expression. Irina was not crying, but her face was contorted in what seemed a paroxysm of extreme embarrassment, even of fear or revulsion. As Franca watched her she moved her left hand, which had been clenched upon her breast, and opened her fingers, spreading them wide in a spiky gesture.

Marcus suddenly said, 'Bring another pillow.' Moxie darted out, causing Jack and Alison to move, and returned with the pillow. Marcus pulled Pat up by the shoulders, pulling him up so that his head was higher, and Moxie thrust the pillow in behind him. Then Marcus became more rough, almost violent, pulling at Pat's limbs, pushing his body about, shaking him, patting and slapping. In the course of this treatment, during which Patrick's eyes followed Marcus's movements, Patrick's face assumed a more alert expression and at last his lips moved and he uttered a sound. Ludens said afterwards that it was a sound of protest at this rough handling. It may have been. Moxie and Franca were both (in retrospect) shocked by the degree of force used. Marcus became gentler, moved to sit nearer to Patrick, ceased his exertions and, after gazing at Pat for some time, began to caress one of his hands, turning it about in his own hands and pressing it. This mode of touching, unlike the previous ones, had the unmistakable air of a personal communication. Alison sobbed aloud, then stopped her mouth with her handkerchief. The priest quietly resumed his kneeling posture. Marcus, still holding Pat's hand, then spoke. 'Patrick, it's Marcus. Any ill thing I said to you I now take back, any harm I meant to you I hereby revoke. I ask you to pardon me. I command you to get well.' Patrick uttered a low whimpering sound and then, quite audibly, 'Marcus.' He tried to lever himself up in the bed. Marcus said, 'Be quiet. You will be all right now. You will get better.'

He released Patrick's hand and stood up. Patrick reached out after him. Marcus said, 'Don't worry, I will come back, I have to rest now.'

After that he turned away from the bed, picked up his jacket which Irina had dropped on the floor, began to put it on, then realising he had no shirt on, dropped the jacket, found the shirt and put that on. Ludens hastened to pick up the jacket and helped Marcus into it. Everyone hastened to stand aside as he made for the door. As he neared it, he suddenly stopped, staggered and sat down abruptly on a chair, leaning forward and holding his head in his hands.

The rapt circle now broke up, several voices were heard, the doctor moved to inspect Patrick, Franca said to Ludens, 'Would he like to lie down? There's a bed next door.' Irina said to Ludens, 'For heaven's sake get him out of here!' Moxie said to the doctor, 'What has happened? What will happen?' The doctor replied, 'Frankly, I don't know!' He tapped his forehead. Alison said to Jack, 'Will Pat recover now?' Jack said, 'Yes.' Irina said to the doctor, 'Could I have a word?' The doctor, who did not know who she was, said, 'Later.' Jack said to Franca, 'Didn't I tell you so?' Irina said to Alison, 'Mrs Sheerwater, I'm sorry –' Alison said, pointing to Franca, 'That is Mrs Sheerwater.' Irina said to Franca, 'I'm sorry to bother you, but could you give me the name and address of that doctor?' Franca said, 'Yes, yes,' and ran into the other room and started frantically looking for pen and paper. When she emerged, Marcus, leaning upon Ludens's arm, was already walking slowly down the stairs. Irina seized the slip of paper, said 'Thanks' and followed. Moxie and the doctor were with Patrick. The doctor said, 'Please be quiet all of you. Go away,' and closed the door. Jack and Alison were having a hasty conversation on the landing. Alison said to Franca, 'I'm going now, dear Franca.' Receiving no reply she disappeared, waving vaguely. The priest, silently bowing farewell, unnoticed, also took his departure. He had many things to ponder in his heart. Tears came again to Franca's eyes, strange tears, tears for everything, for herself as everything, tears out of the terrible cloud of hope and fear that hangs over all things. Jack took hold of her arms but she stood there limply, staring at him with her wet eyes, opening her wet mouth.

Jack said, 'Franca, *be here*.'

She said, 'I am here. Patrick may live, but he may die too. He may lose his mind.'

'I know. But about you and me. It will be all right because it's *got* to be all right, it's *necessary* – without it the world ends.'

'So you think –'

'No, it's what *you* think, you must *think*, now in this moment – of magic – that's not the right word – of spiritual power – it's like a lightning flash – we will be all right, we two, for ever – isn't it? Say so, *say so*.'

'Three – Alison also –'

'Oh hell, yes, her too, but you are the centre, Franca, noble lady, queen, oh my love –'

'Yes,' said Franca, putting her hand up to her tears at last, 'yes, it's a miracle – it will be all right.' She repeated again, 'It's a miracle.'

'Henceforth I shall be his dog,' said Patrick.

'He may not like dogs,' said Gildas.

'He liked one dog,' said Ludens, 'it made him feel relaxed and tender.'

'Did he tell you?' said Gildas. 'What kind of dog was it?'

'No, Irina told me. It was a labrador. She was a child at the time. It wasn't their dog, it belonged to a neighbour.'

'Dogs are enlightened beings,' said Gildas, 'they are saved. Perhaps a dog could save his master. Remember Judas's dog sitting under his chair in *The Last Supper* by Rubens in Brera.'

'What did Irina tell you?' said Franca who had just entered.

'Ludens said Marcus once felt fond of the dog next door,' said Gildas.

'There you are,' said Patrick, who was sitting up in bed. 'I was and have always been his dog. When he is sad because the world rejects him I shall place my paw upon his knee, and he will be moved and heartened and his strength will be renewed. Every great philosopher needs his poet.'

'You mean like Heidegger and Hölderlin?' said Gildas.

'No, not *like* anything that has ever been in the world before.'

'I thought you said –'

'Never mind what I said, I don't *say* things the way you ordinary people do, Marcus and I understand each other, we are folk of the frontier.'

'Would you like some more glucose?' said Franca.

'Yes please. We shall travel the world together as poor beggarly men, carrying our message to the planet, and everywhere we shall be spurned and everywhere we shall be glorified, and a light shall shine about him like to the light which shone upon the day when he raised me from the dead. And I shall write my songs and carry them in a pack and I shall recite them to the people, and sing them too, and I shall tell stories, and the little children shall gather around me, the while himself is in the temple.'

'Why in the temple,' said Gildas, 'are you in India?'

'They are in ancient Greece,' said Ludens.

'We shall walk barefoot and dusty and alone and suffer many things, and within our sufferings we shall find the pearl of great price, the untarnished joy, the secret treasure, and we shall find it because he is a pure saint and the bravest man in the world and I am a simple singer robed in humility, one risen from the dead.'

'Oh do stop, Pat,' said Gildas. 'You are in danger of becoming a Resurrection Bore.'

'Here's your glucose,' said Franca returning. 'Please don't excite him so. Isn't it time you went?'

'At least he maintains our myth about the mission,' said Ludens to Gildas, 'and he's bloody right about Marcus's courage.'

'I don't see why you call *that* courage,' said Gildas to Ludens, 'and the myth is yours.'

'Two angels have I,' said Patrick, 'the Franca angel and the Alison angel. Where is the latter?'

'Out shopping.'

'And the noble warrior?' (He meant Jack.)

'In the studio.'

'He shall paint the story of our wanderings and of our death.'

'What do you mean, "death"?' said Gildas. 'That's new. I thought you had jointly overcome death.'

'We are preserved for a higher ending. When Marcus dies there will be signs in the heavens.'

'What about you?'

'I shall die, as dogs die, in a ditch.'

'In civilised countries,' said Ludens, 'dogs usually die in their baskets.'

'I shall die in a ditch like a poor gipsy man. Franca, when can I have a drink did the doctor say?'

'Pat, dear, can't you just decide to give up drink, can't that be part of the new life you're always talking about? You can do without drink, you certainly don't need it to loosen your tongue.'

'Yes, I must talk,' said Patrick, 'pardon gentles all, I must while the light is with me, while I can see, Oh the things I can see –'

'Such as horses winning races?'

'Those are base matters, I cannot see base matters. I shall write a long poem about what I saw shining from the other side.'

'I gather Irina is out shopping with Alison,' said Ludens to Franca.

'Yes, buying clothes, she's clothes mad. By the way, Alison said, about Heather Allenby –'

'Franca,' said Patrick, 'come and sit beside me, hold my hand.'

Franca came and sat on the bed and took hold of Patrick's hand and they looked at each other.

Ludens thought, why can't I do that, why can't I just ask a woman to hold my hand, why can't I ask Franca to!

Patrick's recovery, soon to be the subject of an article in the *Lancet*, was now, as Ludens pointed out to Gildas, in danger of being taken for granted by them all. Gildas had said that he felt too tired to be continually renewing his amazement, he had other troubles. The recovery had been, though slow, from its inception, fairly steady. Fears about mental damage were soon dispelled. Patrick's weak body slowly resumed its normal functions and its strength. He could even walk about the room, leaning on Franca's arm, and hoped to go, similarly supported, as far as the river when the weather improved. He had also, as Gildas remarked, not lost his ability to talk. The English climate, having given its clients a long series of warm sunny days, had decided that this must be paid for. Rain fell, and the temperature went down to ten degrees Celsius. The women wore warm skirts or trousers, the men put on jerseys. The dank flat occupied by Marcus and Irina, which had no central heating, had become danker and greener, redeemed a little by a contingent of electric fires brought in by Ludens. He, moving between this strange abode and Jack's house in Chelsea, felt as if, wanting to be needed by everyone, he were merely becoming some sort of semi-invisible messenger. After all, he thought, this new scene was entirely, well in a sense, almost entirely, his creation. His faith and determination had saved Patrick's life and brought Marcus and Irina to London. He felt possessive, a bearer of authority and responsibility, as if these people were his children. He wanted them to love him. Yet already they were ungrateful recalcitrant children, escaping from him in all directions, capable of forming new friendships and attachments.

In fact not much of this had yet occurred, though Ludens's jealous mind presaged it. Patrick had of course (yet why of course when he had so nearly died?) resumed his role as poet, jester, teaser, charmer, visited by his old pub companions, and doted upon by Alison and Franca. He had also talked with Father O'Harte. He had given up his lodgings, and all his possessions were in store at Jack's house. It had been suggested (by Jack?) that he might move in with Ludens, an idea which (although he was genuinely fond of Pat) Ludens did not fancy. On the other hand (as Ludens surmised) Jack was not in too much of a hurry to shift Patrick, as Pat was an occupation for Franca, and one which brought her and Alison together. Meanwhile, both Franca and Alison had, after initial suspicion, adopted Irina, at least as far as amusing themselves by helping her to spend money on having her hair done and buying clothes. They treated her, amiably, as a 'little savage' or a 'wild girl', whom they must attempt to civilise.

Ludens, at this time, thought of Marcus as his child. He also thought of him as his father. He felt that his relationship with Marcus was undergoing deep changes willed not by himself, but by him. Ludens found himself watching Marcus, jealously, but with intense curiosity and interest and waiting as for some magisterial dispensation which would mysteriously order his own future, now so completely held in the balance. His precious sabbatical term was being, so far as academic study was concerned, wasted. But Ludens was not concerned now with writing his 'next book', or rushing off to Rome or Paris to read in libraries. Everything, including his next book, his future work and thoughts, his future being, depended upon Marcus. He had even allowed himself to be irritated by Patrick's impudent image of himself as Marcus's dog. If Marcus had a dog, Ludens was that animal. In fact, and at least at present, Ludens had little reason to complain since he remained, with Marcus, the closest person, not exactly the beloved disciple, but the most valuable agent. Marcus in London remained secluded, his chief 'manifestations' being visits to Patrick during which it seemed (Ludens was sometimes present) little was said. Patrick was, and Ludens was touched by this, for all his grand 'impudent' talk, visibly and humbly *afraid* of Marcus. Marcus rather absently, as if all *this* belonged to the remote past, asked Pat how he was getting on, and Pat reported how much better he was feeling. Ludens knew that Patrick longed to touch Marcus, to hold his hand, to stroke his sleeve, but dared not. Ludens was himself in the same situation. Marcus, with Pat, looked tired, resuming the look of weariness which he had worn after the 'resurrection'. Perhaps the room revived a taxing memory of what had happened.

But what had happened? Ludens was right in a way to complain that they were now all taking it for granted. Perhaps that was what one had to do with miracles? The medical profession helped the calming process by 'explaining it all away' in various manners creditable to themselves. Even Dr Hensman, who should have been the most astonished (and perhaps secretly was) joined in the game. Of course, it was now agreed, no one had really felt sure that Patrick was terminally ill, such conditions have their unpredictable aspects, even sometimes of psychosomatic origin (though this side of the matter was touched on lightly). Patrick, on the other hand, Ludens noticed, proceeded in the opposite direction, occasionally speaking as if he had been, when Marcus arrived, not just dying but actually dead. When Ludens cautiously challenged this, Pat replied, 'Well, I should know!' Ludens meditated upon this too.

Marcus, thus present occasionally at Jack's house, where he evidently felt his visits to be a matter of duty, inevitably encountered the women, who treated him with suitable respect and awe, and Jack, who was nervously affable, and even on two occasions Gildas to whom he nodded politely. ('He doesn't remember me,' Gildas said.) There was a simple ordinariness about those brief appearances, during which Marcus enquired about Patrick's health; but how long could ordinariness continue and what would happen next? Ludens's own relations with Marcus might have been called, from Ludens's point of view, promising, even satisfactory, were it not that they were also precarious. He visited the horrible flat every day to see if he could be of use. Marcus seemed to expect this, though usually he had little to say to Ludens. Once or twice they walked together as far as the river. When Ludens tried to ask him about his 'thoughts', he replied that he had 'difficulties' which they might discuss 'later on'. Ludens knew that Marcus had spent part of his childhood in London but could elicit no information about this interesting period, except that his parents had had a flat in Knightsbridge. He showed no desire to rediscover the metropolis; and when not out visiting or walking did, as far as Ludens could see, nothing; nothing, that is, except, presumably, think. He did not read. This continued to amaze Ludens who could not imagine existence without reading. He sat in his room and occasionally made notes on pieces of paper. He was, Ludens felt, *waiting*; and Ludens waited too.

Ludens had not forgotten what Marcus had said to him about Irina. Nothing more had been said on that subject. Ludens, in his present highly textured frame of mind, stowed away this significant memory as not at present relevant to his proceedings. He did not want Irina to become a problem to him, now that he was becoming at least welcome, even necessary, to Marcus. He enjoyed being expected and being useful, providing electric fires, finding plumbers, even tidying and washing things, Irina's efforts in these latter respects being minimal. At times Ludens wondered whether this state of affairs might not go on for ever, whether he might not give up his job and become Marcus's – what? – friend, secretary, servant, dog. Sometimes he ventured to think of his role as that of a sparring partner. He believed, and Irina confirmed this, that Marcus had been, though initially hostile, glad to see him at Red Cottage because he was an acquaintance and someone to talk to. 'He can't find new people at this stage,' Irina said, 'old ones will have to do.' Ludens was not sure about Marcus's ability to find new people, but certainly did not mind benefiting from being an 'old one'. His strange quiet co-existence with Marcus was facilitated by his now surprisingly easy relations with Irina, they even teased each other. She once said, 'We're like two schoolboys!' The odd simile suited her own peculiar mode of speech, so full of girls' boarding-school slang and the coarse expressions which troubled Ludens. Where had she learnt them? He had also come to respect Irina for her ability so rapidly to transform herself into a reasonably well-dressed, reasonably good-looking girl. Her dark hair, cleverly cut and more frequently combed, was soft and glossy, sat tidily, was very faintly curling, flowing abundantly down to her shoulders. She had acquired, with the ready assistance of Alison and Franca, some charming cotton dresses, and also, for the cooler weather, some rather smart dresses of light wool in mistily dark shades of blue and brown, together with a great many silk scarves from Liberty's. It could now become evident that she had a good figure. Ludens also noticed her small feet, clad in expensive discreetly elegant shoes.

Irina, in these days, was often out, shopping, or visiting Pat, or going to see Marcus's solicitor, a Mr Garent, or simply wandering about London being (to use her phrase) a 'mystery woman'. Ludens told her to go to the British Museum and the National Gallery, which she did, though declining his offer to 'show her round'. She also went at least once to see Dr Hensman. She spoke at intervals about moving herself and Marcus out of the flat (which she agreed to be horrid) perhaps to another flat or to some vaguely envisaged country cottage. There was certainly no question (Ludens was glad to hear) of moving back to Fontellen. Nothing was done about this move however except that Ludens collected the names of a lot of house agents. He arranged for Marcus to see a dentist, and took him there in a taxi. So, in a curious lurid calm which could not last and yet, it seemed, could not end, the days went by.

'How I wish I had been there!' said Gildas, not for the first time.

'It was absolutely astonishing,' said Ludens, also not for the first time.

'So you say, but you can't describe it.'

'I have described it! He breathed into Pat's mouth, then he looked into his eyes –'

'Yes, yes, but what was it that *did* it?'

'I don't know. Perhaps he didn't know. It's a fact. Can't you just accept a fact?'

'No, and neither can you. You're entirely bemused. You're under that man's spell. You think he's something holy and mystical.'

'Possibly,' said Ludens, 'but I don't know what that means either.'

'Father O'Harte said Marcus was fighting with a demon, soon he'll tell us he saw the demon. Poor Pat already thinks he's been raised from the dead and is destined for some great thing, to help Marcus to save the world!'

'Well, stranger things have happened. World-changes do suddenly arise. How old was Christ when he began his mission?'

'So you do think he's something holy and mystical?'

'Those are your words. I don't know what I think. Don't be so severe with me, Gildas, I'm under an awful strain, I think something terrible is going to be required of me.'

'Now *you* sound like Christ. I daresay he said that to his disciples, only that bit was censored. I gather you were too busy to see Heather Allenby.'

'Heather –?'

'The girl Alison has lined up for you. She asked you out to lunch to meet her.'

'Oh yes – I told Alison I couldn't come, I had to be with Marcus.'

'You know Alison's play about the ballet school has been accepted by the BBC?'

'Oh really –'

'You see you aren't interested. You ought to be. We need you. Jack needs you. Can't you imagine what strain *he's* under?'

'If he wants to talk to Marcus again I'll arrange it.'

'Boy, you exasperate me! Jack isn't worried about Marcus – he's worried about the women!'

'I can't think about that.'

'You mean you won't. Has Franca spoken to you?'

'No.'

This conversation, occurring shortly after the conversation with Patrick recorded above, was taking place at Ludens's flat, where a scrappy supper had been laid out by Ludens after Gildas's telephone call. It was true that Ludens, though regularly visiting Pat, had seen very little of Jack and had scarcely exchanged any words with Alison or Franca. He felt guilty, then disturbed, by Gildas's words. He also felt a sudden pang, thinking that perhaps Franca, wanting to confide in him and finding him unavailable, had turned to Gildas.

Gildas, smiling his crooked smile across the table and reading his friend's thoughts, said, 'Don't worry, she said very little, virtually nothing, as soon as she started to speak she decided not to. And one didn't need to be told that she's unhappy about Alison.'

'Well, of course –'

'Your best friends are in trouble and you say "of course" and forget them instantly.'

'What can be done? *You* are the one who keeps saying better not meddle, meddling is simply self-indulgence and will to power!'

'I know,' said Gildas, 'you are right to remind me of it. One is never entirely without satisfaction when one's friends are in a mess, one looks at once to how one can enlarge oneself by interfering.'

'I hope you'll do better when I'm in trouble.'

'You are a special case. Anyhow you claim to be in trouble already, but you don't talk to me, I have to ring up. I don't like that.'

'I'm sorry. It's just that I have to look after both of them.'

'They can look after themselves. You fail to realise that Irina is a woman of iron.'

'She is not. You think all women are either little fools or bullies.'

'No. Franca is neither.'

'Irina has had a terrible life.'

'So now she'll get her own back.'

'She's an uneducated child, an *innocent*.'

'You are the innocent.'

'All right, she rushes round buying clothes and –'

'Don't denigrate her now just to please me.'

'Oh get out, go home!'

'Don't raise your voice. I know your nerves are on edge. I'm sorry.'

'I have to *look after* them, I tell you! I have to find another flat, a quiet one, or else a country cottage where Marcus can be a hermit. Irina can't arrange that, she can't arrange anything. And I have to talk to Marcus every day.'

'But you like it.'

'Yes, but it's difficult, it's very tiring. We don't really discuss anything.'

'At least he can shave himself now I gather.'

'Yes. I'm sorry about that, I rather enjoyed it.'

'You are shameless.'

'*You* are!'

'So he still thinks he has a mission. Like you think you're John the Baptist because an angel pointed at you.'

'How did you know?'

'In fact he's just a defeatist, a victim of Jewish masochism. You keep saying Marcus thinks – he doesn't think, he dreams. He hasn't got a philosophical mind. Metaphysics would have been one way out, but he can't take that, so the alternative is to be a persecuted prophet. You've got to think *about* something, thinking is very hard, you can't just *sit* all day and *do* it, even religious solitaries read and say prayers, when the human mind goes beyond anything perceivable there's no proof any more. I'm just not persuaded Marcus has it in him to *be* at that level of intensity.'

'You are trying to provoke me. I don't understand Marcus, I don't presume to.'

'How humble you are. You love him.'

'Yes.'

'Well, let's leave it at that. Now I really am going.'

On the following evening Franca, Alison and Irina were together in what Jack laughingly called the women's quarters, a room just beyond the kitchen which Franca had once designated as her sitting room or 'boudoir', but which, before Alison's arrival, she had not much frequented. Of course Alison was not 'living in' the house, but was often there visiting Patrick (her help as a nurse was no longer required), joining Jack in his studio (where she talked with him about his work), or chatting with him and Franca in the drawing room or kitchen before departing with Jack to a restaurant and taking him on to her flat for the night. Franca guessed that Alison's appearances were part of a plan of Jack's to make Franca used to 'having her around'. Sometimes Jack would bring Alison and leave her with Franca, or Alison would 'drop in' on Franca after seeing Pat. Franca did not initiate any meetings. On these occasions Alison gave Franca some embarrassed or 'significant' looks, but did not renew attempts to have a talk about the 'situation'. Franca led the conversation in a cheerful tone, Irina and Marcus and Patrick providing abundant subject-matter. Pat's recovery, miraculously initiated, had not proceeded miraculously fast. Doctor Hensman was still in charge, making solemn authoritative pronouncements and predictions, and behaving as if it were he who had cured the patient.

What did perhaps seem like a continuation of the miracle was the way in which Patrick had regained his healthy appearance and good looks. He seemed in fact, as many of his visitors remarked, handsomer than ever, possibly as a result of the continued absence of alcohol from his life. The long skeletal head and ghostly hands seemed now to belong to a bad dream. His skin, which had looked so moist and fungoid, was now smooth and clear, his flesh firm. His dark hair, trimmed by Moxie, was curly and glossy, his face with high cheek bones and small nose and small sensuous mouth and dark blue eyes, had resumed its glowing charm; and when his friends (Barry Titmus, for instance, Jerry Locke, Sidney Brett, and Ned Oliver who had recovered from his own ailments) came to see him, roars of laughter could be heard from above. Moxie had early detected Ned smuggling in a bottle of whisky, and had delivered a chastening lecture. It was even possible, Alison told Franca, who already knew, that Pat was actually in the process of deciding to give up drink! He still spoke of how, when he was better, he would 'go to Marcus' or 'follow Marcus'. But Franca believed in none of these things.

Meanwhile, Marcus came less and less often, perhaps 'frightened off', as Alison put it, by Pat's noisy friends, or simply feeling that Pat no longer needed him. Irina, on the other hand, seemed to get on well with Pat, going up to see him with Alison. Franca observed sadly, but without surprise, that her strange feeling of love for Patrick had waned and finally abated as he continued steadily to come to life. She had loved him, she thought now, because, just at that time, she had had to have something else, someone else, to love, a private place for wounded love to go to. But that had been, as she had then suspected and now knew, a device, a dream. Her relations with the real live Patrick were exactly as before. Her presence embarrassed, even bored, him, and his nervous joking and teasing upset her. Alison, Moxie, even Irina, were closer to him now than she was. She thought, I am becoming a recluse. Yes, that's it, that is the way. She began then to feel an odd sympathy and affinity with Marcus, who entered the house so quietly (for now they left the door open for Pat's visitors) and stepped so noiselessly up the stairs. Franca even wished that she could set up a relation of some kind with him. He looked so tall and reliable and gentle and wise, and always greeted her in a kindly way with a little bow and a murmur. Twice she asked him to stay for a cup of tea, but he refused.

Franca was busy. She had, to begin with, colonised the boudoir, rearranging the furniture and bringing down pretty china from the spare bedroom, so as, she planned, to sit there often *by herself*. Lately however Alison, and sometimes Irina, had decided to walk in and join her, no doubt, as Franca felt, to cheer up the 'lonely old creature'; and, in the case of Alison, perhaps to set scenes for some 'statement' which she felt that Franca might wish to, or indeed ought to, make. Meanwhile, with some help from Moxie, (the 'daily' who sometimes 'helped out' was still afraid of infection) Franca continued to run the house, to shop, to clean, to organise, to feed a sick man, to feed her husband, and entertain, as necessary, Alison, Irina, Gildas, Ludens, the doctor, Jerry, Sidney, Barry, Ned, and one or two of Jack's painter friends who, now that Pat was recovering, had decided to come round for drinks. She dressed soberly, changed her clothes less often, coiled her long dark hair into its usual long glossy package which lay so neatly upon her neck. She walked to the shops and back, sometimes walked through the back streets, once almost as far as Marcus's flat (but did not dare to go near it), avoiding the noisy King's Road, and the embankment where Jack often walked with Alison, and as she knew, farther east where Ludens walked with Marcus. The weather had recovered so far as to be rainless, breezy, faintly warm.

And all that time, Franca contained in her breast a storm of anguish and violence so terrible that she had at times, when she was alone and longing to 'break down', to clutch her breast with a fierce answering force to keep the black horror from spurting forth. Her face was calm and benign, always in company, and usually alone too, for she was aware that to *play* such a part properly allowed of no rest periods, no weak moments of unmasking. She must continue, in her deceit, *whole*, like the spy who, in order to go on, has to *become* what he *seems*. She was, daily, amazed at herself, at her self-control; and at the terrible demons which fed upon her, and in doing so, she realised, fed her. She had begun to *need* her rage and her hate, even of late her fierce cruel fantasies. She could not, and did not try to, riddle out, rationally order, explain, least of all banish, these horrible consolations. As it seemed, if she were not to die of her love she had to poison it; and even, over its death agonies, to exult. As the days went by, Franca cherished and nourished and developed her suffering, unable to envisage any change or any plan – any *machine* into which so much relentless force might be fed. Indeed she was afraid to plan or picture a different future of any kind. So long as she stayed silent she had a secret weapon. If she spoke, if once there were the least word, the least crack or fissure, upon which tears and screams could follow, she would have lost her one advantage, her source of ordinary viable life, and would be utterly undone and destroyed.

The vicious force which was now her essence and to which she gave the name of hatred (only this was too narrow and too petty a name to describe it) was directed upon Jack: Jack on whom daily, as he looked at her sometimes so anxiously, so humbly, she smiled the smile of reassurance and of calm. Although she kept Alison so firmly, as in some austere yet not malevolent discipline, at a distance, she could not hate her, even felt a companionable pity observing the discomfort and guilt which proud Alison could not altogether dissemble. At times – and Franca was aware of this as a dangerous weakness – she felt a slight momentary urge to 'talk' to Alison, to give that tiny fatal signal for which Alison was, sometimes so urgently, so breathlessly, waiting. A more immediate peril was her frail stupid desire to ask some sort of help from either Gildas or Ludens. She had, lately, almost come to this point with Gildas, but had checked herself in time. She was less close to Gildas, whom she regarded with some slight awe, for she feared his irony and his sharp tongue, and would not have allowed him the slightest 'liberty' had he not cleverly, for he was very clever, 'set up' a conversation which led her, through a series of exchanges, into the danger area. Here he, ever so slightly, pressed her. Fortunately she retired just in time; and saw his dark eyes, which had been so sympathetic, gleam for a second behind his little round glasses with amusement, with a kind of mockery, as she so promptly retreated. She allowed herself a little to wish that she could sometimes, however indirectly, speak to, even just be with, Ludens; but he was now, as Gildas told her and as she could see, obsessed with Marcus. As for Irina, Franca could not, and did not try to, make her out, but got on with her perfectly well. And all the time the line of force which bound her to her husband stretched and vibrated so that her heart in secret haemorrhage, gushed blood.

Irina was sitting on the table. She liked to do that. She was sitting, that is, on the kitchen table, as the women were, at the moment, in the kitchen. Franca, said to be a good cook, was not a good cook, just an ingenious cook. She did not like cooking. At the moment she was cutting up courgettes and dropping them into a saucepan containing peppers and onions and tomatoes. She was uneasy because Irina was watching her, indeed staring at her. Or perhaps it was just the usual look of her rather weird eyes. Alison sitting in a low wickerwork chair with her long bare legs stretched out, was watching Irina. Irina puzzled Alison. Alison had asked Franca questions about Irina such as: Is she sincere? Is she laughing at us? Does she like us? Does she love her father? Franca could not answer these questions or interest herself in such formulations. She replied that they could only get an 'impression' of the girl and there was no use looking farther. Anyway Irina was just passing by, a fleeting acquaintance. She seemed reasonably harmless and naive and willing to please. The three women could at least 'play tennis', to use a metaphor which Alison had applied to her relations with Irina. Franca thought in terms of a musical trio. They could all three play together. The performance was banal, but there were no obvious discords.

The evening sun, shining at the moment through a side window, over which Franca had drawn a curtain, showed up, glowing like stained glass, a pattern of green and blue leaves and red grapes. The light in the tidy pretty kitchen was subdued and pleasant. It reminded Franca of some old happiness; and she thought I haven't been really happy since that very first day when he said there was someone else but I wasn't to worry.

Irina was wearing a blue-and-brown check low-waisted summer dress with pleats, which Alison had already declared to Franca to be 'too smart, too old, and too expensive'. She was wearing blue tights and sandals and had hitched her dress well up in order to swing her legs. At the same time she kept tossing her head and patting her hair, exploring its new tidied sleekness. Her dark eyes narrowed with the strange squint-eyed intensity which so fascinated Ludens and to which he had drawn Franca's attention. She had not entirely lost the gipsy look of her earlier manifestations, but now, more ambitiously attired, appeared more like some sort of stage character, a dressed-up Bohemian, an artist's model, or an adventuress in disguise. Conscious of being looked at she swung her legs and smiled faintly, twitching her shoulders and arching her neck.

'So your play is going on the stage?' Irina said to Alison.

'No. It is to be on television,' said Alison in her careful precise voice. Alison, always simply and elegantly dressed, was wearing a white pleated skirt and a light green blouse which set off her red hair, 'cooled it' as Jack said. She looked healthy and strong, a fine animal, her skin glowing, her hair radiantly shining. She and Jack now drove out to Chiswick where they played tennis in the afternoons. Alison added, 'They said they would take it, but it is not quite certain that it will be performed.'

'Why is that?' said Irina, smiling.

'Well, those things are uncertain.'

'Haven't you got a contract?'

'Not yet.'

'Of course it will be performed,' said Franca, 'and Alison is writing another play, aren't you, Alison?'

'Another play about a ballet school?'

'No,' said Alison, 'it is about life, about marriage, and –'

'So that's autobiographical too?'

'No, neither is autobiographical –'

'Perhaps I'll write a play. No I won't, I'll be a photographer and roam the world with my camera.'

'How's your father?' said Franca.

'Oh much as usual. He wants to move out into the country.'

'I gather Alfred is looking for a cottage for him.'

'Is he? That's news to me. Anyway we want to get out of that bloody awful flat.'

'Is your father writing a book?' said Alison.

'No. He's existing. Some people live, like the rest of us, like the people in your plays. He just exists.'

'But the people in my plays don't exist,' said Alison, 'they are fictional characters.'

'Is existing better than living?' said Franca.

'He thinks so. He thinks he's more real.'

'And is he?' said Alison.

Irina seemed to be interested in the question and turned a serious face toward Alison. 'I don't know. Perhaps existing is the wrong word. He's like a toad. He's just there.'

'He's a very remarkable man,' said Alison. 'He certainly did Patrick a good turn.'

On this subject Irina affected a little air of scepticism. The other two had not ventured to probe her views on the subject of the miracle.

Franca said, 'Pat says when he's well he'll come to your father and be his servant.'

'Oh great! We could do with a servant like that. He's fantastically good-looking. Don't you agree?'

'He certainly is,' said Alison.

'He is now,' said Franca, 'but, well, as you know, he talks all the time.'

'That's fine. We never talk.'

'You sit like a pair of toads,' said Franca.

'Exactly.'

The door opened and Ludens came in. Alison stood up, Irina jumped off the table. Franca said, 'Hello, Alfred.'

Irina said, 'Hello Alfred, hello Ludens, hello Alfred Ludens, Franca has just compared me with a toad.'

'Surely not. Toads are quiet and harmless and nice.'

'You pig! Isn't he a pig?'

'He's not a pig, he's my friend,' said Alison.

Franca looked upon Ludens with relief. She was used to the 'younger brother' role imposed on him by Jack and Gildas. He was gentle and easy to be with and she liked what Jack called the mad Jewish grin. Only lately Ludens had been preoccupied, nervous, anxious, restless. Now, as he looked round the kitchen, he suddenly frowned and winced, putting on, but only for a second, what Jack called his surly Eastern European sneer. He was known to be 'worried about Marcus', but Franca had not asked him exactly what the worry was.

Alison smiled at him her sunny smile which removed from her face what Franca thought of as her 'legal look'. 'I thought you were trying to find a cottage for Marcus, but Irina says you're not.'

'I'm trying to try,' said Ludens gravely, 'but my clients can't decide what they want.'

'I'm to have Patrick as my servant,' said Irina. 'Isn't that super? He can carry the gear when I roam the world with my camera.'

'Oh, are you a photographer?' said Franca.

'I'm going to be. What else can I become?'

'I've just been hearing about Pat's epic poem about the "other side",' said Alison. 'Has he actually started it?'

'He was writing something when I came in, only he wouldn't show it to me.'

'Can I give you a lift?' said Alison to Ludens. 'My car's outside.'

'Thanks, but my car's outside too,' said Ludens.

Alison said to Franca, putting on her humble ingratiating tone, 'I'm – I'm going back to my flat now.'

'You can give me a lift,' said Irina, hopping off the table. 'Cheerio, Franca. Be nice to me.'

'I am nice to you!'

'Be nice to me *always*.'

Franca, smiling, waved assent. She said to Alison, 'Where's Jack?' She knew that he was painting upstairs.

'He's painting upstairs,' said Alison. 'He's – er – coming on later.' She gave Franca the hang-dog look again.

As Alison disappeared with Irina, Ludens seated himself on the table. 'Can I help? Peel potatoes, clean carrots, slice onions?'

'No, thanks. Jack's upstairs.'

'You and Alison seem to have tamed Irina.'

'Haven't you?'

'No. She's a mad erratic little thing.'

'Are they going to live in the country?'

'She speaks of it, I make suggestions, she ignores them.'

'And he?'

'He's going through some sort of crisis or – metamorphosis. I can't explain. I'm being led – on some dark way.'

'Alfred, I'm worried about you. I feel you're simply being led on a *wrong* way. I think that man's insane, and cunning – and the mixture of insanity and cunning is what you mistake for some deep wisdom. You remember you always thought he had some secret.'

'I still do.'

'I think he's ruining your life, he's taking you away from your work, from *your* thinking, toward something empty and false – he's certainly wasting your time, they both are, they're *exploiting* you.'

'So you don't really like Irina?'

'I don't know. She seems to me terribly unhappy in a way which can make people desperate, spiteful, even wicked.'

'She's certainly unhappy – she's an unhappy lonely child – she's not wicked.'

'No, of course – of course not – What am I saying. *I'm* wicked.' Franca, who had been leaning against the big warm cast-iron stove with a spoon in her hand, threw down the spoon with a clang and marched through the door into her sitting room. Ludens followed, closing the door behind him.

In the sitting room too the curtains had been drawn against the sun. The room was a little dusky, it smelt of flowers which Franca had picked in the garden that morning. Jack did not like flowers, or rather said he was 'bothered' by them, and they were banished from the upstairs rooms. There were two plump 'sewing chairs' and an embroidered hassock and blue china dogs on the mantelpiece, small rugs, a desk below an oval mirror, refugees from other parts of the house. The dogs and the rugs, and the water-colours upon the walls, one by Franca herself, were relics from the days before her marriage. Franca sat down in one of the low plump chairs and began to cry.

Ludens pulled the other chair near to her. Franca did not attempt to wipe away the tears, she let them roll down and drip onto the front of the apron which she was wearing over her brown dress. She sat upright with her hands on her knees. She was thinking, I am doing something terrible and stupid, I am destroying myself even more, I am weakening myself, I am *breaking*. Only I *must not*. She imagined that if she did not wipe her eyes, thrusting in a knuckle or a handkerchief, the tears would leave less trace. She opened her eyes wide, permitting the tears, willing them to cease, breathing deeply. Her bosom heaved, her wet mouth opened, her wide eyes stared.

After a moment or two Ludens reached out and detached one of her hands from her knee. The hand resisted, then after a moment gave way. Ludens held her moist hot hand between his thin dry cool hands, nursing it upon his knee as if it were a wounded bird. He lifted it, as if he were about to kiss it, laid it for an instant against his cheek, then restored it, still captive, to his knee.

Franca withdrew her hand. Her tears ceased abruptly. She drew a handkerchief from the pocket of her apron and very lightly dabbed her eyes. Then she got up and went to the mirror above the desk. Her eyes were slightly red. She opened the desk and took out a powder compact and lightly touched her reddened lids.

Ludens, who had risen, said, 'I'm sorry.'

'Well, it wasn't your fault,' said Franca in a conversational tone.

'Perhaps it was,' said Ludens, 'I wanted to come closer to you and you must have felt it.'

'You wanted to comfort me.'

'Yes. But – I'd put it differently.'

'You wanted me to stop embarrassing you by crying!'

'Franca, *don't*. I just wanted to come to you, to make a little space around you, I don't want to discuss anything, I don't want to do anything, I won't say anything, I just wanted to be *there*, I mean *here*.'

'I understand you,' said Franca, turning round to face him. 'And now, Alfred dear, please go.'

'You're not angry with me?'

'Of course not.'

'You know I'm very fond of you.'

'Yes.'

'You help me too.'

'Goodbye. Come again as usual.'

Alone, Franca washed her face in cold water in the kitchen, washing off the powder she had just put on. Returning to the desk she made up her face, powdering carefully about her eyes. She used little make-up, but the little was important. The sun had gone and there was less light. As she could hear Jack coming down the stairs she returned to the kitchen and picked up the metal spoon and plunged it into the saucepan which she had not yet put on to heat. She stood there awkwardly, incapable of further theatre. Jack came in quietly. Franca turned, bracing herself against the old unthinking uninformed wave of pleasure which, urging her towards him, almost lifted her off her feet.

Jack, in summer plumage, glowed with colour. He had put on weight, but he was taking exercise. His face and neck were reddish brown, his hair was bleached by the sun, his strong arms and hands were brown, looked smooth and warm. He had combed his hair and shaved.

He did not approach his wife, but stood looking at her. Franca turned slightly away and began senselessly to mess the contents of the saucepan with the spoon.

'What's that stuff?'

'Tomatoes and things. How did painting go?'

'Bad. I think I've come to the end of what I can do.'

'You always say that but then you find a new way.'

'I wish Marcus could do something for *me*. Ludens was here talking to Pat.'

'Yes, he dropped in. Irina and Alison were here. Quite a social scene.'

'Ludens can talk to Pat. I hear them chattering. I can't any more. Pat just bores me with his rantings.'

'He can be serious. Perhaps he's serious all the time. One has to argue with him, like Gildas does. I don't mind listening to him. I'm glad he's alive.'

Jack sat down in the basket chair vacated by Alison, making it creak prodigiously, hauled himself up again, found a hard upright kitchen chair and sat on that.

'Franca, don't drift away.'

'Where do you imagine I'd drift to? I live here.'

'Yes, you live here, you do, you do. I don't mean go away, I know you wouldn't do that. But you might become too – sort of quiet.'

'But I'm always quiet!'

'Yes, yes, but I mean remote, passive, sort of dreamy, as if you didn't notice things.'

'I assure you, I notice all sorts of things.'

'Sorry, I'm being stupid, it's just as if you might be too kind, too – you know –'

'I'll be as kind as I please,' said Franca, smiling. 'Isn't that what you want? It comes naturally to me.'

'Indeed, you have a wonderful nature. Almost too wonderful – too unselfish – as if you were – what I meant by remote – sort of sleepy, untouched, abstracted, not really present.'

'Not all there?'

'Forgive me, I'm blundering. You are as wonderful as I expected, and I worship you for it. You do really like Alison?'

'Yes, very much.'

'She adores you. But if you could only be, with her, a little more direct. She feels you're so noble, and apart –'

'I think I'm being direct. I'm just being myself.'

'You see – naturally she wants to talk to you a bit, to talk frankly about how things are, she wants to explain –'

'Naturally,' said Franca, turning towards him now, still holding the spoon, 'but what is there to explain? *You* have explained to me over and over how this thing can be possible. Of course it's possible, we prove it every day. You have quoted many cases, even famous ones. Other people have managed it, why not us?'

'Franca, do you mean it?'

'Yes.'

'I wish you'd say something like that to Alison.'

'I think you've always wanted two permanent women.'

'But I never imagined I'd meet anyone like Alison.'

'You were waiting for the right person.'

'Well – yes – someone who was really *good*, and whom *you* could accept.'

'You've done very well. There it is. We are exceptional people.'

'*You* are exceptional, you are the sovereign, you are the miracle. We shall live openly and speak truth to each other, and create happiness for each other. We can do it. Franca, darling, we must be happy, we *must* be. You will make us happy, you will make us good. We shall arrange things –'

'Yes, I suppose we *will* have to arrange some things,' said Franca, 'like, I suppose you mean, the timetable, which nights you spend with Alison and so on? But you know I shall agree perfectly with whatever you decide.'

Jack looked troubled, smoothing his lately shaven cheek. 'I mean something deeper. It must be a way of life.'

'Ways of life imply times for breakfast.'

'How practical women are, leading men back to simple realities. Yes, the details. But I mean, like the inner and the outer, we must find a rhythm –'

'You mean we three must?'

'Yes, a pattern, of course we may not find it at once –'

'So we can experiment.'

'Not exactly, it will have to be something coming naturally, something intuitive, gradually found out, resting upon our truthfulness and our faith in each other. Sorry, that's not very clear, but you know what I mean.'

'I'm not sure that I do. Perhaps you can give some examples.'

'No, I can't. It's not like that. I can't see it as clearly as that – and perhaps it's better not to see clearly –'

'That is often true.'

'I see, I feel, a direction, an orientation – Help me, Franca.'

'You see strategy not tactics?'

'No, that's too clear and simple. We shall go on living, and changing, together, and this will mean, for all of us, more life, more being, a circle of love, a mystery, a stretching out to each other in the dark –'

'Why in the dark?'

'Because such relations are deep, and depend on faith and love.'

'It sounds rather like the Holy Trinity.'

'I thought that too. With you as the Holy Spirit! But, Franca, seriously, well, all this is serious. I've *thought* about it so much and I feel it must and can be something wonderful for all of us. And it depends most of all on you, in a way you've led us –'

'I can hardly claim to have done that.'

'You are too modest. Your generosity, your goodness, your pure love has enabled this possibility. I *believe* in this happiness.'

'Since we are being so metaphysical,' said Franca thoughtfully, 'I would rather say that the happiness is *your* happiness, the spirit is *your* spirit. *You* are being too modest. You are the enabler, the creative power, the prime mover, the faith is faith in you. To will your happiness is our happiness. And of course you are right that this *must* be about happiness.'

'Don't let's argue like this,' said Jack, 'I'm glad you agree that – I'm glad you *agree*. Franca, darling, let's be simple.'

'And move quietly in the dark.'

'Yes. You know that I love you and am *nothing* without you. So often, in all this, I have felt that I am *nothing*. You give me life.'

'I think you have many sources of life,' said Franca, 'but I am touched by your gratitude.'

'Franca, it's not just gratitude –'

'I know, I know, it's something more mysterious. But about arrangements, the details, what you called the simple realities. I think you have something definite to say – and I hope I have made it easier for you to say it.'

'You have done exactly that. You understand so well. It's this – well
– Franca, to be absolutely blunt –'

'Yes?'

'I want – and I *must have* – both my wonderful women together
under one roof.'

Franca laid the spoon down carefully on the stove. She replied at
once. 'Well, that makes sense. Would Alison like it?'

'Her only worry is that you might not.'

'Then she has no worries.'

'Oh, Franca – angel –'

'Do you mean this roof or some other roof?'

'Oh, this roof – as you said, you live here – I live here – I can't
abandon my studio, it's perfect – here is *the scene* where we must make
our relationship real. If I keep vanishing and having another life
elsewhere, that's inevitably secretive, divisive, insincere, somehow untrue. It's unfair to you, and unfair to Alison. I want you to *know* my
other life, so that really it's *not* another life. I want the world to know
how things stand, and that we're being truthful and open and not
ashamed or in any way put down. I owe it to you. I owe it to Alison,
we owe it to each other, to live this openly and simply. *Here* is our
scene, our home, and you will help us, you will care for us, you will be
the centre. Franca, this isn't madness, is it?'

'No, Jack.'

'Thank God. You know, it hasn't been easy since – since Alison.
Sometimes I imagine I'm crazy. But then I think of you, and I feel sane
again. These things can be *thought* about, moral problems can be faced
and solved, one just needs the will and the courage. Franca, sweetheart,
I bless you, I worship you, you have a great soul, I feel I could serve
you as if you were God –'

'Jack, don't worry –'

'I love you –'

'Yes, good, but hadn't you better go now? Alison will be waiting for
you, and you must be anxious to relieve her mind.'

'Of course. I see it's late, I'd forgotten the time. I must go. I – I won't
say any more now, but you know –'

'Yes.'

'Oh, and – just one other thing.'

'Yes?'

'About the others.'

'What others? Are there others?'

'I mean Gildas and Ludens. I know they wish us well, and they're

151

both wise and reasonable people, they're tactful – but naturally they're inquisitive, they want to know what's happening, and make judgments on it all –'

'You mean they might disapprove?'

'I think they might misunderstand. I'd rather – well, I know how discreet and wise *you* are, I know you'd never say anything to them. I don't imagine they'd actually ask questions.'

'Of course not.'

'I'm sure what I say is quite unnecessary – but they might, you know, sympathetic looks and so on – I'd like you to keep them at a distance.'

'I do.'

'You are so sensible. Later on it will be easier. I'm not going to lose my two best friends. Later on they'll understand, they'll see it as *we* do. Now – my darling – I must go.'

Jack had been sitting in the chair while Franca stood before him. Now he rose and they faced each other across the table. Jack's face, usually so bland and pleased, was, throughout its surface, very slightly dislocated, like a drawing on crumpled paper. He looked himself, yet older, different, an elder brother, his father, or else this future self which he was in the process of becoming. Anxiety, doubt, even fear were very lightly sketched in: an appeal for forgiveness and love. Then, as Franca stared at him, he blushed, a darker redness for a moment suffusing his sun-tanned skin. She could not remember having seen him blush before. He was hesitating, at a loss. To forestall his next movement (such as his taking her in his arms) Franca moved rapidly round the table, took a firm hold of his shoulder, and, as he instinctively lowered his head, kissed his hot blushing cheek. Then she moved briskly away, opened the door, and returned to the stove and picked up the saucepan and the spoon.

She said in a gentle voice, 'Go now, dear Jack, see you tomorrow.'

Jack made as if to speak, then making a helpless expressive gesture, a sort of obeisance, strode out of the door and closed it behind him.

After a moment or two, after she had heard the front door close, she put down the saucepan and the spoon. She waited. Then she pulled up to the table the kitchen chair upon which Jack had been sitting and sat down, placing her elbows on the table and her head in her hands. She was, now, trembling and shuddering, her heart was beating violently, she could feel her scarlet blazing face. Had she blushed earlier? No. He had blushed, not she. She had been, throughout that amazing conversation, perfectly calm. She had looked and sounded rational, kindly, *motherly*. Had she been convincing? Yes. Had she overdone it? No. She had not said 'We'll all be one happy family'. Something quite extraordinary had happened, she had *achieved* something extraordinary. She was amazed at herself, at the weird awful feeling of triumph which was consuming her body, licking up over her like a flame. It was a kind of masterpiece, one of the cleverest, most complete, things she'd ever done. It was a turn of the screw of which she could never have dreamt herself capable.

She sat for a while, becoming quieter, breathing deeply, ceasing to tremble. Then she got up and went to the front door and, as she did every night, and had always done, since Jack never cared about such matters, locked and bolted it. She was alone in the house. She went back into the kitchen and (she recalled this later with surprise), laid a cloth upon the table, set out plates, knives, forks, a wineglass, bread, butter, cheese, apples. She brought out a bottle of red wine from the cupboard. She opened the wine and poured some into the glass. She put the saucepan back on the stove. Of course such a supper, minus the wine, she might have eaten on any of the evenings (and they now stretched back a long way) when she found herself alone. But there was something of an occasion, even a ceremony, even a sacrament, in the way, on this evening, she set out the food and the vessels. She sat down and sipped the wine and contemplated what she had done.

Chiefly she felt that, as in a sudden slip or subsidence, she had become a different person: a worse person, a desperate person, but powerful and free. Or was she simply mad, suffering perhaps from some well-known form of psychosis? *Free?* How could she think that when she had in fact entrammelled herself in terrible evil bonds, luxuriating even in her bondage? She had been really free before. But now had she not, just as she was telling herself that she commanded the game, in fact lost her freedom? Of what value after all is a power which one could never use, or at any rate did not know how to use? She was amazed at herself, *scandalised*, but at the same time could admire the absolutely impromptu fluency of her wicked vicious ill-intentioned lying to Jack. It was true that as she entrapped him she was entrapping herself. She would have to consider later how she would escape from that very complex cage. Surely the very *power* which she now felt she possessed would enlighten her later about how it was to be exercised.

Yes, I *am* free, she said to herself, but it's not like ordinary freedom, it's being in hell, a brilliant lucid hell. If I lose my concentration, if I lose my grip, my *command*, now, I shall fall into despair and humiliation and drivelling insanity. That is what I am escaping from, that is the alternative. I must *think*. I've never been able to think so clearly in my life before. I've never been able to think such extreme thoughts in my life before. It's as if my mind has suddenly broken through into a new area, a space, a vast capacity which I never dreamt I had. The pressure, the *pressure*, cannot crush me, it *forces* me to think. I can now contemplate my experience, my discovery, of how total pure love can be, in all its atoms, converted into total pure hate. I thought those dreadful fantasies I had of killing Jack were the extremity, the end. But I see now that the end is something farther, higher, more utterly frightful. Franca had indeed had those fantasies, and continued to have them, of how she would kill her husband, smashing his head with a hammer, plunging a carving knife into his side, drugging him with sleeping pills and suffocating him. Or she might drown him in the bath or push him under a train. The vivid proliferation of these fantasies had seemed to Franca to represent her final degradation, the end of her sanity, the cell in which her husband would ultimately immure her to whimper away what remained of her life. Her murderous dreams had *then* seemed to her the hallucinations of a soul mad with grief. Now, in the awful clear light which had broken upon her, they appeared as possibilities among others, and not necessarily the most interesting.

How easy it had been to mislead him, as he produced his apologetic arguments and justifications. She could have gone on for hours. She had seen his point of view and expressed it even better than he did. She had made him stupid, and mocked him, and his old assumptions about her docility had blinded him. She had inhibited her sympathy, one genuine sympathetic impulse would have ruined her. For truth, *all* must be false. The enormity of 'one roof' had taken her by surprise, and it was perhaps the way *that* had stiffened her which made her now feel so free, so beyond obligation. There, suddenly, the light had shone. It was as if Jack had driven her, *herded* her into this enlightenment, and a terrible pleasure had come to her aid. Now she could, for a while, rest with her achievement, which was something so much greater and more mysterious than just having uttered a pack of lies, and let what was to happen next gradually formulate itself. She had bought time, a resting-place, a space. There were now many possibilities. Perhaps she would simply lead him on and on into some dark chamber of doubt and fear. Even the threat, the hint, of absolute hate could chill the blood. One possibility which did not exist for Franca, since something in her had already killed it dead, was that one day Jack might tire of Alison, or Alison of Jack. But the quaint idea did occur to her that she might simply go on and on perfecting her role, delighting simply in her ability to deceive, and never, till the end, making any use of her deception. Might not that be the greatest thing? Her work could then remain perfectly complete, unmarred by the unpredictable results of its emergence into the public world. Was not *it* above the banality of revenge? This image of an undamaged whole brought with it a doubt which Franca found piquant rather than disturbing. Was her falsity really so intact? Could she have spoken to Jack so 'sincerely' had she not in some secret part believed what she said? Was she not indeed, not only trapping herself, but deceiving herself, being, to herself, a traitor? Dear me, thought Franca, then perhaps I might be in danger of actually becoming as saintly as I seem! Over this, for a moment, she actually smiled. She ate the contents of the saucepan and some bread and cheese and an apple, and drank most of the wine. Then she went to bed exhausted and, for the first time since her terror started, slept well.

'I think I've found a place in the country.'

'You mean somewhere to live?'

'Yes. Dad says he can't think here. He wants to be settled somewhere quiet.'

'You don't want to go back to Red Cottage?'

'That dump? Bloody no.'

'Irina, how exciting! How did you find it? I would have helped you.'

'I just asked around. I'm cleverer than you think.'

'Where is it?'

'In Wiltshire – a lovely place called Sillbourne.'

'Where Marcus can be a hermit.'

'Well, he can be a hermit anywhere, but he wants to get away from traffic noise.'

'So you've found a cottage?'

'It's on the edge of a village, but quite secluded, there's a little river too.'

'So he can have quiet walks. I'm so glad! May I come there often?'

'Of course, dear Ludens. We can't do without you.'

'I can't do without you either, Irina.'

It was the day after Ludens's visit to Chelsea which had ended with his witnessing Franca's tears. Ludens had reflected uneasily upon this episode. Of course she started it by walking into the boudoir. And then what else could he have done but what he did? Yet she might blame him all the same. Franca had her pride, and part of making her situation endurable must be the fiction that she endured it, if not cheerfully, at least stoically. Indeed Ludens, who had long appreciated the quality of Franca's love for her husband, could, more than other observers, understand the nature of her lack of an alternative. A dash of wry cynicism might have helped another woman, but that was not Franca's way. Now however Ludens had stepped for a moment inside the charmed circle, and things between them could never be the same again. On the whole Ludens decided it would be 'all right'. He and Franca had always been fond of each other. She would rely on his discretion, and perhaps at the same time in some speechless way on his support. He was glad that he had expressed to her, however blunderingly, what he felt. He was glad that he had held her hand. There was nothing here which could mar his relations with her, or of course with Jack.

Irina's news now drove these matters from his mind. He was pleased, excited, also alarmed. Would his 'status' be altered in some way by this new scene, perhaps simply by the change itself? His daily visits to the flat in Victoria now seemed an essential part of his life. He had told the others that he talked every day with Marcus, but this was not strictly, certainly not literally, true. On some days Marcus said nothing to him at all, while at the same time making it, without word or gesture, clear that his presence was helpful. Ludens, arriving, would have to intuit what was required. If Marcus, usually to be found in his bedroom, was sitting upon an upright chair, his back straight, his hands on his knees, staring into space, in a posture presumably connected with some technique of meditation, Ludens would wait outside in the hall, or converse quietly with Irina in the kitchen. If Marcus was sitting on his bed or walking about the room or looking out of the window, Ludens would sit near him either on a chair or else on the floor his knees up, his back against the wall. He liked to sit on the floor, but was careful not to do so too often. He was quite happy to be Marcus's dog, but it was possible that Marcus relied on his assuming some more dignified role. He would wait for Marcus to speak first. At other times he would find Marcus talking to Irina, and ready to go out for a walk. During his conversations with Marcus, when they did take place, Ludens had the impression that Marcus was pursuing a consecutive line of thought, sections of which were randomly surfacing for Ludens's benefit, or even for Marcus's benefit, at moments when Marcus felt it might clarify his ideas to verbalise them aloud, and even to listen to a response. These utterances, emerging from longer periods of silent thought, were often obscure, but Ludens had begun to feel that, not yet perhaps but soon, he would be able to frame a clearer idea of what Marcus was all the time thinking. Ludens now craved for these sessions, and had even instantly, when Irina spoke of the cottage in Wiltshire, decided he would have to move there, reorganise his life, and set up house next door.

'Is Marcus pleased about the cottage?'

'Oh yes.'

'Has he seen it?'

'Not yet.'

'What's it called?'

'Benbow.'

'Benbow Cottage, that's a good name. Could I come when you take Marcus to see it? I could drive you down.'

'Yes, if you like, thanks.'

'I'd love that. Have you actually bought it?'

'More or less.'

'Does it need alterations?'

'It's in very good order, awfully pretty and convenient.'

'When will you move in – if Marcus likes it?'

'Fairly soon.'

'I hope he'll be all right there. He's been so private and solitary here. I hope people won't intrude or think he's odd. Village life can be terribly unpeaceful! I know, I grew up in a village.'

'Did you? Where?'

'In Somerset. My father still lives there in the house where I grew up.'

'What does your father do?'

'He was a schoolmaster, he's retired now.'

'Is your mother still alive?'

'No.'

'Did you love her?'

'I never knew her. She left my father, or he left her, when I was born – or earlier! I'm illegitimate.'

'Are you?' Irina looked at him with interest. They were standing in the kitchen. The sun, managing to slant down onto the red brick wall opposite the window, reflected a hot light into the room. It was a warm day, the noise of traffic came through the slightly open window. Suddenly conscious of it, Irina closed the window, reducing the sound. She came back to stand near Ludens. They had been talking in low voices. Ludens had come early. Marcus was still in the bathroom, probably sitting on the lavatory, where Irina said he liked to spend time.

'Do you mind?' she said.

'Yes. It's irrational, but I do.' Ludens, about to say something more about his mother, checked himself. Better keep such things decently buried.

'Have you brothers and sisters?'

'I have a halfbrother, and a stepmother. They live in Portugal, I don't see them, neither does my father, we don't like them.'

'Do you love your father?'

'Yes, but I don't see him much.'

There was a pause.

'I loved my mother,' said Irina, 'at least I was sorry for her. She was always moaning and complaining, she was always ill with something, then she died of leukaemia.'

'I'm sorry.'

'How can you be sorry? You never knew her, you can't imagine her. Why do people always tell lies.'

'Was your mother Jewish?'

'Why do you want to know?'

'I want to know.'

'Yes.'

'You resemble her.'

'Yes, she was dark, not like Dad.'

'What was her name?'

'Judith. Oh why all this? Her parents were against the match because they thought Dad was a poor scholar. When they learnt about the money they soon changed their tune. My mother wanted to live a posh life and have dinner parties with other rich Jews and cook gefilte fish and wear a wig and dance with fashionable rabbis at weddings, you can imagine how Dad took to that. She never got on with Dad, he was too sublime. We were always hidden away somewhere, I was packed off to various boarding-schools, he gave us piles of money, he just didn't want to see us! My mother thought if I'd been a boy Dad would have lived with us and been grand, or at least people would have noticed us. So that was another mistake I made. As it was we were just too much and he had enough trouble coping with himself.'

'Were your family involved at all in – all that – were any of them in the camps?'

'No! He got it all out of books. Her people cleared off to America. His grandparents were bankers in Switzerland, his parents had a luxury home on Lake Geneva and later on they had a flat in London and another in Paris. I daresay his ancestors were slaughtered in various pogroms somewhere or other, but so what? Do the Jews have a monopoly of suffering?'

Irina, who did not dress up for Ludens, was wearing a simple faded old dress, frail with much washing, the sleeves rolled up well above her elbows. She had been washing dishes when he arrived. She spoke in a metallic tone of almost cynical exasperation, fixing Ludens with her intense dark stare. But her hands sought each other in the nervous wringing motion which he had seen before.

Ludens, very stirred, very touched, by these precious and unexpected outpourings, and hoping to make them continue, said, 'But did you get on well with your father? Like that time when I saw you in Kent, you seemed to be all right together.'

'We co-existed. It's better now.'

'I'm glad –'

'Oh you're always glad about something.'

'Why is it better?'

'I've grown up, and he's more helpless, he's not so powerful and bossy.'

Ludens did not like this picture. He was about to say something when Irina went on, 'You remember the sheep.'

'Of course I do.' Ludens felt himself blushing. He took a pace backward, dropping his eyes and raising his hand to his collar.

'I dream about that sheep. Was it a ram?'

'Was it? I don't know.'

'Didn't you *look*?'

'No. All I noticed was its eyes.'

'I didn't see. But I thought you, being a man, would have done. I suppose if it was there all by itself it must have been a ram.'

'It seems likely,' said Ludens, raising his eyes and lowering his hand.

'And you remember that rotten fence we kept on breaking pieces off the top of.'

'Yes, yes.'

'It had beautiful eyes.'

'Yes.'

There was a sound of the lavatory flushing, then of Marcus emerging and going to his room. Irina picked up some plates from the table and put them in the sink. Ludens moved to the door. It suddenly seemed terrible that Marcus was leaving the flat. Ludens had become used to the flat, it had become home-like and lived-in, Irina had bought plates, table-cloths, bedspreads. Marcus was safe here, hidden from the world. In this village he would be unprotected, misunderstood, a victim. People would gang together to destroy him. And these afflicted abandoned mothers: it was as if his own mother were, for a moment, superimposed upon Irina's mother who was always moaning and complaining and ill. And then the ram: yes, it must have been a ram.

Irina, turning on the hot water and vigorously mopping a plate, said, 'Don't worry. It doesn't matter. Nothing matters much. For instance your being illegitimate doesn't matter. It's rather distinguished, lots of the best people are. Go and see Dad. Knock on his door anyway.'

Marcus said, 'Come in.'

Ludens came in. Marcus was sitting on his bed. On this occasion Ludens decided to sit on the floor facing him, his back against the wall. He pulled off his jacket and folded it up beside him. Marcus was in shirt sleeves, looking rather more dandyish in a clean shirt, indeed a *new* shirt, evidently bought for him by Irina. Ludens studied his face. Marcus had looked, in this latest showing or manifestation, since he came to London, young and alert, not in the long-haired beauty of his very first appearance, but more in a sleek glowing tigerish handsomeness. His reddish-blond hair, slightly faded, evidently not clipped, was a little longer but still close to his head, already curling, giving him perhaps the youthful or angelic look of persons in Italian Renaissance paintings. Ludens, who had been watching this face attentively for some time, could now however read in it signs of care, a wrinkling of the brow, not marked exactly in any lines of flesh but as a cloud poised, the mouth and eyes narrowing as in thought or pain, the hints of a perhaps imminent older face. All this too Ludens was aware of, anxiously, as an aspect of his, Ludens's, presence, and of a frustrated desire to communicate with him. Ludens himself had never felt more alert, more finely tuned. Perhaps in their very silences Marcus had been preparing him, feeding him somehow with his thoughts, with the quality of his deepest reflections. Or am I just imagining all this, Ludens sometimes wondered. When he wondered this he felt a deep sadness.

Ludens was by now, in an ordinary sense, more used to being with Marcus, less afraid of 'saying the wrong thing', and had resolved today to ask a crude question which had been troubling him for some time.

He said, 'Marcus, do you mind if I ask, what really happened about Patrick, I mean, how do you yourself think about it?'

Marcus, surprisingly, smiled at this question, as if Ludens had asked him something rather simple or childish. Gildas had, from the first sighting, maintained that Marcus had no sense of humour. Ludens had replied that Gildas simply didn't understand Marcus's sense of humour. To which Gildas had replied it must be a Jewish sense of humour. Ludens, smiling himself, recalled this as he felt an obscure but reassuring complicity with whatever had made Marcus smile just that smile.

Marcus, now solemn, replied, 'One answer is that I don't know what happened. An unusual power was present. Though what does that mean? The event was important. I was expecting something like that.'

'You mean it was a sign? So in a way I was the messenger?'

'It proved something for me.'

'Do you think he would have died if you hadn't come?'

'I could answer that's none of my business. For all I know he was already dead when I arrived.'

This startled Ludens. 'Pat thinks he was! So it was a miracle?'

'Possibly. If you want to use that word.'

'Could you do it again?'

'I don't know. I hope I'm not asked to.' The smile returned.

'You mean lots of people turning up?'

'I'm not thinking of them. Just that the path now goes on beyond.'

Ludens was about to pursue the matter further when Marcus said, 'I wish I could write poetry.'

'Well, it's something you haven't tried yet!'

'I wish I could *experience* it. But I am afraid that this experience will be denied me.'

'I can imagine, it must be intuitive, like discovery in mathematics. As if poetic utterance were the thing itself. After all, you were looking for a language – Marcus, what *is* it?'

Marcus, not answering this question, said, 'I am confronted by several, quite different, dilemmas. Or, one might say, by a parting of the ways, by several different roads.'

Ludens, tense, said, to provoke him, 'Can't these ways be reconciled and seen to be ultimately only one way?'

'That is the worst temptation. It may even be that just *here* is where I have to stop.'

'Do you mean that if you can just explain what the alternatives are you will have answered the question? Or do you mean that's as far as you'll be able to go – not all the way?'

Marcus reflected. He said, again not answering the question, 'Of course I don't want to stop. I want to go *all the way*. But could I do it without – utterly – *falling*?'

'Into obsession, untruth, vanity, corruption?'

'You know, Ludens, I have had to *learn* to talk, even to you. Of course the thing really worth doing is the thing that is too difficult –'

'I believe you should go on thinking,' said Ludens, 'and I believe you should *write it down*.'

Marcus again smiled what Ludens saw as a mysterious complicit smile, as if Ludens were a talented tempter who was at the same time a fellow initiate. 'In a way it is nothing new, these are the oldest thoughts in the world. To give them life by thinking them again is hard enough. At the one step *beyond*, where one imagines glimpses of a *final formulation*, thinking is no longer a source of satisfaction or even a rational activity, it is a form of torture, a sacrilege which is its own punishment. And if one could even name it, its name would only ever be understood by very few persons. This too is a doom which must be faced, to know that which only few can know, and which cannot be further explained.'

'Mystics evidently felt this,' said Ludens, 'but philosophers usually managed to cover a number of pages! You can't know how many people would understand you, or who these people would be, what they would do, perhaps it's like what you said earlier, none of your business. Surely it's your duty to leave a record, to leave a sign, nothing else need concern you. It's a risk you must take. Even if you only wrote one page.'

'You think it is a little thing to write one page? Such knowledge is an experience which words can degrade. That is part of the problem. You have run after me to find out this thing as if it were just an answer to a riddle, or a joke which you remembered half of. Well, I suppose it is a riddle – and it may be – a joke.'

Marcus, who had been leaning forward, relaxed his pose and began to massage his left hand with his right. He let his left hand dangle, inspecting it as if it were an alien object.

'If I've run after you,' said Ludens with sudden emotion, 'it's not just for that, it's because –' Words failed him. He felt at this moment as if he held Marcus upon a silken thread which he must use all his intelligence and all his courage to keep whole. It was as if Marcus were actually waiting for him to effect some magical release or communication. He said almost coaxingly, 'Come, come, tell me more. We've only just met again after being apart for years. How *can* I know what you've been thinking all this time? Words can do something. What is it *like*, what is it *about?*'

'Oh well,' said Marcus, capturing his left hand again, 'I *suppose* it's *about* what makes human consciousness possible, or rather it's about what human consciousness *is*, which is to say what, and how, the world is, how *anything* is. You see what I mean when I say it's nothing new, it's been endlessly talked *around*. How language makes the world, how thought makes being. But it just may be that *now*, when we've got rid of so many *wrong* ideas, *now*, *at last*, is the moment when we might be able to frame – an answer.'

'Go on, go on – what would be something *like* an answer?'

'It's not anything to do with biology or psychology or any science or the old philosophies – it's something so deep that even the most delicately poised approach almost inevitably occludes it. It is a place covered by a cloud.'

'Language hides it?'

'It is more as if the gods hide it. In mathematics too there are such dark places. One cannot just dig it out of language as I thought once.'

'An experience, an action, a mode of life?'

'True thinking is all of these.'

'But are they alternatives?'

'Wait. I think the sort of answer you want is this. What is sought is a device. Something like an electrical circuit. Something present in a flash, intuitively seen to be necessary, which cannot be otherwise.'

'Marcus, like *what?*'

'Like Gödel's theorem or the Ontological Proof.'

'Oh. How can it be like both?'

'*Crede ut intelligas*! You want me to tell you something and I am telling you something. When I say it's the sort of answer you *want* I mean it's the sort that might help you! Since it is a crude oversimplification it might also mislead you. I could have mentioned *cogito ergo sum*, only I detest that shallow but influential maxim, now I'm glad to say discarded.'

'Oh, is it? But the Ontological Proof is religious, it's moral, it's about how God can't not exist.'

'I said *like*. These are hints, pictures. What is sought is not one thing among others, but the foundation of things. As I said, something *necessary*, something which *must* be so. Such a search cannot but be an ordeal, indeed a metamorphosis. One must be worthy, an intense purity and refinement of thought is required, even one might say a kind of holiness.'

'But you said that morality must be seen to be something superficial.'

'I spoke of what is ordinarily called morality. You see – Ludens, please concentrate –'

'I am concentrating!'

'At a certain point one is compelled to develop a conception of insight, or pure thinking, which is not recognisably "moral", something which simulates, or is, the rising up of man into the divine, as if one were being *driven* into the godhead.'

'I don't think ordinary morality is superficial,' said Ludens, 'I don't think it's just a convention or an illusion. I think it's fundamental and, well, absolute. Of course I'm not a philosopher –'

'If it is absolute, then the occluded particle must remain invisible.'

'Why?'

'Because if morality has a status which cannot be challenged or transcended then the search itself is under judgment.'

'So perhaps we *ought not* to seek – unless we wish to be – what we *can't* be –'

'How do we know?' said Marcus. 'It may be that for a very few the search itself is a necessity.'

'You said we must learn to believe in miracles. But – could one *do* anything with *it* – if you found it? After all, it wouldn't be like a magic ring. It would be more like having a huge diamond on a desert island and sitting there all alone with your diamond.'

'By doing something you mean doing something useful, something good.'

'Coming back to ordinary morality, ordinary people, individuals. It might give one power. But that could be bad. I'm sorry, I'm talking nonsense.'

'We are both talking nonsense, let us continue to do so for a few more minutes. There is something else I wish to say to you, later. Perhaps one could not live with such knowledge. One might die for it, or of it.'

'You mean the knowledge itself would kill one, like a laser beam? Or the gods would kill one?'

'There are no gods unless we become gods. Perhaps if ultimate knowledge is attained it must at once be transformed into a significant death.'

'Do you mean a supernatural event?'

'Those are rather crude words.'

'Wait a moment. If we understood it, the *deep* thing, we'd be gods and above morality. But we couldn't *live*, as gods. We'd have to sacrifice ourselves, to be transformed, instantly. But, Marcus, I'm *lost* – you talked before about suffering, extreme suffering, pure experience of suffering. Did you mean –?'

'Pure, without resentment or hatred. You see, Ludens, if one goes on far enough the thing collapses under its own weight.'

'You mean your thought collapses?'

'One seeks refuge. You see, you see – There are moments when a great meaning, a great new meaning, a meaning for all mankind, comes near to us and can be uttered. To partake in that utterance must demand superhuman courage, courage from the divine, an ability to think so intensely as to die even from pure thought – to die a death ordained, not for self-glorification, a significant and saving death. Only one must be worthy – otherwise – if one attempts and fails – one dies like a poisoned rat, not the best death, but the worst death of all –'

'Marcus, don't talk of death –'

'Or loses one's mind – better to die. Do you believe in God, Ludens?'

'No, of course not. And I know you don't either.'

'Indeed. But is there something where God used to be?'

'No.'

'Well – perhaps we need a new god – not a maimed monster – as any human must become – We need, after the Holocaust, a God that is no god. We must adore emptiness and the extremity of pain. You don't think the Jews have a mission to the world?'

'Good heavens no. Surely you don't think that? I mean, *you* have a mission to the world, every great thinker has –'

'Sometimes I seem to hear my ancestors speaking.'

'Mine are silent.' Or are they?

'You know, my people spoke a special kind of Sephardic Spanish, a language called Ladino. But I never heard that at any time.'

'And now they speak to your soul.'

'I feel their presence. That, which I spoke of just now, gathers us. We stand together under that sign of evil and pain.'

'But these things are everywhere!'

'It is the signal for today, something written in the heavens. How can we sit and think after that –'

'But you are sitting and thinking.'

'I mean, perhaps there are modes of reflection which have become luxuries, ideas we dare not frame, we dare not permit ourselves –'

'I know, I know, Marcus, just don't start on this, *please*!'

'If you have ever been tortured you are tortured forever, you dwell in flames. I, who have lived in peace, know this. The focus of that suffering could maim or kill the contemplating mind. The cries of the innocent accuse us.'

'All mankind is crying.'

'Yes, indeed. Ludens, listen to me. That concentrated evil, that supreme almost supernatural cruelty, *teaches* us that we are at a parting of the ways, man's salvation or man's destruction. That is the omen. The burden of salvation lies upon us, a gathering up of the suffering of all men. It may be, I say it *may* be, that the Jews are once more called to make an utterance to mankind, to manifest, for a new age, a new holiness and a new divinity. Our ancient wisdom is stirred to speech. We have seen and suffered the sign of world change. Because we are homeless, because we are outcasts, beggars, nomads, victims, we are called to witness, to represent the state of man upon the planet. We have always been such witnesses and such representatives.'

'So we like to think. We might just as well say that the Holocaust was God punishing the Jews! He punished us before, why not now! That makes us feel proud. Even if the message is designed for everybody, a warning shot from heaven to warn the whole human race, we're still special! But, Marcus, nothing is more important than that there is no God, and no purpose in history, and no punishments, and no Jewish or any other destiny. We just live in bottomless chaos and have to help each other, that's all.'

'Surely there are times when there are thinkers who think for mankind, and peoples who represent mankind. The Greeks and the Jews have been such peoples and produced such thinkers. The Greeks have gone. The Jews remain.'

'Of course there are remarkable thinkers who emerge in times of crisis, I believe that you are one. But why shackle yourself to *that* horror? It was a particular thing, an episode, a historical event, one can't extract a world meaning from it, or a cosmic signal, history isn't *like* that.'

'You call it an episode –'

'I mean it's an object of historical study like any other. Of course we feel it as a wound. But other people have their wounds too.'

'Why are you so upset?' said Marcus. 'You want me to talk to you. All these days when I have been silent you have stared at me willing me to speak. Now when I speak you are angry.'

'Marcus, I'm sorry, I'm *not* angry, how could I be, I regard you as – you know how I regard you – I just don't want you to waste your time with those old mythological thoughts. You didn't grow up inside that dark house. Don't get shut up inside it now. It's nothing to do with the thing you are looking for.'

Ludens, amazed at his own emotion, found he was kneeling on one knee. He stood up and *shook* himself, like a dog emerging from water. He dragged at his shirt and ruffled his hair and stamped his feet and swung his arms about.

Marcus, who had resumed his composed posture, his hands clasped on his knee, watched this performance with lifted eyebrows. He seemed calm and thoughtful, and throughout his recent eloquent speeches had not raised his voice. He said now, 'You are right to check me. Now please sit down on a chair, sit on *that* chair, please *sit down*.'

Ludens, hot and flushed, sat down, smoothing his hair and running his fingers over his face as if to put it too in order.

Marcus went on, 'My mind is so pressed, so *compressed*, thoughts fight each other like fishes in a net, blood flows. I have deep doubts, deep fears. The spectacle of extreme cruelty appals, it also fascinates, it may obscure the sin, which then acquires the dignity of a mystery. If one thinks of what was done one must also think of those who did it.'

'To forgive them?'

'I'm not sure what that would mean. Rather to join them.'

'To understand them by identifying with them, like you said? To – experience them?'

'To attempt, in some intuition of evil, to understand them, to enact them, and so to activate and *reveal* the evil in one's own soul.'

'To unmask and destroy one's own evil. And so become a just judge – of theirs.'

'To find one's own way to hell, to visit the underworld, one needs a pure heart or divine protection. It is extremely dangerous. My mind is full of dark thoughts and evil yearnings, terrible images which move me to wickedness, as if to some obscure crime which perhaps I have committed already –'

'Demons. How to have clean thoughts. How to separate one's thoughts from one's obsessions.'

'Did I say that? Yes. One might labour for years and then discover that one's thoughts simply concealed some devilish machine.'

'That might not rob the thoughts of value. Artists, and great artists, are often in this dilemma.'

'I am not an artist. I require the clearness of truth and its simplicity. I need daylight. But I wander in the dark.'

Marcus now leaned forward, bowing his head and closing his eyes. A silence ensued. The window was closed, reducing the traffic to a river-like sound of which Ludens now became conscious. He wondered if Irina had gone out, perhaps to buy some more clothes. Or was she listening at the door? The room was tidy. There was a cotton quilt, faded almost to invisibility, upon the bed, Marcus's summer jacket draped on a chair, a shirt folded up, shaving things grouped on a chest of drawers. It was like some anonymous temporary room of an orderly penniless young man. Ludens saw, on top of a closed suitcase in a corner, the curious light-brown cap which Marcus had been wearing when Ludens had seen him first, through the window of Red Cottage. He was moved to ask, 'Marcus, that little brown cap I saw you wearing once, what is it?'

Marcus opened his eyes. 'I got it in India. Someone gave it to me. It's an old Congress Party cap. I used to imagine it helped me to think.'

'A thinking cap!'

The door opened and Irina came in. She carried a tray with cups of tea and biscuits on it, which she laid down carefully on top of the chest of drawers. She said to Ludens, 'You do take sugar, don't you? And I hope you like chocolate biscuits. I have some plain ones too if you'd rather.'

'Sugar, yes, and chocolate biscuits, fine, yes, thanks,' said Ludens.

Marcus, accepting a cup from Irina, said, 'Thank you, my child.'

'Shall I put the biscuits on the bed?'

'Yes, thank you, thank you.'

Irina disappeared. Marcus put his cup on the floor, snatched a biscuit from the plate and held it absently between finger and thumb. He observed conversationally, 'I expect Irina told you we were moving. She has found a little place in the country. Here there is too much noise, as you see one can't even open the window. Red Cottage was unsuitable for other reasons, but there was space and fresh air and I think I need these.'

'I'll hope to see you there a lot. I'm sorry I was so tiresomely upset just now, it's just that I want to protect you.'

'I understand. I'm grateful to you. You're the only person I can talk to. We won't always agree. But look, there is another matter. It's just one more thing – about Irina –'

'Yes.'

'I'm sorry I got angry on that – that first occasion – you know –'

'It is I who need –'

'I think I said to you earlier – I did, didn't I – sometimes I forget what I've said – that I wanted you to look after her.'

'You said that,' said Ludens, 'and I will.' He stood rigid before Marcus, who was now looking tired and relaxed, still holding his biscuit.

'You like her, don't you?'

'Yes.'

'I'm just thinking about the future. You are someone I know and trust. I don't really *know* anyone else. I don't know how she feels about Jewishness. I hardly know how I feel. But – you see – I want her to marry a Jew.'

'Lift your end more to the right,' said Ludens, 'to the *right*, you fool!'

'Sorry,' said Jack, 'I can't think how we ever got it up.'

'Couldn't you just drop it over the edge?' suggested Patrick.

'No!' said Jack. 'We could not!'

'It would simply get wedged between the upper and lower banisters,' said Ludens, 'can't you see?'

'Suppose we lift the bloody thing right up on end?' said Jack.

'Then it'll fall against the window,' said Ludens, 'I can't hold it.'

'I told you to take the feet off,' said Patrick.

'We've unscrewed the casters,' said Jack, 'the feet don't come off, they're fixed!'

'If you turned it *over*,' said Pat, 'you might be able to slide it.'

'We tried that before you came,' said Jack. 'Do get out of the way, will you?'

'There must be some method of edging it round the corner,' said Ludens.

'You keep saying so, why can't you find it!'

'They don't know how to do it,' said Patrick conversationally to Franca. They were standing on the lower landing watching.

'It seems so,' she said.

The object in question was Franca's divan bed, the one she had slept on in the upstairs spare room when she had been looking after Patrick.

It was to be moved downstairs into Franca's boudoir. The mattress was already down in the hall. The bedstead, descending the narrower stairs from the second floor, had become firmly wedged between the banisters and the wall at the point where the stairs turned.

Things had changed at the house in Chelsea. Patrick, much better but still weak, had become a paying guest (Jack paid) at Moxie's house, where Moxie had a self-contained flatlet, often let to a student, and where she could 'keep an eye' on Pat. Moxie, no longer employed by Jack, had undergone a transformation. Relieved of her professional role, she manifested herself as an attractive well-dressed young woman answering to the name of Suzanne. Jack jokingly referred to her as an addition to the family. In the circumstances (that is, of Jack's plan to have his wife and mistress under one roof) it had been necessary for Patrick to move, and Patrick, being distinctly better, had moved, or had been moved. The same circumstances required that Franca should sleep downstairs; Franca had herself, promptly forestalling embarrassment, simplified the rearrangement by announcing that she would now occupy her boudoir; and letting Jack and Alison assent silently, and without having to murmur 'please' or 'thank you'. Irina and Marcus, said to be busy with preparations for their move to the country, no longer visited. Patrick, so he told Franca, had been over to the flat at Victoria and had had a 'talk' with Marcus. He said he had been invited to call upon them at their new house. Meanwhile he turned up daily at Chelsea, sitting with Jack in the studio or Franca in the kitchen. The person who was most patient with him was Alison, who let him read his poems to her and sometimes took him out to lunch. Pat also went to see Gildas and Ludens, both of whom were feeling guilty because they had not offered to 'put him up'. Alison had not yet moved in. The removal of Franca from the upper storey was perhaps the sign that her arrival was imminent. She still slept at her flat, where Jack either spent the night, as under the previous arrangement, or arrived back very late 'not disturbing' Franca, who had until today (also without comment) continued to sleep in the upper bedroom. Alison was in fact often absent, revising her television play and writing her next play. Jack spoke 'casually' of Alison's intention to sell her flat. When Jack and Alison were in the house together by day they were in the studio (where Jack was supposed to be teaching Alison to paint) or else in the drawing room, often watching television. Franca, of course bidden to join them, sometimes did so, but soon withdrew to various 'tasks'. She sat in the kitchen or in her boudoir. She was everywhere, smiling, busy, soft-footed, considerate. Jack and Alison were going for a few days to

Amsterdam. They begged Franca to come too, and she declined so tactfully that they could all, without awkwardness, smile over the plan and even discuss it.

Franca naturally busied herself with genuine tasks, of which there were always plenty. Jack did not like strangers in the house, so there was no regular charwoman, only the obliging person who could be summoned at intervals when Jack was away. Franca *liked* cleaning. She cleaned and polished and tidied and shopped and cooked and washed clothes and sewed buttons onto Jack's shirts. She even once let Alison sew on a button and observed Alison's *gratitude*. She watched herself, she watched them all, with *amazement*. She watched. Often, in her kitchen or her boudoir, she did nothing, she simply sat absolutely still and breathed, sensing her continued existence, preserving herself, taking refuge in a timeless present. This state she spontaneously pictured as if she had become small, about the size of a jar of marmalade (this image appeared with a kind of authority) and had *put herself away* in a small square recess in a wall, just large enough to hold her. The wall was in an interior which was almost dark. It was silent and a little damp. In this recess Franca sat breathing quietly, taking the air in by her nostrils and expelling it by her mouth. In this stillness she recalled how once she had so much loved sleep, half sleep, lying with Jack beside her, relaxing into sleep. This had always been even more precious than love-making, or was its most precious part. And the words 'peace, peace, peace' came to her, as if they were (but could they be?) part of an old prayer, perhaps a prayer which her mother had uttered over her before she could speak. She thought about her mother and her sudden mysterious death. She forbade herself tears. For sleep, she took sleeping pills. Only in this motionless sitting could she now achieve bodily quiet, even sometimes, briefly, mental rest.

She had at times, almost as if it were a comfort, at least something accustomed, run through the fruitless litany of remorse: I ought not to have tolerated his infidelities, I ought to have stopped it at the start, I have colluded with his depravity, it is all my fault. Oh the lies women believe, and will to believe and want to believe! She recalled that fatal time when she had wept because she knew she had diminished Jack, had demoted him, had cracked the perfect image, had lodged in her mind that little black poisonous atom. From this it had all begun. She had thought less of him, he had thought less of himself. At one time, even lately, she had thought that she could bear it, turning it all into pure love. She had imprisoned her anger and hate in a part of her mind, as something unworthy which could be overcome. Jack had said, and said again and again, that all would be well provided no one told lies. But now she herself, her mind and her heart, was composed entirely of lies, the anger and the hate were everywhere, and worse, the calculation, the conspiracy, the dreams of revenge. She found herself thinking, I have held my fire too long and lost the moment of action. I should have *screamed* at the start – whenever the start could now be said to be. As it is – Jack thinks I'm too quiet, dreamy, drifting away, not noticing things. Perhaps he even thinks I *don't care*! And if I were to start screaming now it would be too late. They'd be sorry for me, they'd give me whisky and aspirins and send me to a psychiatrist. The wicked mood of triumphant secret freedom which had come to her after her first *performance* of careful deliberate lying to Jack had, for the moment at any rate, left her. She felt now a dulled sense of degradation: she felt depraved and diminished and shrunken and old. She was, in a house full of strong young people, a little old woman, soon her hair would be white. Only I won't wait for that, she thought, as she breathed quietly, feeling her bosom rise and fall and her heart beat – I'll be dead. I'll kill Jack and myself after. Or perhaps I won't do that. I'll just vanish and live alone in a cottage beside the sea until I go quietly mad and drown myself. And no one will even know. She saw her long hair floating like seaweed upon the waves. How, she wondered, could someone be so unhappy, so tortured by grief, and still not be mad, and still be alive.

Now however she was standing, part of what might be described as a lively merry family scene, upon the landing, watching the descent of the divan bed from the second floor. Suddenly the problem was resolved. The divan, lifted high at one end by Ludens, suddenly began to rush down the stairs, nearly overturning Jack and making a long scar upon the wallpaper with one of its feet. Franca and Pat retired hastily, laughing. Amid further merriment it was carried in triumph down the second flight of stairs, through the kitchen and into the boudoir where Franca had already cleared a place for it. The mattress was brought in. The pillows and bedclothes were already piled on the floor. The badinage continued with Pat, Jack, Franca and Ludens standing round the kitchen table and talking all at once. Franca, who knew that Ludens was looking at her and was determined not to look at him, looked, and a flash of understanding, perhaps simply of remembrance, passed between them.

Ludens said, 'I must be going.'

Jack said, 'Come up to the studio for a moment, I want to show you something.'

They departed. Patrick remained. The morning sunshine brightened the room, embellishing the cups and plates upon the dresser.

Franca said, 'Would you like a cup of tea, Pat, and a piece of ginger cake?' Patrick was still, to the surprise and admiration of his friends, keeping off alcohol.

'No, thanks, Franca, dear, let's just sit down and be quiet together.'

They sat down at the table. Franca wondered if the Irishman had noticed the 'flash' between her and Ludens.

'Will you hold my hand, Franca, like you used to do?'

Franca gave him her hand. She thought, men are always holding my hand these days. What does it mean? Everyone is sorry for me. It will be Gildas's turn next. Then she thought, Jack wants to take me in his arms and I won't let him. If he took my hand I would withdraw it. Yet I am his wife and I desire him. There is something lethal in all this.

'You know,' said Patrick, holding her hand with a steady pressure in his large warm hand, 'I'm very grateful to you, you were so kind to me when I was ill, you were loving to me.'

Franca was touched that he remembered, that he had been aware. She said, 'I cared very much. I'm glad you knew.'

'Oh I knew all right. But you've abandoned me now I'm well, isn't it?'

'I have not!' said Franca, laughing and imitating his Irish intonation. 'It's just that you're well and gone away and you don't need me and that's good!'

'I'm not gone away, sure, I'm here. And I do need you. I've not all that many people. I need you to tell things to.'

'Tell me some then!' she said, squeezing his hand and releasing it.

'You know, I'm to live differently now. I've been talking with Father O'Harte, and I'm come back. I go to Mass and all.'

Franca was surprised. 'I'm glad. So you believe in God?'

'Well, I don't know. I believe in Holiness and the Divine Spirit. Father O'Harte says God can look after Himself. You know, a poet is a religious man. I'm not to drink any more. I want to be a real poet. I can't yet, I haven't got me own voice, the poems are bad, yes, they're bad, little stunted things. But I'll learn. When you've been through death and live again you're changed all through. I'm a new man, I'm a better man.'

'So you think you were dead?'

'I don't know, but I believe it, it's a mystery. I had a vision of Our Lady. I thought I'd go back to Ireland for a bit and go to Clonmacnoise. Do you know it? No? It's a holy place. I had a vision there too once long ago. It's beside the Shannon, in a lovely curve of the Shannon. I'll go there and kiss the stones, and I'll go and kiss me old mother who is living in Dublin with some nuns. But I won't be off for long because I've to follow Marcus.'

'To follow him?'

'I owe him my life so I must give him my life. Father O'Harte says he's a holy person, a sort of saint. You know he's going into the country so I'm to go too and I'll live nearby in a little room or a shed, for I'm going to put my life in order, I'm crazed with living in London and in the pubs and getting drunk every day, no wonder I couldn't write poetry, for I couldn't *think*. You know, the poet is the saviour of the age, *he's* the thinker now, he makes the language of mankind and preserves the experience of wisdom –'

As the rill of Patrick's soft-spoken speech continued Franca was thinking how handsome he was, his clear skin smoothly taut over the bones of his face, his cheeks faintly flushed, his fine ardent eyes dark blue, his thickly curling hair, growing again abundantly, almost black. His small mouth was gentle. She thought, he looks like an angel. Of course he's a wild man, a fox, a seal, a sort of sprite – such a sweet man – I'm glad he spoke to me, I didn't think he remembered.

At that moment the door from the hall opened and Suzanne Moxon, formerly Moxie, appeared in the doorway. In a second, as Suzanne looked at the seated pair, Franca realised something. She thought, she's possessive about Pat, perhaps she's even in love with him!

Suzanne said, now smiling, 'I've come for Patrick, to take him home. He must have a light lunch and then rest.'

Patrick rose obediently and went to the door. Franca said to Suzanne, 'Won't you stay?'

'No. Must go. Must take him back. Car's at the door. Cheerio!'

Behind Suzanne there suddenly appeared the figure of Alison Merrick. 'Oh, are you taking Pat off?'

'Yes. He needs a quiet life.'

'She evidently thinks he won't get one here!' said Alison, after, amid exchanges of greetings, Suzanne and her patient had departed. Alison came and sat down at the table with Franca. 'Is there any of that ginger cake left?'

Franca fetched it. 'Tea, sherry?'

'No thanks.' Franca was relieved that Alison had given up her guilty peepings and hintings and attempts at relevant conversation; only now her calmness and at-homeness were proving equally maddening.

'Is Ludens here?'

'Yes,' said Franca, 'he's upstairs with Jack.'

'I must tell him, Heather Allenby's coming over again. You know, she lives in France during the summer.'

So, thought Franca, all the young people are pairing off, like in a play. Jack is to have Alison, Suzanne is taking Pat, and now Ludens is to marry Heather Allenby. I'm the one who'll be left alone on the stage. Except that I won't be alone. I'll be looking after their babies – including Jack's. And, she thought, I'll *kill* their babies, I'll drown them all in the bath. As she gazed benignly at Alison eating ginger cake, she had a sudden very clear vision of the dead babies floating in the bath.

Alison had seen, through the open door of the boudoir, the divan bed against the wall. She said almost inaudibly, 'Oh –'

Franca got up. 'Do go up to Jack and Alfred. They're in the studio. You can tell Alfred about Heather Allenby.' She went through into the boudoir and began to pick up the bedclothes.

Alison followed her. 'Let me help.'

In silence they spread the linen upon the bed, tucked in the corners neatly, dropped the pillows into their cases, extended the quilt.

When they returned to the kitchen Franca said, with a slight tone of insistence, 'Thank you so much. Now do go up to the others.'

'I don't want to,' said Alison, in a childish sulky voice.

'Well, go somewhere then.'

Alison sat down, spread her legs, put her elbows on her knees, and drooped her head.

Franca said, 'Are you feeling ill?'

Alison in the same aggrieved tone said, 'I fell down on the pavement and cut my knee.'

'Let me see.'

Alison lifted her skirt and extended one brown bare leg. Her knee was covered with blood.

Franca quickly filled a bowl with warm water, poured in disinfectant, found a clean tea towel, cotton wool, and a roll of white absorbent kitchen paper, and knelt down beside Alison. She dabbed at the wound, removing bits of grit, revealing a number of oozing scratches. Alison winced. Franca dried the wound with the paper, feeling as she did so the blazing warmth of the bruised knee, which was already swelling a little. She felt too, as she mopped the trickling water from it, the smooth bronzed skin of the leg. There was a mingled smell of disinfectant, of warm summer flesh, of Alison's bare feet in their open sandals, of the fresh cotton material of her drawn-back dress.

'It's nothing really,' said Alison. 'Thank you so much. It's ridiculous one should be so shocked by falling down.'

175

Franca stood up. 'It'll soon stop bleeding, just dab it occasionally with the paper, here, don't use your hankie. There's blood on the hem of your dress. You should wash it out when you go upstairs.'

'Oh – Franca –'

Franca looked down at Alison, at the brilliance of her red hair, at her long neck and throat, at her bare brown arms, at her white breasts, visible from above, at the glimpse of her paler thigh, still revealed by the disordered skirt. She thought, yes, she is beautiful. And in a moment she'll be holding my hand. I've been elected everybody's mother. Perhaps it's something to do with my desire for Jack which I'm checking at every second. Perhaps there's some sort of aura. What nonsense. I must go away. I won't stay here to have my contemptible revenge on Jack, to see his surprise when I drop the mask. Those thoughts were vile. I'll go to Molly Stein – no, not to her, she hates men, she'd say she told me so. I'll go and stay at a hotel in some quite other place, somewhere I've never been before. And I won't come back. Perhaps I'll find that cottage by the sea and die there quietly.

Alison's wide trusting blue eyes were filling with tears. She took hold of Franca's hand.

Upstairs in the studio Ludens and Jack had been talking.

'What did you want to show me, Jack?'

'Nothing. I just wanted you alone.'

'How's visual art?'

'I can't do it any more.'

'It'll come back.'

'There's no guarantee. Artists do just stop being able to do it. Even Shakespeare did.'

'He decided not to.'

'How do you know?'

'You should change your style.'

'I know, I'm trying to, I can't, the power has been withdrawn. I can't *learn* again now. It's all to do with bloody Marcus.'

'Why blame him?'

The sun was casting a pleasant subdued clear radiance through the brown blinds which had been drawn over the south-facing skylight. Jack kept his studio as empty as possible. His finished paintings were stored at the gallery, or in a room downstairs. The studio contained two easels, chairs, stools, a desk, a bronze dancing Shiva about three feet high over which, today, one of Jack's overalls had been thrown.

'It's probably a delayed curse,' said Jack. 'I expect he cursed me when he cursed Pat, only I was so healthy the effect was delayed, or perhaps my rotten paintings *were* the effect, and I only see it now. I'll get ill, I'll die, he'll have to do another resurrection job. Pat's all right, look at him, he looks like some sort of Irish hero, and he's writing yards of poetry.'

'Have you seen any of it?'

'He read some to me and Alison. She said she understood it. She's very good with him. At any rate it's not like that semi-conscious automatic rhyming stuff he used to spout.'

Ludens had picked up from the floor a sketch, acrylic on paper, representing (perhaps) a pale human figure emerging from a dark marsh or river. 'Oh, a person! I like that.'

Jack snatched it from him and tore it in two.

'I said I liked it!'

'Well, fuck you! I'm sorry, I'm not myself. Or rather I am myself, my new self. Don't worry about me, I'm better than I seem.'

'I'm glad to hear that!'

'I forgot to ask you if your car turned up all right. I suppose I'd have heard if it hadn't.'

'I meant to thank you. Someone drove it right to the door and charged me nothing. I owe you —'

'Nix, nix. How's Marcus?'

'I wish he'd start writing. Maybe he will when he's in the country. You know he's moving, of course I told you.'

'Everyone told me. Irina told me. That was before she got cross with me about her underclothes.'

'*What?*'

'It was just a joke. She'd bought some fancy underwear and was showing it to Franca and I came in and made some remarks. Don't look like that! You know, you underrate that little girl, she's not a naive miss, she's funny, she's witty. She's even not bad-looking. I hope *she'll* be all right in the country, it's not much of a life for her, but she'll look after herself. Are you still having those conversations with Marcus?'

'Yes.'

'You'll miss that.'

'I'll go and see him wherever he is.'

'Ludens, dear Alfred, old friend, don't get fixated on that man, there's nothing left in him, he's an empty shell. The glittering figure who impressed us so much is no more. He's brittle, he's dry, why were we so impressed anyway?'

'You taught him to paint. He taught you to paint. And can't you even remember what you saw with your own eyes in this house?'

'The resurrection scene. That was weird. But there are many possible explanations. You yourself say he's incoherent, and Irina says –'

'Why don't you come and see him? Are you afraid to?'

'Yes. And so is Gildas. He's still got the power to hurt people. He'll probably hurt you. You ought to withdraw honourably while there's still time.'

'Oh Jack, Jack –'

'I don't want you to break your heart over this. I need you, I need your support. Why hasn't Gildas been here lately, is it because he disapproves?'

'Possibly.'

Jack, who had been standing near his friend holding the torn halves of the sketch in either hand, went to the far end of the room and sat on the desk. He tossed away the sketch, kicked off his sandals, then pulled off his socks and rolled up his trouser legs. He undid his shirt.

'Come here, Alfred.'

Ludens went along the room and stood in front of him.

'You look so puritanical today.'

Ludens was wearing a white shirt and black cotton trousers.

'You ought to get out in the sunshine. You're as pale as a nun. You disapprove, don't you?'

'Yes,' said Ludens.

'You think I shouldn't – Well, what the hell do you think?'

'I think you shouldn't bring Alison to live here.'

'You think I should keep two establishments and sneak furtively from one to the other like some sort of guilty adulterous cad?'

Ludens was silent. He raised one hand and tapped Jack on the cheek.

'All right, you think I am a guilty adulterous rotter. Perhaps it's all a matter of style. No, it isn't. I want all this to be in the open, to be *accepted*, I want *truth* to be told. Without truth we shall all sink. If I keep Alison in another place as a semi-secret mistress this house will die, it will die of my untruth – don't you see – I shall lose touch with Franca. Well, no, I *can't* lose touch with Franca, we're eternally connected, but she'd become – sort of holy, frail. I *must* see her every day, she must face it full on and she *can*, I *must* stay here, and so Alison must be here too. Ludens, I'm in love, I'm desperate with love, I'm sunk in it, I'm ruthless, I feel as fierce as hell about this, I could kill anyone who stands in the way, I *must* have both of them, and I *will*, all right it may look like a battlefield, but what has to be done has to be done now and like this. Peace will follow. Then we shall see everything as inevitable and even *good*. It *will* be good, it will be an achievement, they *must* learn to live together, they've got to, and they *can*, they can *already*, they're both so wonderful and so intelligent and they like and respect each other *very much*, that's absolutely clear. I can *make this happen*. Other painters did it, Rembrandt, Rubens —'

'Wait a moment, they didn't have the girls there, at the same time, did they?'

'Maybe not, but they both loved, and greatly loved, two absolutely different types of women. Don't chide me, Alfred, try to *understand*. You look like a young priest in your black and white, no, like a novice, an apprentice monk, you view the world with shocked amazement, you need a real woman in your life.'

'I think you should talk to Gildas, go and see him.'

'Why suggest that, what's the use? You're just a pair of censorious bachelors! If he carps we'll only have a row. I might go and see him all the same, just to *tell* him as I've *told* you.'

That morning Franca had tried to break a cup. She had dropped the cup on the stone floor of the kitchen. She had dropped it, not thrown it. It had failed to break. She picked it up and said 'Sorry'. She thought, I can't even break a cup!

The episode of the divan on the stairs had occurred three days ago. For two nights Alison had stayed in the house, couching upstairs with Jack, while Franca slept downstairs in her boudoir. Nothing was said about this, it just happened. Franca had now perfected a method of smiling at everyone, but never catching anyone's eye. The episode of Alison's knee had been startling, but Franca had somehow shuffled it off, undramatised it. She had behaved like a *sensible mother*. Now, Alison and Jack were away, gone to Amsterdam. Or rather, they would now be on their way back, since they had decided (Franca could imagine the little conversation, she thought of it as a 'little' conversation) to stay away only one night, instead of the three nights originally planned. Franca was sorry about the change of plan. She had said to herself, thinking of that absence, there's my chance! But her chance for what? She could not run away. She *could not*. Jack, at whom now she never looked though she always smiled had, in departing, kissed her. He had hustled her out of the kitchen into the boudoir and kissed her on the lips, slipping his arm round her waist. It's like kissing the housemaid, thought Franca, as she felt his big animal presence. The image gave her an awful cold gratification. Jack, releasing her, had then, almost formally, taken her hand and kissed it. He murmured, 'Oh my love, be kind to me.' Franca replied in a bright clear voice, 'Of course I will. There, there. Don't worry!' This seemed to content him. Perhaps now he was, like a child, content with little, not demanding detail. Or perhaps he had reason to be content, since Franca had been, perhaps visibly, moved, or startled by his sudden gesture of kissing her hand, something which she could not remember his ever having done before. Perhaps this portended some new way of their living together, based upon respect, courtesy, formality, even awe, as if Franca were an abbess, or a dowager empress, and he a local nobleman, privileged to be a frequent visitor. Alison had kissed her too, with a would-be significant kiss, but publicly in the hall. They departed, grinning and waving, in an early morning taxi to Heathrow. Franca imagined their *intense relief* as their taxi turned the corner.

In the time since she had moved downstairs, and Alison had moved in upstairs, she had meditated much, almost as a detached spectator, upon the comparative stability of her incompatible moods, whereby she was, as it were, becalmed. Her great deception, that cruel triumphant power by which she held her husband trapped and blinded, was held in tension between the constant possibility of a devastating revelation, and the equal prospect of an indefinitely continued impersonation of a kind of moral perfection. The weird notion that she might be *in danger* of actually becoming one day as perfect as she seemed added a ghastly charm to her reflections, as she continued to envisage various methods of killing Jack. This psychological edifice, to the creation and maintenance of which she now devoted her energy, she pictured as a kind of large machine erected inside her body, stretching it out and making her tall and rigid like a hard glistening monument. Franca was amazed at her sudden power to develop vivid visual images of her mental states, a power which she had never exercised before, and which she thought of, not without satisfaction, as being perhaps a symptom of incipient madness.

However, when Franca found herself so suddenly, for two days and in such a new way, *alone in the house*, her vast restless self-awareness, her life energy, set her off in a fresh direction. She had not reflected upon what, alone, she would be, had perhaps assumed that she would sit motionless as a statue with vacant eyes. Instead of this, in the very act of shutting the door upon the departing couple, she became intensely aware of the *house*, as if she had now *become* the house. Or rather, as she then, standing tense in the emptiness felt it, she had become something exceedingly small, smaller than the jar of marmalade and more mobile, as small as a mouse, or as an electric spark, which was impelled to run very fast, invisibly fast, round and round the house, altering it in some way which was now imperative. She ran up the stairs and into the bedroom she had shared with Jack. One of the oddities of the situation since her 'descent' was that most of her clothes had remained in the cupboards upstairs, she had felt unable to go and fetch them, and evidently the other two had felt too embarrassed to carry them down, or perhaps had simply not noticed the problem. Alison would have had to decide where to put her own clothes, though perhaps she had left most of them still at her flat. The bedroom was neat, though, as Franca noticed with a little surprise, a bit dusty. Who would dust now, clean the bath, hoover the carpets, now that Franca didn't mount higher than the drawing room on the first floor? Would they clean the place themselves or would Alison employ a maid? (Franca pictured Alison as having a maid, not a charwoman.) Or would they silently assume that Franca would do it, or at least arrange it? Franca's tall glistening machine, still intact and in charge in spite of her having become a running spark, inducted these new, obvious, problems with a certain satisfaction. Alison would have to deal with those matters, it was her task now. Alison's clothes were neatly folded upon the floor or on the backs of chairs. She had not, Franca found on opening it, ventured to hang anything inside the long wardrobe which stretched the length of the big bedroom. Working frantically and fast Franca dragged her clothes out of the wardrobe, carried them onto the landing and threw them down the stairs. In the space thus cleared next to Jack's, she hung up Alison's clothes. She then searched all the rooms where anything could be found which could count as *hers*. There were not many of these things: a few pictures, china, books, letters. The debris of Franca's unhappy childhood had been swept away long ago. She carried the 'things' down and put them in the boudoir, returning for the clothes which she had kicked aside which were still strewn upon the stairs. She did not visit the studio. The little 'writing room' had already been taken over by Alison, her typewriter on the table, her notebooks spread about. This operation took most of the morning. In the afternoon, with continued mouse-like haste, she sorted out the clothes and objects, some to be kept, some to be thrown away, some to be given away. So far as possible she *hid* things, in a cupboard, under her bed, in an old trunk under the stairs. She burnt letters and papers in the big stove. So, she had done it. But what for, to what end? A preparation for flight, for siege, a form of hunger-strike, a form of suicide?

On the following day, the day of their return (only they were not to be expected until the late evening) Franca, who was so used to being by herself, was unable to perform any ordinary activity. She wondered if she should prepare something for their supper. On the previous days they had been out to some meals, but she had also cooked for them. She supposed she had better invite Alison to cook, perhaps arrange a 'rota'. The details were appalling. The quietness of the house, to which she stood listening, was a new quietness with an alien tempo. She recalled with surprise the energy which had yesterday enabled her to race about the house. The little mouse which had run so fast and so far would now sit still in its corner. She saw the little mouse lying dead in its corner covered in dust. She made some coffee. Then washed up and tidied the kitchen. Then she decided to wash her hair, thinking she might derive some comfort from this familiar rite. She filled the basin in the downstairs bathroom and bowing her head plunged the heavy dark mass into the hot water. She washed and rinsed it, dried it with several towels, then with a final towel about her shoulders, spread it out to dry, separating and kneading the long snaky strands. She sat down on a chair in the hall beside the telephone. She thought, I must *do* something, I must *see to* myself. I'll ring up somebody. I'll ring up Ludens. She dialled his number.

'Hello.'

'Hello, Alfred, it's Franca.'

'Oh Franca – Franca –'

'Would you like to come over here for lunch? It's just me. Alison and Jack are away.'

'Yes, I know, they're in Amsterdam –'

'Well, would you like to? Or for tea or for a drink? They won't be back till this evening.'

'Franca, I *can't* – Oh dear – I promised Irina I'd go over and help her pack – I said I'd stay all day – they're leaving, you know –'

'Oh yes. For the country.'

'Franca, I'm *terribly* sorry, I wish I could.'

'Then how about tomorrow? I have to be out doing various things. I could drop in at your place about five or six. I don't want to interrupt your work.'

'Oh dear, oh dear, I *can't*, we're supposed to be leaving tomorrow, or the day after, if we can get everything ready, there's so much to do. I'm driving them down, and I'm going to stay a few days to help them settle in, I'll be staying at a pub –'

'At a pub. How nice.'

'Franca, darling, I want to see you very much, you know that, but –'

'Never mind, later on maybe. I hope everything goes well at the country cottage.' She put down the receiver abruptly and went into the kitchen.

Had something very nearly happened? Ludens had sounded so moved, so stirred by some emotion. Curiosity, pity . . . ? She sat down, spreading her damp hair and squeezing it in the ends of the towel, teasing it out between her fingers. She sat for a while, checking an anguish which made her want to sob.

Suddenly she heard the familiar sound of the key being turned in the front door.

Alison came in.

'Hello, you're back early.'

'Yes, we decided to take the early plane after all.'

'I hope you had a happy time, saw lots of pictures. You should have stayed longer.'

'Jack's gone to the gallery, he won't be home till the evening.'

'Oh.' Franca thought, he's sent her on ahead to fix things up, to have things out, to clarify things, to establish the regime, how things are to be from now on. What have they decided about me, I wonder?

'Would you like some coffee? You must be tired after your journey.'

'No, thanks. What a wonderful lot of hair you have, I've never seen it all down. You look like a sibyl or something.'

'A witch. Yes.' Though her hair was not quite dry Franca began to plait it very fast, letting a long thick plait materialise between her nimble hands, then tossing it over her shoulder and letting it hang down over the back of the chair. 'Did you have a nice flight?'

'Yes, yes.'

'Wouldn't you like something to eat? Good heavens, it's quite late!'

'I'd like a drink,' said Alison. 'No, I'll find it.'

Alison was wearing a dark green shift, rather short. Franca surveyed her long athletic bare legs and the smudge of the scar on her knee as she reached up to the high shelf of a cupboard. She returned with a sherry bottle and two glasses. Alison was bronzed by outdoor life, sunny walks and tennis. She and Jack had been swimming in the Thames near Twickenham. She poured the dark sherry into the glasses, and looked sternly at Franca.

Franca said, 'I'm so glad about your TV play, isn't that splendid. Are you pleased with it?'

'It's terrible.'

'Oh no! But you're writing another –'

'I wish I'd stayed a dancer.'

'You can always go back.'

'I can't go back. There's something so special about being a dancer. But I've lost it forever. Won't you drink?'

'I'll have a little, thanks.'

'You're so *temperate*.' Alison sounded very Scottish, very precise, very censorious, very Edinburgh, as she uttered the word. She drank half her own glass and filled it up.

Franca sipped hers. The strong sweetish sherry with its tawny smell shocked her, running suddenly like fire into her whole body, into her wits. It came with some reminder of youth, of the south.

'Oh Franca, Franca, Franca, what are we going to do?'

Franca decided that Alison had probably been drinking on the plane and was already a bit tipsy. She pushed her own glass away. 'We shall manage, I don't see any problem. I wish you'd let me cook something for you, what about an omelette?'

'Franca how can you *lie* about it! You're not a liar, you're truth itself. *Don't talk to me like that.*'

'Well, don't shout at me. If I could think of something useful to say I'd say it. I don't see anything we can talk about. Whatever it is we are doing, we are already doing it, and it seems to make sense. So why not just let things flow on. And please don't worry about *me*.'

'Of course I worry about you!'

'I'm sure you both wish me very well. I wish you very well. We understand each other. We have already mastered the situation. We can live at peace.'

'Don't talk that non-talk to me! And I'm not speaking for me and Jack, I'm speaking for myself. Don't you see that it's all – well, what is it? What are you going to do?'

'Nothing. Just go on quietly. I suggest you do too.'

'I can't make you out. Do you really feel placid and inert and dozy?'

'What a description! No, I don't think so. Now do tell me what you did in Amsterdam.'

'We fretted about you in Amsterdam.'

'That's thoroughly tiresome of you, I wish you'd stop. I'm perfectly all right, don't you see.'

'You aren't. You feel violent and secretive and full of misery and full of fury. How can you not feel that?'

'Very easily!'

'How can you tolerate me in this house?'

'Oh Alison, don't be such a *bore*! You have a completely wrong picture of me.'

'Well, tell me the true picture.'

'I go on quietly, there's no mystery and no problem, I'm a quiet peaceful person. Do stop being so intense.'

'You're lying again. I'd like to take you by the throat and bang your head against the wall.'

'That would be very unkind.'

'So you've stopped loving Jack?'

'No.'

'You must hate him by now.'

'No.'

'You must hate me.'

'I don't hate you, dear Alison.'

'I'm glad you say that. I love you. I think I love you as much as I love him.'

'Then that makes our *ménage* all the more convenient.'

'You're trying to confuse me, but I won't let you. There's something *definite* I want to say, but I can't get it out and you won't help me.'

'Perhaps it *is* possible,' said Franca aloud, talking to herself. She drank some more of the sherry. Listening to Alison she did, perhaps for a second only, see it as conceivable.

'You mean *it*? Jack is very very determined.'

'Oh yes, he's explained it all to me.'

'He thinks he can just *impose* it. He's like a dictator who's just come to power and does all the awful violent things at once, like changing the laws and murdering people and confiscating everything – then later on it'll all be taken for granted and he can play at being kind and good.'

'What an interesting picture.'

'But just. Isn't it? Have some more sherry.' She filled up Franca's glass and her own.

'Alison, my dear, don't *bother* me so.'

'I will, I will. I care. I can't see this happen to you.'

'You are seeing it.'

'So you admit it's like that?'

'Like what? Don't simplify everything. It's complicated, it's infinitely complicated, we can't analyse it, it's *happened*. Let's just be calm and decent —'

'You think it's something mystical that we have to undergo, I don't! Franca darling, we've got to *think*.'

'No, no, not think, please.' Franca considered saying: if you don't like it why don't you clear off! She decided not to. She felt an affection for Alison, even a kind of relief in the ridiculous conversation.

'Sometimes I hate men.'

'Come, come, Alison.'

'Don't "come, come" me. I hate bullying mannish men. I like gentle men like Ludens and Gildas and Pat —'

'That's nonsense. You love Jack, you love him very much indeed. If you didn't you wouldn't accept his arrangement. In fact it's a perfectly possible arrangement, I think I agree with him, others have managed it, why not us. So he and I are happy. It just remains for you to be happy too. Of course I understand it's most difficult for you, you're struggling with your Scottish Protestant conscience. You're talking to it at this very moment, you're talking it out, you're talking it down, and you want my help. You want me to be angry, which I can't be, and then to be soothing, which I can be. Alison, just *see*, that if you stop worrying all will be well.'

'You're being too clever. *You're* making it too simple now. You *can't* feel benevolent and sympathetic, you *can't* just want everything to be nice, as if Jack were a child, and as if I were a child. Or is that what you *do* feel?'

'Look, at this very moment, by speaking openly like this, we are both doing the very best we can to make it work. Isn't that what you want? Isn't it what we all want?'

'Franca, don't *torment* me!'

'Really!'

'It's the *details*, Franca, it's the *details*. Jack has got some great general idea. I had it too. I *had* to have it. The alternative was leaving him.'

'Not to be thought of, I agree.'

'Don't mock me. I've never loved anyone as I've loved Jack. And no one has ever loved me as he loves me.'

'I'm not mocking, I know. And this great love makes you both *ruthless*. This is simply natural, it's a *fact*, you both *know* that whatever happens, even if God and the Devil were to stand in the way, you will have what you want. *This* is what, out of consideration for me, you are now surrounding with talk about whether and how and why. But let us regard that stage as over, there was a gesture to be made, and you have made it, and I am grateful! I can live with the arrangement, I can live with the general idea, and the details will sort themselves out perfectly well. They will because they must, they've got to. We are all under necessity. Let us be happy with it.'

After a pause Alison said, 'Do you think it will pass and you'll pick up the pieces?'

'No.'

'Are you going to leave us?'

'No! Unless you want me to go, which I think you don't.'

'You are *essential*.'

'Precisely. You'd be miserable without me! I expect, now, I'd be miserable without you, both. So here we are, that's what it's like, and *that's* the deepest we can go and the clearest we can get. So *now* will you stop worrying?'

'I don't know whether to believe you. Why should necessity sort things out? Necessity breaks things. We haven't got *close* to the matter yet, we aren't really working at it.'

'I think we are. When we've come this far, when we've achieved *all this*, including our present conversation, we can take the rest in our stride. By the way, I've brought all my clothes downstairs, and I've hung yours up in the cupboard in the bedroom. I hope you don't mind.'

'But there's nowhere down here to hang clothes.'

'Alison, darling, you are priceless, you illustrate my point! Do you think *that* matters, when we've waded through blood?'

'What I said was stupid. So you admit the blood?'

'Never at all, as Pat would say! It's just an idle metaphor. Of course there are little things to get clear, but they're easy, they're child's play. For instance, you know I don't have regular help, I've usually cleaned the house myself, well now I'm not going to clean upstairs except the drawing room, so you must do it yourself or else employ someone. Isn't that detailed enough and isn't it, when we come to it, as we *have* come to it, a small matter?'

Franca drank some more sherry. The bottle, once full, was now more than half empty.

Alison looked puzzled. She frowned, gazing down at the table, she even bared her teeth. 'You are deceiving me, Franca, and I beg you not to.'

'I am being realistic, I want the best for all of us.'

'You are so calm and wise, you are an angel. For the other two, it's each for self.'

'I think you are both being very considerate.'

'Oh, *Franca*!'

'Alison, you must set your life in order, and that will set *ours* in order. You must settle down here and get on with your *work*. I saw you had put your things in the writing-room. Do type, by the way, it won't disturb me and Jack won't hear it in the studio. So Jack will be working upstairs at his painting and you will be writing plays –'

'And you? What will you be doing?'

'What I have always been doing. Just *being*. I'm good at that. Not everyone can do it. Look, I'll even clean the upstairs rooms after all if you want me to! You see how far we've come!'

'How far *you've* come! Oh, my dear –' Alison suddenly reached out a long brown arm. Franca flinched. Alison had seized hold of Franca's long plait of dark hair and drawn it out from behind the chair. She began to unplait the end of it, moving her own chair closer. Franca watched. 'Franca, you are so beautiful, like an Indian.'

'A squaw?'

'No, an Indian Indian. You'd look lovely in a sari.'

'I'm not slim enough. *You'd* look lovely in a sari.'

'I'm not dark enough.'

'No saris then.'

'I love your hair. What wonderful stuff. It's so dark, yet it's so full of colours, and it's so cool. Can you sit on it?'

'Just.'

'That's wonderful.' Alison stroked the unravelled ends of the hair.

'You have beautiful hair,' said Franca. 'I've never seen such *brilliant* hair, and it will never turn grey.' She touched the red curls lightly with her fingertips.

'Franca, let's run away together.'

'Yes, let's! You mean frighten Jack and then come back again?'

'No, I mean go away and not come back.'

'Go where to?'

'To Heather's house in France. She's often away, she wants me to go and live in it. We could go there.'

'Excellent idea. You are drunk, my child. So am I.'

'*In vino veritas*. Franca, I love you. Let's forget about men.' Jerking her chair further forward Alison put her arms round Franca's neck.

At that moment there sounded the unmistakable click of the key turning in the front door. Alison sat back, shifting hastily away.

Patrick Fenman came in.

'Patrick, dear,' said Franca, 'Alison and I have decided to run away together.'

'Isn't that great?' said Patrick, drawing up another chair and sitting down. 'Can I come with you? Let's go to Ireland.'

'We thought of going to France.'

'I'll come. Except I can't, because I have to follow Marcus and where he is I will be. You could come there too. We could all live together nearby in different cottages and be dear friends.'

'That would be lovely,' said Alison.

'Franca, girl, forgive me for walking in, I had the key, remember, from when you gave it to me when I was staying here when I was getting better. I'll give it back now if you will, here it is.'

'No, no, keep it, dear Pat. We're an open community in this house now and we'd like you to be a member, wouldn't we, Alison. I expect you'd like a drink, oh of course not, you've given up.'

'I have not. I've started again a bit, I'm sorry to say.'

'Then I expect you'd like your usual Irish whiskey, it's still in the cupboard there.'

Franca set out a jug of water and a tumbler, while Pat found the whiskey. Before he sat down he kissed the two women, first on the cheek, then on the lips. 'Here's to friendship. I will tell you – I feel happy. Let us live near together and be kind to each other and love each other. I'm a risen man, risen into a knowledge of God's peace. Will I read you a poem about that that I've written now?'

The front door bell rang. Alison ran out and came back with Gildas.

Gildas, thinner than ever, stood a moment, wrinkling up his face and holding up his drooping hands in a way which Jack called his insect pose. Though it was a warm day, he was wearing his old faded high-necked sweater with a frayed shirt collar showing. He was evidently dismayed by what he saw. Franca thought, he came to see *me*, he thought I'd be alone! She went forward and took his hand. 'Gildas, come and have a drink. We are all friends here.'

'So I should have imagined,' said Gildas, gently withdrawing his hand, 'it's hardly news. I see Pat is drinking, ought he to be?'

'He is going to read a poem,' said Alison.

'Not if I can stop him,' said Gildas. 'All right, Franca, I'll have some whiskey too. What's the matter with you all? You have flames on your heads. Is it Pentecost or something?'

'Yes, it's the gift of tongues. Sit down, man. The girls were telling me –'

Alison and Franca spoke simultaneously.

Jack had entered unobserved. Alison gave a muted scream.

Framed in the doorway Jack stood as a figure of authority, a heroic figure, it was like the return of Odysseus, as Franca said later to Ludens. She had always thought of Jack as a Greek hero, indeed as that particular hero. He brushed his blond hair back from his cheek with a swift gesture, leaving the hand poised on his shoulder as if touching some invisible insignia. Frowning, he surveyed the scene with his prominent blue eyes. How did he know at once that we were guilty, she wondered later, that we were, all of us, conspirators?

'What are you all up to? Why are you letting Patrick drink that whiskey? Franca, you're drinking too, I think you're drunk. You should be ashamed of yourself!'

Franca and Alison burst into wild helpless laughter.

'I want to show you a picture,' said Ludens, 'a drawing.' He put a piece of paper into Irina's hand. 'Now, what is it?'

'It's a bicycle,' she said.

'Yes.'

'So what?'

'Leonardo drew it. Or one of his students did. I copied it for you out of a book.'

'Oh really? So –?'

'So Leonardo invented the bicycle! Or conceived of it anyway.'

'You told me that before. Why do you show me this picture?'

'I thought it might interest you. I think of you as a bicyclist!'

'Well, I suggest you stop doing so. My bicycling days are over. I never want to see a bicycle again, even in a picture.' She handed back the drawing.

Ludens folded it and put it in his pocket. 'I'm sorry.'

'Oh never mind. Shit, hell. Dad's shirts won't be dry in time, they're still dripping into the bath.'

'We can come back for anything that's left behind. We can't take everything in one journey, anyway.'

'I'll never set foot in this bloody flat again.'

'Then *I'll* come back. Don't *worry*, Irina. You're sure you don't want to take anything from the kitchen? That red saucepan, for instance.'

'No, there's kitchen stuff at the cottage.'

'We can buy food on the way down.'

'There'll be food there.'

'Oh – how?'

'The people next door will put it in.'

'That's kind of them. You don't mind if we leave early tomorrow morning? I don't know how long it'll take to get there.'

'All right, all right.'

'And if there's anything you want from Red Cottage I could fetch that too later on.'

'Fuck Red Cottage. I had years of hell there.'

'Oh, how long –? I thought you said a year –'

'Years. I can't remember, it was so awful it seemed a lifetime, why do you endlessly *bother* me, why do you *carp* so?'

'Irina, I'm trying to help!'

'I know. You've been so good, you've worked so hard, I don't know what I'd have done without you, etcetera, etcetera, it's just that sometimes you *exasperate* me!'

'Well, sometimes you exasperate me!'

'I know. I'm awful, I'm dreadful, I'm a drab, a slut, a bitch, a rotten apple, a slug, a black beetle, a beggar maid –'

'Beggar maids wed princes in stories.'

'Yes, in stories! Never mention that again or I'll kill you.'

'Never mention what?'

'*That*! You're *hopeless*. You have no *feeling*, no *sensibility* – Sorry, Ludens, don't hate me.'

'Don't be silly, I don't hate you, I love you.'

The 'packing up' at the flat at Victoria had taken longer than expected, and the departure to the country had been twice postponed. Ludens had been busy helping Irina, what to take, what to buy, how to pack. He had been out shopping to buy suitcases, coat-hangers, stamps, aspirins, tights, umbrellas, electric torches, hot-water bottles. He had bought underwear for Marcus. He had written to house agents about putting the flat on the market. The packing, even with the new suitcases, presented numerous problems. Irina was insistent that there must be only one journey and that everything must fit, with the three travellers, into Ludens's car. Of course Ludens might come back to fetch things. He was also resolved to clear the flat which was now (also to be arranged by Ludens) to be sold. Ludens had, as he had told Franca, booked himself into a local pub, whose existence he had discovered by telephoning the village post office, and was quietly determined to remain there indefinitely. During this chaotic period Marcus stayed in his room and was little seen. Ludens had, however, come closer to Irina. He had, he realised, wanted this closeness. It was not exactly that he had pressed and she had invited. They had simply simultaneously discovered a relaxed and cheerful *modus vivendi* together. They got on well. Ludens had never got on so easily with a woman, not even with Sylvia, who had always been 'playing the feminine'. Ludens and Irina jostled each other, shouted at each other, chattered to each other, argued a lot, laughed a lot. Irina decorated her conversation with the swear words to which he had become more used. (Who had taught her these words? She had surely not learnt them at her boarding-school, whose high-minded staff and prissy pupils she had described to him, and whose old-fashioned upper-classy slang she sometimes employed. He concluded that she must have been reading modern novels.) During this time they had also become accustomed to a pattern of corporeal proximity, nothing like horseplay of course, or holding hands, or significant touching, but just an ordinary sort of being close together like two friendly animals in a stall. During this time too Ludens had been conscious of an unusual sensation. He was happy. He felt needed, he felt secure. He was on good terms with Marcus, content to know both that they would talk again, and that it was impossible to do so at the moment. And Irina, although her speech remained ironic, scolding, teasing, her eyes gave him a welcome which stirred his heart. And more than his heart was stirred. Ludens had not forgotten Marcus's words concerning himself and Irina. He had, however, and deliberately, put these words away as if in a cupboard. They were not yet for everyday perusal.

Ludens had found space and time, amid his new sensations, to feel very sorry that he had not gone to see Franca when she had, so unusually, as he realised just afterwards, invited him. She had even suggested coming to his flat. It had indeed been, as it happened, impossible for him to see her at the times she suggested. But he felt not only a sort of guilt, but a special remorseful intimate pain, to think that he had failed Franca when she appealed to him. This was something which, for his peace of mind, had to be repaired. So, on the previous day, before coming to Victoria, he had called unannounced at the house in Chelsea, hoping to find Franca breakfasting alone. His fastidious imagination shied away from the details of Jack's new *ménage*. He came by taxi (parking his car was always difficult in either place), arrived later than he intended, and was let in by Alison who had been crying. Jack was in his studio, and the two women had been in the drawing room watching a video-recording of Alison's play about the ballet school. Franca explained that Alison had been quite overcome by seeing the familiar school scene and the dancers, some of whom were professionals whom she knew. 'I wish I hadn't given up,' Alison was saying, 'it was just lack of courage.' The women, though rather nervy, seemed in good spirits. As Ludens felt that Franca, who avoided his glance, was unlikely to contrive to talk to him alone, he soon took his leave. Alison accompanied him to the door, where they paused. In that moment Ludens felt sure that they were both remembering the scene beside the lake when Alison had been upset because Jack forced Ludens to behold him naked in her presence. Ludens thought, she's a puritan; and he felt a sympathy with her and would have tarried, as he sensed that she wanted to talk to him. But it was not a good moment, and they parted awkwardly.

Ludens was glad he had been to see Franca and felt sure, as he sat in another taxi bound for Victoria, that she had understood why, and in what frame of mind, he had come. He also felt that Alison had, somehow, understood him, as he had, in some way, understood her. He had, as he returned to looking forward to being with Irina and Marcus, an obscure sense of his life being 'in order', as if deep sources were working benignly on his side. This was a feeling he sometimes had, when he pictured his friends as 'stationed', like auspicious stars, close to him, protecting him, and offering him the privilege and pleasure of performing, in their respect, good deeds. He was sure, at that moment, that he was harming no one, and indeed helping some. Prone to guilt, however, he did wish that he had managed to see Gildas. He often felt in the wrong before Gildas. Something in Gildas accused him. Perhaps it was just that Gildas was closest, he understood most, and although their friendship was impregnable, they could still hurt each other. Something else which was working in Ludens's mind also mani-fested itself before he reached the flat, constituting a darker and more puzzling ingredient in his feeling of reassurance. He was Jewish. Well, he had always known that. If it now came to him in a new way it was no doubt simply an aspect of his belongingness with Marcus and Irina. Yet was this simple? What did Jews do? They observed holy days and rules of diet and put on black hats and went to the Synagogue. Ludens felt no inclination to do these things. They studied the scriptures and meditated upon the history of the Jews and their place in history. Ludens was a historian, but certainly did not regard himself as a Jewish historian. Jews believed in God. Ludens did not believe in any personal God, least of all in the unattractive authoritarian figure of Jehovah. Jews prayed and believed in something sacred and holy. Well. Gildas believed in something sacred and holy, and Ludens felt sure that Gildas prayed, whatever prayer was. Of course, Gildas was a Christian, and Christianity, with its proliferation of images and chatter, made Ludens shudder. Ludens had been disturbed by the strange conversation which he had lately had with Marcus, by Marcus's emotion, and by his own. He had not yet, even, been able to make out how, if at all, Marcus's sudden Judaic piety connected with his original 'quest'. Perhaps it was something which he had discovered *within* the quest. Or perhaps it was merely an accident that Marcus had picked up those utterances of his ancestors. Jews were always prone to irrational guilt; and perhaps especially now. If the Jewish destiny, and the message thereof, concerned suffering, then it must be the duty of every comfortable Jew to fix up some for himself. About the Holocaust, Ludens had prided himself on keeping, as a historian, a cool head. Of course it was the unspeakable thing that it was, about which so many details were now known, about which words failed. Of course it made Jews feel more Jewish. It made Ludens feel more Jewish. But he did not think of it as a cosmic event which must somehow change the whole of human thought, altering philosophy and theology and closing the mouths of poets; such a view seemed to him *superstitious*, a denial of ordinary scholarship and ordinary hard-thinking rationality. Perhaps indeed *it* did, as one thing among others, possibly the most extreme, stir up dramatic reflections about a God which is no god but a significant emptiness full of pain, and so on. But these, he thought, are just pictures out of Jewish religious meditation, recurring under a new impetus, images and ideas also employed by Christian theologians and mystics. Of course they deserve reflection, even a special respect; but they are not more fundamental than the chaos of history and the very various ordinary tasks of truthful thinking. He thought, I must keep Marcus away from this high-temperature religiosity, it will waste his time. As he thought this he felt in his heart a voiceless nameless twinge, like a tiny spark, which he chose to identify as a signal, which very rarely came through, from his ancestors who had lived in the Jewish ghetto in Warsaw.

The words 'I love you' just uttered by Ludens to Irina, had not come to his lips entirely by accident. He had for some time, in the instinctive darkness of his mind in which so many heterogeneous problems were circulating, been wondering how, in what undramatic, as it were casual, not yet significant context he might utter them. He was aware that what exactly the words meant was in a curious way less urgently important than the necessity of uttering them. Now, it had come about. Ludens had, as it seemed to him with helpless fascination, seen, in the last days, perhaps more obscurely weeks, his feelings about Irina undergo a transformation. He recalled with amazement, as if it were years ago, his first shocked vision of the adult Irina, the shaggy, sullen, unkempt 'gipsy' girl standing at the door of Red Cottage who had not spoken to him, and whom he had even conjectured to be mentally defective. Yet had he not had signs enough? In fact Irina at the cottage door had not been his first sighting. He had first of all, as if in some extraordinary dream, after struggling through the dark tunnel, seen her in bed, seen her dark bright eyes, reflecting the candlelight, gazing calmly at him; and he had imagined her to be a child, a boy. The memory of that puzzling experience still disturbed and excited him. And then there were her bare feet in the stream and the tadpoles round her ankles, the cherry blossoms which she had thrown in his face, and above all the walk upon the airfield: there was magic *there* all right. But of course how much better he knew her now, and how changed she looked with her smart dresses and her well-cut hair. Yet all her looks, even the boy, seemed still to be summarised in her present being; even their very first meeting and the dreadful scene at the fence were somehow gathered in, redeemed and graced, as if reflected in the golden eyes of the ram. Irina's intense slightly squinting gaze, the way her eyes seemed to splinter sometimes and crackle with light, her cat-like face, the dark down upon her upper lip, the way she wrung her hands, all blended now into a single presence. Her dark straight hair glowing with its few reddish strands had been thinned and cut shorter in layers to show the shape of her head. She had lost weight, she looked happier. She had, since the resolve to leave London, become happier. Even at home she put on smarter clothes. She was wearing, under a shiny green apron, a simple dark-brown cotton dress with an amber necklace. Bond Street shoes showed off her small feet. Ludens, surveying her earlier, had been ready to laugh with pleasure. Now suddenly his deeper feelings demanded expression.

Irina however had not picked up the seriousness of his last words. Perhaps she had scarcely heard them, or had taken them as a mere mechanical rejoinder to her own 'Don't hate me'. She went on to speak of something else. 'Ludens, please don't mind my saying this, I think you shouldn't get too involved with Dad's theories. I can't help feeling you regard them as something awfully deep, like sort of magical formulae. You ought to relax a bit, that would be better for both of you. He's supposed to have high blood pressure and shouldn't get too excited. I heard you both the other day raising your voices, I think you stir him up and lead him on. If you see something in what he's after, it must be something that you provide yourself. Really what he says is completely muddled, it just doesn't make sense.'

'Who says so?'

'I do. He's talked to me about all that stuff too. I may not be an intellectual but I'm not a fool. You are encouraging him, you're making him feel he's a great man with a message and it's do or die. Whereas really he's a helpless solitary person with a thoroughly confused mind. He imagines he's thinking when he just sits in his room and dreams and mumbles. He *was* a genius, well, I suppose he was –'

'Of course he was!'

'How do you know, you don't know mathematics, do you?'

'Irina!'

'All right, he was a genius, but he certainly isn't now. You're doing him harm, making him think he's so wonderful.'

'I think I am a better judge than you are,' said Ludens. 'You simply don't understand him, there's no reason why you should. But listen, you evidently didn't hear me say something important. I love you.'

'What?'

'I love you, I love you. I'm in love with you.' The third clearer formulation came to Ludens spontaneously. He did not move closer to her. They were standing in the kitchen, she near the stove, he near the door. A slant of sunlight upon the wall opposite reflected a subdued brightness into the room.

Irina, who had been holding in her hand the red saucepan earlier referred to by Ludens, put it down and said, 'Oh.'

'I'm sorry if I startle you.'

'You don't.'

'You mean you expected it?'

'No.'

Ludens smiled a little uneasily. 'Well, I love you. There it is. But please don't worry about it.'

'I won't.'

'Good. There's no need for you to do anything about it. Now or ever.'

They stood facing each other, their hands hanging down, separated by a space of several feet. Irina's face, which had been stiff, stony, suddenly gleamed, her eyes narrowed, splintered and glittered, then opened wide, her mouth relaxed. She looked down at the floor and made the slightest movement with one hand. Ludens instantly knelt down, first gracefully on one knee, then less gracefully on two, his head thrown back. After a moment Irina covered her face. Ludens rose slowly. Then for another moment they looked at each other.

Someone was ringing the door bell of the flat. She darted away past him. Ludens followed. She opened the door to reveal the dark shabby landing, the lift, and Patrick Fenman.

'Oh, Pat, dear!'

Patrick grinned, entered, kissed Irina on the cheek and ruffled her hair. 'How's himself?'

'He's resting.'

'So, well, I shall see him tomorrow evening.'

'He won't be here,' said Ludens.

'I know, I know. I'm coming too.'

'To – to the cottage?'

'Where else – where he goes I go. I'm his jester. Isn't it, Irina? There'll be a little hole for poor Pat to crawl into, will there not?'

'Yes, yes,' she said smiling, half laughing at him.

'And we'll sing there too, won't we? Have you heard her sing? She sings like an angel. Now could you just do me a cup of tea, Irina dear?' He followed her into the kitchen.

Ludens stood appalled. So Patrick was evidently familiarly at home in the scene where he trod reverently as if on holy ground. Where he had timidly knocked, Pat had climbed in. It was for Pat that she had put on that dress, those smart shoes. He had kissed her. Perhaps since she came to London many men had kissed her. She had called herself a drab. Did she know the meaning of the word? Marcus had said she was a 'wild thing' who needed to be 'looked after'. What had that meant? He had said she was a virgin. She had indicated she was not. What, who? Ideas which had already been darkly germinating in Ludens's overcrowded mind came vividly into view. What about the gamekeeper, Busby? She had seemed frightened of him. He had seemed something like her gaoler. Was it perhaps he who had taught her all those words? Or – and this more horrible idea had been very obscurely with him for some time – how had he dared to entertain it? – perhaps Marcus – Marcus had spoken of evil yearnings, of a crime, perhaps committed already, perhaps in a dream – No, that was unthinkable, impossible. Yet might there not have been some confused episode, something which, when Irina was much younger, had distressed her, appalled them both, something which neither of them in their childishness – for here Ludens saw Marcus as a child – had really understood?

These dreadful ideas, horrors from the past now poised to darken the future, occurred to Ludens in a sudden timeless flash as he stood by the still open door of the flat, hearing Irina talking to Patrick in the kitchen. And he thought, I mustn't have these thoughts, I have no status here, I haven't even got the right to be jealous! Anyway, what is it all about, Pat is my friend, when others had given up I strove desperately to save his life and I succeeded. But it does seem so horrible to me that he will be, with them, near them, at the cottage. So, she had sung for Patrick, but not for him. How poisoned all my thoughts suddenly are, thought Ludens. And I felt happy, and I spoke to her of love.

He stepped out onto the landing. He called 'Goodbye, see you tomorrow,' and closed the door behind him and went to the lift and pressed the button.

In a moment he heard the door of the flat open again and Irina was close beside him. She put her hands onto his arms, gripping the stuff of his jacket, then leaned her head quickly forward onto his shoulder. Ludens stood rigid, not attempting to hold her. She murmured, 'Thank you.'

The lift arrived and opened its brightly lit doors. Ludens stepped in and the doors closed, dividing them.

PART FOUR

'You said there's a garden?' said Ludens.

'Yes, a small one.'

'Is there a tree in it?'

'There are trees round it.'

'And other people's gardens?'

'No, just the trees.'

'But it's not outside the village?'

'No, just on the edge.'

'And you say it's furnished?'

'Yes, you'll see, you'll see. And your pub is nice, it's beside the little river.'

They spoke quietly. Marcus in the back of the car, half buried in suitcases, seemed to be asleep. They had made an early start.

Ludens had recovered his spirits. Irina's 'Thank you' had dispelled the clouds of jealousy and suspicion which had so suddenly engulfed him. He felt humbler and more stoical, and so happier. Some of his darker conjectures he now saw as ridiculous. He was glad he had said his 'I love you', content to be uncertain about what it meant and what it would lead to. After that racing start he was glad to find himself in a bright warm interim. He could even feel how touchingly funny it was that Irina had wanted to get her revenge by having *him*, this time, on his knees! The gesture and its reference had been unmistakable. The ritual, with its implication of penitence and forgiveness, made a bond. Also the way they had then, defencelessly, fearlessly, looked at each other. For the present, perhaps a long present, his love was prepared to feed upon silence, upon abstinence and self-discovery, upon a discipline of restraint, as upon nectar. He felt the responsibility which had been put upon him by Marcus, and now tacitly by Irina herself. She was not just a wild creature, she was a wounded creature. He did not know what the wound was, but he had become, as he watched her more closely, increasingly aware of it. She was also of course a free creature, and Ludens knew that his feelings, and his commitment, might well occasion more pain than joy. Now however, sitting close beside her in the front of the car, he felt, together with not unpleasant physical tensions, a sense of hope and joy, even a particular sense of possession. He was carrying her and Marcus away into a new life in which he would share and in which their mutual concerns for each other must inevitably draw them closer together.

They had left London behind. The car was heading south-west. Following a pleasanter quieter route chosen by Ludens, they had left the motorway. The sun shone from a very blue sky in which ahead of them, low down over low green hills, lines of small soft very white clouds were lounging. Ludens thought, we are children going on holiday together, we are good children! Irina was wearing the simple brown cotton dress of the previous day, now with a necklace of brown wooden beads which she had bought in an Indian shop. Ludens had hinted to her that he liked her simpler dresses. (Misled, in his opinion, by Alison and Franca, Irina had made a number of serious mistakes.) She had tucked up her dress and stretched out her shapely brown legs. Responding to the movements of the car her soft thigh sometimes touched his thigh. In low voices they talked continuously, glancing at each other. Once, when arguing a point, she placed her hand firmly upon his on the wheel. He breathed the fresh smell of her new cotton dress: her liveness, her youth, the grace of her slim entire body, her new pleasure in herself which he had had some part in bringing about. He thought, if we were now alone together . . . at least we could *sing*! He smiled, almost laughed, but checked himself; there was so much to be grave about. Irina had made a bold decision and had made it alone. How would it be? Would Marcus settle down? Would the neighbours be friendly? Would there be a good shop nearby? Would Irina be capable of employing somebody to clean? Would Benbow Cottage become a messy shambles like Red Cottage? It won't, he thought, because *I'll* be there. It would be family life. The people he loved were going to be dependent on him! He thought, if they settle down here I'll try to get a job at the University of Southampton. He did not however reveal these remoter speculations to Irina. Their conversation, in so far as it concerned the cottage, had been light and chatty, also including the casual, aimless, almost senseless observations made by happy travellers, such as: What a pretty village. What a silly name. What's that tree? That's an odd number plate. Humpy bridge ahead. Look, goats. There's a nice dog. Mind that police car. Isn't that the spire of Salisbury Cathedral? Would you like a peppermint?

As time passed however, and although they were not yet very near to their destination, Irina's hands came nervously together, seeking each other in mutual reassurance, and they fell silent for a while, awed by the prospect of arriving.

Irina said at last, 'Do you remember the poor pheasant?'

'Yes.' He recalled the crash as the heavy body battered itself on the windscreen, and the storm of feathers, and the blood. When he had, on that day, returned to the car after parking it outside the flat he had found a suspicious policeman inspecting the blood-stained glass. Ludens, who had promptly cleaned the glass, made a joke about this later to Jack. He did not want to remember the pheasant, or Irina's tears. He hoped she would not start to cry now. Marcus's usual nervous humming became audible and Ludens said in a louder voice, 'Not long now!' At that moment, in a sudden flash, as if he had been there, he saw overcrowded cattle trucks packed with terrified Jews trying to comfort each other as the train slowed down and entered the station.

Irina was now directing him, peering at a small local map which she had been given. 'Left here. There's the church tower over the trees. We have to go through the village. Now it's straight on and over the bridge. Look, there's your pub.'

'Yes, the Black Lion!' said Ludens.

'You don't want to stop and unload your stuff?'

'No, not now.'

They passed over the bridge, glimpsing under the shade of arching trees the mirror-clear water of the little river.

Ludens had made his arrangements with the pub by telephone. He was pleased with what he had seen of the wide village street with its square stone-built houses, and the pub, dating from an even earlier century, set in a green garden beside the river.

He drove slowly now along a narrow lane with high hedges, and widened passing places at intervals. The hedges were blotched with flowers of glittering white hawthorn. Beyond five-barred gates the green meadows were peopled by black and white cows. Ludens imagined the pleasant walk from the Black Lion to the cottage.

'Turn here,' said Irina, 'it's just here.'

Ludens turned abruptly between open gates. A large notice of some kind flashed for a moment. The tarmac road continued now between well-kept grass verges and intermittent flowerbeds. A bungalow appeared, recessed from the road. Ludens noticed its name written up: Collingwood.

'Go on,' he heard Irina's voice, 'go slowly.'

The tarmac curved, then divided. 'Left turn here. Slow, slow. That's it. Now turn in onto the gravel.'

Ludens turned the car onto the square of gravel and stopped the engine.

Beyond a smooth unfenced lawn was a small neat bungalow like the one which they had already passed. A white notice said: Benbow. A semi-circle of tall woodland trees framed the house.

Ludens had got out and was standing on the gravel. He said, 'What is this place? Is it some sort of condominium? All this looks like a *park*.'

But Irina had already leapt from the car, helped Marcus out, and was talking to him and leading him towards the house. There were steps up to a small verandah and glass doors, but below upon the lawn, near to the steps was a wooden seat of pale weather-beaten wood, an old seat. Irina had led Marcus to the seat and he sat down.

As Irina turned back towards him Ludens saw three men advancing along the tarmac towards the car. Two of them wore white coats. The third one looked familiar. Ludens recognised him as Dr Hensman. Then he understood. He turned to Irina, whose face was already scarlet. 'You *traitor*! You vile faithless liar!'

Ludens had removed himself well away to the side of the lawn and was standing in the shade under the trees watching and listening and trying to control the anger and misery and *fear* which was now choking him.

Irina had run forward to the trio and had led them back to where her father was sitting. As they neared him Marcus rose to his feet.

Irina said, speaking to one of the men in white, 'Doctor, how kind of you to come and meet us, you've arrived just at the right time.'

'Your arrival was signalled from the gate,' the man addressed replied, bowing to Irina and then to Marcus.

Irina went on, 'This is my father, Professor Vallar. And this,' she said, turning to Marcus, 'is Doctor –' (Ludens could not catch the name). 'And of course you know Doctor Hensman.'

Marcus bowed silently. The man in white introduced his colleague. Dr Hensman said something obliging to Marcus. Ludens turned away and walked for some distance among the trees. He leaned against a beech tree and laid his brow upon the cool smooth grey friendly bark and moved his head to and fro as if he were an animal trying to rid itself of some wounding substance. Desisting from this he became aware that he had almost entered the garden or 'precinct' of another similar villa, this one called 'Rodney'. He retired hastily. He considered unloading *their* baggage from the car and driving back to London. But this idea was absurd. He must stay with Marcus and *protect* him; and for this task he must be intelligent and rational and calm.

He walked back through the trees to Benbow. There was no one on the lawn, but voices came from the open glass doors on the verandah. Ludens crossed the grass and mounted the steps. He entered the room which seemed dark for a moment after the sunshine outside. There was a silence. Then he was addressed by the man in white who had been greeted by Irina.

'Let me introduce myself. My name is Marzillian. I am the head, or I may say the chief, in this vicinity. This is my colleague, or as I may call him my "sidekick", Dr Bland. Dr Hensman I believe you know. And you I think are Mr, or should I say Dr, Ludens? Dear me, what a collection of doctors we have here all of a sudden.'

Dr Marzillian was tall with a dark complexion, very dark hair, eyes which in the subdued light looked black, and a neat rather histrionic moustache which outlined his mouth and drooped below it to points on either side. He spoke quietly, gently, with a slight foreign accent. He wore over black trousers and, just evident at the cuffs, black jacket, a white coat longer than the jacket and buttoning up to a high round collar which clasped his neck closely and over which the ends of his straightish somewhat oily hair neatly rolled. The elegant many-buttoned uniform made him look like an Indian, which he certainly was not. The 'sidekick', Dr Bland, wore a less elegant, crudely starched, white coat with ordinary lapels, revealing his sober shirt and tie. His head and face were round, his hair blond-grey, his lips red, his eyes enlarged and hidden by round spectacles.

The group opened to include Ludens, Irina stepping back a little. Marcus, slightly apart, in an old pale-brown linen jacket and open-necked shirt, looked casual and out of place, as if present by accident, looking, with his head of short curly red-gold hair, bleached by the sun, so young, Ludens thought; yet just now he had been *treated like an old man*, led to a seat and made to sit down. He seemed calm, abstracted, looking out at the garden as if mildly curious. Ludens hoped that he would not start humming again. Irina, who had put on a smart blue summer jacket over her dress, her mouth slightly open, her hand ruffling her hair, looked like someone in a play, the heroine of course, who was just about to burst into some wild activity, like Cassandra before her first scream. She glared at Ludens, squinting at him with her dark eyes.

Ludens, in the second before he spoke, seeing the simpering face of Dr Hensman who was scratching in his ruff of hair, felt a shock wave of fear and anguish. Marcus was among enemies, lesser men who would *never know* . . . In that second Marcus suddenly looked at Ludens, a momentary stern even fierce look which vanished in a flash. Ludens thought, he's warning me not to make a fool of myself. But I *will* make a fool of myself. Anyway he's alert, he's aware.

He had hoped to control his voice, but it trembled nevertheless. He said to Dr Marzillian, 'This place is some sort of institution, is it?'

Dr Marzillian, gazing at Ludens with his clever eyes, and smiling slightly, said, 'The word "institution" sounds rather grim. This is a place of healing, if one might put it so, a retreat house. Every sort of care is available, we tend the body and the soul. There is a peaceful atmosphere and, as you see, beautiful surroundings. It would take time to describe all our functions in detail. I will ask my secretary to give you a brochure. But may I ask if you are a relation, a friend perhaps –'

'Mr Ludens kindly drove us from London,' said Irina. Her thin mouth had grown thinner, her cat-eyes narrower.

Ludens, who thought, So now I'm the chauffeur! was about to speak – he did not know what he was going to say, but words were crowding forward – when Marcus said, in his slow grating voice, 'Dr Ludens is a scholar, he is my friend and pupil. He sometimes helps me with my work.' Here Marcus shot another glance at Ludens, a bracing glance, with even a hint of humour in it.

Ludens was grateful for the word 'pupil' which not only explained him but gave him a certain status.

Dr Bland uttered, 'Wouldn't they like to see round the place?' Ludens, who found he had been assuming for some reason that Dr Bland was Scandinavian, was surprised to hear him speak in a North of Ireland accent.

'Thank you, Terence,' said Dr Marzillian, 'always the voice of common sense. Forgive me, Professor, you must be tired after your journey. Let me show you the rooms, then you and your daughter can be left in peace till luncheon. By the way, the villas don't have ordinary telephones, just one, which connects you with the main house, for use in emergency only, that red thing over there.'

After that they set off in a little column, Marzillian first and Ludens last. 'Benbow' turned out on inspection to be less bijou than it had seemed from outside. It comprised the good-sized sitting room where the conversation had taken place, a small room, study or dining room, three bedrooms, a large smart kitchen complete with gas stove, refrigerator, dish-washer and waste-disposal unit, and a rather gorgeous bathroom. There was central heating, no fireplaces. The furnishing was of light oak with upholstery which looked like hand-woven tweed in a variety of soft colours. There were bookshelves, empty except for some local guidebooks and a manual of suggestions for 'walks'. There was a vase of lilies and daisies on a window-ledge. The house, with the sun streaming in, was certainly pleasant, and Ludens felt with pain how happy he would have been if this Benbow had only been the Benbow of his imagination.

They returned to the sitting room. Marcus sat down on one of the tweedy chairs. Marzillian was explaining to him that 'their maid' would soon arrive and show them the luncheon menu, that vegetarian dishes were of course available, that they might like a stroll in the grounds, but only the staff were allowed to pick flowers. Irina and Dr Hensman were having a whispered conversation, Hensman continually nodding his head. Ludens, standing at the open glass doors, was approached by Dr Bland who said in his Ulster drawl, 'Do you play tennis, by any chance?'

'*What?*'

'Do you play tennis? We have hard courts, and grass if you prefer it.'

'No.'

'Or golf? Only nine holes I fear.'

'No – no – thank you.' Ludens pushed past Bland and, interrupting Marzillian, said quickly to Marcus, 'I'm going to the pub. Goodbye. I'll be back this evening or tomorrow.' He tried to think of something to add, but every available remark seemed fatuous. He turned and darted out of the door, causing Dr Bland to step hastily aside.

He had strode half way to the car when he was overtaken by Irina. 'Where *are* you going?'

'To the Black Lion.'

'Are you taking the car?'

'Yes.'

'Our stuff is still in it.'

Ludens went to the car, hauled out the pieces of luggage and put them on the lawn, then got into the driver's seat. Irina held onto the door, keeping it open.

'Will you come back again?'

'Yes.'

'Will you drive me to London when you go?'

'I'm not going,' said Ludens, 'you can walk to London.' He wrenched the door from her and slammed it. Then he backed the car abruptly out onto the tarmac and drove away as fast as he could, narrowly missing another car which was just emerging from the other branch of the drive. As he slowed down on reaching the road he saw the white noticeboard which he had glimpsed on entering. It said simply *Bellmain. Strictly Private*. Ludens drove back along the lane, over the bridge, and into the yard of the Black Lion.

'Mr Luddens?' said the publican.

'Dr Ludens,' said Ludens. He did not usually sport his doctorate but now it might count as a tiny advantage in the battle which lay ahead in which he would need every trick. He had to get Marcus out of that place *as soon as possible*; it might take days, it might take weeks, but it *must be done*.

The Black Lion was as pleasant inside as it was outside, the oak beams were genuine, the bar was full of 'snugs' and alcoves and ancient country furniture, the small dining room looked out on the garden and the river, as did the pleasant room allotted to Ludens. Once again he felt: how happy I would be now if only it were all true! The sense of the *falseness* of this awful new scene, the *lies* with which it was textured, contaminated any pleasure he might have taken in the old inn, the friendly publican (whose name was Toller) and the delightful river (whose name was Fern).

After sitting for a while in the bar with a glass of the (good) local beer Ludens decided that he would not return to Bellmain that day. Today would be a chaos of settling in, filling forms, meeting people, imbibing information, learning routines, things he shuddered at the thought of. Let them, he thought, face these trials unaided, see how they could get on without him, miss him, wonder about him! He already regretted his brutality to Irina. He even questioned how far she had realised what she was doing. She might have been somehow misled, inveigled, by Dr Hensman and be by now as appalled as Ludens. He felt in any case it was wiser not to appear at once or seem too anxious to make peace. Let her have time to think about making peace. Yes, he loved her, but this love was now a painful bond, an absolute connection with someone and something irresponsibly beyond him. How *could* she! The pain, the connection, had to be endured, it was part of the *work* which had to be done. Going over in his mind the sequence of events since he turned his car into that loathsome 'park' he tried, out of fairness, to conceive that his whole interpretation, his whole reaction, had been wrong. Perhaps it was all really a good idea, Marcus would like it, he would be left in peace, the doctors were harmless, the place was really just an expensive hotel. He reviewed this possibility and rejected it. He did not yet dare to sketch the motives which might have led Irina to make such an arrangement. He knew, from his conversations with him that Marcus, incapable of subterfuges, had had only the vaguest idea beforehand of the 'country cottage', an idea even vaguer than that of Ludens, since Marcus, absorbed in his own problems, had 'left all that to Irina'. He had wanted to leave London. He looked forward to walking in the country. He had certainly not envisaged anything like Bellmain. So might it not turn out to be simple and easy after all? Perhaps Marcus would simply leave the place tomorrow, telling Ludens to drive him back to London? Why was Ludens so frightened? Was he frightened of *that doctor*?

During the later part of these reflections several cars had sailed into the yard and meals were being eaten in the dining room and snacks consumed in the bar. Ludens decided to have lunch late, hoping to get the publican to himself. And so it fell out. After a very tolerable lunch, cooked by the so far invisible Mrs Toller, Ludens, who was surprised to find he could actually eat, invited Toller to join him for coffee. He had already discerned Toller's West Country accent and on enquiry learnt that his host came from Somerset. Ludens revealed that he also came from Somerset. They had a discussion about cider. Ludens, commenting on the charms of the countryside, elicited the information that he had only one fellow-lodger, an American lady, a Miss Tether, who came every year to paint the scenery. How had Dr Ludens found the place? Perhaps Dr Ludens intended a long stay? Would Ludens please call him 'Toller', not 'Mr Toller'? His first name was George but everyone called him 'Toller'. Ludens confided that he too was usually called by his surname. They agreed that there was much to be said for the old-fashioned way of calling men by their surnames, there was something manly about it. Ludens took the opportunity to explain that (contrary to Toller's implied belief) he was not a medical doctor. Toller, who was certainly curious and now encouraged, asked Ludens what he was doing in this part of the world. Just on holiday?

'No, actually – I've just driven a friend of mine down to Bellmain, he's going to stay there for a while.'

'You mean he's an *inmate*?'

'Yes.' The desired flood of information followed.

'Your friend must be a millionaire.'

'He's quite well-off.'

'Is he – you know – a bit odd?'

'No.'

'He soon will be. No, I'm joking. They do you very well. There's a golf course and a heated swimming-pool and a French chef and attractive maids and all. They say it's a place where rich families dump the relatives they can do without, but at least they live in luxury! I expect your friend is elderly? No? Well, I expect he'll get a lot out of it. Is he fond of golf? No? Those two doctors must be making a packet. Is your friend up at the house or in a chalet? Chalet? That costs more. You know, up at the house they've got some real loonies, they lock them up, poor chaps who don't know who they are and just sit and stare all day. God, human life can be sad. Maybe doctors do people some good if they just calm them down and then you don't know how bloody unhappy you are. You know, they drug them to the eyeballs, they've got a drug for everything, if you're miserable they make you merry, if you're too merry they sober you up, if you think you're Napoleon they turn you into nobody —'

'I suppose people just come for short periods for a little treatment?' said Ludens.

'No, when they come they stay! That's the way the doctors like it, when they get onto a good thing. But I shouldn't talk like that. I'm just repeating what people say, maybe it isn't like that at all. It's certainly pretty luxurious, especially if you're partial to golf and swimming and French food. I expect your friend will love it.'

After lunch, reflecting upon what he had been told, Ludens went for a long walk along the banks of the River Fern, examining the wild flowers and observing the dragonflies.

'Excuse me, there's a young lady downstairs asking to see you.'

It was the next morning.

'Tell her to come up,' said Ludens, who had just finished shaving.

A moment later Irina ran into the room and into his arms.

Silently, violently, with closed eyes, they hugged each other.

Ludens released her. He closed the door. Then they held onto each other at arm's length, surveying each other. Then they sat down on the bed. Ludens began to kiss her. She began to cry.

'Irina, don't! Darling, I'm sorry I was so awful to you yesterday. It was such a shock.'

'I know. Give me a hankie, will you. Thanks.'

'Please forgive me.'

'I forgive you. Will you forgive me?'

'No. Sorry, I can't. I mean, I don't understand.'

'Yes, you *don't* understand! You were *awful* yesterday, so rude to the doctors, so rude to my father –'

'Not to him.'

'Yes, when he's just arrived, it's not a moment for shouting at his host.'

'I didn't shout, and he's not a guest, it's not a private house –'

'You jumped to all sorts of ridiculous conclusions.'

'I think I jumped to the right conclusions. I think you've betrayed him.'

Irina jumped up. She stood for a moment opening her hands in the familiar spiky gesture of horror and rage. Then she ran across the room and hurled Ludens's handkerchief out of the open window. She returned and stamped her feet. 'How can you say that! He's very angry with you!'

'Oh God, I hope not!'

'You've upset him, he's in a state, he's afraid you'll go back to London and leave him. He wanted me to come round here last night, only I wouldn't. Oh why were you so awful, you've *damaged* everything so much!'

'You mean I saw the truth and didn't keep quiet! I've been asking about this place, it's a luxury mental home. There are lunatics there who are locked up. Your father will be a prisoner.'

'Who told you that?'

'The innkeeper.'

'What does he know? That's utterly false. I don't think there are any lunatics there. What's a lunatic anyway these days?'

'You evidently think that Marcus is one.'

'Oh shut up! Hell and damnation!'

'You misled me, you misled him, with all that stuff about a country cottage – you *lied*.'

'How could I explain –'

'You fixed all this up beforehand with Dr Hensman.'

'All right, I took Dr Hensman's advice. You don't see the problem!'

'These doctors are onto a good thing. They must have found out that Marcus was rich. I suppose Hensman told them, he probably acts as their scout. They'll *never* let him go.'

'How can you talk such utter piffling rot!'

'Are you just naive, or is there something else?'

'What do you mean?'

'You want to get rid of him, you want to *dump* him. That's what you call the problem!'

'All right, go away, go back to London! We don't want you here! Go to hell!'

'If I go back to London I go back with Marcus. I'm not going to leave him, I intend to rescue him.'

'How can you speak like that, my father isn't a child, anyway it's nothing to do with you, you aren't a member of the family, just because my father wants me to marry you!'

'Did he say that?'

'Not exactly. He wants me to marry a Jewish intellectual, he thinks his grandson will be a genius, and you just happen to be the only Jewish intellectual around. Anyway, I'm not going to marry you!'

'I haven't asked you.'

'Oh *good*. Now look –'

'Irina, please – darling dear Irina, I love you, let's not be angry with each other – I just care so much for Marcus –'

'And I'm just useful to get hold of him!'

'I care for Marcus and I'm *afraid* for him.'

'Well, don't be. You've just swallowed a lot of lying talk and you believe it –'

'I gained an impression of those two doctors –'

'Will you *listen*. The whole thing makes perfect sense if you'll only *see*. That stuff about Marcus being a prisoner is rubbish, of course he can leave, if he hates it we can do something else. But it seems the perfect solution –'

'To the problem!'

'Well, there is a problem, he needs medical care –'

'You mean for his teeth!'

'For his arthritis, and he has asthma and high blood pressure and constipation, all right he fusses, but they can help him, and he wants peace and quiet and not to have to *worry* about anything, you know how he hated London, he wants to work and think, you want him to work and think –'

'I pictured him living free, not in the power of other people, not in an institution.'

'Oh bugger you, use your imagination, you thought Dad and me would live in a romantic little cottage with you next door?'

'Yes. Not *this* anyway.'

'I see. And who does the shopping and the cooking and the cleaning and the weeding and –'

'You do. I do. Irina —'

'Haven't you taken in that I've *had* all that at Red Cottage? I don't want to be poor any more, why should I be? I don't want to have to worry about Dad day and night, what's money for, for God's sake, I don't want to *look after* him and keep wondering whether he's had an accident or set fire to the house! I don't want to have to take him to a doctor and *decide* to take him to a doctor! You talk of freedom — I've never had it! I've been lonely and miserable and in despair, and you want me to consent to all that all over again!'

'It'd be different. I'd be there —'

'Big deal!'

'We could employ somebody.'

'Who's we?'

'We could get people to clean and cook — others can do that, why not us?'

'I'll tell you why. Because we — Dad and me, *and* you — aren't capable of it, we can't do things like that! There'd be nothing but mess and muddle. Dad *hates* strangers in the house. These are the *details* which you won't *look* at. Bellmain is an absolutely respectable and reputable place. Dr Hensman's mother was there —'

'What a wonderful recommendation!'

'Can't you be *serious*?'

'Marcus is young. That place is just a dumping ground. Can't you see it's a perfectly *crazy* idea? We mustn't let it *start*, we must get him out *at once.*'

'Yes, Dad's young, but he's *very* peculiar —'

'You mean mad.'

'Oh stuff it! You know what I mean! He can't, he *won't* live a normal life, he *wants* to be cloistered —'

'Cloistered!'

'Yes, and I don't! He's in perfect health, he'll live to be a hundred, and what am I supposed to do all that time?'

'*Now* you say he's in perfect health! So why does he need doctors? It's all in *your* interest, so you can push him in and leave him.'

'You don't realise how difficult it is to find anywhere —'

'To put away unwanted relations.'

'Anywhere *decent* where someone can live a protected life. He needs *order*, he needs *servants*, he needs not to have to worry about *ordinary arrangements*, he wants privacy and peace.'

'Like in the Bellmain brochure.'

'Stop sneering.'

'I'm not sneering, I'm *terrified*, I'm afraid of those doctors, I wouldn't trust them an inch. How on earth can *you* trust them? They're used to crazy unbalanced people or senile aged mothers. They won't have the wit and they certainly won't have the will or the time to understand that Marcus is a thinker –'

'They're not such fools as you imagine, I've *told* them what he's like.'

'Irina, you don't know what he's like.'

'And you do, wonderful you? Oh, why did you have to get mixed up in all this, I shouldn't have let you come!'

'Just *think*. They'll decide he needs treatment. They'll drug him, they'll give him electric shocks.'

Irina, who had been standing in the middle of the room, paused and stared at Ludens. Today she was wearing a dark red dress with a pattern of large dark green flowers, donned untidily and irregularly buttoned. Her hair was uncombed, or perhaps stood on end by her anxious hands which had been flying about as she talked. She was not wearing the make-up which Franca and Alison had taught her to put on. She seemed, to the eyes of Ludens at that moment, to have reverted to being the gipsy girl of Red Cottage. She said, 'Of course they won't!'

'Look, let's be rational. Sit down, no not here, over there, and let's decide what to do next. I suggest we go along to see Marcus and ask him –'

'I'm glad you think his opinion matters! Why have we wasted time having this argument?'

'And I want to talk to Dr Marzillian or whatever his name is, in fact I'm *going* to talk to him.'

'When you see Dad, be tactful, don't reel out all the stuff you've been giving me. All right, let's go.'

'Wait a moment. There's something else that must be done.'

'What?'

'I said just now I hadn't asked you to marry me. That was a serious omission. Will you marry me?'

She paused, fiddling with the irregular buttons of her dress. 'Are you sure it's me you're in love with, and not just my father?'

'Yes. I love you both.'

'Oh what nonsense you talk! Let's go and fetch your handkerchief, it's out on the lawn.'

'Why did you disappear like that, why did you run away without a word, where were you? Why didn't you come back, why didn't you send a message? We waited for you, you didn't even come and see us last night. Why did I have to send Irina to fetch you? What's the matter with you? If you want to go back to London, *go, go now!*'

Ludens, who had expected a friendly relieved welcome, was stunned. Marcus, standing on the verandah at the top of the steps and glaring down at him, was really angry.

Ludens was speechless. Irina discreetly disappeared toward the door at the side of the house. Marcus turned back into the sitting room. Ludens followed.

'Marcus, I'm sorry, I did say –'

'You were rude to the doctors, rude to me, disgracefully rude to Irina she tells me.'

'I'm very sorry.'

'What came over you? Can't we trust you any more? If you're fed up you can go away.'

Ludens had seen and experienced, in the 'old days', Marcus's coldness, his ability suddenly to freeze people, wordlessly to convict them of contemptible stupidity, to turn his back upon them with exasperation, to drop them ruthlessly. He had never seen Marcus blazingly angry before.

Menaced by his stammer, he trembled. He managed to say, 'I'm sorry I was rude. I was taken by surprise. I didn't expect this place, these doctors. I ran away because I was upset. It was stupid of me.' Knowing how much Marcus despised weakness and confusion, he checked his apologies.

'This new place is enough, without you vanishing. Of course you can go away, but you had led me to expect –'

'Marcus, I'm not going away, not unless you drive me away –'

'All right, all right.' Marcus sat down. 'Sit down, please.' Ludens sat down. 'What did you want?'

This sounded as if Ludens had importunately burst in, instead of arriving in response to a summons. 'Marcus, I'm worried about this place, I don't like it.'

'Why not, what's wrong with it?'

'Well, it's – it's rather like a hospital. Did you expect something like this, did Irina tell you?'

'I thought you had deserted us. As for this place, no, Irina did not tell me and I did not expect it, but I should not have "expected" any place, and in a way it does not matter where I am. In another way where I am is fated. I like this little house. And there is excellent service, as was explained yesterday, when you were not here!'

'Yes, but – it's not a hotel. These doctors have so much power – it's dangerous –'

'Anywhere is dangerous if you carry danger with you. Why are you so suspicious? I have talked with Dr Marzillian who is an intelligent considerate man. I am to have a special diet and I can go swimming every day, which will be good for my arthritis.'

'Diet! Swimming!'

'I need order in my daily life. I feel protected here.'

'Cloistered? Imprisoned?'

'You give a bad sense to those words, I give a good sense. Ludens, I must think, I must be alone. It may be only for a little while.'

'Then we could go somewhere else?'

'No, no. I can't see the future. I don't want another move, another upheaval. This place has many advantages. I propose to stay.'

'But we don't know anything yet, I don't trust these people –'

'I said I propose to stay.'

'All right, all right. But listen, Marcus, and don't be vexed with me. I don't know where you are in your thoughts. You are confronting insoluble problems and ineffable mysteries. Perhaps one day you will solve the problems and penetrate the mysteries. Perhaps one day I may understand more and help more. But now I just want to say two things, and I hope you will excuse my being crude and blunt. First, I think you should stop feeling dramatic about your life and thinking there's some particular role or action which you are destined to perform, I mean like saving people or anything like that. I don't believe in that sort of destiny, and I don't believe in a Jewish destiny either. That's a false path. Thinking about Jewishness, as scholars think, as historians think, of course that's another matter, though I still don't believe that's *your* job. Secondly, the very next thing you ought to do is try to *write it all down*, that is write down what you were telling me about the device, and the electrical circuit, and something intuitively seen to be necessary, not one thing among others but the foundation of all things, and why ordinary morality interferes because it's about individuals and accidents, sorry I'm jumbling all this up – You should write it down, I don't mean solving it, but just *stating*, writing it in a plain rigmarole, as it were, with all the knots and inconsistencies showing. I know you see it as a sort of cosmic game of patience which would one day *come out*, and perhaps it will. But meanwhile you ought to write about the state of the game, about the *kind* of muddle and confusion you're in.

That *must* help you – and it might just help other people, only don't mind about *them*. Please don't interrupt me – and another thing which I've just thought of, do stop thinking about evil, I mean evil in yourself. That's not part of your problem, you are innocent, and if you ever had any bad thoughts they don't matter, and if you think they matter I hereby absolve you.'

Ludens, astonished at himself, for he had certainly not intended or foreseen such a speech, sat back expecting Marcus to be thoroughly annoyed. However Marcus, who had been staring intently at Ludens throughout, suddenly laughed, and having started went on laughing. At first Ludens feared – Oh how many things he feared – that this was a hysterical laugh. But it was not; it was a free happy zany sort of laugh.

'Well, if *that's* your programme for me, you can see how necessary it will be for you to stay and keep me up to it! I am grateful to you for your thoughts, and I thank you for your absolution, a kind act whereby *your* innocence can perhaps lay its gracious hand upon me.'

Moved by Marcus's response to his speech, moved by his laughter and by the word 'gracious', Ludens leaned forward and seized hold of one of Marcus's hands.

Irina materialised on the verandah, dark against the sunlit garden behind her. 'Ludens, Dr Marzillian wants to talk to you *at once*.'

Irina had not been directly entrusted with Dr Marzillian's summons. The bringer of the message was a handsome girl wearing some kind of uniform, doubtless one of the 'attractive maids' mentioned by Toller. She was standing beyond the garden upon the drive, and greeted Ludens with a smile and a slight curtsey and a graceful gesture of her hand, both deferential and reassuring. 'Hello. I am Camilla.' Camilla had loose dark-blond hair and sympathetic light grey eyes, and was wearing a blue-green skirt and high-necked matching jacket with silver buttons over a discreetly visible white blouse. This gear was at once somehow, and rightly, identified by Ludens as 'uniform'. A light-blue enamel badge on the breast pocket said *Camilla*.

Ludens said 'Hello.'

The sun was shining between moving clouds and the air was cooler. As they walked briskly along the flower-bordered drive Camilla, who had now announced herself as his escort, also revealed that she was the 'maid' who was particularly attached to Benbow, and of course to be distinguished from the 'cleaner' called Rosie. She had evidently been introduced, even operational, on the previous day, and referred chattily to the Professor and Miss Vallar. She pointed out to Ludens various features of the scene as these emerged from among the elegant trees. There was the North Pavilion, a sort of communal house, Ludens gathered, with a 'common room' and a 'refectory', a substantial, obviously recent, building with an oriental roof, reflected in a sheet of ornamental water. The South Pavilion, not visible from the drive, was said to be 'residential'. When referring to the refectory Camilla added with an apologetic smile that of course no smoking and no consumption of alcohol was permitted anywhere within the precincts. A group of nurses passed, then two dark-clad figures explained as 'security men', also known as 'bulldogs'. All these persons exchanged waves with Camilla and looked with curiosity at Ludens. By now they had left the smaller tarmac road which led to Benbow and turned onto the main drive. Here, at the end of a vista cut in the trees, and through an opening in a tall dark hedge, Ludens glimpsed an extremely large grey stone erected on some sort of plinth. Camilla said it was called the Axle Stone, she was not sure why. It was a very ancient stone and there was some 'charming legend' about it. She indicated the swimming-pools, one indoor, one outdoor, and beyond them, more perfunctorily, 'the chapel' and 'the crematorium'. On the right, and south, side of the drive some eighteenth-century stables, converted and extended, contained 'offices' and 'staff bedrooms', but were still known as 'the Stables'. Ludens had meanwhile noticed, partly hidden among the trees, three chalets, called Hotham, Keppel, and Boscawen. As they now came clear of the woodland Camilla pointed out tennis courts, and the ('only nine holes') golf course.

Full in view now was Bellmain House, which lent the enterprise its name, and beyond it, partly visible, an expanse of lake water. This main building, always referred to as 'the house', was a long large red-brick nineteenth-century mansion, built on the site of a previous seventeenth-century 'Bellmain Manor' which had been burnt down in 1860. It was liberally covered with long stone friezes of bulky fruits and flowers, and raised upon a terrace, with a hexagonal turret at each end. A dazzling herbaceous border ran along below the terrace, and a path led across a wide immaculate lawn to what was, Camilla said, the back of the house where steps led up to an ornate doorway. As Camilla turned off the drive onto the path, Ludens, who had allowed himself to be distracted by his guide, began to feel extremely nervous. Part of the lawn was laid out for croquet, and an elderly gentleman wearing a waistcoat was actually tapping a ball with a mallet. He paused, then approached, and without more formality said to Ludens, 'I say, does your friend play chess?' Ludens, startled, said yes. Camilla then introduced him as 'Mr Talgarth of Boscawen'; and as they moved on said apologetically, 'I'm afraid this is a very gossipy place.' They climbed the steps between extremely large urns containing lilies and entered, between open carved oak gates and a door of glazed glass, a large dark entrance hall floored with red figured tiles upon which Camilla's smart black shoes with medium-high heels made a sharp clacking sound. She nodded to a uniformed girl who was sitting behind a desk in an alcove. A nurse-like figure disappeared up a staircase. In spite of two immense vases of flowers upon a long table, the hall smelt of something forbiddingly hygienic.

'Now Dr Ludens, what do you make of the names which we have given to our cabins?'

These, after a 'good morning', were the first words uttered.

Dr Marzillian's office was on the ground floor opposite to the entrance. Camilla had vanished. Ludens was sitting on a tall hard elaborately carved mahogany chair and facing, across a large desk, Dr Marzillian, and beyond him a huge 'Gothic' bow window affording a view of the lake, and beyond it a receding undulation of small smooth green hills which (mentioned by Camilla) must be Salisbury Plain.

'I have not reflected on the matter,' Ludens said with cold incisive irritation. He observed the effect of his manner on Marzillian and felt that he had made a reasonably good start. The upper panes of the window contained stained glass tulips whose red glitter distracted his eyes while his hands compulsively explored a swarm of plant and animal forms in the arms of the chair.

'Ah. Then you noticed the names?' This was a swift enough return shot.

'I noticed a few.'

'Tell me the names which you have noticed.'

Frowning Ludens said, for he had certainly paid some attention to the names, 'Rodney, Collingwood, Boscawen, Hotham –'

'Now! Do these names not strike you as having something in common?'

What they had in common had now struck Ludens, who replied coldly, staring at Marzillian, 'They are names of English admirals.'

'Correct!' said Marzillian triumphantly, as if he had pulled off some kind of trick. 'You are absolutely right. "Nelson" we also have, but of course if you had seen *that* you would have guessed at once, wouldn't you?'

Seen in the clear lake light which reflected into the room, aided by a huge gilt-framed mirror upon the wall, Dr Marzillian looked younger, handsome in a rather histrionic way, like a character in an operetta, perhaps the hero's friend. His high-buttoned white coat even resembled a smart stylish uniform, as of a central European military *attaché*. His moustache, smearing the length of his upper lip and drooping markedly on either side, was copious enough to display the glossy health of the long individual hairs. His teeth were very white, his eyes apparently black, his complexion dark, but not so as to suggest that he was an Arab or, as Ludens had earlier conceived, an Indian. His cheeks were perceptibly red. He smiled at Ludens, gesturing towards him as he talked.

'I should tell you that we have a relic of great antiquity here, a great stone, a sarsen, perhaps you saw it on the way.'

Ludens nodded.

'"Sarsen" means "saracen", you know, used in the sense of "pagan". There is a fascinating account of the stone in our brochure, I will send it round. The name "Bellmain" goes back very far, and may have an Arthurian origin. I don't know if such things interest you –'

Ludens thought, he's playing the clown so as to prevent me from saying anything serious. He said, adopting the slightly impertinent style of his host, 'I assume you are an Armenian?'

This question seemed to delight Marzillian. 'Yes, yes! You have noticed the patronymic! But let me tell you, Dr Ludens, that my father was born in Manchester, and I was born in Croydon!' He uttered these facts triumphantly as if they were the termination of some argument.

Ludens, feeling no impulse to inquire about the grandfather, said, 'Dr Marzillian, I would like to ask you a number of questions.'

'Ah! And I would like to ask *you* a number of questions!'

A uniformed maid came in carrying a tray which she set down on the desk. Marzillian said, 'Thank you, my dear.' The maid, not Camilla but equally handsome, wore a badge which said *Maria*. She flashed a smile at Ludens and disappeared.

Upon the tray were cups, coffee pot, milk jug, sugar basin, biscuits, and a note which Marzillian picked up and read. 'Coffee? Black, white? Sugar? A biscuit? Actually these are shortbreads specially made by our chef.'

'No, thank you,' said Ludens, suddenly aware of having had no breakfast.

'Won't you even have some coffee?'

'No, thank you.'

'Well, I shall. I am an early riser and have already spent a busy morning. Now, Professor Vallar referred to you as his pupil. What did he teach you?'

Ludens replied promptly, 'Philosophy.' He had no intention of recounting the long story of his relation with Marcus, which it would have been very difficult, and perhaps now imprudent, to tell.

'At what university?'

This immediately disadvantaged Ludens who had to reply lamely, 'Well, Professor Vallar is, or was, a mathematician –'

'I know, I know.'

'And I have been trained as a historian, but Professor Vallar's later interests have been philosophical, and I have, over a long period, discussed such matters with him since I too am interested in philosophy.'

'So to call you his pupil was a trifle picturesque?'

'I am his pupil,' said Ludens.

'And his friend?'

'Yes.'

'And his daughter's friend?'

'Look,' said Ludens, 'perhaps you could give me some information. Is this place a mental home?'

Marzillian smiled indulgently. 'As I told you, it is a place of healing. There are many kinds of sickness and many kinds of therapy.'

'So as Professor Vallar is neither mentally disturbed nor physically ill there seems to be no reason why he should be here.'

'But, Dr Ludens, Professor Vallar has *come* here, he approached me, I did not approach him, I did not go out and kidnap him.'

'His daughter arranged it. Professor Vallar did not know and I think does not know what sort of place this is.'

'It seems that you do not know either, Dr Ludens. Pray do not be impatient with me. My first duty is to Professor Vallar. As you appear to be a friend of the family, and since you are still here, it is my wish, indeed my professional duty, to find out from you all possible facts which are relevant to his case.'

'But I have told you, there is no case. He needs no treatment. He is perfectly sane.'

'Well, he is here. I have not yet had time to examine him, though we have had a preliminary talk. I gather he suffers from arthritis and asthma, has anxieties about his blood pressure and his diet –'

'Do you *own* this place?'

'Do I own it? Yes. If you mean does it receive money from the state? No. It is a private concern.'

'I suggest that your interest in Professor Vallar is purely financial. You have found out that he is rich, and you intend to keep him here by making him imagine that he is ill.'

'Dr Ludens,' said Dr Marzillian with a gentle reproving smile, 'please be more patient with me. We have a lot to tell each other. Let us be friends, at least allies. No, pray do not interrupt me. I first heard of the Professor, as a potential, let us say, visitor here, from Dr Hensman, whom I have known for some time. Dr Hensman earlier recommended to me the case of – well, let us not go into that. I trust Dr Hensman's judgment and the information he has given me. I did not however rest content with that alone. I made my own investigations, for instance among old friends at Cambridge, a place where I studied once.'

'What did you study?' Ludens asked quickly.

Marzillian smiled a *touché* smile. 'I studied classical languages and archaeology. I pursued my medical studies later in London and then in Chicago. If you like I will give you a copy of my *curriculum vitae*. As I say, I made enquiries in various quarters and have built up quite an extensive picture of my subject, I mean my new guest, and I believe in some sense my patient – in what sense remains to be seen. No, please let me go on. This may seem to you a strange place – it evidently does since you express such suspicions of it – but its nature and basis can be very simply explained. All sorts of people come here for all sorts of reasons. I have some patients, in this building, who are seriously mentally disturbed and whom we treat by the best and most modern methods, aiming to cure them and often succeeding. We are *healers*, Dr Ludens, we, that is Dr Bland and myself, are dedicated men of science, passionately interested in the deep nature of the human mind. Professionally, we are psychiatrists. We are also, in the more general sense, students of humanity. In this field a good doctor must be both. As I say, all sorts of people come here. We have many guests, as we like to call them, who are, let us say, to use a crude dichotomy, more neurotic than psychotic. There are again, when from time to time we have room for them, other guests whose complaints concern the body only and who simply like to stay for a while, enjoying the place as a pleasant hotel which also offers expert medical attention. It is true that our charges are high. But what we offer is very good. I hope you have followed my explanation. Dr Hensman has told me that the Professor desires quietness, convenience, and solitude. I can guarantee that he will not be interrupted, he can be a hermit here. I have even arranged that, except in case of extreme emergency, the neighbouring cabin, Rodney, will be kept empty. I hope this clear account has satisfied you?'

'I'm afraid not,' said Ludens. 'How much do you charge, by the way?'

Marzillian mentioned a large sum.

'Per month, per week?'

'Per day. Let me add that individual insurance can often cover some or all of the expense.'

'I think this is not the right place for Professor Vallar,' said Ludens. 'It is not a matter of money. I daresay you have examined that aspect of his life also.' (Dr Marzillian smiled appreciatively at this compliment.) 'He does not care for luxury hotels, is not interested in food or golf –'

'Ah, but he likes swimming – and he can play chess with Mr Talgarth, whom I think you have already met.'

'Your intelligence service is good.'

'Any detail may matter.'

'I shall hope to persuade Professor Vallar to leave.'

'I confess I am puzzled by your situation, one might say your *locus standi*, in this matter. I mean, how do you come into the picture? The Professor's daughter, who has been here several times with Dr Hensman, seems perfectly happy, even delighted, with our facilities.'

'She is inexperienced and naive.'

'Perhaps you are not on very good terms with her?'

'I am on perfectly good terms with her. I believe she has been influenced, perhaps misled, by Dr Hensman, who appears to be a scout, perhaps a well-paid one, for this establishment.'

'Dr Ludens, I am a patient man, but I must advise you not to let your tongue run away with you.'

'I'm sorry, I withdraw that. There are things which Miss Vallar simply does not understand. I shall explain them and hope to convince her.'

'I wonder what those things are? Professor Vallar himself, with whom I had a valuable talk yesterday, also seems pleased with the little house and all our arrangements. May I enquire, to put it bluntly, what business it is of yours?'

'I am an old and trusted friend and I have his interests at heart. Professor Vallar has always lived simply and humbly. He will be better off elsewhere.'

'Let me say,' said Marzillian, 'in case *that* is something that you need to know, that I am, as a student of human nature and, if I may put it so, not just as a doctor but as a person, *extremely interested* in your teacher. I believe him to be a remarkable man. I desire, as I think you desire, to understand his thoughts and to enable and observe what he will become. In this we can and should be allies. I shall be proud to have him here.'

'As a specimen, as an advertisement.'

'You do me less than justice, Dr Ludens. Can you not recognise the tones of sincerity and the voice of truth?'

'The point is,' said Ludens, approaching the central matter which he had not dared to mention in his conversation with Marcus, 'that I cannot trust you not to drug him.'

'Aspirin is a drug.'

'You know what I mean.'

'I assure you —'

'Dr Marzillian, if you drug him I shall kill you.'

'Thank you, Dr Ludens. I begin to think that perhaps you too are a very interesting man.'

Ludens had left Marzillian almost immediately after the utterance of his threat. He had risen to his feet. His host did not attempt to detain him, but expressed a courteous wish that they might soon meet again. Now Ludens was running across the lawn, ignoring a distant signal from Mr Talgarth, who raised his croquet mallet in salute, or summons. He slowed down and began walking fast along the drive in the direction of Benbow. Why the idea about the English admirals? Probably for no reason whatsoever, a sudden whim, perhaps he thought it would make rich English people feel at home. Ludens was sick with rage and misery, ready to wail with exasperation, he even struck his breast violently with his clenched fist. He had obtained no foothold, established no authority, he had allowed himself to be patronised, led along, treated with humorous condescension. Marzillian was a self-appointed mystery man, a power maniac, a self-obsessed magician. He might genuinely respect, even admire, Marcus, but would he not also wish to dominate him, to change him, to 'do him good'? He would surely want to try out some treatment on such an interesting patient. In *this* place Marcus's eccentricities would attract all the banal semi-senseless labels out of the messy rag-bag of so-called psychotherapy. Of course Marcus was 'neurotic', of course he was 'withdrawn', of course he was 'unbalanced', of course he suffered from some well-known 'complex'. Here the fact that innumerable successful and happy people also did, and that very

clever people were often harmlessly odd, would be passed over in favour
of some more or less violent attempt to restore 'normality'. The mere
thought of Marzillian *talking* to Marcus, probing him, theorising him,
investigating his childhood and so on made Ludens shudder with
disgust. And then there was the other doctor whose appearance Ludens
had not liked at all. The place reeked of drugs and expertise and mental
care. Besides, could Ludens bear to let a clever man like Marzillian
become Marcus's *friend*, as he appeared to wish to be? The whole scene
was awful, the risks were terrible. Marcus would play chess with Mr
Talgarth, bridge with the doctors and Camilla, chat with the other
inmates in the 'common room', become a well-known habitué of the
swimming-pool . . .

Here Ludens suddenly checked his thoughts and actually stopped his
fast walk abruptly. Well, why not? Might not Marcus *enjoy* some
human companionship in this comfortable expensive place? Why
should he have to live like a bear in a cave? He could have peace and
solitude to work and think, then if he wished it a little pleasant
undemanding social life. He could have expert medical care without
stirring a foot or a finger. All this might be *ideal* – neat orderly
untroubled surroundings, so unlike the mess and chaos and anxiety of
Red Cottage. To live without anxiety. This was what Marzillian's rich
clients were buying. Why shouldn't Marcus buy it too? Ludens walked
on slowly. He thought, I'm being possessive, I'm being jealous, my old
vice. I want Marcus to myself, I want to be the only one he talks to.
But suppose he were to stop wanting solitude, or to spend all his time
thinking? Suppose he became soft and corrupted? But that's nonsense,
he's incorruptible. I think this is a vile place, a place beneath his dignity,
which he ought to have contempt for – and yet perhaps in the midst of
it all he'd be safe. He wouldn't see or touch what was awful. And why
do I think it's so awful? Because it might take Marcus away from me?
I'm not just afraid of the drugs, I'm afraid of losing him. And then, he
thought, there's Irina, and her cry of freedom, freedom! Suppose she
goes off to London or Paris – and *why shouldn't she*? My God, it's my
survival that's at stake as well. He thought, yes, I love them both and
I've *got to have them both*. I can't lose Irina, I *won't* lose her. Oh curse
all that money! If only they were poor we could all live together in that
little cottage that I imagined and wanted so much, and I would work,
oh how hard I'd work, to support us all.

His thoughts were interrupted by a scene which was occurring just
ahead. On one of the flowerbeds which bordered the drive at intervals
a man was standing, in the middle of the bed, gesticulating, holding a

bunch of what looked like roses in his hand, while another man standing on the tarmac appeared to be admonishing him. Voices were raised. As Ludens approached he realised, with a new and different pang, that the man on the flowerbed was Patrick Fenman. The man on the tarmac was Dr Bland. They both turned to Ludens.

Patrick extracted himself from the rose bed, detaching his trousers from various thorns. He said to Ludens, 'I haven't got a knife, have you got one? I tried picking off the thorns before I broke the stems, but it didn't work, see, I've torn my hand.' He exhibited a bleeding finger.

Ludens who, ever since childhood had carried a penknife in his pocket, decided against an instinctive desire to hand this tool over to Pat. Clearly its moment had passed.

Dr Bland said amiably, 'Good morning, Dr Ludens. I have been explaining to Professor Vallar's man that he does not need to damage himself, and incidentally mangle the bushes, by picking roses. A word to your maid will bring you any flowers you wish for.'

'I wanted *these* ones,' said Patrick, 'besides it's more genial if you pick them yourself. Of course they're in bud, but they'll come out in water.'

'I venture to doubt that,' said Dr Bland. 'You have made a further mistake by picking them too early.'

Patrick, gingerly embracing the prickly bouquet, addressing Ludens and ignoring Bland, said, 'I'm going to take them to him now. Are you coming?'

'Perhaps I could detain Dr Ludens for a moment,' said Dr Bland.

Patrick disappeared round the corner of the drive. Ludens reflected that he had assumed that the recipient of the flowers was to be Irina, and that he was even more annoyed to find it was Marcus!

'I wonder if you could explain the Professor's servant to me a little. He talks rather oddly. I am not referring to his accent which is that of the Republic of Ireland, somewhere on the west coast I imagine. I mean, for instance, he claims that the Professor raised him from the dead.'

'Oh, that's true,' said Ludens wildly. He was dismayed to find Patrick on the scene, and to hear the role attributed to him. Of course there was nothing he could do about it, he could scarcely denounce Pat, what could he denounce him for. And anyway his own jealous reactions were unfair to poor Pat and contemptible in themselves.

'Are you serious? I identify him as the patient mentioned by Dr Hensman, who gave us a very different account.'

'I mean,' said Ludens, 'Fenman was not actually dead, he was generally thought to be dying, when Professor Vallar arrived and resuscitated him.'

'How did he accomplish this?'

'He looked at him and breathed on him and pulled him about – I don't know exactly what happened.'

'You were not there?'

'I was there – but I don't know. I daresay he might have recovered anyway.'

'And does the Professor believe that he raised a man from the dead?'

'No – of course not – I mean, I don't know what he believes.'

'Haven't you discussed it with him?'

'No.'

'Why not?'

'Oh – he's probably forgotten – I mean he has other things to think about –'

'Hmmm. I thought you knew him very well. Never mind. Perhaps I touch on a sore point. In a moment you will tell me to go to hell.'

'Possibly.'

'So Fenman exaggerates – or is he joking?'

'He exaggerates. His first name is Patrick by the way.'

'May I ask what your first name is, Dr Ludens? We like to be informal here.'

'My first name is Alfred, and I am informally called Ludens.'

'My first name is Terence, and I am informally called Terence – not Terry, please. Has Patrick been the Professor's man for long?'

'Well – he's more like a friend.'

'Oh. I *see*.'

'But Patrick – Fenman – isn't actually *staying* here?'

'Oh yes. Our guests occasionally like to bring their maids or valets with them. Servants are put up in the Stables at reduced rates, and of course to some extent earn their keep by assisting the staff. When Patrick came down with Miss Vallar to view the place I took him to be a family servant, and we have already given him a room accordingly. But if as you say he is the Professor's *friend* perhaps he will be expected to live with him in the house?'

Ludens, wishing to reply, found himself suddenly silenced by his stammer. Checked by his old enemy and by the dreadful mass of information and misunderstanding just conveyed to him by Dr Bland, he walked on in silence, breathing deeply, feeling his face flush, and waiting for the mysterious blockage to pass. He was aware that Dr Bland was watching him intently.

'I'm s-s-sorry, I have a s-s-slight s-s-stammer. It doesn't often happen now – it c-comes suddenly and it p-passes quickly.'

'How very interesting!' said Dr Bland. 'I have already noticed that you are left-handed. We have had one or two stammerers here. It is a strange affliction. I made a study of it myself when I was working in America and developed a theory or two. Have you had any treatment for it?'

'Yes – no – the usual sort of advice. It is certainly better than it was, it hardly troubles me at all now.'

'All the same, any sudden intermittent malfunction can be a serious disadvantage and may always be a symptom. There are many and heterogeneous causal factors involved in stammering. We could have a talk about it sometime if you like?'

'No, thanks.'

'I mean just on a friendly basis, I wouldn't charge you anything.'

'No.'

'Have you had your blood pressure tested lately?'

'No!'

'Well, here we are at Benbow. It has a pretty situation, don't you think? I expect Dr Marzillian mentioned that we are keeping Rodney unoccupied so that the Professor can enjoy quietness and solitude. We hope he will settle down here.'

Irina came out of the house as soon as she saw Dr Bland and Ludens. Dr Bland paused, waved to Irina who waved back, and retreated along the drive. Beyond Irina Ludens could see Patrick and the maid Camilla sitting on the steps of the verandah. Pat was arranging the roses in a vase. Marcus, invisible inside the room, could be heard laughing.

Ludens waited for Irina to approach him. He burst out, 'Look, what's this about Pat being Marcus's servant – and you brought him down here to see the place – and now that bloody doctor thinks he's Marcus's boyfriend –!'

'Ssssh, and don't *look* like that, they may see you.'

'He said Pat was living in the stables. You know Marcus is paying for that! He said Pat could move into the house. You never told me you brought Pat here –'

'Don't raise your voice so.'

'And Pat's been boasting about being raised from the dead!'

'Dad told him not to talk about that. Let's just walk away a little – that's better.' They walked away under the trees. The sun, shining between branches, made little clearings where the grass was vividly green and some permitted wild flowers scattered their colours about.

Ludens felt again that special curious anguish caused by glimpses of a happiness he *would* have felt *if only* things were different – which could be different, perhaps could easily be different – but somehow maddeningly were not. He took off his jacket, which he had kept on to visit Marzillian, and rolled up the sleeves of his shirt. They paused under one of the tall birch trees which here consorted with the conifers. The white trunk of the tree was covered with dark runic lines. Ludens threw his jacket into the grass where their feet had made a pathway. He leaned against the tree and drew Irina against him. She sighed deeply and laid her head against his shoulder. He could feel her soft breasts and her heart beating against his heart. 'Irina, I want to make love to you. Can that be?'

She murmured with her lips against his shirt, 'Please. It's such a great thing. And now – there's so much – to be done – to be settled – you know – when there's peace –'

'Peace – Ah, when will there be peace – Oh Irina, Irina –' He released his hold and she moved away. He leaned his cheek against the runic tree. A great thing, yes. And she, with her one experience – and what was that? Something terrible? Perhaps more than one? Why was he so suspicious? She might be lying, she could lie.

'How did you get on with Marzillian?'

'I don't know, he just mystifies me. Irina, I'm frightened for Marcus. Marzillian is *interested* in him – it's not just money. I think he'd do anything to keep him here.'

'Like what?'

'Drug him, or have him certified.' This last possibility had only just occurred to Ludens. He raised his head and uttered a soundless cry.

'But *you* don't think he's mad.'

'Of course not! But around here everyone's supposed to be abnormal.'

Irina sat down in the grass, hauling up her skirt, stretching out her legs. She said, 'Ludens, I've been thinking about all this. Suppose you're *wrong*. I don't mean about mad or not, perhaps that's not important. What about Marcus's happiness?'

'*Happiness?*'

'Yes. You've been following him round for years trying to get out of him some secret you imagine he possesses. You're always winding him up, driving him on, making him *believe* in his secret. While you're around he feels he's got to go on and on pursuing the great idea or whatever it is. When you turned up at Red Cottage he was just beginning to get over it, to *forget* it, to stop being able to *hold it all together*.

Then when you came you galvanised him, you made him start up all over again. And all that Jewish stuff, you put that in his head somehow, all right perhaps just by being Jewish. Why can't one be Jewish without announcing it all the time and thinking one has some wonderful task and mankind can't get on without one? Chosen, forsooth! But suppose there isn't such a thing as the thing he's after, or suppose that there is but he's utterly incapable of finding it, or suppose that the thing is actually unimportant, or even *bad* – and consider that this *obsession* is making him frustrated and exhausted and *miserable* and unable to live or even meet any other human beings – and damaging my life, and perhaps yours, in fact certainly yours? He's been wretched and lonely and uncomfortable for years, well, you've seen the dumps he's been in, and *I've* had to be in too, and now suddenly everything changes, and here he can have solitude *and* some ordinary life, and I can leave him without going mad with anxiety. *There* I couldn't go away for an hour without worrying. He can learn to talk here, to chat, he's already learning, he'll come to like people and be less peculiar. Why can't you relax your hold a little and let him discover some ordinary enjoyment? You scream because Patrick's here – Patrick amuses him – that girl Camilla amuses him – by the way those "maids" are all nurses, they're trained therapists. Pat picked some flowers for him – that would never have occurred to you in a hundred years. Dad likes it here, he's better already, why shouldn't he stay here, he feels safe, he can notice things, little ordinary things which please and interest ordinary people. We're going over to lunch at the North Pavilion to try the vegetarian menu, he's looking forward to it. You just make him think about Death or the Absolute or something. Why can't you leave him alone, why can't you let him go? You do him harm not good. All right, aren't you going to interrupt me, aren't you going to say something?'

Ludens was silent for a while. He sat down in the grass with his back to the tree. The sun had gone, the grass was cool, a little damp. He felt misery, loneliness, a terrible need for love. He said, 'You do love me, don't you?'

'Yes, yes – but we're *hopeless*, we're incompetent, we're lost – we're babes in the wood – a bear will eat us – no he won't, you'll send him away – but what about all that I've just said?'

'I'll save you from the bear. I'll look after you forever. But – yes – well – what you've said, I understand it and why you say it, I just don't believe it, I believe something else. Irina, what is that strange sound? I heard it earlier this morning.'

There came, seeming very distant, a booming sound, repeated.

'Thunder?'

'No.'

They rose and stood uneasily, listening. She said, 'Let's go back. Come with us to lunch.'

'No, thank you, sorry, I'm going to the pub to calm myself down and think a bit. Tell Marcus I'll be back this afternoon. I want to buy some stuff for him to write with, I want him to *write*.'

Walking back to the Black Lion Ludens breathed deeply and made efforts of will to untangle and tease out and cool down the hot coagulated mass of impressions which he had received that morning. He felt menaced, damaged, defeated. After a while he began to try not to make efforts of will but just to let his thoughts drift quietly apart of their own accord. Then he made himself attend to the various flowers which were growing in the hedgerow: campion, meadowsweet, white flowering nettles, white hawthorn starry with stamens. He thought, suppose I were simply to kidnap him? But then I'd have to kidnap her too. Then he thought, I'm hungry. When he had crossed the bridge and reached the door of the pub and opened the door he met Toller who cried out, 'Here he is!' and 'There's a lady to see you, she's in the lounge talking to Miss Tether.' Ludens ran to the lounge. The lady was Franca.

'Oh, *Franca*!'

As soon as Franca saw Ludens's thin figure, his beaming face, his crazy smile, his evident delight at seeing her, she almost wailed with relief. Tears, instantly mopped away, came into her eyes. It had been right to come.

It had been her idea to leave London, to come to see Ludens and find out what was going on at the 'country cottage' about which those left behind felt such an intense curiosity. The plan had been applauded by Jack and Alison, and by Gildas, who had appeared on two evenings to talk to Jack. Franca was to be their messenger, their mediator and advocate, and was to warn 'the refugees', as Jack called them, that they, the others, would all be appearing shortly.

Franca, though thus approved and mandated, had felt considerable anxiety about her reception. She was frightened of Marcus, whom she had formerly disliked and disapproved of. She felt some vague affection for Irina but was not at all sure that this was reciprocated. Her arrival might simply irritate Alfred, who, busy organising the cottage and 'settling' its inhabitants, might have no time for a visitor and might resent a spectator. Her appearance might be, for all concerned, a thoroughly tiresome intrusion. She had pictured herself approaching the cottage (which she had imagined in some detail), finding the door open, the furniture in the garden, tradesmen trying to deliver things, the 'family' having a blazing row, and a very hot and bothered Ludens saying (to himself) 'Oh *God*, not *Franca*!'

Not of course knowing the address (which Ludens had been unable to give) she had gone first to the Black Lion (Ludens had told Jack where he would be staying) in case (though this could scarcely be hoped) she might find Ludens there alone. She was cheered to be told that, although absent now, he would probably be (assumed by Toller) back for lunch, and she was welcome to wait in the lounge. Moreover if she wished for a room there was one vacant. Franca, who had had no previous plan, and who took this invitation for a sign, promptly engaged the room for two nights. Jack had urged her to stay a bit, if she liked it, and get some country air. Franca was further set at ease (after a moment's anxiety) by the appearance of Miss Tether, introduced by the landlord, who immediately set about making Franca's acquaintance with energy and evident good will.

'Maisie Tether,' said Miss Tether to Ludens after they had all three sat down. She reached out her hand.

Ludens shook it. 'Alfred Ludens.'

Miss Tether, who had neatly waved white hair, wore lipstick, and was wearing a mauve skirt and jacket of what looked like linen but might have been silk. 'I've been making friends with Mrs Sheerwater who has told me so much about herself, and do you know, I have seen her husband's paintings? Isn't that a coincidence? I saw some in an exhibition in Cork Street and found them very interesting. I am a painter too you see, and Mrs Sheerwater is a painter – oh yes you are, once a painter always a painter – and I come here every year, I am a water-colourist and I have exhibited in London and New York. I should tell you I come from Boston. Mrs Sheerwater is, I know, a Londoner, where do you come from, Mr Ludens? You have such an interesting name.'

'My ancestors lived in Poland,' said Ludens, 'but I come from Somerset.'

'Somerset – I used to go down there chasing after Wordsworth and Coleridge! Such a lovely county, I painted in the Mendips, and Glastonbury, that shrine of miracles, I went there once at midsummer. Do please call me Maisie by the way.'

'I'm Franca,' said Franca.

'An Italian name.'

'I'm partly Italian, but –'

'Yes, you look Italian, doesn't she?'

'But I don't know Italy well, I expect you –'

'I've been there *many* times – such a treasure house. I didn't catch your first name, Mr Ludens?'

'Alfred. But I'm usually called by my surname.'

'I shall have to get used to that. Such an interesting name. It means "playing" in Latin, but of course you know that. I know because I had a classical education, my father was a professor of Greek.'

Franca and Ludens, smiling at each other and at Miss Tether, found this amiable flowing chatter utterly soothing, cool, fragrant, medicinal, like a healing herb, like a soft green leaf pressed to a wound.

Franca was very glad to be welcomed, and as it were individuated, guaranteed, by Ludens; and just to be away, on her own, out of the house in Chelsea, Jack's house, her home. As soon as she was on the train she felt, in spite of her fears about her reception, the lifting of a weight. At Chelsea, superficially, things had been 'going on well'. Observing Jack's, sometimes anxious, sometimes apologetic, always watchful face, Franca guessed that he thought that 'the girls were settling down' and 'it's working'. He was particularly tender and loving to Franca, so much so that there were instants when she could not help dreaming that nothing had changed; then she would return to the hopeless darkness and evil of her own heart. The extraordinary drunken scene, the love scene, the treason scene between herself and Alison, had not been repeated. It remained between them as a holy, or unholy, secret, though what exactly it meant, or might portend, neither of them would have explained. They never spoke of it in words; only sometimes in looks was its existence acknowledged as an 'aspect'. In a way, in retrospect, the curious scene (the things they had said!) had been like a secret liberating ritual of some scandalous sort, a shedding of blood, like a magic rite involving the beheading of a cock. (Franca reflected upon this image which had come to her spontaneously.) Perhaps they would not, were somehow bound *never* to, speak of it again. There certainly seemed to be no question of any revolt against Jack. Franca was not appalled or remorseful; on the other hand, the symbolic rebellion had brought her no relief. In a way it proved rather how strong Jack's hold upon the situation really was. If the women could get up to all that, utter those treasonable cries, and still love him, still obey him, still get on perfectly well with each other – did not that simply show that he had won the game? Or had he somehow automatically *not* won it, simply because of the rage and hate which devoured Franca's heart, which had once been so happy and full of love? And if Franca never spoke, never admitted for a second or by an eyelid's flutter, the things that were in her heart, would it still be the case that Jack had not won? She had been glad to leave London, and very glad to see the familiar, affectionate, and as she thought of it somehow innocent, face of Ludens – but she had carried with her those dark awful problems, not even problems, more like heavy poisonous lumps, lethal tumours; and she was painfully aware of them, as she was aware too of the pure beneficence of Maisie Tether's talk and Ludens's smile.

Miss Tether, who was courteous and tactful, did not in fact detain them long. She said she must go and 'tidy her room', hoped to see them both again, even suggested that Franca might like to come painting with her, she would supply the materials. She departed, leaving her listeners with a felicitous space of time before lunch. Ludens suggested they might go for a walk. Miss Tether had recommended a visit to the church, which had a fine Norman doorway. He told Toller they would not be in for lunch. The situation demanded a private meal elsewhere; and for this pleasure, distracted from his hunger by Franca's arrival, Ludens was now prepared to wait. So they set off together along the village street, each of them prudently wondering how much to tell the other.

'What's the cottage like?'

'Well, it's not exactly a cottage, more like a bungalow, and it's on the estate of a big house that has been turned into a sort of hospital.'

'So there's medical help nearby – not that he needs it I imagine. Do they have to buy furniture?'

'No, it's pretty well furnished.'

'I suppose they'll shop in the village, I expect they'll find anything they need, I saw quite a serious grocer's shop as I came through.'

'I forgot to ask how you got here?'

'Train and bus, easy. So they're OK, and you'll be back in London soon?'

'I'm not sure when.'

'By the way, Christian Eriksen is back, he was asking after you, he's got a problem about his flat, I think he's looking for digs.'

'I'm glad he's back. How's Jack, is he painting?'

'He says he can't, but he's doing drawings. He tears them up after-wards.'

'And how's Alison?'

'Splendid. She's very pleased about her play. Patrick hasn't been around.'

'He's down here.'

'Down here?'

'He's come to see Marcus.'

'I'd like to see Marcus – just see him, look at him. I could just pass by, he might be sitting in the sun.'

They passed a small dark pub called the Hedgehog and reached a large florid pub, indeed hotel, called the White Lion, which had already been mentioned to Ludens in disparaging terms by Toller. Although it was now, as Ludens remembered, but a little way on to the church, they decided they had walked far enough and went in. The White Lion, not ostentatiously, or otherwise, ancient, had a large comfortable Edwardian-style bar and a pretentious dining room with white table cloths and waiters. Franca and Ludens decided to eat in the bar and settled themselves in a secluded corner. They ordered ham and salad and cheese and glasses of cider. The ham and the cider were local and excellent. After Franca had drunk a little she became conscious of falling into some sort of disarray. She was sweating after even this fairly short walk, the sun had touched her and made her feel giddy, perspiration was running down her brow and past her eyes, her hair, hastily pinned that morning, was about to come down, she felt an irresistible impulse to touch Alfred. She reached out and took his hand and squeezed it, feeling a responding pressure which assured her that he recalled the previous occasion on which they had held hands. As she released his hand she began to cry. Ludens said in an exasperated rather than sympathetic tone, 'Stop it, Franca.'

Franca, finding her handkerchief and controlling her voice said, 'Alfred, what shall I do? I can't stand it. I must leave Jack, but where could I go? What could I do? Besides I *can't* leave him, I *love* him, except that I'd like to kill him, I'd like to kill Alison, I'd like to kill myself. I have to pretend to be good and kind, or as they see it sleepy and passive and placid, they take it for granted, I don't even get any credit, I can't keep it up much longer, I'll become a wild beast and break out and slaughter everyone. If I had a machine-gun I'd kill them. I am very nearly mad, an evil spirit possesses me, I ought to be shut into a nunnery, shut in like nuns used to be.'

Her hair began to descend, she felt its heavy coolness on her neck and checked its descent, holding it with one hand while the other scrambled for the errant pins. The barmaid bringing the cheese looked with pity at the elderly lady so tearful and red in the face while her hair was falling about her in such a mess.

'Franca, you don't mean any of this, it's wild words, you just are not a violent person. Well, you do mean one thing, that you love Jack and can't leave him. You've simply got to *live* this, *be* kind and good, be what you're really like, be patient –'

'If you mean wait till Jack gets tired of Alison, he won't! He's a man, he wants a beautiful young animal, and she'll never let him go, never.'

'Jack loves you. You love him. You've got to bear it. There's so much suffering in the world, awful senseless insoluble suffering. Your suffering has sense, if you can go on being loving and kind even if sometimes it feels like pretending, it can heal the people about you, it can heal you, and it won't *be* pretence because it's the only *way*, and the only *true* way. If you start hurting people and smashing things every sort of anger and chaos and lies will follow. You *can't* be violent, *you* can't be violent. Franca, darling, don't cry, please, be comforted.' He touched a strand of her hair which had escaped and run down onto her shoulder, touched it with a beseeching gesture as if it were something separate from her, pure and unblemished, like a humble sacred object, or an innocent gentle animal.

She thought, so I *can't* be violent? I tried to break a cup and I couldn't. Perhaps he is right. Or is he? Can one simply, in the name of truth or good, carrying it like a banner, *deny* the existence of such a fierce awful tumult? Then, moved by his gesture, she felt suddenly carried to him by a wave of emotion, as if she could suddenly have clung to him, joining her whole body to his. Now I'm in love with *him*, she thought! Yes, I must be mad, this is madness, this is the violence of the soul. She sat still, feeling weary and emptied, smiling a little at Ludens who was, so kindly and gently, smiling at her.

Ludens had indeed been very glad to see Franca, and had, as he feared she realised, been shocked by her sudden violent talk. Her voice, her face, had changed as if she had actually been taken over by an evil spirit. However she had responded quickly to his pious rigmarole. He was glad she had come; she was for him, as he for her, 'another place'.

He found himself wishing that he had no problems of his own and could give all his attention to her problems. They said farewell outside the White Lion. Ludens said he must do some shopping, Franca that she was very tired and was going back to the Black Lion to rest. Nothing more was said about her seeing Marcus. Ludens did not want her to see Marcus, or to see Bellmain. He hated the idea of the others turning up and tramping about on his territory making jokes and moral judgments. He needed time and *working space* to understand Marcus and help him – not least to find somewhere else for him to live. He could do something helpful at once by providing him with writing materials. When Franca had gone he went into a stationer's shop in the street and enquired after paper and notebooks. The little shop had only writing paper and extremely thin and flimsy 'exercise books' ruled for doing accounts or containing graph paper. Ludens bought a few of these notebooks and some fairly sturdy felt pens. A sense of helplessness and futility swept over him. Could he persuade Marcus to write in these wretched booklets?

The sun had resumed its reign and Ludens, entering Bellmain, was glad to leave the drive and walk through the wood. The curious emptiness of the scene, the silence, the great presences of the trees, the intense summer smell, the silence of the birds in the afternoon, so pressed upon his heart that at last he had to stop, to breathe, to listen. The woodland, seeming man-made, artificial, was so beautiful, so eerie, so frightening. He listened; and then distantly heard a sound of bird song, no it was a human sound, music, perhaps intrusive picnickers with a transistor set? That seemed impossible. Ludens, though so hostile to Bellmain, had already instinctively put together a conception of it as an extremely secluded strictly ordered place with rules which it might almost be death to break. The front gate was discreetly supervised, a high wire fence bordered the road, no doubt surrounded the whole domain. At the same time this austere internal organisation was veiled by the charms of nature and an affectation of luxurious ease. Those charming 'maids', playing at houris and shepherdesses, with their attractive uniforms and their curtseys and their obliging manners, were really nurses, in effect spies, perhaps even budding psychiatrists. They too, no doubt, were subject to the severity of the rules, even to a rule of silence. Speech, here, must be permitted speech, useful purposive speech. So far and so deep evidently did the idea of therapy reach in this establishment as to have already impressed itself upon the vulnerable mind of Ludens.

As he came closer he identified the sound of *singing*, certainly not a radio but nearby human voices singing in unison, no in parts, women's voices, unless that alto were a tenor. A white wall ahead, it could not be that of Benbow, turned out to be Rodney. Ludens approached cautiously.

Sitting on the mown grass in front of Rodney were Irina, Patrick and Camilla. A checkered board with draughts tumbled upon it lay beside them, also a treble recorder. The trio, in full voice, were singing 'The Silver Swan', a madrigal well known to Ludens who had often sung it with Jack and Pat and Gildas and Christian (who was actually a counter-tenor). Camilla was providing a charming though insubstantial soprano, Irina a quite creditable mezzo, Patrick was at his most Neapolitan. Ludens had once more the condensed sensation of something happy and good which had been darkened, defiled, vandalised, utterly spoilt. He was about to step back and creep away when Camilla saw him and pointed. She sprang to her feet, Patrick rose too, Irina still seated, waved. Pat was wearing black trousers and a blue shirt which hung idly upon him. A great smile wrinkled his face, his sunburnt cheek and short nose. He opened his arms wide. 'Come! Sing!'

Irina now jumped up. Camilla adjusted the neck of her jacket. Pat pulled his lolling shirt up onto his shoulder and drew it across his breast. They all, smiling at him, looked guilty, like children whose illicit romp had been interrupted by their father or schoolmaster.

Ludens, skirting round the clearing, said, 'I'm just going to see Marcus.' The damp hot smell of the mown grass was almost suffocating.

'He's asleep,' said Irina, 'that's why we moved here. Camilla has a key of Rodney, do you know it's quite different inside from Benbow, all the houses are different – still, I like ours better.'

Camilla was holding a letter which she now, advancing, held out to Ludens. He thanked her and put it in his pocket. Waving his hand vaguely he went on through the trees in the direction of Benbow. He heard soft quick footsteps behind him but did not look round. Irina caught him up.

'Don't be cross. Do stay and sing. Please don't wake Dad.'

'I won't wake him.'

'Why are you so solemn? Don't be solemn. Help me to be happy, help me to be at peace.'

'Irina, I want to take you and Marcus away from here and look after you. I feel nothing good can happen here.'

'Can't we make something good happen? You make me think we are under a curse.'

'I want to talk to your father when he wakes up.'

'He's exhausted. He's had such a long talk with Dr Marzillian. Well, don't look like that, why ever not?'

Marcus slept. He was lying fully clothed on the bed. A rug had been roughly pulled over his feet. He lay on his back, his face calm, his breathing imperceptible. He might have been dead, as in a picture of a great man lying in state. He looked at peace. How could that calm head contain such a frightening jumble of thoughts? Marcus's thoughts were frightening, they were terrible thoughts which were breaking themselves upon the unrelenting barriers of human capacity, thoughts one might die of, thoughts which might make others die. Ludens suddenly pictured Marcus's thoughts as large black eagles hurling themselves again and again upon a vast opaque motionless sheet of glass. And yet these brave heroic thoughts would be, to almost all people, not only unintelligible but nonsensical, futile, a waste of mental power, a waste of human will – while millions starved. Why does he torment himself so, thought Ludens, why does he torment *me* so? Why can't he and I and Irina live an ordinary cheerful life together? And then there would be the grandson who was to be a genius. Perhaps if that boy existed Marcus would stop battering himself to pieces. But Ludens did not want Marcus to stop thinking. He still, still, wanted, if ever it might be possible, to follow Marcus over the threshold, through the looking-glass.

Ludens had not been unmoved by Irina's accusing cries. 'You've encouraged him, you've driven him on, you've made him believe in his secret – you make him think about death – he's frustrated and exhausted – why can't you leave him alone – you do him harm not good. Why can't you let him go –' And, then, just now, her voice saying, pleading, 'Help me to be happy.' What would become of them all, would they be lost in the wood and eaten by the bears? They were all children, Marcus was a child. And now there were all these new dangers in this place to which Marcus already thought fate had led them, where Ludens must be vigilant every moment to guard the precious clarity of Marcus's mind. And all this time, Ludens was aware, he was neglecting his own work, his own book, using up the freedom which his college had given him for his own studies and reflections.

Fearing the object of his close scrutiny might suddenly wake and resent it, Ludens drew up a chair beside the bed and sat down near to where Marcus's outstretched hand lay limp upon the counterpane. He laid his head down against the side of the bed. Strange waves of calm began to sweep over him. He had had so much anxiety lately, so much struggle. At any rate here he was now, and Marcus was here too, and asleep, and safe. As Ludens began to fall asleep he heard, far away, the high pure sound of the treble recorder which Patrick could play so beautifully.

He woke to find Marcus stirring, and leapt up at once.

'I've been asleep. Have you been here long?'

'No,' said Ludens, glancing quickly at his watch. 'I've only just come.' He had been asleep for twenty minutes.

'I've had a good dream. Where is Irina?'

'She's out in the garden with Pat and Camilla, they've been singing.'

'I'm glad she's enjoying herself. I'll join you in a moment.'

Ludens retired into the sitting room which was heavily scented, not by Pat's roses which were tightly in bud, but by some orange lilies brought by Camilla. Marcus returned from the bathroom.

'Alfred, I've been thinking, it's very kind of you to help us so much, but you mustn't let us interfere with your work. I'm sure you need your own books around you and have your own writing to do. Are you comfortable at the Black Lion?'

'Yes, yes.'

'But it is costing you money. You could come and stay in the South Pavilion, there are rooms there, you could stay there as my guest. Marzillian suggested it.'

'He *suggested* it?'

'He knows how helpful you are to me. He's a very kind man. He said he would charge a reduced rate.'

'Oh!'

'He's a very intelligent man. We had an interesting conversation.'

'So Irina told me. I think I'd rather not live in here. But, Marcus, you aren't going to *stay* here, are you?'

'It solves a lot of problems for me and for Irina. I don't want her to be burdened with shopping and so on like she was before.'

'It's not too late for her to go to the university.' This idea had arrived in Ludens's head lately. He was surprised he had not thought of it earlier; it had evidently taken him some time to recover from his first impression of Irina as an uncivilised gipsy girl.

Marcus seemed taken aback. 'Well, I'm not sure that she'd want to – or be able to –'

'All right, no hurry, it's just an idea, I haven't suggested it to her. Now, would you like us to talk a little, or would you like me simply to sit with you, or shall I go away?'

This list of choices seemed rather to depress Marcus, and Ludens had again the sensation he had had when he surprised the singers, that he was being some sort of pedagogic killjoy. He said hastily, 'Or would you like to go for a walk? We could walk into the village and look at the church, I gather it's Norman, or partly Norman, and we could talk as we go along.'

Marcus replied, 'We might go as far as the Axle Stone, that magnificent monolith, you must have seen it. I walked there with Marzillian after lunch.'

Ludens thought, he's afraid to go out. He said, 'Yes, let's do that. But you must come and visit me at the Black Lion. Would you and Irina come to dinner with me tonight?' He remembered Franca. Well, why not?

'Oh thank you, I don't think tonight, we shall be using our kitchen, Irina and Camilla that is, an experiment –'

As Marcus started fussing about, changing his shoes (he was wearing slippers), searching for a hat (eventually found rather crumpled), and wondering if it was going to rain (which it patently was not), Ludens brought out the 'writing materials' which he had bought at the stationer's shop. 'Look, Marcus, I got you these, so you can start writing if you feel like it. I'm sorry the notebooks are so rotten.'

'I see. So now one has to write on graph paper!'

'Sorry. That must have got in by mistake!'

As he watched Marcus turning over the thin little exercise books Ludens felt, though the thought was ridiculous in a way, that it was impossible that weighty ideas could be written down on such flimsy paltry pages. 'Marcus, I'll get you some decent notebooks in London, and better pens, a fountain pen if you like. Look, I'll drive to London this evening and get them tomorrow morning and be back by lunchtime, and I can bring down some of my own books, and fetch anything you like from your place. I know there are two more suitcases that should come, and maybe other things too.'

Ludens had been reminded by Marcus of something upon which he himself had reflected, the mounting cost of staying at the Black Lion. It had just occurred to him that he could let his flat to Christian Eriksen, who was said by Franca to be looking for lodgings. And he thought too: if I go to London I can see Gildas.

The Axle Stone was certainly an astonishing object. It was roughly rectangular, a flattened rectangle or lozenge of sandstone, standing upon one of its corners and rising to a height of at least twelve feet. It was supported by an oval concrete base which also served as a seat. It was plainly a 'worked' stone, made by man into its present form. It was cut, a yard or so wide, to display two huge surfaces, one mildly undulating, extremely smooth, without sharp projections or cracks, the other deeply scored, criss-crossed with fissures, looking at times (as Ludens thought on improved acquaintance) like an old wise tired sad face, at other times like a mocking or even wicked face. The sunlight constantly altered the appearance of the Stone, slanting to enliven the smooth face with little shadows and to endow the cracked face with its variety of dark significant lines. Ludens had by now read the 'fascinating account' of the stone mentioned by Marzillian, which included the legend mentioned by Camilla. The object, it was agreed, had been in its present position, and erect, for a long time, possibly for a very very long time. An eighteenth-century antiquarian living at Bellmain Manor wrote in a monograph, since vanished but scrappily quoted by a local rector a century later, that the Stone, regarded with superstitious fear by the villagers, was said by local tradition to have been 'always there'. Other evidence was lacking, apart from that suggested by the Stone itself, which bore a marked resemblance to the great stones of the prehistoric temple at Avebury. A fact, quoted by the cleric, was that in 1725 a landowner had had one of the Avebury stones removed to his estate; but the place near Avebury was not Bellmain, and the stone clearly not this stone. There was no record of any such (extremely difficult) removal earlier. The name of the Stone, otherwise unexplained, suggested to some a propitiatory reference to the numerous axles broken during its journey. It seemed a relevant fact that there were no sarsen boulders in the vicinity of Bellmain; though this also prompted the theory that the Stone was actually a facsimile, made for some rich eccentric, perhaps even the very antiquarian quoted by the rector, who had provided a bogus history for his creation. This idea was totally rejected however by 'experts', self-styled or otherwise, who had come at intervals to look at the thing. There were no traces of other similar stones nearby which might have formed part of a significant group. The Stone was a mysterious solitary, not mentioned by either Stukeley or Aubrey. The anonymous author of the brochure gave most of his attention to the 'charming legend'. The Avebury stones (being either pillars or squares) are said to be male and female symbols, suggestive of a fertility cult. It was said that in the twelfth century the incumbent at Avebury church had put a terrible curse upon the stones which were so clearly the work and abode of evil spirits. The legend was that one of the stones, distressed or incensed by this treatment, set off one night and walked to Bellmain where, it was implied, it received the protection of more friendly powers. It appeared that stories of walking stones were not uncommon, a particular stone still at Avebury was said to walk across the road at certain times, and the stones at Rollright went down to the river to drink at midsummer. Avebury was also connected with Arthur's Knights, said to be buried in the vicinity, thus casting another ray of picturesque glamour upon the mystery at Bellmain. Nothing much came of all this for the history books, and local people were free to believe that the Stone was created in 2600 BC by the Avebury men, who might or might not have placed it in its present position. The Stone, the author added, was clearly a female, it weighed thirty-five tons, and had (according to the same legend) a 'dreadful secret name' which would bring either magic power or instant death to anyone who knew it.

The Stone was surrounded by a very tall, perhaps twenty feet tall, thick circular yew hedge, open, toward the drive, just enough to have afforded Ludens his first glimpse of the object, and having two other openings, mere slits a few feet wide. Through one of these slits Marcus and Ludens had now entered in single file. The grass, though mown, permitted a few white daisies. The enclosure, about a hundred yards in circumference, was hot and seemed silent, the thick high hedge perhaps muffling the sound of birds. Marcus and Ludens paused when they entered, looking about, then went to the Stone. Ludens instinctively stroked its smooth benign surface. They sat down on the concrete seat which surrounded the base and had been warmed by the sun.

As they walked along Marcus had pointed out the building which housed the swimming-pool, where he intended to swim tomorrow morning and thereafter daily. He spoke of having swum in the Mediterranean when he was young and his parents had a house near Cannes. He suggested that Ludens might like to swim too. Ludens said he thought not. Did Ludens like swimming? Not much. Where had he learnt to swim, that, in Marcus's view, was always important. At Weston-super-Mare. Where was that? Ludens told him. Marcus, after mentioning that the water in the swimming-pool was of course heated, started to ramble on about other swims which he had had in Lake Geneva and Lake Como, but how on the whole he preferred swimming in the sea if possible, and how it was now some years since he had swum *anywhere*, and so on. This rigmarole, silenced for a moment after their entry into the circle, showed signs of starting up again once they were sitting down. Ludens, aching with anxiety and impatience, and in no mood for this display of ordinariness, cut in.

'Please – I must know where you are.'

'Where –?'

'Where you are in your thoughts. You said you were at a place where the road divided, where there were choices and decisions. I wonder if you have decided, and anyway I didn't really understand what the alternatives were, and perhaps you would tell me?'

Marcus, who had laid his battered white panama hat down beside him, took it up and started examining it. He poked a finger through a hole in the straw. He murmured, 'Do you know, I think I've lost the thread.'

Ludens, ready to scream with exasperation, said, 'You were after a device, I think you used the word "gadget". Something that had to be in order for human consciousness to be, a circuit, I think you used that word too. Something hidden, as if by the gods, and one had to be pure and holy to find it, and above ordinary morality, or what is ordinarily called morality was how you put it, because if morality was not an illusion the discovery would be impossible, but if the discovery was ever made one would become a god instantly and die in a significant manner of pure thought.'

Marcus who had continued to gaze at his hat, said after a moment, '*Well* – if *that* is the position – we are indeed – *dished*!'

'All right!' said Ludens, 'I haven't understood *anything*, I am utterly ignorant and naive, I am a *fool*, I just want to make you talk to me!'

'So, you want to set me off, do you.' Marcus said this as if entirely unaware of the many successful serious conversations he had already had, which had been set going simply by the energy and ingenuity of Ludens.

'Marcus, for God's sake say something.'

Marcus smiled, then laughed, then composed his face. 'I am sorry, Alfred, I am afraid that I have proved, and almost certainly will prove, a sad disappointment to you. You expect some great thing, a great book, a great action, and there will probably be nothing but the dwindling away of what was never really an argument or an idea or a vision at all. Could you bear that?'

'Scarcely. I mean, of course – but I don't want you to give up. I *won't let* you!' Ludens had taken off his jacket and ruffled up his hair and was leaning over and unconsciously pulling up handfuls of grass. His fingernails, scratching the ground, were black with earth.

Marcus sighed, 'All right. But you must ask me clever questions.'

'Damn it, I'm always asking you clever questions! What did you mean about being driven beyond morality into the godhead?'

'Did I say that? Something like that. Partly it's something obvious.'

'*Obvious?*'

'We agree, do we not, that there is no God, no person such as He whom the Psalmist loved and feared, who loved us and required us to be good. Of course our busy human doings need and generate what are called moral rules. These are very various and always tend to obscure what lies deeper.'

'And *it* is deeper.'

'Now, just at the moment when technology seems likely to end what we call our civilisation, human thinking has rid itself of a number of crippling philosophical errors.'

'Like what?'

'Mistakes – old pictures of words as names, old distinctions between subject and object, and fact and value. It's *as if*, just before we plunge into a technological world which will reduce us to imbecile dwarfs, the gods were offering us, at the very last moment, a glimpse of – of –'

'You don't believe in God, but you mention the gods.'

'I said *as if*. Don't you listen?'

'But if we see it, if we find it, will it save us from becoming imbecile dwarfs?'

Marcus paused. He said, 'I don't really know the answer to that question. One would have to die. And never know.'

'You mean the one who found it, who saw it, would die, and this death would bring about the saving miracle you once spoke of?'

Marcus, who had been looking at the yew hedge, resumed his scrutiny of his hat. He said, in rather matter-of-fact tones, 'That would be one line of thought. But to answer your original question, reflections which engage with the deepest and most important matter, the matter of what we are, which we so long used God to answer, must leave the region of values behind. They must also leave behind the region of facts. Science cannot answer that question, nor can our old philosophy answer it, nor of course our moralising. One may doubt indeed whether human thought can find any path to that place.'

'Sorry to be simple-minded, but can't science at least explain the world even if it can't explain us?'

'We are the world.'

'Well, yes, I suppose so – But look – sorry again – you said it had to be something necessary, *like* the Ontological Proof. Why can't it actually *be* the Ontological Proof, I mean what the Proof means, which I take it is that what is desired with a pure good desire necessarily exists – sorry that's a rather crude version but you see –'

Marcus smiled. 'Crude or not it is certainly the only feasible version. I actually considered that long ago but saw it wouldn't do. The conception is not deep enough, too much is left out, it employs the confused concept of desire, and the even more confused concept of love which leads us back towards individuals and accidents, and ultimately requires the existence of God which it is supposed to prove. No, no.'

Ludens, just after he uttered his previous speech, realised that he had never actually thought this particular thought before, it had simply jumped into his head! He was astounded. It represented something which he urgently wanted to say in answer to things which Marcus was saying which frightened him very much. But now he could not clearly remember either what Marcus had said or what he had said. He replied lamely, 'So you don't believe in love. Didn't you love your parents?'

'No. Did you love yours?'

'I only ever had one, my father, he's still alive. Yes, I love him.'

The particularity of this exchange seemed for a moment to break the continuity of the argument. Marcus began to fidget as if, with nothing more to say, he was about to depart.

To stop him, Ludens said, 'But you talk of the purity and holiness required to *think* in a certain sort of way. Isn't holiness the same as goodness?'

'The man who touched the Ark was struck dead. Was that just?'

'It was God who struck him.'

Marcus began to chuckle, then to laugh, then stopped laughing. 'You are right, the episode is irrelevant. And you may say – courage and asceticism and hard work make a kind of virtue.'

'And truthfulness.'

'When one is very close to Truth itself, truthfulness vanishes. One is simply constrained. *That* is the instructive picture. Now let us leave this place, it is rather eerie.'

'So you've let your flat to Christian?' said Gildas. 'I hope there's somewhere to put all those bottles of aquavit. He'll have a Danish party and smash all your *art nouveau* pots.'

'I thought of that,' said Ludens, 'I've locked them all up in a cupboard.'

'And you're going to *stay* out there in the country, in a room in some peasant's hut?'

'Yes, if I can find one. I'm certainly going to stay.'

'Your infatuation will end in tears. What about your mind, your book on Leonardo, your lectures for next term, your *studies* which you are paid to pursue?'

'I'll take some books down with me. Gildas, don't sneer. I'm learning a lot –'

'From Marcus?'

'Yes. I know it's hard for me to explain –'

'I sneer.'

'He forces me to think, his thoughts will help my thoughts, *all* my thoughts. Gildas, I've got to see this through, I've got to help him write this book –'

'You think he'll write a great work because you've brought him a pile of fine hardbacked notebooks with the lines exactly the right distance apart, some blue, some red, some green?'

'Well, decent notebooks help, they help me anyway! And I'm going to buy him a really good fountain pen.'

'That'll cost you a packet. It's like buying toys for a child. Marcus's ideas, according to your account of them, are a total muddle, he'll never see his way through, he'll never emerge, he'll just crumble. There's no centre left, he can't concentrate any more. But I thought your aim was to get him out of that place, not to help him to settle down.'

'I do want to get him out. I thought I might be able to do it at once, but I can't. I've got to have somewhere to take them to.'

'Them – oh yes, the sage and the girl you imagine you love.'

'I do love her.'

'I don't believe it. You love him. The girl is a side-effect.'

'She said something like that. But no –'

'Why can't you get her into bed?'

'The place is too damn public. And I think she's had some bad experience of sex. I can't just seize her and hustle her. She said herself, and I found it so moving, "It's such a great thing." We'll have to wait until there's some kind of peace and privacy, and I can be quiet and gentle and –'

245

'Girls don't want men to be quiet and gentle, I'm told. If you're not panting with impatient lust they think you're not interested.'

'That remark is not up to your usual standard.'

'True. I am declining, I am going to the dogs. I shall soon be lying on the pavement outside Charing Cross Station with a bottle beside me. So you were enraged to find Irina and Pat sitting on the grass and singing "The Silver Swan".'

'Yes! Pat's there posing as Marcus's servant, he has a room there, he's all over the place!'

'Well, why not? He's got a kind of right to be Marcus's servant. My dear boy, seriously, try to be kind to Pat, try to understand him. It's a big responsibility being raised from the dead, it's supposed to change one's life. I hope he isn't drinking?'

'I don't think so. It's not allowed there.'

'He's a homeless man, he lives his penniless poet act for all it's worth, and that's a kind of courage. Now he's got something to do, a place to be, someone to look after. No wonder he's so healthy and beautiful.'

'Why don't you come down and see him, maybe you could share his room.'

'I adore your jealousy, especially when it's so misplaced. I expect Shakespeare wrote a sonnet about that. And I imagine, if I rightly understand your Armenian doctor, that *he* thinks Pat is useful, or else he wouldn't have him there. He must think you're useful too, or he wouldn't tolerate you. You'd better stay useful.'

'I told him that if he drugged Marcus I'd kill him.'

'I expect that delighted him. I don't see how you can stop him drugging Marcus, or even know whether he is. He controls all the food.'

'Well, not all, there's a kitchen and they can buy their own. I must get them out. I'll think how to do that.'

'But they like it there.'

'They'll get tired of it. Or something will happen that will make them stop liking it. There's something about it which they'll suddenly start noticing.'

'It all sounds madly interesting, I wonder what will happen? Something's bound to happen. I must come down and see for myself.'

'Yes, do come. But don't say things —'

'Oh I won't be indiscreet or nasty, I'll be good. You know how good I can be. So Franca's there already. And you know Jack and Alison are coming?'

'Yes, I wish they weren't. Poor Franca! How *can* they?'

'For Jack, it's a matter of principle. He feels he's being truthful, living in the open. He wants to parade his successful *ménage*.'

'It's such a mess. Franca told the landlord her husband is coming – after all *she*'s forced into the open too! – and now he wants me to swap rooms with her because I've got a double room and of course I don't mind, only someone will have to explain to him that her husband will be staying somewhere else with someone else, but they'll all be having dinner together and laughing merrily.'

'The landlord will love it and tell everyone.'

'Don't. At any rate they won't be at the Black Lion, there's only three rooms to let and it's full up. That would be the last straw.'

'You said Franca had made a friend.'

'Yes, there's a marvellously nice American woman, a painter, and she and Franca went out painting this afternoon. Franca painting again! You remember she used to, before Jack suppressed her.'

'You said she was pretty miserable at lunchtime. I ask for no details.'

'She was rather low.'

'I'm rather low too.'

'Gildas, I haven't asked how you are. How are things, are you all right?'

'Your query comes too late, you obviously aren't interested. You don't feel like singing? No, neither do I. Perhaps there will be no more singing. I wonder what will happen to your Master. He may perform another miracle. Christ was revered for his miracles, not his wisdom. Who knows what may happen. I shall certainly come and see.'

'My folks were Quakers,' said Maisie Tether. 'Of course I'm a Quaker too except I hardly ever go to Meetings. I'm at home with these people. I guess we were pretty well among the first in New England – and we never moved on, we liked it there! I'm told there's a place called California where it's sunny all year and humanity has been liberated, but I prefer the East. Not that Boston isn't liberated too, I'm sorry to say, but the countryside is lovely, with the little hills and dales and the little white churches. It's funny that it does look like England in a way – and yet it doesn't. You couldn't mistake it for the Cotswolds.'

'I'm sure you couldn't,' said Franca. 'But have you really never been to California?'

'Oh, I've *been* there, I just don't like it! What did you think of New York?'

'Well, I only saw the Metropolitan Museum.'

'That's great, but there's more to the USA than pictures.'

'My husband loves picture galleries, and –'

'I'm looking forward to seeing *him*, I really do like his work. You know *you* have talent, you studied at art school, why ever did you stop?'

'Oh – well – I got married – I decided I wasn't much good –'

'Oh you did, did you? You let him put you down?'

'What makes you think that?'

'I know about husbands, I know their little ways, I've watched them at work, thank God I never had one. He loves you and cherishes you but two painters in the family won't do. You got married and decided you weren't much good! That's our history in a nutshell! Now isn't it time for you to fight back? Didn't you just love being in that dell painting those trees? Franca, you can paint! I'm serious! You have things to learn, I'll teach you. Courage, that's what makes an artist, courage, boldness, rashness, nerve – like when I got you to let the paper absolutely *swim* with water! We'll try again today. Does your husband paint in oils?'

'Acrylic.'

'Well, it's neater. A bit too neat in my view. When's he coming, this husband figure?'

Yesterday afternoon, when she returned to the pub after her lunch with Ludens, Franca had found Maisie Tether about to set off along the river with her painting gear. She invited Franca to come with her, and Franca came. She encouraged Franca to paint, and Franca painted. She looked at the willow trees and the birch trees and the ash trees and the pink campion and white comfrey and the sorrel and the buttercups and the feathery flowers of the grass and the bulrushes and the shadows and the reflections and the stripy glossy rippling water coloured blue and brown and a subtle yellowish white; and she saw red admiral butterflies and tiny black frogs and a kingfisher and a water rat and a great many aquamarine dragonflies. And she felt a ray which pierced her breast and brought tears to her eyes, making her gasp with an unfamiliar yet somehow remembered emotion composed of joy and melancholy and solitude and space.

The particular emollient pleasure and calm which had, as they agreed afterwards, attended Franca's and Ludens's first meeting with Maisie Tether, had persisted, blossomed as it were, for Franca, into feelings of trust and affection which surely by now amounted to friendship. Miss Tether's presence opened, for Franca, a large warm coloured expanse. She felt larger, stronger, healthier, less scratched, besmirched, bedraggled, plucked at, pulled about. She had seen herself as she emerged (temporarily, she told herself, even momentarily) from the shell or crust of her customary being, sufficiently at least to leave London, as something shrunken, wounded and weak. Miss Tether's company and the river, and the miracle of the colours had detached her from this little bloodstained sack upon which she now looked with amazement, realising *how* much she had been defeated. Why had she broken down so pathetically with Alfred at lunchtime? And what could he say to her except what he had said, what could he do for her except smile at her in the old way? She saw her performance then as soppy, sloppy. She looked down at it as from an eminence. But she knew that this state too was surely ephemeral; and the image came to her of Jack and Alison, as tall as trees, or like the monstrous pictures of dictators carried in public processions, coming relentlessly towards her. So she *reflected* for a time, perhaps many seconds, before she answered Maisie Tether.

'I'm not sure, in a day or two.'

'Maybe he'll come painting with us. Or does he despise water-colour?'

'He used to do water-colour sketches for larger paintings – that was in his first phase – he hasn't done that since.'

'I guess I only know his later work, the mandalas and the eggs and the fishes – what a colourist. What was his earlier style?'

'Oh rather Bonnard–Vuillard.'

'Not a bad place to be. You could do about everything in that place. What made him change?'

'He was influenced by a remarkable man who was a painter but really he was a theorist, a sort of philosopher.'

'Hmmm. I think painters should be influenced by painters and keep clear of theories. Look what happened to Pissarro. Anyway we may be able to have some good talks. I believe you'll be in Mr Ludens's room, it's such a nice room with a view of the river.'

'Maisie, perhaps I should tell you – I live in what is usually called a *ménage à trois*.'

'My poor child, don't say you've got *two* of them!'

'No, no, it's the other way round, which is after all I think more customary – my husband has a mistress, a charming young girl called

Alison. I get on very well with her. It all works very well. I hope I don't shock you.'

'You shock me very much indeed,' said Maisie Tether. Her amiable mouth closed into a hard line, her eyes became steely, even her hair seemed to stiffen. 'You *tolerate* this unspeakable situation?'

'Why not?' said Franca, feeling suddenly intoxicated by the cocktail of her conflicting emotions. 'There's nothing very unusual about a man having two wives. On this planet it is probably more the rule than the exception.'

'On this planet,' said Miss Tether, 'many things are "the rule" which are thoroughly evil and pernicious. So you are a cynic, you no longer love your husband and you don't care what he does?'

'I do love him,' said Franca, still feeling reckless, 'I tolerate it *because* I love him! Can't you understand that?'

'No, I can't,' said Miss Tether. 'You are degrading yourself and you are degrading womankind. He must despise you. You call *that* love? You will be their housemaid. How long has this "*ménage*" existed?'

'Not long – but it's very steady. Before that my husband used to have affairs. Now he's settled down. I'm rather glad, especially as I get on well with the girl. Aren't you being rather puritanical?'

'Yes, I *am*. So you prefer a permanent unfaithfulness to an occasional one, you collude in a situation which demeans you, and exposes him as a rotter! And if the girl enjoys it she must be a vulgar hussy! Are you living in a dream world? I find this disgusting, I pity you!'

They had had an early lunch, intending to go painting in the afternoon, and were sitting over coffee in the otherwise empty lounge. The weather had changed, shiny pewter-grey clouds portended, but had not yet discharged, rain. A silvery light filled the room. Miss Tether, excited by the unusual clouds, had been looking forward to 'having a shot' at them.

Before Franca had time to organise the reply which she was rapidly composing, the door opened and Ludens came in. He was carrying a large blue plastic bag and looking rather tired and distracted, the collar of his shirt standing on end, his dark hair, unkempt, rising into a coronet of little horns and crests.

He waved vaguely to Miss Tether and said to Franca, 'Have they come?'

'Have who come?'

'Jack and Alison. I rang up and they said they were just leaving. I thought they'd be here first. I suppose they've stopped for lunch on the way.'

Miss Tether's mouth became thinner, her eyes steelier, and she gathered her green cotton skirt in more closely about her legs.

'I'm late of course,' said Ludens, as if his hearers had been expecting him hourly. 'I stayed up half the night drinking with Gildas. Then I had to buy these.' He brought out of the large bag several sturdy octavo notebooks with different coloured covers. He held them up like objects exposed for sale. 'I tried several shops. These are the best – just the thing for writing in.'

Franca said, 'Just the thing!' She thought to herself, Alfred is still drunk! 'So you went to London. We couldn't think where you were.'

'Sorry, I went off in a hurry.' He said to Miss Tether, 'I do apologise for rushing in like this, I have to take these to my friend Professor Vallar.'

Miss Tether, releasing her skirt, said, 'Is that by any chance Marcus Vallar?'

'Yes! Why, do you know him?'

'No, but I possess one of his pictures. A remarkable painter. And I knew he was an academic too, and a professor of, I believe, mathematics. Wasn't he Mr Sheerwater's teacher? Yes, there is a discernible influence. Of course Mr Sheerwater's work, though quite attractive, is much weaker. Does Vallar live near here? I would love to meet him.'

'He's in Bellmain,' said Ludens, thrusting the notebooks back into the bag, then combing his hair with his fingers.

'In Bellmain? So he is teaching those poor creatures to paint?'

'He's one of the poor creatures,' said Ludens.

There was a sound as of scuffling in the hall and a loud familiar imperious voice could be heard addressing Mr Toller. Then the door opened and Jack and Alison stood on the threshold.

Franca remembered this moment very vividly later, as if it were a 'still' of particular historical significance, marking perhaps the turning-point between one clearly labelled era and its successor. It was indeed an enactment of the image she had so recently conjured up of the huge figures carried triumphantly upon the placards. But the reality, the incarnation, was at once more impressive and in some way more endearing, more forgivable, in the sense in which dictators are so often forgiven, even loved, by those they tread upon. All this Franca, with a jolt of her heart, took in as she rose instinctively, respectfully, to her feet.

They, the resplendent pair, were taller, seeming larger and more substantial, as kings and queens, in old pictures, are represented as bigger than their subjects. They were healthier, stronger, happier, more brilliantly dressed. Jack was wearing a mauve jacket of very fine light velvety corduroy, an intensely pink shirt, and a purple silk scarf. His blond curls sleeked away down the back of his neck, his commanding blue eyes glowed, his flushed face beamed. Alison, also smiling, her pure red silky hair, grown longer, touching the collar of her dress, was also a little flushed, her usually pale face almost rosy, the faint freckles visible upon her brow like marks of rank. She wore a light-blue cotton coat and skirt the colour of her eyes, and high-necked shirt of dark-blue silk. The gold bracelet, inscribed with a pattern, perhaps even a message, certainly given to her by Jack and never closely inspected by Franca, was prominent on her wrist as she lifted a long hand to her cheek. Franca noticed too that the charming pair were both rather drunk.

Ludens, having taken in the visitation, sat down rather abruptly in an armchair. He seemed, in the new scene, ragged, flimsy, like a damaged puppet. Miss Tether remained stiffly motionless.

Jack spoke. 'Oh goodie, both of you, that's great! We've just checked in at the White Lion. We had the most scrumptious lunch on the way, rather a lot to drink, I'm afraid, we couldn't resist the liqueurs, could we, Aly.'

'My husband,' said Franca to Maisie.

Miss Tether rose. She turned to Franca who was standing beside her. 'You will understand and excuse me. I trust you will forgive my rather intemperate words. Please believe they were uttered by a true friend.' She inclined her head to Franca, then marched towards the door. Jack and Alison stood apart to let her pass. The door closed behind her, quietly, but with a certain censorious firmness.

Jack said, 'What's got into that old bird?'

Alison said, rather solemnly, 'Franca darling, we are so glad to see you.'

Ludens, struggling up from his armchair, said, 'Look, I must run. I've got to see Marcus.'

'Oh can we come?' said Jack, 'could we come just to *see*? We'd love to glimpse him, stare at the cottage anyway, peer over the gate.'

'It's not a cottage,' said Franca, 'it's a bungalow attached to a hospital.'

'*What?*'

'I'll explain later,' said Ludens, 'must go now.' He made for the door.

'Wait a moment – have dinner with us at the White Lion – we're dying to know –' But Ludens was gone.

Alison said to Jack, 'I'm exhausted. We'd better go back to the hotel and lie down.'

'OK. Franca, forgive us. We're dead-beat, we stayed up late last night watching a play on TV Alison wanted to pick up tips from. We'll come and pick you up about seven, well, seven-thirty, actually it's only a step, you can walk, whenever you feel like it, we'll be in the bar.'

As Franca went with them to the door of the inn she was recalling Maisie Tether's remarks. She found them invigorating.

Ludens had been delayed, first by oversleeping after the potations of the night, then by the search for suitable notebooks, then by queues caused by roadworks on the motorway. Now full of anxiety, carrying his bag full of notebooks, he hurried along the lane towards Bellmain. As he enjoyed the walk to and fro he had stationed his car at the inn. The sky had grown darker, the clouds bulging, a dirty luminous black, but there was still no rain. He felt intense anxiety about Marcus, something (but what?) might have happened to him when Ludens was not there to guard him, and it would be Ludens's fault. First he ran, then slowed down to an uneasy jolting fast walk. He had an unhappy stomach and a headache and suspected that his breath still smelt of whisky.

When he had passed Collingwood and had taken the turning to Benbow a figure appeared from among the trees and signalled to him to stop. It was Patrick. He was wearing a trilby hat.

Ludens, fearing something terrible, asked, 'Is he all right?'

'Yes, of course – he was in a bate because he didn't know what had happened to you.'

'I told him I was going to London.'

'I expect he forgot, or thought you'd be back sooner, never mind, he's calmed down.'

Ludens was about to hurry on when Patrick put a hand on his arm. 'Alfred, I want to say something.'

'I hope it's short. I must hurry.'

'It's short. Don't be angry with me, don't be hostile to me, I can't help wanting to be with Marcus, to be his follower, like his bodyguard, I owe him my life forever, and I want to be near him in love and in gratitude, it's a natural urge, I'm a poor man, I expect little, I don't want to live grandly, I can be a poet anywhere, I want to write my poems and go on with my life and enjoy my life, I'm writing a lot now, I'll show you later if you want, I'm a new man, I've got new being, since those hands were laid upon me – don't think I'm potty, I'm telling you as it is, and I'm not costing Marcus a penny, I get the dole money and the Doctor has me free of charge because of the work that I do, looking after the Professor, and I may do work in the garden too, Dr Bland arranged that, he's so nice to me, so I'm part of the family sort of, and Irina cares for me and Marcus likes me there, he said so, and there should be peace round about him and there can be peace, I've not often been happy or thought it was in my stars, but now I could be happy, and I think I ought to be happy since I was saved from death, only if it were not I feel you're against me, don't be against me, if I can do anything for you I will, if I've done any wrong I'll try to undo it, just be my friend as you used to be, I don't forget it was you found Marcus and brought him to me, so I owe my life to you too, and surely a man must be kind to a man whose life he has saved, isn't it?'

This speech, eloquently spoken in Pat's soft confidential Irish tones, amazed Ludens, made him feel shame, and entirely won him over. He realised how much truth there was in the speech, and instantly recalled the words of Gildas on this subject so recently uttered to him. 'Oh Pat, I'm sorry if I've been unkind, I'm so worried about Marcus and I want to help him –'

'I know, I know –'

'But I am your friend as I always was, and you must please forgive me, I'm very sorry –'

'All right then –'

'I'm not against you, not at all, I'm glad you spoke to me so that I can beg your pardon, and –'

'So we shake hands?'

'Yes, with all my heart.'

Standing on the drive, observed by a passing gardener, they solemnly shook hands. Then both, embarrassed, felt they must instantly part company. Ludens, with a salute, hurried on toward Benbow, and Patrick set off into the trees. It was beginning to rain.

Ludens raced across the lawn and leapt up the steps and pulled open the glass doors. It was dark inside and Ludens's eyes, used to the dark vivid light of the storm clouds, blinked helplessly. Then he saw Irina at a table in the corner writing a letter which she put away.

'Where were you, Dad was worried.'

'I went to London, I told him.'

'Well, he didn't take it in. You've been away ages, it's after lunch. Patrick was wanting to see you too, and Dr Bland asked after you.'

'I've dealt with Patrick.'

'You're not fighting?'

'No, the reverse. We're pals.'

'Good. Dad's in there meditating or whatever it is he does. You could look round the door.'

Ludens dropped his bag on the floor. He crept to the half-open door of Marcus's bedroom and tapped softly and then slipped in.

Marcus's room was even darker than the sitting room, the curtains drawn. Marcus was sitting on the bed, not in the orderly upright 'thinking' position which he sometimes adopted, but hunched up, his elbows on his knees, his head in his hands. He had no shoes on and was wearing his pyjama jacket over his shirt. He looked up sharply, as if frightened, and spoke almost in a whisper. 'Where were you?'

'In London. Dear Marcus, I told you I was going, I expect you forgot. Are you all right?'

'Yes, of course.'

'I've brought you some notebooks, you remember, I was to get you some good notebooks to write in.'

'Oh yes. Could you go away, I mean and wait, I'll be with you –' Ludens went back into the sitting room, closing the door, while Marcus retired into the adjoining bathroom.

'Is he all right?'

'I suppose so,' said Irina. 'What's "all right" anyway? How am I to know? How am I to know anything? My life is a puzzle picture with no solution. Whoever created me left out some essential piece.'

She was standing with her back to him looking out at the half-hearted rain which was judiciously falling in large heavy intermittent glittering drops like silver bullets.

Ludens came up behind her and put his arms round her waist. 'I'll supply the missing piece.'

'That's the first obscene remark I've ever heard you make.'

'Oh? Is it obscene?'

'Ludens, I adore you!'

'I adore you, my gipsy angel, my dark enchantress, my sovereign lady –'

'All right, all right. I've got something to tell you.'

A figure appeared in the garden, marching fast under an umbrella. Irina moved hastily away. Ludens pushed open the doors. The figure

255

mounted the steps, folding the umbrella, and entered. It was Dr Bland. He stood for a moment inside the door vigorously shaking the umbrella, opening and shutting it, depositing some raindrops outside on the verandah, some in the sitting room. Irina ostentatiously swept down her skirt with her hand.

'It's cold in here, you should put the heating on.'

'I don't know where the heating is,' said Irina.

'There's a switch in the kitchen. Didn't Camilla show you, or Rosie?'

'Probably. I've forgotten.'

'It's adjustable. Can I show you?'

'No, I daresay even I can understand it. Anyway I don't feel cold. Do you feel cold, Ludens?'

'No.'

'Where were you, why did you run off all of a sudden, we thought you'd jumped ship,' said Bland to Ludens.

'Everyone's asking me this! I *said* I was going to London to buy notebooks for the Professor. I told everyone in sight.'

'You didn't tell me.'

'You weren't in sight.'

'To buy *what*?'

'Notebooks! Look!' Ludens picked up the plastic bag and decanted the thick strong notebooks onto the carpet. Some ink-bottles fell out with them. 'For him to write in!'

'Do you think he'll write in them?'

'Yes!'

'Well, do you mind if I use the telephone? I didn't like to ring here in case I'd disturb the Prof, he might be resting or thinking or something. I must tell the boss you're here.'

The red telephone was on a small low table in the corner of the sitting room. Bland sat down beside it and lifted it up. 'Yes, please. Hello, it's me. He's here . . . He went to London to buy stuff for . . . You're coming over? OK, I'll tell him.' Turning to Ludens he said, 'He's coming over. I'd better warn you he's hopping mad.'

'Oh. Why?'

'Obviously because . . . Good afternoon, Professor.'

Marcus had come in, with shoes on and his crumpled linen jacket. 'What's this?' He pointed to the pile on the floor.

'Notebooks, for you to write in. I told you just now. Sorry, I'll tidy them up.' Ludens, kneeling, began to put the notebooks into a neat pile.

Bland, who evidently felt that Marcus was not his business just then, or was at any rate unwilling to stay to bat civilities around, said, 'Goodbye then. I must be getting along. Why, I think the rain has stopped.' He departed, leaving a pool of rainwater on the carpet which Irina mopped up with a cloth.

She said to her father, 'Do you feel cold in here, Dad?'

'No!'

'Look, Marcus,' said Ludens holding up one of the notebooks, 'that'll be good to write in, better than those other ones you didn't like, strong covers, good paper, lines just right. And there's the ink. And here,' he brought it out of his pocket and out of its box, 'is a fountain pen, the *very best*. I remember you liked fountain pens. Now where shall you write, where should he write, Irina, what do you think, in here, or in the bedroom, or in that little dining room place?'

'I think in the dining room. We eat in the kitchen. In here people might see him. Not that many people go past. But he'd feel safer in the little room, and there's a table.'

'Well, I'll put it all in there.' Ludens carried the notebooks and the ink bottles into the dining room and put them on the table. The table was dusty. Ludens dusted it with his sleeve. Irina had already dispensed with the services of Rosie, the 'cleaner'. He selected one of the notebooks and opened it at the first page. He put the fine shiny black fountain pen with gold-plated adornments back into its velvety box and placed the box open nearby. He drew a chair up to the table. 'There you are Marcus, there is your study!'

Marcus and Irina came to the door and stared in, like animals unwilling to enter a stall.

Marcus said, 'Thank you,' then turning back to the sitting room, 'I'd like to go for a walk before the rain starts again, we could go to the Axle Stone, I like to go there. I was there this morning.'

'It's going to rain again in two minutes,' said Irina. 'You'd better put on proper shoes and a mac and take your umbrella. Ludens has nothing, you'd better take my umbrella, Ludens, your shoes are hopeless but you'll have to put up with that. You'll get muddy walking across that grass. All right, off you go. Will you come back for tea? Oh never mind, what do I care whether you come back for tea.'

Ludens, declining Irina's umbrella, saw that Marcus was pointing at something outside in the garden.

A number of colour patches, resembling a rather 'difficult' modern picture, had materialised on the tarmac. After a moment Ludens was able to 'read' the picture as consisting of two people dressed in brightly coloured mackintoshes, with comical mackintosh hats on. They were waving. The next moment he saw that they were Jack and Alison.

Ludens thought, they must have followed me! He ran out and down the steps.

Jack and Alison had now advanced across the gravel and onto the grass. Jack, who could see Marcus standing at the open door, shouted, 'Hi, Marcus, it's Jack! Hello, Marcus!'

Ludens approached them, holding out his arms wide as a barrier. Clearly they were still drunk, at least Jack was! They must be got rid of *at once*.

This was the moment at which Dr Marzillian arrived. He appeared, a figure in black, loping down the drive wearing a black mackintosh and a black beret and carrying, folded, a very large red umbrella. He at once crossed the grass to Ludens. 'What is this? Who are these people? Did you bring them here?'

Jack had moved forward again, meaning to go to the house. Ludens, perforce ignoring Marzillian, held him back, pushing him by the shoulders. Jack was laughing helplessly. Marcus had retreated and Irina had closed the glass doors.

Ludens cried, 'Jack, Jack, stop, you can't see Marcus!'

'Why the hell not? You're talking nonsense! We're old friends! He'll be delighted to see me! He's not mad, is he? Your landlord told us about this place. Hadn't we better rescue him? Marcus, it's Jack, Jack Sheerwater, your old teacher! We'll get you out of here!'

Marzillian hustled Ludens out of the way, pushing him so violently that he almost fell. He confronted Jack. '*Stop shouting*. This is a private hospital, I do not tolerate intruders. How dare you annoy one of my patients! I can see that you are drunk, disgracefully drunk. Now go *at once*, unless you would prefer to be *ejected violently*. I tell you *go, get out*.'

Marzillian spoke quietly, but his rage was frightening. Jack, daunted and disconcerted, stepped back and started to fumble for words. He raised one hand, perhaps to assist his speech, or to defend himself against physical attack. Alison had meanwhile stepped forward and was plucking at his sleeve, then pulling at his arm. He gave way, and they both retired hastily to the drive and set off walking fast in the direction of the gate. Ludens saw Dr Bland, who had returned to watch the drama, standing under the trees on the other side.

'Did you bring those people in? Who are they, what did he say?'

'I didn't bring them, it was their idea, they're friends, he's Jack Sheerwater the painter, it's true he did teach Marcus painting once, I'll ask Marcus if he wants to see him, but I don't think he will.'

'I decide who sees my patients. You decide nothing here. I know about Sheerwater. He is never to come here again.'

'Oh, all right. Now please excuse me, I am just going to have a talk with the Professor.'

'You are going to have a talk with *me*. Come with me please.' Marzillian turned and strode off. Ludens, after a glance back at the house, followed him.

Out on the tarmac, Dr Bland was still to be seen lurking under a tree. As they passed him Marzillian made a violent dismissive, even menacing, gesture. Bland bowed his head and turned away, walking in the other direction.

As Ludens caught up with Marzillian he became aware that the doctor was still *extremely angry*, and angry with *him*! He recalled Bland saying that he was 'hopping mad'. He was about to speak to him when Marzillian said, in a voice shaking with passion, 'Why did you not *let me know*? I was expecting you for nearly an hour, forty-five minutes of my precious time were *wasted*, and I have two difficult cases in the house – and I reserved that time for *you* – and you failed to come and had not the courtesy to say that you could not come although I *expressly required* that you should tell me if the time was impossible, and that I would expect you if I was not so informed! I honoured you with a confidence which was evidently misplaced! You did not come. *Why not*? And let me tell you this. You are *drunk*. I can smell your breath. You have no doubt been drinking heavily with your disgraceful friends whom you *dared* to bring in here under the influence of alcohol.'

'I'm sorry. I'm *sorry*!' said Ludens, appalled by the ferocity of this attack. 'I went to London last night and drank a lot with a friend there – and I did *not* bring those people in. But look, I wasn't told that you wanted to see me! What's all this about? How was I to know you were waiting for me? I can't read your mind! Nobody said anything about it to me! No wonder I didn't come.'

'I sent you a note, it was delivered to you, into your hand.'

Ludens, touching his brow, suddenly remembered. When he had come upon the singing party outside Rodney, Camilla had handed him a letter which he had put into his jacket pocket. He felt his face become hot and red. He put his hand into his pocket and drew out the envelope. As they continued to walk, he opened it. The note inside read: *I would be grateful if you would come to see me this evening in my office at eight o'clock. Please let me or my secretary know if you cannot come. Marzillian.*

Ludens said in a subdued voice, 'I'm very very sorry. I received the letter, but I was upset about something at the time, and I didn't open it – I just put it in my pocket and forgot it. I am very sorry indeed, I apologise.'

Marzillian said nothing, but made a gesture not unlike the one by which he had (it seemed) savagely admonished Dr Bland. They walked in silence along the drive, across the lawn, up the steps to the house and into Marzillian's office. Maria, who had been working at a word processor at a side table, rose and departed quietly. Marzillian sat down at his desk and pointed to the chair opposite. Ludens sat down.

Marzillian had evidently, as they walked, made a successful attempt to overcome his rage. He said, 'All right, you won't be whipped and put in the cellar this time. Just don't fail again. I have, in the interests of Professor Vallar, extended certain privileges to you, but I shall not hesitate to withdraw them should you prove unworthy. I run a tight ship here – I think that is the correct naval expression – and I expect my people to be orderly and intelligent and to do what they are told. I need, I *demand*, a high standard, I particularly resent a loss of my time. We work under strain here, under great pressure, we work hard. I work hard, I require others to. I have, as I said, two difficult, precarious, cases here in this house. And there are other things. Why do I ramble on. I have made my point.'

'I am very sorry.'

'All right, all right, let us leave that. Do you often get drunk?'

'I drink, I don't usually get drunk.'

'Who was the friend you were drinking with?'

'A man called Gildas Herne, friend of Jack Sheerwater, used to be a priest.'

'What did you talk about?'

'About Marcus.'

'What did he think?'

'That Marcus's ideas are incoherent, that he can't concentrate, that he'll never make any sense of the muddle he's in.'

'Do you think this?'

'No.'

'Did you go to London to ask this man's opinion?'

'No, I know his opinion. I went to buy notebooks for Marcus to write in. I seem to have said this already twenty times today!'

'You believe he will write in them?'

'Yes.'

Marzillian was silent for a few moments. He looked very tired. His next question surprised Ludens. 'What's this *tricotage*?'

'This what?'

'*Tricotage*? What does it mean?'

'It's French for knitting.'

'Yes, but what does *he* mean by it?'

Ludens decided not to tell him. 'I don't know.'

'Some name for – the cosmic matrix – whatever that may be – perhaps a term in physics, or mathematics?'

Ludens shook his head.

'I have talked at length with your professor, also with his daughter, and with Patrick. I am building up a picture. I do this of course with every patient. My aim is to effect a cure and return the person concerned to a better happier life. To effect this I employ many methods including drugs. I am not a friend of electro-therapy. *Pray do not interrupt me.* Every case is different, every mind is unique. Since your professor is my patient I have to ask myself by what methods I can be of assistance to him –'

'He needs no assistance!' said Ludens. 'He is not deranged, he just wants to be left alone to think his own thoughts. It was not my idea to bring him here, and as I said in our last discussion, I do not think he should be here, and I hope to persuade him to leave.'

'Well, let me suggest that you consider the following. Your friend, or teacher, appears to like it here. This morning he enjoyed a swim, beneficial to his arthritis, yesterday evening he attempted a game of chess with Mr Talgarth, less successful since his superiority to his opponent made the game impossible. The situation may be reversed however when they play croquet. I am not being frivolous. He is capable of making friends here, acquaintances anyway, in a situation which will not impair the solitude necessary for his work. This strange and artificial community offers the benefits of communal life without its strains and pressures. The same is true, for instance, of an Oxford or Cambridge college. It may be, for him, certainly for the present, ideal. To be blunt, what is the alternative? To live in total solitude, as he did earlier, or in a noisy London flat, or as an eccentric focus of curiosity in a village, looked after by his daughter or a housekeeper? Wait, wait, let me finish. You said he needed no assistance. But he does need it, as indeed your own activities prove. Let us say that he does not need to be "cured", but does need to be, let us say *enabled*. You provide him with notebooks and conversation. We provide ordinary medical facilities, with privacy, security, and peace. Does this not make sense, and are you not now perhaps convinced that I am a rational well-intentioned doctor and not a demon king?'

'You are a doctor,' said Ludens, 'you are a particular sort of doctor. Your remarks about privacy and peace are designed to mollify and mislead, they are worthy of your brochure. You are not running a hotel. You will crave for something to meddle with.'

'Let me ask you some different questions which may lead to a better understanding between us. I am sorry that I have less time at my disposal now than I had last night, so I have to jump rather crudely from one topic to another. What do you think your teacher is really up to?'

'What do you mean?'

'I can't say more precisely what I mean without help from you. It seems that he wants to solve a philosophical problem about the nature of human consciousness. He also envisages some duty or enactment which is to benefit mankind. He also, and certainly, suffers from deep feelings of guilt. Do these things connect, or are they separate, and how do they relate to the fact that he is Jewish?'

Ludens thought, he wants to have a case he can work upon, something he can classify, some interesting and familiar psychological problem. 'He hopes that his philosophy will benefit mankind, any thinker might hope that. He wants to keep his thoughts away from his obsessions and anxieties, that again is natural. We all have fears and guilt feelings. I know of nothing which he need feel guilty of, I would regard him as exceptionally guiltless. He is aware of course of Jewishness, but he is not particularly interested in Judaism.'

'What about the concentration camps?'

'He has read books about them, as we all have, but he has no other connection, no one whom he knew perished there.'

'What do you think about Patrick's resurrection, I believe you witnessed it?'

'Yes. I think Patrick's illness was wrongly diagnosed, he would probably have got better anyway. Marcus's arrival enlivened him somehow and helped his recovery.'

'Patrick says that Marcus cursed him. So he is capable of cursing people?'

'Pat is a superstitious Irishman.'

'You do not credit Marcus – let us now call him Marcus – with any paranormal powers?'

'Of course not!'

'You would not call him a mystic?'

'No.'

'You make him out, I think you are anxious to make him out, as a very ordinary person. Yet you also believe him to be exceptional.'

'Yes, as a thinker. Not as a psychological oddity.'

'Well, well, I see your line of thought. So though you are not yourself a philosopher, you believe your friend's work to be profound and valuable.'

'Yes.'

'Has he discussed his ideas with any professional philosophers?'

'Certainly not. He wouldn't go near them.'

'Let us leave it there for now. May I hope that we can work together, you and I, and not at cross-purposes?'

'I am prepared to believe that you are well-intentioned,' said Ludens, 'whether you are a demon king remains to be seen.'

Marzillian laughed. 'You know, very much may depend upon you – Talk, talk, yes that's good, and write, write. I believe you intend to stay with us for the present? And Miss Irina too? Excellent.' He rose, Ludens rose, they walked to the door together.

Here Marzillian paused and said in a low voice as if imparting a secret, 'This is a charming place, a beautiful place yet it is also a gateway into hell. The diseased mind is in perpetual anguish, *they* suffer it, the misery and mortality, the hopeless doomed limitation of the human soul, usually hidden from us, audible only as a threatening murmur, a ground bass of perpetual anxiety, the sound of contingency itself. Do you know what it is to abominate the thing that one is, to be afraid of one's own mind, to have a mind which is covered in rats, a mind which continually maims itself and is smeared with its own blood? No, I can see that you don't, you are one of the lucky ones, self-loving and self-satisfied, immured in innocence. For I speak not only of the afflicted ones here, but of many who walk the wide world with smiling masks, but whose souls live in eternal fire, in a shame which robs them of their humanity. Yet all men, even you, carry within their minds some sharp thorn, some bud of cancerous pain, which perhaps will never be activated, but from which, very rarely, they receive some instant spasm of incomprehensible anguish.' Marzillian was silent for a moment, then went on, 'For *him*, there is danger. I cannot understand it yet, but there is danger. I think you have been less than frank with me today. In future please tell me what you think and what you fear. Observe him carefully. There, there, I must not alarm you. Writing, thinking, yes, action, no. Let him take his time. I am glad he has such a good friend.' He squeezed Ludens's arm, opened the door a little to allow him to leave, then shut it abruptly behind him.

Ludens walked slowly away, crossing the grass, not following the concrete path. The rain had stopped but the grass sparkled with rain drops which leapt into his shoes. As he walked he felt a sharp pain which made him put his hand to his heart, something strange, perhaps actually occasioned by Marzillian's words. Some strong emotion shook him. He was deeply disturbed by that talk about 'suffering' – a word also used by Marcus – and by the hint about 'danger'; he wondered what it meant. He was himself not unaware of danger; but he did not let his thoughts go there. It was as if his thoughts, there, would waste themselves, damage themselves, break their wings. He must think, and think hard, about the next *real* tasks, how to persuade Marcus to write, how to help him to *collect his wits*, in fact how to make him *work*. No wonder he, Ludens, must appear to them all as a schoolmaster. He was, as it were, a teacher who has a pupil, an idle and confused pupil, who is far more brilliant than himself and must be coaxed, encouraged, if necessary scolded, beaten. What a strange image! But it came to him more clearly than ever that Marcus had for long, for too long, been collecting and harbouring ideas which must now be classified, organised, articulated, sifted, connected, *written down*. He recalled the word Marzillian had used – Marcus did not need to be cured, but to be *enabled*.

Ludens reached the drive and began to walk, slowly, for he wanted to decide what exactly he was to do when he rejoined Marcus, in the direction of Benbow. Passing Boscawen he saw Mr Talgarth issuing, with his croquet mallet, from his little front door. Boscawen was no larger than Benbow, but differently constructed. Mr Talgarth, seeing Ludens, waved his mallet. Ludens waved back. He thought of Mr Talgarth's dismay, his disappointment, when he discovered that it was *impossible* to play chess with Marcus. So, *tricotage* as the cosmic matrix, the great game. Should he tell Marcus? No, those thoughts of Marcus were too mysterious, too sacred. How had Marzillian got on to *tricotage*? What curious misleading information had he extracted from Irina and Pat, indeed from Marcus himself?

At this moment Ludens suddenly saw Irina sitting under a tree. She was sitting on a seat, wearing a white mackintosh and white rubber boots, a cloud of white cow parsley was spread out in the woodland shade behind her. She sat with folded hands, smiling like the Mona Lisa. Ludens plunged towards her, stepping into the longer grass and soaking his socks and ankles.

'Sit down.'

'The seat's wet.'

'Sit on my mac.' She spread out the skirt of her mackintosh on the seat beside her.

Ludens sat down. He felt the warmth and softness of her body close to him. He said, 'This won't do.'

'What won't do?'

Not answering he said, 'I've been talking with Marzillian.'

'Was he furious with you?'

'Yes. I didn't read his letter telling me to come yesterday evening.'

'I know. He sent Terence to look for you.'

'Who's Terence?'

'Dr Bland.'

'I gather you've been chattering to Marzillian.'

'You talk, I chatter.'

'Never mind. Oh *hell*.' That word too had been used by Marzillian.

'What's the matter? Listen, I've found out things. There aren't all that many people here, at least I don't know how many there are in the house, everything about that's secret, but there's only five in the South Pavilion, and then Mr Talgarth at Boscawen and Lady Barforth at Nelson and Mrs Rydal at Hotham, only she's going –'

'I'm glad to hear they *can* go! That's not bad if they're all paying full price.'

'Oh they are, but really they're on insurance, their health insurance is paying. I wonder if Dad has any health insurance? I must ask our lawyer. We have a lawyer. His name is Howard Garent.'

'The insurance wouldn't pay unless he was certified.'

'What makes you think that?'

'I want to kiss you, only some spy will come past.'

'Who cares? I dare you to kiss me!'

Ludens kissed her. He sighed into her mouth.

'Why are you so sad, Ludens? Don't be sad. I've made friends with the spies. There's Camilla and Anita and Maria and Thelma – and Sandra and Emilia and Barbara and Alethea – they all have to end in A.'

'And Terence, and Patrick.'

'Pat's not a spy. You said you were pals. But look, Ludens, look what I've got.' She reached out her closed hand, then opened it. She was holding a key.

'What's that?'

'The key of Rodney. Camilla gave it to me. It's an absolute secret of course.'

'What's the use of it?'
'Oh, you are so *slow!*'

Franca was listening to Maisie Tether. The words of Maisie were as sweet as honey to her.

It was the evening of the day of Jack and Alison's arrival. Franca and Maisie were sitting in one of the alcoves in the Black Lion bar. The bar, whose small original windows had not been tampered with, was rather dark, resembling a cave honeycombed with other caves. It was raining outside. Franca was drinking lager, Maisie gin and ginger wine. In a little while they were to set off in Maisie's car to have dinner at another pub (called the Lion and Unicorn) in another village where the food, said Maisie who knew it well, was excellent. Franca had left a telephone message at the White Lion to say that she could not come to dinner but would see them tomorrow. This significant defection had been prompted, indeed insisted upon, by Maisie.

'I went to a girls' school and a girls' college,' Maisie was saying, 'there still are girls' colleges in America, though some of them have let in men now, including my old place, I'm sorry to say, it was a fashion of the time, something people felt they had to keep up with, "the will of history" one of my idiotic male friends called it! I can't see the point of co-education, it's always the girls who suffer, they have enough trouble with men without positively asking for it. It isn't as if they'd be cloistered, nobody's cloistered nowadays, more's the pity, not even the nuns – well, a few are, but the nuns I know are all over town in short skirts and smart shoes. I'm not homosexual – or "gay" as they call it now – though why "gay" I can't imagine, it's an odd word to choose – it's just that I've always found myself more at home with women than with men – though I must make an exception for my father, who was clever and good and marvellous company, I miss him to this day. I just think that females are on the whole much wiser and better than males. I should say I'm not against homosexual relations, of either sex, it's one of nature's ways, I rather approve of it, I contribute to my local gay lib at home – *those* people aren't the troublemakers, they're usually quiet and sensible. But for myself, I'm just a free being who prefers her own sex, I'm a solitary who has lots of friends. Really I think that's the best life. My father wanted me to be a college professor, and I could have been, my Latin and Greek were alpha, but I always wanted to be a painter, and he said he'd put up with it so long as I was a good painter – and I believe I am – not great but good! I think it's a happy life being a painter, you've got your art with you all the time, your subject matter, the beautiful wonderful external world waiting around for you – look how lovely that grey light is and the little bit of apple tree you can see through the window. I must teach you how to paint rain, the Japanese are so good at it. You *will* go on painting, won't you, Franca, promise?'

'I can't promise,' said Franca, 'but I'd like to. I think you're right, I think it has a special relation to happiness.'

'How well you put it – yes, and much more than the other arts – as I said the matter, the occasion, is always there, as soon as you open your eyes, and everything you do about it can be art! Think of Constable's sketch-books, Manet's sketch-books, Picasso's sketch-books. The tiniest scrawl, the merest outline or patch of colours is art – and that's true of everyone who has some talent – it may not be good but it's art – not that I approve of Picasso as a man, a perfect cad if ever there was one – and then there's Turner, all those things he called sketches, there's divinity, there's joy, just thinking of those blazing masses of colour lifts up the heart, don't you agree? Whereas if you're a writer, like a novelist, say, and you make notes for your book, *that's* not art, not in itself, the way those sketches are art – and painters can go on painting till they're old, very old – Titian painted wonderful pictures when he was over ninety – the mind doesn't *give out* as it does in other art forms, you see painting's *natural*, it's the oldest art, it's the natural art. My dear mother used to paint a bit and she said it was spiritual refreshment. My mother was a saint really. She was a Bostonian too of course, she used to work with black women in the poor part of Boston – there's hell in Boston like in other cities – I'm glad I was an only child, I guess I did well having the undivided attention of those two superior beings. You had a brother, I think you said, but you lost him?'

'Yes.'

'How sad. You haven't told me about your parents?'

'Not now. Now I want to be cheerful!'

'Not good? I'm sorry. Well, to come back to our plan.'

'Your plan.'

'I want you to come back to America with me. Shake all *that* worthless dust off your feet. I want you to be free and happy and to paint and do *new things*. I put in some do-gooding myself, there's an Episcopalian woman priest, an angel, you'll love her, who's involved with homeless people, you could be in on that – and another thing, I'm connected with the Friends of the Isabella Stewart Gardner Museum, and there's all sorts of ploys and projects in connection with that, not that I want you to do anything but paint and go to that painting school I told you of, it's just that if you want a part-time job there's plenty to do, I'm not trying to put you in my pocket, there's a whole *world* waiting for you over there if only you'll come, and be among good people who will love you and value you. And I'm not short of money, I'm not shy of saying so, it's a fact, my ancestors manufactured chocolate, bless them. You've been living in a dark box – it's time to come out into the light. As for that wretched pair, they're obviously made for each other, I could see that at a glance, they're animals, silly expression, animals are nice and innocent and incapable of cruelty, but you know what I mean –'

'I'm grateful to you,' said Franca, 'I'm *very* grateful to you, I'm awfully glad we've met and you are doing me a lot of good! But I can't come to America.'

'Why not, for heaven's sake? If you're worrying about *their* welfare let me tell you this. They don't exactly wish you dead, they just wish you'd go and be happy somewhere else! When they discover what's happened they'll be opening bottles of champagne. They don't need you, you figure as a duty!'

'It's no good,' said Franca, 'I still love my husband.'

'Words, words! And as for "husband" that's a word I can't stand, I've seen so many places where it fell like a lump of lead! Look honestly into your heart, Franca. You loved him once. You don't love him now. You're just too tired and too silly to realise you are able to *get away*.'

Of course I can't go to America, thought Franca. (Yet why not?) I love Jack. (I do, don't I?) He needs me for his happiness. (What about my happiness?) 'I think I must stay with my destiny,' she said. 'I can bear it all much more easily than you imagine.'

'I despise female masochism.'

'It isn't masochism – it's a matter of – well, of morality.'

'You mean convention, honour and obey.'

'No, something deep, I can, perhaps not yet, but I *can*, accept it, make their happiness my happiness. The notion that it's impossible, unacceptable, *that's* a convention.'

'You want everyone to say, "Look at Franca, way up there on the high wire, everyone else falls off, but *she* doesn't!"'

Franca laughed. 'Well, why not? I'm sure your angelic priestess would agree with me.'

'She certainly would *not*! I won't press my case because I believe that really, deep down, I've persuaded you. Come now, we must go and get our dinner.'

'You hold the torch, *hold* it you fool!'

Ludens held the torch and played the momentary light upon the keyhole of the door of Rodney. Irina inserted the key. The door yielded. Ludens switched off the torch and shuffled cautiously after her into the little house. He closed the door behind him.

'We're in! Now, Ludens, you stay here, don't move. I'll pull the curtains in the back bedroom. Give me the torch. That's right. Stop breathing. I mean stop breathing like that. Are you scared?'

'Yes.'

It was pitch dark. The rain had ceased but clouds covered the night sky. Disoriented, Ludens reached out a hand, could touch nothing, and nearly fell over. Then there was a light ahead.

'Come now – be careful, you'll break something.'

Ludens blundered forward, knocked against a chair, then found the edge of the doorway and stepped through.

'Close the door. Now no one will see any light.' Irina had put a bedside lamp down on the floor away from the window and was covering it with a newspaper.

'That paper will go on fire,' said Ludens, 'and then we *shall* be in the soup.'

'Do you think so? Hell and damnation. What can we cover it with? What about your shirt?'

'We can turn it off in a moment.'

'Can we? Well, I suppose we can. Here, help me.'

Irina began hastily undoing the bed, dragging the quilt, top sheet and blanket down toward the foot. The bed was reasonably wide. She then spread out several large towels. Ludens watched these preparations with dismay. He felt stiff and cold and paralysed by misgivings. Why ever had he agreed to this crazy plan?

'Tuck in your side.'

'All right, Irina! What do you think Marzillian will do if he finds out?'

'He'll scare us nearly to death, and then let us off. He's rather fond of you.'

'You amaze me. What makes you think so?'

'The way he talks about you.'

'Camilla would lose her job.'

'No, she'd just be put in chains. So you think Marzillian would be angry?'

'Yes! He runs a tight ship, to use his expression. He wouldn't care for this sort of private initiative. It might damage his reputation.'

'Don't worry, no one will find out. Do you know, Marzillian's queer. So is Dr Bland. They're a couple.'

'Really? Who says that?'

'Patrick. Actually it's obvious if you come to think of it.'

'It's not obvious to me. Irina, I'm worried about your leaving Marcus alone. Are you sure he'll sleep? Suppose he wakes up and finds no one there?'

'Well, I'll tell you, someone is there.'

'You mean Camilla?'

'No, Pat.'

'You *told* him —'

'No, no, I just asked him to stay till I came back. He obeys me like a dog.'

'But if Marcus wakes up and asks him —'

'He won't wake up. Anyway isn't this what he wants?'

'I doubt if *this* is what he wants!'

The lamp was extinguished. Thick absolute darkness filled the room as densely as if it were stuffed with earth. Ludens could hear a soft slithering pattering sound which must be Irina undressing. He took off his jacket and shirt. He began to undo his trousers. The familiar operation seemed suddenly immensely difficult, as if he no longer knew what was up and what was down. He pulled first one way and then the other, leaning down to feel where his legs were. He tried to kick the trousers off, but something obstructed them, perhaps his shoes. Stooping to find his jacket and extract something important from the pocket, he banged his head against the wall. He sat down abruptly on the edge of the bed.

'What the hell are you doing?'

'Getting undressed.'

'Come on, you donkey.'

Ludens, discovering that he was naked at last, extended himself gingerly on the edge of the bed. Something warm touched him. Her hand, then her arm.

'You're frozen, you're stiff as a board, what's the matter with you?'

'Darling, I'm sorry, I feel giddy, I can't find myself, can we have the light on for a moment?'

'No. Can't find yourself! That's a good excuse. I suppose you have done this before?'

'I haven't done anything yet. Where are you?'

'Here.'

Suddenly as he turned towards her she was present, warming his cold flesh, foot to foot, knee to knee, breast to breast.

'This bed's damp. Don't you think it's damp? Wait while I pull the sheet and blanket up a bit. Budge over, you're lying on my arm.'

'Don't cover yourself. Irina, dearest, you said you'd had – one experience – was it a bad one, one that makes you anxious now?'

'I think you are more anxious than I am.'

Propped on one elbow he began to touch her, stroking her hair and her brow, slowly gently, caressing her closed eyelids, her open lips outlining her magically invisible face, her neck, her small round breasts, feeling her heart beat. It was beating fast. They were silent in the darkness.

She arrested his hand. 'I suppose you haven't any precautions? I haven't.'

'I have actually.'

'So you carry the things around just in case?'

'After you suggested this, I drove to a chemist in the next village.'

'Have you got it on?'

'Yes. Darling, don't resist me. I want you so much, I love you so much.'

'Ludens, sweetheart, oh dear, do you mind – just don't come in – Even though you've got – I don't want – not now –'

'I must – let me – you're ready, I know you are – please –'

'No – I'm sorry – please not –'

'Irina – oh damn –' It was too late. He laid his head on her shoulder. Two hearts beat fiercely against each other.

After a silence, she began to stroke his hair, and touch his face as he had touched hers. 'Ludens – am I awful – have I been beastly to you – are you cross with me?'

'No, angel, beloved, no, no, it's been wonderful, it is wonderful – I'm so grateful to you, so infinitely grateful, so utterly happy. Maybe next time –'

'We may have to wait for next time. We can't do Rodney again, it's too risky. Camilla said it was just for once, she said perhaps later –'

'Then we must –'

'We could go back to your London flat.'

'Yes – oh hell, we can't, I've let it to a friend, he's already there. What about your flat?'

'It's being sold, it may be sold now, I left it to Mr Garent. I suppose the Black Lion –'

'That's no good, everyone sees everything, besides Franca's there.'

'Oh. Franca's there, is she.'

'Yes, I told you.'

'I think Franca's in love with you.'

'Don't be silly. Look, why all this secrecy anyway? I hate secrecy. We're going to be married.'

'Are we?'

'Yes. Let's just go to the nearest registrar's office. Then we can find somewhere to live in the village.'

'You have to wait ages, you can't just do it tomorrow. Besides Dad might want a Jewish wedding.'

'Oh no!'

'*Please* let's not talk about marriage yet, it's too soon, and I don't know what Dad would feel. Put your arms round me, that's right.'

'But he said –'

'Yes, but when it comes to it – he'll feel he's losing me –'

'I'm not losing you, am I?'

'No, no, but do understand, everything is so peculiar at the moment, so *weird* – I don't know who I am or what I'm doing, or whether I should wait –'

'What for?'

'Oh just till everything's clear, I mean – I mean about Dad – he's in an awful state of anxiety or indecision or something – when you come he calms down so you don't know how terribly disturbed he is.'

'Irina, don't keep me waiting till everything's clear. It may never be clear.'

'I know, I know, hold onto me, hold me, hold me, be real, be true –'

'Darling, I am! Oh don't cry so, I can't bear it!'

PART FIVE

It all began about two weeks later. During these two weeks a curious peace reigned. May had given way to June. The sun, recalled to his duties, and sensing his strength at the approach of midsummer, ruled the long cloudless hours. Patrick picked flowers, the 'maids' gave a madrigal concert (attended by the village people) on the lawn beside the North Pavilion, the golf course was patronised by Mr Talgarth, Dr Bland, Lady Barforth of Nelson, Maria, Sandra, and persons, unknown to Ludens, from the South Pavilion. Marcus swam in the open-air pool. Franca and Maisie swam in a beautiful pool which they had discovered far down the Fern. Jack and Alison, who had not dared to renew their visit to Bellmain, settled at the White Lion, armed with learned highbrow guide books, explored the countryside by car, visiting Salisbury Cathedral, Winchester Cathedral, Worcester Cathedral, Tewkesbury Abbey, Avebury, and Stonehenge. They went to Bristol and as far afield as Tintern and Glastonbury. They also became experts on pubs and restaurants for many miles around. Franca quite often accompanied them on these jaunts, Ludens sometimes came too, and twice Ludens and Irina. In their proximity at the Black Lion Ludens and Franca and Maisie were on easy happy terms with each other. Ludens occasionally took Irina out in his car to visit some recommended nearby attraction; but on the whole these two stayed at their post near to Marcus, who declined to go anywhere. Looking back, and discussing it later, Ludens was struck by how, during this interim, everyone seemed to be serene and on good terms with everyone else. Franca consorted cheerfully with Jack and Alison who responded with tactful demonstrations of intense gratitude and love. Maisie Tether, naturally and universally so amiable, provided one exception to the general harmony by refusing to have anything to do with 'that wicked pair'. Irina and Marcus and Ludens even constructed a form of family life which included Patrick, with whom Ludens was now on good terms. Pat was in fact slightly less in evidence, because of a bond of some arcane sort which he had formed with Camilla, with whom he was seen playing tennis soon after dawn. He was also busy writing poems which he took to the White Lion and read to Alison. Mr Talgarth, who turned out to be a retired diplomat, was also a visitor at Benbow and had conversations with Marcus about countries which they both knew, such as France, Germany, India and the USA. Marcus, who now regretted not having visited Japan, showed a tolerant interest in Mr Talgarth's views about that strange country where he had spent several years. Ludens and Irina now shopped in the village for food which Irina cooked with recipes out of a cookery book which Ludens had given her. Fresh fruit and vegetables, including the most delicious asparagus which Ludens had ever tasted, were delivered daily by Rosie. Even Terence Bland, who often looked unhappy, seemed happy. Marzillian was in a golden mood and nobody was in trouble.

Ludens and Irina had had no further opportunity to 'do Rodney', a useful phrase which had now entered their vocabulary. Camilla, perhaps appalled by her own daring, had retrieved the key and refused to risk a second venture. Ludens was impatient but did not press Irina. Twice he had lain with her in long grass not far from the village, but she had been very nervous, and he had not dared to risk the extreme happiness which he felt by demanding too much. He guessed that she had arranged the Rodney episode in order to overcome some anxiety of her own, to 'take it at a run', and prove to both of them that *that* was possible, that it *could* happen. Now she wanted an interval. Ludens could not make out how much she really worried about Marcus's reaction 'when it comes to it'. Ludens did not propose to worry about this. He believed that her procrastination simply concerned the act itself, and that so far was so good. The 'episode' must be rated a success in that it had increased and deepened their ability to communicate, their trust in each other, their ease with each other. Ludens's misgivings during the 'interim' were more concerned with Marcus. He was indeed 'getting on well' with Marcus, Marcus was cheerful, Marcus enjoyed swimming and discussing 'the Japanese character' with Mr Talgarth. He enjoyed eating what Irina cooked for him and being amazed at her skill. He looked healthy and handsome and youthful. His only obvious oddity was that he did not want to go anywhere, even as far as the village. Within the bounds of Bellmain he enjoyed walking, usually with Ludens, sometimes with Pat or Irina or Mr Talgarth. He and Ludens sometimes walked through the woodland, past the North Pavilion and the swimming-pools and the golf course, round the far side of the lake, admiring the huge view over Salisbury Plain, round the far side of the house, past the Out of Bounds garden of the 'house patients', past the vegetable garden, past the South Pavilion, a nineteenth-century folly, resembling a turreted fort, but marred by a large recent annexe, and so, passing the stables (the 'offices') back onto the drive.

More regularly however, with Ludens, Marcus walked only as far as the Axle Stone where they made a morning habit of sitting and talking. The oval seat or base was just wide enough to preclude their actually leaning against the stone, but they frequently, turning round or reaching out behind them, touched it. Ludens might have been relieved by the greater ease and fluency of their converse, which at times amounted almost to 'chat', and by the increased calm and ordinary pleasantness of Marcus's present way of life. But he was not. He felt that Marcus was, in some way that was not good, relaxing, taking a rest. Marzillian had said (and Ludens pondered these words) 'writing, thinking, yes, action, no'. Ludens was not sure what Marzillian had meant by 'action', though he had made for himself some conjectures. Marcus showed no sign at present of 'acting', indeed very much the reverse; but he was not writing either, or, in any lively purposive sense, thinking. When Ludens expressed this anxiety to Irina she ridiculed and chided him. 'Can't Dad have some time off? He's actually quite happy at present, isn't that enough? Don't *bother* him.' Ludens at times ridiculed and chided himself. But mainly he felt an anxiety, a foreboding, even an anguish. It was as if he was waiting for something. Was he simply afraid that Marcus would be, at last, 'cured' of his demon, his demanding questing genius, and become, instead of a tormented monster, a quiet cheerful ordinary man? Or was he afraid that if Marcus did not soon settle down to creative continuous intellectual work he might suffer some sort of collapse? Ludens did not like this train of thought. He considered but dismissed the possibility that Marcus was being given tranquillising drugs. He was prepared to believe that Marzillian was too *interested* in Marcus to wish, at this stage at any rate, to blunt his eccentricity; moreover Irina, Ludens, sometimes Camilla, sometimes Pat, were eating the same food. Whatever the cause, and with whatever import, Marcus showed no interest in the red and blue and green notebooks and the handsome fountain pen. Ludens reminded himself that he, Ludens, who thought habitually through the medium of ink, should not assume that other intellectuals did so too. Irina said to him, 'You, as soon as you have a thought, want to write it down! He doesn't, he's not a writer, he took to painting like a duck to water, that proves something doesn't it?' Ludens found these remarks interesting, disturbing, and singularly unhelpful.

A mathematician is not a writer, neither, in a different sense, is a painter. Plato was suspicious of writing. Perhaps Ludens simply wanted proof that Marcus was having thoughts and trying to clarify them. In any case the thoughts in question were not mathematical formulae or pictures, and Plato did actually write. Besides, Ludens had evidence that Marcus could write and had written. At the house in Kent (the house of the ram, as Ludens named it) Marcus had admitted to making notes, at the flat in Richmond something had been said (though by the Japanese disciple, not by Marcus) about a book, and at Red Cottage Ludens had actually seen Marcus in the act of writing. So the present non-writing could at least be said to be puzzling. If it continued, Ludens reflected, might he not get a machine to record their conversations, which he could then write out? But what Marcus said was often obscure, followed by Ludens in intuitive leaps, and scarcely to be rendered in clear discursive prose. Marcus must invent his own prose as he had invented his own paintings. Jack had taught him to paint. Could Ludens teach him to write?

Ludens, naturally, saw a good deal of Jack during his prolonged stay, with Alison, at the White Lion. Ludens was closer to Jack than to anyone in the world except Gildas. It proved in the event easy for both of them, by a silent understanding, to 'let each other be'. *Later* they would talk, their meeting gaze expressed, *later* they would tell all, recount, explain, bemoan, require if necessary mutual absolution. But now it was better, with so much to say, to be silent; if they began to discuss their massive problems they might misunderstand or wound, and they had each enough unavoidable troubles without adding this avoidable one. So Jack was not a source of anxiety to Ludens. Alison, however, managed to disturb and surprise him by an unexpected conversation which she initiated when they met accidentally in the village street. It was the afternoon, they sat in a café and ordered tea.

'What's up with Franca?' said Alison.

'What do you mean, "what's up"?'

'She seems so relaxed and cheerful.'

'Isn't that good, isn't that what you and Jack want?'

Alison reflected. 'I think that sentence, the way you put it, absolutely shows what's wrong.'

'Oh, how?'

'It suggests that Jack and I are sort of superior beings, like her parents.'

'Well, aren't you?' said Ludens, with a slight edge. It also occurred to him that *he* was worried because Marcus seemed so relaxed and cheerful.

'Don't be hostile to me, Ludens.'

'Alison, I'm not! But look, a relation between two people usually involves a balance of power, perfect harmonious equality is difficult. With three people it's even more difficult. Or do you think you can be co-equal partners like the Holy Trinity?'

'I had hoped so,' said Alison gravely. 'I don't mean who's in bed with whom, I mean at a deeper level.'

'That is deep indeed.'

'And don't sneer at me either.'

'Please – You know I care about your – about your – arrangement.'

'No wonder you don't know what to call it.'

'I think you are all three superior beings, that's what makes it work. You are decent and truthful and generous.'

'Three good adjectives. Yes. But I'm really after some facts. What's that woman Maisie Tether doing with Franca, are they plotting something?'

'Of course not! Maisie's a very nice, very sensible woman, they're *friends*. Franca hasn't got many friends. They go painting together. Anyway, Maisie's going back to America soon.'

'Jack and I are leaving soon too, we're going to stay at Heather Allenby's house in France. I'm sorry you didn't meet her when she was in London, but she'll soon be back. Of course we invited Franca – you know her pretty well, don't you?'

'Yes, we've known each other a long time.'

'Is she in love with you?'

'Alison! No, of course not!'

'Is she in love with Maisie Tether?'

'No! Why can't you take Franca simply without these absurd suspicions? She is doing a great thing for you and Jack. If you accept it you will be doing a great thing for her.'

'It's all so obscene and so painful.'

'It's a pain that can turn into happiness at the turn of a switch. Really you and Jack are happy and Franca is happy too.'

'Do you believe what you're saying?'

'It's shorthand. You know what I mean.'

'I understand you. I think I understand you more than I understand any of them.'

'Then agree with me. Hope calmly and believe in love.'

'You mean in *her* love. You remember that time at Fontellen when you found me and Jack swimming in the lake, and you watched Jack dressing.'

'Yes.'

'You looked at me in that moment in a certain way – as if you understood everything and forgave everything. Do you remember that?'

'Yes, Alison.'

There was a moment's silence. Ludens stirred his tea. He looked at Alison's hand. She was wearing a ring on the middle finger of her left hand, a ruby between diamonds. He looked at the sleeve of her cotton dress, folded back at the elbow. He raised his eyes and found her pale blue eyes staring at him. He thought, we are repeating that moment.

'Ludens, I wish you'd talk to Jack.'

'I don't think Jack wants to talk to me. We'll talk later.'

'I know you have a relation with him which is closer than his relation with any woman.'

'It's different. What you say is a sort of nonsense.'

'I do want happiness.'

'Well, take hold of it. You'll inspire the others.'

'Oh – well – I must go now. Let me pay.'

'No, I'll pay.'

They walked out onto the pavement. 'Where are you going, Alison?'

'To the White Lion. Where are you going?'

Ludens had been going to the Post Office to telephone Gildas, the phone at the pub being too public. 'Back to the Black Lion.' He did not want to walk along the street with Alison.

It was soon after this that it all began. The first intimation was something very simple, almost trivial, and though odd not taken to be important. One morning, when Ludens and Marcus arrived at the Stone for their morning session they found something lying on the oval concrete seat which surrounded the base of the stone, and where they now put cushions to sit upon, brought from Benbow. The something was a bunch of wild flowers, laid down carefully, the flowers slightly separated from each other. Someone had evidently left it behind, perhaps forgotten it. They took the flowers back to Benbow and Irina put them in water where they revived. Two days later there were more flowers there, arranged in a criss-cross pattern, with some pebbles. These they did not take back.

Then something happened which was more disturbing. Ludens, arriving on foot one morning, found three young men standing at the entrance gate, staring at the notice which said simply *Bellmain. Strictly Private*. Of course local people knew what the place was, and regarded it with a certain awe. Other passers-by tended to assume it was a private house and respected its privacy. There was a 'sentry box' among the trees where a 'Bulldog' sometimes sat, but the gates though often closed, were unlocked during the day, and Ludens assumed there was no particular history of intruders.

The young men were standing in the road, not inside the gates, which were open, looking along the drive with an air of curiosity. They seemed to be about twenty, one of them bearded, the others casually shaven, they had longish untidy hair and were wearing shabby jeans and rucksacks. When Ludens reached the gate he slowed down and looked at them, and one of them said, 'Hello.'

Ludens, pausing, said, 'Hello.' Then after a moment he went through the gateway onto the drive. The young men followed him. Ludens stopped and turned and said, 'Can I help you?'

The young men looked at each other, seeming a little embarrassed and shy. Then the bearded one said, 'Is this the place of healing?'

Ludens disliked this terminology. 'This is a hospital and I'm afraid the grounds are private. Sorry!' He turned and moved on.

The young men followed him again, so that he stopped and said, 'I'm afraid you can't come in without permission.'

'Look here,' said the bearded man, who was evidently the leader. 'We've heard something and we just want to know.'

'What?'

'Is there a healer here?'

'There are doctors here. This is a mental hospital. People aren't allowed to walk in.'

'Are you a doctor?' said one of the others.

'No. Look, I don't know what you want here, this place is a *hospital*, if you want to make enquiries you can do so by post.'

The boy who had not yet spoken, who seemed to be the youngest, said in a high clear voice, 'A man was raised from the dead, and we think that someone here did it.'

Ludens said, 'I'm afraid there is no one like that here, just a lot of very ordinary medical men. Now if you want the youth hostel, it's about a mile beyond the village.'

The youngest boy spoke again, smiling, 'Oh we don't go to youth hostels, we sleep out!'

Ludens said, also smiling, 'Well, you have got good weather for it. Goodbye, then.'

He turned and walked briskly away. When he had covered some distance he looked back. The trio had disappeared.

Their enquiry had appalled him. He wondered if he should tell somebody, but decided not to. The wanderers with their rucksacks would probably move on and not be seen again. How on earth had the idea come to them? Had Patrick been talking in the village? According to Irina, Marcus had told Pat very early on to 'Keep his mouth shut'; this prohibition had been repeated by Ludens, and Ludens believed, by Dr Bland who seemed to be in some way Patrick's 'minder'. But could Pat be relied on not to hint at something so remarkable? Ludens did not think that any such rumour could have circulated locally since he had not heard of it from Toller, and Maisie Tether, who 'knew everything that went on', had evidently said nothing to Franca, who would have mentioned it to Ludens.

'Marcus, I want to say two important things to you.'

It was two days later, during which time Ludens had recovered from his extreme alarm at the young men's question. They had not reappeared, and other problems occupied his mind. He was sitting as usual with Marcus at the Axle Stone; as usual, that is, except that Ludens now held a notebook in which he wrote down what he took to be developments or clarifications of Marcus's ideas. He was not writing in the fine hardbacked notebooks he had brought from London, these still awaited the first words to be written on the first page by Marcus; he was using the little limp frail senseless notebooks which he had bought earlier in the village. Ludens wrote a good hand, script not italic, and cared what his writing looked like, but what he had so far imparted to paper were quick condensed scrawls which he had difficulty in interpreting later. Marcus had said that he might take notes; that in itself, inconceivable earlier, was progress. Yet Ludens still felt that this procedure, carrying some taint of sacrilege, must at least be unobtrusive, hence the quick often illegible scrawling. He then attempted, after each conversation, to write out, in one of the other flimsy notebooks, in his own square fair hand, the main points of the conversation. Sometimes, here, Ludens felt as if he were leading a nervous-spirited horse round a course, a terrible course with very high jumps, where there would be dreadful falls and broken backs, only now they were just surveying the course, feeling the turf, looking at the jumps. Naturally in this image Ludens did not figure as the rider of the horse. He was merely a groom or stable lad, always nervously aware of the wild eye, the jerking head, the prancing gait, the strong powerful legs whose kick could be death, the power and dangerousness of the creature, and its beauty. Who the rider was or was to be never, in the development of this imagery, emerged; some god perhaps, Eros himself, or dread Apollo. Or rather, better, Marcus was a centaur, horse and rider in one.

In these last days Ludens had felt encouraged by a sense of greater concentration, Marcus had become a little less relaxed, a little less (as Ludens put it sternly to himself) lazy, a little more tense, more aware of the looming difficulty, the insuperable difficulty which was the only thing worth thinking about. He had rather vaguely assented to, at least had not rejected outright, the idea that Ludens should compose a plan or programme of their studies, almost, as it might be, a synopsis of a book which Marcus would write. At the very least Marcus, in rejecting with horror notions attributed to him by Ludens, would be led to clarify his thoughts. Ludens had decided that Marcus's 'line' might best be made intelligible if treated chronologically as the story of Marcus's intellectual life. Yet he also saw at once that this story, as he proposed it to Marcus, must be selectively edited, omitting certain ideas and stages. One of these was painting: Ludens on reflection thought it wiser not to go on questioning Marcus about what he had expected to get out of painting in case such reminiscences should prompt the sage to return to this time-wasting activity. It was even more important to keep Marcus off the Jewish question, off the Holocaust, off the enlightenment through suffering and the identification with evil and the mission to the world and so on. Marcus himself had said that he feared that his ideas might be damaged by his obsessions. Ludens, now fairly sure that he could discern the latter, saw it as his duty to banish them utterly from the exercises of hard disciplined thinking which lay ahead. Here, recalling what Marzillian had said about 'danger', Ludens found himself craving for another conversation with that ambiguous ring-master. Yet was not Marzillian himself 'danger'? That his enterprise was difficult, dangerous, but not quite impossible was illustrated to Ludens by a dream. He dreamt that he was in a large empty room, lit from above by grey daylight, rather like one of the studios of the art college, only larger. He was alone, standing in the middle of the room, frightened, expecting some person or some happening. A door opened at the far end and Leonardo came in. Leonardo was tall, young, with long pale flowing hair and brilliant luminous eyes. He was dressed in a long white smock or shirt which might have been a painter's overall, but which Ludens realised was the garb of a priest. He felt at that moment a wave of delicious and terrible emotion which almost made him faint, but he was conscious of standing there sturdily, smiling strangely with fear. Leonardo approached him with long strides holding out a paper in his left hand. He said to Ludens in a peremptory tone, 'You must go on your bicycle and take this message to Milan.' He handed the piece of paper to Ludens. Ludens said, 'B-b-but, sir, I haven't got a b-b-b-bicycle.' Leonardo, pointing to the paper, said, 'There's your bicycle!' Ludens looked down and saw the drawing of a bicycle which he had shown to Irina. He cried, 'But, sir, this is not a bicycle, this is a drawing of a bicycle.' Leonardo said, 'You can ride it if you try hard enough.' As he turned to go Ludens called after him, 'What about the message?' The reply was, 'That is the message.'

By this time Jack and Alison had returned to London on the way to stay with Heather Allenby in France, where Franca was to join them later. Franca was at present away too, on a trip to the Lake District with Maisie Tether. Patrick had gone to London to collect some of his gear from the flat of Suzanne (alias Moxie, alias Miss Moxon) where he had left it after his sojourn there. Irina said that Franca said that Suzanne was in love with Patrick, and added that she, Irina, thought that Camilla was also in love with Patrick. This tendency of everyone to love Patrick did not now trouble Ludens too much. Attempting to like Pat's poetry, he had found this easier when (on Alison's advice) he stopped him from declaiming it in a sing-song drawl, and demanded to see the text. The poems, written in Pat's very large legible hand, looked more impressive; and, when Pat announced that one had appeared in *The Times Literary Supplement*, Ludens was able to combine respect with amazement. His amiability, marginally caused by the voice of duty, had increased since Rodney, and because Pat, less often at Benbow, stayed out of the range of Ludens's savage jealousy. Ludens did not in fact believe that Camilla was in love; whatever it was was more likely something engineered by Marzillian. What after all were those handsome houris (who could incidentally sing like larks) up to anyway?

This comparatively empty scene, the weather, the beauties of nature, the orderly routine, the docility of Marcus, the tranquillity of Irina, while on the one hand pleasing to Ludens, also prompted him to resist the temptation to settle down. If this was Lotus Eater land it was time to move on, *this* was not his home. If only, he thought, he could just *get Marcus started*. Irina seemed almost happy. Of course she was pettish, continually complaining and swearing and finding fault with Ludens. But these were little natural mannerisms expressive mainly of the thriving life of the animal, not symptoms of any deep malaise. Ludens meanwhile was experiencing strong and positive desires to do Rodney again as soon as possible. He had (as he felt it) disturbed and dominated Marcus — well, led him successfully forward — and it was now time to disturb and dominate Irina. She had lately heard from the lawyer, Howard Garent, that Marcus had considerable medical insurance which could probably be applicable in the situation in question. If so, one reason, held in view by Ludens's puritanical thriftiness, for hustling Marcus out of Bellmain, was removed. But what about the farther future? Ludens, unless he gave up his job, or found a similar one nearby, which could be very difficult, could not stay at Bellmain indefinitely; he was there on sufferance anyway and could at any moment be banished by an autocrat about whom he knew little and over whom he had no influence. Now, Ludens was deemed 'good for Marcus', next week he might be 'bad for Marcus'. In fact by now one of Ludens's strongest motives for planning to remove Marcus was that such a plan must involve a clarification of his relations with Irina. Was he 'engaged' to Irina or not? Was Irina right to think that 'when it came to it' Marcus might oppose the marriage; either because he would 'lose her', or because he just did not fancy Ludens (even though he *was* a Jewish intellectual) as a son-in-law? Ludens was sure that Marcus, although he had disclaimed any understanding of the concept 'love', was genuinely fond of his disciple and certainly by now dependent on him. Yet was this a point for or against having him also married to his daughter? The fact that Irina was (presumably) a rich heiress weighed of course not at all in his desire for her. He would have been very content with a penniless wife whom he would have worked hard to support. But, to the future containing Marcus, money was relevant. Marcus needed serenity, security, privacy, services which could scarcely be guaranteed in a family ménage supported solely by Ludens's modest salary. Ludens must, of course, hold onto both of them and must therefore settle them in some place of which he, Ludens, was effectively in control.

During this recent period Ludens had also been, he sometimes felt irrationally, troubled by the anonymous flowers, sometimes accompanied by small pebbles, and arranged in patterns which could not be accidental, which were now once again appearing at the Axle Stone. Who brought them and what did they mean? Were they a tribute to

Marcus, perhaps even to Ludens himself? If Camilla could fall in love with Patrick, why could not Emilia or Anita or Sandra or Thelma or Maria have developed a secret passion for Ludens? Or were the flowers intended for some other person who regularly came to the Stone at some other time? Or 'just for fun', or as votive offerings to the Stone itself? Ludens and Marcus now arrived there every morning promptly at nine and were visible much of the time (not all, for they moved round the stone, keeping in its shadow) from the drive through the main opening in the yew hedge. The flowers, evidently put in place earlier in the morning, were still fresh, even damp with dew. For several days now Ludens, who for some reason did not wish Marcus to see the flowers, had made a point of arriving first and removing the offerings, which he 'strayed' inconspicuously here and there in the adjacent woods. The flowers, and the stones, continued to arrive, and Ludens had begun to connect them with something which Marcus had said earlier, to the effect that the place was 'eerie'. He could not help being uneasy, and was now very curious about the identity of the mysterious floriferous person or persons. The gates of Bellmain were locked by night, and opened again at six in the morning by the Bulldogs. On the previous day, entering about seven, Ludens had found the tributes already in place. He was now resolved to get up really early on the following morning and to conceal himself near the Stone to see who came. The high iron gates could not be climbed (he had discovered this on Rodney night) but it was possible (as he had also discovered that night) to get through the well-maintained mix of wall and wire fence which protected the domain, by crawling under some netting through a convenient trench made perhaps by a fox, or perhaps by some miscreant like himself.

'Two important things?' said Marcus looking intently at Ludens. 'What are they?' They were sitting in the morning sun on what Ludens thought of as the 'sinister', much scored, side of the Stone, whose ambiguous message rose up like an altar-piece above Marcus's head. He had been persuaded by Irina to retire his old battered panama hat, and was wearing a smart white sun hat which she had bought him in the village. Under the sunlit brim Marcus's face showed with exceptional clarity in all its detail, the soft lucid light grey of the long eyes, the glitter still of the faded locks now more profuse and slightly curling, and about the eyes and mouth the very faint, very fine wrinkles. The repose of the curling mouth (so Jewish as Ludens had at once seen, though he could not explain this to Jack), expressing authority, austerity, severity, was not reassuring.

Ludens's heart sank. Why was he driven on by this nervous craving, why could he not *wait*? This animal was deadly, why had he ever thought of him as a charming spirited horse which could be led along? He must now collect his thoughts and say *exactly* the right things. Why had he not planned it all, the *exact words*, beforehand? Now as in a crucial exam his mind was suddenly blank.

'Two things –' said Ludens.

'You said two things! Go on.'

'First, I think we should consider moving out of here.'

'Why? Where to?'

'I mean into a house of our own, well, your own. Of course I don't mean immediately, but we should be thinking about it, don't you agree? Of course it's very pleasant and peaceful here, but in the long run we must live more independently, and –'

'Aren't we independent?'

'No. This place is a totalitarian state – a very nice one – but even a nice one is unpredictable.'

'"Totalitarian" is strong language. Are you complaining about Dr Marzillian? What are you charging him with?'

'I'm not *charging* him with anything, he's been very kind to me and I'm sure to you and Irina. But he's a *doctor* –'

'So –?'

'He might want to interfere.'

'In what way?'

'Oh, I don't know –' Ludens found himself up against a barrier of words such as 'drug'. He went on, 'It's just that you'll have to leave here, you can't stay forever in this artificial place, you must live an ordinary life.'

'I have never lived an ordinary life,' said Marcus, 'I don't see why I should start now.'

Ludens said almost angrily, 'You know what I mean!'

'I'm afraid I don't. Let us try the other important thing and see if we can get on better.'

Encouraged by the slight irony in the tone of this remark, Ludens blundered on. 'It's about Irina.'

'Oh.'

'I want to marry her.'

'Does she want to marry you?'

'Yes – I hope so –'

'You hope? Then had you not better sort it out with her?'

'Yes, of course! I just wondered if you had any views on the matter.

285

I mean, I hope, I *assume*, that you wouldn't mind – you did, I think, express yourself favourably, if you remember.'

'If you want me to intervene and ask her to accept you, you are, as they say, barking up the wrong tree.'

'Oh *God*!' said Ludens, exasperated. 'You misunderstand me! Let it go, pray forget it, when and if Irina and I have made a decision we will inform you.'

'What's the matter with you, Alfred?'

'Nothing! I just wish more than anything that we three could live happily ever after in some *house of our own*, and not in this make-believe enchanter's palace!'

Marcus who had been staring at him, first with annoyance, then with ironical irritation, now, after lowering his eyes, gave a grave sad gentle look. He said, 'I am very grateful for your help, very grateful indeed – I think I was once contemptuous of your persistence in pursuing me in order to elicit some secret – but I see now that this was somehow inevitable, even important. I value your loyalty to me, and to Irina. However, let me in turn say two important things to you. First, there is no secret, in the sense in which you used to imagine it. And second, there can be no question of "living happily ever after". I mean simply that we cannot see the future which may contain either happiness or terrible pain. And perhaps a third thing which I hope you will not take amiss. You want – I know you want – something from me, not just the "secret", but – love, or something like that. I cannot give it. I think I said that before. I am sorry – but, as I also said before, infinitely grateful.'

Ludens, who now felt like weeping, said, 'I understand. I'm sorry. We'll say no more about these things. Now let us get on with what we were discussing yesterday.'

Ludens was crawling through the narrow tunnel underneath the wire. It was he decided, probably made by a fox or a badger, or, if by a human, a remarkably thin one. Possibly two species had collaborated. He had already, when finding it (for he could not at first from the other side determine where it was), been thoroughly stung by nettles. Now, within the bounds, he stood up and brushed the dry earth off his shirt and trousers. It was four forty-five a.m. The sun had just risen. The woodland which confronted him was filled with a mysterious powdery pearly light, as if innumerable huge glistening spider's webs were hanging from every tree. Innumerable birds were singing, almost as it seemed to him, yelling. He was at once conscious of being there illicitly. He felt guilty. Suppose he were spotted by a 'Buller' and reported to Marzillian? Also of course he must not be seen by whoever it was, the person or persons he was after, before he saw them. It only then too occurred to him that this person, these people, might be hostile, even dangerous, if disturbed. Perhaps some of Marzillian's 'difficult cases' out for an early morning stroll?

Very cautiously Ludens began to make his way through the trees, keeping within the wood, making a wide arc, clear of Collingwood, behind Rodney, behind Benbow, finally approaching the yew circle and the Stone from the lake side. Here he was not yet in sight of the house, the dome of the swimming-pool and the pinnacles of the North Pavilion appearing some way off on his left. Unfortunately here the trees ended and two or three hundred yards of open close-mown grass separated him from the nearest entrance to the circle. From here the dark hedge, so closely and accurately clipped, looked like an immense object made of metal. Ludens stood here for a while under cover of the trees. He could not, from where he was, see into the circle. In any case the openings on this side were very narrow and it would not be possible to command a view of the Stone without leaving the shelter of the trees. Moreover Ludens did not know from which direction the flower-bearer would come. He, she, it (for he was by now quite ready to envisage a supernatural agency) might come from the house, or across the golf course, which was behind him, or when the gate was opened up the drive. He did not exclude the possibility that, on the occasion when he had come in at seven a.m., he had just missed the creature. Or the approach might be like his own, through a gap in the defences and through the wood. He looked round anxiously. The wood was full of birds, the sound of their song deafening, yet he could see no bird. Perhaps, equally invisible, his quarry was at this very moment watching him. He breathed deeply. Perhaps he had already scared away the mysterious visitant. Was it a *fairy*? What did fairies really look like, how large were they? The flowers, he reflected, were always wild flowers, such as grew in the woodland, though of course also elsewhere. So were they picked on the way through the trees? Picking, selecting flowers was, he reflected, a matter demanding attention, so the, he hoped unsuspecting, picker was not likely to be looking widely about him, he would be looking down at the offerings which he was to bring to the Stone, flowers which Ludens had passed, even trodden on, as he crept along from the road. Suppose the visitant were to see Ludens's track, quite visible, as he now saw looking back, through the dewy grass?

There was a kind of silence which underlay the bird-song, like a clearing under a mist, and Ludens was beginning to feel fear as of something uncanny. He shook himself, shrugging his shoulders and agitating his limbs. The view he commanded from where he was was useless, unlikely to give him any glimpse of his quarry unless the latter actually came up behind him or crossed the grass diagonally from a point nearby. To be sure of success he must secrete himself inside the circle. Not pausing to alarm himself by the prospect of leaving his cover, he set off with long strides across the open grass and slid into the nearest opening in the tall massive hedge. He could now see the Stone, its pointing 'prow' and part of its smooth benign face which in some lights seemed to change from grey to brown. No one. He stood silently in the dark slit for a while. The sun was climbing and he could feel the damp heat rising from the grass. Nothing happened. Perhaps no one would come. Perhaps he had already been seen. His footprints over the lawn were clearly visible in the dew. Standing in the entrance he was in full view of someone coming from the wood. He sat down and managed to wedge himself inside a cleft in the greenery, entering into the interior of the hedge. Here it was very dry, dusty like a dusty room, and full of dead twigs, and branches which, coming at him from all directions, poked him and penetrated his shirt. He felt he was going to sneeze. From here he could see nothing except, through a gap in the foliage, the Stone itself and a small area around it. He sat for some time staring. No one. Why was he so ridiculously concerned to find out who this person was, what did it matter, why didn't he *ask* someone? He had, it seemed, his own reasons for being secretive, as if something disgraceful, or something dreadful, were involved.

The bright light of the sun was making the Stone look curiously pale. As he stared it seemed to be moving towards him like a ship. The bird-song was less. The cries and voices of individual birds could now be identified. It was very hot inside the hedge. He began to feel almost sleepy.

Then suddenly a white figure appeared. Ludens gasped, moved instinctively, then checked himself. His movement had altered his view and he saw now, craning his neck, less clearly. The figure, now with its back to Ludens, was doing something at the Stone, presumably arranging the flowers and the pebbles. The sun, shining onto what must be some kind of pure white robe, made the figure insubstantial, like a moving pillar of light. Then suddenly it was gone.

Ludens propelled himself violently out of his hiding place scraping his face on a branch, he tumbled out, scrambled to his feet, and ran as fast as he could across the grass toward the other side of the circle. He darted through the gap in the hedge, and saw the white figure ahead of him, now running diagonally across the open grass in the direction of the nearest trees. Ludens ran faster. The white creature now looked like a boy. Ludens was catching up until, stretching out his hand, he grasped at the back of the runner. He gripped an arm, and then fell to the ground, bringing his quarry down with him.

It was not a boy, but a girl, down whose face tears were now streaming. There seemed to be round about them a sudden silence, as if, after so much tension and violence, nature had suddenly snapped a string and made everything blank. Ludens quickly let go his hold.

The girl, who seemed to be about fourteen, was dressed in the long white overall worn by the Bellmain domestic staff. Ludens, whose mind had been filled with predatory rage, and the terror and excitement of a hunt, now felt nothing but remorse, contrition and compassion. How could he have been so cruel and so violent to a poor child who picked flowers, what business was it of his, what harm was she doing?

He said, 'Oh, I'm so sorry, I'm *so* sorry, please forgive me, please don't cry, I didn't understand – I'm very sorry I frightened you, I hope I didn't hurt you –'

Still sitting beside him on the grass the girl gazed at him with very large round eyes, like the touching staring eyes of certain gentle breeds of monkey. She gave a little sob or whimper, and produced a handkerchief from the pocket of her overall, with which she covered her nose and mouth.

Ludens rose, then taking her disengaged hand, raised her to her feet. He could feel the very small hand shuddering and trembling within his. They were both of them wet with tumbling in the dew. Her white overall was stained with earth and grass.

Ludens, looking down at her, realised that she was not a child, but a rather short young person who might have been eighteen years old, or perhaps more, but in some ways remained or seemed childish. He thought now that he had seen her before in the village. As this previous half-conscious sighting mingled with his present impressions he felt even more contrite and upset.

He said to her, releasing her hand, 'You won't run away now, will you – you're not frightened of me? Don't be, please. Come now, let's sit down by the Stone and talk to each other.'

He was not sure at that moment whether she would come with him, or dart away. He certainly could not pursue her again. He began to move back toward the Circle, and she followed him, mopping her face with her handkerchief, then brushing down her stained crumpled overall.

The flowers, Ludens saw, were today displayed inside a circle of pebbles. Not disturbing these, he sat down and the girl sat near him and, no longer crying, continued to stare at him with her large amazed frightened eyes.

'There now, let's be friends. My name is Ludens, it's a funny name, but there it is, it's my name. What's your name?'

The girl murmured something.

'What?'

'Fanny Amherst.'

'And you work up at the house?'

'Yes, I'm a cleaner. I should be there now.'

'And you live in the village?'

'Yes.'

Her voice, after the first mumble, was surprisingly clear, with a slight touch of the local accent. She had brown straight hair, neatly cut, encasing her head, giving her, though her hair was not very short, the boyish look which had at first deceived Ludens. Her face, without make-up, was shiny, sun-tanned, rosy-cheeked, tear-stained, her nose was broad, her mouth still tremulous as she continued to bite her lower lip.

'Fanny,' said Ludens, 'I am very sorry indeed that I ran after you like that, and I hope you will forgive me. Let me please explain why I did it. I come here every day with Professor Vallar.'

'I know,' she said in her dignified clear voice.

'And the things which you bring – well, we were puzzled by them, we just wondered what they meant. Because we never saw you, it seemed a bit mysterious, and rather odd, and we were puzzled – you know, it's like receiving anonymous letters, it can upset people. We didn't understand the meaning of those things, perhaps they were for Professor Vallar, or for the Stone, or for some other person, or just for fun, after all why not. Why do you bring them?'

'For him.'

'For the Professor?'

'Yes.'

'But why? You've never met him, have you?'

'Oh no, I've never met him, but I know.'

'What do you know?'

'I know about him.'

'*What* do you know about him?'

The girl, her face now composed, stared at Ludens in silence. Then she said, 'I am late for my work. I must go.'

Ludens felt extremely reluctant to let her depart, but absolutely unable to detain her. The remarkable success of his detective work had not, as he now realised he had hoped, removed his nebulous anxiety about the offerings, it had increased it. He felt even a painful reluctance to question the child (as he still somehow thought of her) further – partly because he felt he had already been quite violent enough without being an inquisitor too – and partly because he *did not want to know* what she meant.

She stood up. Ludens rose too. 'May I still bring the flowers and the stones.'

'Yes, of course, of course,' said Ludens, now taken over by guilt and pity.

'May I ask something else, please?'

'Yes, yes.'

'Might I just once, just for a little minute, come and look at the Professor, I wouldn't come near, I wouldn't disturb you, if I could just come and look at him for a moment? Tomorrow I could come in the morning, I'm not working. Would he mind? Could I come at eleven? I'd just stand over there beside the hedge and see him for a moment, just a moment, could I?'

Ludens was appalled. Whatever would Marcus think? Yet really what did it matter? He'd just have to tell Marcus that some eccentric maidservant wanted to stare at him. After all she couldn't harm him by looking, and was she not herself the most harmless of beings? He had offended her enough already. 'All right, come at eleven, but only for a minute, for half a minute. You see, we are working very hard, the Professor is writing a great book, we have to concentrate and not be interrupted, you do understand?'

'Yes, yes – oh I am so glad – thank you, thank you!' She spread her arms wide apart raising her hands, her large eyes shone with joy.

'I'm sorry, I've made you late, I hope you won't get into trouble. If anyone asks why you're late you must blame me. Look, I'll give you a little note just in case they're cross with you.'

Ludens tore a page out of the notebook which he kept in his pocket.

He wrote: *I was responsible for delaying Miss Amherst. I apologise. A. Ludens. Benbow.* He gave it to her. 'If anyone chides you, show them this, just if it's necessary. Now you must run.'

She put the note away and said, 'Tomorrow!' She uttered a little 'Ah!' expressing perhaps joy or gratitude, then darted off and disappeared through one of the slits in the hedge.

Even before she was out of sight Ludens had realised that he had been foolish to give her the note. It was imprudent to write anything down in this place. And the communication could be variously interpreted. However he assumed that no one would question her and that, in her excited state, she had already forgotten about the slip of paper. He hoped that Marcus would not be annoyed at being put on show. He decided to leave the flowers, which must figure as part of the explanation. He looked at his watch. It was a quarter to seven. He went back to the Black Lion and ate a hearty breakfast.

At Benbow, when Ludens came to collect Marcus for the morning session, everything was as usual. The excitement of his hunt for the flower-bringer had temporarily distracted Ludens from the gloom induced by Marcus's curt reception of his two 'important things'. Ludens had been particularly saddened by Marcus's refusal to tolerate the concept of love. Of course a word was only a sign, the reality could be otherwise; and this particular sign had been so much abused and blunted, it might well be avoided by a scrupulously truthful person. Cordelia really loved her father, she just refused to be effusive about it: rather a tiresome girl actually, Ludens had always thought her, who had caused a great deal of trouble by being so priggishly precise. Still one had to admire such a person and put an extra value upon the love which they felt but did not name. Marcus needed Ludens, he prized him, he missed him; in the case of such a touchy, choosy, ascetic creature, with such high standards of truthfulness and conduct, these phenomena might be taken as evidence of affection of the highest kind.

In the kitchen, while Marcus was having his customary sojourn in the lavatory, Ludens, who for all his wise reflections did retain his attachment to the word in question, put his arms round Irina's waist and said, 'I love you, I love you very much. Do you love me?'

'Yes, Ludens, dear Ludens, silly Ludens, of course.' She began to kiss him quickly all over his face.

Ludens was filled with joy. 'And we'll be married, yes?'

'Well, perhaps, who knows.'

'You're as bad as your father! He says we cannot see the future which may contain happiness or terrible pain.'

'That's true, isn't it?'

'Yes. But we must hope, we must plan.'

Marcus emerged from the lavatory and went into his bedroom. Ludens thought, I'll take her to London. I'll ring Christian and tell him I must have the flat for one night. Perhaps I'll ask him to leave altogether. I must organise *this*, it's time to hustle things. Irina had moved away, but was staring at him, smiling faintly at him with a smile which combined tenderness, playfulness, scornfulness with the superiority of some infinite reserve and the mystery of some infinite sadness. Ludens raised his hands above his head in ecstasy and prayer. Then he left the kitchen and went into the little study where the coloured notebooks were piled on the table. He wanted to be alone for a moment, he felt so happy and so sad, he felt his breast might break open. He felt a strange awful pity, like a pity for the whole world, as he used to feel when he thought about his mother's tears. He opened one of the notebooks, the blue one. If only Marcus could *start* writing, then everything would *move*. If only he can write one sentence, Ludens thought, the first sentence, any sentence, then we shall be off; and *then* all the other problems will be solved as well.

Irina said she was going shopping. Marcus found his new sun hat. He and Ludens set off for the Axle Stone. Ludens was so absorbed in the intensity of his feelings that he forgot about his encounter with the 'visitant' until they actually reached the Stone and saw the offerings. He said to Marcus, 'Oh look, these are for you! You remember someone left some once before, it's a maid up at the house, she's going to be passing by tomorrow at eleven and she said she'd like to step in for a moment just to look at us. I said OK, it'll only be half a minute, she'll just peep in, we don't have to talk to her or notice her. You don't mind, do you?'

'No, no. Are we to take these away?'

'We'll take the flowers, Irina will like them.'

When they had been talking for about half an hour they were interrupted. Ludens's heart sank when he saw Camilla coming across the grass. She handed him a folded slip of paper. It was a note from Marzillian: *Please come to see me at two o'clock.* The secret service had caught up with him after all.

'I wasn't accosting her!' said Ludens.

'There was a bruise on her arm.'

'I ran after her and took hold of her arm, she was running away.'

'Her overall was wet and stained.'

'We fell on the grass.'

'She had been crying.'

'I frightened her, I'm very sorry, I didn't realise –'

'You say you just wanted to question her.'

'Yes, about the flowers and the stones, I couldn't understand them, I was troubled by them. You don't think I –?'

'No, of course not,' said Marzillian. 'The housekeeper, Mrs Singer, was furious, not with the girl of course, but I got you off. She's rather a favourite around here, that child. Now will you tell me *exactly* what happened?'

'I didn't like seeing those flowers and those stones –'

'Why?'

Ludens searched carefully for words. 'I felt it wasn't – proper – I felt –'

'All right, I know why. Go on.'

'I just wanted to know who put them there and what they were for. After all they might have meant anything. I didn't like to ask anyone – they arrived so early –'

'You took them away so that he wouldn't see them.'

'After the first day or two, yes. Then I thought I'd come in very early and try to see who this person was, so I came in about five o'clock.'

'How did you get in, by the way?'

'I crawled under the netting, there's a place by the road where there's a sort of trench.'

'We must fix that, you can tell me where it is later. Go on. I'm not really very vexed with you, I just like to know what is going on.'

'Well, as I said, I saw her come to the Stone, and arrange the things and then I ran after her, I told you, I thought she was a boy, I didn't mean to hurt her –'

'All right, all right.'

'Then we went back and sat by the Stone and I asked her name and she told me and said she worked in the house as a cleaner and I asked what the flowers and the stones were for and why she brought them.'

'And what *exactly* did she say to that?'

'She said the flowers were for Professor Vallar and I said surely she'd never met him and she said she hadn't but she –'

'*Ipsissima verba*, please.'

'She said, "I've never met him, but I *know*." And I said, "What do you know?" and she said, "I know about him," and I said, "What about him?" and she didn't answer that. Then she said she was late for work.'

'And then. Go on, but give me her exact words.'

'She said, "May I still bring the flowers and the stones?" and I said yes, and then she said could she –'

'She said, "Could I –"'

'She said, "Could I come just once, just for a minute, to look at the Professor, I wouldn't come near, I wouldn't disturb you, I'd just look. I'm not working tomorrow, could I come at eleven, I'd just stand over there by the hedge."'

'And you said yes.'

'I didn't like it,' said Ludens, 'but I felt sorry for her and sorry that I'd upset her – and she seemed so innocent and harmless –'

'And you told him.'

'Yes, casually, he didn't object –'

'But you don't like it. *Why?*'

'You said you knew why. All right, I don't want Marcus to worry about other people, I want him to get on with his work and not think he's being given presents or stared at. Quite apart from anything else, it could waste his time.'

Marzillian suddenly laughed. He said, 'You are very good at giving careful well-worded answers which conceal what you really think. All right, I do know why, I just wanted to hear what you would say. I'm very sorry I can't be there.'

'Where?'

'At the Axle Stone, at eleven o'clock tomorrow.'

'Do you think that something will happen?'

'I don't know. But you will come and tell me.'

Earlier, when his morning talk with Marcus had concluded, Ludens had walked back with him to Benbow, where he had given Irina the bunch of wild flowers which she arranged in a vase. She thanked him warmly, assuming he had picked them. Ludens had, on this occasion, left the stones behind on the seat. On other occasions he had 'strayed' the stones together under the flowers, dropping them into the long grass of the woodland. This time, gathering up the bouquet, he had paid more attention to the stones, which he had casually and intentionally disarrayed. They were not local flints, but beautiful rounded sea pebbles, striped and spotted and splashed with various colours; Ludens felt that he had seen some of them before, and reflected remorsefully that they were perhaps treasured possessions which Fanny, realising they had been, like the flowers, thrown away, had lovingly sought for in the woody undergrowth.

Anxious not to be late for his appointment with Marzillian, Ludens had carried off some bread and cheese and an apple from the Benbow kitchen and gone to lurk in the grounds until his watch said ten to two. Marcus and Irina were 'engaged' in the afternoon, first at the swimming-pool, then for tea with Lady Barforth at Nelson. Ludens was surprised, and touched, by Irina's willingness to put up with a social scene which was certainly less than thrilling. He cautiously attributed this tolerance to her pleasure in home life at Benbow, 'playing at house' she called it, which still seemed to amuse her. But he also increasingly felt that this idyllic interval would not last much longer. After leaving Marzillian Ludens went for the usual walk round the grounds, going via the golf course where he met Mr Talgarth and Lady Barforth playing a round. Mr Talgarth greeted him warmly, Lady Barforth more distantly. Perhaps Mrs Singer had already spread the news that he was a sex maniac. The stained overall, the bruise, the tears, could reasonably in any case be held against him, and thinking again of that weird episode he felt an increase of remorse and anxiety. The lake was calm, reflecting the slow progress of a large golden cloud. Moorhens with brilliant scarlet crests and long delicate yellow legs strode daintily about on the verge or clambered splashily in and out of their big untidy nests among the reeds. Ludens thought of the lake at Fontellen and wondered who might be walking beside it now; Busby, surly and alone, with what thoughts, or perhaps Lord Claverden himself? 'That vile toad' Irina had called him. (Why?) All that seemed unreal now, as Bellmain would be soon, perhaps very soon. He stood a while at the great 'view' looking away over Salisbury Plain, which was no plain but an endless recession of small round hills with rounded copses upon their sides. Then he looked back across the lake at the Out of Bounds Garden on the far side which opened narrowly upon the water. He could see the white dresses of nurses, and brownish figures sitting on garden seats. What was *that* like? The perpetual anguish of the diseased mind, the gateway into hell. The murmur of contingency itself. Danger. As he began to walk on he heard suddenly, as if it were rising from the lake water or perhaps happening inside his head, the strange dimmed booming sound which he had heard before. He hastened his step.

The fear which possessed him was dispelled, as he entered the door of the Black Lion, by the sound of familiar voices in the residents' lounge, where he found Maisie and Franca, back from their travels, having tea. Rapturously greeted, he joined them. Mrs Toller, who was fond of Ludens, brought an extra cup and saucer, more tea, more cucumber sandwiches, more of the special cake she knew he liked. Ludens, who had felt himself everywhere on trial, was delighted with his welcome and, as he chatted with Maisie and Franca, with the company of two such charming affectionate women, so sensible and so good-looking. The world suddenly became a pleasant and easy place to live in. The two were full of their travels. They had been to Cockermouth and Dove Cottage and Rydal Mount and Ruskin's house on Coniston, and seen Scafell and Skiddaw and almost *every* lake. Which was Ludens's favourite lake? He scarcely knew the Lake District? He must go at once. Franca liked Buttermere, but Maisie preferred Wastwater, it was so gorgeously sinister; and think, they had found the *very pond* where Wordsworth had met the Leech Gatherer! And the weather had been perfect, slightly misty, slightly rainy, *such* rainbows, and the great place had looked just like a Victorian painting, which was just how it ought to look! And what had been going on at Bellmain while they were away? Ludens was able to inform them that everything had been splendid, Marcus was working on his book, there had been a madrigal concert, and everyone had been feasting on asparagus and strawberries.

On the following morning the weather, though distinctly cooler and menaced by forecasts of rain, remained fairly sunny. Marcus wore his grey cotton jersey over his shirt and Ludens kept his jacket on. They agreed that they would soon have to continue their studies indoors, a change which they agreed might be beneficial. Marcus mentioned, as they walked along, that this afternoon he was to have one of his regular conversations with Marzillian. Ludens, though very curious, did not like to question Marcus too closely about these, and in fact found out very little about them. Marcus implied that they were 'chatty' rather than 'intense'; but this didn't have to be so. Ludens had of course not forgotten that today Fanny Amherst was to manifest herself at eleven. He reminded Marcus of this in a casual tone. He himself, feeling persistent remorse about his rough treatment of the girl, now felt glad rather than otherwise that he could do her this small favour. There were, as expected, the usual offerings at the Stone, laid out this time in neat rows. They sat down, still seeking the sun rather than the shade. Ludens took, surreptitiously, as many notes as he dared. He had already, in his expanded account, which was now more than merely a synopsis, filled two of the local flimsy notebooks. He felt uneasy about what he wrote down, which was undoubtedly in some parts a very rough version, an oversimplification, perhaps even a travesty, of what Marcus said. On the other hand he also sometimes had the impression that they were 'getting somewhere' and that he himself was becoming 'better at it'. As eleven o'clock approached he could not, for all his concentration, help glancing at his watch.

At eleven o'clock precisely Fanny appeared at the large entrance to the Circle, on the side that faced the drive. She was not, as Ludens had somehow expected, wearing her white robe. She was of course not on duty today (it was Saturday) and was wearing a shapeless summer dress of some dark colour which blended into the blackness (now the sun was clouded) of the yew hedge. Ludens and Marcus were sitting, not facing the 'main' entrance, but a little farther round, and Fanny, slinking or gliding along the hedge, took up a position opposite to them. Ludens, intensely aware of the visitor, realised that Marcus was also aware of her and was disturbed. They continued their, for Ludens, difficult conversation. A time passed; surely, he felt, more than the specified half minute. The girl remained motionless. Then Ludens became aware that she had taken several steps forward. She had moved in long cautious tiptoe strides, as in the children's game of 'Grandmother's Steps' where the aim is to advance without being seen. Ludens, aware of the unauthorised movement, did not look directly at her, but made a slight motion of his hand, forbidding further advance and requesting immediate withdrawal. He saw that Marcus had noticed the liberty which had been taken. They went on talking however. Then, to Ludens's horror, the child, walking slowly but with her own ordinary gait, came onward and stood directly in front of Marcus.

Marcus now behaved in a way which surprised Ludens very much. Instead of turning irritably to Ludens, or saying to Fanny, 'Can't you see that we are busy?' or something to that effect, he simply sat quite still, quite silent, and stared at the girl, who was staring at him; and his stare, instead of being amazed, indignant and forbidding, was gentle, thoughtful and troubled. Ludens, annoyed, and bothered by what might develop into some sort of pregnant silence, said in a loud voice, 'Sir, this is the girl I mentioned to you, Fanny Amherst. Now, Fanny, please –'

Fanny, looking very frightened and in a state of controlled excitement, interrupted Ludens by whispering something inaudible.

Ludens said, 'Speak up, Fanny. Then you must go.'

Fanny said to Marcus, 'Will you touch me?'

Marcus, now very faintly smiling, nodded.

Fanny then stretched out, emerging from the folds of her dark-green dress, a very thin arm and a very small hand, palm downward. Marcus reached out his large long hand and laid it on the back of her hand, covering it completely.

The contact was over in a second. Fanny sprang back. She turned a now radiant wide-eyed, shining-eyed, face upon Ludens. 'Oh, can I come tomorrow at eleven, just tomorrow, it's Sunday – Can I, please?'

Marcus immediately said, 'Let her come.'

Ludens said, 'Yes.'

The child scampered away.

Ludens and Marcus then, without comment, resumed their discussion; only Marcus continued, for a short while, to smile faintly.

After lunch Marcus disappeared to see Marzillian. Irina was going swimming in the open-air pool, and then to play croquet with Mr Talgarth. Patrick, not yet back, was now expected, Camilla said.

Ludens, returned to the Black Lion to 'write up' the morning's talk as usual, met Franca who said that Gildas had arrived, had left his address, and asked Ludens to visit him in the afternoon. She also said would he and Gildas please have dinner with her and Maisie at the Lion and Unicorn, the pub near Warminster which they had discovered earlier where the food was so good. Ludens said he was sorry he could not come as he must dine with Marcus as usual. Franca then said would he ask Gildas if he could come. Ludens's thousand-eyed jealousy leapt like a ferocious watch-dog from its lair. Supposing Franca and Gildas were to become intimate friends, excluding him, suppose Gildas were to captivate Maisie Tether? Ludens's stern rational sense of duty, with equally swift reaction, drove the green-eyed creature back to its dark hole. After all, Franca and Gildas had known each other for many years without combining forces against him, and Maisie Tether was shortly going to return to America. Ludens said, yes, of course he would ask Gildas, whom he was going to visit straightaway.

Gildas was staying in a small neat 'bed and breakfast' cottage at the other end of the village, beyond the White Lion, near the church. A youngish woman let Ludens in and said that Mr Herne was upstairs on the right. Ludens found his friend in a tiny bedroom with a pleasant view over gardens and trees toward the churchyard and the just visible church tower. They embraced, laughing, then sat down, Gildas on the bed, Ludens on a rickety chair. Ludens, conscious of looking exceedingly well and exceedingly brown, saw how pale Gildas, who had taken off his glasses, now looked, how tired, how older. He was unshaven, his face dirtied with stubble, his dry parchment skin more wrinkled, his expression in repose more absolutely sad, and his clothes even shabbier. His shirt was torn near the neck and a stringy hole was appearing in the sleeve of his jacket. However, aware perhaps of Ludens's sympathetic gaze, he turned upon his friend his customary bright impish look of teasing affection.

'So how is the great man? Is he filling up those handsome notebooks?'

'Not yet. Gildas, I'm so glad to see you!'

'You look healthy. Have you been playing tennis and golf and sunbathing with Irina?'

'No, it's all very austere, like a monastery. By the way, Franca says will you have dinner with her this evening?'

'What's Franca up to? Is she leaving Jack?'

'No, she'll never leave Jack. She will wash their feet. She's joining them in France at Heather Allenby's place.'

'Isn't that the girl you're supposed to marry, have you met her yet?'

'No, I'm not interested.'

'She might be a better bet than Irina, at least she's a normal English girl, and rich – though I daresay Irina's even richer. Why don't you join them in France, they'd be thrilled.'

'Don't be daft.'

'They haven't invited me. No one has invited me. I have fallen out of society. The landlady offered to mend my shirt.'

'How are you, Gildas, how are things? You wouldn't tell me last time.'

'You didn't ask last time. You are not asking now.'

'God! What counts as asking? If you need money –'

'No, no. I'm all right. Have you been in bed with Irina?'

'Yes. Once.'

'Why only once?'

'Don't torment me, Gildas. And don't mention this to anyone.'

'When have you known me mention anything? But seriously, what on earth are you *doing* here with Marcus? What sort of state is he in?'

'He's perfectly OK, we're working on his book.'

'*We?*'

'We have long discussions and I make notes. Then I write out a sort of summary.'

'Doesn't he write? So *you're* writing the book.'

'No! I don't understand half of what he says, I'm just helping him to think. I've made a sort of synopsis.'

'But if you don't understand him, how can you have the faintest idea whether it makes sense or not?'

'I know it makes sense, I understand that much! Anyway he'll start writing soon.'

'But so far he's written nothing. I think you're wasting your time. The Armenian keeps you on as an unpaid nurse. And I don't believe in the thing with the girl. It's just your old crush on Marcus, you should know by now he's a Sphinx without a secret. You're trying to prove he's still a genius by pretending he's writing a great book while all the time you're writing a nonsensical one.'

'Gildas, stop.'

'Marcus's career, after he left mathematics, has been one long descent into raving megalomania. The fact is, he's incapable of real thinking, he's just staggering from one obsession to another. No wonder he's in a mental home, it can't be an accident, have you thought of that?'

Ludens, who had been staring intently at his friend, said quietly, '*Just don't talk to me like this.*'

'Oh, now you're angry with me! You'll tell me to go to hell.'

'No, but I might tell you to go to London.'

'I don't need telling twice, I'll go at once!' Gildas stood up. Ludens stood up too.

'Gildas, don't be silly, I'm sorry, I'm under a terrible strain at present. I'll explain it all later. Please have dinner with Franca, she's got such a nice American friend called Maisie. I'm glad you're here, I want you to be here, I may need you. Only please don't discourage me and demoralise me and revile me when I'm fighting for my life. You don't understand, you can't understand, you're saying unjust unkind things at random. Don't do it.'

Ludens sat down. Gildas sat down.

Gildas said, 'All right, I won't express my thoughts. I'm sorry you're in some sort of crisis. Of course you won't tell me about it. I'll probably stay here for a while, but I won't expect to see you. I'll let you know when I go.' He gazed at Ludens with his sad pale contorted face. He fumbled in his pocket for his glasses and put them on.

Ludens, distressed, cried, 'Gildas, we're not quarrelling – it's not possible, is it?'

'No, my dear boy, it's not. I'll be here. If you need me you can send a message.'

The next morning, when they reached the Stone, neither Marcus nor Ludens could concentrate. Ludens hoped that it would rain but, though cloudy, it did not. They had brought their cushions to sit on, since, as they had noticed on the previous day, the concrete seat was no longer warmed by the sun. The flowers and stones were there of course, the flowers for the first time woven into garlands. Ludens, pushing them roughly aside as they sat down, saw Marcus frown at the gesture. After his brush with Gildas, some of whose words haunted him disagreeably, Ludens had been unable to compose a coherent version of the previous discussion. This version, usually their starting point, lacking, Ludens found he could not initiate a continuous exchange. He kept asking Marcus questions to which Marcus replied briefly, after which there was a pause, after which Ludens would ask another, often disconnected and no more fruitful, question.

He had left Benbow earlier than usual on the previous evening. Indeed he never stayed late, but he had felt more than usually unnecessary on this occasion. Marcus was silent and rather dour. Ludens kept looking at him. He looked odd, hunched up in an unnatural posture like a sick animal, one hand, drooping as if wounded, held up to his breast, his gaze roving about. At one point Ludens reached out and touched his sleeve, then smiled when Marcus looked at him. Marcus smiled back, then lapsed into his restless brooding. Irina frowned at Ludens's gesture, and gave him a look meaning: leave him alone. Camilla came in after dinner as she sometimes did. She got on well with Marcus, who was enlivened by her charm and by her talent for making an interesting conversation emerge out of anything, however trivial. Ludens and Irina, both by nature taciturn, watched her with glum envy. Ludens found himself wishing that he had decided (why not?) to spend the evening with Franca and Maisie and Gildas. He imagined the happy merry trio at the Lion and Unicorn. He felt himself falling into a state, very common when he was younger, of being totally cut off from the society he was in. He was also aware that if he, now, started a sentence, his stammer would stop him dead half-way through. He got up, waved vaguely to the company, and glided out into the now sunny evening. When he reached the Black Lion he hung around for a while in the bar hoping that Franca and her guests would return, but they did not.

Now he and Marcus had both begun to look at their watches. The time crawled on from half past ten to a quarter to eleven. Marcus had almost fallen silent.

Punctually upon eleven the little figure, in the dimmer light even less visible than before in her dark-green dress against the sombre hedge, materialised, one moment not there, the next moment there. She moved, or travelled, like a beetle walking upon a wall (the image came to Ludens) along the perimeter until she reached her place opposite to Marcus. There she stayed quiet and motionless for some time, and Ludens, still attempting to talk to Marcus, hoped she would simply go away. But she did not, and Marcus, making no pretence of listening to Ludens, was giving her all his attention.

Then once more she began to approach, less tentatively but slowly. She came and stood before him and they looked at each other, he benign and alert, she radiant with a silent joy by which her face was almost contorted. Then she drew something out of the pocket of her dress and said to Marcus in her clear though childish voice, 'Would you please just hold my stone for a moment?'

She held out her hand. In her palm was a black and white stone, rounded and very smooth, about the size of a goose's egg. Marcus's long fingers scooped the stone up. As he held it they continued to gaze at each other, and it was as if, as it seemed to Ludens, in that long moment, they *understood* each other. Marcus released the stone into her outstretched hand. She stepped back, uttering a little cry like the chirp of a small bird. Then she turned and ran swiftly away and vanished.

Ludens, filled with a strange urgent emotion, perhaps fear, perhaps anger, leapt to his feet, intending to run after her and tell her, kindly and firmly, that she must not interrupt them again. But he felt a sudden pain in his arm like an electric shock. Marcus had taken hold of him and pulled him back onto the seat. Marcus's grip was hot and painful upon his arm. Ludens thought at that moment, yes, animal magnetism, that must have been what he did to Patrick, it's a natural force well known to science.

Marcus, evidently unaware of the effect he had produced, said, 'Let her be.'

Ludens, rubbing his arm, said, 'Marcus, we must tell her to stop bothering us.'

Marcus said, 'She is something harmless.' The word 'harmless' had a strange ring.

As it was tacitly clear that they could now do no more work, they set off to walk round the lake. When they had gone some way they met Terence Bland who walked with them, being unusually relaxed and agreeable, pointing out to them a remarkable grotto in a shrubbery near to the house.

'What's the matter, Irina, *what's the matter?*'

'I'm frightened, I'm *frightened.*'

'Please stop crying like that, you're breaking my heart!'

'I'm made for misery, misery, *misery*, I'm made to be *destroyed*!'

'I'll look after you, I'll protect you, I'll save you from anything, Oh don't grieve so, I can't bear it!'

'I'll never be happy, how can you love me, I'm awful, I'm covered with spiders, I'm *doomed.*'

'Irina, *please*, tell me, what's wrong, what is it?'

'Oh everything – Dad, everything –'

'Irina, I think we should leave here, it's time to leave, please let's go, let's go away together, I'll find a house –'

'We can't, we can't move him, you *know* we can't, he's got to be looked after.'

'*We'll* look after him. Irina, we are bound together, you and me and your father. I'm going to the Registry Office in Salisbury to find out how soon we can be married.'

'No, no – I'm all in pieces – I can't –'

'Yes you can. And listen, I'm going to take you to London to my flat, I'll ask my friend to move out. We can be quiet together for a day and a night. Now Pat's back, he and Camilla can look after Marcus just for twenty-four hours, twelve hours. I've *got* to have you with me *quietly* and *alone* – it's hopeless here, no wonder you're in pieces. Let *me* decide things now. Come here and sit on my knee. And please, please stop crying, I love you so much.'

Irina sat on his knee and they wrapped their arms round each other, she clasping his neck, her dark hair, wet with her tears, covering his face. Ludens felt, in the midst of his agonies of anxiety, for a moment, such peace. He held her, he desired her, he loved her. His physical longing merged with such a deep yearning to protect her and cherish her forever. If only they could be alone! Already Marcus was coughing in the next room.

It was two days later. The weather remained cool, some rain fell, grey clouds rushed hurriedly across the sky, east winds shook petals from the early roses. Marcus and Ludens had not revisited the Stone. On the first day they sat instead in the little 'study room' at the table and attempted, at least Ludens attempted, to resume their conversation. Marcus was abstracted, anxious as if waiting for something, Ludens impatient, there was nothing of substance to be written down. More progress was made when Ludens changed his tactics and simply asked Marcus strings of disconnected questions, about his past, about his travels, about politics, about books. Marcus answered readily, briefly, but was somehow 'absent'. On the second day Ludens arrived to find Patrick and Camilla chatting with Marcus and Irina, a scene which was prolonged into 'elevenses' with cups of milky coffee and some special shortbread biscuits which Camilla had brought. Dr Bland also turned up and he and Patrick had a discussion about Ireland which was reasonably friendly, given their extreme tribal differences. Marcus revealed that he had once lived for a time in Dublin, conversing with a man at Trinity College. Ludens resolved to find out whom and why. It had occurred to him recently that it must be part of his programme to establish a detailed account of Marcus's life history, and on this subject he had already started another notebook. At midday Marcus set off with Dr Bland to walk to the house where he was to have his ears syringed by a nurse. Patrick and Irina had started a game of draughts. Ludens went back to the Black Lion where Franca and Maisie were drinking in the bar. Maisie said she *must* see Marcus. In a few days they were to depart, she home to Boston, Franca to France to join Jack and Alison. Ludens was evasive. Returning to Benbow in the afternoon he found that Marcus had been feeling ill and had gone to bed. Patrick was still there. In momentary sunshine Ludens and Irina walked as far as the newly discovered grotto and admired its interesting dampness and the water dripping from artificial stalactites. Meanwhile Dr Bland had visited Marcus and diagnosed the local 'flu. It was on the following morning that Ludens, arriving early, had found Irina in tears.

'Last night I dreamt of the ram.'

'The ram? Oh yes. Well, that settles it. Today I'm going to the Registrar about our marriage. And I'll go to an estate agent and find a house, just somewhere we can move into quickly. We can decide later where we want to live. Oh Irina, there's so much life for us.'

'Is there? I feel I have no life. There's nothing in front of me but a black wall.'

'From now on I'm taking charge.'

'Dad had a bad night.'

'So you told me. But Bland says it's nothing.'

'He was talking all night, I could hear him talking out loud as if someone were there.'

'He was talking in his sleep, everyone does.'

'I'm so *frightened*.'

'But why, what of?'

'I saw a ghost.'

'*What*?'

'Perhaps it wasn't a ghost, after all what do ghosts look like? Whatever it was it was horrible, *disgusting*.'

'But *what was it*?'

'Early yesterday morning, and early this morning too, I was looking out of the window just after six o'clock and I saw this white thing.'

'What sort of thing?'

'White, like a white slug, only standing upright, at the end of the lawn, by the trees by the drive, I suppose it was a person, but it was so still – it could have been a child, a white child – and somehow nasty.'

Ludens, who felt her fear as if it had been poured into his chest, said in a calm voice, 'My dear, that's no ghost, that's Fanny Amherst! She's a cleaner who works in the house, and she's rather fallen for Marcus. She used to come and look at us when we were working at the Stone. She's quite harmless. She's just on her way to work in the early morning.'

'Is she a dwarf?'

'No, just rather short.'

'I think it's something evil, I don't want Dad to see it.'

'Irina, don't be *silly*, we have real troubles, let's not invent imaginary ones!'

Dr Bland was crossing the lawn. Irina sprang off Ludens's knee and smoothed down her dress. 'Here's Terence to see Dad. Please go away for a while.'

Benbow possessed, at the side, an ordinary 'front door', but visitors usually advanced up the steps to the doors of the sitting room. Dr Bland, peering in, knocked on the glass and entered.

He addressed Ludens. 'Already here? I fear you are working him too hard. I am going to prescribe a holiday.'

Ludens, who found Bland physically alarming in some way, said, 'Of course we shall do as you say, Doctor.'

'Terence, please.'

'Terence.' He said to Irina, 'I'll be back later.' The doors were open. He leapt down the steps and ran across the grass.

When he reached the tarmac he slowed down. Irina's fear still filled him to the brim. Her fears, her tears, the soft warm weight of her body. Her extraordinary reaction to Fanny. *How did she know*? he found himself thinking, and was then amazed at the thought. Know what? Surely *he* did not regard Fanny as . . . ? I shall go mad, thought Ludens. Marzillian had predicted or expected that Ludens would come and tell him about Fanny's manifestation at the Stone, but Ludens had not come. He did not want to speak about it, or indeed know what to say. He was thinking *we must get out, we must get out*. He wondered if he should go to see Gildas, but decided not to. So he expected Gildas to stay, unvisited, and to wait? Yes. He wondered, shall I drive to Salisbury, or shall I ring up Christian about the flat?

As Ludens turned the corner and came in sight of the front entrance he became aware of some sort of happening ahead. A number of people were gathered on the drive and he could glimpse stationary vehicles in the road ahead. He thought, there must have been an accident. As he came nearer he saw that a motor caravan was halted with its front wheels just inside the gates and its rear end obstructing the narrow lane. The situation had evidently existed for some time since cars were stopped on both sides of the obstruction. The gates, which could not now be properly closed, had been moved by the security men to form a symbolic barrier touching the nose of the intruding vehicle. A main aspect of the problem, as Ludens took it in, was that the Bulldogs were refusing to let the caravan move forward and the cars in the lane were making it impossible for it to move back. Ludens, who had been walking on the grass verge, had come quite close to the drama before one of the Bulldogs saw him and turned (for they all knew him) to make some appeal, perhaps to ask him to fetch some higher authority. Before this could happen however, Ludens was recognised by someone else.

'Hey, we know you, tell them to let us in. We know this chap, he knows us, we told him all about it!'

The speaker was a young man, the youngest of the shaggy trio who had so disturbed Ludens a short while ago. His two companions were standing with him, together with several other young persons including two girls.

One of the Bulldogs said to Ludens, 'They're hippies, they want to camp here. Are they friends of yours?'

Ludens said, 'No. I just met them once before. I told them not to come in.'

One of the bearded men said, 'We're not hippies.' 'We're on our way to Stonehenge,' said the youngest man, addressing Ludens whom he had evidently elected as his friend and ally. 'For the summer solstice, you know. But we want to stop here first, it is *meant* that we should be here, there are signs, someone who is here has a message for us.'

Three more of the young people had come forward to hear the dispute. A girl in a green track-suit, who was holding some flowers in her hand, said, 'We are not hippies, we are Seekers. We want to see the Healer.'

One of the Bulldogs said to the other, 'I think they mean the Prof.'

'There you are!' said the girl triumphantly, 'he *is* here, we knew he was!'

'We won't cause any trouble,' said Ludens's young friend, again addressing him. 'We are peaceful people, we just want to approach and *look* at him. We don't want to camp here, we just wanted to get our bus off the road.'

A car was approaching down the drive, a BMW belonging to a visiting doctor called Sandburg, whose presence Terence Bland had mentioned. The car stopped and the doctor got out. Behind him Ludens could see Mr Talgarth and Thelma approaching on foot. Cars in the queue on the road were beginning to hoot their horns. He said to the Bulldogs, 'If you let them move forward a few feet the cars outside can pass, and then they can back out. I'll see they don't come in any further.'

'Oh you will, will you?' said one of the bearded men. 'Who are you anyway?' He turned to the Bulldogs. 'Who is this chap?'

The Bulldogs were at a loss. Who was he, how to explain him? One of them said, 'He's nothing to do with us, he's just a friend of one of the patients.'

Ludens thought, I'm blacked because of Fanny!

The bearded man said to Ludens, 'Sorry, chum, I thought you were somebody.'

A policeman had appeared, pushing his way along the side of the caravan and thrusting one of the gates aside. Dr Sandburg, who had left his car and was standing just behind Ludens, said in an authoritative voice, ignoring the others and addressing the policeman, 'Can you get me out, please, officer? I am a doctor and I must get back to my hospital.'

The policeman said, 'I'll do my best, sir,' then addressing the Seekers, 'Who is driving this vehicle? Could you get in, please.'

The taller bearded man said he was the driver and got in. The Bulldogs pulled the gates back, and the caravan moved forward onto the drive leaving the lane clear. The policeman returned to the lane and began marshalling the opposing lines of cars, ordering some to move back into wider parts of the lane. Dr Sandburg's B M W moved past and out of the gates. Thelma had disappeared, perhaps to summon more peaceful helpers.

'Out you go now,' said one of the Bulldogs to the bearded driver, who had climbed out of the van.

'We just want to see *him*. We know he's here. The van's not in the way. I can move it onto the verge if you like.'

'My name's Andy,' the friendly young man said to Ludens, 'we're non-violent, we seek the peace of the spirit, we want to approach those who are wise. We are the people of the New Age. We reverence the simple things of the earth, trees, and flowers, and stones –'

'*Stones?*' said Ludens.

'Yes,' said the girl in green who was listening. 'Stones can become radiant with cosmic power. Some call us the Stone People because we carry stones, we take them to holy places.' She added, 'My name's Miriam.'

Through the gates, now wide open, two more Seekers had entered, there were now about ten of them in all. Another security man had also arrived. The policeman had not reappeared.

'Listen,' said the tall bearded man, whose name Miriam told Ludens was Colin Bassett, 'just let us visit him, he doesn't have to talk to us, we won't talk to him, we'll only stay a minute, then we'll go on to Stonehenge. Or would you rather we all sat down here?'

'Yes, come on, come on!' said a mop-haired youth standing behind him. 'You can't keep us out, you know you can't! Do you want peace or something else?'

'I'll go and look for the policeman,' said Ludens.

'If you involve the fuzz there'll be a riot,' said mop-head.

Ludens went out through the gates and looked both ways, walking along a little. The lane was empty. Its emptiness struck Ludens as sinister. The policeman had evidently decided that this was no longer any business of his.

As he was returning he saw with relief that the caravan was being backed out of the gate. It moved some way down the lane and parked off the road. Colin got out.

'Are you going?' said Ludens.

'No way!'

When, with Colin, he returned to the scene on the drive the situation seemed to have changed slightly. A van from the Wessex Linen Service had driven in and was standing on the drive. The driver and his assistant, together with a villager whom Ludens knew by sight, who worked at the White Lion, had joined the Seekers who had gathered into a little group from which a confused excited chatter was arising. Mr Talgarth and a taciturn male nurse called Lambert were standing by. The security men also seemed to be listening. In the farther distance Ludens was relieved to see Camilla running down the drive.

As Colin and Ludens approached, a long-haired boy cried out, 'Here's the man who was raised from the dead.' In the centre of the little crowd was Patrick.

Ludens said to Colin, 'He wasn't raised from the dead.'

'He says he was,' said Miriam.

'He's a liar.'

'*He* says he's a liar!' cried Andy.

There was a hostile murmur. The little crowd parted and Ludens came face to face with Patrick. Patrick was taller than Ludens. His dark curly hair had grown longer and, tossed back, tumbled down behind his head. His bony face was shiny and reddened with health and sun. His dark blue eyes gazed reproachfully, his small gentle mouth pouted. He spoke, not angrily. 'You should not say that, Alfred.'

Ludens, exasperated, and also now frightened, said, 'Pat, I'm sorry, but you know what I mean.'

'I do not.'

'I mean – I think – you weren't dead – you were just very ill – then you got better.'

'He was dead!' said a threatening voice behind Ludens.

'Oh all right, how can we know!' said Ludens, feeling a threatening pressure behind him.

Patrick echoed solemnly, 'All right, how can we know. But it was a bloody miracle all the same.'

'A miracle, yes!' cried Miriam.

Camilla, who had pushed her way through, appeared suddenly beside Ludens, panting with haste and collecting her flying hair. 'The Doctor isn't here, he's gone to London.' As 'the Doctor' could only mean Marzillian this was welcome news.

'We must get this lot out,' said Ludens.

'Why, pray?' said Patrick. The Seekers murmured approval.

'Look,' said Colin, 'why all this fuss, there's a simple solution which we've already mentioned six times. We only want to *see* him. We come in peace, we are bound for the great Union at Stonehenge. This, here, is a destined stopping place, this manifestation is a part of our pilgrimage, we will *not* go away without our sighting, we won't speak, we won't move, we won't make a sound, one moment will be enough, it may seem short to you, but for us time overflows. If you prevent us now we shall simply wait. We are peaceful, but we are determined. We recognise a deeper law. We are orderly and disciplined. Watch this.' He suddenly shouted 'SIT.'

With a burst of laughter the Seekers moved off the tarmac and sat down cross-legged on the grass, leaving Colin standing with Pat and Camilla and Ludens. Mr Talgarth and Lambert, who had been joined by the White Lion man, stood back. The Wessex Linen Service had driven dutifully on to the house. The Bulldogs were now watching developments with resigned ironical faces. They doubtless recognised a higher authority in Camilla. Over Camilla's shoulder Ludens could see two women standing in the gateway. They were Maisie Tether and Franca.

Ludens said to Colin, 'This is ridiculous, you can't come and stare at someone who is ill! The Professor is unwell, a doctor is with him. Do be decent and go away.'

Colin shook his head.

Camilla, who was now holding Patrick's hand, or rather his wrist, said, 'Why not let them see him? He's not really ill, he's up and about now, Dr Bland has gone. He could stand at the window and they could stand on the drive. I think they really won't go away, and you see they do know how to behave.' She indicated the young people seated upon the grass, making with her free hand the graceful reassuring gesture with which she had greeted Ludens on their first meeting.

The young people replied with cries of 'Yes, yes,' 'Yes please,' and 'We're good.'

Ludens, turning to the security men whom he still felt bound to consult, asked, 'What do you think?'

'Oh anything, so long as you get them out!'

Camilla said, 'I think we should do it at once and get it over. Why are you so anxious?'

Ludens could not explain to her. He thought, I don't want these people to look at Marcus, I don't want him to see them or to think about them, what is happening is *horrible*, but I can't stop it now. 'All right, yes.'

Camilla, looking at him with her persuasive sympathetic eyes, said, 'You know, they won't stay, Patrick will lead them away afterwards, they'll go with him.'

'Like the Pied Piper,' said Ludens. 'But Marcus must be warned, and for heaven's sake keep him inside the house! You go now with Pat. I'll stay here for a few minutes, then I'll bring them through the wood. You'll be silent, won't you?' he said to Colin.

'We understand. We'll be silent.'

Patrick and Camilla ran away, disappearing among the trees. The Seekers, now risen, stood together in silence. Mr Talgarth, Lambert, and the White Lion man made another little group. The Bulldogs said nothing, but exchanged significant glances. There was a reverential pause.

'I say, what on earth is going on?' said Maisie Tether's extremely audible voice over Ludens's shoulder.

He turned. 'They want to see Marcus. I'm going to take them in a minute or two.'

'But who are they?'

'They are Seekers, the Stone People, the people of the New Age.'

Maisie did not laugh. She said in a quieter voice, 'Oh. How interesting.'

'Can we come too?' said Franca.

'I can't stop you.'

'Why should you want to?'

Ludens did not answer this question. He felt, in the very short silence that followed, how everyone was looking at him. He made a signal, raising his left hand. The Seekers stood aside, and Ludens marched forward, leaving the drive and moving in among the trees. He could hear the soft tramp of many feet following him through the grass.

Later on, looking back at that extraordinary march through the wood, it all seemed like something vastly extended in time and space, as if, in some dense but silent tropical forest, he had been leading a native tribe toward some place of fateful sacrifice. In fact, as he soberly remembered later, the whole episode from the first moment of seeing the intruders to the moment of reaching Benbow could not have taken more than twenty minutes. Perhaps it was a case of time over-flowing.

As they reached an open space near Rodney, Ludens glanced back at the orderly curving file marching in pairs with solemn faces. Rodney was screened by trees, but Benbow was closer to the drive, and before approaching it Ludens led his pilgrims out onto the tarmac. He thought, perhaps it will only take a moment and we shall get away with it after all, if Pat and Camilla haven't upset Marcus. Perhaps I should have gone, but I didn't want to leave Pat with that lot. What a perfectly insane business!

Just before the little house became visible, Ludens paused to let the tail of the procession catch up. He then addressed the group who gathered round him.

'The Professor's house is just here. I want you to stand on the drive, not on the lawn. I will go in and ask him to stand at the window for a few moments.'

Ludens walked slowly on. Benbow behind its lawn and bushy shrubs came into view. The Seekers and their camp followers, including Maisie, Franca, Talgarth, Lambert, the man from the White Lion, and a gardener who had been picked up on the way, spread out along the edge of the grass, facing the house. Ludens moved quickly on to the lawn, intending to go into the house and conduct Marcus briefly to the window. But he was forestalled.

As soon as the pilgrims were in place, indeed sooner, the glass doors of the sitting room opened and Marcus emerged. He was wearing a white robe. He stood quite still at the top of the steps gazing down the garden at the row of onlookers. There was a sudden absolute silence and stillness. Moments passed. Ludens was aware of Lambert's face, rapt and wide-eyed. The first movement was made by some of the Seekers who, with slow almost surreptitious fumblings, drew stones from their pockets, laid them in the grass, and resumed their immobility. Ludens himself, a little ahead of the line, was held as in a trance. Then he said to himself, it's Marcus in his dressing-gown, oh *hell*, Pat and Camilla have messed things up properly. He coughed, shook himself, pulled at the collar of his shirt, then began to walk toward the house. Behind him there was a faint audible sigh.

As he came nearer to Marcus, Ludens saw his face more clearly. It was, in that instant, scarcely recognisable. Marcus, gazing at his visitors, had assumed an expression of serene brooding solemnity which had in it something sullen, even something dangerous. His eyelids drooped, his mouth drooped, his face was as smooth and still as that of a statue.

Ludens had intended to mount the steps and hustle Marcus quickly back into the sitting room. But this would have been ungracious, and was in any case, as he approached, suddenly impossible. He stopped, and stood there helplessly, as if rooted to the earth, vibrating with amazement, exasperation, fear and awe. The next moment Marcus turned his head, looked at Ludens, and smiled. The spell was broken. Ludens ran forward and up the steps. Marcus turned and went back into the sitting room, followed by Ludens. Behind them there was a strange sound which Ludens could not at first recognise. It was the sound of clapping.

Inside the room Ludens quickly closed the doors and pulled a curtain across. Patrick and Camilla materialised beside Marcus. In a strange moment, as Ludens remembered it, they all stood round Marcus *holding* him, holding his arms, holding the folds of his gown, surrounding him as people behind the scenes might surround an actor who had just moved off the stage leaving behind a rapturous audience.

Recovering Ludens said to Patrick, 'Go and take them away, get them out quick, they'll follow you, go on.'

Patrick left, opening the doors and leaping down the steps. Ludens caught a glimpse of the 'audience' now broken up into groups, presumably talking. He said to Camilla, 'We don't have to report this to anybody, do we?'

'Well – I must talk to Maria and Anita.'

'Where's Irina?'

'Outside. She wanted to watch it all from the front. She's probably walking along with them, she was curious. Look, they're going already.'

'Just make sure Pat sees them all out of the gate.'

'I will. Goodbye, Professor, you were *wonderful!*' Camilla then did actually kiss the shoulder of Marcus's white towelling dressing-gown. She vanished.

Ludens found himself left, still holding onto Marcus's sleeve. As soon as he was alone with Marcus he felt as if some great hot wet tropical storm were breaking over him. He felt he wanted to weep, to wail, to hug Marcus, to shout at him, to kick him. He gripped Marcus's other arm with his other hand and shook him. He cried, 'Marcus, Marcus, you mustn't do it.'

'Do what, my dear? Now let's sit down quietly, shall we?'

They sat down together on the small tweedy sofa. Sitting beside him Ludens realised that Marcus was trembling, and that he too was trembling.

'Marcus, I'm terribly sorry, I couldn't stop them, they would come and see you. I hope Pat and Camilla explained. They're sort of harmless loonies, young people going to Stonehenge, you know how they go every year to some sort of festival at midsummer. They'd somehow heard of you and wanted just to have a look. It was very kind of you to come out like that. Thank heavens it's over! They'll clear off now. You aren't upset are you? Don't be upset. I'll look after you, I'll go with you anywhere, I won't ever leave you.'

'Could you pull back the curtain?'

Pulling back the striped curtain Ludens saw that the bottom of the garden was not yet entirely empty of people. Franca and Maisie Tether were still there, examining the various 'offerings', stones and flowers and a few leafy twigs, which had been laid out at the end of the lawn. Ludens opened the door and made a 'clear off' gesture, almost as ferocious as that by which Marzillian had dismissed Dr Bland. Maisie hastily put down the flowers she had been holding, and she and Franca hurried away down the drive.

Ludens stood looking down at Marcus, who was breathing deeply. 'Marcus, are you all right?'

'Yes, of course.'

'Will you get dressed, shall I help you?'

'No, I think I'll just sit quiet for a while.'

'Would you like me to stay? Would you like to sit in the study? Would you like us to talk?'

'Not now. Alfred, I must tell you –'

'What?'

'I must simplify my life.'

'But, dear Marcus, it is simplified already!'

'No, I mean – suppose I were to take up painting again?'

Marcus, now rubbing his throat and his chest, looked up with an air of child-like innocence which filled Ludens with fear, exasperation, almost rage.

'Why shouldn't you paint if you want to,' said Ludens, controlling his emotions, 'but wouldn't that be just play, something that belonged to the past, a stage you went through –'

'I wish I could compose music.'

'Well, you can't! What you *can* do is *think*, and you must go on thinking, go on with what you've really been doing and what you're really good at. Don't you see that when you went in for painting, when you met Jack and me, and Gildas Herne, remember him, you were just searching for a way – and when you found the way you stopped painting. Now you've been following the way and you've discovered what you were looking for all those years, and now you've got to *clarify* that discovery, you've got to *go on* –'

'Is it like that?' said Marcus, looking up as if he expected from Ludens some great decisive saying.

'Yes! And *that*'s not simple – but your mode of life is simple – and it can be even simpler if we can just get ourselves out of here –'

'Oh, isn't it all right here for the present?'

'Yes, yes, we'll stay – Marcus, you are driving me mad!'

'I'm sorry –'

'I'm sorry too, forgive me, let's not work this morning, let's have a day off, we could go for a walk – I could take you out in the car, I know you haven't wanted to, but maybe now –'

In a jabber of conversation Irina and Patrick burst in through the doors of the verandah. Behind them the sun was shining on the garden.

Irina, who did not usually manifest such affection in public, ran to her father, plumped down beside him on the sofa and hugged him. 'Dad, you did so well, it was just right!'

Marcus, smiling with pleasure, put his arm round her. After the curious absent vagueness of his talk with Ludens he looked alert and self-possessed.

Patrick, kneeling on the floor, patted Marcus's feet. 'It was great!'

Ludens said, 'I'm going to the Black Lion, I've got to write some letters, I'll be back later.'

Looking down at the enlaced trio Ludens felt that he too must touch Marcus. He stretched out his hand. Marcus took it and they shook hands formally. The gesture was suddenly ridiculous. The other two laughed. Ludens departed, closing the glass doors behind him.

When he had walked quickly some way along the drive, he was overtaken by Irina.

'Alfred, what's the matter, you're cross, you're in a huff, what have we done?'

'I'm not in a "huff", and who's "we"?'

'Oh don't be *silly* – what is it?'

'I don't want you and Patrick to stir him up so.'

'"Stir him up"? What on earth do you mean? Anyway, wasn't what happened this morning stirring, wasn't it exciting?'

'I found it disgusting. It was an act of violence. Those crazy people imposed themselves on us. And they upset Marcus. I don't want him upset.'

'He doesn't belong to you.'

'Yes he does. He belongs to me and to you. You belong to me too.'

'Oh really, big deal! All right, I'm only teasing.'

'*Teasing*!'

'You're so solemn. Dad *loved* it.'

'That's what terrifies me. You and Pat seemed to think it was just a bit of theatre.'

'Wasn't it?'

'I hope you saw that horrible gang off all right.'

'I think they were nice people. I had quite a talk with them. Yes, they went off.'

'Irina, please, don't *discuss* it with Marcus, I want him to put it away into the past, it doesn't *concern* him. And we must get him out of this place, it's awful, it's full of bad vibrations.'

'So you believe in vibrations?'

'Irina, just try to *help* me, will you?'

'I will, I do, though you're so *hopeless*. Look, someone's coming, I think it's Anita. Come back soon, won't you!' She ran off.

Anita, who was as tall as Ludens and wore her hair in a long thick plait, was approaching from the road. Ludens scarcely knew her except to say 'good morning'. He found her rather forbidding. If there was a hierarchy among the 'maids' – which he had not so far detected – she must certainly be at the top. She smiled and would have walked by, only Ludens, pausing, said, 'When is Dr Marzillian coming back?'

'This evening.' She smiled again, waved a vague hand, and moved on.

Ludens thought, they disapprove of me. Then he thought, of course he'll have to know, I'll have to explain it all to him, and he'll think it's my fault!

He felt a strong desire to return to Marcus and drive the other two away, but he kept on walking; it was as if he wanted to punish Marcus by his withdrawal. Let Marcus realise how essential Ludens was!

The sun was winning its friendly game with the running clouds. It shone, through shifting layers of green leaves, onto the wrinkling surface of the River Fern, covering it with flashes.

As Ludens approached the Black Lion a bearded man emerged from the courtyard. It was Colin. They met on the pavement.

Ludens said, 'Well, *bon voyage*.'

Colin said, '*Bon voyage* nothing. We've decided not to go to Stonehenge, we're staying here. This is where it's at.'

'You don't think we said too much to that reporter?' said Franca.

'Not at all,' said Maisie. 'If we'd refused to talk he would have invented something and been nasty as well. As it is, we gave him a very sober dull account.'

'I'm surprised the press got onto it so quickly. I suppose that waiter at the White Lion must have been saying things.'

'The tiny local rag hardly counts as "the press". They don't know what news is. I don't suppose anything much has happened in this place since the Romans left.'

It was the late afternoon of the day after the Seekers' invasion, and Franca and Maisie who had gone on a shopping expedition to Salisbury were sitting in the Close and looking up at the Cathedral spire which the fast clouds were making to fall earthward in a way which, they agreed, made them feel quite giddy if they watched it for long.

Franca, although her mind was full of pain and almost any mental movement was anguish, could not help having some vague mechanical sense, funded by nameless memories, of being on holiday. She seemed somehow to 'enjoy' eating the tea-time tomato sandwiches which Mrs Toller had packed so neatly in grease-proof paper, and watching the innocent tourists sitting on the grass and crowding into the church. Earlier, standing inside the Cathedral, she had felt a strange pure grief which brought tears to her eyes, as if some huge looming total impression were submerging her and removing her identity. Maisie was moving busily about, 'doing' the scene, her sharp well-informed eyes appreciating every charming detail. Franca, overwhelmed, blinded, felt faint and sat down, then hurried out into the sunshine. Then watching the playing children and the frisking dogs and the summer dresses of the girls tugged at by the breeze, she tried vainly to repeat the experience. What came to her instead, as a sort of consolation prize, was a sense of, perhaps just an idea of, living in the present. If only she could resort to that at will, like a shot of morphia. Yet what was living in the present, could it be done, was it what she was doing now?

Maisie had put off her return to America, Franca had put off her departure to France. That morning Franca had received a letter from Jack. The letter ran as follows:

My dearest one, how is it with you? *Please, please* come soon. I need you, we need you, I mean Alison and I and also Heather, who is an angel, you will love her. (We now have a definite plan for bringing her and Alfred together!) We've done a lot of the usual eating and drinking and jaunting about which I won't bore you with accounts of. My dear, my eternal love, I miss you every moment, I yearn, *I thirst*, for your presence. You are my wife, Franca. If I were blind you'd read to me, if I were paralysed you'd dress me and feed me and push my wheelchair. You have always comforted me, your kindness, your goodness, have never wavered, even when, indeed when I look back *especially when*, I was in the world's eyes a most imperfect husband. You understand this, you understand *my intent* never to be separated from your love. You have in your keeping the greatest gift which I can receive, the *grace* which I demand. Franca, *we know* about love and about the opening of one soul to another. I speak to you now like a sinner addressing God, and contending with him. (I suspect there's something like that somewhere in the Psalms!) I believe in you so much that you must do what I want. I am appealing to the sacredness of our marriage bond. Some would think this appeal, in this context, insane, even blasphemous. I think, I believe, that you will see it as simple, natural, even proper. You must make me happy. All difficulties can be smoothed away if you will only trust both my love and your love. Real love is boundless. The fact that you give some to one person does not mean that you have to take it away from another. Jealousy is not only a sin, a vice, but a perfectly *irrational and unnecessary ailment*! Good and generous people move beyond that petty area. I know I wrong you when I even mention this here. *You* are far beyond, far above. I have always looked up to you and revered you. Please come soon, my darling, and have a happy holiday with me and Alison and Heather. Alison of course joins me in longing for you to come. She understands. Note our telephone number above – the telephone has only just been installed – Heather hasn't had the house for long, it's an old farmhouse which she has rebuilt, designing everything herself, you will love it. I rang our home number, but I expect you are still in the country. I won't ring the Black Lion, as the phone is so public. Come, my Franca, my dear love. Believe what I say, it comes from the heart, and as you believe it you will see it is right. I trust you. Always your Jack.

Franca, after shedding tears over this letter, showed it to Maisie, being perfectly well aware of her motives for doing so. Maisie's predictably hostile reaction was even more extreme than Franca expected. Franca had to snatch the letter back or Maisie would have torn it to shreds.

'I've never read such vile cunning hypocritical stuff in all my life!'

'But he's *sincere*,' said Franca, 'that's the *point*, I know him, he is absolutely sincere, it *does* come from the heart!'

'Of course he sincerely wants you back, entirely on his terms – he feels, even he, a monster like him – feels some tiny discomfort, some tiny trace of guilt at ditching you, and he wants you to remove that little stain upon the perfect happiness he keeps talking of, *his* happiness of course, *his* happy life with another woman! He wants you to forgive him, to be smiling around the place, to be *seen to consent* to his disgraceful arrangements. Can't you catch the tone of ruthlessly selfish anxiety in all this foul talk about love? He needs you, oh yes he needs you, simply to ratify the whole thing, and then when it's public and everyone can see how wonderfully it works and how civilised all three of you are, far above petty conventions and bourgeois pretences, then he'll change his tune, he'll let you slip quietly away into the background, he'll let you *diminish*, and you'll let it happen, and he knows you will! Oh he won't plan anything, it'll just be instinct, just natural, coming "from the heart", and *then* of course he and Alison will be asked to the dinner parties, *they'll* go on the holidays to Greece and the trips to Nepal, you won't go, you won't *want* to go, you'll wave goodbye to the young people and plan little treats to welcome them home and they'll hug you and say you're wonderful, and they'll despise you, and everyone will despise you, and you'll *grow old*!'

'I'll grow old anyway,' said Franca.

'You know what I mean. And he dares to speak of the marriage bond, *he* talking of the marriage bond, and of the Psalms, and of how you'll read to him when he's blind, I suppose he thought all that stuff would move you.'

'It did.'

'Then you're a silly little goose and I'd like to shake you and I'm not going to let you be made the victim of such a heartless rotter! Anyway he's not blind or in a wheelchair, he's having the time of his life getting drunk on the best wine and falling into bed with a beautiful woman.'

'Yes, she is beautiful, isn't she.'

'So you have some spirit left. Jealousy is not a vice, it's a natural instinct, at least it shows you're still alive! And let me tell you something else, a girl like that would never have taken Jack on unless she was sure she'd started a process which would end in your annihilation. But Franca, dear, concentrate. If you want proof that he's a mean calculating sod this letter is it. If you imagine that there's a wonderful role for you as an exemplar of perfect love you're an idiot. There can't be love on those terms. He'll just get bored with you, in the end he'll hate you, and you'll hate him.'

'Well,' Franca had said, murmuring it as if to herself, 'I *do* rather think in terms of perfect love.' Meanwhile, although she wanted very much to reply to Jack's letter, even to ring him up, she decided to wait. And Maisie, who may have felt she had said enough, dropped the subject.

The letter had shaken Franca very much. Jack's voice, his will, made her realise what an extraordinary and wonderful refuge she had found with Maisie, and how precarious this shelter was. It had seemed, dreamily, possible to go to America. Now it seemed utterly impossible. What indeed was left to 'show that she was still alive'? The energetic rage which she had felt against Jack, which had drawn its power from its secrecy, its *did they but know*, seemed now merely a useless self-torment. She owned no threatening weapon. If she wished Jack dead, she must wish herself dead too. She would never have the strength to punish him. She would go to them in France, return with them to Chelsea. And after that – how terribly, to stir her, Maisie had discerned it – her great secret rage would slowly be transformed into a small secret hatred, whose miserable attrition would diminish Franca, shrink her, until she became a very small animal, scarcely visible as it scuttled here and there in the house. How can I even *think* of such a fate, Franca asked herself. Better to commit murder. Yet she knew that when, after reading the letter, she had so much wanted to telephone Jack, it had been in order to reassure him.

As they drove towards Salisbury they had discussed Gildas, who had dined with them on the day when Ludens brought him their invitation, but who had declined further meetings, though they had glimpsed him later in the village, always by himself. The evening had not been a great success, since even Maisie who could usually (a gift she shared with Camilla) rouse a lively and interesting conversation out of any triviality, had not been able to dispel the melancholy with which Gildas himself was evidently struggling in vain. Maisie said he must be heading for a serious depression, she hoped he would not commit suicide. Franca said he had always been like that. They both deplored the absence of Ludens. Maisie, who thought of herself as a natural therapist, remained sure that she could do Gildas 'a world of good', but had not yet had the chance to try again. Now however, as they finished their sandwiches and engaged with Mrs Toller's special cake (the one which Ludens liked, as Maisie pointed out) they returned to the inexhaustibly fascinating topic of the manifestation at Benbow.

'The thing about the stones was so strange,' said Franca.

'Oh I don't know. There are tribes of Indians who venerate stones in that way. Men have always been bowing down to stones. I daresay anything can be made holy by being sincerely worshipped. I love stones – perhaps I'm a natural Stone person myself – I collect them from all over the world and they inhabit the house – *they* are like a tribe. There were some beautiful stones which they put there on the grass – I wonder where they found them.'

'Perhaps in Dorset on the Chesil Bank.'

'Let's go there. I was awfully tempted to take a particular one away with me.'

'Why didn't you?'

'Oh it wouldn't do. One doesn't disturb offerings which people make at a shrine.'

'But it's not a shrine, and they were just dotty young people. You can't call *that* a religion, it was just a game.'

'Well, I'm a Quaker, a bit lapsed but it's gotten deep in my soul, I believe the Inner Light is everywhere, and it can take some pretty weird forms.'

'They gave me the creeps,' said Franca. 'Anyway you saw Marcus.'

'Marcus in Majesty, I really think it was a religious experience – yes, *and* Irina, *and* famous Patrick who was raised from the dead. Why was Ludens so cross with us?'

'He's very possessive about Marcus, he's helping him to write the great book, he doesn't want him distracted by that sort of nonsense.'

'I wonder. I do like Ludens, he's innocent, he has such an open nature, one could trust him. You know, he's very fond of you.'

'I'm fond of him too, I've known him for ages.'

'Hmmmm. A pity you didn't marry *him* instead of that so-and-so. Franca, let me give you a piece of valuable advice. The best way to rid yourself of a bad useless craving is to open your heart to other people, find new people to love.'

'Maisie, you know I'm doing that!'

'Yes, and thank you. But have a look at young Ludens. I believe he's in love with you.'

'Why did you let her in?'

'She just *came* in!'

'You mean, what, pushed open the doors?'

'Yes! It was daytime, they weren't locked.'

'Where was Marcus?'

'In his bedroom, but he came out when he heard us talking –'

'*Talking*, you *talked* to her?'

'Of course I did! I said "What is it?" or something, then when I saw the child I knew.'

'What did Marcus do?'

'He understood at once.'

'He didn't hesitate?'

'No. He sat down *there* and beckoned the woman and she came and pushed the child forward –'

'What did she say?'

'Nothing, she just pointed to the little girl's funny-looking hand, and Marcus took her hand between his and looked very hard into her eyes, and then they went away.'

'Irina, you shouldn't have let them in, you shouldn't have let him see them.'

'What could I do, they walked in, he appeared! They were perfectly harmless, perhaps Dad can do people good in some strange way, anyhow there's faith healing, that's real. And those Seekers were back, they were here just after seven, they gave us a serenade.'

'A *serenade*?'

'They chanted some kind of hymn. Then they left some stuff and went away.'

'I saw the stuff, I removed it.'

'And you took away those stones they left yesterday. I liked those stones. What did you do with them?'

'I just hid them in the wood. I'll show you where if you like. We mustn't let this sort of thing begin. Did Marcus hear them?'

'This morning? Yes, he got up and came to the verandah, then he went back to bed. Why are you so bothered, why not let it all happen, it's very touching, it's interesting.'

'It's all false! Marcus could be forced into living a lie. It could look so awful.'

'You care about how it *looks*!'

'We must get out.'

'Well, you started it all, you thought he would save Pat's life, and he *did* save Pat's life!'

'That was a special case. Pat thought Marcus had cursed him –'

'Oh look, someone else is arriving.'

In fact several people were now standing on the grass and looking at the house. They stood apart from each other, standing erect like posted soldiers: an elderly man, a middle-aged woman, two young men in jeans, a smartly dressed girl.

Leaving Irina in the sitting room, Ludens opened the verandah doors and descended to the lawn. Addressing the group he said aggressively, 'What do you want?'

There was an awkward silence, then the elderly man said, 'We want to see the Master.'

'You mean the Professor.'

'Yes, we want to see him,' said one of the young men.

Ludens said, 'He is not a healer. He is a patient. This place is private. Please go away.'

The persons stared at Ludens. The youth repeated, 'We want to see him. We'll wait.'

'We'll be quiet,' said the woman, 'we'll be patient. But please don't ask us to go away. We *cannot* go away.'

'Well, move off!' said Ludens.

The persons looked at each other. The elderly man produced a camp stool from a bag he was carrying, moved a little way into the woodland and sat down on the stool with his back against a tree. The others retreated and stood together on the drive, conferring. Ludens returned to the house.

'When will Marcus be back?'

'He'll be swimming now, and then he's going to see that nurse and get some more pills.'

'They won't go away.'

It was the afternoon of the day following the arrival of the Seekers. The previous day had been, for Ludens, full of annoyances and omens. He had returned to the Black Lion, indeed 'in a huff', as Irina had said, and feeling 'it's all too much'. He felt he was being devalued, rejected, losing control of the situation. After his horrifying encounter with Colin he tried to find Franca, but was told by Mrs Toller that she and Miss Tether had already gone off painting. He then decided he *must* see Gildas. But supposing Gildas had gone? Why had he, Ludens, been so unkind to his best friend, and so arrogant in expecting Gildas, who had his own troubles, to hang around just in case he should deign to see him? He ran along the village street to Gildas's lodgings, where his landlady announced him not at home. He had gone out early, she did not know where to. Ludens immediately concluded he must have gone on the painting trip with Maisie and Franca. After this, in no very good mood, he returned to Benbow, where, before entering the house, he removed the stones and flowers which the Seekers had left, and distributed them here and there in the darker parts of the wood. This counter-ritual cheered him up a bit. He returned to find Irina out shopping and Marcus sitting in the study. This seemed a good omen, but the notebooks were untouched, and Marcus, declaring himself still 'under the weather', declined any discussion. They walked as far as the Axle Stone where they found the concrete seat entirely covered with stones and flowers and twigs. After gazing at these portents they turned away, and Ludens, thinking he must take the opportunity to point a moral, even to 'teach Marcus a lesson', said, 'I suppose these people are harmless, but one does hate bogus religion.' Marcus said nothing and conversation lapsed as they walked back. Ludens, still annoyed with Marcus, himself and Irina, went back to the Black Lion and started drinking in the bar, after which he had a large lunch in the restaurant, after which he went to sleep. When he returned later to Benbow Camilla and Pat and Mr Talgarth were there, there was general conversation, in which Ludens did not join, and everyone went to bed early. On the next morning Ludens hurried round to Benbow and found Marcus still in bed and Irina having an argument with Rosie, who was sometimes now allowed to come and clean when Irina had let the place become too dusty and dirty. He returned to the pub, missing the departure of Maisie and Franca on an 'all-day jaunt'. He walked to Gildas's lodgings, Gildas was again 'out somewhere', Ludens again assumed with Franca and Maisie. He went to the post office and rang the number of his London flat but got no reply. He tried to ring the Registrar in Salisbury, but the number was engaged. He walked back again to the Black Lion and started writing an emotional letter to Gildas but tore it up. He tried Christian's, that is his own, number again, but no luck. He decided to go for a walk along the river Fern where he ran into Andy and

Miriam who were very nice to him, but were evidently bound for some secluded spot to be alone together. This glimpse of young love did him no good. He returned too late for lunch at Benbow to find that Marcus had gone to the swimming-pool. Irina had set out some bread and cheese and a tomato for Ludens to eat, when he had been appalled by her casual reference to the episode of the woman and child. And now there were these new intruders.

Looking out again there was no sign of anyone on the drive, though Ludens was sure that the man on the camp stool was still at his post in the wood.

'What shall we do now?' said Ludens. 'I must go and tell somebody up at the house.'

'Why are you in such a state? A few daft people turn up. It'll all blow over.'

'It won't unless we stop it now. Marcus mustn't see that lot.'

'They've gone away.'

'No they haven't, they're waiting out of sight.'

'I can't stop Dad –'

'No one left a note for me? No? Where's Camilla just when we need her? I'm going to the house.'

As Ludens crossed the lawn he saw, as he expected, the elderly man sitting on his stool under the tree, and when he reached the drive the others were still there confabulating a little further away. They fell silent when he passed and the two women nodded their heads to him. When Ludens reached the main drive which ran one way to the house and the other to the gate he paused. He had expected, indeed wanted, to be summoned by Marzillian, who must surely know all about the Seekers episode by now, but no summons had come. Did this mean that Marzillian now regarded Ludens as ineffectual, expendable, useless? Ludens reminded himself that Marcus was not the only weird and wonderful person in Bellmain. There were the 'difficult' cases in the house of which, so strict was security, he knew nothing. There were others, even Mr Talgarth, whose inner life might terribly belie his urbane surface. Yet Ludens could not help thinking that really Marzillian was far more interested in Marcus than in his other patients. Perhaps on the whole it might be wiser to wait a little to see if Marzillian would declare his hand. If he went to the house now he might not find Camilla, might fall into the hands of Anita. Perhaps the whole thing would really blow over in a day or two. As he stood there hesitating he saw a familiar figure coming towards him from the direction of the house, Fanny Amherst.

Fanny, who was carrying her white overall over her arm, was evidently coming off duty. Ludens had thought a lot about her, recalling their first meeting with shame, and their two subsequent meetings with a different distress. He wondered whether he were now seen as a child molester. How old was Fanny anyway? Ought he to seek her out or write to her to apologise again for his roughness? He decided this might simply embroil him even more and prolong an embarrassment which was now better forgotten. Besides he felt (and felt some shame about this too) a certain horror of the girl, as if she were something uncanny. Now however, seeing him, she was waving in a friendly manner and he was waving back.

As he walked along with her towards the gate, it occurred to him that there was something which he ought to say. 'Fanny, I hope you don't mind my asking you, but please don't come in the early morning to look at the Professor's house. It just upsets him and his daughter, they want to be left alone.'

'All right, I'm sorry. But I must come – sometimes –'

Ludens, having failed to produce an answer to the implied question, now felt it his duty to go on walking beside her until some pleasanter moment of separation would be reached. They came out of the gate and walked in silence as far as the bridge. Here they might have parted with some amiable greeting, but Ludens said, 'Fanny, could we talk for a minute or two, will you come with me? Let's sit *there*.' He indicated a seat, which he had noticed earlier, down on the bank of the river and out of sight of the road.

She turned obediently and followed him down the slope of thick grass and they sat together on the seat.

'I'm sorry I was so rough when I ran after you and we both fell on the grass, I hope I didn't hurt you.'

'No, no, not a bit, not the least little bit, I was happy about it afterwards.'

Touched by this little speech, which he felt he understood, Ludens smiled at her. They smiled at each other. 'Fanny, I've been wondering – could you tell me – you brought flowers and stones to the Axle Stone, and you brought a special stone to the Professor. Are you connected with those people who have just arrived, who are going to Stonehenge?'

'Yes, yes, I am.' She had thrust her short brown hair back behind her ears, giving herself the boyish look which had deceived him when he first glimpsed her. She gazed at him now, her large brown eyes shining, as if Ludens were giving her some extraordinary treat.

'You mean you belong to their sect, or whatever it is, they call themselves the Stone People.'

'Yes. They often come past here in the summertime. And I went to Stonehenge once too at midsummer, only we weren't allowed to go near the Stones.'

'And you believe in something, some creed, is it like religion, is it religion?'

'Religion?'

'Yes, like Christianity. Are you a Christian?'

'Oh yes, I went to the bishop, I go to church, to the communion.'

'And this belief, the stones and going to Stonehenge, is that part of Christianity, or is it different?'

Fanny, wide-eyed, smiling, biting her lip, then smiling again, stared at him as if she were taking part in some delightful game, or else in some wonderful ceremony, an initiation or a catechism. She said with her clear-voiced precision, 'It's all together, everything like that *must* be, because there are these rays everywhere, these forces that gather into Holy Places, and into Holy Things, like the Great Stones –'

'And *our* Stone, Fanny, here –?'

'Yes, it is a great precious thing, a diamond of power, a very special high thing like a great prince, but what is in it is in all things, only more gathered, as in people, in some people, and when the forces pass through these people they do so much good, they spread out so that many others can feel them, there are such wonderful people –'

'So these forces, these powers, do *good*?'

'Yes, I know, for only good is everywhere, and we see that all things are holy, all the little accidental jumbled things, like little stones, like bits of earth and dust, like little nothing – things –'

The river Fern had made, just below where they were sitting, a little beach of small pebbles. Ludens got up, selected one of these at random, gave it to Fanny and sat down watching her.

Very seriously, gazing at him, she held the stone enclosed in her hand, then held it to her breast, then to her brow, then without looking at it handed it to Ludens with a radiant smile.

Again it seemed to him like a game, but a mysterious game upon which many things, of which one knew little, might depend. He did not look at the stone but put it in his pocket, smiling at her. For a second, silently, they both almost laughed.

Ludens, feeling that their conversation was about to end, said, 'So this belief, your Stone belief, is not new, it is something very old.' It did not sound like a question.

Fanny, not replying, sustained his gaze, then said, 'I must go.' They rose, and with a little quick salute, she turned and scuttled up the bank like a small animal and was gone.

Ludens waited, then followed slowly, scrambling up the steep bank, clinging onto the tough grasses. What will happen to her, he wondered, what dark force, what vile man, perhaps, will destroy her and ruin her life? Or will the holiness, which she finds in all things, continue to protect her? Then he thought, does *she* know the name of the Stone? If so it proves the Stone is innocent. He went on into the village and down the village street, and this time he found Gildas at home.

'Is that all?' said Gildas.

Ludens had recounted the phenomena to date. 'Isn't that enough?'

'I feel inclined to say you have seen nothing yet.'

Ludens was lying on Gildas's bed. He felt entirely relaxed, his limbs heavy and at rest. He felt intense relief at being in his friend's presence. He felt safe.

Gildas was sitting on an upright chair beside the bed, somewhat in the attitude of a doctor. He said, 'Look at this.' He held out a newspaper.

Propping himself up, Ludens looked at the proffered page.

HEALER DISCOVERED IN MENTAL HOME

A 'holy man' has been discovered living in seclusion in the quiet village of Sillbourne. He is 'Professor' Mark Valler, who has spent many years in the East perfecting the secret healing arts of the natives. He has it seems, established himself as 'alternative medicine man' at Bellmain luxury mental hospital owned by Dr Marsillon. The 'Prof', as he is called, has various successes to his credit, including having raised a man from the dead. This latter-day Lazarus, alive and well to prove the point, is one of his benefactor's many disciples, who form a group known as the 'Stone People'. Now that the Prof's healing skills are more widely known many other 'patients' may be expected. What does that saintly figure charge for his services? Nothing! The Healer was not available for interview, but our reporter talked to ex-dead Mr Fenman, and to American tourist Mrs May Tether, who lately witnessed a mass gathering at the 'shrine'. 'I believe in his powers,' said Mrs Tether, 'there are more things in heaven and earth than are thought of in modern philosophy.'

The article was accompanied by two photographs, one of Benbow, captioned *Little House of Healing*, and one of Patrick, captioned *Raised from the Dead?*

'Oh *hell*,' said Ludens, 'I'll *kill* that Irishman.' He perused the article again. 'And Marzillian will kill me, he'll think I somehow started it.'

'But you didn't.'

'I led that crazy Life-Force mob to Benbow, I thought it was the best way to get rid of them.'

'They'd have found Marcus anyhow, your little friend Fanny Amherst would have shown them the way.'

'Yes – I suppose she put them onto him in the first place. But how did she know? Not that there's anything to know –'

'Are you sure?'

'Don't you start, Gildas. Fancy Maisie being such a fool as to talk to a newspaper. Still, it's only the little local sheet, and the stuff is such evident nonsense, I don't suppose anyone will pay attention.'

'I'm afraid they already have. A London journalist tracked down Maisie at the Black Lion. He rang her up this morning. Of course she wouldn't discuss it. But the trouble is, they know who Marcus is.'

'You mean the London people do?'

'Yes. Of course the local man didn't, but he didn't get Marcus's name wrong enough, and someone spotted it. You must admit it makes a wonderful story. The journalist who talked to Maisie said he was coming down at once.'

'Gildas, we must get Marcus away, we must *kidnap* him and Irina and take them to some secret place.'

'And keep them prisoner there? According to you, they like it here. Look, I want to see Marcus.'

'*What?*'

'Everyone else is seeing him, I don't see why I shouldn't.'

'You want him to take off the curse?'

'Something like that.'

'You're mad! Oh God, if only Jack were here! He's a man of action, he'd think of some way to rescue them.'

'Talking of Jack and kidnapping, I think Maisie Tether is planning to take Franca away with her to America forever.'

'Franca won't go, she'll *never* leave Jack, no matter how many wives he has. I'd better go back and see what's going on. Oh God, why did this have to happen?'

'It's not the end of the world. Perhaps Marcus will carry it all off somehow, he'll ride the storm. And I want to see him do it.'

'So you want to take him away?' said Marzillian.

'Yes.'

'Why?'

'You must know why, in fact you always know why. You saw the scene this morning. He's being entangled in a charade, he's being treated like a saint, like a healer, people will be coming to him to be cured, he's being vulgarised, victimised, forced into a false position, it's all supposed to be *religious* – of course it's only starting, it may die out quite soon, but if we don't stop it now it will do him so much harm, perhaps irreparable harm – and the only way to stop it is to remove him to some place where he can't be found.'

When Ludens had returned to Bellmain after leaving Gildas his worst fears were realised. The news had evidently got around. He saw people walking boldly in through the gates. The security men were not in evidence. Invaders were being controlled, in so far as they were controlled, by the Seekers who, wearing green armbands, had stationed themselves at strategic points, and appeared to be directing some at least of the arrivals toward Benbow. However, not everyone who had walked in knew what was going on or had any particular aim in view. The privacy, the out-of-bounds nature of Bellmain, was well-known and respected in the locality. Outsiders were allowed in only on rare special occasions, as for the madrigal concert, or on a few particular days to view the gardens. Local people, seeing others freely entering the magical forbidden domain, followed them, thinking that this must be some unscheduled 'open day'. Some people were standing around on the drive asking each other questions. ('Can we go anywhere?' 'Is there some performance?' 'Are those girls singing again?') Some were wandering away into the woods. When Ludens, almost weeping with anxiety and chagrin, reached Benbow he found a group of about twelve people standing in orderly fashion upon the drive opposite the house, and conversing in whispers. Three others, favoured for unclear reasons, or simply bolder, were standing on the lawn. The glass doors were shut. Colin Bassett seemed to be in command of the situation, marshalling the onlookers, questioning some of them. A man declaring himself to be a journalist was asked to lower his voice. Ludens was about to push past the pilgrims and run to the house when someone caught his arm. It was Camilla. 'Please, Dr Marzillian wants to see you at once.'

The sun was shining through the huge Victorian window of Marzillian's office, turning the stained-glass tulips into fiery jewels, while beyond, revealed in quieter shades of English watercolour, the gentle hills, tufted with copses, elegantly rolled away into a blue distance. A curtain had been drawn across part of the window leaving Marzillian in the shade and Ludens blinking against the sunlight and the red glitter from above. He was seated on the tall mahogany chair, his nervous fingers returning to explore the invisible bulges and recesses upon its arms. Marzillian opposite, behind his desk, was at first a blurred shadowy figure, his attention manifest only in his attitude as he leaned a little forward, his hands clasped upon the surface of the desk. As his face became more visible it seemed to Ludens that the dark moustaches had grown bigger and the dark hair longer. Marzillian was wearing his smart high-buttoned Indian-style white coat, but slightly open at the neck, and resembled now some raffish stylish Eastern pirate in command of some sleek fast well-ordered dangerous ship.

'That might be difficult,' he said. 'Have you any such refuge in mind?'

'Yes, I have!' It only at that moment occurred to Ludens that, of course, he could take Marcus and Irina back to Red Cottage!

'Have you suggested such an abrupt departure to the Professor and Miss Irina?'

'No – but of course they'll agree, I mean they'll agree when they've taken in what's really going on.'

'So you think they have not yet understood what that is. Perhaps you will explain to me what it is.'

'What what is?'

'What is really going on.'

'Well, all those people marching in, and – Someone showed me a newspaper.'

'I have seen it.'

'I gather that the London papers are sending journalists. You don't want that do you? This morning a woman came to Marcus with a sick child and expected him to cure it. Then some people stood in the garden and wouldn't go away, now there's more of them outside the house. Of course all this started when you were away, but you must know it all by now. I thought those Stonehenge Seeker people would go away, but now they've made this place their Stonehenge. I suppose they heard about Marcus from Fanny or from someone that Patrick babbled to in the village.'

'Well, go on.'

'Go on? Where to? Here I am!'

'You haven't told me what you think is really going on.'

'But I told you that! Marcus is being upset by a lot of crazy young people who think, or pretend to think, that he has magical powers and can raise the dead, and a lot of other people who want to come and gaze at him and bother him, and it has become impossible for him to work. He must be taken away to some other place, this situation is intolerable. Anyway I can't understand why you seem to be putting up with it, why are the gates open, why have the Bulldogs been withdrawn?'

'As you know, our Stone has a little fame –'

'You mean something like this has happened before?'

'Not like this, but something less extreme. When people are profoundly attracted to something they will walk through fire. Please excuse this somewhat tautological sentence, but you see what I mean. Our fences are little better than a symbolic barrier, all that is required is a pair of wire-cutters or even physical strength or will power. It is a credit to our locality that we have had in fact very few trespassers and vandals, the place is respected, perhaps also feared.'

'You mean you *can't* now keep people out? I don't believe it.'

'Of course one could keep out casual inquisitive tourists. But not the, admittedly various, interested parties.'

'But you must do something! Can't the police help?'

'I happen to know that the local police are anxious not to be involved. Anyway what could they do, who could be charged with what? A few people might be proved to have damaged a few plants or cut a hole, in some wire. There is a law about mass trespass, but it would be a long and tiresome business to invoke it effectively. I thought it more prudent to make friends with your Seekers.'

'Yes, I saw them in charge, they even had armbands on! You evidently don't think it will all blow over in a day or two?'

'Not in a day or two, no. For the moment, for the moment I say, our best policy is to let it run, and control it as best we can. Now let us move this admittedly interesting conversation on a little faster.'

'I'm sorry. Anyway you dictate the tempo not me!'

'I cannot keep them out. Now why is this so? Because there is a very powerful magnet here.'

'You don't mean the Stone, you mean Marcus. But what sense does it make to call him a magnet? It's all just the result of idle talk, rumours, curiosity, he has simply become a *tourist attraction*! There's nothing serious, there's nothing *deep*.'

'Well, let me ask you this. You suggested that the Seekers found out something from Fanny or from Patrick.'

'I suppose it was Fanny's idea, she knows the Seekers, in fact she's one of them. No one would be likely to take Patrick's chatter seriously.'

333

'Why not? Patrick was cured in a way which surprised Dr Hensman. He witnessed that scene, so did you.'

'Yes –'

'And you were surprised.'

'Yes. But what are you getting at?'

'Let us say that Patrick was not raised from the dead. But something very unusual happened – which you for some reason are anxious not to remember. What is that reason?'

'I don't understand –' Ludens paused. He inspected Marzillian's fierce intent face, his dark almost black eyes. He went on. 'The reason. Well, I don't want Marcus to think that he has any special – miraculous – sort of powers. All right, why don't I. Firstly, because I don't believe he has. I think the Patrick thing was a fluke. Patrick is a superstitious Irishman, he really imagined that Marcus had put a curse on him. The medical profession was wrong – they often are after all – in believing that Pat was irremediably ill. The shock of Marcus appearing and touching Pat and saying he removed the curse, quite accidentally gave Pat some impetus, the will to live, which made him get better. That's point one. Obviously if Marcus has no such powers he ought not to imagine that he has. Secondly, imagining that he has would not only be believing an untruth – it would confuse his mind and *waste his time*. You know how much he cares about the book he's writing –'

'I know how much *you* care – and are you not writing it?'

'Don't start that. You've picked that up from Pat or Irina. You said writing and thinking, yes, action, no. You said there was danger. What was the danger, what is the danger?'

'I want you to tell me.'

'I – I can't –'

'Ludens,' said Marzillian, 'you and I have been, since we first met, playing a kind of cat-and-mouse game. You are aware of this?'

'Yes.'

'You remember that I said that you were less than frank with me; and that you were good at using words to conceal what you think. Well, this must now stop. What is it that *you* are afraid of?'

Ludens was silent. He was, of course, once more, searching for the words to conceal what he thought. He was also, and he was conscious of this at once, being authoritatively and *completely* silenced by his old complaint. He *could not* speak. Marzillian, watching him, said nothing.

After a while Ludens, released, said, 'I'm s-s-s-s-so s-s-s-sorry, I have a –'

'Dr Bland told me. Now, please –'

'I am afraid that it may turn out that Marcus is really completely and incurably insane.'

'Precisely.'

There was another silence. Ludens was now aware that he might soon start to shed tears. He covered his face with his hands.

'Now listen, Ludens,' said Marzillian in his gentlest and silkiest voice, 'I will in a few minutes stop tormenting you. You gave me two reasons just now why you were unwilling to remember Patrick's resurrection. One reason was that you thought it was a "fluke", the other that if Marcus were to reflect upon it it would confuse him and "waste his time". You have been, as we all know, very diligent in keeping Marcus occupied and encouraging him to pursue what you see as his life-long philosophical quest. You believe that Marcus is in possession of some deep understanding which he is capable of clarifying and giving to the world. You have also, as you have now courageously admitted, at least entertained the idea that your belief is unfounded and that Marcus is simply deranged – the view, incidentally, held by his daughter. Don't interrupt me. You do not believe that he has paranormal powers, you believe that he is a sane person and a deep thinker, you fear that he may be a crazy person and no thinker at all. You envisage two possibilities, sane thinker, or insane fantasist. But is there not at least one other possibility?'

Ludens had uncovered his face and had seemed disposed to interrupt. He had been following Marzillian carefully. Now he was at a loss. 'I can't think – I don't see –'

'Is it not possible that Marcus is not insane, and not now (though perhaps he was once) a deep thinker, but simply a sane, eccentric, neurotic person who happens to have paranormal gifts?'

Ludens stared at Marzillian with amazement. 'No! Are you, a scientist, seriously suggesting –?'

'I am not "suggesting" anything. I am trying, as you are trying, to understand "what is really going on". I have followed, with the greatest interest and sympathy, your attempts to awaken a great thinker and persuade him to clarify deep thoughts so that they may be written down. This enterprise has seemed to you the best way, not only to convince yourself and others that Marcus is not mad, but also to convince Marcus himself. You are a brave soul struggling for the mind, perhaps for the life, of someone you love. How far you may have succeeded I cannot tell, but I believe you have found your task no easy one. Now a crisis which neither you nor I could have foreseen has, I am afraid, put a stop, perhaps temporarily, perhaps for good, to your

335

attempted rescue. Other considerations are forced upon us. This must bring us back – for I am afraid the time I allotted to this conversation has run out – to the practical matter with which we started. You want to remove him. I said that might be difficult. In fact I am sure that he would refuse to go.'

'You mean because he has by now become convinced that he can work miracles?'

'Let us not quibble about terminology. The term "miracle" is emotive, and "paranormal" advisedly vague. We are dealing with a border area of human capacity about which we scientists, though we rarely admit it, still know very little. Perhaps we should think here not just or primarily of "events" or "powers" but of states of being which are not as rare as we imagine. Techniques of meditation are associated with an extension of normal powers – in other cases the gift may seem more like a physical endowment. These may in effect be modest matters, such as an ability to heal or alleviate certain ailments. Persons so endowed often attract other people, not only by their usefulness, but by a kind of psychosomatic magnetism. This "aura" may not be associated with the religious attributes of holiness, though a consciousness of such a condition may well make its bearer feel himself a man apart.'

'I don't understand you,' said Ludens. 'Do you see him, *him*, settling down to a rewarding life as a quack healer, attracting a lot of silly unbalanced people and crazy followers?'

Marzillian said patiently, 'You have been anxious to steer Marcus away from any consciousness, or illusion, of having unusual powers, and you are dismayed by what you call a charade which may lead him into believing a lie. All right. I am indicating an alternative way of thinking which may help us to understand what is happening now, and may or may not concern what happens later. I do not yet know "what is really going on". I just think that for a while, perhaps a short while, we must simply wait.'

'You want to wait because it all interests you, it's something you simply *can't miss*, it's a clinical spectacle from which you want to learn something, you want to let the whole thing run riot – and if Marcus is destroyed in the process –'

'I am concerned about my patient. I am not concerned with your desires and ambitions except in so far as I can relate them to him. I want "the best" for my patient. What is the best? No doubt that is a metaphysical question. But what is presented to us now, this "unexpected phenomenon", raises questions which we must face head on.

Marcus's problems may be quite different ones from those you have envisaged. It is indeed an unhappy fate to be a failed philosopher. I am simply trying to see. There is a whole other matter, a dark matter, which we have neither of us mentioned –'

'What –?'

'But now we must stop. I am tired and expect you are too. I must proceed to my next mystery and for the moment forget this one completely.' He stood up.

Ludens rose. The dazzling sunshine, the glittering tulips, Salisbury Plain bleached and misted by light, of which he had been oblivious, became suddenly visible. He felt giddy and had to press hard upon the arms of his chair.

As Marzillian walked towards the door he said affably, 'I noticed, didn't you, in that newspaper article, that Miss Tether was quoting Shakespeare. No doubt she quoted correctly, and was incorrectly reported by the journalist. They are so unlettered these days. It goes, does it not, "There are more things in heaven and earth, Horatio, than are dreamt of in your philosophy." Now perhaps you can tell me, I believe it is a disputed point, is "your philosophy" simply an idiomatic way of saying "philosophy", or is Hamlet referring to Horatio's own philosophy?'

'Now listen to me, Marcus and Irina, I think we should leave here at once and go back to Red Cottage.'

It was the evening of the same day, a day upon which Ludens looked back with amazement and shame. He had been unable, after leaving Marzillian, to obtain any private communication with either Marcus or Irina. When he reached Benbow he found a group of people still outside, and inside Colin and Patrick and Camilla talking with Irina. Marcus had shut himself in his bedroom. Ludens was immediately involved in 'arrangements'. Even if the intruders, partly sightseers, but also devotees and 'the sick', did not increase in numbers, some sort of order must be established, notices posted, barriers put up, timetables established. Camilla was to report to Anita, who would report to Dr Bland, who would instruct the security men. Ludens took part in these discussions, suggesting this, rejecting that, while at the same time feeling that he was surrounded by lunatics. He even agreed that Irina should ask Marcus to go out to show himself to the watchers so that Colin could tell them all to go home. He stood aside with lowered eyes as Marcus marched through and stood on the verandah for two minutes during which there was silence inside and outside the house. When Marcus walked back through the room and returned to his bedroom it was impossible to speak to him and no one spoke. Ludens, feeling he must not look at him, for he was terrified by the idea of 'catching his eye', did look quickly and saw Marcus's face serene, exalted, grim. This face filled him with horror. Meanwhile the pilgrims outside, who had stood so motionless in spellbound silence, were relaxed, shaking themselves like dogs, stretching like awakened sleepers, murmuring to each other in low tones. When Colin went out to them they followed him with docility; Colin returned to report that the Bulldogs were already back on duty and the gates closed. Patrick and Camilla said they must go, but stayed on for a while, eating some sandwiches which Irina had made and talking over the events of the day in an electric atmosphere of excitement and pleasure. Ludens, though he was very hungry, refused the sandwiches, wished to leave but could not, and stood beside them in silence. When the visitors had gone and Irina had gone back to the kitchen and Marcus had not yet emerged, Ludens went out and stood in the garden. He went as far as a tree and touched it, and leant his forehead against it. He was bitterly regretting the admission which Marzillian had forced from him.

The light was darkening into a vivid intensity, though the sun had no intention of setting for some while yet, in fact it proposed to be up until well after nine. When Ludens returned to the house he found the table in the sitting room set out with more sandwiches, fruit and cakes, for what Irina called a 'picnic supper', to be eaten on the verandah as it was such a lovely evening. He was touched that she had noticed that he had not eaten, and was now urging him to do so. Marcus came out, and they sat on chairs on the verandah, replenishing their plates from the table. Marcus seemed serene and pleased. He and Irina talked about the events of the day as if it had been an ordinary day, even containing amusing episodes. Ludens's outburst produced a moment's silence.

'That's a daft thing to say,' said Irina. 'Hell's bells, we put a lot of energy into getting out of that ghastly hole, why ever go back to it now?'

'I only mean because it's a place we can go to immediately – then we'd find somewhere else, I'd find somewhere else. I suppose we might go to London – but you said your flat was being sold, and my flat is rented to someone else. Of course we could go to a hotel. Anyway I think we should leave here *at once*.'

'Why ever? We thought we'd settled down, didn't we, Dad?'

'We can't *settle* here, obviously. I did think after all we could stay in peace, just for a little while, and get going on some work – but even that's impossible now, everything's changed. We can't stay and be victimised by these Stone People and exhibited to gaping crowds. We'd be involved, we're already involved, in a false degrading charade. I think we should get out quickly before it gets any worse and go where no one can find us.'

'What's a false degrading charade?' said Irina.

'All this cult stuff, these bogus acts of worship, this stuff about rays and forces and about healing and so on – we're being made to play a false role, it's all false, it's a lie.'

'Who's being made to play a false role?' said Irina, looking at him fiercely with her intense eyes. She had just washed her hair, which was in its frizzy bushy state, as on the occasion of Pat's resurrection.

'Marcus is.'

'No he isn't. *That's* a lie.'

Marcus had listened attentively but calmly to these exchanges. With his shirt wide open and his sleeves rolled up and, Ludens noticed, barefoot, he looked handsome and full of being. Patrick had trimmed his hair, in which the luxuriant evening sun was finding many different shades of red and gold and orange.

Ludens now addressed him. 'I had a talk with Marzillian this afternoon, that's why I didn't arrive sooner. What's your impression of that man? I can't make him out. It's occurred to me that he may even be a little mad. People in his job often are. Or is he just a bit of a charlatan putting on an act?'

Irina said indignantly, '*You* dare to call that man a charlatan? I think he's the most impressive and charming man I've ever met!'

'Oh you do, do you!' said Ludens. 'I gather you have secret conversations with him.'

'They're not secret! Do I have to tell you every time I have a conversation? Of course he talks to me. I think he's a wise good man.'

'All right, all right. Now please, Irina dearest, would you mind going away, go and wash up or something, I want to talk to Marcus alone.'

'I'm damned if I will! *You* go and wash up!'

Marcus said, 'Please go, I want to talk to Alfred.'

Irina went into the house banging the glass doors behind her. Ludens gazed at Marcus with sudden fear, feeling that *this* was to be their *first* real conversation. Indeed he felt at that moment so frightened of Marcus and of the things he proposed to say to him that he plunged in at once,

'Of course I don't really think Marzillian is mad or a charlatan. He may be a very brilliant doctor and man of science. But he's someone who likes drama and mystification, he likes to think that things are complicated and deep.'

'And aren't they?' said Marcus, watching Ludens and smiling. 'Isn't that what you think?'

'No,' said Ludens crossly, 'some things are simple. You said you'd like to simplify your life. What did you mean by that? If you mean leave this bloody awful place and mysterious Dr Marzillian, then I'm with you! Why can't we go to Red Cottage? Then I will find us another place somewhere else. And Irina and I will get married and bear you a grandson who will be a genius.' That was not at all the speech which Ludens had planned and he groaned to himself even as he uttered it. He added lamely, 'And we'll all live happily ever after, all three of us, I mean all four of us.'

Marcus did not comment on this touching picture. He said gravely, 'No. I think it must happen here.'

'What must?'

'Whatever is going to happen.'

'So something is going to happen?'

Marcus did not reply to this. He said, 'About simplifying my life I will tell you in a minute, but first let me say this. I don't want to go on with that book.'

'I was afraid you would say that.'

'I can't do it, Alfred. *You* must write the book. You evidently think you can make something out of all that stuff. You tried to put it all in order as if it were a single argument, but all I can see is old thoughts placed end to end. You think there's some great further philosophical step, some ultimate move, some ultimate *place*. But it's no good, we can't get there, human beings can't get there, you can't leap over your own shadow.'

'You're tired,' said Ludens cautiously. 'Let's have a rest from the book. You may feel better about it later on. Yes, we need an interval. We've been too mechanical about it, we've been in too much of a hurry. Later it may fall naturally into a different pattern. Surely you don't believe that all that *thinking*, all that *concentration*, the things you studied, have led you nowhere?'

'They have not led me to any conclusion which I could write down in a book. Whether they have led me to where I am now, I am not sure. Perhaps that is something which I shall know later. It may be that all that striving was nothing, and that finding out that it was nothing was the point. Or it may have been simply a series of moods, ways by which it occurred to me to spend my time. In any case, I must now rest from multiplicity and from the frenzy and agitation of thinking, and enter an empty space where I must wait for guidance. I know you always thought I would discover some final secret.'

'Yes. I am sorry you seem to have given up desiring it and seeking it.'

'Oh but I have not given up. I have simply come nearer.'

'My dear Marcus, whatever can you mean?'

'We spoke of a device, or gadget, contraption, a place obscured.'

'You said we can't get there, humans can't reach it.'

'I don't think they can. Maybe someone could. It may be thought of in a certain way, but that is the thought of it, not the thing itself. However this may not matter.'

'What does matter, what matters more?'

'A state of being.'

'Marzillian used that phrase, I thought he'd taken you over, perhaps you've taken him over! We all have states of being. You mean a special one, like being a saint, or being able to raise the dead or walk on the water?'

The garden was in shadow as the sun descended behind the trees and the dense warm air seemed itself to become visible, a soft hazy prelude to the dark. Ludens could not see Marcus's face clearly, but his sense of his bodily proximity was increased as Marcus leaned forward, putting his hand to his brow. He murmured, 'These things mean something, they are signs, but –'

Ludens, now very much alarmed, but keeping up a brisk even jocular tone, said, 'You talked about being above ordinary morality and how someone could find out something which would make him a god, when he would instantly die of pure thought! Is that the line?'

'Oh well, not by discovering *that*, the old thing – I mean –'

'But the new thing? Marcus, please, do you now think of yourself as a holy man, will you go round touching people, *do* you think you raised Patrick from the dead?'

'No.'

'I'm relieved to hear it!'

'But something did happen that day. I felt as if a streak of lightning had come from above and passed through my body and on deep into the earth, and I felt as if I had become some quite other kind of being –'

'You mean a sort of divine being. That *must* be the beginning of an illusion. Marcus, *don't go down that way.*'

341

'I am not a fool, Ludens,' said Marcus, raising his head and suddenly speaking sharply, 'I have reflected upon that experience – and upon other experiences which have occurred since. Such things demand reflection.'

'They are signs.'

'Yes. It was as if, I say *as if*, an expression which you sometimes fail to note, a higher power had for a moment violently shaken me, as a warning –'

'A warning?'

'Warning me to change, to find a new way, *the* way –' Marcus paused, Ludens was silent. 'You see I have never really seen, and do not yet see, the *essential* place of suffering in all this –'

Ludens thought, I hope he's not going back to the destiny of the Jews! He said in his most unmystical voice, 'Suffering, and death, these come to all of us. But do go on. I want to hear about the new way.'

'You know, Alfred, you have played a part too – you took me away from Red Cottage, you led me to Pat. Then you forced me to make some final attempt to collect all my thoughts together, you *taught* me my thoughts, all my old thoughts, you rehearsed them and set them in order as it were pointing forward, pointing toward the hidden conclusion which you wanted me to reach.'

'Yes, it was like that,' said Ludens, 'it was just like that.'

'That was very kind of you. You worked hard. But you know – for me, it was a nightmare – it was like walking barefoot on sharp stones, or breathing black dust with a sack over one's head. I endured it stupidly because I felt I had to, it was a task ordained, a punishment or penance to be got through – as if in hell, being unable to *think* any more, one had to keep rehearsing all one's old dead thoughts. Sometimes I felt it might just go on uselessly for years until I died. It made me somehow lose what had happened with Patrick, and even Patrick couldn't help me to recover it. I even began to feel that it was an isolated episode, a gift from elsewhere, not meant for me at all –'

'But then?'

'But then you helped me again, inadvertently of course, you ran after Fanny Amherst –'

'You mean that – surely –'

'I am speaking of experiences. At that point, when our work, my penance, was interrupted, I felt a change, as if – it's hard to explain – as if I had regained a simple purity of vision – something like intuition in mathematics, when you are suddenly *there*, when there is nothing between you and what you seek, nothing, nothing general, nothing pictorial –'

'Pure cognition?'

'A misleading term. I sought it under such guises, and became entangled in concepts – that was the long way round, or rather the wrong way in. No, not like that. But I can tell you what they say in the trade. Intuition in mathematics is a sense of beauty. Don't misunderstand me. Gushing about beauty may be just a cover-up for not knowing what to say about the feelings people have about knowledge and ignorance in maths. But this way of putting it has struck an echo.'

Ludens was touched by the word 'trade' coming so oddly from Marcus's lips, a faint signal from his mysterious anterior life as a mathematical genius, which he had led before Ludens met him. 'And this was what you felt you were recovering – different and as it were farther on?'

'I am talking too much.'

'I can see something has happened to you,' said Ludens, 'and I think that, just now, you are, somehow, happier, and I'm glad about that – and I'm sorry about the sharp stones. But I wish – I just wish I could see more, and understand more, what this state is like –'

'You want everything to be like something.'

'Well, that's how we think, with pictures and in general terms – we, I mean, not you! I suppose the magnet is different from the magnetised, the sun is different from what it reveals. But what will you *do*? I can't help hoping, and believing, that later on, in a new way, you will want to write about it all, surely you will want to *explain* – but never mind about that. How will you live, how will you occupy yourself?'

'I don't know, Alfred, I shall know when the time comes.'

'How will you know? Will you be led or told? What will lead you or tell you? Is it religion, is it God?'

'I can't answer these questions.'

'Do you think you can cure people or make them happy or make them good? Or is it not to do with people at all?'

'Alfred, please be content with what I've said – I found it quite difficult to say it to you.'

'Yes, and I'm grateful. And I'm also extremely puzzled and upset and alarmed. And *please* don't let this now pure intuition get mixed up with life-forces and miracle cures and going to Stonehenge and so on. Where you are, *wherever* you are, is far above all that. All right – I am prepared to see what I shall see. Can I ask one more question?'

'Yes.'

'What about me and Irina?'

'What about you? I believe you will be happy.'

'You don't object?'

'Of course not. I said, you have played an important part –'

'All right. Whatever was leading you has evidently been leading me. I just hope it will continue to do so. I'm just rather shattered, I don't know my way about any more – but, Marcus, you know it's strange and – maybe it's that magnetism – I feel very close to you now. All that time when we were walking on the stones and breathing the black dust I felt a continuous pain of being cut off from you. I *knew* I was trying to drag you along where you didn't want to go. But now I feel we are both together in a sort of good space, an open air of reality, almost as if *this* was what I was looking for, to be *with* you, and talk to you in this direct way. Well, perhaps this is just a moment, and there is still, on your way, so far to go and so much to learn, and whether I can come – but I will come, I *will*. Look, would you hold my hand just for a moment. You hold other people's hands, I don't see why you shouldn't hold mine just for once.'

Ludens held out his hand. Marcus took it in a firm hold. Ludens withdrew his hand and held it with his other hand.

The sun was setting, the long shadows of the trees had covered the lawn, the sky was intensely, densely, darkening its blue.

Ludens was suddenly aware of a movement. On the other side of the drive, among the trees, something, some figure, had moved. He looked, straining his eyes, into the obscure powdery twilight. A dark figure was moving at the verge of the wood. There was something uncanny there; he thought of satyrs, trolls, wood spirits, dangerous things. Marcus had seen it too. They watched.

The figure moved out onto the drive, stood a moment, then slowly crept forward onto the lawn. It moved awkwardly sideways, creeping, more like now to a large black caterpillar. Then, nearer, it declared itself as human, a man. Ludens rose to his feet. He had recognised the visitant. 'Gildas!'

Gildas who had been moving along the edge of the grass beside the woodland, now approached cautiously and stood in the open at the foot of the steps. Marcus had remained seated.

Gildas, having stood for a moment in silence, murmured, addressing Ludens, 'I'm sorry, I had to.'

Ludens said to Marcus, 'This is Gildas Herne. You remember him. He was a friend of mine and of Jack Sheerwater in the old days.'

Gildas said, now in a firmer voice addressing Marcus, 'I'm sorry. I felt I had to see you. I would like to talk to you, if I may, for a short while. Do you remember me?'

'Of course I do,' said Marcus. 'Alfred, you go and see Irina. He can sit here with me.'

Ludens turned and as he entered the sitting room and closed the door saw, in the increasing dark, Gildas sitting down in the chair which he had vacated.

He went through the dark sitting room and into the lighted kitchen. Irina was seated beside the table. The unwashed dishes were still piled up beside the sink. She looked at Ludens with histrionic contempt.

'What are you doing, Irina?'

'Sulking. Thinking about death. There's the washing-up.'

Ludens ran hot water into the basin and began to mop the plates and cutlery.

After a while Irina said, 'Who's with Dad?'

'Gildas. You remember Gildas Herne.'

'The man with the crooked face, yes. Do you think they want coffee or something?'

'No. Even if they want it they can't have it.'

'Why not?'

'Because it's too late. And we can't be bothered.'

'We?'

'We who are going to be married.'

'You think so.'

'Yes.'

Irina was silent, scratching a mosquito bite on her arm. The lake was a breeding place of mosquitoes, as everyone was now telling everyone else.

After a while she said, 'I don't think I can marry, I'm not fit for it, I'm not real enough. That's the trouble. I'm a puppet that's realised what's wrong with itself, and it's *horrible*. I'm propped up somewhere all alone, watching the real people go past. I'm propped up crying in a corner.'

'Oh shut up. What do you think of what's happened to your father?'

'Has anything happened? I hadn't noticed. Oh you mean becoming a god or something. At least he's cheerful. He's almost happy. At any rate he's stopped imagining that he can think. He's just existing. I wish I could.'

'Irina, I'm afraid for him. What are we to do?'

'I suggest we clear off.'

'*What?*'

345

'Let Marzillian look after him. He's the expert. What's this place for, after all, why did I bring him here? I think he's got into a place, and into a picture of himself, that suits him down to the ground. So he's lucky. All those batty people will go away – *they're* unreal all right – he'll be a nine days' wonder and that will set him up, then he'll be happy here in a dreamy state of quiet self-satisfaction. I don't know what he thinks he is, Jesus Christ or the Messiah or something. The main thing is that at last he's *pleased with himself*. I've never told you, I've never bothered you with this, how depressed and miserable and beastly he's been for so long. I've had a terrible time with him. Perhaps I deserve it, perhaps I'm under a curse, perhaps I'll always be a moping wretch. But at least I could get away from him now.'

'Irina, we can't go away and leave him behind.'

'Why the hell not?'

'He depends on you so much –'

'No he doesn't.'

'Well, he depends on me.'

'Let your soppy friend Gildas take over. He and Marzillian could make a good working partnership, they could calm him down. You do him no good, you're always exciting him and bothering him. Of course you're in love with Dad, I've known it all along. You regard him as your occupation, your life's work. For two pins you'd give up your job and stay with him forever. Now you're whingeing because he won't write that book for you. But you'll find another way of manipulating him I expect. All right, you stay here, but I'm going, I've had enough. I want to have some *fun* at last. Fun – what's that?'

'Irina, stop –'

'At least *now* I hope you'll admit that he's mad, mad as a hatter.'

'Please don't speak about him like that.'

'I'll begin to believe *you're* mad quite soon.'

'Darling, come here. Come to me. We'll sit on the table together. That's right.'

'That's typical of us. Sitting on a table. How romantic.'

'Kiss me. You love me, don't you?'

'Yes, Ludens, but we're doomed. I am anyway.'

'Don't be silly. I love you, I'll look after you and protect you till the world ends.'

'Perhaps it will end tomorrow.' She began to cry, leaning against his shoulder, her warm tears soaking into his shirt.

Half an hour later Ludens and Gildas were walking down the drive in silence. It was dark, yet, as is the way in June, somehow not really dark. The moon had not risen. A few high stars were large and yellow but gave no light, rather were decorations in the dusky vault of the sky. The darker darkness of the woodland penned the drive. Ludens took hold of Gildas's unresponsive arm, then released it. They walked on.

'How did you get in?' Ludens asked at last.

'I just kept walking round the fence till I found a place where someone had cut a hole in the wire. How do we get out?'

'I've got a key.'

After another silence Ludens said, 'How did you get on with Marcus?'

'Very well.'

'You won't tell me.'

They reached the gates. Ludens unlocked them, then locked them. The lane, arched over by trees, was very dark. He took Gildas's arm again.

'At least,' said Ludens when they reached the bridge, 'I hope he took the curse off.'

'Oh yes, very satisfactory.'

When they reached the Black Lion Ludens made as if to continue down the street with his friend, but Gildas checked him.

'No, you stay here. I go on.'

'Good night then,' said Ludens. They stood silently together.

Gildas then said, 'You know – Marcus has become something absolutely extraordinary.'

'Yes, but what is it?'

'I don't know. But whatever it is, I believe in it. Goodnight.'

'How did you find out?' said Franca to Jack.

'Christian Eriksen sent us a newspaper cutting complete with pictures of Marcus and Patrick! The article couldn't say positively whether Marcus had turned into an incarnate god, it was more interested in reminiscing about his days as a mathematical genius.'

'It's very distressing,' said Alison, frowning and narrowing her lips.

347

She evidently felt that Jack was taking it all too lightly. 'There was poor Ludens thinking he would write a great philosophy book, and the poor man has just crumbled away into insanity.'

Several days had now passed since Franca and Maisie had sat eating sandwiches in the Close and watching the spire of the Cathedral falling to the ground. During this time the crowd of devotees and sightseers at Bellmain had not abated, swelled now by journalists and photographers. A television crew was threatened.

'He may come back to the book later,' said Franca. 'Alfred thinks that after midsummer the mob will melt away. Apparently they're expecting some sort of manifestation at the solstice.'

'Manifestation?'

'Some happening, a great scene of healing, or signs in the heavens!'

'That's mass hysteria,' said Alison. 'There is such a thing.'

'Well, there's still a bit of time before midsummer, and I certainly can't imagine that poor Alfred is enjoying it.'

'No, but Patrick is!' said Franca.

'I'm sorry to hear that,' said Alison. 'But of course he's so kind and sympathetic, he's probably just pleased that Marcus is happy.'

'You say Marcus is in a state of weird euphoria?' said Jack.

'Yes – and yet it's not weird, it's not like frightening or uncanny, it's like warm sunshine or radiant heat or –'

'Franca has been taken over!' said Jack to Alison.

'But do you get it just by *seeing* him?' said Alison. 'Or do you have to talk to him?'

'How many yards does it reach?' said Jack. 'Could we feel it here? Do you feel anything, Aly?'

'Just seeing him seems to do it,' said Franca, 'but he does now see some people individually. Colin Bassett says it's to do with holiness.'

'Who's Colin Bassett?'

'He's the leader of some little sect which has attached itself to Marcus.'

'So he gives audiences? I don't think I want one,' said Jack. 'I don't really want to be face to face with that old enchanter again.'

'He's not old. He looks quite young now.'

'He's found the elixir of eternal youth. *That's* what he was after all the time! I wonder if he'll give some to Ludens.'

'Have you had an audience?' Alison asked Franca.

'Well, I didn't actually speak to him. I went along with Maisie Tether. Maisie was so *determined* to see him I was afraid she'd just rush in, so I got Patrick to arrange an appointment. We only stayed ten minutes and he talked with Maisie all the time about painting.'

'So that witch hasn't gone back to America? And Patrick's in charge! How comical.'

'Yet how right,' said Alison. 'If you owe your life to another man – Pat always said he wanted to be Marcus's servant.'

'What about Ludens, is his nose out of joint?'

'Rather. Of course he's not a believer, like Colin and Patrick.'

'So our Alfred doesn't feel the rays? He hasn't run away sobbing?'

'No, he hangs around, looking rather pathetic and out of things. I think he feels the rays but they just frighten him. Irina is there too of course, she seems a bit embarrassed by it all.'

'Embarrassed, I should say so! If your parent suddenly turns out to be a god!'

'You mean Ludens thinks these "rays" are an emanation of mental unbalance, perhaps mental chaos?' said Alison. 'Of course the presence of a mad person is very disturbing. Marcus is probably an extreme manic depressive, gone over the edge. It's a psychotic spree.'

'Poor Ludens,' said Jack. 'But Heather's coming back to England quite soon. What he needs is a dose of Heather Allenby!'

'What impression did you get of Marcus,' Alison said to Franca, 'when you saw him at close quarters?'

'I didn't think he was mad,' said Franca, 'it wasn't like madness – or how I imagine madness, I don't really know much about it. There was a sort of electricity in the air, but it was enlivening, if you know what I mean.'

'Were you frightened?'

'Only to begin with. Maisie did all the talking, he asked about her painting, and she said she'd got one of his pictures and she described it and asked him about it, and he couldn't remember the picture but he said something about how you can paint your mind by visualising, I didn't really understand –'

'I bet you didn't! But I suppose *she* was spellbound? Another believer.'

'Not exactly. That reminds me, there is a genuine believer here whom you know – Gildas! He's staying in a lodging quite near the White Lion. He's met Marcus, and according to Alfred he was quite bowled over, he saw the light or whatever it was. It's no good going and calling on him I gather, because he spends every day walking about alone.'

'He didn't dare to try a second dose? Well, I'm absolutely fascinated,' said Jack. 'I'll squeeze Gildas and Ludens till they tell me *everything*. Come on, what's stopping us, I can't wait, the rain's over, the sun's shining – let's go to the fair!'

Franca had been very surprised by her brief visit to Marcus. They sat at the kitchen table. Irina brought them glasses of orange juice. Franca had sat, her body faintly shuddering as if it were very close to, or indeed *was*, a silently pulsating machine. Even her teeth tended to chatter, but perhaps that was only at first. Her mouth, she remembered afterwards, had stayed slightly open throughout the short interview. She sat very upright staring at Marcus's face: it was as if it had been peeled, a mask removed, it glowed with cleanness, radiantly smooth, like a face in an illuminated picture. Marcus sat at the head of the table, with Maisie and Franca on either side. There was some bread on the table and a bowl of apples, then Marcus's hands with their pale skin and long fingers. Franca, automatically thinking of Christ at Emmaus, banished the image or rather stored it. Marcus's hair, as bright, she thought, as when she had first seen him, fell in curling tendrils. Franca felt an extraordinary desire to laugh. She was only vaguely aware of his conversation with Maisie, secure in the knowledge, which came to her almost at once, that he would not address her. Yet he included her, turning to her at intervals, and smiling as at an old friend.

Afterwards, of course, she and Maisie talked a great deal about it, and then Franca did laugh, feeling, as she had said to Jack, enlivened and in some way cheered. It was not exactly happiness, it was not exactly an enchantment, rather a sense of detachment, which Franca was eager to test against the return, announced by telegram, of Jack and Alison. So far it had stood up. She felt her separateness from them in a new way. Perfect love? Not quite, certainly not as she had previously enacted it, thinking in terms of silent suffering, the thrill of concealment, the discipline of conscience and the voice of duty, nun-like austerity, the agony of sacrifice, and a purification by fire. What she felt now was more like a simple, sensible invulnerability. Why should *she* be hurt by *their* happiness? She examined, in this new clear bright light, her old love for Jack. It appeared to be intact, even, as she oddly thought it, cleaned up, unmasked, peeled. All right, she loved him, he gave her delight; yet she was no longer tangled into him or bound round him in such a way that his every movement could cause her agony. But would this detached state last, and was it anyway a good thing or a bad thing? Perhaps it simply meant that she had suddenly cut through the centre of the bond between herself and Jack, like cutting a vital artery? Snap. The results, not yet evident, might be deadly. Franca decided not to speculate about the future, but to enjoy for the present her unexpected access of calm benevolence; and she felt too that her liberation, however brief, into the land of unpossessive generosity, had been occasioned not only by Marcus, but by Maisie Tether, by her discovery that, even now, she could make a friend.

The atmosphere of the 'fairground' was indeed unusual. The sun, shining upon vegetation still wet with rain, produced a steamy moist warmth, the woodland was like a tropical forest, full of exotic flowers and the screeches of birds. Visitors or pilgrims, grouped near to the gate, produced a genial hum of soft amicable conversation. It was not really like a fairground gathering. Some sort of single mood possessed it, friendliness was ostentatious, strangers looked directly at each other and smiled. Jack said, 'It's like a blooming church fête.' There was in fact no dense crowd, only an intermittent trickle of arrivals. Notices which had been up saying *No picnics please* were obeyed, the barrier placed on the main drive at the Benbow turning was respected, the signs to Benbow were followed. A path had been made beyond Benbow through the wood (even at the expense of cutting down some bushes) to enable the devotees, after staying a while in front of the house, to return by a circular route to the gate without colliding with the entering stream.

The approach to the house was made by all comers in silence. Jack and Alison, following Franca, had stopped talking. Jack took Alison's hand. Everyone was walking slowly, with a certain solemn dignity. When they neared Benbow Franca looked back with a significant look. A group of people were standing quietly upon the drive and upon the grass verge of the woodland. By some wordless convention a few people felt moved, or privileged, to stand upon the lawn, but without coming near the house. The group shifted a little in an orderly way as people left or arrived. The gazers dispersed themselves considerately, stepping aside so that others could see. Franca, followed by the other two, stood boldly in the front row.

Marcus was at the top of the steps, standing very erect and looking at the crowd. Behind him, in the shade of the verandah, was Patrick. Both of them wore, over cotton trousers, long Russian-style shirts, unbelted, of some white heavyish woven material. The shirts had high collars but were open at the neck. Patrick, though evidently 'on duty', was standing 'at ease', his feet apart, his hands loosely clasped in front of him. Marcus, hands hanging, was in repose yet not quite still. His eyes roved, his head moved slightly, he seemed to be scanning his visitors intently, as if anxious to meet the eyes of every individual. Sometimes he looked away, into the wood or up at the sky, occasionally he put a hand to his throat. Minutes passed. Some of the people moved on, others arrived. After some time Marcus made a sign to Patrick who placed a chair behind him at the top of the steps. Marcus, without looking round, sat down on the chair, stretching his hands out along its arms, and continued his gazing. The end of the lawn was marked by a line of offerings, flowers, sometimes fruit, the usual stones, which arrived every day and were, in the evening moved by Patrick and a Seeker to the sides of the lawn, where mounds of variegated donations stretched away under the trees. The withered flowers were removed. What happened to the fruit no one knew. Perhaps, as the donors hoped, it was eaten by the sage himself.

After a short time, for they all three felt somewhat disturbed, almost guilty, facing Marcus's searching gaze, Franca motioned to the others and they withdrew, not passing on toward the Way Out, but retiring again to the main drive. When they were well away from Benbow Jack said, '*My God!*'

'Yes,' said Franca, 'it is amazing, isn't it? Whatever can one think?'

'Fancy old Marcus carrying all *that* off!' said Jack. 'It's a bloody marvel. I feel quite shaken!'

'So do I,' said Alison, 'but it's a crowd effect, like at a football match. I've seen evangelists do it too, in Scotland. Patrick looked beautiful, didn't he.'

'I think it's hypnotism,' said Jack. 'We used to think Marcus had that talent in the old days. But he doesn't do it all day?'

'Oh no, only at intervals, people may have to wait for a long time. Some of them can't stand his gaze, others become addicted to it and are rooted to the spot.'

'I couldn't have stood it for long,' said Jack. 'I'd have been tempted to shout "Hi Marcus, it's me!"'

'Look,' said Franca, 'don't disturb him, let's just watch him, over there, it's Alfred.'

Some distance away, just beyond the barrier which said *No Entry* and prevented visitors from going on toward the house, Ludens was standing in the shade at the edge of the wood, leaning against a tree.

'He looks like a poor Jewish refugee boy,' said Jack.

'He looks so unhappy,' said Alison.

'He's moping,' said Franca, 'because Pat has taken his place with Marcus. Pat does everything now. Poor Alfred is out in the cold.'

Ludens was indeed cast down. He still saw Marcus every day, coming in early in the morning as usual, hoping on each occasion to be able to continue the 'real conversation' which had taken place on the evening when Gildas had appeared and when Ludens had held Marcus's hand. It was of course impossible to have the old 'book' discussions, but Ludens kept trying to lure Marcus into talking more about a 'simple purity of vision' and 'new intuition' and 'a sense of beauty'. These scenes however consisted of Ludens rambling round those topics, Marcus smiling, or frowning and saying 'No,' and increasingly often telling Ludens to stop. Sometimes Ludens felt that he had 'gone too far' and might even be in danger of being banished forever. However Marcus continued to want his company, and they even developed a new style in which they conversed about plants and animals, and even about books and pictures. Ludens recalled how on *that* evening he had felt dismay yet also elation, as if he were actually witnessing the metamorphosis whereby Marcus could recover, after a long journey and in a new way, the pure intuitions of his youth. He had felt then that he and Marcus together were being lifted up into a pure *more real* region high above the world. During the days that followed however he found himself watching helplessly while Marcus was taken over by what Ludens increasingly saw as vulgar theatre and dangerous depraved magic. With the abandonment of 'the book', Ludens now realised, he had lost his authority. He had failed, he had fallen, and Marcus's continued kindness to him, seemingly like a consolation, made his lot more bitter.

Ludens's time with Marcus was also curtailed because Marcus often wished to be alone to prepare for, or to recuperate from, his public sessions. Ludens, though he detested and disapproved of these performances, did eventually watch some of them, out of loyalty to Marcus, and out of curiosity. This 'facing the crowd' seemed to him not like an instant act of triumph but more like an ordeal or 'work', whereby Marcus on every occasion transformed a potentially hostile mob so as actually to commune with a number of individuals, leaving no one out. It was as if the crowd, at first, might have been ready to throw stones or fire bullets, so great was the degree of change which was required of them. Of course in fact the people who turned up were mostly extremely amiable, *wanting* to be changed by Marcus's laser beam into creatures of a quite different kind. When Ludens, in one of the few 'live' conversations which they had during this time, described his impressions, Marcus shook his head and said, 'It is difficult, but it ought not to be, sometimes it isn't. One has to be empty yet attentive, that ought to come naturally.' When Ludens asked whether looking at people in silence could do them good, Marcus said, 'I believe so, there is much to learn,' and told Ludens to go away. After the 'lookings' Marcus was certainly extremely tired. In the afternoons Ludens always absented himself as he had done before. Marcus then occasionally saw individual people, or 'penitents' as Patrick called them. Who chose those people Ludens did not know, perhaps Pat, perhaps Colin, perhaps even Camilla who was now more than ever in evidence at Benbow. Ludens was no longer 'in the picture', nor did he strive to be. Some natural force, like the movement of a big animal, gently pressed him aside. In the evenings, he came again to Benbow, but now there were 'supper parties', Pat always, Colin and Camilla often, Andrew and Miriam sometimes, other Seekers, and Mr Talgarth who was taking a great interest in the whole phenomenon and was much enlivened by it. Of course Ludens saw Irina every day, and sometimes walked or shopped with her in the afternoons, but she too was now part of the 'machine', not actively, but allowing herself to be controlled. He was cheered by her irreverence when they were alone together, but there were no more of the 'domestic scenes' which he had loved so much. He had visited the Registrar in Salisbury and found out how to get married. But such planning seemed for some reason to be impossible just now. He dismissed, as one motive among others and an unworthy one, the idea that when he was married to Irina he would have more power over Marcus! The 'religious mania' surely represented an interim, a 'silly season' which would probably end at midsummer. With what to follow? Ludens felt that everyone around him was living in the present, a place where he certainly could not live. A last straw had been those white shirts which Patrick had suddenly produced. Marcus had put his on with docility. Ludens even saw him looking at himself in a mirror.

Leaning against his tree, he scratched his back up and down like an animal. He was without occupation: no more philosophical discussion, no more 'writing it up', afterwards. His 'own work', his book on Leonardo, his pursuit of Bruno, his projected studies of Ficino, Pico, Aretino, Alberti, Savonarola, Machiavelli, these seemed dead things now, the dreams of a deceased self. Gildas had withdrawn from him into some form of meditation which involved long solitary walks. Of course Gildas could not now endure Ludens's scepticism, as before Ludens had not been able to endure his. Well, at midsummer things would change. Or would they simply become more established and institutionalised? Gazing at the, at that moment fairly small, file of people who were turning off the main drive toward Benbow, Ludens saw the figure of Geoffrey Toller, the landlord of the Black Lion. Toller had recently, and with trepidation, 'gone the round' to look at the Professor; now become an addict, he went every day. 'It's like going to church!' he told Ludens. 'It does you good, you can feel it!' His wife, who was more sceptical, had so far refused to go. She said it must be 'something oriental, something to do with that wicked Stone'. Not far behind Toller was Mr Talgarth, accompanied by a tall man wearing a dog collar. Seeing Ludens they left the stream and walked past the barrier to join him.

'Good morning, Ludens,' said Mr Talgarth, 'may I introduce Mr Westerman. Dr Ludens.'

'Hello, I'm your parson,' said the tall man. 'I think I've seen you poking your head into our little church. It's quite a gem, isn't it?'

'It's a beautiful church,' Ludens agreed.

'Well, what do you think of all this business, Dr Ludens? I understand you know him well.'

'It's remarkable,' said Ludens.

'Of course, it's unusual in England,' said Talgarth, 'but it would be an everyday sight in India. In that country there are gods everywhere – a saying of Heraclitus incidentally – they live with a concept of holiness which has vanished from the West. They can smell it and taste it. They seek out holy things and holy places and holy men and venerate them wholeheartedly. Here we find such excesses embarrassing.'

'One must distinguish of course,' said the parson, 'between a genuine sense of the holy, which promotes unselfishness and virtue, and an intoxicated hysteria which is a holiday for egoism.'

'I don't think they bother about these distinctions in India,' said Mr Talgarth.

'I believe the Professor has been in the East, Dr Ludens?'

'Yes,' said Ludens, 'but I think he invented all this stuff himself, or perhaps it came to him as a divine gift.'

'Someone told me a light can be seen shining round his head.'

'I haven't seen it,' said Ludens, 'but some people can see auras which are hidden from others. Why don't you go and look?'

'I am just taking Henry along,' said Talgarth. 'He has not yet had the Experience.'

'Perhaps you know Fanny Amherst?' said Ludens to the parson. 'Does she come to your church?'

'Indeed, a church-goer, and a communicant, I prepared her for confirmation – a quiet innocent girl, though – you know –' He tapped his brow.

Ludens deduced that Fanny's 'excesses' as a Stone Person were not known to her pastor.

Mr Talgarth smiled at Ludens. 'Coming with us?'

'No, thanks.' Ludens had come to like Mr Talgarth, but was puzzled by him. Mr Talgarth rarely left the precincts of Bellmain, no one visited him. Yet he certainly did not seem in any way 'unbalanced' or 'odd' or even neurotic. He held friendly, interesting, even learned conversations with Marcus and with Ludens. He had a calm clever face. Ludens, recalling what Marzillian had said about 'perpetual anguish', studied that face; and thought that, at rare intervals, for a second, for a mini-second, it winced or shuddered as at some dreadful secret pain.

'Why, there's Mrs Sheerwater!' said Talgarth. He waved. Ludens had introduced Franca and Maisie when, walking with them, he had met Talgarth on the drive. As Franca advanced with Jack and Alison, Talgarth and the parson disappeared along the way to Benbow.

Ludens was startled. 'So you've come back!' He shook hands with Jack and kissed Alison and Franca with enthusiasm.

'Yes, we felt we had to come and support you, didn't we, Aly. And Heather is going to come too, she's got the builders in at the moment. We're all thrilled about Marcus!'

'Thrilled? Why?'

'Well, who would have thought dear old Marcus would turn out to be an incarnate god?'

'Who indeed. Have you seen him?'

'Yes,' said Alison, 'we stood in the crowd and were looked at. It was rather sort of electric — but of course we were expecting to feel something. Is it hypnotism?'

'I don't know. It appears to make people happy.'

'Yes, but does it make them good?' said Franca.

'It makes them good-tempered.'

'It hasn't made *you* happy,' said Alison.

'I'm told that everyone has a bud of cancerous pain in his soul,' said Ludens. 'Mine gives a twinge now and then, but I can live with it. I'm glad to see you lot.'

'We're glad to see you, my dear fellow. Now what you need is a *drink*. Come along with us, we're installed in the White Lion as before, and have a good stiff drink and a slap-up lunch.'

'No, thanks,' said Ludens to Jack, 'I'm afraid I have an appointment here. But I hope I'll see you later. You know Gildas is around?'

'Yes, Franca told us, he's saved. We must do something about him.'

'Come and see us *soon*, be *with* us,' said Alison, gazing at him with affection. She was standing in her familiar pose, one foot set sideways, stretching her slim muscular body and her long neck. She held out her hand gracefully, graciously, and he took it.

They turned away down the drive, receding, Jack in the middle with his arms round both waists. Ludens, who of course had no appointment, sighed. He thought, I wouldn't mind being in bed with either of those women, but they're not available, and anyway I love Irina, deeply, deeply, with a destined love, even if she is, and indeed she is, and because she is, all those things that Jack said, barbarous gipsy, wild animal, abyss, hell, danger, chaos, night, demon and priestess. And she had said, she had actually *said*, 'Let's go away together,' and Ludens had said 'no'. He hunched himself in anguish over this thought. He could not leave Marcus; he felt, and it was as if he alone felt it, that Marcus was daily and hourly in terrible danger, as if he were climbing up a tall tree, a steep cliff, the spire of Salisbury Cathedral, and *must fall*.

He watched the enlaced trio until they were out of sight. Why had he not accepted Jack's invitation to a stiff drink and a slap-up lunch? Wasn't that precisely what he wanted, what would cheer him up and do him good? Why hadn't he gone, why could he not run after them, why was he feeling so leprous and accursed? He walked slowly back toward the barrier. Almost at once he saw a stout man in black approaching him and waving. He recognised Father O'Harte. The priest positively rushed at him and began shaking both his hands.

'How good to see you here, what luck, I'm so glad. You can tell me how he is and what is really happening, it's all over the newspapers, you know – has he done any more cures – what a lot of people – he's become quite famous – can I get to see him – can I find Patrick?'

Ludens was touched, also alarmed, by the priest's enthusiasm. He found himself hoping that Father O'Harte would not be disappointed. 'Yes, Pat's here, he's very well, so is Marcus of course. I don't think he's done any more cures, well he may have done for all I know. He sees people every day, that is he lets them look at him, that seems to do something for them and he sees a few people individually. But really I'm not the expert, you must see Pat. If you go down there you'll come to the bungalow where he lives, he may be standing on the verandah with Pat, being looked at, or he may be inside. Pat would probably see you in the crowd. If they're not visible you could tap on the door at the side.'

'Yes, yes, I'll go at once, thank you so much. You're at the Black Lion, aren't you? I want to see Gildas too, I've got his address.'

'Gildas – how did you know?'

'Oh I know a lot, Patrick rings me up. And Suzanne is coming, I expect you know, you remember the nurse, Miss Moxon. He rings her up too. Well, I'll go, thank you, thank you. What strange times we live in.' He hurried off in the direction of Benbow. Ludens waited a while to let him get ahead.

Near to the Benbow turning he met Dr Bland who was just coming up from the gate. During the recent days Ludens had become almost friendly with Dr Bland, whom he had disliked so much at first sight. Perhaps it was simply that, seeing him wandering about unemployed and useless, Bland had felt sorry for him. On the other hand, perhaps he too was now being treated as an interesting case.

'Well, Ludens,' said Bland, 'how is it with you, my boy?' Bland, staring through his thick round glasses, looked, Ludens thought, even odder and wilder than usual. Perhaps he was, as doubtless so often, in trouble. His short faded blond hair, which usually lay sleekly on his large round head, was disordered and unkempt. He spoke loudly, almost aggressively.

'I'm fine,' said Ludens.

'Right as a Ribstone pippin?'

'Yes.'

'You don't look well. Perhaps you need sex. You don't seem to share the general euphoria which has so suddenly overwhelmed our quiet scene.'

'No. You don't either.'

'Happiness. What's that? I don't know. How can one be happy when one loves a demon?'

Ludens was startled by this confession. He thought, it's the atmosphere, it's all that electricity, we're all a bit on edge, ready to blurt out our secrets. Not that this is exactly a secret. He said, 'But he's a good demon.'

Bland made a snorting noise. He touched Ludens's shoulder and went on towards the house.

Ludens looked at his watch. He began to walk slowly toward Benbow. In about ten minutes the 'show' (or 'showing', as Colin called it) would be over. He would slink in by the side door, see Marcus and Irina, and hear Pat and Colin discussing, though not for Marcus's ear, the success of the performance, the number and behaviour of the devotees, and what was being said in the village. He would help Irina to set out a 'picnic lunch' in the kitchen. When the others sat down, Ludens would stand, joining in the conversation in a friendly manner, for he did not of course express overt hostility. Though not pointedly excluded, no one urged him to sit. He could however hope for certain significant looks from Marcus and Irina intended (he thought) to reassure him. He did not, felt he could not, eat with the others, but gathered food from the kitchen which he consumed privately elsewhere, in the woods or at the Black Lion. After lunch, when Marcus was resting, he could go shopping or walking with Irina. He would have found the situation intolerable had he not felt certain it was transient. When he reached Benbow the little crowd was still there, attentive and silent. Ludens glided round it to a point where he could see Marcus sitting, Patrick standing. Ludens looked round for Father O'Harte. Then he observed a new phenomenon. Several people had moved onto the grass and were kneeling there. He saw the priest upon his knees, his hands clasped in prayer, as he had been on the occasion of Patrick's resurrection. Then he saw another familiar form. Gildas too was kneeling, with clasped hands and closed eyes.

In the next days the routine continued, people came and Marcus stood before them wearing the white garment which now reminded Ludens of the smock worn by Leonardo in his dream. Looking for familiar faces Ludens saw the waiter from the White Lion, and Lambert, the taciturn nurse. Toller still came, his wife still declared it to be 'pagan'. The euphoria persisted, more devotees knelt on the lawn. The Seekers said, 'We shall see great things at midsummer.' There was, Ludens agreed with Mr Talgarth, a certain vulgarisation of the scene attendant on publicity, the occasional vocal sceptic or 'rough element', but such disturbances were peripheral. Journalists and photographers were orderly, the press more sober. Marcus's past was raked over, his career as a mathematician, later as a painter, photographs of his paintings were published and people who owned some hastened to send them to Christie's. Of his private life, and of his later struggles with philosophy (or whatever it was) little seemed to be known. References to cures and healing continued, but without sensational evidence. Articles hostile to Marcus naturally appeared too, denouncing him as a charlatan or a blasphemer, or suggesting that the whole thing was being engineered by the doctors in order to advertise their clinic. In fact, rather to Ludens's surprise, Marzillian himself, surely the most picturesque object after Marcus, scarcely figured at all in these speculations. He kept the 'fun-fair', as Terence Bland described it, at a distance, well away from his own quarters, and remained wrapped in a cloud, defended from the idly curious by his disciplined and iron-willed staff. By now the Bulldogs and some sturdy Seekers were operating a discreet check-point at the gate, necessary to prevent an influx of local pedlars attracted by the crowd. Outside in the lane, where a farmer had opened a field as an expensive car park, lemonade and ice cream were on sale. Ludens was glad to notice, that in spite of promised midsummer treats, the numbers were now steadily diminishing. He was also pleased that Colin and Patrick being so talkative, he was left alone.

One day he made an expedition into Salisbury and bought an expensive Japanese camera for Irina, for which she expressed gratitude, but with which she had not yet experimented, although he had bought her quantities of film. Ludens had not forgotten her saying more than once (though perhaps it was a joke) that she wanted to be a photographer and roam the world with her camera! He thought, after handing over his gift, that it was a mistake to encourage this ambition. However, he did not take it seriously, and had simply been seeking a pretext to give her a handsome-looking present. Gildas continued to come, occasionally, to kneel on Marcus's lawn but was more usually invisible on his long sessions of walking meditation. He avoided Ludens, or rather told him that he did not want to see him at present. He conveyed this information gently, adding that of course they would talk again 'later on'. Ludens, who now craved for conversation with his friend, had to accept that. He would have liked also to talk to Marzillian, but received no summons, and was also, he realised, frightened of what such a talk might elicit or reveal. Franca and Alison and Jack, wearied for the moment of the spectacle at Bellmain, drove about in Jack's car. They invited Ludens but he refused. They also invited Irina, who also refused. Maisie Tether had gone to London preparatory to her return to America. Father O'Harte had also returned to London, but saying he would be back soon. Suzanne Moxon, 'in pursuit of Patrick' as it was assumed, had not yet appeared. Pat's relations with Camilla remained obscure. In fact he sometimes went jaunting with the trio, or read his poems to Alison at the White Lion. Ludens was glad of these absences, though they did not mend his deep sense of separation from Marcus. He recalled the way in which, when he had said to Marcus, 'What about me and Irina,' Marcus had replied, 'I believe you will be happy,' as if Ludens were being set aside as the convenient Jewish boy who would take his daughter off his hands, and look after her decently somewhere else. It feels like being separated from God, he thought. A little singing occurred, some of the Seekers were singers (a girl called Kathleen had a particularly good voice) and they joined Ludens, Pat, Camilla, and

Irina in rendering some folksongs and familiar rounds and madrigals. But Ludens's heart was not in it. The weather continued fairly fine and the evenings were long, and they sat outside enjoying the quiet of the garden, after the worshippers, to whom they were now so used, had retired from the scene. What is this, thought Ludens, and can it go on?

The idea of 'doing Rodney' was of course all this time disturbing him; but it had become a part, a condition, of the enchantment which paralysed them all, that Rodney seemed, for the moment, pragmatically out of the question. Irina's talk of 'clearing off' had not meant a one-night scurry to London. Ludens did not venture to suggest anything clandestine. He felt he was being, by the situation, perhaps by Marcus, required to *wait*, like Ferdinand until, by an ordeal of chastity, courage and pure love he should deserve his Miranda. Something would change, something new would happen, and in that change would lie his reward: at least where Irina was concerned. He tortured himself by wondering whether perhaps he had lost Marcus forever. One thing which he could and did do during this spellbound interim was to watch Marcus closely. Was he the helpless captive of a senseless situation; or was he rather embarked upon some deeply understood, deeply experienced, mystical enterprise? Was Marcus *thinking*? Sometimes Ludens simply hoped that Marcus would collapse and begin to need him again.

Shortly before the fated something new began to happen Ludens had a harmless but also disconcerting visitation from the past. One morning when entering the gate of Bellmain he was stopped by an elderly woman who looked familiar.

'Why, Dr Ludens! Surely you remember me. I'm Helena McCann. You remember when the Professor was living with me in Richmond, with the Japanese gentleman? I've left London now, I live with my sister in Amesbury. I read about the Professor in the paper and so I came over on the bus to see for myself, I've just been there looking at him. Oh the poor thing, the poor mad thing, how can the doctors let him do it? Of course when he was living with me he was a little bit out of his wits, wasn't he? But it wasn't ludicrous and horrible and sort of weird, he was quiet then. But now, Oh the poor man – I'm quite upset. I thought in our society poor mad people were kept privately in hospitals and not put on show. I'm really shocked; they'll be charging admission next! I shall tell my sister all about it and we'll come over again together. She could hardly believe what it said in the paper. I expect you've come to have a look at him too.'

Ludens parted from her with friendly exclamations and hopes to see her again and meet her sister. He walked away with black thoughts.

Much as he detested Marcus's mission, he in some way respected it and felt a kind of admiring awe at the silent devotion of the worshippers, as if he were almost proud of Marcus for being so impressive. For some reason it had never occurred to him that a great many of those who came and looked at Marcus in what Ludens took to be reverent silence were in reality gaping at some kind of monster, a freak of nature, rather uncanny, rather extraordinary, very pathetic. He felt a wave of awful sadness. Why indeed did Marzillian allow Marcus to make such a fool of himself, for perhaps after all that was what it came to? Ludens, trying to read the mind of that 'good demon', had assumed that Marzillian looked upon the 'phase' as a kind of malady to be fairly rapidly 'worked through'. But perhaps that eminent magician was getting more than he bargained for? The idea that things were out of hand and Marzillian had lost control worried Ludens a great deal. Of course he was never likely to know what Marzillian intended, since the worthy doctor would not admit to a failure. Meanwhile an aura of respectability had been conferred upon Marcus from another quarter, since Mr Westerman, the parish priest, had suddenly, evidently convinced of something, sent one of his more neurotic sheep, an eccentric middle-aged spinster, to have a talk with the Professor.

Miss McCann may or may not have returned to the 'fair' to display the 'monster' to her incredulous sister. In any case, Ludens did not see her again. He had however, shortly afterwards, another visitation more mysteriously portentous and disturbing. Upon the drive one afternoon he was accosted by a young man in dark narrow trousers, with a smartish striped shirt open at the neck. The young man's face was smooth and lean, his hair dark and straight, his eyes brown and clever, and he was carrying a parcel. He smiled at Ludens in a polite and friendly manner. 'Dr Ludens I believe?'

'Yes.'

'Good afternoon. I am your rabbi.'

'I have no rabbi.'

'It's a mode of speech.'

'You mean a kind of idiom, as in "your philosophy"?'

'You jest. I mean I am the local rabbi.'

'I see, as in "I am your parson", which someone told me lately.'

'Precisely. Only my claim is of course stronger than his.'

'Why?'

'Because you are Jewish.'

'What makes you think I'm Jewish?'

'A number of things, your face for instance.'

'Mention others.'

'I have heard about you from your friend Gildas Herne.'

'Oh have you. What do you want?'

'Why are you so aggressive? Were you not polite to the parson?'

'Yes.'

'Then why not to me?'

Ludens did not propose to answer this question, the answer being clear enough. 'So you've got to know Gildas Herne.'

'I hasten to say he had nothing but praise for you.'

'I don't need to be told that.'

'My name by the way, is Daniel Most, spelt M.O.S.T., pronounced to rhyme with "cost", not "coast". My name means bridge in Russian. A good name for a teacher, don't you think?'

'You haven't told me what you want.'

'I want to see the Professor.'

'I am sorry to tell you he is not the Messiah.'

'I know that, well, I surmise it. I have something I want to give him.'

'Is it that parcel?'

'Yes.'

'You can give it to me.'

'Why should I? It is not for you. I want to see him and give it to him personally.'

'What's in the parcel?'

The young rabbi hesitated at this point. He said reluctantly, 'A prayer shawl.'

'*A prayer shawl?*'

'Why take that tone?'

'Look,' said Ludens, 'I'm sure you mean well, but the Professor has never been near a synagogue in his life –'

'Neither have you, I imagine.'

'Right. He has no connection with the Jewish religion and desires no connection. Your gift could have no meaning for him except that of a superstitious object.'

'Why do you deride religion?'

'I don't deride religion in general.'

'I see, only your own. There's a Jewish joke in this somewhere.'

'Don't tell it please.'

'So you actually admit that it *is* your religion?'

'Look,' said Ludens, 'I'm sorry to be, or to seem, bloody-minded, but the Professor has no interest in Judaism –'

'Ah, now you say Judaism.'

'Of course he's fully conscious of being a Jew, I mean he's not interested in Jewish religious ceremonial.'

'He doesn't keep the holy days.'

'Of course he doesn't! Innumerable Jews don't!'

'But he is a religious man.'

'What does that mean? Not in your way. That's his business. I'm sorry.'

'Well, may I please see him? Other people talk to him, why not me? I want to give him the shawl. He can use it as a tablecloth if he likes.'

'He is not available.'

'What are you so afraid of?'

'I'm not afraid! I just don't want him to be disturbed by irrelevant matters. Look, if you'd like to give me your parcel I will give it to him.'

'You want to get rid of me.'

'Yes.'

'All right.' The rabbi handed over the parcel. 'Perhaps I could see him later.'

'Maybe – I don't know –'

'I'll pray for him, and for you.'

'Oh – thanks!'

The rabbi turned back toward the gate. Ludens, who had been making for the gate, turned back toward the house. He was extremely upset. He had been disgracefully, vulgarly rude to an innocent kindly man. He had felt, on Marcus's behalf, sudden uncontrollable fear and hostility. And he had not failed to be wounded by the reference to Gildas. So Gildas, who would not talk to him, chattered to someone else! On the other hand, having manifested these unworthy emotions, he had been fool enough to accept the wretched parcel which now he was bound to deliver. So he had the worst of both worlds. He tried to console himself by thinking that Marcus would not know what the object was. But should that be so, would it not also be Ludens's duty to inform him? Oh *hell*!

When he had encountered Daniel Most, whose name rhymed with 'cost' not with 'coast', Ludens had been on his way to the Black Lion to say a previously arranged goodbye to Jack and his women who, regarding the 'show' as effectively over, were about to return to London. After a suitable interval Ludens resumed his walk to the pub. As he went he was reminded of another, though not the gravest, of his numerous troubles. The Black Lion, though less expensive than the White Lion, was rapidly depleting his modest savings. Christian Eriksen was paying a (suggested by Ludens) ridiculously small rent for staying in his flat. Ludens might soon be eating dangerously into his next salary cheque. He could not hope, or wish, to live free in Bellmain as Patrick did. He was certainly doing a job for the place, but the job was *essentially* unrewarded. Borrow from Irina? Impossible. From Jack? Conceivable but unpalatable. He really ought to look for a cheaper lodging in the village (an attic at the Hedgehog?) but he was reluctant to do that yet, since the Black Lion had become his home. Reflecting sombrely he crossed the bridge and was entering the yard of the pub when a woman barred his way. It was Alison, and it was soon evident that she had been waiting for him.

'Hello, Alison. Shall we go in?'

'No. *They're* in there. Ludens, I must talk to you. Where can we go?'

They walked out of the yard and back across the bridge. Ludens led the way off the road and down to the seat by the river's edge where he had talked to Fanny Amherst. They sat down.

'What's the matter, Alison? Why you've been crying.'

'Yes, damn it. I hope they won't notice. I've got some dark glasses in my bag.'

'My dear, don't look like that. What is it?'

'I'm just torn to pieces.' She held out her hand and Ludens took it for a moment, pressed it and caressed it. Her large long hand was pale in colour, slightly freckled, the back of it gleaming with a scatter of tiny red hairs. She gripped him firmly.

'I wish you could be happy,' said Ludens. 'You *ought* to be happy. You're so strong. You're as strong as a panther.'

'I wish I were a panther. I wish I could be ruthless. Or rather, I wish I could be ruthless without suffering so much pain.'

'But what's happening?'

'Can't you understand? What was bound to happen. Listen, Ludens, if I say it to you I can do it. You must help me, you must *support* me.'

'I'll do anything I can for you.'

'I've got to have Jack all to myself, I've *got* to – anything else would drive me mad, *is* driving me mad.'

'I thought you were all discovering how to be happy together. It's not impossible.'

'Oh don't be a *fool!*'

'After all, you're in the stronger position. Can't you be generous?'

'I'm surprised at your cynicism.'

'It's not cynicism! I'm trying to understand. Jack loves you, he's mad about you.'

'Yes. And I'm mad about him. And I'm not going to share him with anyone else. Listen, *listen*. Franca tried to poison my relation with Jack by sort of criticising him and suggesting we could be in league against him.'

'You and Franca against Jack? It might do him good!'

'It was poison, it was evil, it was separating me from him.'

'Are you accusing Franca of doing this on purpose, in cold blood?'

'No, I suppose not. I suppose it was impulsive or instinctive.'

'But did you go along with it?'

'For a moment or two – perhaps it amused me, or I felt sorry for her. Then I saw – it was then I *saw* – that I must get rid of Franca. I know she's an innocent person, a decent person, an absolutely victim person, she's put up with so much, I think she'd put up with anything. But I've got to destroy her.'

Ludens, who had seen this coming, said, 'But you like her.'

'Yes, that's the point, or part of it, oh why can't you *think* –'

'Sorry, I want to help you, I am thinking, I'm just trying to get it clear, to get the possibilities clear.'

'I'm going to tell Jack he's got to leave her, he's got to send her away, he's got to divorce her and marry me.'

'Otherwise you'll leave him.'

'No! I can't leave him, I'm bound to him, I'm made of him, I am him! I'm just going to . . . force him to . . . do that.'

Ludens thought, poor Franca. And poor Alison. And poor Jack. Though so racked by his own woes he saw the whole thing, the whole web of torture. He said in a reasonable tone, 'Isn't it possible that Franca may, perhaps not at once, go away of her own accord?'

'I used to think that, I used to hope it – but now I see she *won't*, she'll hang on like a limpet, she'll have to be torn off, she'll have to be kicked off. He's so charming with her, he's so considerate, he's so loving, you can see her absolutely *cleaving* to him. She'll *never* go, unless she's *slaughtered*.'

Ludens sighed. He looked down at the beach of pebbles, the little accidental stones of which he had picked up one. He thought, and it's still in my pocket, and he put his hand in and touched it. Oh the awful randomness of human life, the suffering, the remorse, the cruelty, the inescapable cruelty. He said, 'Look, Alison, have you considered this. You are very young. It's possible to stop being in love, to fall out of love, people do it, people who have thought it impossible have found that they can do it. Indeed this is happening all the time. You feel this to be inevitable, this carnage, this slaughter as you describe it. But suppose you just gritted your teeth and *left Jack*, cleared off and found another man, a younger man without a wife, without a woman, whom you could love and be loved by happily in freedom without all this bloodshed.'

Alison stared at him, thrusting back from her brow the silky drift of her red hair which had by now grown longer, longer the way Jack liked it. She stared at him with her pale blue eyes, her young sincere eyes, faintly red-rimmed by recent weeping. She murmured, 'Ludens, I can't, I'm his slave.'

Ludens considered saying, but did not say: if you make Jack divorce Franca, or if you drive Franca away by persecuting her, that too will poison your relation with Jack. Instead he said, 'Couldn't you just wait? Time may solve the problem somehow. I've already suggested one possibility. But – oh Alison, can't you just endure it, do what Jack wants, since you love him so much?'

'I can't bear it. Just now in these last days, I can see that he imagines it's all right at last, he thinks he's got us both *exactly where he wants us*. He *does* love her, he *does* need her, she's his mother! And she's convinced of it now, that he really absolutely loves her. I think she doubted it earlier, she might have run away then, but not now – he's charmed her, he's hypnotised her, he's turned her into an animal – a sweet little animal – which I've got to kill.'

'He doesn't know yet –?'

'How I feel? No. I'm deceiving him, I'm deceiving them both, you'd be amazed how well I can do it! I'm all smiling and loving, I kiss Franca and then I smile at Jack, and he smiles at me, and he smiles at her, and she's all smiles too, and he *approves*, it's horrible, it's obscene, I'm degrading myself, it's got to stop.'

'You're just going back to London?'

'Yes, thank God. I couldn't do anything in France, or here. When we get back there, into that *nightmare* house, I shall be able to act. Do you understand, Ludens, do you *understand*? I want you to understand, I want *you* to understand, when it happens.'

'I understand,' he said.

'Thank you. I don't mean forgive me or absolve me or anything like that. Perhaps what I'm going to do is unforgivable. Or rather – Jack will have to forgive it – and he *will* forgive it, and that forgiveness will be the steely centre of our marriage bond. Now I must bathe my eyes.'

She left him and went to the edge of the water, standing upon the little stones and bending to dip her handkerchief in the quick glittering stream, and dabbing her eyes repeatedly. She squeezed the handkerchief, then lifted the skirt of her blue dress and patted her face dry with the hem of it. Ludens watching thought, that's the dress she was wearing that day beside the lake – Alison returning to him, had put on her dark glasses.

'What do you want me to do now, Alison? I think they were expecting me. Shall I go away or what?'

'No, no, you must act in the play too. Please come with me, support me. It helps me to know that you know. I must pretend – it hurts so – I must keep it up until we get to London.'

Ludens went with her back to the inn and round into the garden, which was flanked on one side by the Fern reappearing beyond pollarded willow trees. Here, at a table, with a snow-white cloth, Franca presided over a silver teapot, cups of thinnest china, slim limp damp cucumber sandwiches and tomato sandwiches and lettuce-and-marmite sandwiches, and home-made curranty scones, butter, jam, cream and lemon sponge-cakes. Jack was seated beside her, huge, his whitest of white shirts unbuttoned, the sleeves rolled up, his strong brown pleasantly hairy forearm laid along the back of Franca's chair. Franca in neatest lightest white-trimmed brown cotton, her dark hair tucked into a long sleek glossy bun, had her Ingres look. She looked prim and gracious and in charge. The approaching pair were greeted with cries of welcome. Jack kissed Alison and embraced Ludens, Ludens kissed Franca. Chattering, they sat down to tea.

Watching them from a window of the inn were Mr and Mrs Toller.

'You know,' said Toller, 'he's pulled it off, he's got away with it! He's got them both. They're all happy. Just look at them! The women love it, they *love* it.'

'I doubt that,' replied his tough knowing little wife. 'And don't let it put any ideas into *your* head, Geoffrey Toller!'

'My dear love, how could I want anyone but you!'

All the same, he thought, as he lingered at the window, if it were possible, it would be very nice indeed. And why stop at two?

'Hello, donkey,' said Irina to Ludens when he returned to Benbow. 'Where have you been, donkey?'

'Saying goodbye to Jack and the girls.'

'Oh them. Look, I've been picking daisies in the wood just here – aren't they pretty?'

'We're not supposed to pick the flowers.'

'Oh, and who says so?'

'Marzillian.'

'Well, he isn't God.'

'Isn't he?'

'Have an apricot. One of the worshippers brought them, they're delicious. What's in that parcel?'

'A shirt.'

'Let me look.' She seized the parcel from him and opened it. 'It's not a shirt! What a lovely velvet bag, and this pretty thing inside! Look, it's rather nice, what charming stripes and tassels. Shall we hang it on the wall?'

The change which Ludens was expecting, desiring and dreading began to show itself soon after the events just recounted. It should be mentioned that the prayer shawl, in appearance a small blue and white striped blanket, with pendent tassels, *was* hung up in the study room by Irina, who of course did not know what it was. Ludens, thereby breaking faith with Daniel Most, said nothing about it to Marcus who, not particularly aware of his surroundings, ignored it. Ludens, who had many other anxieties, had decided to surrender the object into the hands of fate, here appearing in the person of Irina. If Irina had not seized it he would have given it to Marcus. As it was, he decided to 'give it up'. At least it was visible, not hidden in a drawer, and if it was able thence to exert some magic power, that was its affair. In any case other more urgent problems were now arising.

In retrospect, it seemed surprising how much Marcus's way of life, in what Ludens thought of as the first phase of his mission, was taken for granted by all. Marcus's 'showings' occurred with a sober regularity, as if they were daily tasks of a priestly kind like the saying of a liturgy. The devotees, now much reduced in number, contained many regulars, but new pilgrims, and inquisitive outsiders still turned up. Offerings of stones and flowers continued to appear at Benbow and at the Axle Stone. The piles of stones, now mounting up in the woodland as they were removed to make room for more, were beginning to pose a problem. A gardener, directed by Camilla to take some to the grotto, had announced there was no more room there. Ludens suspected that the security men had told the workmen who were renewing the fences to use the stones to fill in holes round the concrete posts, and probably a few barrow-loads disappeared in this way. Irina, who did not share

Maisie Tether's respect for votive offerings, regularly selected the prettier ones and brought them into the house. Camilla, Anita, Sandra and Thelma also took their pick. Ludens, who had superstitious scruples about the stones, took one and gave it to Mrs Toller. He found himself curiously unwilling, faced with a pile of individually interesting stones, to decide to pick up one rather than another. He did succeed in selecting one to give to Gildas but felt it somehow improper to take one for himself. After all, he already had a stone given to him by Fanny, and this stone might resent the appearance of another one. When he had a vivid image of the two stones fighting in his pocket Ludens decided to close down this line of thought unless he wished to become one of Marzillian's patients.

Patrick continued in his position of acolyte and poet in residence, busying himself with self-appointed tasks, proclaiming himself Marcus's valet, washing and ironing the ceremonial 'shirts' and shaving his master daily. He also helped Irina in the kitchen, being especially fond of washing up, and flirted with the cleaner Rosie whom Irina had by now learnt to tolerate. His situation had moreover lately been further enriched by the arrival of Suzanne Moxon at the White Lion. She now attended regularly at the 'showings' and was seen about with Patrick. It appeared that she had originally provided the 'shirts', had perhaps even made them, according to Pat's instructions, and he had been to fetch them from London and had stayed the night. Where Camilla now stood was unclear; but Ludens and Irina agreed that Camilla's interest in Patrick had probably been more professional than romantic and that she had been using him as an 'eye' kept on Marcus. Ludens was now less irked by Pat and less worried about his status, and was even able to contemplate the Irishman's extraordinary handsomeness without either jealousy or envy, though he could have done without the poetry readings to which Marcus and Irina listened politely, as Alison had been used to do before her departure. On one occasion Ludens was even sharply chided by Marcus for suggesting to Patrick that they had all had enough. Ludens certainly thought often and anxiously about his friends in London. He had had no news and expected none. Alison might well have changed her mind. If she had not, some terribly agonising bloody scene must now be going on at the house in Chelsea upon which none of the victims was likely yet to report. He thought a lot about Franca. Poor good dear quiet innocent Franca, so little worthy to be the target of murderous hate. He was sorely missing and needing Gildas and decided to go round to his lodgings and demand a restitution of his rights. However, when with this in view he presented himself at the door, the landlady said that Mr Herne had returned to London. He wrote Gildas a peevish indignant letter which he later regretted, and to which he had had no reply.

After Marcus had given up philosophy for holiness Ludens had at first not known what to do with himself. This was the period when he would be seen moping about and leaning against trees. Before long however, deprived of his struggle with Marcus's ideas, he began to feel a natural impulse to return to his own. He had, when at first (how long ago it seemed, though in reality it was a matter of weeks) he had driven his master and his dear girl to the 'country cottage', brought with him several books including a large new work on quattrocento Italy by an Italian scholar called Matteo Fabriani, whom Ludens admired and had met. He had recently taken to reading and annotating this book in his room at the Black Lion (he had moved into the smaller cheaper room with no view of the river). He had learnt by experience that he had better not 'hang around' too much at Benbow, receiving imagined slights by which he was made unhappy. There were times when his presence irritated Irina or when he could not get near Marcus. He came now in the early morning, again at lunchtime (not a great festival at Benbow) and then for the long evenings, often now without Pat. Mr Talgarth too came less; meeting Ludens on the drive he explained that he was now 'in eclipse' but would see them again when he felt better.

On one such evening Ludens and Irina were sitting outside upon the seat made of much-weathered blanched teak to which Irina had led Marcus, 'as if he were an old man', on his first arrival at Benbow. Pat and Camilla had 'liberated' two smart cast-iron chairs from the garden of Rodney, but Ludens and Irina preferred the old seat. Rodney, whence, Irina discovered, an ailing Mr Rampton had been hastily removed just before their arrival at Bellmain was, as promised, still empty. Irina speculated that he had died from some terrible infectious disease. 'As things are here, we shall never know.' Ludens had murmured, 'Better not to know.' Watching her now he was thinking, as he often did, about that one previous, clearly disastrous, experience of sex which had left her so wounded. Would she ever tell him? About that, at present, it was probably also 'better not to know'. He did not touch her but enjoyed the particular intimate pain of the tension between them. The sun was behind the trees and new minty herby smells were coming from the woods.

Irina, who had been shifting about restlessly, leaning down to pluck tufts of grass, said suddenly, 'I'd like a dog.'

'We shall have a dog.' The idea of the dog they would have came to him as a healing dart sent from the future. Ludens loved dogs. He was considering how to pursue this promising subject when she spoke again.

'You know, I think Dad is breaking up.'

'What do you mean?'

'He's upset, haven't you noticed? He didn't want to tell you. You haven't heard anything in the village?'

'No.' Ludens had indeed noticed a change in Marcus's mood but, without perceiving any reason for it, had been waiting to see what it meant. What had happened was, as Irina explained, this. Mr Westerman, the parson, had sent to Marcus for 'counselling' the neurotic spinster lady aforementioned (her name was Miss Tillow): a token of confidence which had reassured many of the local people who regarded Marcus as 'barmy'. However Mr Westerman, and evidently Marcus, had reckoned without the creative imagination of the lady's neurosis. Soon after her meeting with Marcus (though not at once) she began to say that Marcus had made sexual advances to her. Of course it was generally agreed, at any rate declared, that this was obviously untrue; but a few genuine doubters remained, and not a few malicious tongues. A youth who had read about Tantric Buddhism in a magazine reported that gurus often went to bed with their disciples of either sex. The word 'Tantric' was then a reminder of Marcus's mysterious paintings, photos of which had appeared in the London papers. Marcus, to whom Patrick indiscreetly reported some of this, was extremely distressed and had (this was now two days ago) cancelled his afternoon meetings with individuals, much to the disappointment and even annoyance of those who were hoping to be 'counselled', or perhaps 'cured'. Marcus had in fact seen comparatively few people at these *tête-à-têtes* which were kept very brief. Ludens had listened in to one or two of the early ones and been impressed by how little Marcus said, and how simple and sensible and even obvious was what he did say. Those who later proclaimed themselves edified or healed had evidently benefited from the sage's presence, perhaps his gaze or his touch, rather than from any admonitions or verbal teaching. Ludens did not know whether Marcus touched his afternoon clients, but Irina had seen him touch the crippled girl, and Ludens had seen him touch Fanny Amherst. Of course, he thought, they'll all want to touch him, they won't be able to stop themselves, and he, feeling that force, whatever it is, within him, will want to touch them! He's so naive and innocent, no wonder he's in trouble, after all people misunderstood Jesus too! According to Irina, who had learnt it from Pat, Marcus's sudden cancellation of his afternoon 'service' was said (by some) to be a case of wounded vanity. The blow to Marcus's *confidence* had clearly been a grave one. Of course his whole extraordinary mission rested upon confidence, his confidence, their confidence, in his power, his truthfulness, his goodness. So, could Marcus now simply be losing his nerve? It appeared that he had not actually asked Irina to conceal this set-back from Ludens, but she had intuited that he did not want Ludens to know, and she would have said nothing, only Marcus continued to be very upset and now, this afternoon, had said that he ought to cancel his morning sessions also.

'Just after he said that,' said Irina, 'he asked where you were, because he wanted to talk to you. He said you were avoiding him.'

'Good God!' said Ludens, now extremely disturbed. 'Why didn't you fetch me?'

'I said I would, then Pat arrived to walk him to the swimming-pool, and he said to leave it, and he'd see you this evening anyway. He seemed to cheer up and went off with Pat. Since then he's been as usual, he was perfectly O K as you saw at supper, he can't be very anxious to talk to you, or he'd have done it now. I just felt I should tell you. Really I don't know what he'll do next.'

Ludens had leapt up. 'I'll go and ask him.'

'Better not, he's settled down, you'll just excite him. He needs more ordinary company. Mr Talgarth is having one of his things, and the Seekers have gone to Stonehenge.'

'*Have* they? I thought I hadn't seen them.'

'Only for a few days, they felt Stonehenge might be hurt if they didn't visit it, him, so they've gone to pay homage, but they're coming back to arrange midsummer here, they're being allowed to have their ceremony at the Axle Stone, and other people can come too. Maybe Dad will last out as long as that.'

'But Irina, we mustn't let Marcus be upset by stupid rumours and lies, he must go on, he must simply ignore them, the whole thing will blow over, I can't *bear* him being put down by this nonsense —'

'Why not? This holy man act has to come to an end. Better let him end it quickly in his own way.'

'Oh Irina, how dreadful!'

'What's dreadful? Do sit down and stop looking so intense. He's not being disgraced or anything. Everyone knows that woman is lying or off her head. You were always against this cult business. Perhaps when it's over he'll become more normal. He hasn't made his great philosophical discovery, and now he's found out he isn't God. So what? He had to do it all himself, not like other people who take it for granted they're not superman. He had to try it all and fail it all. He's got enough mind left to accept that. He's had a good run.'

'Don't talk like that. We must tell Marzillian.'

'I'm always telling Marzillian, except I haven't seen him just lately, I told Camilla. Marzillian always knows everything anyway. There's some crisis up at the house. Oddly enough we aren't the only daft people around here.'

'So Marzillian put all that stuff into your head?'

'What stuff for heaven's sake, my dear animal?'

'About his trying and failing and so on, and then becoming normal.'

'Well, it's just obvious, isn't it? He's letting Dad *run*, I mean like a fish on a line. He can't treat him yet, it's too dangerous. He's letting him work out his own escape route.'

'What do you mean "treat" him?'

'Give him drugs. I suppose he isn't on drugs, we'd know.'

'And you mean he will be later.'

'It might help, mightn't it? At the moment he's manic, he has to enact his own mythical destiny. Then he'll calm down.'

'Oh – Irina –!'

'Don't be so tragic! I've got to bear all this too, I've got to understand it! A stupid ordinary doctor would just give Dad a few injections and make him into a cabbage. Marzillian sees that Dad can do it all himself. In the end he'll *think* his way through, he's still got lots of mind left, he'll think himself out of it all. Perhaps I'm not putting it very well – but isn't this how *you* see it?'

Ludens was silent. He sat down and held his head in his hands. No, this was not how he saw it. But how did he see it? Was he disappointed that Marcus was losing confidence in his magic powers? He was appalled at Irina's picture of a normal Marcus settling down to ordinary life on tranquillisers. He said, his voice trembled: 'I'm sorry he thought I was avoiding him. I imagined he preferred having Pat around just now, I didn't want to press my company on him. I *want* to be with him, I want to be with him all the time.'

'Well, we'll get rid of Pat and you can be with him again, only for God's sake don't try to get him back onto that ghastly philosophy game. Anyway, we haven't got through the miraculous healer lark yet, it may go on for ages.'

'You don't think he has any special unusual powers?'

'Of course not! And neither do you! I never saw *you* kneeling on the lawn with Gildas and Father O'Harte.'

'You don't think I should speak to him now?'

'NO, please not. You might annoy him, you're so bothered yourself. I want a peaceful night. Ludens, darling silly beast, I'm *tired out* with *acting* all this business. Let's leave it now, I'm too tired, you're tired too, it's all such a damn strain. Just say goodnight in the usual way, I'm sure he won't ask you to stay. Then turn up tomorrow as usual, just be around a bit more, *watch* him.'

'I *do* watch him!'

Ludens went, with Irina, to say goodnight to Marcus. He hoped that Marcus would ask him to stay and talk, but he did not.

Ludens, deep in slumber, was having a dream. He dreamt he was up on some high mountainside, the air was darkening, perhaps twilight, perhaps a gathering storm. He was walking with difficulty up a steep path covered with small sharp stones upon which he often slipped, falling forward and jarring his hand upon the unstable surface. On either side of the path grey jagged very hard rocks rose up, and he was aware of a vast landscape of such rocks stretching away into mist or darkness. Ahead of him, above him upon the steep path, an animal of some kind was walking, also slowly and with difficulty. Ludens could not make out what kind of animal it was – it was dark and shaggy, about the size of a small pony. He thought, is it a llama? He felt anxious about the animal in case it should get lost, or fall, or be without food. He wanted to catch it up, but his feet kept slipping upon the river of stones. Then he saw a light further on ahead, as of a lantern illuminating a large flat ledge and the mouth of a cave. He was afraid, but also very eager to reach the ledge. He hurried, now using his hands to balance himself upon the steep path, trying to scramble up the slope on all fours. As he came near to the ledge he saw that a man was there, a bearded man dressed in a long whitish robe and looking, as Ludens saw him in the dream, like a figure out of the Old Testament. The dark shaggy animal had arrived upon the ledge, and as Ludens, still below, watched and scrambled he saw with horror that the bearded man was covering the animal with a cloth and leading it into the cave. Ludens thought, *He is going to kill it!*

'Dr Ludens, Dr Ludens, wake up!'

Toller was in the room, pulling back the curtains to reveal the daylight outside.

Ludens sat up. 'What is it?'

'I'm so sorry to wake you, but Miss Amherst is downstairs and wants to see you urgently.'

Ludens leapt out of bed. The dread enactment of the dream had turned into a waking horror. He looked at his watch which said just after six o'clock. He dragged on trousers, desperately buttoned a shirt and ran down the stairs barefoot.

Fanny was standing in the hall dressed in her white uniform. When she saw him she reached out a hand holding a letter. 'Please, it's for you, it's from Miss Vallar, she said I must give it to you at once, it's very urgent. Now I must run or I'll be awfully late, I'm sorry I must run –'

'Fanny –'

She was already gone, running fleetly out of the open door. Sick with alarm he tore open the letter. Its message was simple. *Please come at once.*

Ludens rushed back upstairs, completed his dressing and left the inn, running as fast as he could over the bridge and along the lane. The gates of Bellmain stood open. Panting and having to slow down he went on with long strides taking the short cut through the wood. The morning was still faintly misty, the trees strange presences, the grass soaked with dew. He dreaded utterly what he would find.

When he reached Benbow he saw the glass doors open and Irina standing on the verandah. When she saw him she ran down the steps and into his arms. He held her violently, hugging her, his eyes closed.

'What's happened?'

She detached herself. 'Well, nothing much has *happened*.'

'Marcus is all right?'

'Yes, but – Perhaps I shouldn't have sent you the letter. I was running out to find someone to take it, I didn't like to leave Dad alone, then I met Fanny just coming in to work. I've been up all night, he's been in such a state, he's never been like this before, moaning and saying he's unworthy, he's a sinner, a blasphemer, a broken vessel, he used those words, and so on and so on. He wanted to run out in the middle of the night to find something or do something! I kept trying to get him to go to bed but he wouldn't until about four o'clock and we were both utterly exhausted and he fell asleep then lying on his bed and I sat on a chair outside his door because I was afraid he'd run out and I think I did sleep a bit. He was still asleep when I wrote you the letter and went out and gave it to Fanny. Then when I came back he was awake he'd even got up and put a kettle on the stove! He said he was so sorry and he felt better now, and I made some tea, and now he's sitting in the little room with his tea.'

Ludens kept her close in his arms. She was weeping now, sobbing. He led her to the wooden seat and they sat down clutching each other.

'I'm glad you sent for me – there now, there now – I'll look after him, I'll look after you.' Ludens felt such an agony of love for them both, he gasped with it, he moaned with it, covering her with his embrace.

Gradually they let go of each other. Irina mopped her face with the sleeve of her dress. Ludens's face was wet, perhaps with her tears, perhaps with his. 'I'll go in to him.'

'Yes, do. I'll stay out here and calm down. Stay with us, won't you.'

'Of course.' He went in, leaving her sitting on the seat, her skirt spread out and her hands folded, amid the raised arms of the peaceful trees and the interwoven song of the birds and the summer light clearing the mist away.

Marcus was sitting in the study with his cup of tea, a spoon inside the cup, his elbows on the table, his forearms outstretched. He looked calm and turned his head gravely toward Ludens.

Ludens ran to him, sat down on the chair that was next to him, and seizing both his hands began kissing them. Marcus withdrew his hands and thrust Ludens away, but gently. 'Come now, Alfred, come now.'

'I'm so sorry –'

'I'm sorry. I'm afraid I upset Irina and she sent for you. Thank you for coming.'

'But, dear Marcus, what is it, what was it that was grieving you so in the night? Please tell me, *please*.'

'I think I told you – or did I just tell Irina – I think I must stop what I've been doing, seeing people and all that. It seemed to be the thing to do, as if I had to do it.'

'It was, it is, the thing to do –'

'You don't really think so, I know you don't. It seems strange now that I could do such things, like being possessed by a spirit.'

'A good spirit. I think you should go on. You don't harm people, you do them good. Don't change suddenly, don't do anything suddenly, we'll think it out.'

'Yes, we – I – must *think*. I *can* think it out, there's a way through, like a narrow way, a narrow narrow way, so thin, like a – like a tightrope, like a fine taut wire over, over an abyss –'

377

'Yes, yes, a path, a way through, we'll find it, won't we, I'll go with you, you and I and Irina –'

'In the night – I was overwhelmed – it was as if some evil being came to me and overthrew everything and accused me of everything and made me see myself as something terrible, something loathsome, a monster. And yet it is true, I am a monster, the being that came cannot have been evil, it was a good being, but cruel.'

'You are not evil, Marcus, you are not a monster, come back to reality, come back to ordinary *sense*. You're not perfect, nobody is, but you're a good man, you harm no one – your feeling that you could help people, even heal people was a good truthful feeling – now perhaps you feel that that time is coming to an end, that may be right too, but you mustn't lose it, the hope, the faith, the sense of direction, the sense of a mission – I feel sure about this though I don't know what it is, what it will be –'

'You don't still want me to write that book?'

'No, yes, it *doesn't matter*. I want you to be at peace and to be yourself. I want you to be happy. Marcus, you're *young*, you're just beginning to find out, you can *think*, you spoke just now about thinking – you're tired now, you've tired yourself out trying to do everything – you need to rest, reflect quietly, slowly, and rest – then you'll see later on what to do, where to go – you said there was a path, a way, you'll find that way, perhaps you can't see it at present – now you need a time of blankness and silence and attention and patient waiting in which you'll learn what you must do next. Be guided by me, dear Marcus – I see now and I think I understand, the spirit that visited you was a wise spirit – all this time you've been pushing at things, at great things, at the deepest problems of mankind – like a – like a bull, and battering yourself at the barriers of language and thought, at the very edge at the perimeter of human knowledge. Of course you're exhausted, of course you feel despair – rest now, sit still, wait. You haven't wasted it, all that time, all the things you've tried to find out – they're in your mind all those things, they are a part of your wisdom – perhaps you can't formulate anything now, you can't find a synthesis – perhaps there is no synthesis – but all that you know, all that you've *experienced*, is with you, it's in store, and you'll understand later, there'll be an intuition, that intuition that you told me about – you'll see – you know how these things come, after you've tried for a long time and waited for a long time, and after you've rested and been silent. Now is the time when you must rest. Do you see what I mean, Marcus, do you see what I *mean*?'

Marcus, who had been listening attentively, nodded his head. 'Yes, yes – I see – but – yes. I see. Where is Irina?'

'Sitting in the garden and breathing the lovely warm air and becoming calm. Listen to the birds singing.'

'Yes, I hear them. Do you know what that is?' He pointed to the striped tasselled prayer shawl which Irina had pinned up on the wall.

Ludens, taken aback, shook his head.

'It's a prayer shawl. I remember my grandfather had one. My mother's father, that is.'

Ludens was silent. Marcus went on. 'I understand you, at least I see what you're getting at. And I am very grateful to you for thinking about me so much, so exceptionally much, and taking so much trouble. I know Irina is grateful too. But I am not exactly – where you think I am. No human being can see another's mind. It is a matter of experience. I seem to myself to be moving slowly, not in haste. I felt lately that I was being led – now I feel I am still somehow being *taught*. Only now – there are things which I somehow abandoned – like abandoning children, like abandoning sheep – in the wilderness – and I must find these things again. I must find my own way to the pit, to the dark place – and not, when I know so little, seem to live like a god.'

'You think what you've been doing lately, seeing people like you have and letting them come, was living like a god?'

'Yes, what else. I saw them kneeling. Did you not see them kneeling?'

'Yes. But, Marcus, listen. People kneel in a holy place, confronted with a mystery, confronted with they know not what. It was not *you*, Marcus Vallar, they were kneeling to. They knelt to something which was revealed to them, something which you enabled them to see, to feel the presence of –'

Marcus seemed interested in these words. He said, 'As a spectator, you speak reasonably. But I, in myself, must judge. I had no pure experience, I was no clean vessel, I enjoyed it. I enjoyed power, I felt a force coming out of myself to them which made them tremble, which made them kneel. I am not worthy to be such a medium. And you, Ludens, have been thoroughly unhappy about the whole thing, as I know. You have even punished me with your absence!'

'Marcus –! Listen. Perhaps no man is worthy – yet you might be humble enough to be the vehicle of a power which is purer than you are! Yes, I have felt unhappy about this business – then I came somehow to believe in it too just because I believe in *you*. I think you can give people something real, some spiritual thing, some peace – but I think also that your feeling that it should now come to an end is right, and it is as if you are being led and being taught. As for my absence, I felt I ought to withdraw a little and not trouble you, I thought you would summon me back again, and you have done so. I am sorry if I seem to preach to you and exhort you – I think I am simply offering you your own thoughts.'

Marcus smiled at this. He reached out and touched Ludens's hand which was lying palm upward on the table in a gesture of supplication. 'Not quite. But you are eloquent. You spoke of happiness, and of giving peace and forgiveness to people, which now seems to me blasphemous. And I have indeed felt a joy, a kind of rapture, but that was just what made me forget.'

'Forget what?'

'The suffering.'

'Oh Marcus, for heaven's sake, the world is full of suffering, what you were doing was alleviating a little bit of it, what else can anyone do. I understand what you say about blasphemy. But don't make a drama of it all. Sometimes we forget the suffering of other people, sometimes we remember it, sometimes we do something about it. You speak as if one really did have to become God!'

Marcus looked thoughtfully at Ludens, staring at him. 'You may be right after all about telling me my thoughts. Only it's as if you turned them round to show another face. Never mind. I have to return to it, to *that*.'

'Marcus, I shall scream! Everyone suffers, not just the Jews, to think *we* have a special mission to the world is just megalomania. Of course one stays with *that* – it is *exceptional* – but there are a lot of different conclusions which are all reasonable ones.'

'I mean, I must not become confused, it is a privilege. I mean, what happened there, you know, what happened to them, to *think* about it. All right everyone suffers. But sometimes a thought, an *experience*, can rise right up, as if it were breaking the surface, breaking the waves like a fish leaping into the air, into another dimension. And not just *them* but the wicked people too, they must be carried up, inside a thought, in an experienced shaft of being, in an attempted understanding –'

'You say attempted. Yes, ultimately one cannot understand, it's no use asking why –'

'You know the famous poem about the rose, that it is without "why", *ohne warum*. I read in a book that someone *there*, in one of the camps, asked a guard "why?" and the guard answered "*Hier ist kein warum*", here there is no why. This – as it were it makes a circle – it is one of those things –'

'Devices? Intuitions?'

'The rose is without why, it has no foundation, no justification, no cause, it just exists, its simple being is what it truly is, there can be no further questions. The camp, too, in its own terms, is without why, it has put itself beyond the reach of justifications or causes, it cannot be questioned, it is outside rational human discourse. It cannot be described, scarcely thought about. One may say too that a description of the rose means nothing unless, as in poetry, it can *be* the rose.'

'I don't follow, how does this connect –?'

'When words, even thoughts, fail, one might attempt, as it were an identification, something one might die of –'

The door opened suddenly and Patrick entered. He had come in by the side way, not across the lawn, and now stopped, surprised to find Ludens there, as it was still before his usual time of arrival.

Ludens said, 'Pat dear, could you go away for a bit, I want to talk with Marcus.'

Marcus said to Patrick, 'Don't go, Alfred and I have finished our talk. Let's go to the kitchen and make some more tea.'

'Yes,' said Ludens, 'let's do that.'

Marcus and Ludens followed Patrick into the kitchen. Patrick filled the kettle and put it on the gas-stove. Irina, who had evidently been in the sitting room, came in too. Ludens wondered if she had been listening at the door. He felt suddenly exhausted as if he had been shouting for hours. His whole body felt pain. What terrible things Marcus had just said. Ludens could not decide whether they were deep things or mad things. He wanted to go away but could not leave Marcus now. He exchanged glances with Irina. She looked exhausted too.

Marcus sat down at the kitchen table, the others stood. He addressed Patrick. 'Pat, I am going to tell the people this morning that I will do no more of it, no more of that standing and looking at them, that time is over. I shall tell them so.'

Patrick took it well, he said, 'That shall be as you will, sir.'

'Perhaps it would be better if you warned those other people, the religious people, the young ones –'

'You mean Colin Bassett and the others?' said Ludens. 'I think they're away.'

'They got back last night,' said Patrick. 'I'll tell them.'

'I want everyone to know, so that it can be over. I'll go out this morning as usual at eleven and announce it to anyone who's there, I'll just tell them it's over.'

'They'll be sad,' said Patrick. 'But so be it, sir.' He looked at Ludens.

Ludens, anxious not to seem to return any significant signal, looked down. Irina said, 'I think Dad is right. It has been very tiring for him.'

The time between then and eleven seemed interminable. Marcus said he would lie down and rest, and retired to his bedroom. Patrick went to find Colin, who was lodging at the Hedgehog, failed to find him, but found Andy and Miriam who were living in the motor caravan which was parked on an old gipsy site beyond the church. Camilla arrived, was told what was going on, and went away again. Irina did a lot of washing dishes and washing clothes and dusting and cleaning and tidying. Ludens, unable to return to the Black Lion, went into the garden and sat on the seat, then walked about under the trees where he fell over a heap of stones. He hid from Patrick who came back to the house. He returned to the house himself as a lot of people were starting to arrive. Commenting on the crowd, which was larger than usual, Irina remarked that it had been foolish to tell the Seekers, who had evidently sent the news quickly around, and now a lot of nasty tiresome people had turned up simply to see the 'final performance'. Ludens said something soothing but privately agreed with her. Meanwhile the spectators were filling the drive opposite the house, standing among the trees opposite and at the side, and spilling over onto the lawn, trampling on the offerings, and coming a little nearer than usual to the house. No one was kneeling. Ludens had wondered if Marzillian, who undoubtedly knew, would come discreetly to watch. There was no sign of him, but at the last moment Dr Bland arrived and stood obscurely on the fringe of the gathering. Ludens thought of running out to him, but it was by now somehow impossible to do so. Camilla and Thelma were visible. The Seekers were in evidence, having spread themselves out here and there among the people. The crowd, murmuring a little at first, fell silent as eleven o'clock approached.

At eleven Marcus issued from his room. He was not wearing the long white mantle which Patrick had procured for him. He was dressed rather shabbily in his baggy brown cotton trousers and brown shirt. He looked like a workman or an off-duty soldier. Pat, who had automatically donned his white garment, had hastily taken it off again. Marcus marched quickly to the doors, threw them open and advanced onto the verandah. Patrick followed and stood behind him as usual. There was a silence which lasted so long that Ludens began to believe that Marcus had decided not to end his 'showings' but to continue as usual.

At last Marcus spoke, 'I have to tell you – I have to tell you – that these meetings are now at an end. It has been a strange time – for me – and I don't want to explain – I can't explain – what I think was happening – in that time.'

Ludens, standing with Irina well back behind the glass doors which he had carefully closed after Marcus and Pat, shut his eyes and held his brow. Marcus was speaking helplessly, lamely.

After a pause Marcus began again. 'I shall not see you in this way any more. Nor shall I see you – in the other way – as when I had people to – to see me for advice – or just to tell me things –'

Someone at the back of the crowd shouted, 'Speak up, please, we can't hear.'

Raising his voice a little Marcus went on, 'I am sorry, and feel I must ask – your pardon. I was encouraged to think – I mean I thought – that I had a message – a mission – to be fulfilled in that way – in what I have been doing among you. I now realise – that the time is not yet. I thought that I could – somehow – establish holiness – make a place that was holy – even heal people – bring peace to the minds of – But I was wrong, I was not worthy, I am not worthy – what I was attempting – has now come to an end.'

A voice, perhaps the same voice, said, 'So you never raised a man from the dead.'

'No, I never raised a man from the dead.'

The crowd had begun to move restlessly, some in evident embarrassment bowing their heads, just wishing it could end, others, amused and excited, yearning for more. The presence of the 'rough element' was also making itself felt. Irina said to Ludens, 'I think we should stop him.'

Someone else in the crowd, in answer to Marcus's admission, said audibly, 'So he lied,' and someone repeated, 'He lied.'

Marcus suddenly advanced, moving down the steps, not yet onto the lawn. He cried out, 'No, I did not lie. I helped to cure a man. This man here!' Still facing his accusers he pointed back at Pat. 'I never said I raised anyone from the dead!'

'But you let other people say it!' another voice piped up.

The crowd was now visibly disturbed and divided. Some people were talking raucously and pushing their way to the front, others saying 'Stop!' 'Be quiet!', or 'Don't speak to him like that!'

Patrick had moved down onto the steps next to Marcus and was saying something to him. Ludens opened the doors. Marcus, pushing Patrick away, cried in a now ringing voice, 'I am unworthy, I have evil thoughts, I live with horrors, you must pardon me, you must forgive me, you must pray for me!'

Above the increasing hubbub in the crowd a woman's voice was raised. 'You deceived us, you pretended to be good but you weren't!'

Marcus, who had been unconsciously undoing the buttons of his shirt, perhaps in an instinctive gesture of baring his breast, called out, now in a frenzy, 'I am sorry, I wanted to help you all, I wanted to save you all – only this was wrong – what I've been doing – it was the wrong way –'

There were now derisive catcalls from the drive and someone shouted 'Sex maniac!' which raised a sort of laugh, and then, 'He has the girls in the back room,' 'Look out, he's undressing!' Then, 'What about Miss Tillow?', and even louder, 'What about *Fanny*?' 'What goes on at the Axle Stone?' 'Ask Fanny.' Patrick was now visibly restraining Marcus who was shouting something inaudible. Ludens ran out and grasping at Marcus got hold of his flying shirt. Then someone threw a stone. A shout, half of malicious triumph, half of shocked indignation, went up from the crowd where a number of scuffles had already broken out between the 'rough elements' and the burlier Seekers. The stone hit Patrick on the shoulder. The offerings of the devotees, laid out in rows at the end of the lawn, provided a ready arsenal. More stones followed. One struck Marcus on the hand as Ludens and Patrick pulled him back into the house. As Ludens got his last glimpse of the scene outside, Bellmain security men were arriving on the scene. He locked the doors and pulled the curtains, then ran to lock the back door, while the other two persuaded Marcus to sit down on the sofa.

One thing which amazed Ludens in retrospect was the calmness displayed by Marcus immediately after the drama. At one moment, with his shirt half off, he was shouting at a hostile crowd, the next moment he was sitting upright, buttoning up his shirt and tucking it into his trousers, smiling faintly, and telling his distraught entourage that he was perfectly all right, they were not to worry or make a fuss. He even seemed to be taking a certain satisfaction in what had happened. Ludens heard him say, 'Well, *that's* done it!' Possibly Marcus, having decided to abandon his mission, or at any rate *this* mission, was glad to have ended it in such a thorough way. The idea that in doing so he had surrendered his dignity, destroyed his prestige, and made a complete fool of himself did not seem to occur to him, or if it did, did not seem to trouble him. He asked Ludens to pull back the curtains, went to survey the scene outside, now totally deserted, counted the number of stones on the lawn, and said it was rather distinguished to be stoned. He enquired solicitously about Patrick's shoulder, and with rueful pride, displayed the bruise on his own hand, the right one, remarking that the Lord who had struck him on one hand, had now struck him on the other. He then explained (news to Ludens) that a congenital stiffness in his left hand had been exacerbated by an accident in California involving a feat with a rope. He expressed the hope that no one had been hurt in the scrimmage which had seemed to be occurring. He asked for more tea to be made and they all sat in the kitchen and drank cups of tea. Irina too behaved calmly, speaking quietly to her father, uttering no exclamations, shedding no tears. For a while they 'made conversation' about the happening as if to ease it into some sort of manageable ordinariness, speculating about who the stone-throwers were, how the security men had cleared the scene so quickly, and finding it funny that no one had come from 'the house' to find out if they were all all right! In fact Camilla did then arrive, and rapidly satisfying herself that they were, went away again. Patrick took the opportunity and followed her. He had been rather silent during the chat, mainly expressing the wish that he had been able to join in the fight. But Ludens knew, looking at him, how deeply wounded he was, and how, probably, he simply could not bear at present to be with Marcus or to hear a trivial discussion of the terrible thing that had occurred. Marcus asked Irina what was for lunch, and then at last said he would like to lie down for a while.

Ludens, of course simulating calm, was in a state of extreme agitation and shock. He felt that his whole relationship with Marcus had that day been violently jolted, even dislocated. Gazing at him, he marvelled at the man, at his composure, at his appearance, now suddenly that of a youth who has been in a 'scrap' and is exhilarated, proud to show himself without a ruffled feather. Ludens, remembering too his own words about a vessel of holiness and a vehicle of power, measured how far he had respected, even somehow believed in, Marcus's august state of being, and how upset and disappointed he was at this wanton act of public self-defilement. He understood not only Pat's grief, but also Pat's sense of shame. He was shocked by the stone-throwing, and even more shocked by the outcry at the end, which he hoped that Marcus had not heard. It was a bitter detail that even his own boorish encounter with Fanny had been garbled in. But what perhaps hurt him most was that unforgettable picture of Marcus, who had been such an impressive figure of silent dignity and magical power, absurdly shouting and waving his hands about, and having to be removed like a poor madman with his shirt-tails flying. Some curtain between himself and Marcus had this day been torn, partly, by way of prelude, in their conversation, later more dramatically in the dreadful crowd scene. Was it possible that, by so undoing himself, Marcus had damaged, perhaps forever, some precious tension of awe and fear which had always existed between him and Ludens? Ludens chided himself for this thought. Surely Marcus's courage and his truthfulness mattered more than his loss of face! What was to be wondered at was Marcus's extraordinary power of *metamorphosis* which he had possessed all his life. Ludens was touched, and also dismayed, by one or two glances which had come in his direction during the 'chat', looks which seemed to suggest that Marcus was wondering what Ludens had made of it all. As Ludens reflected on those matters he had in mind also the dark words which Marcus had uttered that morning about the 'experience' and the 'leaping fish' and the lethal tension of thought. Marcus had seemed at that moment confused, continually rephrasing what he was saying. Had he simply been rambling, or was he speaking about something, some definite new phase, which was to come next, and to be made possible, even energised and enabled, by the destruction of the lofty prophetic personage whom he had with an obscure inevitability become? Did Marcus really not care about the fall from that eminence, indeed was rejoicing in it? It could be that the 'fall', with its scattering of all solemnity, had actually removed the danger, the menace, the 'dark matter' of which Marzillian had twice spoken, creating a fresh simplicity, an interim, a new start of various thoughts. Alternatively, that clearing of the space might have a more sinister significance.

When Marcus had retired to rest and Ludens and Irina were left alone, she said at once, '*Now* are you convinced?'
   'Convinced of what?'
   'Oh, do stop living in a dream!'
   'You're not going out, are you?'
   'What do you mean? No.'
   'He mustn't be left alone.'
   'He's never left alone, there's always you or me or Pat or Camilla.'
   'I'm going to look for Dr Bland.'
   'Why him? He's nothing.'
   'I want a second opinion.'
   'You won't get one.'

'Irina, you do love me, don't you, you won't stop loving me?'

'Of course I do, of course I won't even though you're so silly and so bad, you're all I've got! All right, all right, off you go.'

Ludens walked to the house. On the way he saw Mr Talgarth who, about to emerge from Boscawen, stepped back and closed the door. Perhaps he had been there. In any case the news would be everywhere now. He mounted the steps into the hall, where he was immediately stopped by the uniformed girl who ran out of her alcove like a spider. 'Excuse me, Dr Ludens.' He thought, everyone has been warned against me!

The girl went on, 'I'm afraid Dr Marzillian is not available today, he has a conference of visiting specialists.'

'I don't want to see him,' said Ludens, 'I want to see Dr Bland.'

This seemed to surprise the doorkeeper, who of course said, 'I'm afraid Dr Bland is also engaged with our visitors.'

Ludens stood a moment or two in the dark hall breathing the hygienic smell which was mingling with that of the lilies which was wafting in through the open door. 'I see. Thank you. Please could you let Dr Bland know that I would like to see him as soon as he has a moment?'

The girl nodded, saying nothing. Ludens departed, resisting as he crossed the lawn, the temptation to turn back and see all the windows filled with faces looking at him. He thought, when *I* go mad I won't be able to afford this place. Then he thought, what am I saying, am I mad already, or worse still, a traitor? He felt very miserable and also extremely hungry having eaten nothing that day, and decided to go back to the Black Lion. He was alarmed by a disinclination he felt, just at the moment, to return to Benbow.

At the pub – of course he should have expected this – he was upset by the behaviour of Mr and Mrs Toller. Toller was embarrassed, clearly upset himself, distinctly sorry for Ludens. 'Well, Dr Ludens, who could have expected it. I'm very very sorry. What a dreadful scene.'

'Were you there?'

'Yes. I hope the Professor was not hurt, or Mr Fenman?'

'No, not hurt.'

'I'm sorry the Professor was so – overwrought – a lot of people will miss his – his being among us in that way. I hope he's well and not – I hope he's well?'

'Yes, he's well. Could I have some breakfast?'

'Yes, but it's lunchtime –'

'Of course, how stupid of me. Could I have a sandwich in the bar?'

Mrs Toller, serving the sandwich, also said how sorry she was, but could not conceal an I-told-you-so air of triumph. The bar was full of holiday people who were all (Ludens imagined) staring at him, so after gulping some beer he took his sandwich upstairs. As he stood eating it and gazing out of the tiny window of his small room under the eaves which looked out on the car park, he was conscious of a kind of lightening of the darkness of his mind. Scrutinising it he realised that it was an awareness that *others were in trouble too*, notably Jack and Alison and Franca. He thought, my God, what a contemptible worm I am to be *consoled* by the troubles of my friends! How can I go to Marcus, how can I help him, how can Irina love me? However, in spite of self-castigation, he continued to allow himself to be distracted by his curiosity about what was happening in Chelsea. He could not ring up Gildas, who had given up his telephone some time ago, he rang his own flat, which Christian was still renting, but got no answer, he could hardly ring Jack's house to enquire! It was on the following morning that he received Alison's letter. *I have done what I said I would do. Forgive me. Love, A.*

'Why are you still here? Why haven't you gone back to Stone-henge?'

On the evening of the day after the stoning of Marcus, Ludens was surprised to see Colin, Andy, Miriam, Kathleen, Max, and other Seekers emerging from the bar of the Hedgehog. Ludens had been (rather hopelessly) to call at Gildas's lodging to find Suzanne Moxon installed. Suzanne spoke to Ludens very sympathetically, very sensibly, obviously aware not only of Ludens's distress, but of his shame. How are the mighty fallen, was the hidden theme. Suzanne however embroidered this into the calm explanatory diagnosis of a professional nurse. She did not exclude the 'paranormal', all sensible people in medicine were aware of its 'fringe', but in fact Marcus's case was a simple and typical one. She had felt a good deal of mistrust of Marzillian's methods – he was quite well known in his field, by the way – but she believed that in this instance, though not exactly vindicated, they had certainly proved lucky. Marcus had enacted his deification, his role as a god, omnipotent, benevolent, loved and worshipped by all, and had then also 'engineered' a satisfactory martyrdom to close it down. Had he seemed remarkably calm and pleased afterwards? She thought as much, it was a classic pattern. Now having lived his religious myth to the full, he would be quiet, and more amenable to conventional methods of treating his condition. He might now be regarded as a sick man among others. Suzanne's own view, prior to the crisis which in fact in such cases was also typical, was that Marcus was a sufferer from Asperger's Syndrome, a particular form of autism characteristic of very clever children, wherein a specialised brilliance (in music, mathematics, or 'uncanny' powers of calculation or memory) was combined with a complete inability to feel affection for other people or even to communicate with them. A detailed case history of Marcus would be of considerable interest to the profession.

Ludens listened gloomily, with a polite appearance of interest, to this stuff. The conversation was closed by the entrance of Patrick. Suzanne then announced that she and Patrick were going to London, she did not say for how long. Pat avoided Ludens's eye. Ludens now found something else to blame himself for. Pat had been, as he had been himself, very shocked and upset by the ending of Marcus's 'mission'. Pat of course had believed in it. Ludens too, as he had realised later, had also, in another way, believed in it. He had failed to talk to Pat, to support and console him, partly because he had so much shared Pat's feelings. They had crept away each to his own corner to hide their wounds. Pat with his great debt to Marcus and his simple faith had been a significant figure, something essential. Now perhaps Suzanne, with her dreadful 'scientific explanation' of it all, was about to carry him away forever? There had been no opportunity to clarify the matter, and Ludens had left at once, then falling in with the Seekers.

'Oh, but we're not going,' said Miriam. 'Why ever should we?'

'We've decided to stay with you,' said Andy, reaching out and touching Ludens's sleeve in a shy sympathetic gesture.

Ludens felt like saying they needn't stay to console *him*!

Colin said, 'Of course, we shall stay on till midsummer. We decided that earlier, and nothing has happened to make us change our minds. In fact we feel even more strongly that spiritual forces are at work here. Isn't that so?' There was a murmur of assent from the others, including a tall burly fellow whom Ludens had last seen seizing a 'rough element' by the collar.

Ludens, not sure what to reply, murmured, 'I see – well – I think everything will be rather quiet now.'

'We are expecting something at midsummer,' long-haired Kathleen said.

'Don't expect too much,' Ludens said in a jocular tone which was sadly out of key with the solemnity of the young people.

Ludens had in fact already noticed a phenomenon which might have suggested the continued presence of the Seekers. On the afternoon of the stoning, when Ludens returned to Benbow, he noticed that some person or persons had removed all the stones and offerings from the lawn, together with the flowers and twigs which had increasingly surrounded the house. Many stones had been removed from the near woodland too. Walking in the park later Ludens, moved by some sudden magnetic ray, went to the Axle Stone, a close proximity he had been strictly avoiding, and found that a great many stones had arrived there, piled up around the base and arranged on the seat, together with fresh flowers and twigs. Evidently the main focus of spiritual energy had moved from Benbow to the Axle. Ludens felt a wave of deep mysterious sadness which perhaps had many causes. What was going to happen next? Perhaps nothing would happen next, perhaps the drama of Marcus and Ludens was over, and Marcus would now become an ordinary person, living quietly, reading a few books, going swimming, playing croquet with Mr Talgarth, and taking a benign interest in Irina's photography. Must not something like that be reasonably hoped for? Such a picture might well include a few discussions of philosophical matters. Did Ludens really want Marcus to go on performing these amazing Protean feats of change, continually becoming something entirely new and unexpected, perhaps able to engineer some miraculous phenomenon to delight the Seekers at midsummer? Nothing could be more idiotic!

Ludens had not given up his idea of consulting Terence Bland, though he had done nothing more to promote a meeting. Marzillian was silent; it was, he agreed with Irina, typical of his 'style' that when something astonishing happened he should make no comment. Ludens had been interested, perhaps unreasonably surprised, to learn from Suzanne that Marzillian was actually well known and his 'methods' discussed. Ludens had assumed, he now realised, that Bellmain was some unique secret community, rather like an enclosed order, ruled over by a mysterious potentate who was a law unto himself! The hand of the potentate was evident in the reassertion, even reinforcement, of privacy. The gates were now manned by Bulldogs who vetted all entrants. In fact, as in some palpable change of atmosphere, very few people now appeared who had to be turned away. A few newspapers briefly reported or misreported the scene at Benbow, but the matter was not discussed or followed up. Ludens noticed that the Seekers were not subject to the ban on pilgrims. This privilege was confirmed to him when, on the afternoon after the encounter outside the Hedgehog, he met Miriam and Kathleen on the drive, carrying flowers and evidently bound for the Axle Stone. They had, it appeared, been told by Camilla that they could come in to visit the 'Axle' as they familiarly called it, and could be there, with others, to greet the dawn at midsummer. Miriam also revealed that the Axle, a famous stone, a 'high being', among 'those who knew', had always been known to the Stone People, but till now they had not been able to come to it at midsummer 'like people used to'. The new dispensation was doubtless a result, though she did not say so, of Marcus's presence. The two girls, in the sunshine, in their summer dresses, laden with flowers, looked so enchanting, Miriam with dark curly hair, Kathleen with long flowing golden hair, that Ludens felt a sudden and quite precise desire to kiss them, and intuited for an instant their desire to kiss him. Nothing of that sort occurred however.

Ludens, not expecting any signal from Dr Bland, had assumed that the doorkeeper had not passed on his request. However, shortly after the meeting with the damsels, Ludens, nearing Benbow, saw a figure standing, possibly hiding, under the trees beside the drive. For a moment he hoped it might be Gildas, then recognised Bland. As he hurried towards him Bland turned about and disappeared into the wood. Ludens followed. When Bland reached a clearing where a fallen tree provided a seat he sat down, not in the patch of sunshine, but in the shadow. Ludens sat beside him; he thought, this is an illicit conversation, Bland doesn't want Marzillian to know.

'Well, my child, you wanted to see me?'

'Yes. I don't know what to do. And I don't know what *you* are going to do.'

'If you mean the Doctor, why ask me?'

'You're easier to talk to, when I'm with him he puts thoughts into my mind, I'm hypnotised.'

'You're not the only one. The answer to both your questions is probably that there is, at the moment, nothing to be done. Ideally people cure themselves, others stand by and pray, that is best, though the best is not always possible. How is the Professor?'

'It's about time someone asked. Just after the stoning business he seemed quite calm, even pleased. But I think he's very disturbed, I think he's frightened, he must be. He just talks in an ordinary way, but he's thinking about something else. Anyway *I'm* frightened. I talked to a nurse, a friend of Patrick's —'

'Suzanne.'

'Yes, of course you know everything. She said she thought that now Marcus had acted out some sort of megalomania he could be treated by more "conventional methods", I suppose she meant drugs. I can't make out what your policy is. Are you, is *he*, just letting Marcus drift to see what he does next – so he's just a pet monster in your zoo –?'

'A striking image, though not quite apt. Do you want us to use "conventional methods"?'

'No, of course not – I want Marcus to *get through* it all, and *understand* it all, I want him to be *enlightened*, I see him moving toward some great, not theory exactly, though I used to think that, but form of being –'

'So you're not discouraged by what happened the other day?'

'I was to begin with, now I'm not. I see him as having achieved something, and going on. But I'm afraid too. I feel so alone. I want help. I just wanted to talk to you.'

'I'm flattered. You are a brave boy, you hold on, you endure. What does Miss Irina think?'

Ludens hesitated. 'I think she wants doctors, treatment, care of the sick.'

'Nothing fanciful, not like your vision.'

'Not like my vision. But supposing I'm wrong? Whatever that might mean – which I can't imagine –'

Bland, who had been sitting very upright with his hands clasped on his knee, staring intently at Ludens through his thick round glasses, suddenly sighed, raising his hand to his brow. His rather puffy face had been made rosy by the sun. Here in the benign tree-shadow which softened every outline he looked younger, gentler, like a young schoolmaster. He resumed his posture. 'I'm afraid I can't help you, or indeed make any comment on what you have said. I must not influence you. Just stay near him. Go on believing in your vision. It will probably do no harm, it may do good.'

'But supposing –'

Bland sighed again and rose to his feet. 'We are surrounded by horrors. The human soul is full of foul and dreadful monsters. Just stay with him. Hold his hand, stroke his brow, kiss him. Do you kiss him?'

'I kissed his hands once.'

'Do so again. I'm sure *she* does not. He needs love. Ah, love, yes, we all need that. As I'm sure you understand, this conversation did not take place. Not that it contains any inflammatory matter. It is rather, if anything, disappointing. Goodbye, my dear boy.' He touched Ludens's cheek lightly with three fingers, then disappeared among the trees.

Ludens, returned to Benbow, found Irina sitting on the steps. He sat down beside her. She had washed her hair and was alternately rubbing it with a towel, dragging it with a comb, and teasing out the locks between her fingers in the sunshine. It was quickly becoming, as usual just after being washed, a heavy frizzy shapeless fuzz, which with her flushed dark complexion, made her look primitive and exotic. She sat with her feet wide apart, the skirt of her cotton dress plunging between her knees. She had an old sloppy pink bed-jacket over her shoulders. Her present indifference to her appearance both touched and irritated Ludens. She had rarely worn at Bellmain the smart clothes which she had bought in her 'spending spree'. 'Who looks at me here?' In fact Ludens loved her wild native appearance, the intensity of her dark squinting eyes, her contrariness, her bad language, her fretful bounding flight from him, the quality of her impatience with him. Everything about her which had once seemed unkempt, careless, graceless, dowdy, rude, was changed for him into the attributes of absolute charm.

'Hello, good animal, you're late.'

'So I'm good today.'

'So far.'

'I was talking with Terence.'

'Who's Terence?'

'You know, Dr Bland.'

'You like him, I don't, I think he's creepy. What did he say?'

'Nothing.'

'I told you so. Guess where Dad is.'

'Where?'

'Talking to the Demon King.'

'It was just about time he took some notice of us.'

'Well, it may be about money! Someone came to see Dad this morning from Mr Garent, the lawyer. Anyway *he* has other troubles, we're minor. When he does see Dad they just chat about Zen and chess. He's going away.'

'Marzillian? *Going away?*'

'Yes, only for a few days, not forever. I suppose he's allowed to take a holiday.'

'*Holiday?* Him?'

'I know it's hard to imagine – where would he go? St Tropez, the Lake District? Albania would suit him, he'd like it there, he could become the leader of some brigandish hill tribe.'

'I'm glad he's talking to Marcus.'

393

'I thought you and he disagreed about Dad's condition.'

'He hasn't got a condition.'

'Oh don't start that.'

'Well, don't *you* start it.'

'He's got asthma and arthritis and high blood pressure and thinks he's God, otherwise he's OK.'

'You know what I mean.'

'I'm afraid he'll relapse. Suppose he starts up all over again and runs round the village naked telling people to repent? He needs to be quietened down, he's working himself up for something else, I can feel it. You simply excite him, you egg him on. I think you should stop seeing him.'

'Oh shut up.'

'All right, but don't encourage him, you're always urging him to go on, *avanti, avanti, excelsior, excelsior*. You think there's something wonderful ahead, some new apotheosis, some great discovery, that magic formula you think he's got hidden away. For heaven's sake let him *rest*, he's just an ordinary confused elderly man. Well, he's had his fling, he's had his moment, he's seen people kneeling at his feet – I think he just wanted to be famous again, to be *noticed*. He should be content now, he should relax and realise it's all over. He needs to be told *that*, instead of being made to believe that the great thing is still to come. You don't tell him the truth. He mustn't go on thinking. Alfred, you must *give up*.'

'You mean he should be given soothing drugs so he can sit quietly in a corner and wonder why he can't do anything or think anything any more? You'll break his heart.'

'Oh, if it's all in aid of his heart not breaking! He hasn't been able to do anything or think anything for years. It's all in *your* mind. Those years, well they seemed like years, at Red Cottage he was just scribbling nonsense, he was sitting and dreaming, at least he was quiet. Then *you* arrived. And I thought you were the liberator!'

'You don't understand him, you don't love him.'

'How dare you say that!'

'I'm sorry, I'm sorry, of course you love him. But you *can't see his mind*. There's something which he must – overcome – he has to see his way through – and I – I may not be much good – but I am the only person who can help him.'

'You don't care that he's ruining my life – he's probably ruining yours too –'

'Irina, darling, *we*'re all right, we're together, we're young –'

'I'm not young. I've never had any youth. So you think we're to go on tending a sick man and wondering what ghastly thing he'll do next? Is that the future we're promising ourselves? Look, let's talk plainly, bloody hell, why can't we just leave him here, let the doctors control him – and then we can *get away*. Isn't that what you want, to be with me? Or do you just want to be with him? I'm *tired* of it all, I'm tired, I'm miserable, I'm fed up –'

'My dear love, my sweet love, don't be angry with me, I can't bear it, just be patient –'

'Oh patient! I've *been* patient – I've kept hoping – Oh you don't know what I've hoped for, such great great things, such impossible things – but I'm just trapped and caged – and *you* won't get me out, you're just in the cage too! Now you'll say it's nice to be in the cage together – I know you – you're a disaster. All right, no you're not, but I want so much to get out – it's *my* heart that's breaking.'

Irina began to cry, uttering long wailing sobs and drawing her fuzz of hair down over her face.

'Irina, get up, come inside.' He stood and pulled her to her feet. She stumbled up the steps after him. As Ludens, having pulled her inside the room, was closing the doors, he saw Marcus on the drive approaching the lawn. 'Here's Marcus. Don't let him see you crying. Just be in the kitchen. I'll talk to him.'

'Let's both go out the side door and into the wood.'

'No, we must stay, we can't leave him alone.'

'Why not? Or do you really think he's daft after all? And he's seen me crying before, I cried all the time at Red Cottage. Little you care! Anyway I'm going.' She ran from the room and out of the side door banging it behind her.

Ludens came out onto the verandah. He was very upset by what had just passed, but he knew Irina would forgive him, and he now had to give his full attention to Marcus.

'Oh, Alfred, good, you're here, let's sit inside, it's getting hot.'

'Irina's just out –'

Marcus came in and sat down on the little tweedy sofa. He was wearing the brown 'battle dress' shirt and trousers he had worn on the day of the stones. He sat staring ahead and frowning a little, his face not exactly wrinkled but as if lightly written over, scrawled with thoughts. Ludens sat beside him watching him. He felt an urge to embrace him, to hug him as he hugged Irina. But he sat quiet, quite still, waiting for him to speak.

'Where's Patrick?'

'Still in London. He'll be back.'

'I miss him. Are his poems good?'

'I don't know. I can't judge poetry. Maybe they're good. They're certainly better.'

'Well, poetry – perhaps it is the highest thing. I think Pat was very sad about – what happened –'

'Marcus, what did Marzillian say to you?' Ludens tried to speak casually, but the question sounded portentous.

Marcus did not respond at once. He looked at Ludens, at first sternly, then with a slightly mocking gaze. 'What do *you* think of that man?'

'I think he's wise,' said Ludens. 'Perhaps he's good. But he may not always be right.'

'He asked me if I would permit him to give me a certain drug. He told me the name of it – he even wrote it down – I have it somewhere –'

Ludens was startled. 'What did you say to him?'

'I said no.'

'Thank heavens!'

'It was good of him to ask me, was it not.'

'It was his duty. But Marcus, you're not *tempted* –?'

'To let it all pass from me? Occasionally.'

'What you called the tension of thought, or the leap of the fish. When you said that I turned your thoughts round and showed another face – perhaps it's my task to do that, my role in your life. Not breaking the tension must be a matter of seeing a light ahead, seeing *enlightenment* ahead – I don't mean that word in a technical sense but in a general spiritual sense, as *you* can see it – a place where thoughts are free and at peace at last – and surely *that*'s the experience, the act, the precious treasure, to get there and live there and *be* there. That's the other dimension. That's the right way.'

'And the wrong way?'

'Drama, pictures, thinking too much about evil, whether it's done or suffered. Of course one *will* think – but that thinking must happen later when you've reached a place which is further on, and thinking will be different there. And the leap is not – is not what I think you sometimes see it as – as breaking, as acting. It's something much more like a quiet transition after a lot of patience and – tension of thought, yes – but with *that* as its discipline, its orientation, its truth. Not confusion and chaos and immolation and pulling the house down, not something experienced as a great significant moment. You've just had an experience and a lot of great moments and you've come through it and left it behind you and seen it as a lesson. Passing through the fire, yes, if you like, and through the fire *ahead* too, but the truth of it is the peace and freedom beyond. The fire is not an end in itself. The truth is something which you don't know yet, something that will be lived later on, lived as humans live through time, perhaps over a long long time, for that's not an end point, but the beginning of the real journey.'

Ludens spoke fast, scarcely knowing what he was saying, amazed at what he heard himself say, trying in an agony of concentration to hold it all together. He paused, trying to assemble his thoughts, to compose, before it vanished, a better way of putting it, to try to see the point, the absolute *point* of his idea.

Marcus did not speak at once, as if waiting for Ludens to continue. Then he said, 'Did I say that about your showing me my thoughts and turning them round?'

'Yes. I believe, I feel, that I am very near to thinking your thoughts now –'

'I doubt it. Don't try, Alfred, *don't try*.'

'Marcus, please listen to what I say – about the peace later, the freedom, the *goodness*, the life to be lived, the open space and the *light* –'

'I think you mean happiness.'

'No, I don't mean happiness. I mean –'

'I can see that you are trying every argument. But for you it is still all romanticism.'

'*Romanticism!*'

'You warn me against pictures and drama – but you are painting pictures – and the thing itself is not there.'

'The thing itself –'

'You want to console me, to justify me, to preserve me, to rescue me. Here indeed your thoughts are not my thoughts. Perhaps I was wrong to let you come so close, I wronged you, I hope I have not damaged you – will not have damaged you.'

'I'm sorry. You think I am talking nonsense simply in order to – I don't believe it's nonsense but never mind. I'll try to say it again differently later. All right, you are travelling on. Just please *take me with you*.'

'You don't know what you are asking. There is no light where I am. If any comes it is not enlightenment but lightning. Tell me, where did the prayer shawl come from? Irina said you brought it –'

'A rabbi gave it to me to give to you.'

'Why didn't you tell me? Well, why do I ask, I know why. It doesn't matter. And here is Irina. What have you got there, some flowers, a cake for our tea? Let Ludens put the kettle on. You come and sit with me.'

Irina ran to her father, kneeling beside him on the sofa and burying her head in his shoulder while he put his arms around her and bowed his face into her hair. Ludens, who had so rarely seen moments of overt affection between these two, turned away. Putting the kettle on he thought, will it be like this, *can* it be? Romanticism, happiness, perhaps Marcus is right! Domestic happiness. Why not? That *wasn't* what I meant then – But then I was intoxicated by Marcus's thoughts – Perhaps I can't see them, but I can *smell* them. Terence said go on believing in the vision. But what is the vision and what is being true to it? Of course I want to preserve Marcus, to bring him through – is that itself a kind of treachery? I want to see light ahead, but perhaps I should close my eyes. Who knows. Well, there in the future, *he* will be there too, the grandson. Perhaps he, *that*, will prove to be *the thing itself*. The longed-for boy. Ludens, through the mist of the future saw him, looking back at Ludens with his big wondering dark childish eyes, his clever genius eyes filled with compassion and with understanding. Then as the kettle boiled he thought: well, supposing it's a girl?

As he made the tea and set out the tea things on the kitchen table he heard another voice in the sitting room. Patrick had returned. There were exclamations and laughter. Irina called out, 'Pat's back, lay an extra cup. And make some toast.'

'Perhaps I shouldn't have run away,' said Patrick to Ludens. 'I just couldn't bear it. I felt my heart would break.'

Tea was over. Marcus, who had missed his swim because of his meeting with Marzillian, had set off for the swimming-pool accompanied by Irina, and by Camilla who appeared in time for the toast. She had evidently already encountered Patrick and they exchanged the usual banter. Ludens, obeying Irina's mute signals, had announced he was going back to the pub and would see them later. He thought to himself, perhaps Irina will hold onto him better than I can, her instincts may be cleverer than my ideas. She doesn't really want to hand him over to the doctors. Anyway that's not in question just now, since he said no to Marzillian.

Patrick, surrendering Marcus to the two women, had said he would walk with Ludens to the Black Lion. Ludens, as they walked, looked at his tall companion and saw how dejected he looked. His handsome bony small-mouthed face had subtly altered its lines, transforming its usual jaunty playboy expression into some ancient mask of bitter sorrow. His eyes, cast down, looked an even darker blue, not reflecting the heavens but gazing down into the cold depth of a sunless sea. His curly black hair had lost its gloss – perhaps it simply needed washing. Ludens felt a special new companionship with him as if they were both vagabonds, even hunted men, tramping the roads together. He thought of Patrick as he had first known him, playing the drunken Irish poet in the pubs of Soho, unemployed, unpublished, living on the meagre 'dole', handsome, merry, generous, pursued by women but living a life which, while probably not entirely chaste, was not disorderly or promiscuous. The whole mystery of Pat's being seemed to rise up beside him, enclosing the striding man in a dark luminous cloak. Then he remembered Pat dying, the wasted emaciated doomed figure descending into death, which had sent Ludens away upon his quest for Marcus, which had brought with it so many strange and wonderful and awful things.

'Pat, why did Marcus curse you?'

A slight look of animation changed Pat's face. 'I told him off!'

'Really! Whatever did you say?'

'I was drunk. He'd said something critical about how I should stop playing the stage Irishman and wasting my time writing rotten poems when I knew I'd never really be a poet. That upset me terribly, it was like a punch in the face. So I went crazy and I told him he didn't understand poetry and he never would and how poetry was the highest thing a man could do and was the only place where we could see and say what was the meaning of ourselves and why we're here, which I said he would never know, and anyway he was just playing at being a painter himself, and he'd go on playing at being this thing and being that thing and imagining he was destined to be something great when really he was just a blown-up ball of vanity and when he'd tried everything and failed everywhere he'd realise he'd been a charlatan all his life and he'd shoot himself.'

'Pat!! He must have felt you were cursing him!'

'I regretted it at once of course, and I've regretted it ever since and wished to blot those words out of existence and they remain burning in my mind, though he must have forgotten them long ago because I am nothing and he is all.'

'He was angry.'

'He was devilish.'

'What did he say that constituted the curse?'

'I won't repeat the words. I'm superstitious about words.'

'But then he cured you, he really did cure you.'

'Yes. And I suppose I wasn't dead, only God knows if I was, I just felt as if I'd been dead, and I wanted everyone to know and to reverence him, and I couldn't help boasting everywhere and sort of letting on I'd been dead, and other people were saying that anyway.'

'But you didn't ever believe what you said to him then?'

'No, of course not, it was the devil in me speaking.'

'Speaking to the devil in him.'

'I always loved the man. And when he was revealed here for what he truly was I felt justified myself, you understand, I felt finally forgiven. And then he tore it all up, he tore it all to tatters. And why? Why should he not heal people, heal the body and the soul, when he has the power to do it? There's people in the village say they've been cured, and their life has been changed. He's a healer, sure that's a holy man, how can he deny himself?'

'He thinks people would misunderstand and be misled, he thinks there's something higher, some other form of witness and he's not worthy yet. Do you still go to Mass?'

'Yes. And to the pub.'

'You've started drinking again?'

'I got blind drunk on the evening of that day when he destroyed himself. People were calling him a liar and calling me a liar.'

'I know. I felt – terrible – on that day too. But I think I knew –'

'I felt everything I believed in was made foul –'

'But you believe in God?'

'In God, yes. But He's far away. And there's so much sorrow here. You know what's happened to them at Chelsea, the three of them?'

'I heard something –'

'Alison wrote me a letter and I called to see them. Franca is a saint.'

'I know.'

By this time they were standing on the pavement outside the Black Lion.

'Pat, he asked after you, he said he missed you.'

'Ah, yes, well, I owe him my life – and that's forever. I'm off now to the Hedgehog to see Colin and them. It's great things they're expecting come midsummer. They're getting fireworks to let off so at least something will happen.'

The next morning about half past seven Toller knocked on the door of Ludens's room to say that 'a gentleman was waiting for him downstairs'. Ludens hurried down. His heart sank. The gentleman was Daniel Most. Today he was wearing a dark suit complete with waistcoat and tie. He looked sombre. (Was it the Sabbath?)

Looking down on him from the stairs Ludens got a slight shock. In the half-light Daniel Most resembled somebody. Ludens thought, he resembles me! Of course the resemblance was slight, consisting merely in the same height and build, the same narrow face and dark hair, similar lips, and a rather sad reflective look. Ludens suddenly thought, it's a centuries-old look, there's something suspicious in it, intense, withdrawn, even frightened.

Most said at once, before Ludens had left the stairs, 'Let's go outside.' He walked out of the door and across the courtyard into the garden. Ludens followed. They sat down on a seat beside the river, where it turned in a loop, circling the Black Lion and going on to the bridge. The sun today was, as far as shining on England was concerned, having a bit of a rest. It was occluded, hid in a uniform greyness, traversed by a film of mist. The temperature had gone down. Ludens was glad of the jacket which he had hastily put on. The two stared at each other.

'You know, you look a bit like me.'

'Really?' said Ludens.

'Where did your people come from?'

'Warsaw.'

'My people came from Kiev. Actually it's just that we both look like someone else.'

'Who?'

'Kafka.'

'Hmmm. What do you want?'

'What happened to the prayer shawl?'

'I gave it to his daughter who hung it on the wall. He saw it and knew what it was. He asked where it came from. I told him a rabbi gave it to me to give to him.'

'Did he chide you for not giving it to him?'

'Oh really,' said Ludens, 'I can't explain all these things. It's none of your business anyway.'

'It is my business. I want to see him. Tell me why you don't want me to.'

'We've got enough trouble without rabbis.'

'Tell me.'

'He's upset about various things and doesn't want strangers blundering in.'

'He's upset about what just happened? I wasn't there.'

'That's not important, I mean it's over. He's worried about his thoughts and his work.'

'I must ask. Did he lose any family?'

'No.'

'Did you?'

'No.'

'I didn't either. But he thinks about all that?'

'Any Jew does. But *that*'s not it.'

'I wonder how you can be sure. Are you afraid he'll commit suicide?'

'No! Of course not! Do you think every Jew is suicidal? He's a philosopher, a thinker, he's worried about theories, about deep matters, *that*'s the sort of trouble he's in. I want him to get through his difficulties and think free peaceful thoughts and not be burdened –'

'You said he was upset, you think he is burdened and has difficulties and needs peace. Perhaps what disturbs him is precisely the need to make peace with his Jewishness. That too is thought, is philosophy, is a deep matter. Especially now.'

'Why especially now? Judaism is a dark place. One doesn't have to live there. I don't want him to. I want him to be out in the light.'

'But evidently he is not in the light. You think he is surrounded by demons.'

'Well –'

'I know about demons. I think I know about his demons, or their close relations. I feel sure I could help him, that is I could bring him help.'

'Where from?'

'From God. From the Wisdom of God.'

'I find you impertinent. God is a private matter. What is God anyway?'

'A dark place –'

'Marcus hasn't got "religious problems", you couldn't even interest him in them.'

'I want to try, that's all. He has read a lot about the Holocaust.'

'Who says so?'

'Gildas Herne.'

The demons of jealousy plunged their pitchforks into Ludens's heart. So when Gildas, shunning Ludens, was supposed to be having long meditative walks, he was chattering to this rabbi! 'I don't want to continue this discussion.' He rose and began to walk away.

The rabbi hurried after him and stopped him, pulling at his coat. 'The prayer shawl meant something to him.'

'He just remembered that his grandfather had one.'

'You can't simply leave out his Jewishness as if it were a disease.'

'Look,' said Ludens, facing him, 'why can't you leave us alone? I think you're just curious, you just want to gape at him like everyone else.'

'You don't think that. You're afraid of me.'

'Oh go to hell.'

'Please, I have heard about his long pilgrimage. I too want him to reach the place of peace where thoughts are free, though perhaps too there is no such place or we cannot get there. There is a pain which is our awareness of the God from whom we are separated. This is not superstition or the worship of idols, you *know* that. Why cannot our pains and burdens be spoken of in this way? Prayer is thought also, our deepest thought. I could speak to him in the language of his heart, an old language which he will remember. He needs that remembrance too. It can do him no harm. I shall bring food for his thoughts. Oh taste and see that the Lord is good. At least ask him if he would like to talk to a rabbi.'

Ludens hesitated. He felt at that moment *confused* by what, in his gentle confident cultivated voice, Daniel Most was saying. He felt too tired and too worried to understand. His thoughts kept slipping away to Gildas, and what Gildas might have said to this man to make him so persistent. Or perhaps it was nothing to do with Gildas. Ludens did not want Marcus to be stirred up in just this way, he did not want someone else, *anyone* else, to probe that mystery.

Most spoke again. 'You may be rightly offended by my assumption that I would be bringing him a message. Let me add that I feel, I hope, that he may have a message for me. I want that message. It's not idle curiosity, Dr Ludens.'

Ludens thought, yes, of course I am offended by his assumption, though it has only now occurred to me that I am. Ludens did not like the word 'message'. He thought, they all want that. If I just reject this man he'll run straight to Marcus anyway. He said, 'All right, I will ask him. If he says no I hope you will respect his wish.'

'Thank you – thank you – I will come to you again.' Most turned quickly and walked away, perhaps fearing that Ludens might change his mind.

Ludens thought, I'll mention it casually to Marcus, he'll say no. Of course that man means well, I don't dislike him. He'll believe me and stay away. And as he walked back to the inn he reflected that perhaps he did resemble Kafka, and that cheered him up a little.

As he entered the door he was met by Toller. 'Dr Ludens, it's your visiting day! There's a lady to see you, and guess who it is!'

The lady was Franca.

My dear, my very dear, I have to tell you the truth. Alison has presented me with an ultimatum. She cannot any more endure the situation in which we have placed her. She loves me and wishes to be my wife. I love her and I *cannot leave her*. She alone, of all the women whom you have so generously and so understandingly tolerated, I *cannot leave*. What she demands is, then, that I divorce you and marry her. I have to tell you this, I have always told you the truth, and you in your deep wisdom and your deep compassion have enabled us both to live with it. For this I revere you, I worship you, I kiss your feet – Franca, I can't find the words. And now – do I now ask of you the impossible? Sometimes in life one is confronted by the impossible – the unthinkable, the insuperable – which, if it is faced truthfully, fearlessly, reveals itself as a bright blazing light, a reality of being not imagined before. So – you know what I am going to ask – you have already guessed. *Our* bond is unbreakable and old. We have been together since we were children – well, since I was virtually a child. We are of one substance. I am encouraged here by the fact that *already* you have accepted Alison as a permanent fixture in my life. You have done this with a nobility and a grace, so exceptionally yours, so wonderfully you. You have, to put it grossly, swallowed half, and I am now asking you, *begging* you, to swallow the other half. What would my life be without you? How could I *be* without you? And – why can I not *continue* to have everything I want? This is my childish, my outrageous, cry, which I think, I feel, you at least will perfectly understand. I must do what Alison wants which is in itself reasonable. I know how much you have liked and understood *her*. Our mutual situation as a trio will not be in any way altered except for a conventional formality – I mean the divorce. This is a piece of paper – valuable to Alison, harmless to you. You are I know,

I *know*, above conventions as you are above the vulgarity of jealousy.

The house in Chelsea will be yours – I will for the present still use the studio – your life there will be, under the new regime, in many ways easier. Sharing it between the three of us has been (you understand me?) awkward for you in many ways. I will be with you often, as I have been in our recent mode of living, perhaps more often, and in a more convenient and carefree way. Alison, I may say, has agreed to all this, she is generous and is grateful. Franca, can I rely on you for this final forgiveness, this final toleration of me, this final proof of your love for me? Others may think this crazy. I know you will not. I cannot live without you – your enmity would kill me. Let us not speak of that, it is impossible. I *must* have you in my life, as you have been for so long, pardoning me and loving me, breathing being into me, continually creating me. *Oh my dear.*

It may seem cowardly to tell you this in a letter – but it is, I think, wise, since I can make matters absolutely clear. I hope you will credit me here with truthfulness and with courage. Alison and I will be away now for two or three days. I think it is better so. I feel confident that you will not only succeed in carrying me through this ultimate trial – but will also see the *sense* of what I say. I may telephone you – but on second thoughts better not – the telephone is not right for such speech as we must now have with each other. I will write to tell you when I am returning and I will come to you alone. I too need courage, I too am in travail. *I love you*, Franca, sweetheart. Your Jack.

Franca, sitting on Ludens's bed, watched him as he read Jack's letter. He read it carefully, slowly, frowning slightly. Franca studied his narrow face which resembled the face of a fox, a dear good wise fox.

When the trio had returned to London, Franca had felt, sitting in the back of the car, a despair so terrible that the idea of suicide, which had never before come near her, actually appeared, showing its wicked dreadful face, peering at her through a slit in the real world. But what was the real world, and had she not, she herself, irreparably deformed and corrupted her world by this awful lying charade? Now, sitting in the car and hearing their merry chatter in which, regularly turning round, they included her, she felt that her place had been, by cruel and unjust judges, finally and relentlessly fixed. She was mother, they the happy spoilt irresponsible children. Mother stayed at home, glad to receive the glossy postcard which assured her loving heart that her children were having a wonderful time. How had this, which they, in their unconcealed satisfaction, made to seem so natural, come about, and how had she, at every step, aided and abetted their triumphant progress? She had spent her time, as on a survival diet, analysing her reactions while, with an ease which appalled her, playing her compliant role. This deception, if it was a deception, this dense strange state of being, had been made possible, as she reckoned it, by two factors, one her love for Jack (which, mauled, maimed, degraded, still lived), and the other her vicious hatred of the unspeakable pair: her gloating sense of her one advantage, her secret weapon, so precious that she felt she might never use it, her ability to turn into a furious beast which would hurt, damage and destroy what it had loved and cherished and preserved. Of course the secret weapon would also annihilate its user. If ever she were thus to savage Jack with an anger as strong as her (by him) imagined love she would, after her brief wicked joy, be tortured to death by remorse and regret and the impossibility of undoing what she had done. The common-sense idea that she did not have to choose between sacrificial love and self-destructive hate, but could gently and ironically withdraw from Jack and let her famous 'love' die quietly of starvation did not appeal to Franca. Meditating upon her feelings she thought about her mother's miserable docile life with that cruel man; and perhaps some old fierce Italian instinct for revenge now lent its fire to her rage. How could she simply *let them get away with it*? Supposing she were just to keep her two alternatives with her, to brood over them, pretending to comply, indeed complying, while nourishing her hidden anger as a source of power? But then, for how long, for years, for all her life, would she tell him on her death-bed? Would such a long deception *be* a deception? Franca had at times allowed herself to be charmed by 'absolute love' as by an innocent gentle entity, perhaps an angel, but appearing more often as a kind sweet animal, like a graceful gazelle. Jack's letter, with its hideous ruthless finality, had banished that gracious thing and probably killed it.

Yet *was* the letter so final? Did it not after all make, in terms of the mad world they had been living in, a kind of sense? Would they not all be happier if Alison were Mrs Sheerwater and Franca the ex-Mrs Sheerwater still maintaining, as senior member of the harem, her old well-known bond with her prince, whose durable guilt feelings she could playfully and spitefully exploit? People could and did live exactly thus. Could she live on in the house in Chelsea as a gay divorcee with a famous salon? Would Jack's earnings be enough to support her indefinitely in such a role? In fact Franca had been, before she found Jack's letter upon the kitchen table, dimly aware of a 'light elsewhere'.

She had made no conscious effort to discover this 'other place'; but in one case chance, and in another her recognition of a bond which had long existed, now led her toward a consolation which was not part of the huge machine of her misery.

Franca was confident that she knew, roughly or generally, what Ludens's reaction to the letter would be, though she wondered what would be the first thing that he said when he stopped reading. Perhaps Ludens was wondering too.

He ventured a quick glance at her, a calculating surmising glance. He looked again at the missive, as if to gain time, then said, 'How utterly – how – how *rotten* –'

'Oh but one can understand it all,' said Franca in a light tone. 'Don't you think? Given that the whole situation is pretty mad, there's logic in it. In a way, Jack and I are already divorced. I'm the ex-wife, she's the wife. As he says, the formal divorce is just a piece of paper.'

'Franca! You don't think that!'

'Because I must be hoping that Alison will disappear? I have no grounds for such a hope.'

'Not just that, not that at all. It's just too much. It's breaking-point.'

'Yet you can surely understand, after all he's your best friend, you must understand how much Jack wants and needs – what he has asked for.'

'Yes, but –'

'You won't abandon him, will you, *you* won't break with him because of this – it's not *your* breaking-point?'

'No, I suppose not, but –'

'So you envisage it as, even though rotten, possible.'

'Franca, don't play games with me. You say he left the letter in the kitchen. You don't know where he and Alison are?'

'No idea. You think I ought to be waiting at home in case he rings up?'

'No!'

'What *do* you think I should be doing?'

'I don't know,' said Ludens, almost in a tone of exasperation. 'I can't advise you. I'm terribly shocked by that ghastly letter. On the other hand, as you say, it has its own logic. I think your reaction is *heroic*, I think you are *wonderful*. So you'll go through with it, divorce and all, and Jack turning up now and then and sending a cheque? I suppose you won't want to see much of Alison – so it won't be quite the *ménage à trois* which Jack thought he could fix up – poor old Jack!'

'I don't think Alison will want to see me – it's rather the point that

---

I cease to exist. I think she imagines I tried to alienate her from Jack.'

'She said something like that to me.'

'What? She told you about it?'

'I shouldn't have said that. She said you'd tried somehow or other to make her join you against him.'

'That was a joke of course. I'm surprised she took it seriously. She was just protesting against the whole thing.'

'Jack says here that she "can't endure the situation in which *we* have placed her"! I can't make out whether this letter is a naive blurting out of the truth or a most ingeniously constructed trap.'

'Oh I think it's naive and truthful.'

'I bet he made several drafts. Look at the writing. He must think you're a fool.'

'But I am, precisely that, I'm uneducated, untalented, I lack substance, I lack presence, in short I'm fitted, don't you think, for just the role he is preparing for me. I deserve this. I feel it. Naturally he must feel it.'

'Franca, darling, *stop it.*'

'Stop what?'

'Stop saying these provocative things which you don't mean.'

'I see. You want me to be outraged, to be angry, to weep, on your shoulder. You want me to *break down!*'

Ludens, who had been sitting on a chair in front of her, dropped Jack's letter on the floor. He moved to the bed and put his arms around her. Franca began to cry, pressing her wet mouth and eyes against his jacket.

'Sorry, my darling, I didn't want to bring it on – I just couldn't stand being teased like that.' He thrust her away a little, stroking her brow and her hair, then dusting her face powder off his collar. Then her hair began to come down and fall about her shoulders and onto Ludens's knees, and he helped her to collect it together into an orderly tail.

'*Teased!* Well, I know whatever Jack does you'll go on being his friend. Men always stick together against a woman whatever the rights and wrongs.'

'I mean, you were pretending, leading me on, to see if I'd agree with a lot of nonsense and believe you were just accepting it all. But, my dear, what *are* you going to do? It's so *awful*. Maybe the best thing is to keep quiet for the present –'

'You mean – just accepting it all?'

'No, I mean wait – see what will happen – things may change –'

'What things? What will happen will be divorce and Jack and Alison living happily ever after in France. You *do* mean accept, and you *do* agree with what you just called nonsense – that I just say it's all right, and of course I understand, and of course I know you need me, and I'll just sit quiet and be so glad to see you when you drop in now and then.'

'Listen. Jack's madly in love. He's mad – he may recover –'

'He won't recover, *they suit each other perfectly*, he should never have married me – no wonder everyone was so amazed – actually all this was clear to me long ago. But you think I should just smile and wait?'

'Honestly, Franca, being realistic, and you did talk about logic, what else can you do? You may as well stick it out calmly, I mean accept it with a smile and not a scream.'

'Suppose I want to scream.'

'Inhibit it.'

Franca, who had dried her eyes and face with the back of her hand – she could not find her handbag which she had put down somewhere in the room – stared at him. She had of course been 'teasing' him but in the hope of evoking a spirited response. She felt disappointed, she felt an anger which made her toss her head and shake it, unsettling her liberated hair. She welcomed the anger as a sign of life, of the new life.

'Look here, Ludens, you ask what else can I do. In a moment I will tell you. But you shock me. Everything you say assumes that there is nothing in my life except my love for Jack.'

'Well, you do still love him, and you've endured so much –'

'Whether or not I still love him has become unimportant, there isn't any point any more in asking about that love or trying to test it. It belongs to the past. I am absolutely through with Jack, I've *finished* with him. Yes, I've endured so much, and you seem to think this means I will endure anything. It does not. This letter is the end.'

'Franca, dear –'

'You're on his side.'

'No, I'm on your side! I'm not insisting, how can I, that you love him and forgive him – though now I've had a little time to think I do actually believe that would be the best course – I just don't see any sensible alternative to simply saying yes, and waiting to see if he changes his mind. All right, you feel at the moment that you're through with him, whatever that means. But assuming that you have to put up with the divorce you may as well do it with dignity.'

'*Dignity!*' Franca's Italian ancestors, so long dormant, arose in her so violently that her eyes flashed and she felt her long heavy hair lifting as if it wanted to stand up on end. 'You see *no alternative* –!'

'Franca! You're not thinking about suicide?'

'No, you fool, you *idiot*! Listen to me, Alfred, my dear, just listen quietly. Do you remember how you took hold of my hand on that day in my sitting room, in my little servant's room off the kitchen, when I was crying, remember, and you said, "I wanted to come closer to you and you must have felt it."'

He said, 'Yes – Franca – I remember.' He took her hand now, which had been lying near to him on the counterpane, and held it firmly, caressing it with his other hand.

'Well, now – let go, please, I want to sit back and look at you. Maisie Tether – she's gone back to Boston, by the way –'

'Oh, yes, I'd forgotten her – there's been so much going on –'

'Yes, evidently, you have forgotten her! But now – I'm afraid I can't say all this slowly, I'll have to say it all at once. Maisie wants me to go and join her, and I'm going to go, I'm going to America to live in Boston – and I want you to come with me.'

'You – Franca – I don't understand –'

'It's simple enough. I'm going to America, to stay there, and I want you to come with me and stay there too. She'll get me a job, and you –'

'My dear, I understand the bit about Maisie, but why me?'

'Because we've known each other a very long time, and I've suddenly *seen* this, I've seen it in a great shaft of light, I love you and I think you love me. When I'm divorced I'd like to marry you.'

Ludens's face, which had been only a little touched by the sun, became red. A great flush blazed up from his neck to his brow. He put his hands over his eyes.

Franca went on. Now that she had spoken the light glowed brighter in which she saw it all. 'You could get a university job in America, why not? It's just – it's like an idea of genius – for both of us. You want to be married, I want to marry again, I want to marry a loyal truthful man. And I *do love you*. I've felt this love, like an angel standing beside me – for a long time – and I do believe – that you care for me, that you feel something very special and particular – Do I surprise you, do I shock you? Please think about this. I feel it is destined. I don't want to go to America and leave you behind. You are, I realise you have always been, a pillar of my world. Maisie adores you, by the way. Am I mad? Can you, will you, *think* about what I have just said?'

Ludens suddenly began to behave very strangely, shaking his head and gasping, and jerking his arms as if he were trapped or tied. He dragged at the neck of his shirt, he jumped to his feet and walked to the window and struck the glass, then opened the door and banged it, he shook the table, the chair.

'Alfred, are you all right?'

'Franca – it's just that I'm so moved – so surprised – so *deeply* moved, and I can't help being glad, so glad, so grateful, but then I'm not glad, I can't be, because I can't come with you to America and I can't marry you.'

'Well,' said Franca. She felt calmer now and liberated for the moment from the burden of anger and frenzy and despair and pain which she had carried with her since she had read Jack's letter – and prophetically from earlier. 'It's possible, you know. There's time, think about it. I threw the whole package at you because I wanted you to know *how much* there was in it. Let me be near you. You see – I haven't got anybody in the world now, except you and Maisie.'

'But, Franca, I can't, I can't even think of it. Dreadful things have been happening here – I have to look after Marcus.'

'Oh Marcus, yes. But you can't stay with Marcus for ever. His daughter's with him, it's her job. I told you what I think about him, that he's damaging your life and wasting your time. You must have given up thinking he has some magic formula by now. You must want to escape from him. I'll help you escape. Now he's in a proper hospital being looked after surely you can get away.'

'But, Franca, I love him – and I love her too.'

'You mean Irina? I remember you were sorry for her.'

'I'm going to marry her – I think –'

'Don't be silly.'

Franca now sitting back relaxed upon the bed, leaning upon pillows which she had pulled towards her and holding her snake of hair in one hand, watching Ludens in his torment of surprise, felt herself filling up with a new life, a new power: power over her future, over this man for whom she felt, even as she witnessed his strange distress, an increase of love. She went on, 'You say "you think". So it's just an idea.'

'I mean, she may decide against me – but I don't believe she will.'

'Alfred, you *can't* marry *her*, the notion is absurd, she's a wild irresponsible uneducated barbarian, you yourself described her as a mad erratic little thing, she's not quite human, she'd run away. She's already led quite a wild life I gather.'

'No, she hasn't, I know –'

'She couldn't settle down with you. You like order, she likes disorder. It's as simple as that. You're utterly unsuited to each other. I can't think how you can ever have imagined marrying her. No – I can't think it's serious. It's just that you're sorry for him, and so you're sorry for her. And you're disappointed in him – and you'll be disappointed in her, when you just *wake up* and see how impossible she is. I'll wake you up, I'm doing so now. And you needn't even be sorry for her, she can look after herself! You remember I said Marcus was cunning. I think she's cunning too. She'll want a husband very different from you. Now stop acting like a man having a fit, come and sit beside me. Nothing awful has happened. You don't have to come to America and marry me. You could just do one of these, or we could live part of the year in America, or – we can see, we can see. What I want, what I must have, is you being the most important thing in my life from now on. You said you wanted to be closer to me – you are closer to me. Come and sit beside me now.'

He sat down beside her, ruffling his hair and shaking his head and gasping. Franca, overtaken by the tenderness of her desire, which made her certain now of every movement, certain of her power, enclosed him in her arms, kissing his cheek, then his lips. He responded to her kisses, closing his eyes, awkwardly clasping her. Then they held each other quietly.

They moved apart and looked. Ludens, still flushed, combed back his dark straight hair with his fingers, his other hand covering his mouth. Franca murmured something.

'What?'

'Hairpins. I think they're all over the place.'

Ludens began to search the bed, then the floor, crawling near her feet. He handed her some of the pins, and she began the swift mysterious business of suspending her hair. He sat before her on the floor. Then knelt before her, placing his hands on her knees.

'How did you get here?'

'Early train to Salisbury, then taxi.'

'When did you find Jack's letter?'

'Yesterday afternoon.'

'How did you spend the rest of the day?'

'Crying, then thinking. Oh *how* I thought! I've packed four suitcases. I've got one with me, it's downstairs. Molly Stein will pick up the others. I'm not going back.'

'But, Franca, how about money, I can give you some, where will you live?'

'I've got quite a lot in the bank. I can stay in hotels. Molly or Linda could put me up. Linda has a cottage in Surrey. *You* could put me up! Maisie says she'll send me an air ticket any time. Don't worry about that, I just want *you* to do some thinking.'

He got up slowly, and spread out his hands in an ancestral gesture.

'I can't be what you want. I am bound to Marcus and Irina. Please don't stay here, I mean now in these days, there's a crisis, I've got so much on my hands, I've got such awful problems –'

'Can't I help you?'

'No, you're another problem! Please go, Franca – I'm very very sorry – of course we love each other, and you're right, we always did, and now – now *this* has happened – and I'll be close to you and in your life if you want me to – but not in *that* way. I am so grateful to you, and I *am* glad too like I said – though it seems like a dream which we have both had. But – Franca – isn't it perhaps what you've suggested, isn't it somehow an act of revenge on Jack? I've just thought – it's the thing that would hurt him most of all.'

Franca, who had finished coiling and pinning her hair, reached for her handbag and her coat. She gazed at him with an intimate ironical tender look. 'So after all, your loyalty to him is greater than what you feel for me?'

'No, no, I'm just thinking – it's not for his sake that I can't be as you wish – oh dear Franca, I'm so upset, I'm so sorry –'

Franca got up and put on her coat. She felt dazed but calm. She tested her being to see if the new life was still in it. It was. She thought, I've said enough, I've done enough, if I stay now I shall become confused. I have taken *the step*. She said to Ludens, 'Don't be upset. I'm glad I've spoken to you and I know you will think about what I have said. You have made me happier, you have made me better. Don't worry. I can't believe in your other attachment. It's the old man you're in love with and when you've got past your awful problems and when he's acted out his fantasies and is having some proper treatment you'll see how empty it all is – empty and vain. I think you see this already, you're just being loyal and brave. I don't believe in either of them. She'd never live in your quiet world, she'd be bored, when she's got rid of him she'll want to race about and spend her money – in London she was spending money like a mad thing. I'm sorry, I shouldn't speak about them. I'm glad to have seen you and delivered my message.'

'Franca, I must go now, I've got to see Marcus, I always go at this time of day – dear Franca, thank you – and do please understand –'

'All right, I can wait. And you think a little. Have you so much love that you can afford to do without mine? So, we'll meet again. And when your crisis is over, try to be quiet and by yourself for a little. I may go to America just for a short time now to see Maisie. I'll be back. And tonight I'll give myself a treat, I'll stay in a hotel in Salisbury. I've hardly ever stayed in a hotel by myself and I'm looking forward to it intensely.'

A taxi had taken Franca away. Ludens was walking to Bellmain. He paused on the bridge and looked down at the busy glossy wrinkling shining water. Franca's visit had been something amazing, astonishing, menacing, distressing, and beautiful. That Franca, wise good sweet Franca, should have come to *him*! He could not help feeling, like a bright recurrent spark in the darkness of his mind, so glad that Franca loved him – and that he loved her. Had he been firm enough, clear enough, about the impossibility of her absurd but wonderful plan? Perhaps they had disbelieved each other. She could not credit that he could love Irina – and thinking of the impression Irina had made, even on him, in London he could understand that. He could not believe that Franca really wanted to marry him. He saw it as a 'rebound' fantasy, a plan really manufactured to hurt Jack. It was an episode, a test of a certain freedom. After it Franca would probably return home, she would smile, she would assent. The painful death of her love for Jack might occur over a longer period, perhaps years. Or else she might actually 'pull it off', really achieve a pure selfless attachment, love him and endure it all.

As he left the bridge and made for Bellmain he thought, she'll come back and we'll talk of it again and she'll understand. Other more urgent thoughts now crowded him. He had, after his yesterday's conversation with Irina, conceived a plan which he now felt resolved to carry out, which was to *move into Benbow*. Why had he not decided this before? There were many reasons. He did not want, as things stood at the moment, to press his company on those two. His coming and going gave them more space, while making up a reassuring routine of activity. He did not want Marcus to have to make conversation. He did not know what view would be taken by Marzillian. He was reluctant to bring the problem of 'Rodney' back into the picture in this particular way, arising as it would seem inevitably in such a context. What had changed now? Chiefly the quality of Ludens's anxiety. He had taken to heart Bland's words, 'stay near him'. Patrick was now less in evidence. Marcus was, indeed must be, in some state of shock after the dramatic end of his 'showings'. His dark strange brilliant mind must be brooding upon whatever was to come next. Ludens wanted to be, if not with him more, at least available more. More complex considerations concerned Irina. He did not believe there had been any 'wild period'. He thought it possible that something upsetting had occurred in some schoolboy–schoolgirl context which had led Irina, though actually still a virgin, to 'feel' that she was not. He had also ventured to think about her father. He did not of course imagine that Marcus had violated his child except in fantasy. This might indeed be the 'sin' of which he sometimes accused himself. He might however have frightened Irina by some outburst which could account for her fear of sex and for the laconic yet tender aloofness between them. These were uncertain speculations, concerning which he did not feel anxious or able to ask questions. What he did feel was that it was time to move nearer to Irina, to obtain both more trust and more authority, and if possible to get her properly to bed. He thought, I have been cautious, I have been prudent, I have been patient, I have waited. But I must not wait too long.

When he reached Benbow Irina came out to meet him upon the grass.
'Dad's busy. He's talking to a rabbi.'
'*What?*'
'I saw this man outside, he was sitting on the grass across the drive, so I asked him what he wanted. He said he'd seen you and you were going to ask Dad if he wanted to see him. So I said I'd ask and Dad said yes, so I brought him in. That's all right, isn't it, why look like that?'
'Well, it's happened, so I suppose it's got to be all right. I wanted to ask Marcus if he'd like to see the chap.'
'So why, what's the difference?'
'You asked him in a way expecting the answer yes, I would have asked him in a way expecting the answer no.'
'I don't understand. Why are you so grumpy?'
'I'm not "grumpy" my darling, I just feel – Oh never mind what I feel. Could I have some tea and some bread and butter? I somehow forgot about breakfast.'

'He told you he had terrible dreams? He never told me that.'
'He keeps up appearances with you. I'm a stranger.'
Marcus had spent an hour with Daniel Most, an hour during which Ludens's morale had continued to sink. He tried listening at the door, but could make nothing of the swift soft sounds of the conversation. It even occurred to him that they were talking in some foreign language. Yiddish? Hebrew? Ludens intensely resented, when it came to it, the crude interference of this self-appointed 'expert'. He dreaded its effect, at this crucial time, upon the direction of Marcus's thoughts. Marcus's

thoughts! He pictured them now as huge looming animal-like forms slowly performing mysterious gyrations in a mist.

Ludens had wearied Irina by his restless marchings to and fro and utterance of regrets and forebodings, and she had finally turned him out of the house. He waited on the lawn, grinding his teeth, and when Most emerged leapt on him almost ferociously. After that they decided to go for a walk. They had reached the far side of the lake where there was a seat placed conveniently for the view, and where, through the jumpy diamonds of the wire fence they could watch the restless shadows of small clouds passing over the little empty hills. Not even a church spire was visible. There was a sound as of distant thunder. A cool breeze was bending the long grass beyond the fence and Ludens wished he had put his jersey on. He leaned forward awkwardly with his elbows on his knees, drooping his head. He felt like tearing his hair.

'You don't look as if you slept well either,' observed Most.

'What about – I mean what were the dreams about?' said Ludens.

'Imprisonment, torture, death, what else.'

'What do you mean "what else", what sort of way to talk is that, he wasn't there, he read about it, reading is a different experience, night-mares are about trains or exams or losing things –'

'All right, all right, you asked me! Are you suggesting his dreams are waking fantasies?'

'I don't know what I'm suggesting. I don't want this business to overwhelm him, I want it to be something he can think about among other things and not as *the* thing. He said once that it was an icon of all human suffering.'

'A touching image, but one must beware of images, they console and are made to be destroyed. It was a technological achievement, it was a particular event in the history of our race.'

'"Race", what do you mean "race"? I'm English. All right, we're different, we're special, we're the universal conscience of humanity! I just don't want you to worry Marcus with all that or bring him Jewish objects or talk about Jewish mythology or Jewish God. He hasn't got the concept of God, you'd be talking nonsense to him. He's at a crucial stage in his life, in his thought, he's been thinking for years and years, he's in an *agony* of thinking, you can't come suddenly to someone like that and imagine you can "discuss his work" or "offer him ideas"! Apart from anything else it's damnably impertinent. Philosophical thought means thinking the whole of philosophy and then moving on from there. You have to think beyond and behind every formulation, take the *whole* thing to pieces, reduce it to raw material, get at it in a raw state. It's a long long pilgrimage, a long path. I've tried to follow, to understand, of course I can't, but I've worked with him and for him for a long time. I want him now, at this particular special moment, to be able to work in his own proper silence and be quietly alone with his own thoughts. Anything you could thrust upon him would be trivial, irrelevant, just utterly tiresome. I hope you understand what I say and will have the decency not to worry him again.'

'He asked me to come back.'

'He was being polite.'

'I have listened to you carefully,' said Most, 'but I have not changed my mind. I think I did communicate with him, as I hoped and expected to do. You sneered just now about the conscience of mankind. Now when wickedness is so educated and so well armed, it may be the task of innumerable people and peoples to be that conscience, and to preserve the memory of what evil is and what good is. Do not forget the things which thine eyes have seen, tell them to thy sons and to thy sons' sons.'

'For the Lord thy God is a jealous God, who destroys his enemies, which here below means do not forgive but requite evil with evil as soon as you have the power! All right, I'm sorry, I am simply trying to offend you, I hope I have not succeeded.'

'No,' said Most gravely, 'you have not. Listen. You think I am an ignorant blundering intruder. I must risk seeming or even being that. I believe that your friend is trying to remember things which I can help him to find.'

'Old Jewish things.'

'Old human things. He confronts a darkness, perhaps a crucial darkness, upon the long path you spoke of, he confronts an abyss which he has always known of and perhaps can now name.'

'Don't tell me!'

'He said to me that he had always felt that he was engaged in a dialogue –'

'Please not that sickening banality.'

'Why are you so afraid of the name of God? Is not that something that human beings should remember and are in danger of forgetting? *He* has the concept, and so have you.'

'The concept is empty.'

'If it is empty it is there. Nothing could be more important to this planet than preserving the name of God, we must not abandon it, it is entrusted to us in this age, to carry it onward through the darkness –'

A shadow fell upon the grass nearby. 'May I join you?' said Marzillian.

Ludens and Daniel Most stood up. Marzillian seated himself and motioned the other two to sit with him. Most sat down. Ludens stood in front of them with his back to the landscape. He thought, he must have seen us from the window of his office.

Marzillian, seen in the bright light, looked slightly older but suntanned and relaxed. His moustache had been discreetly trimmed, his hair made sleeker though no shorter. In a white shirt and creamy flannel trousers he looked more like a kind of exotic cricketer than a pirate. He crossed his legs, smiling amiably.

Ludens, intending to introduce Most, said to Marzillian, 'This is –'

But Marzillian interrupted him. 'Oh I know Daniel. He has been of assistance to me before in more than one difficult case. Isn't it so, Daniel?'

Most gave Marzillian a quick glance and a brief ambiguous smile.

The information he had just received enraged Ludens so much that he felt like turning away from them without a word. So the rabbi had been 'put up to it'! Everyone he met turned out to be a spy. He stepped back and said to Marzillian, 'I am going to move into Benbow, to live there. I will pay you rent of course. I imagine there is no objection.'

'Oh no objection at all, and of course no rent. I was about to suggest it myself. Now please sit down again, there is room for three.'

Ludens turned, without replying, and set off back across the grass in the direction of the golf course. He found himself literally shuddering and trembling with anger and with the impulse to weep with rage. His fury was partly directed against himself. Even here, now, in the midst of the most serious and awful problems he had ever faced, he could still feel idiotic puerile jealousy! He felt possessive about Marzillian, he even, evidently, felt possessive about Daniel Most! He detested the idea that Marzillian had encouraged, no doubt asked, the rabbi to interfere. Most, though certainly unwelcome, had appeared like something uncontaminated and pure, absolutely well-intentioned, coming from outside. Instead of which he was just part of the local plot, the Bellmain network, invited, perhaps begged, to 'have a go' at the Marcus Vallar case! I must get Marcus and Irina *out*, he thought. Of course I've told myself this before, but now it's urgent. It's *this place* which is rotting his mind and making calm peaceful thinking impossible. I'll buy a house somewhere in the country, and have Irina and Marcus there, and Irina can have a dog like she wants, and I'll commute to London by train. Or perhaps I'll get a job out of London. What about Exeter University?

We could live in Devon. But how the hell am I going to buy a house? I suppose I could get a mortgage. Or I could borrow from Jack. The thought of Jack returned him to Franca, who had this morning proposed marriage to him! Dear dear Franca. No wonder Jack wanted to keep her. Was his letter really so awful? It simply stated exactly what he so understandably wanted. Perhaps every man should have a wife and a Franca as well.

'You're sure you don't mind my being here?' said Ludens to Irina.

'Of course I don't mind, I'm glad, I said so! But there's just *so much* – and now – I don't know what to do.'

'Shall I go away, go back?'

'No! Don't *madden* me! Dad doesn't object, Marzillian doesn't object, you want to, it may be a good idea – I just can't manage new things in this little place, it's a strain, it complicates everything at every point, we've never settled down here – but it's all right, it may be better, anyway here you are and it's a relief in a way.'

'I'll help you.'

'*You – help* – dearest donkey, don't make me laugh! You don't realise how difficult it is just to *exist* with Dad in this mousehole – one has to have a routine –'

'But we have a routine, we've always had a routine. I won't be in the way.'

'But you *are* in the way. You're a large animal. Pat's bigger than you but he knows how to fit in, he's more tactful and graceful, though I suppose he's abandoned us now, since Dad was so disgraced, or humiliated or martyred or whatever it was.'

'Pat's still here, he's staying with the Stone People, or maybe with Camilla or Suzanne. He'll turn up again. I think he felt ashamed because he ran away.'

'You'll run away next.'

'Irina!'

'Well, I wouldn't blame you. Yes, I'm glad you're here, but it's a nuisance because I'll have to tell you things about Dad, for instance he's always getting up in the night to go to the lavatory. And he moans and cries sometimes.'

'Oh – dear –'

'You know *nothing*. And he snores. And he gets up very early in the morning and goes for walks, it's light so early and the curtains are hopeless.'

'All by himself?'

'Yes, you fool!'

'Are you sure he's asleep now?'

'Yes, it's after his bedtime, and he's taken his sleeping pill.'

'Sleeping pill?'

'Yes, it's harmless, it's the one everyone uses, you're so suspicious! He takes pills for his blood pressure doesn't he? He'll sleep soundly now for several hours, then he'll probably start to be restless, sometimes he sleeps longer. Sometimes he calls out to me and I go in to him. He has terrible dreams. He talked about his dreams to that rabbi. He's an awfully nice man, isn't he, I like him and I think he does Dad good, he's coming to see him again. Perhaps if Dad could believe in God he'd calm down a bit! Thank heavens it's not long to midsummer, after that there'll be less tension, even I can feel the rays!'

'Well, if that rabbi asks for me say I'm out! Irina, I'm going to buy a house.'

'Oh really? Where? What about us?'

Electrified by anger and fear, Ludens, after leaving Marzillian and Daniel Most to their conversation (he looked back but they were talking to each other, not looking after him), had gone straight to the Black Lion and announced to Mr and Mrs Toller that he was leaving. There was surprise and regret. He paid his startlingly large bill, packed his suitcase and books, and arrived at Benbow with the news that he proposed, if they had no objections, to stay. The proposal was warmly received, and although Irina began at once to make petty complaints, Ludens could see that she was really glad. Marcus said, 'So you'll really be with us,' and that pleased Ludens very much. He had not, during the day, had an opportunity to speak to Marcus at any length alone, but planned to have a serious talk with him on the morrow. Now that Marcus had gone (early as usual) to bed another problem, of course, confronted the pair in the sitting room.

Ludens had been startled into his flurry of decisive activity most immediately, as he was well aware, by the appearance on the scene of Daniel Most, and the instant sense that the unexpected intruder was in danger of *usurping his place*. The possible extent of this usurpation, rapidly dawning upon Ludens, was indeed appalling. Daniel Most: friend and ally of Marzillian, preferred confidant of Marcus, possible pet of Irina. Marcus wanted his daughter to marry a clever Jewish boy: well, here was *another* one, just as clever and certainly Jewisher. Ludens was unnerved by the speed with which this stranger had pushed his way in. He had even appropriated Gildas. It was time for Ludens to assert his rights. But what exactly were his rights? Had he perhaps by being too respectful, too tactful, too gentle, forfeited what he thought of as his rights? He must now hasten to make unambiguously clear to all interested parties that (whatever that might mean) *he was the one*. Ludens was of course also affected by pressures which had been independently building up, not least his desire to be again, and more successfully, in bed with Irina. He had begun to think that she too wished for this, for a more forceful and authoritative taking of possession. He had for long enough respected her anxiety, the wound left by the unhappy experience about which he had decided he must soon question her more closely. There was also the problem of privacy, but about that, now that he was on the terrain itself, he felt more confident or more careless. He had, as he packed his things, paid Toller's bill, and driven his car to Benbow, decided that he would let a little time pass, perhaps two or three nights, before making his firm move. But now, left alone with Irina in the sitting room, he discovered he could wait no longer.

The little spare bedroom, where with some ceremony Irina had made up Ludens's bed, was next to the side door, on the other side of which was the study. Irina's bedroom, which faced the back of the house adjoined the bathroom, and the kitchen and Marcus's bedroom, which faced the lawn, made up the other side of the house. Ludens had said, half questioning, half commanding, 'You will come to my bed tonight.' Irina had looked at him gravely and said nothing. Ludens rushed to his room, pulled the curtains, undressed with feverish speed, then sheepishly donned, in lieu of a dressing-gown, his mackintosh. He had put the bedside lamp on the floor so that it gave a dim subdued light. He pulled back the sheet and blanket which had been so neatly tucked in. He waited, containing with the pressure of one hand the audible hammering of his heart. He could hear now, farther away, the soft regular sound of Marcus's sibilant snores. Suppose she did not come? But she came; startling him because he heard no sound, sliding silently in through the door like a snake. She was wearing a long silky dark blue robe, unbuttoned and unbelted, which hung loosely about her. Her head was bowed, her dark hair falling to conceal her face. Ludens's mackintosh fell off, taking itself away. He slid his arms round her, thrusting them in under the robe, and drawing her up against him. They stood thus motionless with closed eyes. Then Ludens helped her to shed the silky robe which fell with a swift sighing slither to the floor. They sat down awkwardly on the narrow bed, then stretched out, pressing and kneading each other as they struggled to lie at full length face to face. He could hear her sighing. She murmured, 'Don't make any noise,' with her warm lips against his shoulder. Ludens, lying beside her now, burrowed one arm beneath her, drawing her closer to him. He felt deeply blissfully happy, and could have cried out aloud or burst into sobbing laughter. But he was silent, holding her firmly, adoring and commanding her whole body, and with his free hand caressing her lightly. He sighed too, controlling his impatience, wanting the long minutes to pass slowly which were so full of pure delight.

They continued, not in a whisper but in magically low tones as if their very thoughts had tongues. 'Oh my Irina, my dear girl, I love you so much.'

'Dear Ludens, dear dear good Ludens, don't be cross with me.'

'That's the silliest thing you've ever said.'

'I'm still – you know – anxious.'

'I've got that thing on, don't worry.' And yet why have I got it on, he thought. Isn't this the very moment to begin another life, to procreate that genius that Marcus wants, that we all want, the beautiful brilliant boy with the large thoughtful eyes? But he knew that it must not be, the solemn act must wait, he would lead Marcus and Irina along, faster, now, and faster, but at a pace which was for them just right.

Ludens, beginning to cover her, felt her slight resistance, and paused. 'Irina, will you tell me? What was that thing that happened in the past, the thing that upset you so? Could you tell me now? Or would you rather tell later?'

He felt her suddenly shudder, and when she spoke it was in a tearful voice. 'It made me very unhappy.'

'All right, don't say more, you can tell me later. Don't grieve, my love, that's the past. I love you and I'll make you happy, I'll mend all, I'll heal all. I worship you with my love, I give you my whole heart, for ever and ever. You do love me, don't you.'

'Yes, yes – but –'

'But what?'

'I'm sorry to be just me – there's so little of me.'

'Oh – you – silly – darling –'

'Now you'll start up about how I ought to go to the university!'

'I'll say that tomorrow. Oh you dear sweet creature, my creature – now will you let me?'

But she did not. And Ludens had to be content with what had happened before. But, overcome by love, he was content, and fell asleep at last, falling into a deep dark pit of happiness.

Later on he awoke, instantly conscious of where he was and what had been happening. Irina had gone. The lamp had been put out, the door was ajar. He listened for a while, and heard her talking softly to her father in his bedroom. Ludens thought, she won't come back here, that's all right. I'm so happy. I'll go to sleep again now. I'm at home.

He slept, and when he woke again it was dawn, the early dawn of the short summer night. He got up and put on his mackintosh. He went into the sitting room, intending to go outside and walk on the dewy grass with his bare feet. But when he reached the uncurtained window he saw a figure standing on the lawn. It was Marcus, fully dressed, standing with his back to the house. He stood very still, then suddenly moved and seemed to glide away, fading into the grey shadowy powdery crepuscular light and disappearing among the trees.

Ludens stood at the window for a while, and the mystery of the solitary walker came over him in a wave of sadness and heart-rending care.

In the days that followed Ludens himself did a good deal of walking. His mind, divided between happiness and unhappiness, hope and fear, was extremely distressed. He realised now that living at such close quarters with Marcus and Irina was indeed, as Irina had indicated to him, difficult, a strain, complicating everything at every point. He soon became aware of the things which Irina had concealed from him, because, as she said, she didn't want him to 'fuss'. 'Dad puts on a show for you, he pulls himself together, he's dafter than you think!' He realised that, in some partly literal sense, Marcus had 'tidied himself up' for his conversations with Ludens, which had had, as he now saw, a certain formality. The 'domestic scenes', to which Ludens had attached so much importance were also, he could see, 'social occasions', and so virtually 'put up jobs'. All three of them had, hitherto, followed a certain instinct in not seeing too much of each other and following the particular routine to which Ludens had referred. Now meeting each other unkempt, in the case of Marcus and Ludens unshaven, competing for the bathroom, dressing and undressing and sharing meals, in a tiny space where speech was everywhere audible, gave them mutually new impressions. (Like early days of married life, Ludens thought. But he was not discouraged for he knew that love conquers all.) He was often in trouble for breaking rules which had never been explained to him, such as to use special forks and spoons for eggs, to put the honey and marmalade jars onto saucers, not onto tablecloths, to keep the wet garbage separate from the dry garbage, and to shut the kitchen door at night because the fridge made a noise. Marcus was sometimes irritable, often depressed, Irina was sharp-tongued and quickly exasperated. It was soon agreed between Ludens and Irina that Ludens should simply absent himself at certain periods of the day, following his previous pattern. 'Go to the office!' as Irina put it. Only now, when exiled from Benbow, Ludens had nowhere to go. He did not want to go to the Black Lion, although Toller, with a remarkable and touching kindness, had told Ludens he could come and sit in the bar or the residents' lounge any time to 'do his work', of which Toller had some vague and respectful idea. He could not settle down to read or think at Benbow where his tiny room contained only a bed and a chest of drawers and where he had always to be anxiously listening to what Marcus and Irina were saying. He was quite glad when Irina sent him on shopping expeditions. He also went on long walks out into the countryside along lanes where red poppies and white daisies and purple clover and meadowsweet and foxgloves and flowering elder had already replaced the cow parsley and the hawthorn.

Aspects of Marcus, now seen continuously at close quarters, worried Ludens. Marcus certainly looked older, not just in the rather dignified sage-like manner he had sometimes observed earlier, but in a wilder more untidy, as if disintegrated, way. His face sometimes expressed an extremity of grief which made him look almost grotesquely haggard. Irina, when Ludens spoke of this to her, said that her father looked 'much as usual', 'always looked like that', and had only put on a different face for Ludens when Ludens was a 'visitor', which now he was not. Ludens was also worried by the dawn walking, which Irina said he 'always did', and which, as Ludens had felt on the first morning, seemed to remove Marcus into another realm, a realm of danger. There was also the weird question of what Marcus did all day. He swam, he saw the physiotherapist for his arthritis, he went for short strolls with Ludens, or with Ludens and Irina. But mostly he simply sat either in his bedroom or in the study. Was he *thinking*? Ludens, who could not imagine thinking unaccompanied by at least *some* writing, was not sure. He was clearly, with some kind of intensity, *existing*, perhaps entering a form of being of which Ludens knew nothing. During these sittings, when Ludens was occasionally able to observe him, Marcus's face lost its haggard look, assuming an expression of calm, even of shrewd satisfaction, which was not reassuring either. On two mornings, during Ludens's prescribed absence period, Marcus saw Daniel Most, as reported by Irina. Marcus said nothing of this; and Ludens had decided, for a short time, to abstain from the 'serious talks' which had for so long constituted their closest mode of being together. Ludens was, in this respect, not exactly sulking; he just felt that he, they, must for the moment *wait*. The same instinct made him steer clear of Most. In this abstention Ludens was supported, perhaps also prompted, by his new relation with Irina which now so filled his consciousness and nourished his being. In the midst of the painful web of uncertainty presented by every day, Ludens and Irina pursued their secret intimacy, something almost entirely unspoken, except in the sense that, as Ludens felt, it transformed all ordinary discourse into the language of love. At night it was the same as before. Ludens had not questioned Irina again about the 'wound'; and he had accepted her prohibition as a temporary barrier which would before very long, perhaps for some unknown reason, be suddenly withdrawn. Meanwhile he was prepared to wait, and enjoy the much that was granted, not complaining because it was not all.

On one of these days Mrs Toller, whose disapproval did not preclude curiosity, came over to bring a letter to Ludens, and was rewarded by a glimpse of the Professor sitting in the study, whose door he usually kept open, carefully examining, then biting, one of his fingernails. Mrs Toller said how much they missed him, and was Mrs Sheerwater coming back, and that they had had a postcard from Boston from Miss Tether. Ludens escorted her politely out and walked with her to the junction with the main drive. He had wondered whether the letter might be from Franca. He still observed in himself the unworthy pleasure felt at the thought that others were in trouble too, a pleasure which could co-exist with sympathy, even with love. But the letter was from Gildas and ran as follows.

I am sorry not to have written. I have been suffering a small domestic upheaval. And I wanted to recover from the extraordinary effect of Marcus. I still can't make out what *it* is about him, where *it* lies in the field of force of the spirit – let alone of morality. (Ah

... morality ...) Whatever he did for me (which you called lifting the curse) took place without words – we did talk, but that was just a superficial murmur which created the time in which something else could happen. I can't describe it. He looked so sad. I never saw him look sad before, he was always so superior, everywhere the king. You once called him a god from elsewhere who had lost his way. Perhaps he has realised now that he's trapped here and has to suffer with us and become mortal and die. Not supreme power after all, but having to give everything away. Sorry, this is becoming sentimental nonsense, like what you talk.

Daniel wrote to me about Marcus abjuring his godhead and being execrated by the populace. Daniel thinks you are hostile to him because you don't want him to talk religion to Marcus. I make another diagnosis, having reference to an ungenerous trait in your character upon which I have had occasion to comment. Never mind. I would like to see you, not least to hear from your lips a description of the abdication scene – though I am afraid to come in case I meet Marcus again! You see I am still frightened of him. I will tell you what I decide. I expect you know what has been going on at Jack's place.

Yours G.

This letter exasperated Ludens. He was not in a mood to be castigated or patronised by Gildas, and he found the reference to Marcus conde- scending and frivolous. Moreover what *was* going on at Jack's place? About which Gildas must know more than he did. Above all, the letter was not affectionate enough. He tore it up, regretted this and tried in vain to reconstruct it, having decided that its chief message was that Gildas was unhappy.

Ludens continued to be worried about Marcus's dawn walks. Where did he go? Suppose something were to happen to him? He wondered if he ought not to follow Marcus surreptitiously so as to guard him. He was reluctant to do this because there was something so purposeful and mysterious about these disappearances; to spy upon them would be blasphemous and to be discovered spying might attract some serious penalty. However anxiety and curiosity triumphed over piety and the next morning Ludens was already dressed, waiting in his bedroom when Marcus emerged from his. He watched from the sitting room while, as before, Marcus stood motionless upon the lawn. Then when he moved he vanished so quickly that Ludens feared he might have lost him already. However when he reached the drive he could see Marcus's figure ahead of him walking on the tarmac. Ludens followed, treading on the wet dewy verge. At the main drive, Marcus turned towards the house, and Ludens was not surprised when he turned off to the left and crossed the grass to the yew enclosure and the Axle Stone. When Marcus had entered the enclosure Ludens ran lightly over the grass and, circling the outside of the yew hedge, introduced himself into the slit-entrance nearest to the wood. He moved forward cautiously. Marcus was on the concrete seat, in profile to Ludens. He had cleared a space in the pattern of pebbles and was sitting motionless, his back to the 'broken' side of the Stone which, assembled now into a face of profound sadness, towered above him. Time passed. The birds sang. The sun rose. Marcus sat. Ludens moved slightly forward. He had a curious sensation as of an almost, yet not quite, audible rhythmic beat, as if a large distant machine, deep inside the earth, were pulsating, something felt perhaps rather than heard. Ludens felt calm, then almost dazed as if a great space were opening up about him. He felt curiously sleepy and had to concentrate to focus his eyes on Marcus. He began to blink, screwing up his eyes then rubbing them. When he looked again Fanny Amherst had arrived and was standing facing Marcus, not near to him but a little way out on the grass with her back to the hedge. They stayed thus facing each other, for several minutes. Ludens could not see what that gazing was like, but it seemed to him not to resemble an ordinary encounter of two human beings. Then, as he blinked again, Fanny vanished, flitting away through the opening from which she had come.

Ludens suddenly thought, suppose I too were to go and *look* at Marcus? On the occasions when Marcus had 'manifested himself' to the devotees outside Benbow, Ludens had been either behind him in the house or at the fringe of the crowd and watching them rather than him. He stepped backward, then ran swiftly round the outside of the yew circle. He entered now as Fanny had done and moved along the wall until he was directly opposite to Marcus, then turned to face him. Ludens remembered later that at that moment he had expected, and feared, some terrible look of recognition. But there was none. Marcus's eyes stared, large and empty, more like holes than eyes. Ludens stared back. He began to feel again the soundless rhythmic beat which he had felt in his hiding place. He felt the yew wall against his back as if he were pinned against it and was aware of its darkness towering above him. After a while the empty eyes seemed to have acquired a cold glow. Ludens was now able simply to stare without being conscious of blinking, perhaps without blinking. He looked into those eyes, and then, with a slight effort, managed to focus his attention on the face. He was enabled to do this because of a curious phenomenon. It was as if Marcus's head, leaving his body and very much enlarged, had advanced towards him, hanging in space at a point half-way from the yew wall and the Stone. The face that he saw was contorted with grief, and not only with grief but with some other emotion which at once seemed to Ludens like fear, the most dreadful fear. He thought, it is the face of a prisoner waiting to be tortured, *waiting* . . . The face was so painful that he felt he could not endure it and tried to move and look away; but it was as if he were pinned to the wall and his head clamped into a metal vice. He felt like crying out but knew that he could utter no sound and could not even make the attempt. Then gradually he was aware of a relaxing of tension, the dreadful head withdrew and diminished. Then he was looking at Marcus sitting opposite to him, and Marcus's eyes had become the blank eyes of an abstracted thinker, or of a meditating mystic, his eyelids drooping a little, his mouth pensive and sad. Ludens thought, did *she* see *that*? He did not know what Fanny had seen, but was certain that the worshippers at Benbow had seen nothing like it.

Marcus suddenly rose. He turned and stooped and pushed the stones back, not arranging them but scattering them roughly. Then he turned and began to walk toward Ludens. Ludens, petrified with fear, thought at first that Marcus was going to walk straight up to him as if to meet him face to face and breast to breast and walk straight through him. But Marcus was simply making for the opening in the hedge near to which Ludens was standing. He passed fairly close to Ludens, not looking at him or seeming to be aware of him. He passed by and disappeared. Ludens sat down on the grass.

Everything now reappeared. The birds, which had been silent, were singing. The handsome sarsen was catching the rays of the sun which was shining through one of the entrances. The votive pebbles were disturbed where Marcus had been sitting. The panic fear was over. Ludens, attempting to collect himself, felt a stale aching emptiness, a futile accidental desolate feeling, and a hurt sense of loss. He also felt, as if this were a refuge, extremely tired, and he lay down for a while upon the grass which the sun was already drying. He looked at his watch. It was nearly nine o'clock. Had he been asleep?

He rose up quickly and set off in the direction of Benbow. He thought, I must make sure Marcus went back there and didn't go wandering off somewhere else. I ought to have followed him. But I couldn't, I was *too tired*. He hurried, approaching Benbow through the woodland. The doors were open and he could hear Marcus's voice, so familiar, so ordinary. Ludens felt unable to go in. He turned back along the drive. At the corner of the main drive he met Daniel Most.

Most said, 'Hello Ludens, I've been looking for you. So glad to see you – good morning. How are you? Look, I've been wanting to say this to you. Marzillian didn't send for me, he didn't ask me to see Marcus or anything like that. I came on my own just because I'd heard of him. I thought you might –'

'All right, all right.'

'And another thing. My wife and I would be so pleased if you and Marcus and Miss Vallar would come to dinner with us some time in the next week or two.'

'*Come to dinner?*' So the world of 'dinner parties' still existed, did it, far away, somewhere. Ludens was astonished. He was also annoyed, for a moment almost enraged. He could see through the specious words. So Most had noticed that Ludens was made jealous, at any rate was offended, by the idea that Most and Marzillian were working together against him. He had also evidently noticed that Ludens resented Most's acquaintance with Irina, and was aware that Irina thought Most 'awfully nice'; hence the blatant phrase 'my wife and I' to inform Ludens that he was married. The apparently friendly speech was simply a ploy to remove impressions which might impede Most's access to Marcus. Ludens glared. 'No, I'm sorry, we don't go out to dinner.'

'Oh – too bad –' Most seemed relieved. Perhaps the invitation had been prompted after all by Mrs Most's curiosity. 'How's Marcus? I thought I might see him this morning.'

'Have you arranged to?'

'Well, yes.'

'Go ahead, then.'

'Don't be so angry. Be calm. Talk to me properly.'

'Something awful has happened. No it hasn't. Nothing has happened. I've just understood something. I must have help.'

'What is it? Let me help you.'

'He's thinking about *that*, Marcus is, he's removing himself, he's –'

'I know he's thinking about that. You kept him off it so it accumulated. Wait, wait, please understand. We've all got to do it, *we*, I mean perhaps everybody, weave the past into the present, work at it, like endlessly imagining, not just falling into it like into a pit, but surrounding it, I don't mean in a theoretical way, like discussing whether it was unique or what exactly caused it and so on, but connecting it, a sort of

Midrash, like people in the camps telling the stories of their lives, like someone said –'

'All right, but I'm just a historian. Look, this is worse than you think, it's worse than I could imagine.'

'Steady on. Let's go and sit somewhere.'

A group of young people was advancing along the drive, Colin, Andy, Miriam, Kathleen, the red-headed boy called Max, and two other youths whom Ludens knew by sight. The girls had made a garland of flowers which they were swinging between them. Most said, 'Hello, Colin, hi kids!' He evidently knew them well.

Colin said, 'Hi!' to Most, then to Ludens, 'Look, we've been talking – I wonder if we could come and see the Professor? There's not so many of us now, the rest have gone to Stonehenge. We've never really talked to him and we feel it's such an opportunity, such a, you know, privilege, we'd feel, if we didn't see him again, that something that was sort of *meant* for us hadn't happened. Do you see what I mean?'

Ludens said to Most, 'You look after them, you decide.' He said to Colin, 'Do whatever he tells you.' He said to Most, 'I'm going to see Marzillian.'

'Has he asked you?'

'No.'

'He won't see you, you know what he's like.'

'You go to Marcus, try to see what's in his mind.' He said to the Seekers, 'If you see Patrick tell him to go to the Professor.'

Ludens turned and hurried away, running at first then walking fast along the drive in the direction of the house. When he got as far as Boscawen he met Mr Talgarth. Talgarth stopped him, touching his arm. 'Have you heard the news? Lady Barforth is going!'

'Going –?'

'She's leaving us. She's going to live with her daughter in Berkshire. She said she was only here for the golf. By the way, a nephew of mine is coming on a visit, he used to be in the English chess team, perhaps he could give the Professor a game – you might tell him.'

'I will. Excuse me, I've got to see Marzillian.'

'Marzillian – I haven't seen him for months – can't stand the beggar – see plenty of Terence though, he's a real doctor, he can make a *diagnosis*. He does all the work. Marzillian just talks soothing nonsense.'

Ludens ran on. Although the sun shone a cool wind had risen. He leapt up the steps and strode into the hall.

The door-keeper stood up, then advanced as soon as she saw Ludens.

Ludens said, 'I must see Dr Marzillian.'

The girl said, 'He is in conference. I'm sorry. I will tell him you called.'

Ludens walked past her, knocked on Marzillian's door and walked straight in.

Marzillian was in his place. Dr Bland was sitting near him at the side of the desk.

Marzillian, expressing no surprise, said amiably, 'Sit down, Ludens. Sit *there*.' He pointed to the chair opposite to him.

Ludens sat down. Dr Bland had risen. Marzillian said, 'Don't go, Terence,' and Bland sat down. 'Now, my young friend, what is it, what can I do for you?'

Ludens had not planned or even conceived of what he was going to say. He simply felt, as he had expressed it to Most, that he must have help. He said, 'I'm very alarmed about Marcus's state of health. Were you talking about him?'

'No, about another case, but go on, what alarms you?'

'I – I have seen – oh, never mind what I've seen, I think that Marcus is destroying himself, he's being eaten up by – by his own thoughts, by some awful imaginings, by terrible grief – he's going to destroy himself by some sort of internal combustion.'

Marzillian exchanged a look with Dr Bland. He said after a moment, 'Thoughts, however terrible, are not necessarily destructive – they may be a path, a way – they may represent a progress, even a therapeutic process. We are way-using creatures. You yourself have followed Marcus on a path, indeed a long path, over many years. Your interesting friend has, with a most exceptional intensity and continuity of thought, continued his quest. Even in the short time that he has been here he has moved on, he has changed and made experiments and made discoveries. The psyche is a vast space within which we seek for God – you understand my use of that word – a space of which most people are unaware, crouching as they are in some tiny corner of it, living the life of a beetle in a hole. Marcus has travelled far into remote and strange regions, not just as an objective scholarly spectator but as one who lives and *becomes* what he knows. He has the godlike power of metamorphosis, he participates, he tastes. It is impossible to travel so far and live so completely without enduring the black contingent grief which underlies all human existence, without taking the pathway into the most extreme places of human suffering. That price is paid for other knowledge, the knowledge of God, the energy of pure creation, the infinite possibility of the soul, the joy and pain of power and of the necessity of laying it aside. Much of this you yourself have perhaps seen and in part understood. You have tried to check him, to contain him, even to guide him, but you have failed, and may have learnt something from the failure. I hope that you will go on, I hope you will continue to have faith in him and in the part which you can play in his pilgrimage.'

Ludens, listening to Marzillian, sat crouched in his chair, feeling himself shrinking, as if he were veritably turning into one of the beetles of which Marzillian had spoken. The feeling of insipid futile senseless accidentalness returned to him. Why argue, why answer, why do anything? He felt cold, he was conscious of hunger, he felt faintly sick, faintly dizzy. He said, 'I don't understand your use of the word "God", and I don't think that Marcus knows what he's doing or where he's going, I don't think he's in control. I think he has gone too far. I am *terrified*, and I have seen a terrible thing, and I want you to do something.'

Marzillian, staring at him, said thoughtfully, 'Well, I won't ask what it was you saw, but let us say that for a moment you looked into hell, you were *enabled* to look. But that was *your* experience. Of course it frightened you.'

Ludens thought, he'll leave me with *this*, if he can, I must keep on talking. He said, 'Have you talked in those terms, I mean about the vast spaces of the psyche and so forth, with Marcus?'

'He knows all these things. I have spoken with him, hoping to learn something.'

'But he is *ill*.'

'You say this at last.'

'You are just watching him.'

'What do you want me to do?'

'I want you to give him something to calm him – to remove this awful intensity – like a – tranquillising drug –'

'You said once that you would kill me if I gave him drugs.'

'I've changed my mind.'

Marzillian and Bland again exchanged a glance. Ludens thought, they're probably already giving him something – and if they are I'm *glad* – I just must *share* it with somebody – I can't carry all this alone. He added aloud, 'I can't carry all this alone.'

Marzillian said, 'I assure you that I share your reverence for that extraordinary mind.'

'You'll look after him, won't you?' said Ludens. The words sounded weak and pathetic, old familiar desperate words so often uttered to doctors.

'We will do our best,' said Marzillian. He sat back in a manner which suggested that the interview was over.

Ludens rose. As he approached the door Dr Bland, reaching it before him, opened it. Ludens looked at Bland. Ludens's eyes expressed mortal anxiety and supplication. Bland's eyes expressed a mournful sympathetic understanding. Ludens walked out through the hall onto the terrace. He was amazed by the bright sunlight, he had not been conscious of any light, as if he had sat in darkness. He crossed the lawn. Two people he had not seen before were playing croquet. They nodded to him as if knowing who he was. He began to walk along the tarmac more slowly toward Benbow. Well, what *did* he want? Did he really want Marcus to be drugged into some quieter, calmer, safer mode of being? Did he want him to be confined in the house, put in one of those terrible 'cots' which Patrick had described to him, after he had once been smuggled 'inside' by Camilla? How could one look after someone like Marcus without damage: like trying to contain some wild thing which would smash itself against bars, or bite off its own trapped foot? He wanted to feel that Marcus was safe – but could Marcus ever be safe?

As he took the turning to Benbow he heard a loud chattering which was not that of the midsummer birds. The group of Seekers appeared, coming towards him talking and laughing loudly. They hailed him with waves and cries. Yes, they'd seen Marcus and it was *wonderful*! He'd lectured them about education and work and going back home and meditation and quietness and holiness and pureness of heart, and as Kathleen put it was really just like 'the nicest of uncles'.

Ludens was astonished. 'How long were you with him?'

'Oh about twenty minutes or so,' said Colin, 'but it seemed like much longer, didn't it?'

'We were very nervous,' said Miriam. 'When we used to see him on the steps, you know, he seemed so remote, so unearthly, he made us feel good and happy, but we wouldn't have dared to come near him, we didn't even venture onto the grass, remember, though some people did, there was a kind of electrical barrier like in science fiction. We had to pluck up our courage to ask to see him. We discussed it a lot and we decided we must try, we'd think later what a loss it was, and it's been so perfect –'

'He made a great point about going on with our education,' said Andy, 'and getting the best education we could, and going on learning all our lives, and how we ought to be quiet and meditate every day, and how we ought to go home and get on with our studies and –'

'And *are* you going home?' asked Ludens.

'Oh yes, after midsummer,' said Colin, 'we've changed our plans about that. We'd bought a lot of fireworks to let off at dawn, but we've decided not to, it'll be very quiet, we may sing a little, it'll be in *his* spirit.'

'Where do you live?'

It turned out they all lived near Birmingham and had known each other a long time and had thought of 'dropping out', but now they would go back to their training and education like *he* said.

'But wherever we are,' said Miriam, 'in times to come, he will be the centre, he has changed our whole lives. We've left our addresses with Irina so she'll tell us where he moves to if he leaves here.'

'I think,' said Colin, 'that we shall always *know* where he is somehow.'

Ludens said farewell to them and walked on slowly. How amazing that Marcus had been able to communicate with the young people in that way! Had he actually *said* all those edifying things? Or had he really said very little which had expanded automatically in their minds under the influence of his presence? The meeting had been organised by Daniel Most. Ludens now wished that he had organised it. But mainly he felt glad that it had happened. How very strange that the Marcus whom he had seen in such a travail of agony at the Stone should have gone back to Benbow and become at once like 'the nicest of uncles'! But what had happened at the Stone? Ludens was assailed by a curious doubt. Had he actually seen that strange and dreadful thing – or had he in fact fallen asleep and *dreamt* it? He thought, if Marcus goes out before dawn on midsummer day I'll go with him – and it will all be quiet and peaceful like they said. I'd like to be with Marcus then and to hear them singing.

As he neared Benbow Ludens felt an anxiety composed of fear and shyness. Had Marcus, he wondered, actually *seen* him earlier that morning? And what sort of state would Marcus be in now? As he crossed the lawn and mounted the steps he could hear the sound of animated conversation coming from the kitchen. Nervously he opened the kitchen door.

He was welcomed by exclamations of cordiality and pleasure. Seated round the remains of breakfast were Marcus, Irina, Most and Patrick. Another chair was brought, a cup and plate, Irina made more tea and toast, he was quickly included in the conversation and surrounded by sympathetic and amiable faces. Irina gave him an intimate and loving smile, Daniel Most a quizzical grin, and Patrick an apologetic old-friend-back-to-the-fold look. At first Ludens did not look directly at Marcus, but when, among all the renewed chatter, he ventured to do so, he received a curious amused ironical forgiving dart of a glance, rather like what a headmaster might despatch to an erring pupil whose discovered misdemeanour he proposed to overlook. Ludens smiled back with his broadest crazy smile. A great surge of relief and comfort came over him as he looked around the table, he was among friends, he was safe, he was loved, he was real, it was a happy domestic scene, it was, it came to him, just like *family life*, something which it occurred to him, not for the first time but now with a particular poignancy, he had never had.

The conversation was still about the Seekers, about whom Daniel turned out to know a good deal. He had, he said, come across them last year at Avebury where they had caused surprise and amusement by going round kissing the immense stones. He revealed that Colin had been a theology student, Kathleen was a painter, and Andy and Miriam, who were playing truant from a polytechnic, were shortly going to get married. The talk then got onto Stones in general, Marcus spoke of the stone circles in Brittany which he had visited with a mathematician who had theories about them, and Patrick recalled dolmens in Ireland which were venerated by Catholics who then got into trouble with their priests.

At last Daniel Most rose and said he must go. He offered to help Irina with the washing-up, an offer which she refused with ironical comments about others who didn't even offer. The gathering disintegrated, with Marcus retiring to his study, Irina staying in the kitchen, and the other three walking out onto the lawn.

Daniel Most said to Ludens, 'I think he's all right.'

Ludens, who did not want to talk to Most who was evidently anxious to talk to him, said curtly, 'Yes. Good.'

Patrick said to Ludens, 'Alfred, could I have a word with you?'

Ludens gave a vague valedictory wave to Daniel who then, saying 'See you soon,' set off along the drive.

Ludens and Patrick sat down on the wooden seat.

'What do you think, Pat?'

'What about?'

'Marcus of course.'

'I don't know, he changes so much all the time.'

'Yes,' said Ludens, 'he has the god-like power of metamorphosis.'

'But God is always the same.'

'Well, real God is, but I was thinking of the Olympian gods.'

'I don't know about them. There are weird beings in Ireland, but they're mostly making mischief.'

'Perhaps Marcus makes the higher mischief.'

'Don't you jest.'

'Pat, I don't feel like jesting, I'm worried about him.'

Ludens had decided not to say much to Patrick. He wanted to reflect.

'I should have stayed with him, now I feel cut off, I feel I let him down, I feel like St Peter.'

'Don't worry, you're back now, he kept asking about you, you calm his nerves.'

'I don't know. I was so terrible to him that day long ago I told you of, I called him names, hollow and vain and that – he can't have forgotten. I think he's a man would remember an offence all his life, and keep smiling at you.'

I hope not! thought Ludens. He said, 'No, no, he's forgiven you long ago, and he cares for you because he saved your life. Pat, please stay around now.'

'I thought you were against me.'

'I'm not, we need you, I need you, you feel things I can't feel. What *do* you think?'

'I think he's gone too far.'

'Too far?'

'He's thought too much, like into a kind of doom. If you think too much it's intolerable, it must be, you see all the horrible things that are hidden away, the world's so vile really, there's just little bits are nice, and if you really think you can hold a thousand things in your mind in a second, like you or I could hold three. It's a great pain to try to imagine what such thinking could be, it stands to reason if things are mostly bad and you think them your mind must be full of horrors, as I think his mind is. I thought this earlier once you know, but then I sort of thought he was God, you'd have to be cruel and have infinite love and, well, I don't know what else, some great wisdom and other things to be able to see the whole of sin and evil and all the tears and not go mad. And of course God would be seeing it all, our poor little planet and all the other planets and the stars and the galaxies and the whole cosmos may be in the whole of time dripping with tears and the blood of the innocent ones. Well, of course I don't think he was God but I thought that for him it was like that, that he could see it all and understand it all and somehow just by understanding and being there and being himself make it better. Now I don't think that.'

Pat was silent. Ludens said, 'So now –?'

'I don't know. I thought he was on top of it all riding on a cloud. Now I think he's a victim.'

'A victim, like –?'

'Like Christ on the cross all for nothing, like if Christ was just an ordinary man, a good man but full of sins as every man is, and a deceived man, who was wonderful but not as wonderful as he thought.'

Ludens said after a moment or two, 'But even if it had been like that with Christ, even if it *was* like that, as I believe, it was *not* for nothing.'

'Well, if it's human things it's all accident, maybe good comes, maybe bad, maybe nothing.'

'That's not an argument against trying to be good – one must try to be good – just for nothing.'

'You talk! I used to think he was a good man, then I thought he was a saint, now I don't know maybe he's some kind of magician. Sometimes I think there's evil there.'

'He thinks about evil –'

'Maybe only God can do that without being darkened. You remember how beautiful he was – and he's still beautiful. It's uncanny, like the black arts. But what do I know, I know nothing. He saved my life and I thought he could save my soul too. As it is my life is worthless, I'm drinking and I can't write poetry and there's the women – Suzanne's in love with me, I want Camilla but she's just an agent of His Nibs, I haven't even been to bed with her. I think I'll go back to Dublin.'

'Pat, don't give up. Are you still going to Mass?'

'That, yes.'

'That's good.'

'Why should you care? It's not logical. All you've got left is empty pious talk. Now I'm going to get drunk at the Hedgehog. Will you come?'

'No. But please stay with us.'

'Oh go to hell.'

After Patrick had loped away down the drive Ludens sat for a while thinking. He decided not to torment himself by trying to make sense of what had happened at the Axle Stone. The more his thoughts touched it, the more he felt they ought not to. It was even possible that he would soon *forget* what had happened. He did not want to think, in connection with Marcus, about the 'uncanny', the word which Pat had used, and which Gildas had once used too. And that very morning he had begged

Marzillian to put a stop to it all! He had felt relief, he still felt relief, to think of someone else being responsible! Thus far had his faith in Marcus, his idea of Marcus, slipped and become incoherent. He had been pleased to hear how sensibly Marcus had talked to the Seekers, glad to see how readily, in the kitchen, he could join in a conversation. So was Ludens now content with 'family life', treasuring evidences of Marcus's ordinariness, and defending him by empty pious talk? *Where am I* now, he wondered, have I committed an act of treachery? Now I am even consoling myself by thinking that Marzillian probably understands the situation better than me, and that he will do, or will have done, what is wisest without any reference to what I say.

He felt very tired. He had scarcely slept. When Irina had left him, as she always did about midnight, it had been almost time to watch for the dawn and listen for the sounds of Marcus's departure. His eyes closed now. When he opened them Irina was sitting beside him.

Irina was wearing a brown dress which she knew he liked, her legs, outstretched beneath the tucked-up skirt, were bare, her feet, in sandals, dusty. She had some sewing on her knee, another dress of which she was shortening the hem.

'Hello, beastie, you've been asleep.'

'Hello, queen and empress. Where's Marcus? He seemed all right at breakfast.'

'He's resting, he says he's tired.'

Ludens thought, no wonder he's tired! It must be hard work doing whatever he was doing this morning! People in Tibet take years to learn it. Then he thought, I shall have to talk straight to Marcus, or I shall become a traitor or a madman.

Ludens said, 'He wakes up so early, the sun rises at three something. It'll be better after the solstice. You know, midsummer is the day after tomorrow.'

'Is it? We seem to have been doing nothing but wait for it, it's been getting on my nerves. I hate this interminable daylight. And after that those exhausting Seekers will go away. It's lunchtime now. You don't want any lunch do you?'

'I certainly do!'

'I think it's too hot to eat. I'll make you a sandwich. Dad says he wants to talk to you this evening.'

'Damn it, he can talk to me any time! He doesn't have to make appointments!'

'I wish he'd stay in bed. He's so strung up and restless, he won't keep still. I know it's his illness, but –'

'He's not ill, he's perfectly well.'

'You don't believe he is. You said just now that he "seemed all right", as if this were unusual!'

'Oh, darling, don't torment me!'

'Whenever I try to make you *think*, you say "don't torment me!"'

'I'm going to fix up about the marriage licence.'

'Yes, and you're going to buy a house.'

'Yes, and we'll live there, Marcus and you and I and our son. Dear sweetheart, what's the matter?'

Irina was in tears. Her sewing fell to the ground and she buried her face in his shoulder.

The 'evening talk' which Marcus had so unnecessarily 'booked' took place in fact very late, partly because they had again had 'company' at Benbow. Marcus's rest had continued until tea-time. Ludens had sat in his little bedroom trying to read Fabriani's book about the quattrocento, but he could not concentrate. Then Pat and Camilla arrived, then Mr Talgarth bringing his chess-playing nephew, then Irina put on a second tea which lasted till supper-time. Ludens, who liked regular civilised meal-times and was dissatisfied already with his sandwich, resented this disorder. It seemed to amuse Irina, however, and Marcus tolerated it and even had an animated conversation about chess with Mr Talgarth's nephew. No match was suggested however, Ludens thought because the young man was afraid, Irina later said because Marcus had probably just realised that he had forgotten how to play chess. The genial family atmosphere was absent, and the guests (as it seemed to Ludens) stayed on out of desperation, feeling they ought at last to be able to make things jollier. Marcus and Irina and Ludens had a late scrappy supper, after which Marcus disappeared into his bedroom and stayed there so long that Irina said he must be asleep and they might as well go to bed. Ludens said he would wait up all night if necessary. Irina then said that in that case she, being exhausted, was going at once to her bedroom and did not want to be disturbed. Ludens, upset, went out into the garden.

The long warm summer evening was relinquishing its 'interminable daylight' into a clear moonless night, the sky a transparent darkness, the milky way arching in a dense band of gold which vouchsafed to the earth its dim illumination which was like no other light. Nearer to the horizon the more domestic constellations were visible as jagged splashes. Everywhere stars were falling, solemnly, soundlessly, restlessly, carelessly, out of the vast generous over-production of Nature or God. The heavens were silently alert, but the obscurer earth was mysteriously just audibly busy. There was no wind, yet the trees seemed to be stirring, breathing, as if turning to each other. There were occasional rustlings in the undergrowth, and more distantly the hooting of an owl and the melancholy unearthly bark of a fox. Ludens, sitting on the seat, noticed a dark patch near to him moving upon the lawn, the humpy gliding form of a hedgehog. Then Marcus materialised in the dark warm air and sat down beside him.

After conversing for a short while in low tones they decided to walk, and set off in the direction of the house. Ludens, allowing himself to be guided, wondered if Marcus wanted to go to the Stone, but he showed no sign and marched on past the darker darkness of the yew circle. A vague human shade appearing suddenly upon the grass verge took shape as a security man who saluted them and faded again. Avoiding the turning to the house they walked on as far as the golf course where they stood a while in the openness, smelling the dewy grass and a heavy loaded perfume which they agreed must come from the innumerable roses now clambering on walls and drooping on trellises or bushily in evidence in the herbaceous border. They turned back, walking more slowly. All this time they talked in low tones of nothing in particular. Ludens said that the grounds, which were full of, occasionally visible, foxes, were, he was told, full of badgers too. Had Marcus ever seen a badger? No? Neither had Ludens. Was it not amazing how animals could conceal themselves so completely? And why did one never see a dead animal, except on a roadway? They discussed the probability of there being 'monsters' in Loch Ness, then moved to the probability of there being innumerable planets elsewhere in the cosmos, even locally in their galaxy, where something like human life existed. Before they reached Benbow Marcus suggested that they should go and sit in the garden of Rodney, where they could talk more at ease without disturbing Irina. Ludens reminded him that Pat and Camilla had stolen the garden chairs from Rodney to bring to Benbow. Marcus said there were two folding chairs on the verandah at Rodney which would serve them well. After this they fell silent. Even as they were talking Ludens had begun to feel an overwhelming sensation, not unlike feelings which he had had before, but more huge and uplifting, as if he were literally being lifted off his feet. As they walked in silence, it took the form of a sense of unity with Marcus as if Marcus had taken him up into a cloud and were conveying him gently and purposefully along toward some place, so long desired, and now so close. What it was that so enthralled and took him could not be simply Marcus's will or any emotion of his own; it was as if they had happened upon one of the great warm streams of the ocean of the cosmos and were, for a moment, being carried onward by it.

Now, as they sat side by side on their chairs, placed upon the star-lit lawn, like two solemn deities, Ludens felt quiet, restored to his own steady breathing, as if whatever power had granted him his union with Marcus had now gently set them both down, settling them firmly in their earthly proximity, so close yet so completely separate. Now Ludens could name it, but only with crude earthly names: fate, sex, love, death – or the dream of death. The world to which he had now returned was the world of technology and separation, where steel compartments made impossible the larger movements of the spirit. It was as if they were packed in boxes wherein they could move their eyes only. The boxes touched, but not they. All this came to Ludens in a second. Accustomed to the dark, he could see, from the corner of his eyes, Marcus's hand, laid upon the arm of the chair next to him. With deliberation, overcoming the opposing force, he lifted his own adjacent hand and placed it on top of Marcus's. Marcus's warm hand reacted at once, like a small animal suddenly disturbed. It twisted itself away, so that for a moment Ludens thought his gesture was being violently rejected. Then he felt his hand clasped in Marcus's hand, en-closed, held, gripped hard; and then released with a kind of finality which returned them both to their respective boxes. Ludens felt his body convulsed with grief and joy, a desire to weep, a desire to faint.

As they sat, however, exercising the amazing ability of the mind to think several things at once, Ludens was trying to think of something simple and ordinary to say.

Marcus spoke first, with suitable simplicity, as if he too were playing the game. 'So you will buy a house.'

'Oh yes,' said Ludens in a casual tone, 'this has been a useful phase, but it's time to move on, don't you think. We shall be more comfortable, the three of us, living in our own home. We'll have to think where we'll be, of course. I mean, if you wanted to keep in touch with this place we could live near here. We'll have to discuss it all. But you do agree in general? I do think it's time to move.'

Marcus, though raising no objection, did not pursue the matter of the house. He said, 'And Irina –'

Ludens interrupting said, 'Of course, we shall be married, I shall look after her.'

Marcus went on. 'This place has helped me, it has done me some good. Please know that I am very grateful to you.'

'I am grateful to you!' said Ludens. 'I am glad, I am infinitely glad, that we are friends. But I am afraid I haven't been much use to you so far.'

'You mean you tried to make me write a book and I wouldn't!'

'I'm sorry I was so persistent!' said Ludens, echoing Marcus's light tone.

'I think that many things would not have been possible without your help. It is as if the gods sent you.'

Ludens was overjoyed at those words. 'I must warn you that I still hope you will write a book, not now of course, but later on. Yes, it has been good here, perhaps in ways which I do not yet understand. You have had necessary experiences. But this is just the beginning. I see your passing beyond these happenings into another realm of possibilities and powers – new things which I can't imagine now, but I believe you can.'

'You want my life to have been significant.'

'It has been, it is, and it will be. You must by now have a sure and tried faith in – in your quest – in *it* whatever it may be.'

'*You* have always had faith, and perhaps you were not wrong, though you may well be disappointed.'

'I cannot be disappointed. I'm sorry about what I tried to do, I mean to persuade you to do, it was, I see that now, a blunder, it was unsuitable and premature. But you are guided by a star, and you will know your time.'

'Human life is very short, Alfred, it is a short walk.'

'Yes, but for what you are destined to do, long enough. You are young. You will travel on, and I will travel with you.'

'You are very kind. You say that I am guided by a star. What I feel I must do may not be what you want.'

'Oh, I know, I know. But I am the slave of your wisdom and I shall always understand later. I can endure strange judgements and steep paths.'

'I want you to believe that my life, though it may be a failure, is not just an accident. I'm afraid I put this badly.'

'No, no – but say more.'

'You want me to do something "for the human race". That is a large saying. What can it mean? As for thinking, I have tried, but I cannot go all the way.'

'You have gone far, very far, you must rest, you will go further.'

'In this matter one cannot rest, if one rests all is lost. When one comes near to those things –'

'To the mystery, what the gods conceal.'

'And to the evil which only God could forgive or understand – there are no words, the spirit faints, one must try to think on, *onward*, in silence, with no God, just through a persisting tension of being.'

'You must make all that into *work*,' said Ludens, 'you must find out how to achieve continuous *work*.'

'You have come farther than I realised. Yes. But by "work" you still really mean ordinary thinking and making of books. It is more as if, perhaps suddenly, all one could do would be to offer it – one's whole being becoming it – as a sacrifice –'

'Finding one's way to hell and back.'

'Is there a way back? Finding one's way to – "hell" is not really the word – to the flames – as if – to find the right way to annihilate oneself by thinking, as a marathon runner dies doing, to the utmost, what he *must* do.'

'I don't like these metaphors! This is only the *beginning*, as I keep telling you. All right, you reach, farther on perhaps than other people have ever been, the impenetrable and the unthinkable, and now you can say nothing. But this is not like having to die at the feet of some dark thing. By "work" I don't mean ordinary thinking like what has gone on for such ages. I believe that at a crucial moment you are a crucial person. You yourself said that now was a time, the *first* time, when human thought could move beyond the errors of the past. So, in the place in which you stand, in what you *experience*, you should simply *wait*. The mystery cannot be revealed, the riddle cannot be answered, the ultimate thought cannot be thought, the evil cannot be understood – but *something*, perhaps *only by you*, and many years later, can be *said*. You must, please, become calm and not think about it as a sort of drama. You must forge a method, a medium, as a great artist does, utterly forgetting himself – and in the end you will have a message for our poor world, as great human beings have had in the past. This is what I believe in for you.'

Startled by his speech, Ludens was silent. He heard Marcus sigh deeply. Then he said, 'Thank you, Alfred, thank you. How solemn we are! Human life is short, we don't exist all that much. A pale brief flicker in the dark. Well – let's go back now, shall we? The air is colder. We must put the chairs on the verandah, otherwise they will be rained on.'

They put the chairs back, then walked in silence the short distance to Benbow. As they went the first blackbird awoke and uttered his word.

The next day was chaotic. Ludens, unable to go to sleep at once, lay for some time rehearsing the conversation and weighing every word. He was very disturbed, yet also reassured. He could sense Marcus moving in the dark, like a great frightening animal, a Loch Ness monster. He felt that, in a confused instinctive way, he himself had spoken well, returning indeed, it might be, some dim simple echo of Marcus's own silent thoughts, the thrust of his being. He felt that, somehow, progress had been made, time had been gained, there would be a wholesome interval. Farther than that he did not dare to press his speculations. What reassured him was Marcus's kindness to him, his *thanks*, his reference to Irina, his assent to the house. These were real 'ordinary' foundations upon which their life, the life of all three of them, must rest in the 'next phase'.

He slept later than usual. He had decided in any case not to try to follow Marcus on his morning peregrinations; once was enough. As he woke up he now heard the squeak of the kitchen door, the plop as the gas was lighted, and the sound of Marcus filling the kettle and putting it on. In terms of the morning ritual, this was the signal for breakfast. Irina, not an early riser, who found getting up something of a trial and was accepted as being 'grumpy' in the morning, usually stayed in bed until Marcus decided he wanted his breakfast and signalled this by going to the kitchen. Ludens usually stayed in his room also, sometimes now reading in the mornings, and waited to hear Irina emerge. Today he dressed quickly and darted into the bathroom to shave, hearing Marcus and Irina already talking. Breakfast was late, conversation, usually conducted rather lamely by Ludens, was unusually relaxed and animated. Honey from Bellmain bees (the hives were in an enclosure near the grotto), brought yesterday by Rosie, was on the menu, and Irina put out the 'better plates', which she had bought in the village, which had pictures of butterflies on them, each plate being different. They discussed butterflies, counting how many different kinds they had seen in the park. Ludens was relieved to see that Marcus, who had lately looked anxious and tired, now seemed calm, authoritative and benign, somewhat resuming his original 'Renaissance prince' good looks. Only today, Ludens thought, perhaps more like some successful artist, a famous young pianist perhaps, with that particular well-defined haughty curling of the lips. Ludens was usually wary of catching Marcus's eye, or being noticed looking at him, but now, feeling empowered, he gazed more confidently, and Marcus returned an amused ironical complicit smile.

After breakfast Marcus had retired to his bedroom and Irina had washed up the breakfast things, together with last night's dinner things which were always left till after breakfast. She refused Ludens's offer of help, which she called 'feeble and hypocritical'. She was now established in the sitting room, wearing her red dress and continuing to hem the other dress which she was shortening. He stood watching her, aware that she would soon send him away 'to his books' or 'to the office'. He thought, can I be happy? Can I, Alfred Ludens, be happy? Why not?

The sun was shining and the doors were open. Irina, lifting her head from her sewing and looking towards the garden, suddenly cried out, 'Oh *no*! Oh *really*! Look who's here!'

Ludens looked. Alison Merrick was standing on the lawn.

She stood in her tense yet easily graceful attitude as of one about to leap into action, her long neck craned, her head thrown back, one long pale hand, having thrust away her mane of red hair, still poised at her brow. She was wearing tight white trousers and a green shirt. A blue and grey plaid shawl which she was holding in her other hand trailed down onto the grass. She looked to Ludens's startled eyes immensely tall, immensely strong, immensely there.

Irina, quickly gathering up her sewing, said, 'I'm not here. She can't see me, can she? It doesn't matter. I don't want to talk to her. *You* deal. Just get rid of her, get her away from here. As if we haven't got enough trouble! Oh buggeration!' She vanished, and Ludens heard her bedroom door slam.

He advanced onto the verandah. 'Alison!'

'Oh thank God!' She relaxed, gathering up the shawl, and advanced with long strides.

He came down quickly to meet her. 'Let's walk a bit. You don't mind, do you?'

'I don't mind so long as I can talk to you. I'm so glad. I looked for you at the Black Lion, but they said you were living here. Oh I am glad to see you. What a relief!'

'Yes, I'm living here now. Let's go this way.'

445

'And Marcus? He's still here?'

'Yes.'

'Is he better, any less batty?'

'He's fine.' He walked Alison away from Benbow toward the main drive. 'Let's go to the golf course. I bet you play golf.'

'Yes, I was a junior champion.'

Steel, thought Ludens, that's what she's made of, very flexible steel! He glanced at her as they walked on. The sun, which had not altered the fresh pallor of her skin, had covered her visible parts more liberally with freckles. The sleeves of her shirt were rolled up, the buttons considerably undone. Ludens could not help glancing. 'Is Jack with you?'

'No, no, he's in Paris seeing some gallery man. Look, let's go the other way, I've seen golf courses. This is all so public. Let's walk to the river. I suppose you know what's happening?'

'I know nothing, not since we last met.'

'I thought Patrick might have told you.'

'No – well, he said something about Franca being a saint.'

'Yes, that's it. But I'd better tell you everything. Well, it's all come out, I can't think where to start, though actually in a way nothing's happened. God, I'm glad to see you!'

Mr Talgarth and his nephew, who resembled him except for being slimmer and younger, approached, said 'Good morning' and passed. Ludens noticed the nephew appreciating Alison.

'How do you mean nothing's happened? You said you were going to tell Jack he must divorce Franca and marry you. Did you decide not to after all?'

'Oh no, I told him, he said yes he would, he told Franca, he's even got a lawyer to fix it all up and he's bought us, him and me I mean, a luxury flat with a view over Regent's Park.'

'So what are you complaining about?' said Ludens. Lambert the male nurse who had been one of Marcus's devotees, met and passed them, looked at Alison, then looked at Ludens not exactly with a wink but with something like it.

'It's not what I expected.'

'Why not? You've got what you wanted.'

'I told you I was going to kill Franca, I had to, I had to pulverise her, to destroy her, but –'

'But what?'

'She's indestructible.'

'Really? You've got Jack, divorce, marriage, even a luxury flat. Isn't that enough? Haven't you humiliated her sufficiently, haven't you *disposed* of her – do you want to drive your car over her?'

'*Yes*! Oh Ludens, you don't understand –'

'No, I don't.'

'She ought to be furious, she ought to be in tears, she ought to *clear off* – but there she is, smiling and agreeing and wishing us happiness and telling Jack how much she loves him and pretending she loves me too – and perhaps she really does and that's worse – you see, I think it *isn't* a lie, it's genuine – genuine goddamn *unselfishness*!'

Ludens felt exasperated. Yet at the same time he couldn't help being interested. He said cautiously, 'If you just wait, she'll probably decide to go away.' Perhaps, in fact probably, Franca had decided not to run away after all. He, Ludens, who had formed a part of her running-away plan, had failed her dismally, and though she had put a brave face on it she must have been disappointed – indeed disappointed would be too mild a word. How little thought he had given to her since, how little imagination of her feelings – and after the great honour which she had done him. She had offered him herself and said she loved him. She had said they loved each other, which was true. Oh poor Franca. Now perhaps she had decided to give in after all, to *assent* – to do in fact what he himself had advised. She had said at the end that she was going to 'carry on the charade a little longer' before 'choosing her moment' to depart. But now, and in view of Ludens's defection, poised between the appearance and the reality, might she not, confused, despairing, or with a higher wisdom, have decided that she must now *really* do what she had *said* she was pretending to do – or have realised that her pretence had been a reality all the time?

Alison said, 'No, she won't go, she'll never go. You see, Jack is giving her the house, and the studio. He *says* he'll get another studio, but I'm sure he won't. I thought divorce would be *it*, I thought marriage would be *it* – but she'll still be there, being so brave and so kind and Jack will be running to see her several times a week, like he used to see me when it all began. And she'll be *there*, eternally there, I can't stand her *existence*, I can't stand her being in Jack's life, to me it's death, I want to obliterate her, I want to make her *nothing* to us any more, like what happens in a *real* divorce. But in fact it'll be just exactly what *he* wants and absolutely not what *I* want. He's always wanted a *ménage à trois* with Franca as the dear old senior wife who's no good for bed any more but is a wise much-loved mother figure and –'

'Well, can't you put up with it?' said Ludens. 'If Franca is kind to you instead of tearing your eyes out can't you be grateful? Jack's madly in love with you and you're madly in love with him, you suit each other perfectly. Maybe he should never have married Franca at all. Anyhow if you're patient and ingenious you can probably freeze her out as the years go by. You'll destroy her in the end. It'll give you something to do.'

'Oh shut up Ludens, don't *disgust* me! For Christ's sake let's have a drink. I *must* have a drink, I've been drinking like a fish ever since I realised what a swindle it all was. Let's go to the Black Lion. Would the bar be open yet?'

'I'm sorry,' said Ludens, as they turned out through the gate into the lane, 'I see your difficulty, though it seems to me to be one you can live with. Compared with the problems other people have it's not so grave. After all what's the solution? You don't want to transfer your affections to someone else, you can't. You've got the man you love, Jack will be your husband, he adores you, he'll do what *you* want. You can leave London, you can live in Paris, in Rome, anywhere. You are young, and Franca will very soon be old. She will fade and you will watch her fading and enjoy feeling pity for her.'

'You're on her side.'

'She's the victim.'

'Oh *hell*. There's much more that I've got to say to you but I must have a drink first. Tell me about yourself. How's the old man?'

'He's not old. He's all right.'

'Then why are you still hanging around here? He's surrounded by doctors, isn't he? Why don't you come back to London?'

'I must stay, I'm like his research assistant. I'm helping him with his work.'

'So he isn't mentally deranged?'

'No!'

'And the daft Irina, where is she?'

'She's here too.'

'Ah, here's the dear old Black Lion, thank God.'

They went into the bar, where Toller greeted them with discreet cordiality.

Alison asked for whisky and soda and Ludens, after a moment's hesitation, followed suit. She insisted on paying. They went out into the garden and sat on the seat, near the river bend, previously occupied by Ludens and Daniel Most. Since Ludens had moved to Benbow he had given up alcohol. He had not missed it. Now the whisky and soda was running through his veins like warm molten gold. He felt rejuvenated, renewed, filled with energy and understanding.

'That's better. Let's have another.' They had another. 'Now, my dear Ludens, I can tell you what I came to tell you. I've decided to leave Jack.'

'Alison! But you love him! You said you –'

'Yes, I said I was his slave, yes, I'm desperately in love, but I've just been realising, for all sorts of reasons, just in these last few days, that I *could* leave him. After all women do give up the man they love. And the best way to do it is to learn to love another man. You said I didn't want to transfer my affections and that anyway I couldn't do it. I do want to and I think I can.'

'Well, congratulations,' said Ludens. 'Look, let me buy this round.'

'You don't believe me because you can't see that precisely *because* I love Jack so much I *won't* share him with someone else. I'd rather kill him, or myself. When I came to *that* point I – well, I just thought there might be another way –'

'My dear Alison, it must be the drink. You don't want to leave Jack and I don't see any good reason why you should. You can't magic yourself out of the situation, you've got to live it as decently and as grimly as you can. Wait, let time come to your rescue. Of course in a way I'm on Franca's side but – what was I going to say – it seems to me –'

'You're drunk. So am I. *In vino veritas*. You believe I can't magic myself out? Listen. I think I've found him.'

'Who?'

'The other man!'

'What other man?'

'The man I'm going to transfer my affections to!'

'Alison, don't be silly –'

'I can't go on in this degrading situation – that's what it essentially and eternally is, *degrading* – it degrades me, it degrades Jack, it degrades her. What Jack wants is *essentially rotten*. It's a rotten prison, a rotten *pit* we're in –'

'My dear, please be calm, and please don't raise your voice. You can't think clearly in this storm of emotion. As I see it, the main point is that you love Jack, you *love* him –'

'Yes, and I'm ready to wade through blood for him, but there is no blood, only a false sickly slime – I can't do it, I can't live in fogs and falsehoods, I must live in the open, I must find my way out, I must find someone else, and I have found someone else.'

449

'So you imagine. Who is he?'

'You.'

'*Alison* – you're *mad*! *Please* go away, go back to London, go back to real life, go back to *Jack* – you can't be serious –'

'Yes, I am, and it's all your idea. *You* told me, I can remember your very words, that it is possible to stop being in love, to fall out of love, people do it, people who have thought they can't have found that they can. Suppose I were just to grit my teeth and leave Jack and find another man, a man without a wife, without a woman, a truthful good man whom I can love and be loved by in freedom, in daylight, without all this torture, this *hell* –'

'But, Alison –'

'Why not? For I *do* love you. I took a fancy to you on the day we first met. Do you remember that day? Of course I was already in love with Jack, I was his property, but I certainly noticed you. And you noticed me. Do you remember that day by the lake at that place, when we looked at each other and *understood* each other? Then when you gave me that lecture about finding another man, an unattached man, whom I could love in honesty, you were – perhaps it was unconsciously – pointing straight at yourself. Perhaps you didn't expect anything then. But you can expect anything you like now.'

'Alison, darling, I'm stunned, of course I didn't mean to suggest myself, that's crazy! I never dreamt – Oh I'm so moved. I'm so touched, I'm so grateful, but it's impossible!'

'You mean loyalty to Jack –'

'No, no – well, there is that – but –'

'Don't say you find me unattractive. All right of course you don't – Ludens, forgive me, I'm distraught, I've been in anguish about all this for so long, really from the start, there are so many pains, so many wounds – I can't bear seeing Jack trying to hold it all together and make sense of it and, not exactly lying, but it's all half-truths, it's a *mess*, and I hate messes, it's just not the sort of thing I can accept or live with. Of course Jack goes on saying it's all right, it's working, it's fine – God, he loves me so much, how can it be so terrible, but it *is*. It's not that I sympathise with Franca, I don't, I feel absolutely ruthless about her, it's just that her existence makes mine impossible, she's just eternally there, with her kind good smiling face and her wise looks – and Jack depends on her, I can see that dependence, that look in his eyes, his *relief* when she's nice to him, of course she's always nice to him, and to me – and her having the house, that's somehow the last straw, after all they've been married for years and years – sorry, I'm becoming incoherent. Look, let's have one more drink and then go somewhere where we can really talk.'

Other people had come into the garden, filling up the picnic tables near the house. Ludens fetched another drink. After that they left the pub and crossed the bridge and started to walk along the path on the other bank of the river. Ludens said to himself, this is something amazing and frightful, and I'm drunk, and I can't think clearly. Ought I to tell Alison that Franca told me she was going to leave Jack? No, I don't think so. Franca *hasn't* left Jack, she may well have changed her mind, in fact she almost certainly has. After all she was expecting something wonderful from me, *I* was to pull her out, she was able to resolve to leave Jack because she could run to me. And, good heavens, that is exactly what Alison has done! And I can't help her either! Two beautiful women declaring they could love *him*: of course they were simply using him as an emotional rest-home, a stepping-stone perhaps, they didn't really mean it. And yet – surely they *did* mean it! What a waste of love it all was, why can't I love them, he thought. But I can't, and when they need me I must send them away. And Alison, so young, so beautiful – alas . . .

'My God, you haven't said *this* to Jack?'

'No, not yet. It's the details, it's the timing. *When* can I leave him, at what hour, on what day, saying what? You must help me, you must love me, you must *rescue* me. We can love each other, we *do* love each other, and my God what a *relief* it'll be to be out of that cage – outside, loving freely, loving innocently! Oh what an ill fate it was that has made me love that man. Look, let's go and sit in there.'

They left the path through an opening into a glade, at the far end of which, shaded by trees and surrounded by saplings and bushy brambles, was a smooth grassy bank upon which they sat down. Alison immediately put her arms round his neck. Ludens put one arm round her waist. They held each other closely in silence for a moment.

Ludens said, 'Alison, this won't do, I'm sorry.'

'It will do. It will do very well. We've just proved it.'

He thrust her away a little and they sat holding hands and looking at each other. Ludens groaned. 'Alison – no, let me talk. Two things. First, it's possible that Franca *may* leave Jack, I mean go right away, she has this friend in America, you met her, Maisie Tether –'

'She'll never go away, never, never.'

'Second. I love someone else and am engaged to be married to her.'

Alison squeezed his hand, released it, then took it again.

'Who is she? Can't be Heather? No, you've never met her.'

'It's Irina.'

'*Irina*? Are you *crazy*?'

'Alison, I love her, and we'll get married – probably.'

'You say "probably".'

'I hope we will.'

'You sound pretty doubtful. Are you having a love affair?'

'Yes – sort of – it's difficult.'

'Ludens, don't deceive yourself and don't deceive me. You're just obsessed with the old man – all right he's not old – he fascinates you, he hypnotises you, he dominates you. Evidently he wants you to marry his daughter, perhaps to take her off his hands. It's *his* idea, you're just going along, she's going along, you're both reluctant really. I can see it all, it's a forced thing, a shadowy thing, it's "probably", it's "difficult", it's "sort of". That's not how things should be. There's no *blood* in it, it's *childish*, it's *flimsy*, it's not like *this*. Don't tie yourself up, just to please *him*, half-heartedly, to a half-hearted girl, and, as you must know, and really think, a very silly shallow girl. Wake up my darling, that's all a shadow, this is a reality. Can't you see the difference?'

'Forgive me, Alison. I'm drunk, so are you. You're in a wild crazy state, you're unhappy, you're in pain, you turn to me. You don't know what you're doing. Your reality is with Jack, however difficult it is, or now seems. You've taken him on, you must live your love for him bravely. I can't help you. I'm very sorry, I wish in many ways that I could. I'm very moved that you have trusted me and spoken to me as you have done. I'm very very grateful, I care for you and I wish –'

'You love me. Kiss me, Ludens.'

He found himself kissing her. They rolled against the bank, then down onto the level grass, and lay there clasped together. Ludens sat up. She lay beside him holding his hand against her cheek, against her lips.

'Alison, I love you, I desire you at this moment, but we're in an illusory world, as if a magician had suddenly put us in a beautiful tent in an enchanted landscape, all by ourselves. But the real world is somewhere else and we must go back. I really do love Irina and she really loves me, all my loyalty, my true happiness, all the real stuff of my life and my future is there with them –'

'You say "them".'

'With her and with her father. I am committed to them both. Now you must go back to London. I advise you, I advise you very strongly, to stay with Jack and *wait*. You're in a frenzy, you want to be rescued, you want to invent a new person and a new place, but it won't do, any move you made now would be quite wrong and much regretted later. Now we must go back. Come, dear dear Alison.' He rose, pulling her up with him.

'No. Stay here. Ludens, please. Don't abandon me.'

'We must go.' They walked back to the path and turned toward the village.

Ludens thought, if only one had two lives, if only one were two persons! Well, that was what Jack was attempting to have and to be. What a waste . . . and that too was what Jack thought, and refused to countenance. But, here, how inevitable, how impossible, Ludens told himself as he walked beside Alison. He did not look at her for fear he might see her crying. How *could* she leave Jack? If she really did for a moment she would run back. This was just a wild momentary impulse, something perhaps that she would later feel relieved to have attempted in vain. He had no doubts and would have no regrets, only he felt at present an acute mental and physical pain.

Alison rubbed her eyes. She said, 'Well, I don't accept this, I don't believe you really want to marry that hopeless ridiculous girl, I don't believe you *will* marry her.'

'I do, I will. Alison, how will you get back?'

'Taxi to Salisbury.'

'I'll order you one from the Black Lion. No, we'd better not go there. I'll order you one from the White Lion.'

They walked along the village street side by side. Whatever do we *look like*! he wondered. Colin and Kathleen appeared in the distance but fortunately disappeared into the Post Office. At the White Lion Alison went into the bar and Ludens rang for the taxi. When he joined her he found she had ordered two whiskies. They sat down in a secluded corner. Lunch was in progress and the bar was almost empty.

'Alison, thank you. I'm so – well – pleased, grateful, you understand. I wish I could be better, more useful.'

'You're a fool, darling. Don't marry that girl, she's unreliable and dotty, she's *insubstantial*, she's capable of all sorts of spitefulness. And as far as I can see you're the only man she's ever met! You're shut up with her and that hermit, you're a captive. Her father thinks you're respectable and Jewish. It's all artificial. As soon as she meets a few other men she'll leave you. Sorry, but you know what I mean. She's uneducated and barbaric, she hasn't seen the world, what she really wants is a dominating tycoon who'll show it to her. No wonder she's "difficult" with you! Ludens, come with me, come in that taxi, just *jump in*, let me take you away to a new world. You'll feel such relief, such joy. Don't you want freedom, don't you want *happiness*? Don't run back into that snare.'

'Look, the taxi has come.' They went out together.

'Goodbye, dear Alison.'

'I don't believe what you say, I warn you!'

'Alison, forget all this. It never happened. Go back to Jack.'

'Kiss me, Ludens.'

He kissed her. The taxi drew away. He went back into the bar and finished his whisky.

Ludens, sitting there in the corner, feeling that he was red in the face and being stared at, thought: what on earth have I been doing this morning, where have I been, what have I done? I've been away in some other world, a traitor, a deserter, I've listened to wild untrue statements about people I love and not denied them, I've been kissing another woman and telling her I desire her. That place in the wood – was it visible from the path? We didn't even bother! Suppose someone did see us, suppose they told Irina, or told Marcus? Of course she won't tell Jack and of course I won't. She's had a lucky escape, especially if Franca does decide to leave. Oh, what a rotten mess, why did I let her lead me on, why did I get involved in such an awful situation, I'm drunk, I'm a disgrace, it's late, it's lunchtime, and they'll be wondering where I am. I must run – but I can't. I can't turn up like this. I'm still drinking, and what's more I want another drink! Should I confess it all to Irina? I can't, it's too bad, and it would *sound* even worse. God, I probably even smell of Alison – she doesn't wear make-up – she doesn't seem to anyway – but her hair smelt of something, some shampoo I suppose, and it's bound to have got onto me, onto my clothes, into my hair. What can I do? If I don't turn up they'll get worried, they're so used to my always being there, always turning up punctually. What *can* I say, will all this folly have terrible consequences? Why have I put everything I love and value into this danger? How could I even for a second contemplate such a *slip* that would alter my whole life? Supposing Marcus is furious with me, supposing Irina thinks I love someone else and have been deceiving her? Suppose they *throw me out*? I'd die, I'd die at their door like a dog. Why was I so disloyal? For this most of all, and most deeply, disturbed Ludens. He had listened to Alison reviling Irina, calling her unreliable and spiteful and shallow. And he himself had encouraged her by using words such as 'difficult' and 'sort of'. He ought to have stopped Alison at the start, he ought to have asserted his position absolutely. Alison had dropped poison into his ears, she had said that as soon as Irina met other men she would leave Ludens. Could this be true – and was he, Ludens, now actually considering it as if it *might* be true? And – what he had said to Alison about his desiring her and about an enchanted tent – he had been there, in that tent, where he never ought to have been.

'But whatever were you doing?' said Irina. 'Naturally, I thought you were running off with Alison.'

'I just couldn't get away from her, she just wanted to go on and on about her and Jack, and how they'd bought a flat near Regent's Park, and Jack was going to have a show in Paris, she simply went on talking, I couldn't get a word in, I think she wanted somehow to let us know, in case we were suspecting otherwise, how wonderful it all was! Then I tried to get a taxi for her but I couldn't, then we had a sandwich at the Black Lion and she would drink whisky and I'm afraid I had one too, then it took ages to get the taxi and she'd started talking about Franca –'

'Yes, what about poor old Franca?'

'Oh poor old Franca is putting up with it bravely just as everyone expected, she's being very kind, very rational, accepting all the arrangements – of course she has to, but I do believe she does it out of love, she's a wonderful person –'

'She's spineless. If I were Franca I'd kill them both. Let me see, which would I kill first – I'd kill Alison first, then I'd torture Jack and kill him afterwards.'

'Irina!'

'I think they're awful people anyway. What's the matter with you, why are you so restless, why are you opening your mouth like that and fiddling with your hair?'

Ludens had found Irina sitting in the garden, and was making the most of his chance to avoid proximity. He kept opening his mouth to let the air in to take away the fumes of whisky, and spreading his hair out in the sunshine hoping to remove any telltale perfume. He was relieved, so far, by Irina's fairly matter-of-fact greeting, and her trustful acceptance of his rotten story.

'I'm sorry I was late. Was Marcus cross?'

'You weren't late, you were absent! No, he wasn't cross, but he's been rather tense and excited all day. He asked where Patrick was, he said he had something to say to him. What did you talk about last night, out under the stars? I heard you coming in awfully late.'

'We talked about how we'd have a house and live together and how you and I would be married –'

'Did you then!'

'I told Alison about our engagement, I hope you don't mind.'

'Engagement! What a word. You'll be giving me a ring next!'

'Irina – yes, of course, I *will* give you a ring – you'll accept it, won't you, you'll wear it? Please – we'll go to Salisbury and choose one!'

'There you are – you hadn't even thought of a ring! You're *hopeless*!'

Marcus came out of the house. He stood for a moment on the verandah looking at Ludens. Ludens at once saw what Irina called the excited look, Ludens saw it more as a distraught nervous triumphant look, as of a tired wary commander on the day after the battle. He was wearing a white shirt with a blue scarf hung round his shoulders, grey flannel trousers, and athletic running shoes which Ludens had not seen before. The blue scarf, having some resemblance to a priestly stole, gave him an authoritative formal look as if he were about to declare or inaugurate something, an international fair or a new era. Yet also he seemed to Ludens's eye, wild somehow, detached, lonely, in danger from incomprehensible forces. He looked away from side to side as if seeking enemies, then came down the steps, the sun seizing upon his bright hair, producing, Ludens thought, the halo effect which had impressed the Seekers. For a moment Ludens felt something of the feelings he had experienced last night, together with a desire to run forward to him, to hold him and shield his body as if from an arrow or a bullet. As he looked, Marcus took control of the blue scarf, tucking the pendent ends inside the neck of his shirt. He said to Ludens, 'What were you up to?'

'He was getting drunk with Alison Merrick!' said Irina. 'You remember her, Dad?'

'Of course I remember her.'

'I wasn't getting drunk,' said Ludens, 'I just had to listen to an interminable story about – Oh never mind, here I am.'

'Here you are.' Marcus's statement consigned Ludens's putative misdeeds to the past. He continued to look at Ludens however, not sternly, nor with the forgiving irony which he sometimes employed, but with a mournful almost woeful stare, which Ludens, distressed, could not interpret. As he hesitated, he felt the total strangeness of the man, and of the destiny which had made him, Ludens, his follower and companion over so many years.

'It's teatime,' said Irina. 'Is it teatime? Do we want tea?'

'I do,' said Ludens. He thought, tea will do me a lot of good! And I'm very hungry too.

'Look, I've finished shortening my new dress, I shall wear it tomorrow. Isn't it pretty? It's blue and green which should *always* be seen!'

'I shall look forward to tomorrow,' said Ludens. 'And tomorrow we will buy a ring.'

Marcus had turned back into the house. Irina was shaking out the altered dress and holding it up to herself. Ludens took a few more mouthfuls of the warm summer air. As they moved toward the house Ludens thrust his hand in under her hair and round her warm neck gathering up the mass of dark locks. They mounted the steps together. On the verandah Irina, turning round, exclaimed, 'Oh dear, we've got another visitor, this seems to be visiting day at Benbow. Or perhaps he's just a tourist.'

Ludens looked. An elderly man with copious grey hair and heavy grey moustaches was standing at the far end of the lawn. Ludens at once thought, he looks like Einstein. Then he said, '*Good God! It's my father!*'

Ludens strode down the steps and across the lawn and, as it seemed to him afterwards, collected, or swept up, his parent without pausing, propelled him back onto the tarmac, and set him in motion toward the main drive and out of sight of Benbow. Ludens senior submitted to his removal without resistance, even hurrying his pace, as Ludens gripping his arm as if making an arrest, marched him smartly along.

'Alfred, I'm sorry to appear suddenly like this, you see I didn't know your address –'

'How did you know I was here?'

'It was all in the paper, about Marcus Vallar and how you were his disciple. It all sounded so odd –'

'You thought you'd come and see!'

'Yes, but there's something else I have to tell you –'

'It *is* odd. Let's go somewhere and have a short talk. Then I must go back to them.'

'Was that Marcus I saw going back into the house?'

'Yes.'

'Look, can't we go to your lodgings, can't we just have a sit-down in peace somewhere, need you walk so fast?'

'Sorry. I haven't got a lodging. I live in here with Marcus.'

'I'd like to meet him.'

'It's impossible.'

457

'Why is it impossible? Am I so unpresentable? He's Jewish isn't he?'

'Yes, but what the hell has that got to do with it?' Why is it impossible, thought Ludens, why am I so rude and cross? It's just that with so many awful pressures and problems I just can't stand my father too!

'Look, Tuan,' he said. A secret well kept by Ludens from his friends was that he called his father 'Tuan', an honorific title derived from a novel by Conrad. A part of Ludens's childhood revolt against the situation in which he found himself an outsider was his refusal of proffered names: Dad, Daddy, Pa, Papa, Pop, Father, Pater, even 'Guv' all went on offer and were rejected. His halfbrother Keith accepted 'Dad' which was also used by his stepmother. 'Look, Tuan, I'm sorry to be so rough, and of course I'll introduce you to Marcus if you wish, only not now. It's just that it's all a bit difficult.' Yet why was it difficult, why didn't he just bring his father along to have tea with Marcus and Irina, why were they all so unlike ordinary people?

'I imagine your guru is a bit odd? This place is a mental home, isn't it?'

'He's odd, but he's perfectly sane. I'll explain. Look, when are you going back?'

'I've just arrived and he says when am I going back! I've booked a room in a little pub called the Hedgehog. I thought I'd stay a day or two. I want to tell you about –'

'All right, then you can see Marcus tomorrow. I'll call for you at the Hedgehog after breakfast. I'll say goodbye now –'

'Can't you give me twenty minutes now, can't we sit down somewhere and talk properly? Why are you so damn rude and in such a hurry?'

'I'm sorry, Tuan, I beg your pardon – it's just that – I'm sorry – All right.' Ludens overcome by an intense desire for tea, had realised that it could be had in the village. He had been walking his father as fast as he could toward the gate; now he slowed down a little. As they turned into the lane a familiar figure was visible coming towards them. A meeting was inevitable.

'This is Mr Daniel Most, he is a rabbi. My father.'

'How do you do, sir.'

'How do you do.'

'Are you going to see Marcus?'

'Of course.'

'Is he expecting you? Oh, hell, what does it matter. Tell him I'll be back soon.'

'Certainly.'

'Nice-looking boy,' said Ludens senior as they walked on. 'Looks a bit like you.'

'Oh really.'

'So Marcus has returned to the fold?'

'No, he's just interested in Judaism, he's interested in everything.'

'What was the chap's name? How do you spell it?'

'M.O.S.T. It means bridge in Russian. It rhymes with cost not coast, bossed not boast, tossed not toast, lost not –'

'I sometimes wish I hadn't lost touch. I suppose I could still turn up at a synagogue. Sometimes I'd like to. I'd have to ask people what to do.'

At the Black Lion they installed themselves in the residents' lounge where Mrs Toller hastened to bring them a splendid tea consisting of ham sandwiches, tomato sandwiches, scones with raspberry jam and cream, and three kinds of cake, all home-made. These delicacies, together with fine strong Indian tea, were to Ludens as the food of the gods, pure innocent nourishment bringing healing and absolution. His headache vanished, his field of vision cleared, he began to eat heartily. So did his father who, as he explained, had had no lunch. Ludens had presented his parent to Mrs Toller, and Toller soon arrived to pay his respects. Ludens was touched to see how pleased his father was by the welcome he received, and by the kindly speeches offered in praise of his son.

'I must be getting back,' said Ludens, 'you said you wanted to tell me something.'

'Yes. Grave news I'm afraid.'

'What?'

'It's about Keith and Angela. Angela's man has left her. They're both coming back to England.'

'Oh? But does that concern us?'

'Yes. They're coming back to me.'

Ludens, still not thinking very fast, took a moment or two to understand the appalling enormity of the situation. 'You mean to *live with you?*'

'Yes. They haven't anywhere else to go.'

'But – only for a short time – they won't stay, they'll move on?'

'They're penniless. There's nowhere they can move to.'

'I thought Keith was making millions with computers. He can get a job, then they'll go.'

'He made some money, but it all went. He might get a job, but I rather doubt it. He's got what people now call a drug problem.'

'So you mean you'll have to support them.' Ludens paused for a moment. 'Oh. I see. You mean *I*'ll have to support them.'

'I certainly hope you'll help.'

'But I'm just going to get married.'

'*Are* you? Who to? Was that her?'

'I'll tell you tomorrow. Of course I'll help, don't worry, Tuan. Where are they now?'

'At home.'

'You mean at our house?'

'Yes.'

'And there they'll stay.'

'They'll have to.'

'Oh *God*.' In recent years Ludens had not often returned to the cottage in Somerset, but he still regarded it as home, where his father was. But now . . . Hideous thoughts pressed upon him as he gradually assembled the new picture. *Those two* had returned, his enemies, who had ruined his childhood. *They*, the spoilers, the destroyers, would be there now, forever. An old familiar anguish, not recognised at first, declared itself: Keith too was his father's son.

Ludens stood up. He left some money on the table. They went out into the sunny courtyard. Hoping to strike a lighter note, Ludens senior asked his son if he liked the moustache, which was new. Ludens, who thought it messily disfigured a handsome face, said it was fine. He mentioned Einstein, hoping that was tactful. He said he would accompany his father to the Hedgehog. An awful rift had opened in his mind and hideous things were emerging. He felt suddenly, distinctly, a yearning for his mother, a grief for her, the mother he had been cheated of, and given a false mother and a false brother instead. He found himself saying, 'Tuan, did you leave my mother, or did she leave you?'

'I left her.'

'I thought so somehow. Never mind – oh – never mind. Here's someone I know.'

Colin Bassett had just emerged from the Hedgehog. Ludens made the introductions. After he had greeted the older man with suitable respect, Colin said to Ludens, 'We'll all be at the Stone at dawn tomorrow.'

'Oh, I'd forgotten, it's midsummer.' He said farewell to his father, promising to come about nine the next day, left him talking to Colin, and set off back to Bellmain. Grimacing with rage and hatred he groaned aloud. That horrible *ménage* in which he had suffered so much was to be reconstructed. An even more terrible thought struck him.

Suppose his father were actually *pleased*, suppose he were lonely, suppose they were all to love and cherish each other and live happily together ever after *excluding Ludens*?

A figure whom he had been vaguely aware of as walking behind him caught him up. It was Gildas.

They walked on together, silently at first.

'My stepmother and my stepbrother have come back and are going to live with my father.'

'Wasn't that your father I saw with you just now? He looks much older, of course it's years since I saw him. And by the way, Keith, if I remember his name correctly, is your halfbrother, not your stepbrother. A stepbrother is –'

'Oh shut up. What brings you here?'

'I want to find out something.'

'What?'

'Do you really intend to marry that girl?'

'Yes. I'm going to take them away, I'm going to buy a house where we can all three live together in peace.'

'I see.'

'Gildas, don't you abandon me!'

'I won't. I'll turn up occasionally and play with your children.'

'You know what I mean. I need you absolutely. It's been such a terrible day. I'm frightened of everything.'

'Then it's time to hurry on into the rosy future you just mentioned.'

'Yes, but it's all falling on *me*, I have to make the decisions, I have to set the pace –'

'Get on with it then. Buy the house and remove them. We're *all* waiting for you, to know where we stand! I think the pubs are open, can't we have a drink and a talk?'

'No, no. I must get back, I've already been drunk once today. But please, you're staying aren't you, we can meet tomorrow.'

'All right. Have you heard the news from Chelsea? The girls have settled down. Jack has won the great game.'

Back at Benbow Irina was sarcastic. 'How kind of you to visit us. Why don't you stay with your friends and relations? Who will you dart off after next? Your admirer Gildas Herne was here asking for you.'

'I met him in the village.'

'What's your programme for tomorrow?'

'I have to see Gildas, and my father. My father wants to see Marcus –'

'Doesn't he want to see me?'

'Yes, of course.'

'Do you call him Dad? Then we shall have two Dads around.'

'No – I –'

'What do you call him?'

'I call him "Tuan".'

'What's that?'

'It's out of a novel by Conrad.'

'By who?'

'Joseph Conrad. It's some sort of African word. It means chief, or lord.'

'Good heavens. Does he deserve it?'

'Yes. What's for supper?'

'There is no supper. Dad's gone to his bedroom already, he's been meditating all the afternoon, now he's retired with cheese and biscuits. If you want any you can get them from the kitchen.'

'Irina – be an angel –'

'And what?'

'*You* get me cheese and biscuits – and some other nice things. I was upset and I couldn't eat my tea –'

In the end Ludens got a good supper of poached eggs on toast with grilled tomatoes, biscuits and cheese, an apple and a banana and a piece of cherry cake.

Irina, indicating that it was a bad time of the month, retired early, declining his bed. When Ludens asked tenderly if she had a pain, she said crossly yes, and disappeared. Ludens himself went to bed soon and lay awake for a while listening to the owls. He now *very much* regretted having forced his father to answer that question which had travelled with them for so long a time. What did it matter now, what spirit had moved him to open that wound? Was it some sudden desire for revenge, a desire to hurt his father whom he loved? He wondered if his father were, at this very moment, lying in bed in his attic room at the Hedgehog, remembering what he had done to Ludens's mother, and thinking perhaps that Ludens would now think ill of him and withdraw from him. Whereas it's the exact opposite, thought Ludens, I absolve him, I love him more. Why haven't I seen more of him, talked to him, looked after him? For ages now I haven't written to him properly, I've sent him postcards, rung him up sometimes, been to see him now and then for half a day. Now *they'll* look after him. I can't bear it. I wonder if he could come and live with me and Marcus and Irina? Of course that's absurd! And Ludens thought then of how much, as the years went by, Marcus had become his father. So, he thought, I have two fathers and two mothers – only the mothers are one true and one false, while the fathers are both true. He fell asleep and dreamed a happy dream, that his father and his mother had met again and become reconciled.

He awoke in the early light of dawn and was immediately wide awake. He sat up, remembering his dream, then remembering that it was midsummer day and the Seekers would be gathering at the Stone. He dressed quickly, deciding he would go there to see. Presumably Marzillian had given them permission; he could afford to be generous sometimes to his unpaid assistants! Ludens opened his door cautiously. The other doors were closed except for the door of Marcus's bedroom. Ludens glided over and peered in. Marcus was not there. He tried the bathroom door. Not there. He stood a moment or two listening to the faint mumble of the fridge in the kitchen and the soft sound of Irina's sleeping breath. He sighed deeply. Rodney was still not all it should be. He crept out of the house and began to run soundlessly over the grass along the side of the tarmac. As he approached the yew circle he slowed down. There was no one about. The birds were singing, not in the jumbled unison of earlier months, but piercingly, individually, as if in turn. The sun had not yet risen but the pale greyish air was already trembling with atoms of light. Perhaps the Seekers had not yet arrived, or had not been let in after all? He walked quickly to the yew hedge and slipped in between the high dark green walls into the circle.

The circle was full of people. Ludens stopped, feeling the dismay of someone blundering carelessly into a large solemn unexpected scene: indeed in this case a religious rite. He was tempted to back quietly out again, but as this would attract even more attention he decided to stay, and after a few moments moved a step or two, keeping his back to the yew wall. Becoming calmer he was able cautiously to look around. The silence was impressive, also the immobility. There were in fact fewer people than at his first impression but enough standing back against the yew, to form an even ring about the Stone. A few stood in the open, as if posted, nearer to the centre. Ludens thought, Marcus is here somewhere. He did not like to be seen to stare curiously about, but managed in the still uncertain light to see some familiar faces. Camilla, Anita, Thelma and Maria were standing together on the far side. Fanny Amherst was standing out nearer to the Stone, so were Miriam and

Kathleen, and on the farther side Colin. Ludens was surprised to see Terence Bland with Patrick beside him. Marzillian was of course not to be seen. Ludens thought, he wouldn't risk his magic in a crowd or be somewhere where he was not evidently the master! He recognised some of the hospital staff, the nurse Lambert and the girl Rosie, and a few villagers, the waiter from the White Lion, and Mr and Mrs Toller who had the air of shameless tourists at an ethnic ceremony. Mrs Toller even gave Ludens a discreet little wave. Conscious of being looked at nearer at hand, and hoping to discover Marcus, Ludens turned his head and saw Gildas. He was in process of smiling at him when he noticed Daniel Most standing with him. Most, his attention drawn to Ludens by Gildas, smiled and Ludens smiled back, then looked quickly away composing his face and overwhelmed for a moment by an amazingly physical spasm of jealousy. After a minute or two he ventured another look. Most was standing soberly, his hands clasped, looking ahead. Gildas, who had been waiting for Ludens's glance, gave him a special wry smile and a small gesture of his hand which Ludens, understanding the language of their long friendship, took to mean that Gildas, aware of Ludens's ailment, sympathised derisively with his condition.

The hazy light was gradually clarifying itself. The smooth kindly face of the Stone, opposite to Ludens, looked still entirely flat, as if blank, like a sheet of glass with a grey curtain behind it. There was a slight movement of expectancy. Ludens thought, of course there's a watcher outside, looking out toward the hills, waiting for the sun to appear over the horizon. He saw Miriam turn toward Kathleen. Then the silence was broken by a very high very pure and sustained sound. Ludens, realising what it was, thought, I didn't know Kathleen could sing so well and produce such a great volume of sound! The note was being taken up, he could see that Anita, Camilla, Thelma, Maria, and Miriam were also uttering the high wordless sound. Then the sound or cry of joy was swelled by many voices, creating a vast complex impromptu harmony, like the crescendo of an organ. Ludens found himself singing, uttering a spontaneous thrilling note which it would have been impossible to repress. He felt at the same time an expansion of his body as if some new emotion or captive spirit were attempting to break out of its mortal bones. He thought, this is religion, and Oh how strange it is, we are worshipping something we know not what and being lifted up by forces which we cannot name. It is a visitation of gods. It was like this in ancient Greece. The great outcry, which seemed at its climax more like a great shriek or superhuman roar, gradually faded and died away into a long audible sigh; and out of this there came a sound of chanting. The Stone People, standing together, were singing something which sounded like a plainsong chant. Ludens could not make out the words, but felt he understood them. He thought, it's a deification of language, it's the language of something higher, the original voice of poetry, we are surrounded by spirits.

When the song ceased the crowd, which had been so still, became capable of motion and, in low tones, of ordinary speech. Dr Bland had disappeared and the hospital staff were quickly leaving, returning no doubt to duties from which they had been officially excused. Ludens, still near to one of the 'gates', decided it was time for him to go too. He dreaded, after such an experience, having to chat with the Tollers. He did not even, just now, want to meet Marcus. He moved away, giving Gildas a signal which he knew would be understood. Gildas nodded, accepting the postponement of their conversation. Ludens wanted to be alone. As he was about to leave he turned for a moment, conscious of some magnetic ray, and saw Fanny Amherst not far off looking at him with her huge eyes. She raised both hands, turning the palms towards him. Ludens replied with a similar salute, and then slipped out and began to walk fast, then to run, across the grass in the direction of the golf course and the lake. The sun, symbolic hero of the recent scene, had now risen clear of the hills and was shining in a clear blue sky, dazzling, blinding, blazingly pure, visible yet invisible, a triumphant transcendent presence: how can he not be taken for a god, thought Ludens, and used to symbolise perfect goodness, as indeed he was by the greatest of philosophers. After crossing the golf course and skirting the end of the lake Ludens, hurrying now through longer grass, came to the high fence of netted wire which marked the border of Bellmain.

He wanted to get out, to run out into the countryside. He walked along the fence, shielding his eyes from the sun. At last he found what he was looking for. Some wildness had invaded, crossing the border in the shape of nettles, ground elder and high grasses now rising into pink feathery flowers. In this neglected spot he discerned a shallow dip, a channel, a tunnel, like the one he had used once, seemingly so long ago, to enter Bellmain from the lane. He knelt and scrabbled into the grass, then snake-like wriggled under the wire and out the other side, where, as he stood up, he realised he had been made rather wet, the ditch being evidently the abode of a little spring. He walked on, rejoicing in the dampness. He was on a hillside of long grass, soon to be hay, lightly dotted with buttercups and blue cranesbill. Turning his face away from the sun he saw above the hills a buzzard with spread wings rising in spirals upon an air current. At that moment, dimly, he heard, or perhaps felt, the faint distant booming sound which might have been thunder. He went on a little, then in an ecstatic surrender to gravity, fell prone upon the ground. An extraordinary happiness possessed him. He thought, today I shall buy Irina a ring. And Marcus, he must have been there at the Stone, how much he must have rejoiced, how much he must have *understood*. If such a thing could ever be, it was a message from *it*.

Ludens, still damp and faintly muddy with leaves and grasses adhering to his clothes which were rapidly drying in the sun, made his way back to Benbow. Irina was sitting in the garden. When he saw her Ludens suddenly felt guilty. Surely he ought to have taken her with him to that amazing experience. And yet – she had been asleep, she had never shown any interest in the Stone People, she would have laughed at it all. Guilty all the same he approached. She had not yet seen him and he thought how beautiful she looked, her expression in repose so intently grave, her hair framing her face in an abundance of dark orderly locks, one hand with fingers spread out at her neck in a gesture seeming to signify some sad yearning. She was wearing the new dress, blue with green, which she had recently been shortening. When she saw him she sprang up, her face resuming its bright restless impish look.

'Where have you been, you silly useless goat?'

'Oh Irina –' He was about to tell her that he had seen something wonderful, but as she had not seen it and would probably not have thought it wonderful, he said, 'I've just been to look at the Seekers' midsummer day jamboree.'

'Oh, that nonsense. I'd forgotten. I suppose Dad was there. Have you seen him?'

'No, but I expect he was there.'

'I couldn't think where he was, he's usually back by now.'

Ludens, looking at his watch, saw that it was later than he had imagined. He had evidently stepped out of time. He was about to explain that Marcus had probably, like him, wanted to be alone for a while, again checked himself and said, 'I expect some of those people wanted to talk to him.'

'Well, he'll miss his breakfast, and you don't deserve yours. Needless to say I haven't had mine, I've just been waiting for you.'

'Well, here I am, I've come!' He sat down beside her and held her, clasping his arms round her waist. 'Irina, we're going to Salisbury today.'

'Oh, are we?'

'Yes. To buy a ring.'

'That's old-fashioned. People don't wear rings now.'

'I'm old-fashioned, you're old-fashioned, we are made for each other.'

'I don't think we're made for each other, we're just accidents, we couldn't be more different, and our differences don't fit either. We keep falling over each other and butting each other out of the way. It's just that we get on somehow. I tolerate you though you're so daft, and you tolerate me though I'm so awful.'

'We *do* get on, don't we, and I'm sorry I'm daft, I'll try to do better, and you're not awful, you're my priestess, my goddess, my gipsy queen, my absolute witch, my —'

'Oh shit, let go, you're dirtying my dress, what have you been doing, you must have been rolling in the mud somewhere.'

'I'm so sorry!'

'Now I'll have to wash it. Never mind, it'll have to get used to being washed. I do wish Dad would come back. I hope he hasn't got into a dream and wandered away into the countryside. Suppose you go and look for him, see if he's still at that Stone.'

'All right, but there's nothing to worry about.'

He left her and walked as far as the Stone. He met no one on the way. He thought it possible that Marcus might be there, and as he entered the yew circle expected to see him sitting on the seat where he had so often seen him before. But the place was empty, curiously and uncannily empty as if, after so much tumult, having returned to a repose that it did not want to be disturbed. The only trace of the festival was that there were more flowers than usual around the Stone, and more stones had been added to those that usually 'lived' there. Ludens retreated quickly and made his way back to Benbow hoping to find Marcus there, but he was not. Irina, who was still sitting in the garden, exclaimed at once, 'Did you find him?'

'No.' Ludens was now slightly infected by Irina's anxiety, but spoke cheerfully. 'He's probably walking about in the grounds and thinking. We mustn't fuss about him so. He'll soon turn up.'

'I hope so. Suppose you make yourself useful by going and putting the kettle on?'

Ludens crossed the grass and went through into the sitting room. His sun-accustomed eyes found it dark inside. The bedroom doors were open, the kitchen door as usual shut. He went first into his own room and took off his damp shirt and trousers and put on dry ones. Then he went to the kitchen. He opened the door.

Marcus was lying on the floor. At his first look Ludens did not realise what it was that was lying there, some amazing bulky thing taking up the space, an object grasped at once as strange and horrible. He stared down at it with terror and astonishment. Then his eyes assembled it and he saw it. He had at once on entering been aware of a strange smell. The door of the gas oven was open. Marcus's head was not in the oven but lying beside it on the floor. He was lying on his side, his face turned towards the door, his head slightly tilted back, one arm outstretched beside the stove, the other bent over his breast, the fingers touching the neck of his shirt. He was wearing the white shirt and flannel trousers which he had worn on the previous day. He wore socks but no shoes. His eyes were closed, his mouth slightly open, his face seemed calm but exceedingly remote. The striped prayer shawl was draped over a kitchen chair. Ludens had never seen a dead man, but he knew at once that Marcus must be dead.

He closed the door behind him and knelt down. He said, 'Marcus!' though he knew that it was useless. It was hard to utter a sound and he was not sure he had uttered one. He shook the shoulder, instinctively undid a button of the shirt, dislodging the arm slightly, felt the naked flesh of the breast and quickly withdrew his hand. He leaned down over the mouth and nose to detect any lingering breath, but the remote still face appalled him and he rose to his feet. The thing was motionless. There could be no doubt. He stood for a moment, then turned off the gas.

He walked out of the kitchen and closed the door behind him. He felt sick, a darkness descended on him, he felt he might faint, he reached the sitting room and sat down on a chair. He sat there shaking with grief and horror and a strange repetitive sound now issued from his lips. A black anguish stiffened his body and he kept uttering little high-pitched cries. He got up, staggered, and stood with his feet wide apart, moaning and reaching out his arms. He heard himself mumbling: help, help. He must find help, he must tell somebody, he must not be the only person to know, he would die of that knowledge. He blundered towards the doors and out onto the verandah.

Irina was standing on the lawn brushing down her dress. Looking up she said, 'What a time you've been, can't you even boil a kettle?' Then, seeing Ludens, she said, 'What's the matter?'

He sat down on the steps. She came to him. '*What's the matter?*'

Ludens said, 'He's dead. He's in the kitchen. He's dead.'

Irina made no sound. She walked past him, brushing him with the skirt of her dress. As he got to his feet again he heard her open the kitchen door and then close it again. She sat down in a chair in the sitting room and uttered a loud cry like a shout, then a shriek, then another shriek.

'Irina, stop, *stop*, I can't bear it.' He went to her and tried to take hold of her head, but she thrust him away, flailing with her hands, punching. She began to sob and tears spurted from her eyes.

Ludens said, 'We must tell somebody, I'll go, I'll run –' He thought he must run to the house. Then he remembered the emergency telephone which had been pointed out to them when they arrived at Benbow. Oh, where was it? He found it, a small red telephone on a small low table. Kneeling on the ground he lifted it. A calm female voice at once said, 'Can I help you?'

Ludens said, 'I'm speaking from Benbow, *Benbow*. Professor Vallar is dead, I think. Please could someone come here at once?'

The voice said, 'I will see that somebody comes to you at once.'

Ludens dropped the telephone. When he turned round Irina had gone. He ran to the door and could hear her sobbing and moaning in her bedroom. He looked in. She was lying face down on the bed, her head deep in the pillow, her sandalled feet kicking rhythmically at the counterpane. He closed her bedroom door and went back to the sitting room. He put the telephone carefully back in place and sat down on the sofa facing the window. Now tears came, great tears rolling down and dripping off his chin. There was a kind of silence, the distant sobbing seeming like a sound inside his head. He sat still, time was passing, he thought no one will come, I shall have to run there after all. He thought of going back to the kitchen but could not.

Then as he stared out into the garden he saw almost with surprise a car drawing up beside the lawn. Marzillian, Dr Bland and a male nurse got out. The nurse stayed beside the car, inside which there was some sort of machine. Bland ran across the lawn and leapt up the steps. Marzillian followed more slowly. Ludens, feeling suddenly that he and no other must show them, hurried to open the sitting-room door, then the kitchen door. Bland and Marzillian pushed past him. Bland knelt down beside the motionless form.

'He is dead, of course,' said Ludens in a strange high voice.

Bland said, 'Yes.'

Ludens said, 'He gassed himself.'

Bland said, 'That he did not do.'

Marzillian took hold of Ludens's arm and gently directed him out of the kitchen and shut the door. Irina's sobs and cries were audible. There was no need to explain that she was there and that she knew.

Ludens went into his bedroom. The arrival of the doctor had checked his tears which now began again. He found a handkerchief and thrust it into his mouth to stop himself from sobbing. He sat on the bed, then lay down, but found the position intolerable and sat up again. He began to say to himself that he must be composed, that he must think, that there would be things he must say and things he must do. The sound of Irina's weeping, a quieter sound now, was terrible to him. He wanted to go to her, but her grief appalled him. There was nothing he could say to her, nothing he could do for her.

After a short while Marzillian appeared at the open door and said, 'Alfred, could you come with me? Let's go outside.'

Ludens followed him. They went into the garden and sat on the seat where such a little time ago Ludens had sat with Irina and talked about buying a ring. The male nurse was sitting in the car which had backed onto the gravel next to Ludens's car. Marzillian put his arm round Ludens's shoulders for a moment, then withdrew it and said, 'Compose yourself, my dear. I just want you to tell me what happened. Did you find him, and when?'

Ludens, pocketing his soaking handkerchief, tried to reply. But the demon of speechlessness sealed his mouth and he could utter no sound. He put his finger to his lips, shaking his head.

Marzillian said, 'All right. Take it slowly.'

After a few long moments Ludens said, 'I went out very early to the ceremony, the thing at the Axle Stone. His bedroom was empty then, and I assumed he'd gone too. He often went walking early in the morning.'

'You didn't go into the kitchen.'

'No. We always keep the kitchen door closed because – because the refrigerator makes a noise. Well, after the Stone business was over I went walking for a while. I came back here and went into the kitchen, then I telephoned.'

'And yesterday and last night, how was he?'

'He was quite ordinary – a bit tense, but he often was. He went to bed early.'

'Irina was not with you this morning?'

'No. She was asleep. And then – she was waiting for breakfast till I – and he – came back, so she didn't go into the kitchen. You see – Irina sleeps late – he was usually the first to go to the kitchen in the morning – to – to put the kettle on.' The terrible thought had occurred to Ludens that if he had not gone to the ceremony or if he had not run out into the countryside afterwards he might have saved Marcus's life. He moaned, closing his eyes.

Marzillian, who knew what he was thinking, said, 'You could not have saved him. He has been dead for some time.'

'I oughtn't to have been away so long, I ought to have watched him *continuously*. I might have woken in the night, I might have smelt the gas.'

'About the gas, I doubt it, the kitchen is well ventilated. Besides –'

'What did Dr Bland mean?'

'It was not the gas.'

'Then how did he die?'

'I don't know yet. Now I want you to go for a while and sit with Irina. Talk to her if she wants to talk. But I think she will still want to cry. Just be with her. I am afraid that in a case like this we have to involve the police, and the sooner and more thoroughly we involve them the sooner we can get rid of them. I think we had better move you and Irina to another chalet for the moment. Perhaps you could pack a suitcase with some things for both of you. It will give you something to do. I'll send Camilla to help you. Would you like that?'

'Yes.'

'And Patrick?'

'No.'

'I don't think the police will bother you much. He left a note, it was lying beside him, it was not addressed to anybody and I have taken the liberty of reading it. Here it is.' He unfolded a sheet of paper and held it out.

Ludens read, in Marcus's odd curly writing, *I die by my own will. No one is to blame in any way. I wish my body to be cremated. Marcus Vallar.*

'I shall need it to show to the police. Thank you. Now go back to Irina. Pack suitable things, you will be staying elsewhere overnight. We'll send a car to collect you.'

'And – Marcus –?'

'The police will want to see the scene. Then we shall take him to the mortuary. Do not blame yourself my dear child. I think this had to be. We shall talk properly later, you and I.' Marzillian rose and went to speak to the male nurse, who immediately drove the car away.

Ludens went into the house. The kitchen door was shut. Behind him he could hear Marzillian talking on the emergency telephone. He went into Irina's bedroom and closed the door.

To his surprise Irina was no longer lying on the bed. She was bathing her face in the washbasin and patting it dry with a towel. She said, not turning to him, 'What are we supposed to do?'

'They're moving us to another chalet. The police have to come, and Camilla is coming to help us pack.'

'Why?'

'Just to help. Marzillian will arrange everything.'

'What's Camilla got to do with it, I don't want to see her.'

'Marzillian just thought you might like –'

'I might like?'

'He said did we want Pat or Camilla and I said Camilla.'

'I'd rather have Pat if we've got to have anybody, but why have we got to move?'

'They just want us out of the way, when the police are coming, and after that they'll be – moving Marcus – to the mortuary –'

'We won't be in the way, we won't scream or anything.'

'I suppose the police will want to look at – what's here – and they'll want to see us – and it'll be easier if we're somewhere else – I suppose –'

'They'll want to see me. You don't exist.'

There was a sound outside. Ludens opened the door. A car had returned. Camilla was in the sitting room. As he stepped out Irina closed the door behind him.

He came to Camilla who put her arms around him and kissed him. She had been crying. 'Oh, I'm so sorry –'

'Camilla, dear –'

'How's Irina?'

'Bearing up.'

'She's a strong brave girl.'

'I think we're to move.'

'Yes, just for the moment, tonight anyway, or for longer if you like. You're to go to Collingwood. It's empty now. You'd better take some clothes, night things, toothbrushes, anything you need. Sorry about it, but it's better for all concerned, when we take him out, and so on.'

'I understand. Can I help?'

'No, I'll, we'll, do it all quickly. Could you wait in the garden, do you mind?'

He returned to Irina's room and tried to open the door but it was locked on the inside. 'Irina, we're to go at once, to Collingwood. Could you pack a few things, we'll be staying the night there.'

'Go away, I'm washing my hair.'

He went to his own room and put a few things in a suitcase. He thought, she's washing her hair. I'd better do something, like shave perhaps. But he could not. He put pyjamas and shaving things into the case, also a bottle of whisky which he had brought from London.

Irina emerged and went to the airing-cupboard for a dry towel and rubbed her hair with it. She went back to the bedroom and came out with her coat and handbag and a small case. 'Let's go then.'

Ludens paused. He wanted to look at Marcus once again. He said to Irina, 'Do you want to –?' She walked past him. Ludens turned back to the kitchen door. But at once he heard voices, the soft low sound of Marzillian and Bland talking to each other. He hurried through the sitting room and out of the house.

Outside Irina was sitting in the back of the car, Camilla in the driving-seat. Ludens got into the back, separated from Irina by her bag and case and coat piled on the seat. They proceeded in silence. As they turned right and drove along the main drive a police car passed them.

Collingwood, farther back in the woodland than Benbow, was reached by its own gravel drive. Ludens remembered having seen Collingwood and read its name when he first arrived at Bellmain, before he *knew*. Oh why did we ever come here, he thought, to this cursed place. If we'd been living in an ordinary house and I was working and earning a living for them and we'd been ordinary people it couldn't have happened. If only I'd been more afraid, if only I'd really looked after him, if only I'd stayed with him all the time . . .

The door of the chalet was open. Irina jumped out with her belongings and went in. Camilla and Ludens followed.

Camilla said to Ludens, 'Shall I tell Patrick or will you?'

'You tell him. Go now. And thank you so much.'

'I'll just come in and make you some tea.'

'I can make the tea.'

'Well, I'll show you where it is.'

Collingwood was similar to Benbow but differently designed. The only entrance was by a door at the side, there was no verandah, but a long large bow-window. The sitting room was larger, the bedrooms smaller. There was a genuine garden with flowerbeds and roses in bloom, and two cast-iron seats painted in white.

Irina had gone into one of the bedrooms and closed the door. Camilla showed Ludens the kitchen, the larder and refrigerator already supplied, the emergency telephone. She turned on the gas stove and put the kettle on.

'I'll go now, but I'll come back later. A policeman will come, but it'll be quite simple. Patrick will want to come. Shall I tell him not to?'

'No, let him do what he wants.' Ludens thought, now everybody, one by one, will have to know. The world will have to know. Then he remembered his father who would be expecting him. 'Camilla, could you send a message to my father, he's staying at the Hedgehog, tell him what's happened and that I can't come to see him.' He thought, everyone will know, everyone will interfere and want to talk. Oh if only I could take Irina right away, and we could be alone together and mourn and bear it together. Then he thought, but I *can* take her away, and soon, when these horrors here are over, we'll go away and *hide* and endure *that* horror and weep and comfort each other. Oh God, why has it happened, how could it happen . . .

When Camilla had left he went to the bedroom. Irina had got into bed and pulled the bedclothes up to her neck. She was lying on her back, not weeping. She said, 'It's cold here, I'm cold.'

'I'll get another blanket.' He ran into the next room and hauled a blanket off the bed and laid it carefully over her. 'I'll see if I can find a hot-water bottle. I'm just making some tea, I'll bring you some tea.'

'I don't want any tea.'

'Whisky then, some whisky?'

'No. Nothing.'

He drew a chair up beside the bed. He wanted to hold her hand, but her hands were hidden. He touched her hair, it was still damp. He touched her cheek and she shuddered.

'Oh my darling, my darling – I'll look after you forever. We'll have our house together soon.' He thought suddenly about his son, their son, and it was as if once more he could see the child, looking at him steadily, with grave thoughtful eyes. He groaned, bowing his head.

Irina, lying on her back, her eyes wide open, gazing at the ceiling, said, 'Oh, the vulgarity – the vulgarity of it –'

'What do you mean?'

'To do it today, mixing it up with all that midsummer thing, as if it *meant* something.'

Ludens, confused, did not know what to say. 'Well – it does mean something – not *that* of course – and I suppose – I suppose a time has to be chosen –'

'He could have done it any time with sleeping pills.'

'Sleeping pills –'

'He's had them for ages, he had them at Red Cottage, he was saving them up, I thought he'd do it there, do it quietly, I've been waiting for this for years, in a way I'm so relieved it's over at last.' Tears now came into her eyes and rolled sideways into the mass of her damp hair.

'Oh Irina – my love, my dear –'

'And to gas himself – like putting on a show for the newspapers – like showing off and making it symbolic and that – it's so mean and pathetic – it's kitsch, it's absolutely *kitsch* –'

Ludens did not tell her what Dr Bland had said and Marzillian had confirmed. He said, 'Irina, he's dead, these things don't matter, why do you think such things –'

There was a sound of knocking. Ludens left her and went to the door. It was a policeman.

'I'm sorry to trouble you. I believe Miss Vallar is here? I wonder if I could have a few words with her? Would she be able to talk to me?'

Ludens ushered the policeman into the sitting room. As he did so he saw through the window Patrick sitting on one of the white seats in the garden. He went to Irina who was already up, combing out her hair. She found her handbag and quickly powdered her face and examined it in a mirror. 'Yes, I know, police.'

She went to the sitting room and closed the door. Ludens turned off the gas in the kitchen and went out into the garden and sat beside Patrick. They sat together staring at the ground.

Pat said, 'I should have been with him all the time, I should have slept outside his door, I should have slept under his bed.'

'I should have,' Ludens murmured.

'That's what I *intended* to do when he raised me. He'd have let me too. He cared for me. Didn't he care for me?'

'Yes. He asked for you yesterday – Oh God, yesterday –'

'*Christ*, and I didn't know, I didn't come, I *curse* myself –'

'Pat, it would have happened anyway. He wanted to go.'

'That's what we say to ourselves now.'

'Yes.'

'I feel – you know – that he died for me, instead of me, he took my illness when he took back the curse into himself. The devil that came out of me went into him. When he saved my life he condemned himself to death, he is for me Christ crucified. I don't know what I'll do with myself now. He was the meaning of my life. Not the women. I loved him long ago when we first met him. He gave me a place in the world. I've always felt I was an animal, a weird strange animal like no other animal, not really a man, but like a poor unhappy animal with no mate, just looking for a master. Then I found him – and when he rejected me it was the eternal fire, I thought I'd die, and I nearly did die – and when it was he cured me I felt I was the son of a king. But then I wanted him to be God and that was wrong, that was my fault, I didn't understand when he gave it up, I didn't see that he was going for something higher – and now it's all over.'

'Yes, he *was* going for something higher. Perhaps he achieved it. Perhaps that's the meaning.'

'We want it to be. But I tell you there's no meaning. It's just death. It's what we're feeling now that's the truth. It's all accidental after all, we're accidental, perhaps there is nothing higher, and no difference in the end between his death and that of a fox.'

'Pat, don't despair. Go on writing poems. Remember that we're friends. Remember like we used to be.'

'We shall never be like we used to be. I think I'll go back to Dublin. Maybe I'll go back to the West.'

'Where the seals are.'

'That old joke. And maybe it's true too. I don't feel human. I'm a poor lost animal, everything's weird to me. And now living without him. Oh Christ, Christ –'

The policeman emerged from the house and stood looking at Ludens. He got up. 'Don't go, Pat.' He went to the policeman and walked with him to the police car which was standing in the drive.

'You're the young fellow who found the body?'

'Yes.'

'Could you describe what transpired?'

Ludens described how he came to Benbow and what he found.

'Did you know the deceased? You were visiting him?'

'Yes. He was writing a book which interested me, and I came here to discuss it with him.'

'Any theories about his death?'

'No.'

'Would you kindly write down your name and address?'

Leaning against the bonnet of the car Ludens wrote his name and London address.

'Profession?'

'Teacher.'

Ludens thought, Irina is right, *I don't exist.* When he returned to the garden Patrick was gone.

Irina stayed in bed and would not talk to him. She refused tea, whisky, food. He tried vainly to find her a hot-water bottle. He made himself some tea and drank a little whisky. Camilla came back accompanied by a nurse with offers of sleeping pills and tranquillisers. Irina refused to see them. Ludens and Camilla sat in the garden. Clouds covered the sun and there was a cold breeze. Ludens kept thinking where is he now, what have they done with him. He kept imagining that he was still alive, that he *must* be, that it was all a bad dream. He had been alive yesterday, how could he not be today, what *was* this terrible change, what was this *absence*, this eternal and irrevocable absence? Ludens felt cold and sick, amazed that he was able to sit on a chair and speak rationally to Camilla. Camilla said did they want the maid Rosie to come? Would they mind staying at Collingwood at least till tomorrow, perhaps a little longer? Ludens said no, they wouldn't mind. Would they like anything fetched from Benbow? Ludens said he thought not. He thought of asking Camilla to bring them a hot-water bottle, but could not bring himself to mention anything so trivial. He wanted very much to talk to Marzillian or Bland but dared not ask for that either. Camilla told him to use the emergency telephone if he or Irina wanted anything. Then she went away. He went back to Irina who was, or pretended to be, asleep. He poured the whisky out of its bottle into a jug. He boiled a kettle, and when he heard Irina get up and go to the bathroom he poured the hot water into the whisky bottle, wrapped it up in a tea towel, and put it into Irina's bed. But she said it was too hot and she didn't want it so he took it away again. She again refused tea, food, whisky. Ludens sat on a chair in the sitting room near to the bow-window with his hands folded on his knee. He was conscious of himself sitting quietly, looking out at the trees and the flowers. He was conscious of his body as a heavy cold horrible container. He had the feeling, coming to him as the memory of a dream, of being a prisoner waiting to be tortured. The extremity of pain was yet to come. And even now he was denied the comfort of self-pitying misery and warm tears. He saw his father, Gildas and Daniel Most standing in a row in the garden, and felt a dismay amounting to anger. He went out to them and even said to his father, 'What is it?'

Gildas said, 'We met by accident, we thought we'd come together.'

Ludens's father said, 'Alfred, I'm very very sorry. I can imagine – and I hope your fiancée is not too –'

Ludens thought, what an odd word, 'fiancée', nobody has said that before. He said, 'She is taking it bravely.'

Daniel Most said, 'Is there anything we can do?'

'No. Thank you for coming.' He made a movement as of returning to the house.

Most said, 'I'll leave you. I'll want to talk to you later and I hope you'll want to talk to me. Please. Here is my address and telephone number.' He held out a card to Ludens who did not take it. He handed it to Ludens senior who passed it to Gildas who put it in his pocket. Most went away.

Ludens senior said, 'I must be getting along, I have to get back and fix up the house. I'll give your love to Keith and Angela. I hope you'll visit us.'

Ludens said, 'Thank you for coming. Goodbye.'

His father hesitated. What did he want to do, shake hands, embrace, kiss? He did none of these things, but put his hand to his brow in a gesture of distressed confusion and marched hurriedly away.

That left Gildas. They looked at each other in silence. Ludens felt he was remembering another dream. Gildas said, or whispered, 'I'll stay, I'll be near.' He stretched out his hand, which Ludens automatically took, then realising that Gildas was giving him Daniel Most's card. Their fingers touched clumsily and the card fell to the grass. Ludens saw an expression of exasperated misery on his friend's face. He also saw, over his shoulder, Camilla approaching, her footsteps audible upon the gravel of Collingwood's private drive. Gildas retreated, saying 'Good afternoon' to Camilla. Ludens thought, so it's the afternoon now. He picked up the card from the grass and began reading it. The frightful contingent unreality of his being made him feel sick. He thought, I suppose it's shock, like soldiers have when a limb has been shot off and they make jokes and ask for a cigarette and then suddenly fall dead. He turned back toward the house. He thought, I feel faint, I wish I could faint, I wish I could be with Irina only she doesn't want me yet, she hates my presence.

Camilla, whom he had forgotten, caught up with him. He said, 'Have they taken Marcus to the mortuary yet?'

'Yes.'

'It's ridiculous to say "Marcus". There is no Marcus now. He doesn't exist any more.'

Camilla, after a moment in which she evidently tried and failed to find some consoling reply, said, 'Before I forget, I've brought you this, it's a photocopy, the police have to have the original.' She handed Ludens a copy of Marcus's letter, which he put into his pocket together with Daniel Most's card. 'I'm sorry to trouble you and Irina with practical details, but there are one or two matters. First, are we to take it that his wish to be cremated is to be fulfilled?'

'Yes, of course.'

'Jews are generally against cremation, but since he specifically said —'

'Yes, yes.'

'And in the case of cremation we have to bring in outside doctors, so we'd like to know now –'

'Yes –'

'Are you sure Irina agrees, has she said so?'

'No, but of course she agrees.'

'Perhaps you would ask her, just so as to be sure? There's also the question of the funeral service, but –'

'All right, all right.'

'Irina's solicitor has been on the telephone –'

'So he knows already?'

'We informed him. He urgently wants to talk to her. Could she ring him or take a call from him? The call can be made or received through the little red telephone.'

'I should have thought he could wait till tomorrow.'

'Indeed, but perhaps you would tell her.'

'Yes.'

'And another thing, if you could ask her tactfully, whom should the bill be sent to now?'

'What bill?'

'Well, for his board and lodging and medical care up to the date of death, and for the board and lodging in respect of you and Irina and Patrick.'

'I thought we were free. And there isn't any board, we paid for our own meals.'

'There was produce from the estate.'

'All right. But who's been paying the bills till now, I suppose they have been paid?'

'Irina told us to send them to the solicitor. I suppose we still should, but we'd like her to confirm.'

'Yes, yes, yes. All right.'

Camilla disappeared, running away along the gravelled track.

Ludens went back to the house and cautiously approached the door of the bedroom. Silence. He cautiously opened it. Irina was sitting on the bed. She said, 'Where have you been? I've been calling you. I must telephone our, my, lawyer, at once.'

'Darling, I'm sorry, I was in the garden –'

'Never mind where you were, you weren't here, I must telephone my lawyer –'

'He's been trying to telephone you.'

'Then why the hell didn't someone tell me?'

'They thought – I thought – you were resting, perhaps asleep –'

'Perhaps asleep – as if I could sleep! I'll go up to the house now and ring him.'

'You can do it from here on the red phone, it's in the –'

Irina darted out, found the telephone, lifted it and said in peremptory tones, 'I want to talk to my lawyer.'

The person at the other end evidently understood at once, since in less than a minute Irina was saying, 'Is that Mr Garent? This is Irina Vallar, my father is dead . . . Yes, yes, I could come at once . . . Then tomorrow morning . . . You've got the will of course . . . Good . . . Oh – oh really – for heaven's sake don't forward anything – you haven't forwarded anything, have you? . . . Yes, keep them. I'll see you tomorrow at eleven. Thank you. Goodbye.'

'Irina, Camilla wants to know –'

'Oh bugger Camilla.'

'She wants to know where the bill is to be sent.'

'What bill? Oh the bill. Send it to Mr Garent, I don't want to see it.'

'And also whether – whether it's to be cremation like he said.'

'Like he said? He never said, never to me anyway, we weren't given to chatting about it.'

'It was in the letter – Oh of course you haven't seen it – here it is, it was beside him. This is a photocopy, the police have the original.'

'You mean you had this all the time and you didn't show it to me?'

'I'm sorry, I saw it this morning only they took it away, and Camilla's only just brought it –'

'I should have thought I was the person who should see it and have it!'

'I'm terribly sorry, I forgot to say –'

'You forgot! God!'

'I'm sorry, I'm sorry, anyway I suppose cremation is OK, since he –'

'Cremation is OK! All right, he's dead, anything is OK!'

'So I'll tell them –'

'Anything you like, just don't *bother me*. Oh rot it all! – I suppose I can get to London by eleven tomorrow, maybe I'd better go up this evening.'

'I'll drive you.'

'No, I want to go alone. I'll go by train.'

'I'll look up the trains. Where is your lawyer's office?'

'Why do you want to know?'

'To reckon how long it will take you to get there.'

'It's in Victoria Street. Now leave me alone, will you? I'm ravenous. No, I'll make myself something in the kitchen.' She went into the kitchen and closed the door.

Ludens lifted the telephone and was supplied, by the calm anonymous voice, with a list of evening and morning trains to London and afternoon and evening trains back to Salisbury. He wrote the times out clearly on a sheet of paper, opened the kitchen door, put the paper on the table, and closed the door again. He sat in the bow-window looking at the rain fretting the garden. He kept thinking about Marcus's closed eyes. He went to the kitchen again and opened the door. Irina was sitting at the table eating a poached egg on toast.

'Please go away, I'm eating something.'

He came in and sat beside her. 'Irina, I can't bear you being so cold and hostile, please stop it.'

'Stop what? I'm not being cold and hostile. I'm just in a terrible awful state, I'm torn to pieces, everything has changed, do you want me screaming?'

'I understand, forgive me, yes everything has changed, except one thing. I love you, you love me.'

'That's two things. Thank you for finding out about the trains. I think I'd better go up this evening.'

'I must come with you. Please let me drive you. I won't bother you. I just want to look after you, we must comfort each other.'

'No. Just try to *see*. I have to make this journey *alone*, I've got to deal with these things by myself. I've got to *think* by myself. I've got to *get away* by myself. It's the first time I'll be really – just me. I've got to prove that I *can* be.'

'I do see, all right, yes – but I'll worry all the time till you're back. Where will you stay? At the flat, it's not sold yet is it?'

'I'm not a child, I've lived in London, I don't know, maybe I'll stay in a hotel. Just don't torment me!'

'You'll come back tomorrow afternoon, won't you, keep that list of trains, you can let me know by telephone what train you'll be on and I'll meet you at Salisbury. And I'll drive you to the station in good time for your train this evening. I do wish you'd let me drive you to London. All right, all right. Just please look after yourself, it'll be such anguish being parted from you, I can hardly bear it. You do love me, don't you.'

'Yes, yes.'

'And we'll be married and live in that house.'

'What house, there is no house.'

481

'Don't, please – Irina, I'd die of grief, only there's you. Put your arms round me and kiss me.'

She put her arms round him and kissed him.

PART SIX

Dear Dr Ludens,

My wife and I would wish to send our deepest sympathy and condolence to you concerning the shocking death of your friend the Professor. We are very shocked and upset indeed. What a surprise, and I suppose he did it as part of that midsummer business, perhaps he was overwrought. We are very sorry, please give our sincerest condolences to Miss Vallar. We quite miss you at the old Black Lion.

With kind regards,
Yours truly,
Geoffrey Toller

Dear Mr Ludens,

I was so sorry to see in the press that 'our professor' as I always think of him, has committed suicide, and fancy gassing himself, a horrible act. I wonder why he did it, do you have any clue? I always thought he was overloading his poor mind, and I suppose it just gave way suddenly, he did nothing but work and think and that's bad for anyone. It is very upsetting for all when people take their own lives, sometimes it is meant as a revenge to make the others guilty, but I'm sure you did all you could to help him and you must have had the very best doctors at that expensive place, so you need not feel you did badly. I still recall with pleasure your visits to us at Richmond. I am very happy now with my sister in Amesbury. She joins with me in sending sympathy and good wishes.

Yours faithfully,
Helena McCann

My dear Ludens,

Just to say how very sorry I am to hear about poor Vallar. He came here, perhaps hoping to be 'cured', poor fellow. I suspect he had too large a dose of the 'exaltations' of the East. His brief appearance in the role of 'sadhu' was indeed impressive and he could no doubt have had a following had he wished it. In this godless age people will follow anyone. But Western rationality broke in and mental conflicts were too much for him. I knew him very little: but I would surmise that he lived a noble and courageous life, and died the death of a stoic. On a more mundane level, I doubt whether our Armenian friend's fancy methods were the right thing: down-to-earth modern medicine in the form of strong drugs might have done more good. But suicides are mysterious, and one must respect their mystery. I send my sincerest condolences and best wishes.

Yours sincerely,
Richard Talgarth

Ludens, I am most terribly sorry and shocked to hear of Vallar's suicide. What caused it I wonder? I fear he was, in his post-mathematical period, a great man *manqué*, and may have been but too conscious of that. Or are we to see him as one of Hitler's victims? When will the lethal effects of that monstrous crime ever end?

Thank you very much for the loan of your flat. I am now, as you see, established elsewhere. Quite a lot has been happening in my life of which I will tell you later.

I know how terribly you will miss him. With love and all sympathetic wishes,

Yours, Christian

Dear, I am *so sorry*, I do hope you got my telephone message, I couldn't get through to you, I just *have to* stay in London a bit longer, there are *endless* legal matters and I have to keep signing things. Not quite sure where I'll be so write to me c/o Mr Garent's office. I'll let you know. With all my love to you.

I.

I'm sorry I was so nervy – it has all been so terrible.

My dear Freddie,

Jake has told me of the sudden death, by his own hand, of this philosopher who meant so much to you. I believe he had some great theory, but I'm afraid such things are beyond me! I really am so sorry. As Jake will have told you we are out of Portugal. (Thank heavens!) Mario ran off with an attractive young Spanish lady and that was that! (She had lots of money *of course*!) It's a great relief to be back in our dear little cottage where we were all so happy when you and Keith were kids. As I think Jake hinted to you, Keith has some problems, but the local health and social people are very helpful and he may go to a clinic in Bristol if we can afford the fare! I'm afraid we're skint, we were awfully cheated by Mario who left everything for us to pay. We're settling down here well and will of course be glad to see you if you are ever in this vicinity. With sympathy and all fond wishes, and love, and from Keith,

Yours truly,
Angela

Dear Ludens,

I cannot sufficiently express my sorrow and my feeling for you in this awful loss. Of course I feared it, as I am sure you did. But the shock of the reality is terrible, indeed unspeakable – I know how much you loved him and how hard you tried to help him to order his mind. (Sorry, this is badly put, but you understand me.) He was gifted with an exceptionally intense capacity for sympathy and compassion in the most literal sense of these words. We have all thought about that horror and that evil which is greater than can be conceived, and which those who survived it tell us cannot be communicated. We are, we others, in a deep and strange way, ashamed that we were not there. We shall continue to think about that inconceivable suffering for very many years, no doubt for centuries, that is a part of our destiny and our docility. But as time passes, and even now, it will become, however much we grieve and mourn, an object of thought, a theme of meditation. We shall not allow it totally to invade and overwhelm our minds and our hearts. With him it was otherwise – it was given to his great soul to open itself to that absolute, to experience the inconceivable and to perish by it. This meaning must attach itself to the mystery of his death. We shall revere him as one who faithfully and fully lived out his role of prophet and martyr.

Daniel

There are *many* other things which I want to say to you. Please let me talk to you *soon*.

Dearest Ludens, I am *very very sorry* to hear about the demise of your guru. Perhaps you expected him to go? It sounds like a dramatic and carefully planned departure. I am truly sorry and I imagine your grief. I am glad that I came to you as I did and that we kissed each other as we did. I shall not ever forget that, and I do love you. However – that sad stern word – I think you may be right, I mean in thinking that I

485

can't leave Jack. (Of course he doesn't know I came to see you, that must remain for ever our secret.) Sometimes I feel devastated, humiliated, corrupted, disgraced – sometimes that I am, through tribulation, gifted with some almost superhuman energy and insight – and that my new life with Jack is just starting and will be an achievement, a creation, something wonderful. The kind of ruthlessness I feel about Franca is now more of a scar than a sin. She remains in our (my and Jack's) world like a Cheshire cat, continuously present, smiling – and fading. Oh heavens, look after yourself, don't marry that girl, your relation with her is childish, not grown-up, not really deep. I am so sorry about your teacher – you know, you must know, it was him you loved, not her. I send you my love, very much of it.

Alison

My dear, I am so very sorry not to see you during this time. I had hoped to come back but *I simply can't*, I'm involved in endless mysterious legal mysteries, muddles about insurance, I have been all over the place sorting things out, I may even have to go to Switzerland! Thank you for arranging the funeral and *everything*. Excuse this scrappy note, I have to rush. *Sorry*. My much love to you.

I.

My dear, my dear old friend, what terrible news about Marcus. I can't quite believe he has actually left this scene, left *our* lives, wherein he was always so significant! How we tracked him, you most of all of course, and lost him and found him. Surely he'll turn up again in a few years with some new brilliant idea! I am so sorry. Why, why? Well, even I can think at once of hundreds of reasons, an overloaded mind, a sense of failure, a Newton complex like we used to say, fear of losing his wits, loneliness, guilt – Why wasn't I in a gas oven? Is it true that he gassed himself? I find this a little *too* picturesque! I look forward to discussing it all with you. I do hope you are not too devastated, don't be. Perhaps you saw it coming and are in a way relieved? Did he actually get on with writing the great book, and have you now got it? Ludens, I am very sorry that I haven't been in touch. Well, you can imagine . . . However my *ménage à trois* is now at last firmly established, mostly owing to the high and indeed *noble* characters of the two ladies. They have been *wonderful*. There were no illusions on either side, they *saw* the difficulties, and *suffered* them, and *overcame* them. From all our pain and tribulation together we have evolved, I believe, a new and vital creative energy. Will you please come and see? Please ring up. I gather you have no telephone at that place. We are all thinking about you. With much love, ever

Jack

I didn't communicate earlier because I wanted the thing to be settled, but also because I feared that you disapproved! Perhaps you still disapprove. But I feel sure you will overlook the sin since you love the sinner.

Dear Ludens,

I'm very sorry I didn't write sooner. We were all absolutely in shock. It just seemed like something crazy, violent, even cruel. How *could* he leave us? How *could* he give up his mission to mankind just when it was starting? We felt the world had ended, we felt he had negated himself, and somehow us as well. That's why we cleared off so quickly without seeing you or Irina. We sort of felt ashamed! But now we see it *quite differently*, we understand it as a symbolic act, an immolation to whatever gods there be, like Christ, like Shiva leaping into the fire, like a total experience of the suffering of the Jews, that sort of thing. And he bound it into *our* ritual, made it part of *our* seeking, to show somehow the unity of all the spiritual world and how everything really can symbolise everything else. It's not as we expected, we thought he would somehow be with us for years as our special guide and inspiration. As it was – we happened to be there, and he in some sense deemed us worthy, and we are humble and proud. I would like to feel that he died just at the rising of the sun when we all cried out, and with that great cry his immaculate soul left its earthly abode. I send much sympathy to you, and I hope you will find your way to participate in the echoing of his message. We all think of you and hope to see you again soon. Miriam and Andy send love, they will invite you to their wedding. Kathleen sends love too. I am going back to my theological college. I may even end up as a Buddhist-style Anglican priest. With most loving greetings,

Yours,
Colin

My dear son,

What a terrible tragedy, I am very shocked by it and very sorry about it. I am glad that I was able to see you, just before and just after it happened. It was important to me to see you. I think of you very much, all the time, and imagine your deep sorrow. I wish I had met your great professor. After all, he has been with you, and you with him, for many years of your life – and I cannot help feeling that you found in him a

487

father who was more worthy of you. Please think of me and please write to me. Angela and Keith are here. I think Angela is writing to you. It's strange to be together with them again, and not as awful as I expected, though Keith is in a bad way. It has been a bit lonely here. Angela is having all sorts of ideas about improving the house — it certainly needs some attention!

You told me that you were going to get married, and I rejoice heartily at that news, and look forward to meeting your fiancée. Perhaps you will write to me soon about that? Do come and see us, come and see *me*. I wish I could do more, be more, for you. You understand. Ever your loving,

Tuan

Dear Alfred,

(if I may), I heard the news with great sorrow, grieving for you and for him; a great, perhaps saintly, man has been taken from us and we must mourn. I feel especially close to this sad event having witnessed, I should say *experienced*, in two successive scenes, the exercise of his spiritual powers; once when he drew Patrick back from the brink of death, and later when he manifested as a healer and a vehicle of grace at Bellmain.

There can be no doubt about the genuineness of his gift. His mission was short, but its significance and its results will spread in widening ripples. Great mystical beings are rare indeed and we must stand in awe before the silent authority of their mystery. In his mode of death he signalled his identification with the sufferings of his people and through them with the sufferings of all creation. Christ was admired for his miraculous powers, but chose instead the helpless humility of death. Marcus's *imitatio Christi*, if we may reverently attach the phrase to him, offered in sacrifice both the satisfaction of a great intellect, and the spiritual happiness of a holy healer. He preferred the *supreme act*, opening the door wide upon darkness, being conscious, in his meditation upon the destiny of his people, of the suffering and the sin of the whole world; and that consciousness destroyed him. He died at midsummer so as graciously to mediate his death to those he left behind. His message will live, not least through you, his beloved disciple. May your tears be dried as you meditate upon the power and meaning of this life, this death. Please come and see me when you return to London.

Most lovingly, in Christo, yours
J. O'Harte, OSB

I'm sorry I had to go without talking to you properly. I won't (can't) write you a long letter. I want to see you as soon as you want to see me. At that time come to me please.

Gildas

My dearest Alfred, I can imagine how terribly shocked and grieved you are by Marcus's death and how terrible a loss it is – and what a nightmar- ish business. I hope Irina is being some support, though she is such a frail girl, I sympathise with her too. As for me, I am preparing for my departure to America. I haven't told Jack yet. I am waiting for his next trip abroad with Alison. I don't see that I need to go through the ordeal of telling him face to face. He is so pleased with himself, thinking he has his two women securely settled in their places. For a while it gave me an awful satisfaction to think how grossly I was deceiving him. Now I pity him. Not that he will grieve for long – he and Alison will heave a sigh of relief – this thought almost persuades me to stay! Really the whole thing is agonising, and I know how much blood will flow – mine, not his – when we are at last definitively wrenched apart. But I know that I must do this violent thing, or lose myself, fade, shrivel, and cease to be. But I do long to get away. I still hope you will come with me – *please come*, now or later. Maisie asks after you in every letter. I can't believe you will marry that poor child – you are simply sorry for her. I'll let you know when I'm going, address and telephone number. *Oh God*, what a mess life can become. But beyond – there is true happiness, goodness, joy. My dear, ever my love to you,

F.

My dear Alfred,

I have heard from Franca about your bereavement, and hasten to say how very much I sympathise with you in this dreadful loss. Perhaps he was committing the suicide he felt his parents ought to have committed. I hope you, who loved him so much and have known him so long, are able to transform your grief into some kind of consoling understanding. Do not feel remorse. He did what he had to do and was determined to do – heaven only knows what it means, but it *has* meaning and is not just an ugly senseless accident. Perhaps he was a magician who, forswearing his magical powers, chose Goodness, and was destroyed by his own magic – as he foresaw and expected. What a great man, and a holy man. It was better that he should not grow old. *Come to see me. Franca is coming!* With much love,

Maisie

Dear Dr Ludens,

We were sorry to hear of the death of Professor Marcus Vallar. It is rumoured that he left behind an almost completed philosophical work, which is now in your possession. If this is so, the Cambridge University Press would be very glad indeed to see this manuscript with a view to publication. With kind regards,

Yours sincerely,

R. F. Schutz

PS I knew Marcus when he was a Senior Wrangler at Cambridge. You may not remember but we met briefly when Marcus was living in Richmond. I was very shocked to hear of his death. I have long since given up the agony of mathematics for the easier life of a publisher!

Dear Mr Ludens,

We believe you were a close friend of the late Professor Marcus Vallar, and we wonder if you would be interested in writing his biography for us? If you would prefer, J. P. Banstead, the experienced biographer who publishes with us, would gladly collaborate with you on this important venture. We cannot reach you by telephone, so perhaps you could ring us? Hoping to hear from you,

Yours sincerely,

Miles MacAdam

Dear Mr Ludens,

I believe you are in possession of a secret discovered by your father-in-law Professor Vallar, which is to be passed on to mankind. I should be most grateful if you would let me know it. You see – I am in possession of the *other half*. When these two formulae are united a new age of the world will begin, including the ultimate spiritual union of East and West. *A god must die*. I am sure that you understand me, and I anticipate hearing from you at once.

(Dr) P. L. Changku

My dear, I am so sorry to have been so elusive, I have had to be all over the place. I picked up your sweet letters from Mr Garent. Thank you for arranging all those things, I would have been no good, I would just have cried. And now, I do really have to go to Switzerland! It's unbelievable! I don't know how long I'll be away, I'll let you know, you are kind and good.

Love from I.

Dear Mr Ludens,

I enclose a photocopy of the will of the late Professor Vallar, in which he names his daughter Irina Deborah Vallar as his sole heir, and, as you will see, names you as his literary executor. Also enclosed are: a sealed letter addressed *To my literary executor*, and three keys, two of these for Miss Vallar's London flat, the other that of the Red Cottage, Fontellen, kindly lent to us by Lord Claverden. I should say that although a literary executor is usually also a beneficiary, you have not been otherwise mentioned in Professor Vallar's will, or in any papers we hold of his. However, your railway fares, or cost of petrol should you drive, to and from Fontellen, will be reimbursed by the estate. May we request you to perform your duties, that is the perusal of all relevant papers in respect of the wishes of the deceased, as quickly as possible and return the keys to this office, since the flat is to be sold and Lord Claverden wishes to renovate the cottage. I should remind you that all papers and writings left behind at whatever place are the property of Miss Vallar and must not be removed by you. You are required now simply to peruse them, and, as it may fall out later, represent in respect of them the wishes of the deceased.

Yours truly,
Howard Garent

To my literary executor
Please destroy everything.
M.V.

My dear dear, In haste, *so sorry* I have to be away from you. Love – I.

'I hope you don't mind,' said Marzillian, 'we're really short of space now.'

'So you think the publicity did the place no harm?'

'None at all it seems, rather the contrary!'

'Perhaps Camilla could help me pack up Irina's things and you could store them till –'

'I'm sorry. Camilla is already assigned to one of our new patients, and we cannot take responsibility for the belongings of previous inmates. We had to introduce this rule because people sometimes left us trunks full of stuff which they never called for! I gather you have now kindly moved to the Black Lion? Good. And Collingwood is already cleared, you have moved everything to Benbow? Excellent. I would be most grateful if you could pack *everything* up, ready to be moved out of Benbow as soon as possible, so that we can get the cleaners in. We shall have to charge rent, not to you of course, until that is done. Could you do it by tomorrow afternoon?'

'But where am I to move the things to?'

'Oh sorry, haven't they told you – Irina's solicitors will send their removal men immediately when everything is packed – just do try to pack it securely. After that please return the keys of Benbow, just leave them with Julie at the desk. Thank you for the Collingwood keys. That's all I think.'

The funeral was over. No inquest had been necessary since it appeared that, in spite of the suicide note, Marcus had actually died from natural causes, in fact from a sudden heart attack. It appeared that he had suffered for some time from a serious heart condition. The police surgeon, and no less than three outside doctors who were called in, confirmed the opinion of Marzillian and Bland in respect of the cause of death. It was unfortunately by then too late to prevent the more interesting story of suicide from spreading. In Irina's absence, Ludens was accepted at Bellmain as being chief mourner, and in charge of the funeral arrangements. There was no Jewish ceremony since Irina had told Ludens before she left that she was sure Marcus would have hated it. Ludens allowed Daniel Most to choose and read passages from the Old Testament. For music Ludens chose the slow movement from Beethoven's Quartet, Opus 127, remembering that Gildas had said once that Marcus liked the late quartets. Present were Ludens, Most, Talgarth, Marzillian, Bland, Lambert, Camilla, Mr Westerman (the parson) and Fanny Amherst. Ludens had expressed the wish, which accorded with the custom preferred at Bellmain, that the ceremony should not be publicised. He dreaded the idea of an influx of inquisitive villagers, or acquaintances arriving from London. Marzillian's office informed Garent's office and Ludens of course wrote to Irina. He did not inform Jack or Gildas feeling, for different reasons, that he could not deal with either of them at present. Patrick had evidently left, anyway no one knew where he was. The only 'outsider' was Mr Westerman who, according to Camilla, came to all funeral services uninvited. No one conducted the ceremony, there was no ovation or spoken prayer. During the music which preceded and followed the disappearance of the coffin, people sat or knelt. Ludens wept silently and continuously. Daniel Most covered his face. Camilla and Fanny were crying. Marzillian and Bland, who arrived last and sat at the back, slipped away quickly when all was over. Ludens, kneeling near the coffin, was glad that it was cremation not burial. He shook with agony at the proximity of Marcus's body. He did not want to think later that it still existed, disfigured and decomposing. Daniel Most said something to him afterward about 'first the gas then the fire' and Ludens nodded. Before the funeral Camilla asked him what was to be done with Marcus's ashes? Ludens said he would take charge of them and probably scatter them in the little 'garden of remembrance'. However, when he was given the casket he took the ashes very early on the next morning and scattered them around the Axle Stone. There were no flowers now, only the little stone offerings which had been neatly piled in under and around the circular seat. Ludens performed his task rapidly and at random. Only later did he learn that someone had observed him. He had decided not to worry Irina with this problem. In any case he did not know where she was.

On the day after Marcus's death Ludens had very much wished, and also expected, to be able to talk at length with Marzillian. But although he more than once asked Camilla, this audience was not granted. Perhaps, he later thought, Marzillian was not yet ready to see him; and indeed he was not yet ready to see Marzillian. Ludens had failed. Was it possible that Marzillian felt he had failed too, could Marzillian feel this? It was something Ludens did not want to see. It was as if Marzillian needed time to put his case together. Yet, Ludens decided on further reflection, Marzillian had other troubles, was used to suicides, and had probably expected this one. It was not his business to grieve and speculate and explain: that belonged to Ludens. Ludens also made efforts to see Terence Bland, but these were also unsuccessful and Ludens soon concluded that Bland had been instructed to say nothing until Marzillian had spoken. The newspapers had little to say about Marcus's death, beyond announcing that he had committed suicide by gassing himself. There was a brief obituary, evidently composed and filed many years ago, dealing with his work in mathematics. Someone who wrote to *The Times* about his pictures appeared unaware that he had done anything else but paint.

When Ludens took Irina to the station that evening, and took leave of her with many kisses and embraces, he had completely assumed, and thought he had agreed with Irina, that she would return from London on the following afternoon. He gave her a list of the afternoon and evening trains, and told her to telephone him to say what train she would be on, and he would meet the train. He informed Camilla and Maria who said that of course the call would be put through to him, and if by any chance he was not there, the message would be conveyed to him as quickly as possible. He spent the afternoon beside the telephone, then unable to bear this silent vigil drove to the station, meeting all the London trains, and telephoning Bellmain at intervals to ask if Irina had arrived or sent word. He gave this up at midnight, after getting no answer from the special number which Camilla had given him, and raced back to Collingwood, where he spent the night on the floor in the sitting room beside the red telephone. Early the next morning he ran to the house in case any message had been overlooked, but was told that none had come. He went into the village and telephoned from the post office the number of the flat in Victoria, but the number was unobtainable. He ran back to Bellmain in case she had meanwhile arrived by taxi. The following morning he received her first letter saying that she had to stay longer in London. That afternoon he was told to return to Benbow bringing all his and Irina's belongings. He wrote to Irina every day care of the solicitors. He decided to telephone their office, but could not find it in the telephone book, as it of course turned out that Garent was not the first name in the title of the firm. He thought of telephoning Garent's home, but found no Garents of any kind in the telephone book. He asked Camilla to give him the office number which after some delay (perhaps difficulty) she was able to do. Trembling with anxiety and distress Ludens, again at the post office, rang the office and, being requested to give his own name, was told that Mr Garent was at a meeting. He rang again and was told that Mr Garent was away. When Garent was a third time not available Ludens asked if there was anyone in the office who could tell him how he could get in touch with Miss Vallar. A silence followed, then an anonymous voice told him she was involved in arrangements concerning her father's estate and it was impossible to say where she was. Irina's second letter arrived, and then her third, allaying some anxieties but also stirring up terrible impatient longings and dark thoughts. All this while, before and after the funeral, he was grieving for Marcus, looking for him, feeling his absence as a great open agonising wound, tortured by misery and remorse, sometimes feeling half-mad with pain, moaning aloud and weeping, sitting on the floor beside the telephone with wet, swollen eyes and lips, not checking his grief but indulging it like a frenzied child. He longed for Irina, for her voice and her hair and her soft body and her dark teasing eyes, for the comfort of her presence, like morphia, bringing relief and hope and less dreadful tears, he longed for a union with her wherein as one body and one soul they could survive, a union without which he would die. He lived each minute, each second, as penultimate, herald to the sudden sound of her voice, or her appearance on the lawn, in the room, the return, the embrace, and each minute and each second brought disappointment and despair and a growth of black fear. So he lived at Benbow, buying himself a little food in the village and sleeping beside the telephone, until at a hint from Camilla, he moved to the Black Lion where he continued to wait. The telephone call which for an instant shocked him with hope and insane joy had turned out to be only the summons from Marzillian.

There was a pause during which, without showing any signs of impatience, Marzillian continued to stare at Ludens who was sitting opposite to him. It was a dark day, rain was falling, the room was sombre. Ludens, suddenly unable to think of anything to say, felt a panic fear that Marzillian would now tell him to go, deliberately leaving unuttered all the things that needed to be said. He tried to clear his mind and find the next question.

'What did he die of?' said Ludens.

Marzillian, as if expecting this question, said readily, 'Oh, not gas, of course.'

'I heard Dr Bland say that.'

'Yes. It's not at all easy to gas yourself. It takes quite a long time, and you have to make the room airtight and get your head well inside. Also, if you've succeeded you look pretty odd. And with this sort of gas —'

'Marcus looked calm — quiet anyway.'

'Indeed. The gas was symbolic. Rather touching.'

'*Touching?*'

'After he had travelled so far and risen so high, it was a homely touch. As if he had come home.'

'I don't understand. What *did* he die of?'

'On the death certificate I put heart attack.'

'And was it?'

'He had high blood pressure and could be described as having a "heart condition".'

'But you don't believe that killed him?'

'No.'

'What did then?'

'I don't know. It was an unusual death. I decided not to puzzle the police or my medical colleagues with any interesting conjectures.'

'But you think he really –?'

'If I rightly anticipate your question the answer is yes. I think he enacted a psychological experience which killed him. This is one rather crude and uninformative way of putting it.'

'You believe such things can occur?'

'I believe so. There are cases – and no doubt more than one knows of – because they are hushed up.'

'By the doctors?'

'We are reluctant to admit that there are more things in heaven and earth – I recall that we discussed this quotation on a previous occasion.'

'You think he was determined to die?'

'I never had any doubt of it.'

'He once said that there could be such a death which would be significant, a sort of act of salvation, but one would have to be worthy of it, otherwise one might die the worst death of all like a – I forget his words – a poisoned rat –'

'One worries about one's state of mind, about one's motives, and these are rarely clear, and rarely pure. Many suicides are vindictive, acts of revenge. Or one may prefer death to madness.'

'But I wanted him to live. And when you said there was "danger" I thought you meant danger of suicide. But perhaps you meant danger of a bad death. Whereas you wanted to steer him toward the good death. Oh what nonsense this is –'

'Perhaps you would rather not discuss it –'

'No, no, I'm sorry, please go on.'

'I think we both have reason to assume that your friend was an exceptional man, possessed of an outstanding intellect, and also surrounded by, indeed full of, forces which he did not entirely understand.'

'He called himself a maimed monster and said he felt he was crammed with demons.'

'Put it this way. He had discovered that he had magical powers, paranormal powers as people say. He was a magician. He wanted to be a good magician. But is there such a thing? What mortal can have such power and not be corrupted?'

'When he found he could heal people he stopped.'

'I think that phase had to come, to be experienced, and rejected. The danger of it was that – how can I explain it to you – it might be as if having conjured up and used these powers, let the demons out as it were, and having then opted for – let us say for the moment something higher – he might be overwhelmed by forces which were still his own, but now alien and hostile.'

'And be destroyed by his own magic. Somebody suggested this to me in a letter.'

'These are picturesque metaphors. But then the unconscious mind lives by metaphor. To die overcome by guilt and fear and helpless remorse, having made of one's own psyche a vile wicked omnipotent Enemy – I have seen such cases.'

'He wondered whether the holy and the good were the same, or whether they were enemies.'

'Many men have died clutching that problem to their breasts.'

'He sometimes spoke as if he'd committed some great sin, or imagined or desired it, and said it was necessary to identify with evil people so as to understand them, and he spoke of an experience, or a place, where the terrible suffering of the innocent and the terrible sin of the guilty meet each other –'

'The notion that you have committed a great sin, like the sin against the Holy Ghost, is a familiar symptom among disturbed and alienated people. But one must try to see in each case what it means – and let me say before you interrupt me that I am not classifying Marcus as mad, but rather thinking of him as a sort of psychical genius, who was able to *think* about the arcane forces of the mind and confront them. This, and no less, was the danger he was in. Great saints and mystics have written, often most poetically, about such states and about the sense of guilt and peril which can accompany them. As when visions of the divine, intimations of perfect goodness, seem suddenly to shatter the life of reason and of ordinary morals.'

'A friend of mine said of Marcus that a dose of ordinary morality would kill him.'

'A shrewd saying, it stirs the imagination.'

'But you don't think Marcus – well, I'm certain he didn't *do* anything, but he may have had obsessions which he was ashamed of, some repressed sadistic tendency – no that's putting it too strongly, *I* never saw anything like this, it's just that he talked about it –'

'We all have obsessions which we are ashamed of and which ordinary moral common sense buries at an appropriate level. Some explorers of the psyche recommend deliberate evil-doing so as to shock and fracture the conscious mind into some state of greater enlightenment. I would not recommend that. The discovery that we are capable of extreme cruelty is one we are better without. But these are dark regions where doctors too can make mistakes, Freud thought that children's stories of being sexually abused were all fantasies. I am sure your friend neither did nor thought any remarkable evil, but that what he was seeing was the shadow of his own peculiar feelings of guilt.'

'You mean guilt for not having died in a concentration camp.'

'You told me, and he told me, that he had read a lot about these things. I see in his life an increasing sense of his Jewishness which constituted for him a profound psychological drama. Survivors from those camps tell us that they feel terrible guilt and shame – let us not pause here to discuss the interesting difference between these concepts – so much so that some of them committed suicide just after being liberated, and some did so many years later. This particular guilt is great and deep in proportion as the evil which occasioned it is great and deep, unique in the history of mankind, a subject for grave meditation and the most scrupulous study for innumerable years to come. I am not Jewish but my people too were slaughtered, and my heart has knowledge of these wounds. Then it is said, why do the innocent feel guilty, should they not rejoice in their innocence and point furiously at the evil ones? But, when the body and the soul is stripped, who is innocent? Where is ordinary morality then when what is required is the courage of the saint? Absolute misery and absolute fear quickly reduce men to the instincts of self-preservation at their most gross and graceless. The evil men knew that their victims would not survive without co-operating with them, and the knowledge of that, perhaps infinitesimal, degree of co-operation, the simple obedience that kept one alive when another, a braver one, had died, demoralised and shamed those who continued to live, destroying their sense of themselves as free worthy beings. How are we to judge even those who quietly, readily gave in, co-operated, became the tormentors of their fellows? And even the courageous ones, the pure ones who at risk to themselves gave aid and comfort to others, can say later that they might have done more, and will think all their lives of some small good act which they failed to perform. Those who survived tell us these stories which are uttered against the background of that terrible silence of the great majority who travelled dumb from the railway station to the gas chamber. This scene, exhibited to our knowledge and never to be forgotten, is like an allegory, a picture of purgatory, where we see too the brilliant light shed by the saints, those whose faithful goodness or virtuous anger brought them soon to terrible death; and, beside them, the extremity of the human condition which is usually concealed. The torturer strips his victim naked. In religious images God strips the soul and purifies it by fire and hides it in Himself. But here below the poor imperfect psyche must travel on, carrying this experience, daily relived, of the absolute of human frailty, this *secret* which he is not able to convey to any other person.'

When Marzillian paused Ludens, who had been listening with rapt attention, said, 'So you think Marcus somehow entered into this secret, this consciousness, and was able to raise it to such a degree of intensity that it killed him?'

Marzillian, not answering the question, said, 'Who can feel innocent? Great pain, the pain of others taken on in imagination, may seem like a punishment, may be a punishment, but then where there is a punishment there is a crime. This is one of the dialectical games which is played by the soul, it can be a very destructive game, it can be a source of energy, good or bad. It concerns too the mystery of how the suffering of expiation can be transformed into the suffering of redemption.'

Ludens, struggling to follow, and wanting to connect all these ideas with Marcus, said, 'He said once that only a god could suffer purely and that if some ultimate knowledge were attained it must be turned at once automatically into a special sort of death – I thought he meant a sort of saving redemptive death, when one would die simply by not being immune to the suffering of others – and that this would cause some sort of cosmic shock which would save the world from destruction. I couldn't understand this. But you said something about the drama of his beginning to feel Jewish – maybe he saw *that* as the more real or incarnate meaning of what he thought earlier – as if the extreme goodness of the saints, and the guiltiness of the innocent if you see what I mean, would somehow generate a great spiritual energy for the salvation of mankind.'

Marzillian was looking at Ludens now with a kind of gentle weariness. His hands, which had been tensed, were relaxed upon the desk. He sighed, then actually closed his eyes for a moment, then rubbed his mouth and ruffled then smoothed his dark hair. He said, speaking in a different tone as if to calm the exalted intensity of their recent discussion, 'Well, who knows. All that was a historical phenomenon with causes, something contingent, subject to accident. As for your friend, perhaps something of the kind was the case. His farewell note said that he died by his own will, not by his own hand. The body gave no clear clue, exhibited no clear cause. As I said I have known other cases – very different ones, yet with some similarities. He was a very remarkable person. The power of the mind over the body has limits which are uncertain, the serious study of this subject is in its infancy. We have much to learn.'

Ludens, feeling that Marzillian was now tired of talking to him and would soon terminate their conversation, said hastily, 'But supposing he hadn't really seriously intended suicide, suppose he had changed his mind at the last moment, but the shock of all the preparations, turning on the gas and so on, sent up his blood pressure and brought on an attack so that if –'

'I don't think so. Let us say that he found his own peace in his own way and did not just what he wanted to do but exactly what he wanted to do. Please do not blame yourself, my dear boy. You could not have prevented this, you were fighting a losing battle all the way. You wanted him to live and he is dead. But you were, in this whole story, the essential thing, the catalyst, the saving and enabling figure. Without you he might have sunk into that dark sea. You stirred his mind, you made him *think* at a time when just this was necessary. He could not have *talked* to anyone else. With a sure instinct you led him on, not as it happened where you wished, but where he wished. You took care of him, you cherished him, your love gave him quietness and order and calm and space.'

'Yes, I loved him,' said Ludens, 'but he said he didn't understand love, he said it was an incoherent concept. He said this when he was worrying about philosophy smashing itself on ordinary morals. Perhaps what he really felt guilty of was not being able to love.'

'We must not torment his mystery, but leave it alone. You must be content that such a man walked to his death with his hand on your shoulder.'

'But – but did you *want* him to kill himself?'

'Listen,' said Marzillian, 'if I had taken him into the house and watched him and looked after him and drugged him I could have preserved his life for a time. But his mind would have quickly clouded over and as he became aware of his condition he would have lived in torment, and destroyed himself either mentally or physically. As I told you once, I wanted him to take his time, to work it out for himself, not to disappear, as so many do, in a poisonous cloud of self-hatred. Of course I could not be sure what would happen. I wanted him to find his own way. Now tell me, when are you going back to London – soon I imagine?'

'Yes, when I've packed all that stuff.'

'How is Irina?'

'Oh – Irina –' Ludens had expected this question, and prepared a reply, but now could not speak. He put his finger to his lips.

Marzillian nodded.

'Irina has had to go all over the place to arrange things about the estate.'

'Where is she now?'

Ludens hesitated. 'I don't know. I don't know where she is.'

'I thought so,' said Marzillian. 'And I don't know either. We also have been trying to get in touch with her. But let me tell you something. Mourning and grief can take the form of flight. We even have a technical term for it, we call it *fugue*. The shock of something terrible, such as a violent attack or a bereavement, produces a kind of shame, people can be terribly ashamed of their wound, their loss, they cannot face the world, they need to hide. In such states of mind they wish to recover alone and they run away, leaving those who are closest to them, and travel to a distant place and live in a hotel, or with an acquaintance whom no one near them has ever heard of.'

'You think she may have done this?'

'It is possible. Well, we have had a good talk and now you must be off. Call in again before you leave just to say goodbye, and I'll see you if I can.'

Ludens opened the side door of Benbow with the key which was still in his possession. It was the morning after his conversation with Marzillian. He had meant, after seeing Marzillian, to go to Benbow at once and start to clear up and pack. But it was still raining a little and the sky was dark and his heart failed him and he returned to the Black Lion. Mr and Mrs Toller were endlessly kind to him, and although also endlessly inquisitive had by now learnt to leave him alone and not offer suggestions and conversations and sympathy. He went upstairs and threw his mackintosh and umbrella on the ground, sat on his bed, took off his shoes, lay on his bed, sat up again. The room was cold. He did not think about what Marzillian had said about Marcus, he would think about that later. He remembered how beautiful Marcus had looked when he was young. He felt giddy with grief, there was a black pain in his breast like a black stone. He found himself hunching his shoulders and wrinkling up his face into a sneer and crooking his fingers inward under his chin as if he wanted to shrivel himself up. He would become a small animal and scuttle away into a dusty corner, he would become a beetle encumbered with dust, he would become a black speck, moving, then still. He shook himself, agitating his hands and throwing back his head. He thought about what Marzillian had said about 'flight'. Perhaps at this very moment Irina was sitting on her bed in a hotel room in Geneva and thinking about him. He had added his London address and telephone number to all his letters. Perhaps her letters were waiting for him there. Surely this absence would end and be forgotten, when she was with him again, hugging and kissing him as she had done upon the station at Salisbury. Oh why had he let her out of his sight! Why had he let Marcus out of his sight!

Now at Benbow he stood in the hall, smelling the silence and the emptiness and looking at the suitcases in which he had brought back his and Irina's things from Collingwood. He went to the kitchen. The room seemed curiously empty without Marcus lying in it. He saw again the heavy limp bulk of that large body, one arm outstretched, the head thrown back as if its owner had fallen at the end of a long journey at some destined goal at some shrine upon some threshold. But of course there was nothing, no journey and no arrival. What had happened to all that great quantity of being? He closed the door. The kitchen had been tidied and cleaned. He opened the other doors. Someone had evidently been in, probably Rosie. The rooms were clean, the beds stripped, the wardrobes emptied, the clothes folded and placed in neat piles. The prayer shawl, removed from the kitchen, had been placed with Irina's dresses. The velvet bag in which it had arrived was on the dressing-table. It now contained her necklaces. In the study the notebooks which he had bought for Marcus were placed together, with the expensive fountain pen still in its box. He looked at the notebooks. They were blank except that in one, so touchingly, Marcus had written his name like a schoolboy. He went into Marcus's bedroom. He searched the room. Marcus's clothes were on the bed. Quickly, holding his breath and screwing up his eyes, he thrust his hands into the pockets of Marcus's garments. Nothing, except a handkerchief. Keys and a wallet lay on the dressing-table. The wallet contained some bank-notes. Marcus travelled light. There was nothing for a literary executor to do at Benbow.

He went into the sitting room and opened the glass doors. The rain had stopped, the sun was shining through a misty cloud, the warm jungly smell of the woodland entered the room. He thought, I am leaving. He returned to the hall. He noticed that some thoughtful person had provided extra suitcases, rather battered ones, to assist the packing, together with a roll of stout string. Unavoidably he remembered that someone had told him that the most awful and affecting thing in the 'museum' at Auschwitz was the huge pile of suitcases, cases of all kinds covered in labels, which represented the illusions of those who had arrived imagining that they would now rest from their nightmarish journey, sleep and change their clothes, and prepare for the hard but endurable work that awaited them in this labour camp. He started to pack and felt a sort of relief in performing a routine task at which, with a mind used to sorting and placing miscellaneous data, he was quite good. He worked quickly, concentrating first on Irina's and Marcus's belongings, which included things which Irina had bought in the village, dresses, scarves, also the 'special' plates with butterflies on, which he packed carefully inside Marcus's more substantial clothes. He packed the camera which Irina had never used. In fact Marcus had brought very few garments. In one of the drawers he found the curious light-brown cap which Marcus had been wearing when Ludens saw him through the window at Red Cottage, and which Marcus had vaguely told him someone had given him in India. What had Marcus been up to in India? Why had Ludens not *questioned* him? He folded up the two long white shirts which Marcus and Pat had worn during the showings. He folded up Irina's blue and green dress. Blue with green should always be seen. He packed up his own belongings including the notebooks in which, for that short time, day by day he had written his own orderly understanding of Marcus's thoughts. He was disturbed by a sound on the verandah. Daniel Most was standing at the door of the sitting room.

'I hear you're leaving.'

'Yes.'

'I'm glad I found you. Can I help?'

'No thanks.'

'Are you going today?'

'Yes.'

'Could we have a talk, not long just a – necessary – talk?'

'Thank you for your letter. I'm afraid I've got to see Marzillian now, he told me to call in before leaving.'

'I need to talk to you.'

'If you mean do I blame you, no of course I don't.'

'It's not just that. It's – do you think we could sit down for a while – perhaps in the garden on that seat.'

'I'm sorry, I must get on with what I'm doing, I'm in a hurry.'

'Please –' Most had advanced into the room. Ludens backed away. He thought, this man does think I blame him – and he thinks all sorts of Jewish things which I don't want in my mind at present – and he wants to take my hand, even to embrace me, he wants tears, he wants to console me and to be consoled by me. But I can't do anything for him and he can't do anything for me. We must wail in our own corners.

Ludens said, 'Sorry.'

Most was looking at him sternly, almost angrily. He said, 'Later then – we've *got* to talk. Something devastating has happened to me too. I've got to think about it. I want your help. Perhaps you need mine.'

Ludens said, 'There's enough drama without this as well. Perhaps you think he's become a sort of saint of Judaism, an icon of the Jewish destiny. I wanted him to write a great book, to find a universal language of philosophical understanding, that's what the world needs, not just something – particular.'

'You mean thinking about the Holocaust?'

'Of course it's a great sign of some kind – but I don't understand it – I don't know *how* to think about it – I feel it crushed him like the fall of a huge stone. He was obsessed by it, it wasn't just your arrival, perhaps you were right to try to talk him through it, which I couldn't do. I expect it was all inevitable anyway, and for reasons I couldn't even glimpse, and I was living in a state of total illusion from the start. Now I just feel that the plough has passed over my back and my bones are broken and my heart is broken.'

Ludens, who had not intended to display any emotion to Most, turned away, retreating into the hall. The rabbi followed him however, standing in the doorway, looking at Ludens who was now putting some of Irina's shoes into a suitcase.

Straightening up Ludens said firmly, 'Thanks for coming. Goodbye then.' He looked at Most, who was dressed in a respectable dark suit and spotless white shirt and sober tie. Was it the Sabbath once again? Ludens had lost count of days. Most's dark sleek hair was combed back behind his ears, it looked as if it had been lacquered, he was exquisitely shaven, he looked like a bureaucrat. Ludens was conscious of shaggy uncombed hair, a visible beard, an open shirt, a stained face, for although the gift of tears had, perhaps temporarily, left him, he felt that his face was darkened, smudged, perhaps bruised. He glared at Most whose face expressed pity. Ludens endured the pitying stare. Then as he looked, seeing that Most wished to say something but could not find the words, he saw the face rather as a face of grief, of pain, of affliction, somewhat lost, even somewhat mad. The exchange of looks liberated Most who then made an odd gesture. For a moment it seemed as if he were going to kneel or prostrate himself. But all he did was stoop and touch the floor with the palm of his hand, then, standing back, stretch out his arm with the hand open as if he were begging or else making a way for someone to pass. He said, in an ordinary tone, 'We must meet again. We *will* meet, won't we? In London.'

Ludens said, 'Yes. Yes. In London,' nodding his head several times. The rabbi disappeared. Ludens finished his packing, closing up the suitcases, securing some of them with string. He carried his own cases out to his car which was parked at the end of the lawn on the square of gravel. He went back to the house, locked and bolted the glass doors, then, emerging from the side door, locked that and pocketed the keys. He set off on foot toward the house.

Marzillian had told him to 'call in before he left' but Ludens, with no appointment, imagined that he would not be admitted or might at best receive a quick handshake. He had already resolved to make a certain detour, and was approaching the yew circle when he saw the flutter of a girl's dress among the nearby trees. He stopped, pierced by the familiar agony of a terrified hope. But it was Fanny Amherst. He went on and entered the circle and waited for her near the Stone. He was upset because he had wanted to be alone.

Fanny was wearing, on this occasion, not her uniform, or her green dress, but a straight loose shift of a subdued saffron colour. She ran towards him across the grass. He looked down at her, feeling a sad pity and awe, as if she were some fairy creature outside the family of mortality.

She spoke first, looking up at him with her large eyes of a gentle animal, speaking in her clear unhesitating voice; and he thought, after all, she speaks with authority, she is some kind of priestess! 'At first I could not understand, but I know now that it was for salvation, and I am so glad that it was given to me to meet him and to touch him, here in this place. I *know*, but I go on weeping for him, isn't that strange!' Large tears came from her eyes and moved slowly down her cheeks. She let them flow, then closed her eyes for a moment and they ceased. Leaving the tears wet upon her face she patted back her smooth brown hair with one hand as if adjusting a cap.

Ludens said, 'I feel as you do, something strange and holy has visited us, we must be glad that we were able to meet such a person and we must respect the mystery into which he has passed – and still continue to mourn him.'

'You are going away now?'

'Yes.'

'May I give you this?' She placed a smooth grey sea pebble into his hand.

Ludens, startled by the solemn gift, put it hastily into his pocket, where he heard it touch the other stone which he had picked at random from the river beach. The little sound seemed to be echoed by a faint booming in his ears. 'Thank you. Fanny, what is that strange sound? I have heard it several times. Am I imagining it?'

'It is the artillery school on Salisbury Plain exercising their big guns.'

'Oh –'

'Not everything here is without explanation.'

'Goodbye –'

'I'm sorry you are going.'

'I expect I shall come back.'

'People don't come back here. Goodbye.' She made a quick gesture, touching her brow then raising her open hands, and turned swiftly and darted away.

Ludens waited a moment; then, feeling a presence, he turned and not raising his eyes, quickly touched the great thing first on one side, then on the other. Another final farewell. He walked quickly away. The encounter with Fanny had disconcerted him, he was not pleased with the words he had used, and he was troubled by the two stones, which reminded him suddenly of Dr Changku's two formulae which if united would change the world. He had not answered any of the letters he had received, but he had kept them all, including that one. He thought, that's magic, and it's nothing to do with Marcus, nothing at all. He then, by some arcane connection, recalled the eloquent almost rhetorical words of sorrow which he had uttered to Daniel Most. Where had those words come from – and surely it was a harrow not a plough. It must be from the Bible. But all he could think of as he walked on quickly to the house was that David had put the conquered Ammonites under the saw and under the harrow. It is everywhere, he thought, and certainly there, man's inhumanity to man.

He hurried up the steps. The roses, whose scent had come to him and to Marcus on their last nocturnal walk together, were disordered by yesterday's rain. Julie, the porteress, installed in her alcove, no longer formidable, greeted him and asked him to wait. He gave her the Benbow keys and sat down on a tall-backed chair with a seat embroidered with a white hand rising from water. He heard Marzillian's door open, and a man emerged who crossed the hall in haste. Ludens caught a glimpse of his face and shuddered. He waited a little longer. Julie told him to go in and he went in.

Whatever it was that had been tormenting his previous visitor had left no mark on Marzillian's face. He looked less tired than at their last meeting, and seeing Ludens looked almost jaunty. He twirled the ends of his moustaches and gracefully tossed back the raven locks which brushed the spotless collar of his high-necked white coat. His dark eyes rested upon Ludens with lively sympathy, almost with satisfaction. Ludens thought, he's glad *our* thing is over. No more worry about Marcus, no more arguments with me, and no anxiety about the bill either!

'Well, it's departure day, is it? I hope you managed to pack everything up? Sorry we couldn't spare Camilla.'

'Yes, I've packed everything up. I gave the keys to Julie. I'm just leaving for London.'

'Have you seen Daniel?'

'Yes.'

'Good. He very much wanted to talk to you. Now, before our farewells, just one more thing, a strange thing.'

'What?' Ludens felt alarm, fear. He sat down in the mahogany chair.

'Just listen to this and tell me what you think.'

Marzillian was fiddling with a small recording machine on the desk. He turned a switch. Ludens heard Marcus's voice, that slightly rasping, slightly foreign, rather Cambridge, slow crystallised honey voice which had for so long made Ludens's heart turn over. Shocked, he stared at Marzillian who was staring at him.

Marcus was speaking in a rambling way as if to himself, stopping, then starting again, then making little humming sounds or sighs. But what was most strange was that he was talking in a language which Ludens could not at all recognise and which he had certainly never heard Marcus speak.

Ludens and Marzillian continued to gaze at each other. Then

Marzillian switched the machine off, the voice ceased. 'What do you make of that?'

Ludens, overwhelmed by the sense of Marcus's presence, then absence, could not reply at once. Marzillian waited. Ludens said, 'It sounds as if he's talking to himself. But what's the language? It doesn't sound like Yiddish, in fact it's certainly not Yiddish. Could it be Sephardic Spanish? His parents spoke that old Jewish tongue, but Marcus said he never knew it. He could have unconsciously remembered it. But it doesn't sound at all like Spanish.'

'Yes, he's talking to himself,' said Marzillian, 'perhaps when falling asleep. As I think I told you when you arrived – how long ago that seems – or perhaps I omitted to tell you – there are listening devices in the chalets for use when necessary – which in my experience is all the time. This, in a situation where some of our patients are living free, I mean at liberty, as it were, is a sensible indeed essential precaution. The greater part of what we hear is without interest to us, and of course we destroy the recordings unless they contain matter of clinical importance. What you have just heard is certainly interesting. The language is indeed not Yiddish, nor is it Sephardic Spanish, nor is it a Slav language. Finnish, Hungarian, Greek? No!'

'Japanese or Chinese?' said Ludens. 'Marcus attempted to learn both those languages.'

'Naturally I thought of that,' said Marzillian, 'and consulted Chinese and Japanese colleagues, but they recognised nothing. An Indian language? I know Marcus visited India. But apparently not. I have sent tapes of this speaking to several distinguished linguists of my acquaintance who were all completely baffled. You never heard Marcus utter anything like what we have just heard?'

'No, never. Could it be just nonsense noise, like infantile babbling? No, surely there was a linguistic structure – But didn't you *ask* Marcus?'

'*Ask* him?' said Marzillian, frowning. 'One does not silence the bird that sings by asking it questions. Of course the world is full of languages, but we are also dealing here with probabilities –'

'I'm sure Marcus never learnt any African or Polynesian language.'

'Quite. In any case my experts have busied their computers with all such questions.'

'Perhaps he discovered it after all,' said Ludens.

'Discovered what?'

'The formula, the message to the planet, the universal understanding. At one time he was searching for some original language which lay at the root of all languages, east and west, and I suppose if anyone mastered that no one would understand him! But later he started talking about suffering as if that were some sort of universal language. It's certainly a universal condition, so perhaps it's a sort of language, I mean, we all experience it but we don't understand it, the meaning of it lies beyond us, something like what you called the murmur of contingency. I never made any sense of this, or of what you said either, it's too picturesque. As if the planet, talking to itself, cries out and complains. Perhaps when distant people on other planets pick up some wave-length of ours all they hear is a continuous scream. Anyway, what Marcus was uttering certainly sounded like a human language, something which made sense. Perhaps he had passed some barrier – he was talking in a sort of dreamy reflective tone, not like someone frightened or hysterical.'

Marzillian, who had been listening carefully, said, 'Yes. Marcus talked to me about these things – but I doubt if what we have just heard – and there is more of it – will enable us to look beyond that barrier, if indeed such a barrier exists. You spoke of a continuous scream. Saint Paul spoke of the whole of creation groaning and travailing in pain – though it is true that he optimistically added "until now". He also mentioned "speaking with tongues", the sound of ecstasy, the voice of the spirit not of the reason, and he warned the Corinthians against this sort of private language. Magic besieges the religious life and men yearn to speak the language of angels. I have met with such phenomena myself, I mean the weird babbling of some deranged people. There is a technical term for it in the medical profession, which is indeed the word originally used by Paul. But I have never encountered anything like the sound and the tone of this impenetrable speech. As I have said to you before, our knowledge of the soul, if I may use that unclinical but essential word, encounters certain seemingly impassable limits, set there perhaps by the gods, if I may refer to them, in order to preserve their privacy, and beyond which it may be not only futile but lethal to attempt to pass – and though it is our duty to seek for knowledge, it is also incumbent on us to realise when it is denied us, and not to prefer a fake solution to no solution at all. But more briefly, some matters resist inquiry and remain mysterious, and I suspect that what we have just heard is one of them. I wanted you to hear it as I believe you will appreciate it as one more strange and wonderful thing which remains the private property of that strange and wonderful man. You understand.'

'Yes –'

'Well, it only remains for us to say farewell and wish each other a happy journey through the hazards of our future pilgrimage.'

'I want you to have this note of my London address and telephone number,' said Ludens, handing over a card which he had written earlier that morning.

'Thank you.' Marzillian laid the card on his desk and stood up. Ludens stood up. He felt a sudden wave of coldness and fear. He thought, is there no more to be said, no more to be *done*? Am I really *leaving*? It was as if he were leaving Marcus behind, a finished case with no problems except one or two insoluble ones. He also felt another, and new pain. He tried to find the right words. 'I thank you very much for what you have done for him, and for me. I hope that – I hope that we may meet again at times in the future. I would like to think that we are, or could become, friends, and could meet as friends. I expect you are often in London. I wish I could believe that sometime somehow, I might be able to help you. I doubt if I have the capacity, but I certainly have the will. Anyway, all I am saying is that I hope we may, at not too distant intervals, be able to meet and talk again. I would value that privilege very much indeed.'

Marzillian looked at him intently, gravely, with his dark wide-open eyes which could express so much sadness and so much irony. He said, 'I come to London only on medical business. My place is here where I can concentrate my attention wholly upon my patients. I have, to be quite frank, no time for anyone else. In my trade one must forgo the luxury of becoming fond of people. I would mislead you if I did not, in answer to what you have just said, make this clear. I'm sorry.'

Ludens could not check a sudden silent look of appeal, in answer to which Marzillian, returning his gaze, very slightly shook his head. Then he smiled his usual rather coy sceptical smile. He came round the desk, made for the door and opened it wide. Ludens followed him. They shook hands in silence. The next moment Ludens was outside and the door closed behind him. He reflected, as he walked back toward Benbow, that the card with his name and address on it was probably already in the wastepaper basket.

He got quickly into his car, started the engine and set off, casting no glance at the little house. When he slowed down at the corner of the main drive he saw Camilla who was walking toward the house. By mutual instant agreement they waved a wordless farewell and the car turned towards the gate. Just before he reached it, where the drive widened, Ludens saw Dr Bland who had just appeared from the lane. Ludens drew into the side and Bland came across. He opened the passenger door, removed a suitcase which was on the seat, put it on the tarmac, got in and closed the door.

'So you're leaving us?'

'Yes.'

'You've said goodbye to our lord and master?'

'Yes.'

'Well, goodbye then.'

'Terence, don't you too.'

'Too what?'

'I said to Marzillian I hoped I'd see him again. He said he wouldn't have time and couldn't afford to be fond of anybody.'

'Well, if he says that, what do you expect from me?'

'Oh just some human feeling.'

'What makes you think he hasn't any?'

'All right, he's being professional. I'm just in such misery. I suppose I want a kind word.'

'What about *her*?'

'I don't know where she is.'

'So you're off to London?'

'Yes. I said I'd like to see him in London. I'd like to see you in London, if it comes to that.'

'He'd kill me.'

'I suppose he would. It's just that I feel I'm leaving Marcus behind, as if it's goodbye to him too. I know this is nonsense – in a way he doesn't exist any more, in another way I'll be thinking about him and living with him and living him for the rest of my life, so it doesn't matter where I am, and he isn't anywhere. But it's the end of an era, I've had a sort of home here, and Marzillian and you have been kind to me and comforted me and we have talked about him and looked after him together. I wish there could be some continuing bond.'

'I know. But it is a professional matter, it's not personal, it's not hardness of heart. Besides, he's so addictive, if he didn't throw people out they'd all be swarming back. I suppose I should be pleased he keeps them all away, indeed I am pleased. He got fond of you, I've got fond of you, but there it is. Goodbye, look after yourself, don't let that bitch break your heart. I imagine he didn't kiss you, but I will.' Bland put his arm round Ludens's shoulder and kissed him on the cheek. He got out of the car, replaced the suitcase, closed the door, raised a hand in salute and turned away towards the house. Ludens drove out, turned right, crossed over the bridge, passed the Black Lion, the White Lion, the Hedgehog, the church and started following the signs to the motorway.

I write to say that I have decided to leave you, finally and forever. It has to be. You may feel surprised, you will probably, when you think it over, feel relieved. I am doing you a last good turn. I think that you have really believed it possible to have two happy cheerful wives. You relied upon me to accept anything, even divorce, and still remain as, through all your infidelities, I have always been, your loving and adoring Franca, poor Franca who is so unselfish, being really without a self and able to bear anything like a mindless dog or a pathetic ageing mother. I have in the past, it is true, loved you absolutely, and you are the only man whom I have loved so much thereby proving to myself that such love is possible. For a time, during your final outrage, I did imagine that my love was indestructible, and that I must stay with you, stay near you, do your will, or die. I have lately woken up to the fact that something indeed has died – my love for you, which you have at last succeeded in beating to death. I can recall, over years, the touching complacent childish look of gratitude with which you greeted my ever-renewed toleration of your relations with other women. They came and went, you told me, I was eternal, I remained, much higher, much more loved. And when you said, well, I'm afraid *this* one is permanent, and when you then said she was to live in our house, and then of course I wouldn't mind being divorced, everything would be really just the same – I think you genuinely imagined that I would 'not mind', that my adoration for you was infinitely expansible, and that I would settle down to being in some vague sense still your wife, a benign presence guaranteeing your complete happiness with another woman. You really believed in the 'happy trio' – without that naive belief you could scarcely have behaved with such thoughtless cruelty. You may briefly regret my defection, but will soon be consoled by Alison's joy, and will feel relieved, as if some old ailing animal which you had to look after has at last died. I have felt for some time now that my old love for you was turning into hatred, the energy of love into the energy of hate, and I have felt that hatred poisoning my soul. Then I began to wonder why I should be not only trodden on but poisoned, corrupted, forced into living on untruth. Now my love for you is gone, it is absolutely over, and I am *glad* that this is so, do not imagine that I shall come weeping back. I said I was spending the day with Molly Stein. Well, I am not. I am leaving the country for good, and when you read this I shall be gone. The divorce proceedings will be arranged through our lawyer. I assure you that I want to *get rid of you* now with all possible speed. Do not try to write to me. If any letter of yours ever reaches me I shall destroy it unread. Goodbye.

Franca.

Dear dear Alfred, I am writing to your London flat as I imagine you will be back there very soon. I have left Jack. I have written him a savage letter of farewell. I think I really hate him now. Oh it's so terrible. But honestly I've had enough. He hasn't had the letter yet, I shall leave it on the kitchen table, he's away with Alison at the moment, they're going to Scotland together. I feel I must, before it's too late, *save my own life*. Why should I go on living in misery and humiliation and fear? I have decided to go to America to join Maisie. I believe I shall be able to work there. Why not choose freedom and love and happiness? I wish that you would come with me, I mean come to me, come soon. I want to talk about that. I love you very much, and I want very much to see you before I leave England. I'll be at a hotel, I'll send you a note of where, and I'll keep on ringing your number. Everything I said to you at the Black Lion remains in place. I love you and I want you in my life.

Franca.

The letter to Ludens had been posted on the previous day. By invoking this witness Franca had proved to herself that it was not just a dream, she could actually do it, the die was cast. She had an aeroplane ticket with a date upon it. Now it was the last day, the final morning at the house in Chelsea. She had packed her bags, the things to travel with her, the things to be left with Molly Stein. It struck her as she packed them how few these things were. So much that had seemed to belong to her she could leave behind without regret, together with the largest part of her life. Jack was away with Alison. Franca had booked her hotel. She had placed the letter to Jack in an envelope on the kitchen table. Now all she needed was a taxi.

The farewell letter had cost her several tearful drafts, but the fair copy, neat and unstained, was written in a clear hand in the beautiful italic script which Jack had taught her, and her tears had dried. Franca had, in the very composition of this message, the instrument of her liberation, hardened her heart. The plan of escape, in its true envisagement, had taken her several days during which she had realised that she could go, she could go to America, *that* far she could go. She had, after many telephone calls, stopped fearing that Maisie 'didn't really mean it' or 'would find her a burden'. She even had the money to go and had paid for her own ticket, she had her own bank account into which Jack had, since forever, been paying money. And she was now confident that she could work in Boston, she could earn her living as a dressmaker. Maisie had assured her that dressmakers were precious as gold in that city!

Jack, who was living at Alison's flat (the luxury flat was being altered), had still appeared on most days at his studio and had set up a custom of having simple scrappy lunches with Franca. These lunches had had a curious surreal atmosphere. They had seemed relaxed, merry, full of jokes. No 'business' was discussed, no divorce planning, though Franca knew it was going forward, Alison's name was freely mentioned, Franca inquiring about her new television play, Jack telling little affectionate stories about Alison as if Alison were Franca's daughter or younger sister. But there was a kind of conniving slyness in the glances which they occasionally cast at each other, particular ways of smiling, he humbly, or ruefully, she reassuringly. She resisted the temptation to break it all down into honest wails and tears. She must not be tempted by truthfulness, she must play the game out to the end. The act of leaving itself would be the ultimate truth.

Ludens arrived at the flat in St John's Wood at about two o'clock. The journey, which had briefly seemed like an escape, had become a nightmare. Ludens had felt sick, felt faint, wondered if he were going to have some kind of fit. His lips trembled and he kept blinking his eyes, and looking down at his hands to make sure they were holding the wheel. It was as if someone else, over whom he had no control, were driving. He began to have the illusion that Marcus was sitting in the back of the car, a big inflated body with open eyes, half alive, pitiable, dangerous. At one point he actually had to stop the car and look round. As he neared London he began to drive very fast, longing to arrive, yet fearing to arrive, consumed by a fierce craving for Irina. Surely her letters would be waiting for him. Of course, he should have realised, she was still in Switzerland, while his letters to her were being kept at the solicitor's office, and she had been writing to him at the flat, thinking that he must be back there by now. Perhaps she had been telephoning his London number. He imagined the letters, now much longer, full of explanations, of accounts of what (which Ludens could not conceive of) was happening in Switzerland, of longings to see him again. How easily, he thought, by the merest touch, by the merest gesture of tenderness, she could allay his pain. On this diet of expectation, he had fairly frenzied himself by the time he arrived. As he got out of the car he was shuddering and his teeth were chattering. As he fumbled with the keys at the front door he heard the telephone ringing in his flat. He dropped the keys, picked them up, raced up the stairs, found the key of the flat and jammed it into the lock as the telephone stopped ringing. He had difficulty pushing the door open as it was buttressed by a pile of letters which had been thrust through the letter slit in his absence. He ran to the telephone and picked it up, insanely hoping that, though it was no longer ringing, he would hear a voice. Then, moaning aloud with exasperation and anxiety, he knelt on the floor and began scattering and sorting the mound of letters. He set aside any typed envelope which might contain a communication from the solicitor. He went through the pile twice. There was nothing from Irina. He hastily opened the typed letters: nothing. *Where was she?* He ran back to the telephone and dialled the solicitor's number. Sorry, Mr Garent was away at present. Ludens thought, now they recognise my voice. He left his telephone number.

He sat on the floor holding his head in his hands. He felt as if his whole body would burst open with anguish and lacerated will. Where was she and why didn't she write and what was he to do with himself, with his mind, during the next hours which would have to be lived through, how could he continue to exist in such a state of tension without going mad, screaming, mutilating himself? He thrust one of his hands into his mouth and bit it violently. Then the telephone rang.

It must be her. He leapt up, knocked the phone to the floor, retrieved it, and tried in vain to speak into it. Before he could regain his utterance a loud clear familiar voice said, 'Hello. Is that you, Ludens?'

After a moment Ludens said, 'Hello, Jack. Yes, it's me.'

'Are you OK? You sound a bit out of breath.'

'I've just arrived back this moment, I ran up the stairs. How are you?'

'Oh fine, everything's very OK except that I haven't seen you lately and we haven't had a real talk for ages. I'm so glad you're back in London, I've missed you a lot, London has had a hole in it which I've kept noticing.'

'I've missed you too,' said Ludens.

'Why don't you come over? Franca's spending a day or two with her wild women friends, you know, Molly Stein and co. Aly's gone to Edinburgh, I was going to go too but she decided after all she'd better go alone, she wants to soften her father up a bit before I meet him! She'll be back tomorrow, so I'm all alone till then. I'm just going over to Chelsea to mess about in the studio, do come round and have a drink. I want to work for a bit, so come about five, that's not too early for drinking.'

'I'll come,' said Ludens.

'Splendid. I'll leave the downstairs door unlocked, just come up. I want to hear all about – you know – Marcus – I'm so terribly sorry. I hope you're not too smashed up.'

'No, no.'

'Good. Well, longing to see you. Cheerio.'

Ludens sat down again on the floor. He looked at his watch. How was he going to live with his mind until five o'clock? Anyway, ought he not simply to stay faithfully beside the telephone, like some loyal dog, hour after hour, day after day? He thought, this is hell, not being able to live with oneself, like Marzillian said. He got up slowly and went to the bathroom and dashed cold water on his face. The telephone rang.

Ludens raced back, slipping on the sea of letters, kneeling on the floor beside the table and seizing the instrument with wet trembling fingers. He uttered a low cry into it.

Franca's voice said, 'Oh, I'm so glad, you're back.'

'Yes. I've got back.'

'I wonder if you could come and see me?'

'Yes, I expect so. How are you, Franca?'

After a moment's silence Franca said, 'Alfred, have you read my letter?'

'I've only just arrived, I haven't had time to look at letters yet.'

'Oh well – Look, could you see me this evening? I've got to go shopping in the afternoon. Could you meet me at a bar at about half past six or so?' She gave an address in Kensington.

'Yes, good, I'll look forward to seeing you.'

'And you'd better read my letter first – of course it may not have arrived – never mind, come anyway, I'm longing to see you.'

Ludens put down the phone. The voices of two friends had been welcome. Seeing them would at least make him affect some sort of composure and stop him from tearing at himself with grief and apprehension and painful hopes. He must not indulge the contemptible weakness of his misery. He thought, I'll try and see Gildas tomorrow, I can't ring him, I'll just go over. Anyway, by tomorrow – perhaps she . . . He had eaten nothing since a hasty piece of bread at the Black Lion. (The Black Lion already seemed a remote imaginary place in an ancient legend.) However, eating, envisaged, seemed impossible. He thought, I'll go and look at the flat in Victoria, in case there are any papers there I ought to destroy. I'm sure there aren't, but I must go sometime and I'd better get it over. He had not, since he received this charge, thought seriously about his task as literary executor. He had kept the keys sent him by the solicitor wrapped in a handkerchief in his jacket pocket, two small Yale keys for the flat, one larger old iron key for the cottage. He left the cottage key on the mantelpiece. He decided, I'll walk to Victoria, it will pass the time and make me tired. He was about to go when he remembered that Franca had said something about a letter. He kicked the envelopes about until he saw her writing. He picked up the letter and put it in his pocket. He went downstairs and out into the sunshine.

He walked down Wellington Road, down Park Road, down Baker Street, along Park Lane, down Constitution Hill, past Buckingham Palace, along Buckingham Gate, and across Victoria Street. As he walked his mind was full of flashing lights and vivid instantaneous pictures of how it had been, what it had been, how it would now be well, how it would now be ill: what it would be like to live without Marcus. He thought about Marcus, and his body ached for him and his mind searched for him. Nor did Ludens, as he passed the Palace and saw the Royal Standard flying, exclude the possibility that when he arrived at the flat he would find Irina waiting for him. The letter in which she told him where she was might have gone astray or still be in the post. But this image, often occurring, was most speedily banished. He had trained his marching step to represent the absence of any hope. Later there might be a time which would utterly annihilate this time as a brief period of senseless anxiety. But he must not think of that now, and he imagined himself as he walked as a prisoner walking to Siberia or a guilty man starting a long penance.

He entered, travelled up in the lift, put his key in the door, opened the door. He could not prevent the picture of her welcoming cry, of her arms about him, even in the moment of its destruction. As the door opened he groaned aloud. The flat smelt of emptiness and desolation, it had returned to its sullen past, its twitching slumber out of which it had been ill-temperedly awakened by that short sojourn.

The tormented enchanted furniture still stood silently on guard, its contours clearly designed to resist any companionship with the human form. The fungoid smell was stronger and the murkiness and the greenness knew nothing of the sunshine outside. The place had, as at Benbow, been tidied, the drawers emptied, clothes and bedclothes piled and folded. The china, removed from cupboards, was set out on the kitchen table. Of course there was nothing for Ludens, literary executor, to find in that unhappy space. He went into the bathroom and looked at himself in the mirror and recalled how he had shaved Marcus on the day of Patrick's resurrection and how, their eyes meeting, Marcus had smiled, and Ludens had put his hands on Marcus's shoulders, and how just after that Marcus had said, 'Look after Irina.' Ludens now gazed at himself and thought how thin and wild and frightened he looked, and he recalled the word 'homeless' which had been uttered by both Marcus and Most, and he thought of the bag always packed for departure, and he thought, in a moment I'll be remembering the Warsaw ghetto. Removing himself quickly from the shades of his ancestors he hurriedly left the flat. When he came out of the building he recognised a new sensation identifiable as hunger. He had intended to walk on to Chelsea along the embankment, but time had passed and he would now need a taxi to reach Jack by five. He started walking toward Victoria Station. He stopped on the way at a shabby café and bought a sandwich. He found his taxi.

'So the great incarnation ended in tears.'

'It ended,' said Ludens, 'in what it might be more accurate to call a symbolic martyrdom.'

'Some stones were thrown and some louts belaboured the righteous.'

'One stone struck Marcus on the hand.'

'That was lucky. He had a bruise to show for it. But I don't understand what happened next. Was he terribly ashamed, did he think he'd made a fool of himself?'

'No, he was relieved it was over. He felt he was in a false position.'

'You mean with people coming to be healed and he knew he couldn't.'

'Not exactly – you see, in a way he knew he could. At least he could cure some people.'

'Come, come you don't believe that!'

'Jack! You saw him cure Pat!'

'Well, I've thought about that a lot. We never really knew how ill

Pat was – Marcus just gave him some kind of shock which renewed his energy, his coming gave Pat the will to live.'

'All right, but that's a cure, isn't it? And it's well known that there are people who can cure things which doctors can't just by touching or breathing – particularly psychosomatic things of course.'

'Oh, psychosomatic – Anyway you are determined to think he was something wonderful.'

'He was something wonderful.'

'But he couldn't write that book for you.'

'He didn't want to.'

'He wanted to kill himself.'

'I suppose so. I was reluctant to believe this.'

'You were reluctant to believe he was raving mad. Do you admit you were wrong?'

'No.'

'Well, the symbolic martyrdom was not a real martyrdom, but the symbolic death was a real death. You say he didn't gas himself?'

'The doctors said not. They said it was a heart attack.'

'But you think he was magically translated, like Jesus.'

'Something of the sort!'

'Anyway he *didn't* kill himself. Perhaps he was trying to fake a suicide attempt, turning the gas on a little, and he accidentally set off a heart attack and got more than he bargained for.'

'Maybe.'

'You remember all those books about the concentration camps? I suppose he was rather manic-depressive even before that started. That he was sado-masochistic we all knew from the very start, look at how he treated Pat and Gildas! He would have smashed us too if he could, only he couldn't! You must admit he was a monster!'

'A holy monster, a wounded monster.'

'Oh you are so romantic! Sorry, poor chap, you have been through it!'

Ludens, coming in at the open door, had at once heard Jack singing upstairs in the studio. The song Jack was singing was 'Voi che sapete'. Ludens listened as he mounted the stairs. *Voi che sapete che cosa è amor, Donne, vedete s'io l'ho nel cor . . .*

As soon as Ludens saw Jack he felt for a moment a relief from pain. He almost staggered, then sat down on a chair near the door of the studio. Jack bounded towards him, pulled him to his feet and hugged him. There followed the interrogation which was for Ludens almost a narcotic, a soothing litany, as if he were almost pleased to hear Jack's blunt reasoning reduce all Ludens's mysteries to a uniform level of banality.

'And Irina? Is that still on?'

'Yes. She's away at the moment, gone to Switzerland to sign things.'

'All that money! But are you sure you really love her? Aly and Franca can't believe it.'

Ludens waved the subject away and asked Jack about his painting. 'I see something surprising over there – a human figure!'

'Yes, I'm going through a crisis, a metamorphosis, it's quite grim, I don't know whether when I come out of it I'll be able to paint at all!'

'What does it represent,' said Ludens walking over to the canvas, 'or what will it represent?'

'The raising of Lazarus.'

'So Marcus did something to you?'

'Someone as crazy as that sends out vibrations.'

Ludens looked at a pale wavering figure against a background of red, a red wall perhaps, and some people – were they people? 'Where's Christ?'

'Well may you ask!'

'I like it, it's got something!'

'It's awful, but at least I can try, I work every day, I feel I've got to fight my way out of a sort of charmed circle – maybe it really is getting away from Marcus at last! There's some kind of simplicity and truth which I can just intuit – it's somewhere there – it's as if I were *blind*, as if I'd discovered not sight, but blindness, I keep praying to the great painters, I feel like a *worm* –'

'You look extremely well, crisis suits you.'

The pale-brown blinds had been drawn over the skylights and the brightness outside penetrated as a lively subdued glow which favoured every colour. Jack in his blue smock, his mauve shirt just showing, was striding about as he talked, making the boards creak. Paint streaked his smock, smudged his hands, his rosy well-shaven cheeks, even adhered to some locks of his blond hair. His prominent blue eyes gleamed with amiable satisfaction. He was, Ludens thought, even as he proclaimed himself a worm, eminently at home in himself, in his trade, and in the world.

'And what about the girls,' Ludens went on, 'how is life with them?' He recalled the last time he had seen Jack, sitting in the garden of the Black Lion with Franca and Alison, and then the receding trio, Jack in the middle with an arm round each.

'Oh, it's settled down, I knew it would, it's splendid, it just feels ordinary and natural now. I think Franca likes being here and living a bit of her own life seeing Molly and Linda and that lot and going out to exhibitions. And we have lunch together most days. I'm encouraging her to take up dressmaking again, she's rediscovering her talents, she's got more time and space of her own, and she and Aly are genuinely fond of each other.'

'Two exceptional women,' said Ludens, 'I congratulate you.'

'Look, what about a drink? What would you like? I must look after you, you look a bit pale and wan. Did you have lunch after that long drive, would you like something to eat, can I make you a sandwich or something?'

Ludens hesitated. He still felt a bit hungry, but said, 'No, don't bother, yes, I'd like some white wine.'

The reference to Franca, which almost made Ludens say jocosely that he was to see her this evening, probably with her women friends, also reminded him that he had a letter from her in his pocket. As Jack disappeared downstairs, Ludens took Franca's letter from his pocket. He opened it and read it. He put it away again.

He sat down on a chair near the easel, removing Jack's polychrome palette to the floor. He felt a flush rise up into the roots of his hair. So, he had arrived at a terrible moment, a moment of absolutely hideous catastrophe. There could be no doubting the total final seriousness of Franca's decision. How would Jack take it? It was obvious that Jack, arriving from Alison's flat after their change of plan, and going straight upstairs to the studio, had not found the fatal letter. Jack was not one who would or could dissemble in such circumstances. Now, this very moment, he would find it. Would Ludens hear a strange cry from below? Of course he might not go into the kitchen, indeed why should he, since the drinks and the glasses were kept in a cupboard on the landing outside the drawing room. Ludens went to the door and listened. Silence. Perhaps Jack had found the letter and was sitting at the kitchen table reading it. Would he feel relief: thank God she's gone? *Impossible.* He absolutely needed Franca, he absolutely believed she would never leave him. A letter expressing not only farewell but terminal hatred would wound him very deeply and forever. That he might deserve to be wounded was neither here nor there. Ludens felt an impulse to run down the stairs and, if Jack had not found it, to seize the letter: let Franca think again. But this would be wicked, dreadfully unfair to Franca, who would have to perform the terrible act once more, and of no help to Jack. And suppose Franca, wantonly disturbed and confused at her moment of escape, did feel bound to think again and fell into some miserable mixed-up indecision, she might well regret later that she had not made the clean clear departure which it must have taken so much courage to plan.

Ludens now heard Jack ascending the stairs. His footsteps sounded ominous, until suddenly he began to hum and then to sing, 'Braid the raven hair', clinking two glasses against a bottle as he entered the room.

'I hope this stuff is OK, I'm afraid it will be a bit tepid. Shall I get some ice from the fridge?'

'Oh no, no thanks, certainly not, no no, I quite like it tepid.' Ludens thought, I must get away quickly now. He drank a little of the warm wine.

Jack sitting down and gulping the wine, said, 'Yes, I feel with painting that I'm back at the beginning again. Perhaps in art one always has to try to get back to the beginning, to feel that one might do *anything*, and that every sort of excellence is possible. I've been sleep-walking for years. Do you know, I actually *hate* all that stuff that made me so famous? I've got to start again. I'd like to show you some of the things I've done lately –'

'Jack, dear, I must go, I'm terribly sorry, I didn't realise it was so late, I must get back to the flat. I'm expecting a telephone call.'

'Ah, from Switzerland! I won't keep you.'

'I'll leave you here to meditate on your art. I expect you want to work and I'm interrupting you.'

'No, no, not at all –'

'I must be off, I'll ring up soon.'

'Do that. Have you seen Gildas? No? Do look him up. He's got a pack of troubles. Goodbye then, and come again *soon*.'

Jack showed no sign of moving, and Ludens hurried away downstairs. He realised it was almost time to see Franca. He dreaded this encounter which he would have to conceal from Jack. He wished he could just *not know*.

He reached the hall. The kitchen door was ajar. He pushed it open and saw Franca's letter lying on the table. He closed the door, as if that meant something, and went on to the front door.

He was about to open it when he saw a letter lying at his feet. It had evidently been delivered since he came in, or more likely not noticed, either by himself or Jack, entering from the bright sunshine into the darker house. He recognised the writing on the envelope as he instinctively picked it up. It was addressed to Jack. He noticed that the flap of the envelope was scarcely sealed, and was gaping at one side. Impelled by a sudden curiosity and a strange anxiety he carefully eased the flap open and took out the letter. It was from Alison. Ludens read the letter through, once fast, then more slowly. He stood quite still in the hallway. He listened. There was no sound from above. Jack had stayed with his art. Ludens stood for several minutes thinking. Then he put the letter in his pocket. He went into the kitchen and picked up Franca's letter and put that into his pocket too. He left the house and soon found a taxi in the King's Road.

The 'bar' mentioned by Franca turned out to belong to a small hotel off Gloucester Road. Ludens, arriving in his haste a little early, found Franca already sitting there in a corner with a drink in front of her. She waved to him.

'Hello, Franca, what are you drinking? Can I get you another one?'

'Whisky and soda – no, I'm OK, what would you like? I'll get it for you.'

'I'll have some wine – no, don't get up, I'll get it.'

'No, let me –'

'No, no, sit down, do what I tell you!'

Standing at the counter Ludens was conscious of extreme distress. He ordered a whisky and soda. What wicked sardonic god had suddenly presented him with so much power over two women? He did not want it, but could not refuse it. Or could he refuse it? Unfortunately, now, to refuse it was to use it. He felt desperately tired and began to think about Irina.

He put on a calm face and returned to Franca. 'So, now you frequent bars?'

'Oh yes, I love bars, I love hotels, I'm staying here till I leave. Look, here's my ticket!' She drew an aeroplane ticket out of her handbag and put it on the table. She said, 'You know I want you to come.'

'I can't.'

'You haven't *married* her?'

'No.'

'I'm terribly sorry about Marcus. I know how much you cared, you had really *given* yourself to that man, you believed in him and he did save Pat's life, and he was a wonderful man but somehow so sad, one might say doomed. He must have known his life, the life of his mind, was over, he couldn't write that book you wanted him to, he hadn't got any secret knowledge like you used to think. He must have felt it was time to go. You don't blame yourself, do you, you did everything possible.'

'I tried. But – oh – Franca – how beautiful you look. I'm so glad to see you.'

She had become slimmer and was wearing, over a white blouse, a high-necked dark-blue dress he had never seen before, with a golden brooch on the collar. She looked composed, *smart*. Her pale sallow face glowed like ivory, touched too by some colour, whether from the sun or from some minimal careful use of make-up. She was also, he noticed, wearing smart shoes. Her dark gentle eyes gazed searchingly at Ludens, gazed with a kind of sympathetic authority, an intimate caressing appeal. Ludens thought, how could I ever have thought this woman pathetic, weak, a victim, a charming failure? He thought, why can't I feel happy for once with a woman, with this woman? He said, 'You look perfect. You've got your Ingres look.'

Franca smiled faintly. She leaned over and tapped his hand with the aeroplane ticket. 'Have you read my letter?'

'Yes.'

'I had to write and tell you. I didn't want you to hear it from anyone else. You know, I feel so much better now, so *free*, I know I'm doing right. I hope you think so too, actually I know you do. That time at the Black Lion with you and Maisie, I think I made up my mind then. Between you, you lifted me up and made me able to decide, able to *see*. How could I go on living with Jack and living for Jack when he was married to Alison? Only a lunatic would have conceived such an idea or endured it. I was not only beginning to detest him, I was beginning to despise him. I was suddenly able to see our marriage as a phase, after which something else, something different, would happen. I realise now how unhappy I was married to Jack even before *she* came. And it has dawned on me – and so much because of you – that there's another place where there is happiness and another me who can go there. I've also realised that I can love another man – I love you. And I'm sure that you love me. I want us to talk about this in freedom.'

'Franca,' said Ludens, 'listen. Oh Franca, I do love you, and I want your happiness so much. But before you go I think there's something you ought to know, something you ought to see, just so that you can be sure that, taking this too into account, you are still right to choose freedom. And I think you *are* right. Just look at this.' Ludens put Alison's letter into her hand.

What Franca read was this:

I've decided to leave you. I'm sorry that, since I had to conceal my feelings until I was sure of them, this may come as a surprise. It's not just that I can't bear to go on accepting Franca's kindness and goodness, if that's what it is, and her detestable patience. I've decided I can't after all go on accepting you, there's no way in which I can adjust to the situation – perhaps the deep thing is that, as it turns out, *you can't make me happy*. It appears that I just don't love you enough to carry on. I was deliciously happy with you when we first met and loved each other and I was able not to care a fig about Franca, or to judge you, or to see what I was doing. Now I'm afraid the party's over. Since that time I've become steadily and fundamentally unhappy. I only half-imagined that if you were *married* to me Franca would dissolve or disappear. But really why should she? She loves you, and she has got a humble, I suppose saintly is the word, *courage* which enables her to stay in place. Also, as I began to realise, she knows that you love her and need her. After all, your needing both of us was the doctrine which you were always trying to teach! The necessity of leaving came to me absolutely when I thought about explaining you to my father. I vaguely told him I was 'involved with a married man' and left it at that. I knew he didn't like it, I suspect he assumed it would pass. I couldn't have faced him with the whole picture. Of course I have been, and literally still am, in love with you. But one can recover from being in love, it is sometimes one's duty to do so, and indeed as I write I am already recovering. It's not in itself a very valuable state of mind, and for me it has become a positively bad one. I'm sorry, Jack, I feel very sorry for myself, and for you, and for prim gallant Franca, whom you will no doubt continue to torment and deceive. It was just a rotten scene and I am very relieved indeed to be out of it. I am glad, for your sake as well as mine, that I can make a clean break. This writing to you is a last connection and it is very painful indeed, as I write, to *feel* that connection even as I end it. I shall send this letter to Chelsea to be sure you get it sooner, as you said you might stay there while I was away, and you are sure to go to the studio. Oh God. My dear, the awful pain. But cutting and running is the only thing. I'm sorry I had to lie to you about going to Scotland, at least at the last moment it was a lie. I didn't go to Edinburgh, I went to Heathrow. When you receive this I shall be in Ireland with Patrick. I don't plan to stay there, or with him, I don't *plan* anything just now, so who knows, but he is someone I can innocently love and be friends with, a good dear being, a sort of child, perhaps he really did die and go to paradise and come back. We shall be somewhere near Dublin, then maybe we shall go to the west and become seals. I need calmer air, and after feeling so Scottish a dose of Ireland may do me good. Don't blame Pat, it was my idea. This is goodbye, Jack. I have shed many tears which I have concealed from you, but I am not crying now. *Don't run after me.* I am sure you won't after reading this and taking in that I *mean it.* Let us be thankful that we can leave each other so cleanly and so quickly.

Alison.

Ludens, watching Franca as she read the letter, felt a little lightening sensation, which was his relief at finding that he was interested enough in someone else's problem to forget for a few seconds, the agony of his own. He watched her, wondering in extreme sympathetic anxiety what it was right to do, and what she would do.

Franca read the letter slowly, frowning slightly, breathing deeply, then read it again. Before she spoke Ludens felt impelled to say something which he felt he might later regret not having said.

'Franca, don't be hasty. Well, I'm sure you won't be. As I said just now, I personally think you may well be right to go away in any case – I mean you may reasonably judge that this news makes no difference. I don't think that Jack will pursue Alison or that she'll come back. I don't know. But he may still look for another woman. At this very moment you're out in the clear, you're emotionally disengaged. You have *made* this space, this freedom, it's precious, it's an *achievement,* and you should think carefully, perhaps for some time, before deciding what to do with it.'

Franca looked at him. Her face was tense and flushed. She drew back her lips and showed her teeth. She put the letter down on the table and put both her hands to her cheeks. 'I don't understand – why have you got this letter?'

'Oh, I'm sorry, I should have explained. I saw Jack this afternoon at the studio, he said Alison had decided she wanted to go to Edinburgh by herself. Then when I was leaving I saw this letter, which had evidently just come, lying in the hall – it was badly sealed and I picked it up and read it and took it away. Jack hasn't seen it.'

'You saw him at our house this afternoon.'

'Yes. And he hadn't seen your letter.'

'But he'll have seen it now.'

Ludens took Franca's letter out of his pocket and laid it on the table. 'He'd gone straight upstairs, he didn't go into the kitchen. After I'd seen her letter I removed yours.'

Franca closed her eyes for a moment and put a hand over her mouth as if to postpone speech. Then she said, 'What are you going to do with Alison's letter?'

'He must have it,' said Ludens, 'mustn't he, and not know it's been tampered with. I shall seal it up and take it back to Chelsea late tonight, so he'll find it in the morning. Isn't that what we must do?' As he spoke Ludens began to see more clearly, what he had unreflectively understood earlier, that of course he too had had a choice, and still had one. He was offering to Franca a knowledge and a freedom which he was denying to Alison. He could even have done it the other way round! *What's involved here*, he thought. Of course Alison has actually run away, and Franca, at present, has not. I don't know where Alison is, Franca is in front of me. Am I favouring Franca because she's an old friend, or because I think she deserves to be able to choose? I am gambling with her happiness – and also with Jack's. What *is* the right choice?

In answer to Ludens's spoken question Franca, looking at him intently, simply said, 'Yes.' She handed back Alison's letter.

Ludens wondered whether she had fully understood what he had done. He thought: I hope she won't want to be fair to Alison! And I hope she won't think that what I've said and what I'm going to say amounts to pleading Alison's case. Oh God! He said, 'Do take time to think. You've found something else, which you *want*, and it may be the better thing. I'm weighing this side of the balance because I don't want you to regret later that you didn't *run* when you could. I'm not trying to persuade you, I just want you to see both sides and not just follow a blind impulse.'

Franca gave a very long slow sigh. She was now sitting in a composed attitude with her hands folded. She said, 'I think I'll have another whisky and soda.'

Ludens went to the counter and ordered two whiskies and soda. He thought, if Alison had known that Franca was going she would have stayed. If Franca had known that Alison was going she would have stayed. If Franca left now would Alison come back? Suppose they both go – it would serve Jack right. There would be time to console him later. What am I at? Do I want both Jack and Franca separately turning to me, am I pleased to think of Franca on her own at last? Then suppose Alison comes back and they both stay and it's all as it was before only more awful? Can I even try to calculate their happinesses? And wait – how important is happiness anyway? What about virtue, duty – oh, those things . . .

He returned to the table. Franca's letter still lay there, but it had been torn in two.

'So what does that mean?'

'What do you think it means,' said Franca, 'how can you have any doubt, how can you have had *any* doubt about what I was going to do?'

'Very easily. What are you going to do?'

'Go back of course. I'm going back now.' She moved to get up.

'Wait, *wait*! Sleep on it. Let him read her letter first. He may leave instantly for Dublin.'

Franca sat back. 'You're right, I must wait till he's seen the letter, I mustn't be there when he finds it.'

'It's also possible that she'll be back tomorrow!'

'Many things are possible. You take her letter back late tonight. I'm not supposed to be returning till tomorrow evening, so I'll come back then.'

'And find him longing to be comforted?'

'I don't know. I'll manage whatever I find. He may simply not be there. I'll wait. I'm eternally grateful to you for intercepting my letter.'

'Oh – well – all right.' Ludens felt his own miserable anxiety claiming all his attention. He thought, there *must* be news of her tomorrow. He went on, 'Maisie will be disappointed.'

'I shall see Maisie again.'

'And all that brave resolve to save your life and do your own work, and live in freedom and happiness? Oh please don't lose it. All right, go back to Jack but somehow hold onto freedom too –'

'Alfred, I don't think you really know what love is like. The things you mention are *shadows*, *fantasies*, they are *nothing*, Jack is reality, to consider leaving him, to plan to leave him, was to tear myself out of myself.'

'You may have to do so again.'

'Perhaps. But don't speak blasphemously of the future – in fact there is no future – I feel as if I might die tonight, I am ready to die. Even if I knew he would kill me, or whatever sorrow awaits me, I must return, now that I can return – I feel as if I've been separated from him for a thousand years – and now I am *permitted* to go back. That's how it feels. I am not sacrificing *anything* except some restless uneasy dreams. But – I do thank you and I do love you, dear dear Alfred. Now – I'd meant to ask you to dinner here – only now I have to be alone. I hope you will be very happy with Irina.'

'All right. I'll go. Needless to say I won't speak of this to anyone. I'll take Alison's letter back. But don't forget about, I don't know what to call it – you should live in a larger space, and pull Jack into it, go and see Maisie and take him along. Oh hell – sorry – I'll take myself off.'

As she now stood beside him he lifted her hand and kissed it. She kissed his cheek. He felt the radiant warmth of her hand and her lips. It was true that she seemed now like one who had been dead and now lived. The next morning Ludens received a letter from Irina.

Ludens was on the telephone to the solicitors. He had decided to telephone first and if he learnt nothing go round to their office.

'Hello, I wonder if I could speak to Mr Garent?'

'Who is speaking please?'

'My name is Ludens, Dr Alfred Ludens.'

After a pause a different voice said, 'I'm afraid Mr Garent is not here.'

'Perhaps you could help me? It's about his client Miss Irina Vallar. I just wondered if she had returned from Switzerland.'

'Switzerland?'

'Yes. I believe she had to go to Switzerland on matters concerning the estate.'

'Excuse me.' After a silence the voice said, 'I am very sorry, I cannot help you.'

Desperately seeking an identity, Ludens said, 'I am Professor Vallar's literary executor, and in this connection I urgently need to contact Miss Vallar, I need her address.'

'One moment please.' A faintly audible conversation took place in the background. Then, 'You may write to Miss Vallar care of this office, and if you have any queries about your role as literary executor I suggest you write direct to Mr Garent.'

'Do you know where Miss Vallar is?'

'Sorry not to be more helpful.' This, which closed the conversation, was uttered as if the question had not been heard.

Ludens put down the receiver and sat for some time thinking. Then he looked again at the note from Irina which had just arrived and which he was holding in his hand. This read: *Forgive me for not being able to be with you.*

The envelope bore an English stamp. He had, with a magnifying glass, studied the smudged postmark in vain. He had read the maddeningly ambiguous missive over and over. He could not catch the tone of the words. It was a note which somebody might write who had been *kidnapped*. She was 'not able' to be with him. Why? She was reluctant to say, she did not dare to say. Perhaps she was ill and did not want him to see her in some helpless or unseemly state? Should not the message end with some other word or words, such as 'now' or 'just now' or 'yet'? Was 'forgive me' a mere turn of phrase equivalent to 'terribly sorry', or had it some deeper and graver content? Such reflections had, in the interval between the arrival of the letter and the time the solicitor's office opened, reduced Ludens to a state of frenzy. Should the words prompt compassion, rage, despair? On the other hand, it was a letter, a message, she was thinking about him. Perhaps, indeed no doubt, she was a hopelessly awkward and incompetent letter-writer. Perhaps 'the estate' was presenting her with grave problems, difficult decisions, which she wanted to be free of before seeing Ludens again. The solicitors were obviously withholding knowledge which they possessed, but that could be simply professional discretion. Why should they give information to a shadowy person who rang demanding an address and saying he was a literary executor? There was no reason for Irina to have mentioned him as being her special friend, let alone her fiancé, there was nothing necessarily sinister in the refusal to inform him, though Mr Garent's persistent absence might seem significant. These were matters upon which Ludens had reflected, and might have long continued to reflect, had he not received a little glittering nugget of suggestion from the scarcely audible background conversation which had taken place after he had asked for Irina's address. He had heard, or was pretty sure he had heard, the word 'Fontellen'.

Ludens now seemed to perceive a clearing in the mist. He had been impressed by, had indeed treasured, what Marzillian had told him about 'flight', how shocked and bereaved people, feeling 'ashamed' and wanting to hide, run away to distant places where they can rest and recover alone. Of course, it was now suddenly obvious, Irina had gone to Red Cottage. Why had he not thought of it before? He felt now that he had not sufficiently imagined her shocked unhappy state of mind, how desolate she must be feeling after so many years with her father, how maimed, perhaps how guilty, thinking, as bereaved people do, of the things she ought to have done. She had wanted to conceal from the world, perhaps especially from Ludens, these crippled and humiliated conditions. She might have been carried along for a time by the *sheer* business of her survival, the 'signing things', the going to Switzerland. Back in England she felt unable to face the world, needing even to put off her next meeting with Ludens. She wanted to meet him with her usual brave unconquered face. Yet, he thought, all the same, though she does not summon me, she will be very glad when I appear! Perhaps it has even become by now a sort of test!

During the interim Franca felt as if she had been metamorphosed, every atom of her body cleansed and energised, her blood drained away and replaced by some pure beatifying liquid; she had been translated to a plane of being where everything was extremely brilliant and clarified, clearer than the clearest air, brighter than the brightest colours, vibrating with a supernatural energy. She thought, it's 'pure cognition', like Jack used to say Marcus was after! Perhaps a sacrificial victim in a cult in which she heartily believed might feel like this before her death. After Ludens's departure, her appetite unimpaired, she scrutinised the dinner menu, chose a wine, and enjoyed a leisurely meal. After dinner she went for a short walk in the blue warm London evening through streets lined with enormous plane trees, smiling at passers-by and dogs. Returned to the bar, she sat over a liqueur, playing the mystery woman and conscious of some appreciative attention.

On the following morning she made some practical moves. Her planned departure was still some days distant and she was booked into the hotel till then. She cancelled her flight, and her booking at the hotel. She considered telephoning Maisie but decided to wait. She had already left her more substantial luggage with Molly Stein, where it could stay for the present. She packed the small suitcase which she had with her, and left it with the porter. She then went for a long walk through Kensington Gardens, Hyde Park and St James's Park and on to the National Gallery where she contemplated some ecstatic paintings by Duccio, Simone Martini, Giotto, Sassetta, and Fra Angelico. She had lunch in an Italian restaurant in Soho, then took a bus back to Kensington and sat in the lounge in the hotel. Time still remained to be lived through. As she waited, the concept of her death, which had been so felicitously dissolved in the ecstasy of her hope, floated free and took on a grimmer form. The sense of 'now it's all or nothing' which had comforted and released her lost its charming vagueness. Franca had never contemplated suicide, but now the idea presented itself. Win or lose. If she lost *now* could she reanimate those shadows and fantasies which had composed her idea of freedom? The notion that one will not survive a particular catastrophe is, in general terms, a comfort since it is equivalent to abolishing the catastrophe. Franca, giving her death a sideways look, was conscious of this too. She had hitherto refrained from listing the possibilities, but now, as she looked at her watch, this agnostic serenity could not be sustained.

What she must rate as most likely was that Jack would simply not be there. She then might or might not find Alison's letter lying on the mat in the hall. If there was no Jack and no letter this could mean either that Jack had carried off the letter to Alison's flat or to the airport on the way to Dublin, or that Ludens, who after all had his own troubles, had simply forgotten to deliver it. Or of course that Alison, repenting of her act, had returned during the day and removed it. If there was a letter and no Jack this could mean that, contrary to Ludens's expectations, Jack had not come to the studio during the day. It could also mean that Alison had telephoned, or had returned and was with him at her flat. In either case Franca would have to put the letter on the hall table and sit out the time before whatever might happen next. If Jack was there, upstairs in the studio cheerfully painting, welcoming her with his usual affection, this could again mean that Ludens had forgotten to deliver the letter. It could also mean other things, such as that, for some strategic reason, Jack was concealing his distress; perhaps had invented some lie to cover his imminent departure to Dublin. Alternatively if Jack were there, overcome by grief, having read the letter, Franca might simply be required to console him by assurances that Alison would be back at any moment, or else by facilitating his departure to Ireland. There was to be considered too not only Jack's misery and his love for Alison, but also his anger directed not at her but at Patrick. Franca would be welcomed as a research assistant, likely to uncover clues as to Patrick's whereabouts, old Irish addresses, names of friends who might be in the Dublin telephone directory. Among all these numerous (for there were certainly others) variations of outcome, some involving prolonged uncertainty and agonising waiting, Franca had not dared to dwell upon the one she so desperately hoped for in any detail. Hope itself, in the garb of life or death, had hitherto sufficed.

She had planned to return to Chelsea at the hour of her presumed return from Molly Stein. This would allow ample time for Jack to have turned up and digested the letter. Now however, unable to wait any longer, she ran out of the hotel and hailed a taxi.

She thrust her key cautiously and quietly into the door and pushed it open. She stepped carefully inside and closed the door soundlessly. There was no sign of the letter, and no sound in the house. She went into the kitchen and sat down at the table and panted and listened. No sound. Perhaps nothing had happened at all, Ludens had forgotten to bring the letter, Jack had not come. She went into her boudoir, now less in use since Jack and Alison had moved out, and put down her suitcase, took off her coat, looked at herself in a mirror, tidied her hair, adjusted the collar of her dress. She went out into the hall and listened. Nothing. She put both her hands to her violently beating heart. She began with quiet steps to mount the stairs. On the first landing she paused and looked into the drawing room. Empty. Then as she climbed the second flight of stairs she heard a sound from above, the familiar noise of the creaking floorboards in the studio. She quickened her pace, but soundlessly, sped up the third flight and reached the door of the studio. She heard another footstep and a sigh. She quietly opened the door.

Jack was standing with his back to her at the far end of the studio in front of the canvas upon his easel. He was painting. He moved back, studied the picture, then began intently mixing paint upon his palette. She thought, Ludens forgot the letter, it is all to do again! Then she thought, Alison came back and retrieved the letter before he saw it. Or, Alison telephoned to tell him she had changed her mind. Oh *God*. She moved slightly and Jack turned, he smiled at her and waved his brush. 'Just a moment.' He turned back to the picture, intently applied a small touch of paint, then stepped back again. Franca sat down on a chair. Bitter tears were gathering but she controlled them, breathing deeply and swallowing. She thought, I'll just say hello and escape.

'There. Now.' He picked up a chair, brought it near to her and sat down, pulling the chair forward until their knees nearly touched. 'Dear Franca –'

Franca rose, moving away. She said, 'I'm rather tired, I think I'll lie down for a while, I expect you'll be going soon, I just wanted to look in for a moment, I hope the painting's going well.'

'Franca, don't go. You do look tired. Do sit down, *sit down, please.*'

She sat down again, staring at him, rigid, anxious only to get away.

To retain some air of composure she studied his face, his head, how he looked as he now bent forward towards her, how well he looked, his aquiline nose reddened by tennis court sunshine, and his muscular arms, covered with golden fleece, emerging from the rolled-up sleeves of his shirt and smock.

'I hope you had a nice time in Edinburgh.' Fancy thinking of that she reflected, it's exactly what I ought to say!

'I didn't go to Edinburgh,' said Jack. He was staring at her intently with his blue Duke of Wellington eyes, slightly frowning, slightly surprised, as if he had not seen her for a long time.

'Oh? I thought you were going –' She paused, not sure what she was supposed to know.

'Franca, listen,' said Jack, 'I want – I want your attention.' He seemed for a moment at a loss. 'There's a lot I want to say to you, there are questions I want to ask you.'

Franca thought, perhaps someone has told him I'm leaving, perhaps he has made it up with her and she has suggested –

Jack went on. 'But I'd better just, at once, show you this.' He put Alison's letter into her hand.

Franca held the letter and feigned to read it. In fact she found that she *was* reading it, and felt almost *interested* in it as when one rereads a well-known text, finding it different. Franca's kindness, her detestable patience . . . you can't make me happy . . . explaining to my father . . . I don't love you enough . . . the party's over. Franca became absorbed in the letter, holding it for a long time. She looked up at Jack and found his eyes blazing at her as if with anger. She thought, he can't bear it, he is going to Dublin.

She said in a calm sympathetic tone, 'Oh Jack, I am so sorry – what a terrible letter to get – but you must know that she doesn't mean it. She'll come back – or else she'll be waiting for you to come after her, you can get her back with your little finger. We can easily find out where she is, Pat's old friends are sure to know, like Ned Oliver and Barry Titmus, I'll find out for you, don't worry, don't. She loves you so much, you love her so much, it can't end, you know it can't.' And now it was as if Franca really did not want it to end, so absorbed was she into Jack, his familiar presence and his being, his need for her comfort. Yet of course, and she knew as she spoke, she was saying what she *had* to say, playing the part which she *had* to play.

Jack, sitting back in his chair and studying her face, said, 'Thank you Franca.' He took back the letter which she offered to him and put it into the pocket of his smock.

Franca felt giddy, was she supposed to go now? She felt an uprush of emotion as if she might faint. She turned her head away. She rehearsed things she might say like, I want to help you.

Jack scraping his chair back got up and began to walk about. He kicked a pile of sketchbooks violently out of the way. He said in a loud voice, but in a conversational tone, 'I saw Ludens, he's back in London.'

'Oh really? I hope he's not too awfully upset about Marcus.'

'Of course he's upset, he's devastated, it's the end of his world.'

'But isn't he going to marry Irina? That must be a consolation.'

'Oh fuck, I don't know what he's going to do.'

'Well, I think I'll go and rest now,' said Franca. 'I don't want to interrupt your painting.' She did manage now to get up and move towards the door.

Jack got to the door first and stood before it. 'Franca, don't do this to me.'

'Do what to you? You want me to be kind to you, I *am* being kind to you! I feel sure Alison will come back. How can she leave you just when everything has settled down? Any moment she'll ring up and say she's coming back.'

'I don't understand you. You *terrify* me.'

'Jack, really –'

'You're so calm and cold.'

'I'm usually calm. I'm not cold.'

'You're very fond of Alison, aren't you.'

'I can't exactly –'

'Are you fonder of Alison than you are of me?'

'No.'

'It sounds as if you want us to go on, all three of us.'

'You'll find her and bring her back. That's how it will be. What are you so annoyed about?'

'You mean you don't care?'

'I don't scream at you. In the situation in which you put me I try to be gentle and helpful and not otherwise.'

'Franca, Franca, is your heart dead, have you lost your soul?'

Franca, amazed herself at the coolness which had come to her, wondered for a moment if it was, if she had. Had her long play-acting, which she thought of as a blazing furnace of wickedness, simply cut her off from the reality of her love and from the torture which it had undergone? Where was she now?

'Oh maybe,' she said, and pushed past him to open the door.

Jack seized her clumsily, banging the door shut and crushing her against it. He shook her, his hand on her shoulder, gripping her violently. For a moment they struggled, Franca trying to thrust him away while her head knocked against the wood of the door. She cried, 'You haven't told me what you're going to do!'

Jack let her go. 'What do you mean?'

'Oh you *fool*! What about Alison? Are you going after her?'

'No! You saw her letter. How can I go after her!'

'If it's like *that* the answer is of course you can. You want to. Off you go. I'm not stopping you. I'll help you!'

'Franca –'

'Or if you prefer to wait for her, I'll wait with you!'

'Franca, come back, sit down, we're both mad!'

'Or if you don't want me to be with you while you wait I won't be. I'll do whatever you want, I always have.'

'Please don't speak in that tone. Come.' He went back to the two chairs and sat down. Franca stumbled after him. She didn't cry but for a moment wailed aloud. All purpose, all sovereignty over her own fate, all 'pure cognition', the fierce clarity of just anger, all was gone. It had been too long and too much and she had made a stone of her heart and she would never be able to justify herself, and never be able to explain. Whatever happened now he would despise her, even pity her. The power which she had had once she had dispelled by mistakes which she could not even remember. She sat down facing him, staring at him, with a strange strained mask of a face concealing grief and remorse and rage.

'Franca, please talk sense to me, try to see what's happened.' He leaned forward and tried to take her hand, but she withheld it.

'I will, I do. If Alison were to walk into this room now you'd take her in your arms, and I'd go quietly downstairs and make some tea.'

'It's over, it's all *over*. That's what I thought you'd understand as soon as you came in. Of course I was in love with her.'

'She's just testing you. You are in love with her.'

'I am recovering. We were both realising it was impossible.'

'I don't believe you. If it seemed difficult, it was because of me. And that's easily rectified. I can go. I can unmake myself. I very nearly *did* go, Jack. I didn't mean to talk to you like this. I thought it would all be much simpler, one way or another. But just now, just at *this* moment, we are balanced on a knife edge.'

'I told you I would love you for ever and it is true.'

'It's not "true", where we are now such words are burnt up. You must decide whether or not you really want Alison. You are in a state of shock and you are consoling yourself by exhibiting your desolation to me. But why not work on the situation? Why not admit that you *will* work on it? Don't you realise that if you were to whistle to Alison and say "The coast's clear, she's gone", Alison would come racing back? As I told you, I can go, I can go and stay with Maisie Tether and get a job in Boston.'

'You couldn't do that.'

'I'm just telling you that as far as you are concerned I can vanish. I won't die of grief. I can make myself another life. You needn't feel any guilt about it.'

'But – do you *want* to go?'

Franca told herself, I am getting a grip on it again, I must say just the right things, produce just the right words, it's all far more complicated than I thought, there's a whole other dimension, a whole other game to be played out. But what is this game, this inevitable necessary move, is it a search for truth or a cunning manoeuvre? Can this be right, is this love – or *is love really over*? 'I don't know Jack. I want to see into your mind. I don't want to wreck your happiness. Perhaps by doing what you asked and staying here and being patient and tolerant I *have* wrecked it – or almost. But there's still time. If you run after Alison now at once you will get her back. You still love her, she still loves you. I'm the problem. My kindness to you which we pretended made things possible has made them impossible. Perhaps if I had really loved you I would have been even more heroic, I would have left you. But, as I say, I can go now, and I am beginning to feel that I must go – not just for your sake but for my own. You say "it's over", as if this is something simple and obvious, you even assumed that I would immediately take it for granted, you assumed that I'd just give one cry of joy. But what does it profit me if you hate me later because, at the moment when you could still retrieve her, I clung on to your hand?'

Jack was looking puzzled, confused, almost frightened. He looked at her warily now, exasperated, trying to think about what she said and discern what she meant. He dragged his hair back, gripping it hard, and shook his head violently to and fro. 'Franca, this *is* something simple. You are making it into a stupid drama and I can't see why. I can't argue with you this way. I thought you accepted it all – and that you'd accept what's happened now! All right, it was crazy –'

'No, it was a possible situation.'

'You're tormenting me, you're leading me into some trap, don't do it! I had to believe that you would always be there, I have always believed it.'

'Yes, and I have been, I even am – but I will not be at the cost of making you lose what you prize more. Jack, I'm not playing a game with you. I want you to have time to decide, and you must decide *alone*. All this has happened suddenly, neither you nor Alison know what you really want. I am going to *withdraw*. I'm going away. I can go to America to see Maisie, or I can stay with Molly, or at Linda's cottage, or at a hotel, or go on a tour. After all it's my life that's at stake too. If you lose *her* because of *me* you may detest me, and take your revenge by finding someone else. You'll probably find someone else anyway!'

Jack had undone his shirt at the neck. Undoing another button he threw away a coloured scarf which was lurking inside. In a sudden movement which made her quickly shift her chair he stood up and tore off the painting overall, tearing it roughly over his head, bundling it up and hurling it across the room. He sat down again running his hand round his neck and down onto his chest. 'Answer me. Do you want to leave me? Is it simply that?'

'No! Don't be a fool, Jack! Try to understand what I'm saying. I didn't rehearse this or intend it. When I read that letter I felt happy for a moment. *You* thought I'd just feel I'd won. But it's not so easy. Indeed, let us not make a drama of it. I'll just go away for a while, perhaps a short while, I'll tell you where I am, then you can decide quietly. You can spend the time examining your feelings, and possibly trying out Alison's – it won't be difficult to find her. She is probably expecting you! As for *us*, there's no point in romancing about it is all now as it once was. It can't be that. We don't want to hurry into an unhappy relationship in which you are full of regret and resentment and remorse, and I feel guilty at having somehow compelled you by being so relentlessly patient and nice. You see – wait, let me talk – this thing of Alison is unique. The other ones were different, your heart was not engaged. Now, you see – oh even if you give *her* up, you'll want another like her – anyway let's not think about that! It all proves that I *must* go away for a time so that we can both see what has happened to us.'

Jack murmured, 'You terrify me.'

Franca rose to her feet and moved away behind her chair, holding onto the back of it. She said, 'So let's do it quickly. We must be brave enough to do it. I'll go away now and you stay here. I won't go far. I'll let you know in a day or two where I am. You know what I say is wise. And when I've gone you'll feel much better. Stay here, Jack, stay and paint. I'll go away quietly.'

She began to walk towards the door, moving as in a dream. She felt, some spirit put all those extraordinary words into my mouth. I have used my power, I have said exactly what I had to say, and what had to be said. Now let me go away and rest.

But again he pursued her, this time seizing her strongly and gently, holding her shoulders and turning her towards him. 'Franca, all this is nonsense, it's unreal stuff. Or if you like, it's a play which we had to enact, or you to enact and I to undergo. You are my wife and I forbid you to leave me. Franca, here, let me hold on to you properly, do you love me?'

'Yes.'

'Don't leave me. I love you, I love you. Here come back, sit down again.'

She sat down and Jack, kneeling at her feet, leaned his head against her side, against her breast.

'Franca, darling, I beseech you, don't go away – you won't go away, will you, not even for a moment?'

'I won't go away.'

'I can't live without you – you will stay with me forever, won't you?'

'I will stay with you forever, Jack.'

She thought, more than that I can't fight, not against *him*, whatever pains there be, for I do love him eternally. As for the future, there might be bitter tears, but she felt that whatever the suffering she had fought the battle of it already. She had fought rightly, and been perfectly defeated, and that was right too. She stroked his hair and felt the warmth of his neck. Tears came from beneath her closed eyelids, and as she caressed his head she smiled, not the triumphant smile which she had sometimes pictured, but a relieved exhausted defeated smile.

FREE BICYCLES. The notice was still there, a little dirtier and more askew. The gates however had been set up more firmly on their hinges and the gravel mounds into which they had been sunk cleared away, the drive levelled and the number of weeds reduced. The gates were padlocked together on a chain long enough to admit a human being but not a car. Ludens, having parked his car on the verge, slipped in through the gap. The place seemed as deserted as ever. The bicycles were much as before except that two or three of them had been cleaned, if not painted, and had viable tyres. Ludens chose one, and set off along the cycle track.

Various birds were singing but Ludens soon stopped hearing them. Or perhaps, now that he had reached the darker denser woodland which made a tunnel of the drive, some spirit silenced them. Ever since this journey had become inevitable Ludens had been sick and faint with the hopes and fears which were fighting savagely within him, fighting, it seemed, actually inside his heart which had distended with grief and now filled his whole diaphragm. His heartbeats came like blows. He thought continually about Marcus, rehearsing it all, trying to remember significant things which Marcus had said, seeing that weird fallen empty body, blaming himself. How could he have let it happen, why had he trusted Marcus not to do it, why had he not been beside Marcus always as his dog, his slave, sleeping at his door, in his room, holding onto his garments? How could he have *lost* Marcus so carelessly, so wickedly, after having spent so much of his life-energy seeking him and finding him in a way that had seemed predestined? And now he had lost Irina too – Marcus had told him to look after Irina and he had lost her. Why had he let her go away alone, why had he not *insisted* on going with her, why had he not used his authority? When she went to London that evening, when he drove her to the train, he was too crushed to think and blindly assumed she would be back on the following day. Of course, surely, he would find her again soon and all his terrible agonising fears for her and about her would vanish utterly and be forgotten, as he would be with her, hearing her tell him all about what had happened in Switzerland, how difficult and incomprehensible and ridiculous it had all been, and how glad she was to be back with him. But meanwhile, until that blessed moment of relief had come, he was tortured by the agony of separation and by every sort of imagined terror. He had been thinking that perhaps in some mysterious way her father's death might relieve Irina of the sexual inhibition or phobia which had so far left his joy in her incomplete. It had now occurred to him that Marcus's death might simply teach her too a way of death. How little he knew of her, how little perhaps he had been able to interpret her wilful moods which concealed or expressed some dreadful inward despair. He had even at last begun to imagine that she had run to Red Cottage simply to kill herself, and he pictured entering the house and finding her lying dead upon the floor, or upstairs upon one of the beds. How deeply, since *that* upon which Marcus had so long meditated, did the virus of suicide pervade his people. Perhaps it has always belonged to us, Ludens thought, remembering Masada. Yet what nonsense it was, Gentiles were killing themselves all the time, only when a Jew did it, it seemed to have some special racial meaning. And as he thought of Irina lying upon her bed having destroyed herself, he recalled how he had first seen her there in the darkness of the night, peering round her door and meeting her bright eyes and thinking she was a boy.

It was the afternoon of the day after Ludens's conference with Franca, and after he had, late at night, delivered Alison's sealed letter to the house in Chelsea. Probably by now Jack had read the letter and was perhaps already in the forgiving arms of Franca, or else on a plane to Dublin. Ludens's departure had been delayed by a number of telephone calls, each one of which he expected to be from Irina. He dreaded having to leave his telephone and imagined how she would ring him in vain just after he left. He wasted some time in indecision about whether he should tell the solicitors, whom he now regarded as his enemies, where he was, at last telephoned them, realised it was Saturday and there was no one there, and left a message on their answering machine. Then Father O'Harte rang up and said at length how sorry he was about Marcus and how Ludens must regard his friend as a holy man, a kind of saint, and his death as a spiritual mystery. Ludens, though he could hardly get the priest off the line, realised that the good man's aim was to comfort Ludens and so to receive comfort himself. Christian Eriksen rang up wanting Ludens to come to dinner to meet someone or other. Suzanne rang up asking where Patrick was. Dr Hensman rang up asking where Irina was. Gildas rang up wanting to see Ludens. A journalist rang up asking questions about Marcus. At last he left, listening till the last moment for the next, perhaps crucial, call.

The wood became less dense, light showed ahead, he came out into the open confronted by the view of the house and the silvery streak of

lake water beyond. In the rich afternoon light, beneath a sky, blue at
the zenith, embellished beyond by motionless rounded white clouds
tinged by a fierce pink, the domed house looked majestic, formidable,
like some palace of judgment. The grassy meadow, across which the
cycle track continued, which had been green and flowery, was now a
jaded yellow, the flowers were over. Ludens decided to leave his bicycle
at this point rather than walking it over the bumpy path toward the
cottage, and hid it, entering the edge of the wood and laying it flat on
the ground in long grass beyond a screen of saplings. He returned to
the path and began to run along it. Now he heard the birds again,
especially the strident but musical song of a certain bird. He thought,
in a few minutes I shall be there and I shall have gone through the
looking-glass into another world, of horror or of joy or of deeper
desolation. He had tried not to think about what might be there:
perhaps nothing.

The woodland trees withdrew, the grassy clearing revealed the cottage. The two doors were closed. Ludens already held the key in his
hand, but he hoped to find the door unlocked. He ran as fast as he
could across the grass and blundered against the nearer door. It was
locked, the other door was locked also. He unlocked the nearer door
which gave onto the main part of the house. He stumbled through the
doorway and stood still. Then he called several times 'Irina! Irina!' The
house returned a wave of silence. Time, *time* was so terrible, he
experienced it now as a vast spongy grey wall which slowed his
movements wilfully withholding from him the emergence into nightmare or into the vast sunlit land of relief. He looked quickly into the
downstairs room, then ran up the stairs, his feet scarcely touching the
treads. The upstairs landing was dark, a curtain had been pulled. The
bedroom doors stood open. He looked into the rooms. Nothing, no
pale ghastly figure lying upon a bed. There was something odd about
the landing. He realised that the door into the cupboard, through which
he had struggled on that first night, was open, and there was light
beyond. The cupboard had been cleared and the doors were open at
both ends. He ran through the cupboard and into what had been his
own room, examined the tiny room next door, and then the two rooms
downstairs. He hurried back again, through the cupboard and down
again to where the sunshine was coming in through the open door. He
ran out onto the grass and called her name. There was something so
strange in the utterance of that cry, not like a summons uttered for a
human being. Silence. Then he heard again the harsh musical warbling
of the bird, now nearby. After that he examined the house more

carefully. Was it inhabited? The beds had been tidied but not stripped. All the furniture was in place, the kitchen fully equipped. There was a cup in the kitchen sink, a broom in the hall. He went upstairs to Marcus's 'study' and was here forcibly reminded that he had an additional reason for being there. *Please destroy everything.*

Ludens had, because he feared it and because of Irina, not reflected on this duty. He had thought, probably it will be simple when the time comes. Deliberately he did not go beyond this thought. Had he not seen for himself, after all, Marcus's inability to write anything down. It was true that at the very beginning of his final adventure, he had had his first sighting of Marcus sitting on the bed in the downstairs room writing something. But he had never seen piles of notebooks or a sea of papers scattered on the floor. What he had seen was Irina burning various things including papers in the incinerator behind the cottage on the day of their departure. He had not asked or discovered whether Marcus had told her to burn them. He had not thought about that either, and the shock which he had felt at the time had quickly vanished among other intenser worries. Now he recalled that scene almost with relief. He had not now, in his quick race round the house, seen any writings, but then he had not been looking for them either. The downstairs room had been swept and tidied. Ludens looked into a cupboard and under the bed. Nothing. He went to the upstairs room in which Marcus had said to him: there will be no writing. What is written will be written in blood. A pure experience will save the world. The suffering will be the message. Seeing nothing, Ludens stood rigid in the room, suddenly cold as if some slow awful refrigeration were diminishing him, thinning him, until he should become as thin as a needle and then vanish. He thought, and how have *I* survived, why am *I* not dead too. Why was I not with him, why did I not stay with him. And now I shall *never know*, and for the rest of my life I shall mourn and diminish. He stood, his jaw trembling, his body trembling as with extreme cold. He was awakened from this lethal trance by a distant sound like a cry. He moved, stood, seeing the room, listening. The cry was not repeated.

He looked about him. The room was as before, the two chairs still in position, one by the window, one by the bookshelves, the small table in the corner, the old oak rocking-chair. This room too had been swept and tidied, the empty bookshelves had been dusted. There was nothing on the shelves or on the table. He noticed a small cupboard. It was empty. He was about to leave the room when it occurred to him to investigate the rocking-chair. The capacious lower part of the chair beneath the seat revealed a handle. He pulled. A large box-like drawer fell out onto the floor. It was full of papers and notebooks. These had evidently escaped the destruction by burning, with or without Marcus's command, of all the other writings. Ludens, kneeling, spread them out on the floor. Moreover there were a number of different scripts, some no doubt just an earlier hand, some perhaps an assumed hand, some in what might have been Japanese, or else a private code. A battered ancient-looking notebook appeared to contain poems of which Ludens could only read a word or two, another notebook contained disjointed illegible statements, perhaps aphorisms, perhaps jottings of ideas, many hastily scrawled sheets of paper looked like first drafts. There were also, on separate sheets, sequences of mathematical symbols. What was here, he wondered – the tragic fragments of a weary bewildered mind which the world must never see – or a dense treasure-house of profound secrets by which people now and in the future would be inspired and enlightened? Perhaps the very secret that would save mankind, written down after all, and not enacted?

Ludens sat back on his heels. His historian's instinct abominated a destruction of evidence. Suppose he were to gather it all up and take it back to London, attempt to decipher it himself, bring in one or two experts to help him? But then who would these experts be, and could he trust them? Could he trust himself? If there were a rumour about 'papers' or 'strange original ideas' all sorts of people would be after them. Ludens in defending them would be appropriating them. Suppose something were stolen and published and seen to be vacuous nonsense? Perhaps Marcus felt that any future interpretation of his ideas would certainly be corrupt and wrong. Better to destroy them than let them fall into the hands of fools and knaves. All the same . . . Was there a dilemma or was there no dilemma? If only Marcus had spoken to him directly and bound him by a promise! Marcus had named him as his literary executor, but the envelope had only said 'To my literary executor'. *Could* people order other people to do such things? Ludens suddenly remembered Kafka. Had not Kafka told Max Brod to destroy all his manuscripts and had not Max Brod decided not to, and was not that the right decision? True, what lay in Max Brod's hands when Kafka was dead included the manuscripts of *The Castle*, *The Trial* and *America*. Ludens had never read a complete account of that situation. Did Kafka want the books destroyed because they were unfinished, or for some other deep hidden reason? Ludens felt sure it was the latter. How can survivors measure such reasoning, ought they not simply to obey? Of course Max Brod was sure he could measure the value of what lay before him. Whereas Ludens could not now, or perhaps ever, measure the meaning or the value of what Marcus had left behind. All that was clear was the trust which had been laid upon him, the expression of the 'deep reason'. Or of some obviously sensible consideration, such as a wish to obliterate rambling juvenilia.

Suddenly Ludens heard again, more distant, the strange cry that had disturbed him earlier. It sounded now familiar, as if it were something which he knew and ought to recognise. He stood up hastily and thought, anyway I'll put the stuff together, I'll find some bags somewhere, something to put it in. He ran down to the kitchen and found several plastic bags which he brought up and, kneeling once more on the floor, began roughly to sort and to pack up the scattered writings. Occasionally he looked at a sheet or a page but could not make out any continuous sense. His mind was already distracted by something else: he thought, Irina *must* be here, I feel it, she must be nearby. I must hurry and decide and *get this over*, I must *find* her. The man at the solicitor's office said something like 'at Fontellen'. She might be staying in the house with the housekeeper, or perhaps in the village, perhaps it was she who had tidied up the cottage and stripped it, arranging what was to be sent to London. She must be here somewhere. How likely that seems now. Oh God, I must go and look for her. He completed his packing and carried the heavy bags down the stairs. As he remembered it later, he actually got them to the bottom of the stairs without having made up his mind what to do, whether to burn them at once or carry them to his car. He staggered out of the door, left two large bags and went back for the others. Then when he reached the door a second time he walked round the side of the house to the incinerator. Returning for the remainder, he picked up some matches in the kitchen.

The incinerator was almost empty, a small debris of ashes at the bottom, the space round about unlittered. A long iron rod lay on the grass nearby. Ludens began frenziedly to thrust sheets of paper in through the bars, tossing the notebooks in over the top. He paused to light a match. He recalled how Irina had thrown paraffin on the smouldering fire to make it blaze. He thought, I must find some paraffin. But it was soon clear that this was not necessary. The dry air, the gentle warm breeze, took care of the little flame, and the papers flared up at once. Ludens now fed the blaze with frantic haste, inserting the papers and ramming them with the iron bar into the depth of the conflagration. He took off his jacket and threw it behind him. Soon there was little left except a small flickering fire at the bottom of the tall radiantly hot pillar. Ludens's face was running with perspiration. Some remnants of white paper were still smouldering. He belaboured them with the rod, which was almost too hot to hold, until they too had become black and beaten to pieces. He threw the rod down, picked up the bags, put on his jacket and returned to the kitchen. He put the bags and the matches back in their original places. He stood confused in the doorway. Was there no more to be done, had he left anything behind? No, nothing was left, all was burnt.

He emerged into the sunshine. The key was still in the door. He locked the door and pocketed the key and set off at a fast pace toward the meadow. Here he began to run along the bumpy path, upon the dry yellowing verge, disturbing the seeds of the grass, which made him sneeze. He found his bicycle, safe where he had left it, and wheeled it out onto the cycle track. He set off along the track in the direction of the house, noticing that the sun, now obliquely in his eyes, was lower in the sky, and the air and light were denser, hazier, with a sense of evening. From the point where the track divided Ludens could see the brick pillars of the wistaria walk where he and Marcus had trodden on flowers and where now the fallen lattices had been put up again. He turned to the left, crossing the drive swiftly at the place which said *Dismount*, and came down to the edge of the lake. Here he deposited his bicycle on the grass beside the track and walked back toward the house. He stood for a while in the warm silence looking at it, studying the windows. Most were shuttered though two or three had curtains visible. Probably it was just as before, possibly a housekeeper was there. He did not feel able to walk across the very large lawn and up the stone staircase to the front door, if it was the front door. The place looked closed up and sleepy. Lord Claverden was hardly ever there. In any case Irina was not on friendly terms with his Lordship, whom she had referred to as a vile old toad. 'Irina at Fontellen' could mean Irina at the Claverden Arms in the village, coming in every day to sort and strip at Red Cottage; and surely to walk about in the gardens, performing her mourning, overcoming, alone, her horror and her misery, enduring the days of her flight which were perhaps accomplished, and now waiting to be discovered. He turned and walked back to his bicycle, seeing now the little grove of cherry trees whose petals Irina had once, so long ago, thrown into his face. Nearby a cuckoo was calling out its stuttering farewell. Then he heard another sound.

This was the sound he had heard at the cottage which, now close at hand, he recognised as the bark of a dog. Far off it had sounded weird, even menacing. Now it was welcome, friendly. Then he saw the dog standing in the long grass, gazing at him and wagging its tail. A golden labrador. It came towards him, gazing at him with its loving eyes. Ludens did not need to speak aloud to it, his soul spoke. He stepped forward into the grass and sat down. The dog came to him and caressed him. It was a young dog, though well out of puppyhood. They caressed each other. Ludens put his arms round the smooth warm furry neck and rubbed his brow against the loose muscular shoulder. The dog, excited, began to lick him, his cheek, his ears, its warm damp tongue passed over his closed eyes. Ludens could feel his heart beating against the dog's heart. After a little of this loving he calmed the dog down, told it to sit, which it did, and they contemplated each other with delight. They smiled, they laughed, Ludens gently stroked the dog's beautiful head, and the dog put its paw up to touch his arm. At last Ludens sighed. He shifted, knelt, made as if to rise. The dog, attentive to his mood, moved away a little, turning back towards him, standing now upon a path of mown grass among the taller grass. It waited for Ludens.

As he looked at it he suddenly thought: a dog, a labrador. *Irina.* Had not Irina said that she wanted a dog, and said it should be a labrador? Or had *he* said that? She certainly wanted a dog. The dog went on, then paused, looking back again. Leaving his bicycle, Ludens followed it. *Of course.* He knew now where that path led and whom he would find at the end of it. He said aloud to the dog, 'Are you the messenger?' The dog wagged its tail enthusiastically. Ludens walked on, or rather seemed to fly quietly at a gentle steady pace, just above the ground, watching the dog who at intervals turned to look at Ludens with love and approval. So they went on until they reached the edge of the airfield.

The summer day showed no sign of ending, but the sky, a thick sleepy blue above, was faintly greenish at the horizon, entertaining some thin horizontal wraiths of cloud. The lake, as Ludens turned for a moment to look at it, was a pale motionless silver-blue mirror. As Ludens stepped off the already dewy grass onto the warm concrete he felt a wave of emotion like a blast carried from some great explosion far away; and felt again as if he were entering a vast domed silence. The dog padded on and Ludens followed it, loping slowly, easily, upon the hard warm flat surface which seemed, as if misted, to have no edges. The dog stopped, and Ludens stopped too. Then it began to run.

A figure had appeared far away upon the great grey surface, a figure upon a bicycle. The sun shining obliquely into Ludens's face dazzled him. Shading his eyes he began to run too. He so desperately hoped, then became so joyously certain, that it was Irina. *It was Irina.* He ran, he waved, he tried to shout but could not. The dog, racing in front of him, drew ahead. They came nearer and nearer.

Then slowing his pace, panting and shading his eyes more carefully, he became aware of another figure. Two people, two bicycles. He slowed down a little more until he was walking, his heart struggling in his breast, his mouth gaping with apprehension. Through the looking-glass. Now.

At last he stood, letting the two cyclists approach him. The dog was running in ecstatic circles round the advancing pair. They were quite close now. One of them was certainly Irina. The other was a young man whom Ludens had never seen before. Close to him they dismounted and came towards him, wheeling their bicycles and smiling. Irina turned and said something to her companion beside whom the dog was jumping up and uttering yelps of joy.

The young man spoke first. He said to Ludens, 'So Sidney found you, did he?' And to the dog, 'Good boy!' The young man was tall and very blond, wearing a white shirt and grey flannels, his tweed jacket over the handlebars of his bicycle.

Ludens did not, could not, reply. He was staring at Irina.

Irina looked amazing. Ludens could not later determine what it was that made her look, in such detail, so startling and extraordinary. She seemed to stand forward from her background as into a larger brighter dimension of being. She was like a perfected idea of herself, of which the other was a messy degraded sketch or image. She was wearing smart tight trousers with a dark-green and black check, a dark-blue shirt and a knotted green silk scarf. Ludens had never seen her in trousers before. She looked elegant, slimmer. Her face radiated the sort of wild gleaming glaring joy which now illuminated the face of the dog. Only Irina's human joy was more intense, brimming over with authority and significance. She stared back at him, her lips parted, her dark bright faintly crossed eyes shining with fierce rapturous consciousness. Her smile trembled under a magisterial restraint, checking perhaps some terrible disgraceful helpless laughter.

Then she uttered these words. 'Hello, Alfred, I'm so glad to see you. May I present my fiancé, Lord Claverden.'

Ludens was amazed to recall how perfectly he had behaved, as if he had foreseen it all, as if he were acting in a play and with calm certainty remembered all his lines. He said, looking toward the young man, 'I'm so pleased to meet you. May I offer my congratulations.'

'Oh thanks,' said the young man, in his pleasant public-school voice.

'That's great. I'm so glad to meet you, I expect you've been down at the cottage, we saw your smoke signal.'

'Yes,' said Ludens, 'I was to deal with some papers, there wasn't much to do. It's all finished there now.'

'No problems?'

'None at all.' They smiled at each other.

The young man had kindly cheerful blue eyes and floppy straight hair and an amiable grin. He went on, 'I should explain in case you don't know, but I expect you do, that my father died lately and so I've got this new name. My real name, if I may put it so, is Adrian Sedgemont.'

Ludens, nearing the end of his repertoire, smiled again and said, 'So glad to have met you both, I hope you'll be very happy. I'm sorry that I have to clear off in a hurry, I've got to get back to London. It's lucky I was so enchanted by your dog.'

'Wouldn't you like to come up to the house and have a drink?'

'No thanks, I must take myself off.'

'Would you like to borrow my bike?'

'No, I have one down on the track. Goodbye, Irina, I congratulate you too, I wish you joy. Goodbye then.'

'Goodbye.'

'Goodbye, Alfred. And thanks.'

Ludens turned quickly away. The dog followed him for a little distance, then turned back.

PART SEVEN

'So you're not too terribly upset?' said Franca to Ludens.

'Of course he isn't,' said Jack. 'He put up with her because of Marcus.'

'He had a lucky escape,' said Gildas, 'and is congratulating himself.'

'Anyway you saw it coming?' said Franca.

'Well,' said Ludens, 'she told me there was "someone in her life" –'

'And you guessed who it was?'

'I'm glad to think that she'll be happy,' said Ludens.

'As for her being happy,' said Jack, 'that's another matter. That place is falling to bits. All her money will go on mending the house and sprucing up the decaying park. And she'll be stuck in the country with a dull fellow.'

'Could he be marrying her for her money?' said Franca.

'No,' said Ludens.

'And she's marrying him for the title,' said Jack, 'so they're both satisfied!'

'No, no,' said Ludens, 'he's a very decent man and good-looking too. They're just in love, no need to impute sinister motives.'

'Not sinister, sensible,' said Jack. 'Such acts have many motives. They may fancy each other too.'

'You say Irina looked happy?' said Franca.

'Radiant, transformed.'

'She needed a bit of transforming,' said Jack, 'she was such a little drowned rat.'

'Wasn't it strange,' said Franca, 'the two obstructive fathers disappeared together! Lord Claverden didn't want his son to marry a Jew, and Marcus didn't want his daughter to marry a Gentile. Then suddenly the way was clear.'

'If they'd really been in love they'd have run away,' said Jack.

'Easier said than done,' said Franca. 'She had to stay with Marcus, and *he* would have been disinherited. His father was that sort of

550

monster. He'd have left it all to the Communist Party! Perhaps they had a pact to wait.'

'So you knew?' said Jack. 'You were very discreet about it.'

'But you imagined you were in love with her,' said Franca.

'I did for a time,' said Ludens, 'but she never encouraged me, and of course nothing happened. It was all my dream.'

'Exactly,' said Franca. 'Maybe you wanted to secure her so that Marcus could never sack you!'

'I've said so all along,' said Jack. 'It was all part of your obsession with Marcus. You'd been after Marcus for years, trailing him from place to place, then at last you really got hold of him. She was just part of the scenery.'

'Don't grieve too much about Marcus,' said Franca. 'He lived his own life and chose his own death. You supported him, you were his companion on the pilgrimage, you did nothing but good.'

'You enabled his mind,' said Jack. 'He'd probably been thinking it all out, gas and all, for years. He was an artist. You helped him to see how it could be done perfectly.'

'I think we should go home,' said Franca. 'It's very late. Come on, darling.' They rose.

They were *chez* Gildas. He had insisted, although Franca had immediately suggested dinner at Chelsea. There could not but be, as they all felt, something symbolic about this reunion. 'Home is the sailor, home from the sea, and the hunter home from the hill,' as Jack vaguely yet aptly quoted. Marcus was dead, Irina disposed of, Ludens was back in London, back with his friends, his quest over, his obsession ended. Jack too, who took this optimistic view of Ludens's condition, was, as he felt and declared, definitely *back home*. Gildas, the enlightened spectator, had never been away.

'At our place next time,' said Franca. 'We must be oftener together.' She kissed Gildas, squeezing his hand. She kissed Ludens and hugged him, ruffling his hair. Jack too hugged Ludens and shook him. They went away down the ill-lit rickety stairs.

Sitting in the Bentley, as it purred its confident way through the empty rainy streets which gave back fleeting reflections of the bright lamps, they discussed the evening.

Franca, her arm along the back of the seat, her fingers lightly touching Jack's shoulder, said, 'Well?'

'Well what, angel?'

'Did you believe Ludens?'

'Yes, why not? He couldn't really have been in love with that poor child, he was sorry for her. He's escaped from both of them now, thank God.'

'You may be right that he was sorry for her, to begin with anyway.'

'It's all simpler than you think,' said Jack.

It's all far more complicated than *you* think, thought Franca. But she did not pursue that line of thought, she was far too happy to speculate about the misfortunes of others.

Jack went on, 'You were so right to say we must all meet oftener. They're like our family, those two. They're good for us. I think we're good for them.'

'Yes. We must look after them.'

'Franca, I want to tell you –'

'What?'

'Don't be alarmed. I just want to say how happy I feel now, so calm and unafraid. I feel like someone who's been having brilliant hallucinations, and when they cease one is tired and relaxed and returned to health and reality. It's like seeing real colours after seeing television. As I always say, television is a sin against the visual world. I've been in a dark place looking at dazzling images. Now I'm out in the lovely gently lighted real world under the cloudy sunny open sky.'

Franca said, 'Good.' Then 'But perhaps you'll run away again into those dark places.'

'I don't think so. It's a fever that has run its course, more like a play in which I had to act, all the way through, until what was so plainly the end.'

'The stage full of corpses.'

'No, I've just walked out of the theatre.'

'I'm not sure about that metaphor. No more Alisons? We can't know.'

'As you said, she was unique. I tried it and it was a disaster, we were degrading each other. I've learnt something, I've been ill and I've really absolutely recovered. I love you, Franca, darling, sweetheart, wife, old friend – when I thought I might lose you I felt I was dying.'

'Hmmm. I don't think you ever felt that. Never mind – dear best sweet Jack. And we'll go to Boston and see Maisie?'

'You think she'll tolerate me?'

'She will *now*. We've discussed it all on the telephone. Jack, I love you so much, what a relief, when I wake in the morning it's joy not nightmare.'

'You've been so wonderful, so good, so steadfast, so perfectly forgiving, you've stayed in the truth – and that's where we'll live now. And I'll learn to paint all over again.'

'Yes – your painting will come out into the light of day too.'

Did I stay in the truth? thought Franca. No, I didn't! I wandered away into oh such strange and awful places about which I shall never tell anyone. I have escaped a terrible punishment, and one which I deserved. That I'm back again and have a dear husband and a home – that's pure luck really. Will it last, will Jack not find another Alison, even the same one, and do the job properly next time? I don't think so, but I don't know, I can't know. And I feel now it's like any other not-knowing – we may be dead tomorrow or maimed or mad, but today is true and real and to be lived well in the clear light and the fresh air.

They were able to park the Bentley just outside their front door. The rain was stopping. They opened the door, and closed it and bolted it, and went upstairs to bed.

'Discretion is one thing, lies another.'

'All right, all right.'

'It's another evidence of decay.'

'They made it out themselves.'

'With my assistance! I just couldn't bear to tell them what really happened, I couldn't bear to tell anyone except you.'

'I appreciate the compliment.'

'I've been telling lies and I hate it. Oh hell, what does it matter. I wish we hadn't talked about her, but I had to say something. I keep seeing her on that bicycle. I've never seen such incarnate joy – and triumph.'

'You feel moved to add "triumph".'

'She couldn't help it. Of course it was accidental, and just as well – a stylish leave-taking, no doubts or shadows, everything conveyed in an instant, so clear and bright – and brief. She couldn't conceal her happiness, it was so spontaneous and true, the final real truth at last.'

'She never gave up hope. You can't blame her for that.'

'I don't blame her for anything. How could she recover from such a

Prince Charming? I didn't suspect, I didn't dream, of course I didn't know he existed until that moment on the airfield. Then I saw it all in a flash – her happy life with him, the two of them together in that Eden, in those woods, beside the lake, until the two fathers interfered. I wonder if they were together in Paris? There was some story about her going to Paris.'

'You suspected others – Busby, even Marcus. You know, all that bad language you so much deplored, she must have picked it up from Busby. I see him as a go-between, liberally tipped by the young master, then perhaps becoming too familiar and turning nasty.'

'When she said there had been something I got the impression it had been something awful, when in fact it had been something wonderful, but lost.'

'I wonder if it was just the fathers. There may have been more to it, he might have left her for someone else.'

'I don't know. Anyway, how could she even hint at anything so precious, especially when she thought it was all over, all a lost paradise. She said once she was a beggar-maid, and I said beggar-maids wed princes, and she said she'd kill me if I said that again. Poor child – how she must have suffered, swallowing down that bitterness and trying to stop thinking about him.'

'She evidently didn't stop. No wonder she wouldn't let you in. If she'd become pregnant that would have been the end. As it was she could say –'

'I don't want to speculate about what she could say. But how extraordinary, the two fathers dying at the same time. When did she know, how did she know, were they in touch all the time? I don't think she went to Switzerland at all, she went straight to him.'

'They made a beeline for each other.'

'She said, "I've hoped for such great things, such impossible things, oh you don't know what I've hoped for", and she said, "I'm made to be unhappy!" And she said to me, "You're all I've got." I didn't realise it was a cry of despair!'

'I don't think you ever stood a chance, even without him you were always a *pis aller*. Sooner or later she'd have danced away. I really do think you've had a lucky escape.'

'But Gildas I could have persuaded her – you know, she even suggested, twice I think, that we should leave Marcus and go away together.'

'But of course *you* couldn't leave Marcus.'

'Then she said it was him I loved and not her. We couldn't have left him, I don't think she meant it. But – oh I could have persuaded her, we talked of marriage, I was going to buy her a ring –'

'Yes, you *talked* of marriage, and you did *not* buy her a ring. And you let her come to you "like a ghost in the night" I think you said.'

'I was so anxious not to coerce her. Perhaps I was too scrupulous, too timid. I thought I was Ferdinand and she was Miranda.'

'And you were afraid of Prospero. But you said he wanted you to marry her?'

'She said he wanted her to marry a Jewish intellectual, and I was the only one available! He thought his grandson would be a genius. Yes, I ought to have rushed things. But all that time I was out of my mind with anxiety about Marcus. Of course I ought to have gone with her to London – I thought she'd be back the next day – anyway it was too late by then.'

'But you believed she loved you.'

'She did love me. I thought for a moment it might have been revenge for –'

It occurred to Ludens in time that he had never told Gildas, or anyone, about his rejection of Irina's childish love for him, the scene at the fence with the ram. He was certainly not going to tell it now – and how he had just for a second imagined that it had all been an ingenious plot, a punishment for that act of cruelty which led Marcus, so Irina said, to reject her as a 'failure'. He had not really ever measured how much she must have suffered from that double rejection. That was another knot of horrors which he would have to live with. He said, 'Oh just her general lack of success. But no, she really did love me.' He recalled how Irina had summoned him from the Black Lion and how she had hugged him on the lawn when she had been frightened by Marcus's crisis of guilt and fear, and how she had cried out, 'Stay with us.' He recalled her endearments, how she called him 'beastie' and 'donkey' and all their teasing companionship and how she had so shyly and so tenderly come to his bed where even her prohibition which gave him such distress also made him glad because he was obeying her. They had been happy and unhappy together, they had suffered like animals together in a pit, they had been like merry loving children. But, he thought, we never made love properly, I was like a novice. And would she ever call Lord Claverden a silly useless goat? Surely not. For her, I lacked dignity, I lacked authority, I lacked substance. We were indeed like hapless babes. And now – how much I wish I did not know where she was! The curtained windows at Fontellen, and those two wandering beside the lake hand in hand.

'You don't feel resentment against her?'

'No.'

'Good.'

'I love her – I loved her –'

'Hang on to that past tense. You're well away. You would need an intellectual girl, a girl with an intelligent soul. Anyway I share her view that it was really Marcus you were after. As it is, however much pain you're in, you can congratulate yourself that you harmed no one.'

'I didn't save Marcus. I didn't keep him alive.'

'You served him, you did what no one else could have done, you helped him to make sense of it all.'

'You mean I helped him to resolve to die. No wonder Marzillian wanted me around.'

'He saw Marcus as a suicidal type, and –'

'Not *type*. Marzillian's not a scientist. He enjoys studying individuals over whom he has power. When they're no longer with him he forgets them.'

'I wish I'd met Marzillian, I saw quite a lot of Terence.'

'*Did* you? I suppose he had some scientific theory. Like Suzanne, who explained to me that Marcus was a case of someone-or-other's syndrome, brilliant people who can't communicate or feel affection!'

'You wanted Marcus to live on and on and write great books. But, you know, one of the problems was that he simply *couldn't write*. He knew the language of mathematics, but he wasn't at home in any ordinary language.'

'He was so brave, and so selfless –'

'Scarcely selfless – rather more like hubris.'

'He was *heroic*. He worked so hard, he wanted so much to *learn* –'

'Whether he studied Chinese and Japanese and Sanscrit all at the same time I don't know, but that can certainly serve as an image of his industry. Any report must say "he tried hard".'

'Somehow he acted out the whole pilgrimage of modern man – to know almost everything, and then to want that one thing more, and perish trying to find it.'

'Yes, greed, pride, power. All right, courage. He thought he had a mission to mankind. He thought you were the messenger – and evidently you were, you set it all going. Then he cured Patrick, that must have influenced him a lot, it was another sign. Then he discovered Judaism –'

'I didn't set it going, and he didn't suddenly discover Judaism, it all goes years and years back, you remember he was reading about the Holocaust –'

'That was a terrible historical event, Judaism is a religion.'

'It wasn't a lot of accidents and false starts, he was on a path, he spoke of a tightrope, a narrow path, having to find one's own way to hell –'

'He certainly persevered, but he lacked the intellectual or spiritual energy to keep it all in focus. His presence could produce in people a sense of significance, understanding, vision, even well-being, he was *impressive*. But he was fundamentally muddled.'

'So you think his life and death meant nothing, you think he died in despair and confusion and –'

'Perhaps Christ died in despair and confusion. Any death is essentially accidental. As for meaning, that is our affair.'

'Irina said his death was vulgar, that it was kitsch.'

'She found a good word. Christ's death has probably collected more kitsch than any other happening in history.'

'But, Gildas, Marcus did something for you, when he talked to you that day on the verandah, he must have said something that –'

'He said nothing, he talked kindly of trivial matters.'

'But, like with Pat, he lifted the curse –'

'Simply being with him did that. I said he was impressive.'

'You knelt down to him in the garden, I saw you kneeling.'

'One may kneel down anywhere in front of anything or anyone, the impulse to worship is deep in human kind, it is a natural right.'

'You recognised him as something holy.'

'I think you've had enough to drink and had better go home.'

They had been sitting facing each other at the table, which Ludens had strewn with little balls of bread which he had been nervously and unconsciously kneading. Gildas got up and went to the piano. He struck a few sombre chords.

'I've only been drinking the wine,' said Ludens humbly. 'I'm not drunk. Let me stay a bit longer. There's something you know which I want to find out.'

'My dear, that's exactly what you were always saying to Marcus! Do you think I've got it now?'

'There's something about him which you've understood –'

'Nothing particularly obscure. He was attempting the impossible.'

'You were the one who was always quoting "a difficulty is a light, an insuperable difficulty is a sun".'

'A poet said that, it's different for poets. The kind of thinking Marcus aspired to cannot be thought.'

'You mean it's not permitted. You said he was *unheimlich*.'

557

'Beyond a certain point metaphysics is all the devil's.'

'Well, he wanted to get beyond the bounds of traditional philosophical thinking and discover some new kind of thinking, the thinking of the future. But isn't that what great men have always been doing? And if he failed, at least he indicated the places where failure was inevitable.'

'The missing link which the gods conceal. Yes. He should have been content with that and not meddled with other things.'

'How do you mean? He said something about philosophy being shipwrecked on ordinary morality.'

'So he shouldn't have started thinking about the Holocaust.'

'Because it captured his mind, it made him think about other things like suffering and guilt and pity – and so on?'

'And so on. He caught a glimpse of quite different problems and lost his nerve, he saw how dangerous it was to go on.'

'Because only God can be just?'

'Meditation on the Holocaust is not at all like meditation on Christ's passion, but the temptations are similar, the difficulty, the impossibility is similar.'

'Don't bring in Christian images. As far as I can see, meditation on Christ's passion is pure self-indulgence!'

'One would have to become God, or return to the simple moral values of the world. He was not equipped to do either.'

'Gildas, do stop!'

'He told you he found the concept of love incoherent. Of course I know Jews find the Christian idea of love soft, handed out on a plate, I know what you mean. But Marcus despised the whole messy sentimental muddle of ordinary morals. To put it another way, as Jack said as I recall, he was a cold fish –'

'No – he was certainly able to love –'

'Whom did he love? His daughter, his parents?'

Ludens said, 'I think he loved me.'

'How touching! What you saw was your own love reflected from a hard surface.'

'Don't mock, and please stop speculating about him in this hostile way.'

'Well, let's think about *tricotage* – you remember how he puzzled over that word as if it were a mysterious talisman.'

'Marzillian picked it up somehow. All the rooms are bugged. He thought it meant a cosmic network, something out of physics. I didn't argue.'

'It was a little fragment of real speech. I don't know what it means.

Most people didn't live long in the camps. But I see it as improvising, making things for others, being practical and unselfish in *that* situation, the mystery of goodness. It disturbed Marcus.'

'All right, it disturbs me. So you think you can explain why he failed.'

'Who says he failed? Perhaps time will show. I'm sure he didn't kill himself because he couldn't invent a metaphysical system or make a great synthesis. He might have been afraid of insanity, that his mind might give way under the strain. He might have realised that he couldn't express what he experienced, or experience what he conceived of. He began to fear the degradation of his thoughts, perhaps that shipwreck he spoke of. Whatever the reason he reached the point where the only thing available to him was the act.'

'Something wordless and senseless.'

'No, the culmination of his mission, what gave sense to his life, what would make him remembered.'

'I suppose if Christ hadn't been crucified, but had died of old age – but you're being too ingenious. You think *amo ut intelligam* is the key.'

'Well, and perhaps it is. What I am really worried about is you!'

'I'll survive.'

'I mean, what are you going to do about him?'

'What can I do?'

'You might write a book about him, of course that wouldn't be the book you wanted him to write, but it could be a book about his path, his way. I'm not suggesting you do this, I'm just wondering whether you're thinking of it.'

Ludens stopped crumbling up the remains of the bread and moved from the table, drawing up a chair close to the piano, looking at Gildas's abstracted profile. His friend looked older, dirtier, shabbier, sadder. Ludens touched the piano, a high note. He had never learnt to play the instrument and regarded it with respectful timid humble awe. He had not told anyone, not even Gildas, of the burning of the papers. He was already regretting it bitterly. He thought, I wanted to carry out his wishes, but what were his wishes? I ought to have tried to find out when he wrote that note. It might have been years ago, he might have forgotten, he might have changed his mind. I ought to have waited and thought about it, I ought to have *looked* at the stuff. I just wanted the pain to be over, I wanted not to have the indecision and the responsibility. And I wanted to rush out and look for Irina. I'll tell Gildas about it, about the burning later on. He said, 'Writing about Marcus could be a life sentence. You may be right that his presence produced an illusion of understanding. How can I think about the Holocaust if he couldn't?'

'I don't know what you should do. I'm just trying to think your thoughts.'

'So am I!'

'Marcus's story may disappear without trace. On the other hand, he could become a cult figure, a Jewish hero.'

'You know what Midrash means? Commentaries on scripture, interpretation of stories, weaving and connecting up of sayings and stories, a kind of continuous making of history –'

'I know that – I'm surprised you do.'

'Daniel Most spoke about it, he said someone said that the stories people told each other in the camps were like that. I think he thought that Marcus might be worked over and woven in and assimilated in that way.'

'Of course you'll wait and see. You wouldn't like people to get things wrong. On the other hand –'

'I wouldn't want simply to write the biography of an eccentric. I'd have to write as an historian –' And what am I to do with *my* notebooks, he thought, my records of those conversations, my attempts to interpret his ideas? He thought, I *can't* write about him. Anything I wrote would be untrue, would be a betrayal. 'You told me to go home some time ago. I think I'd better go now.'

'You're not angry with me?'

'No, I'm just so bloody miserable and smashed up, I feel like Petrushka, made of sawdust but in agony.'

'You used to boast you'd been pointed to by an angel in a picture by Leonardo!'

'He meant "destroy that one". I dream of words and blood. I feel that my thoughts will never be at peace, never again in my life. I'm sorry to be so spineless. Let's talk about you for a change. How are you getting on?'

'Well, if you'll excuse an expression I use –'

'Gildas, please –'

'*If* you'll excuse an expression I use, I think it's *about time* you asked. How am I getting on? The bookshop has closed and I have no job, this building has been sold and is to be pulled down, so I have no home. I propose to live on social security in a small room in the East End of London and try out life at the bottom and see if it is possible to help other people, a thing incidentally which *he* never tried to do.'

'Oh, Gildas, forgive me, I'm so sorry –'

'Of course there will be no space for my piano.'

'I'll look after your piano. And why don't you come and live with me? There's plenty of room.'

'A tempting idea, but no, no, it wouldn't do. I'm better alone. I may even try to creep back into some cranny in the Anglican Church when the theologians have dismantled it all a bit more. I'd like to get hold of a choir again. I might try to organise my own.'

'I'll come and sing in it. I'm glad you're coming back into religion.'

'I never left it. I *know* that my Redeemer liveth. I know that if I ask for what I love I shall receive it. *Da quod amo. Amo enim. Et hoc tu dedisti.*'

'You think you can make God be.'

'My dear, there is no other way. The soul should stay at home.'

'I envy your certainty. *Statuens in parte dextra.* You know how to pray.'

'Anyone can do it. You move effortlessly into another dimension of being.'

'You'll have to pray for me. I think I *will* go home now. I don't want to disintegrate before your eyes or start to weep or curse. Anyway, one thing is certain, I'm through with women.'

'Would it were so, but I doubt it. You remember the prophecy, that you would only be in danger of matrimony when three women desired you. That is yet to come.'

'Oh but –' Ludens was about to say, as he had that moment realised, that it had already come! Three wonderful women had loved him! But one was a witch, and so he had received nothing but a curse. And that was another thing which he could never divulge. He said, 'With Irina, it's like having slept with the priestess, I feel no other woman will do.'

'Oh rubbish!'

'I suppose there's still that girl Alison was so keen I should marry. What was her name – Hilda Wetherby?'

'Heather Allenby. I'm afraid you're too late. I kept this cutting for you from the *Times*.'

Ludens read: *The engagement is announced of Miss Heather Jessica Allenby, daughter of Sir Maurice Allenby and Lady Allenby, of the Willows, Hexton, Gloucestershire, and Dr Christian Valdemar Eriksen, son of Dr and Mrs Eriksen, Valkendorfgade 78, 1153 K, Copenhagen.*

'Good heavens, how did Christian pull that off?'

'She came to your flat looking for you, and he was there.'

'Well, farewell matrimony. All the same I'd like to have a son. Marcus thought his grandson would be a genius.'

'He still may.'

'His Lordship may be charming but I doubt if he's clever.'

'Sorry to disappoint you again. I made a few enquiries. The Honourable Adrian Sedgemont, now Lord Claverden, is a physicist, Cambridge and Princeton.'

'Damn. At least he's not a Jew.'

'It is true that he has not that advantage.'

Ludens sighed, and for a second the mists of the future parted and he saw once more the longed-for boy, gazing at him with great dark intelligent eyes. The vision faded.

'Gildas, it has just occurred to me, that person you talked to when you found a Sedgemont in the London telephone book, the man with the pleasant voice who gave you the address of Fontellen, that was probably him.'

'I've thought of that.'

'And if he hadn't been there, you might have changed your mind, none of all this would have happened at all.'

'Don't let's play that game. Innumerable things could have altered other things. Everything is accidental. That's the message.'

'Well, you won't abandon me, will you.'

'Don't be silly, Ludens, you are buckled to my heart. I will come *con scarpe o senza scarpe*. You must be feeling pretty feeble even to mention it.'

'Perhaps I'm not made for human communication anyway. I think I communicated better with that yellow dog than with any being I've ever known except you. I think I shall run away. Marzillian said something about flight, fugue, it's a technical term, it's something desperate people do, when they run away and hide and don't tell their friends and live secretly in lonely hotels. Well, that's what I'm going to do. I've just thought of it.'

'Not for long, I hope.'

Yes, that's what I'll do, thought Ludens, I'll run away. I'll find a little hotel somewhere in the north of England, beside the sea, and I'll walk on the beach and pick up stones and meet friendly dogs and no one will know me, and I'll gradually come together again and I'll think it all and endure it all and survive. But Oh my dear monster, my friend and my master, my dear dear wounded monster, my poor dead monster.

'I'll come back,' he said to Gildas, 'I'll leave now, I'll walk home.'

'Let's sing before you go. Let's sing our evening hymn, the one you like.'

They sang.

> The day Thou gavest, Lord, is ended,
> The darkness falls at Thy behest.